THE EDGE OF THE CHAIR

. . . .

Harper & Row, Publishers / New York, Evanston, and London

THE EDGE OF THE CHAIR

Edited by JOAN KAHN

. . . .

FIRST EDITION

Library of Congress Catalog Card Number: 67-22500
Designed by The Etheredges

H-R

ACKNOWLEDGMENTS

"The Sixth Capsule; or, Proof by Circumstantial Evidence," by Edmund Pearson. Copyright 1926 by Doubleday & Co., Inc.; copyright 1925, 1926, by Condé Nast Publications, Inc. (*Vanity Fair*). Reprinted by permission of Mrs. Edmund Pearson.

"Fool's Mate," by Stanley Ellin. Copyright © 1956 by Stanley Ellin. Reprinted by permission of Curtis Brown, Ltd.

"The Axeman Wore Wings," from *Ready to Hang* by Robert Tallant. Copyright 1952 by Robert Tallant. Reprinted by permission of Harper & Row, Publishers.

"Stone from the Stars," by Valentina Zhuravleva. Reprinted from *More Soviet Science Fiction*, translated from the Russian by R. Prokofieva, introduction by Isaac Asimov. Copyright © 1962 by The Crowell-Collier Publishing Co.

"The Queen of Spades," by Alexander Pushkin. Reprinted from *The Queen of Spades and Other Stories*, translated by Rosemary Edmonds, by permission of Penguin Books Limited, Publishers.

"Billy: The Seal Mission," by Stewart Alsop and Thomas Braden. From *Sub Rosa: The OSS and American Espionage*, copyright © 1946, 1964, by Stewart Alsop and Thomas Braden. Reprinted by permission of Harcourt, Brace & World, Inc.

"A Watcher by the Dead," by Ambrose Bierce. From *The Collected Works of Ambrose Bierce*, published by the Neale Publishing Company in 1909. Reprinted from *Ghost and Horror Stories of Ambrose Bierce* by E. F. Bleiler, copyright © 1964 by Dover Publications, Inc.

"Tea Party," by Harold Pinter. Originally appeared in *Playboy Magazine*; copyright © 1964 by Harold Pinter.

"Death Draws a Triangle," by Edward Hale Bierstadt. Copyright 1934, by E. H. Bierstadt.

"Prisoner of the Sand," from *Wind, Sand and Stars* by Antoine de Saint-Exupéry, translated by Lewis Galantière. Copyright 1939, by Antoine de Saint-Exupéry; renewed, 1967, by Lewis Galantière. Reprinted by permission of Harcourt, Brace & World, Inc.

"The End of the Party," from *Twenty-one Stories* by Graham Greene. Copyright 1947 by Graham Greene. Reprinted by permission of the Viking Press, Inc., and William Heinemann Limited.

"The Last Inhabitant of the Tuileries," from *The Turbulent City: Paris 1783-1871* by André Castelot, translated by Denise Folliot. Copyright © 1962 by André Storms. Reprinted by permission of Harper & Row, Publishers, Incorporated; Barrie & Rockliff, Publishers; and Vallentine, Mitchell & Co., Ltd.

"Jesting Pilot," by Lewis Padgett. Copyright 1950, by Henry Kuttner. Re-

To Bennett Cerf
but for whom . . .

CONTENTS

. . . .

THE EDGE OF THE CHAIR

INTRODUCTION

OR SOME NOTES ON BECOMING AN ANTHOLOGIST

. . . .

I have been an editor for a long time, but up until now have been the kind of editor who, having found a manuscript (fresh from the author's typewriter) that pleases, helps turn it into a book and sees it safely out into the world, hopefully in its best possible shape to meet as wide an audience as possible.

I have always enjoyed being that sort of editor, but a little while ago found myself agreeing to put an anthology together. The prospect was interesting, but a whole new thing for me. The material I would be working with would have already been discovered and edited by somebody else, so the primary responsibility would not be mine. I enjoy assuming primary responsibility usually, but this seemed a nice, temporary change. Then took a look at the amount of competition around and got nervous. There was *lots* of competition, much of it very good, but I decided I'd try to meet the challenge, see what would happen.

Planned to produce an anthology in which not only each entry was good and exciting reading but which would read well as a whole, front to back, one in which there'd be a constant change of pace, impact, and taste, so that a reader's interest would be held all the way through. Wanted to have as much variety as possible, so hunted (it seemed as if the hunt went on for a million years, but I guess it wasn't quite that long) for material that would be fresh (even when the authors were well-known) and different. Wound up with quite a batch of splendid reading—from Pushkin to Pinter via Sir Arthur Conan Doyle, Kipling, Faulkner, Christie, Saint-Exupéry, and twenty-seven other first-rate writers, with backgrounds ranging from New Orleans to Russia through New York, London and Le Mans.

Decided not only to vary the flavor of the entries by alternating fact and fiction but also to provide constant surprises and even shocks as the reader moved from one selection to another.

1

Worked out the juxtaposition of the entries carefully, though this doesn't mean a reader can't plunge in briefly, read one piece, wander off, come back and plunge in again. A nice thing about anthologies—they can be go-and-stop reading for the free moments a reader has between chores or just before falling asleep.

The over-all theme of this collection is suspense. Suspense often means suspense of life and death, of murder mysteries. But there's suspense in all good fiction and much good fact. Suspense can be anything from will a small boy be rescued from a well to will a big boy get a girl. Suspense is wanting to know what is going to happen next to the people on paper.

I hope that while they read this book readers will be held in suspense, even on the edge of their chairs. That's what the collection was planned to do, and I hope it will succeed. Guess I'll find out eventually—I'm in some suspense right now myself.

JOAN KAHN

New York City
April 7, 1967

THE SIXTH CAPSULE;
OR, PROOF BY CIRCUMSTANTIAL EVIDENCE
By Edmund Pearson

. . . .

*One of the greatest of true crime writers reports
on the tragedy and scandal that made the Comstock School
for girls unenviably famous.*

At about half-past ten, one Saturday evening in the winter, some thirty-five years ago, a small procession of schoolgirls streamed through West Fortieth Street in New York. They had been listening to a symphony concert, and now, with the teacher, who had been acting as chaperon, guide, and guardian from whatever evils infest symphony concerts, they were returning to their boarding school. This was at 32 West Fortieth, which must have been at about the site of the present Engineers' Club. It was called the Comstock School; the principal was Miss Lydia Day.

There were nine girls in the group, and they came back under the mild but pleasurable excitement of an outing which was of a thoroughly improving nature. Probably even Miss Prism, in *The Importance of Being Earnest*, who bade her pupil, Cecily, in reading political economy to omit the chapter on the fall of the rupee, as "too exciting"—probably even Miss Prism could have taken no exception to the evening's diversion. Modern music, with its distressing tendencies, had not arrived in this year 1891. Nevertheless, the girls, as they approached the door of the school, were coming near to a passionate tragedy, a mystery and a horrifying scandal.

The names of six of them are lost to history. Somewhere or other, middle-aged matrons, they probably survive today, and their memories must often turn to that night in January. Three of them, Miss

3

Carson, Miss Cookson and Miss Rockwell, were to be brought even closer to the pathetic events of the next few hours, and the results which were to make the Comstock School unenviably famous.

These three young ladies went upstairs to their room, which they shared with another pupil, Miss Helen Potts. She had been spending the evening quietly indoors with the principal, alternately reading to themselves, or aloud, from John Brown's short stories, and his *Talks about Dogs*. When her roommates came in, she had already gone to bed and was asleep. After a while she woke, and said:

"I have been having such lovely dreams . . . such lovely dreams about Carl. I wish they could have gone on forever."

Carl—so her roommates understood—was Helen's fiancé, or sweetheart (his exact status was not clear), and he was known to some of the girls as an occasional caller at the school.

Within half an hour, all of the girls were in bed, and one of the teachers had been in to turn out the light. A few minutes later Miss Carson heard a moan; she got up and went to Miss Potts, who said in a muffled voice:

"I feel numb; I feel as if I were choking."

She asked her friend to rub her head, which Miss Carson did for a while, and afterward returned to her own bed. Presently she was called again, and soon all three of the girls were aroused. Helen now said that she could not feel their hands when they rubbed her head. She added that she felt as if she were going to die. When her roommates advised her to go to sleep, she said, speaking with difficulty:

"If I do, it will be the sleep of death."

She presently added: "Do you suppose that that medicine Carl gave me could do me any harm?"

After that, she spoke no more; her breath came with great difficulty, and as she slowly drew it in, made an alarming sound in her throat. The girls, thoroughly startled by this time, called the principal of the school. It was now nearly twelve o'clock. When Miss Day came, she soon found that Helen was not only unable to move, but that she was unconscious. Dr. Fowler, the school physician, was sent for; he lived but three doors away so that he arrived in fifteen minutes.

Dr. Fowler was an experienced physician who had been practicing medicine more than thirty-five years. He found Helen in a state of profound coma; her skin was cold, pale and of a bluish tinge. She breathed in a very labored manner, and only twice to the minute. The pupils of both eyes were symmetrically contracted so as to be hardly visible. He sent for his assistant, Dr. Baner, and toward morning, when both men were thoroughly tired by their efforts to resuscitate the girl, a Dr. Kerr was summoned. Dr. Fowler, who had seen many similar cases, began at once to give the treatment for narcotic poisoning. All of the restoratives were administered, and all the methods tried, to keep up artificial respiration. About three o'clock in the morning there were some signs of improvement, but these did not last for more than half an hour.

While one or two of the doctors were working over her, the other began to inquire what she had taken, and how she came to have access to such an apparently large dose of poison. In the room was a pill box—empty—and written on the cover the words: "C. W. H. Student. One before retiring."

There seems to have been little doubt who C. W. H. was; possibly Miss Day knew that Helen had been taking medicine, and by whose prescription. He was a young student at the College of Physicians and Surgeons; his name, Carlyle W. Harris. Dr. Fowler promptly sent for this gentleman, and he arrived about daybreak, while the doctors were still rather hopelessly working over the dying girl. Said Dr. Fowler:

"We have a frightful case here, and there must have been some very great mistake. What did those capsules have in them?"

Mr. Harris said that he had prescribed them "for malaria, for headache, for insomnia and the like." He had ordered twenty-five or -six grains of quinine, and one grain of morphine to be equally mixed and to be divided into six capsules, so that each should contain four and a half grains of quinine, and one sixth grain of morphine.

Dr. Fowler answered: "One sixth of a grain of morphine or even one grain of morphine could not produce this condition. We have here one of the most profound cases of morphine poisoning that I have ever seen."

He further advised the young man to go at once to the druggist—Ewen McIntyre & Son, at the corner of Sixth Avenue and Fifty-sixth Street—to see if there could have been some mistake; if the proportions of the drug had been reversed. Mr. Harris soon returned, saying that he had been to McIntyre's (which was untrue) and that they declared that there had been no error.

Dr. Fowler asked of him if he were a physician, licensed to practice. He replied that he was a medical student and had signed the prescription in that manner. More than once, he asked: "Doctor, do you think anybody can hold me responsible for this?"

Dr. Fowler replied that he was not then concerned with responsibility, but with his attempts to revive the patient. Mr. Harris stood about, for the next three or four hours, showing no great concern for anybody but himself. He helped the doctors in some minor way, and made the brilliant suggestion of the operation of tracheotomy—cutting into the windpipe, for the purpose of inserting a tube, which aids breathing in cases of obstruction. The doctors ignored this as useless; in Dr. Fowler's opinion, expressed later, it would probably have killed the girl.

Dr. Fowler at last gave up, and said: "Well, it is no use; she is gone."

Harris asked: "Is she dead, Doctor?"

To the doctor's affirmation, he exclaimed: "My God, what will become of me?"

He had told Dr. Fowler that he was "somewhat interested in the girl," and that he might have become engaged to her after his graduation. So the three men moved away from the bed and stood at the windows, to allow him to take farewell of his intended wife. He did not improve the opportunity, however, or show any signs of affection.

He did say to Miss Day, who entered the room, that he was sorry for her. And a few minutes later, as the three physicians and the medical student were on the sidewalk outside, he renewed his inquiry:

"Doctor, do you believe anyone can hold me responsible for this?"

When, later in the day, Mrs. Potts, the mother of Helen, arrived from her home in New Jersey, she told the schoolteachers of an incident of the day before. In tragic irony, it matches some of the events in Hardy's novels. She knew that Mr. Harris had prescribed for her daughter's slight illness. She did not know that the original prescription, as made up by the chemist, was in six capsules. Two of these, for some reason unexplained, the young student had kept, as the box contained only four capsules when Helen received it. Shortly after giving the box to Helen, Harris had gone to Old Point Comfort for a few days. Helen, on three successive nights, took the third, fourth and fifth of the capsules, and as they were not only harmless, but nonbeneficial, wrote to Carl that they had done her no good whatever. He replied, urging her to go on with them. One capsule—

the sixth—remained. On the Saturday morning before her death, she showed the box to her mother, remarking that she had lost faith in the medicine and would throw it out of the window. That poor lady, her mother, restrained her, advised her to take it that night, and she promised to do so.

Mr. Harris was reproved by his teachers for his conduct in prescribing medicine when he possessed neither a degree nor a license to practice, although matters were more lax in his day than they are now. For the most part, however, he was the object of much sympathy for the unfortunate death of a patient through some other person's "dreadful blunder."

The body of Miss Helen Potts was buried near her home in New Jersey; Carlyle Harris prudently absented himself from the funeral, "for fear he might break down."

Everybody but a few of the newspaper writers seemed, in the course of the next few weeks, to have forgotten the case.

There are two kinds of "yellow journalism": one which results in outrageous invasions of privacy, and one in the furtherance of justice. Pursuing the latter course, the *World* made some investigations at the City Hall and elsewhere. One of the results was the publication of the fact that on February 8, 1890—a year before the death of Helen —two young people, calling themselves Charles Harris and Helen Neilson, had been married by an alderman. Neilson was Helen Potts's middle name; Charles Harris was the medical student, and his bride was the girl at whose death he had been present. Much other information was gradually coming to light; until it was possible to reconstruct the biography of a young man in whom the police began to be deeply absorbed.

Carlyle Harris was the grandson of an able surgeon, who was paying for his education; and the son of a woman who enjoyed a little celebrity as lecturer and writer. He had seemed assured of a successful career. In a competitive examination, he won a desirable appointment; his own personality was unusually winning. A lady who knew him, and remembers him well, has told me that there was no exaggeration in the contemporary descriptions of him as an attractive fellow: good-looking, frank and honest in manner, he was so engaging as to be popular with girls and with older women, and not at all disliked by men. There was, indeed, some aura of the model young man about him; his mother, who lectured to Sunday schools and temperance societies, used to introduce the subject of "Carl" as an example of what might be accomplished by proper religious training to develop a really good boy.

There were a very few persons who knew that if Carl died young it would not result from the love the gods bore him for his extreme rectitude. His excursions into primrose paths showed some precocity; they must have begun well before he was twenty, when he decided that wealth, fame as a physician and a fashionable marriage might all be attained without missing any of the fun of the fair as he came along the road. He was at that age of cruelty, between eighteen and twenty-four, when many clever egoists blossom into their greatest activity. As much as any other class of youth, perhaps a little more, the medical student is apt, at this age, to take a genially pagan view of women: girls exist for his amusement, and he fancies he is well equipped by his knowledge to avoid any troublesome consequences.

It should not be thought that Carlyle Harris was concerned only with girls; he had more manly diversions. In his extra-academic hours, he and some other merry boys went down to Asbury Park and founded the Neptune Club, which existed neither for yachting nor swimming, although it was wet enough for both. The police of Asbury Park were shocked at the unholy activities of the Neptunes; and Mr. Harris, as secretary-treasurer, spent a tedious night in the lock-up, and was finally indicted (although never prosecuted) for keeping what the constabulary, in their coarse manner, described as a blind pig and a poker joint.

The secretary of the Neptune Club, taken from a county jail, pursued the study of chemistry both in and outside the walls of the medical college. He discovered that rye whisky not only mixed agreeably with ginger ale, but that so mingled it produced a sweetish drink very pleasant to young ladies of his acquaintance. It had, moreover, the further merit—from the point of view of the complete amorist—of masquerading as nonalcoholic, and of being imbibed as such by girls who had not, hitherto, been sufficiently responsive to his advances. Modestly describing his adventures as a great lover to a casual acquaintance, Carlyle Harris mentioned four or five successes, but said that in two instances he had been forced to satisfy the whims of the lady by a marriage ceremony.

In the summer holidays, following his second or third year at the medical college, he met, at a hotel in New Jersey, Miss Helen Potts, then a pretty and unsophisticated girl, not much over seventeen. The prospective Dr. Harris apparently did not prescribe for her the whisky and ginger-ale recipe. The friendship of the two—as long as it remained merely a friendship—was not disapproved by the girl's mother. That lady, for a considerable time, seems to have liked Carl. Her daughter, fond as she became of her suitor, declined to accompany him on an informal elopement. She was, however, persuaded to go with him on a morning excursion, ostensibly to see the New York Stock Exchange at work. Actually, they went to the City Hall, where, under various misrepresentations, they were married by the alderman aforesaid. The affable Harris, no doubt, made promise of public acknowledgment of the marriage with almost all the holy vows of heaven.

In the following spring his medical skill not only failed to relieve his wife from the embarrassing situation in which she found herself, but put her life in danger. Helen was sent away to Pennsylvania, to a relative who was a physician. This man delivered her of her dead child. She stayed in Pennsylvania during the summer and recovered her complete health. Except for Mrs. Potts, who had been taken into confidence, the marriage remained a secret. The elder woman urged upon Harris a public acknowledgment of his wife, and a marriage before a clergyman. The young man pleaded his career and his dependence upon his grandfather, and, instead, prevailed upon his mother-in-law to send Helen to the Comstock School. Some deception was practiced by Helen's mother, since the principal of the school would have refused admission to a girl whom she knew to be married. Carlyle Harris had a certain facility in getting others to assist him in spinning webs.

As the anniversary of the marriage approached, Mrs. Potts became more and more insistent for a public and religious ceremony. She besought Harris in conversation and by letter to rescue her daughter from her questionable position. Carl finally agreed to do this, if "no other way can be found to satisfy your scruples." He had no intention whatever of acknowledging his wife; he had already been considering other plans, and they were based upon his knowledge of *materia medica*, his confidence in his own cleverness, his appreciation of the advantageous position of the doctor and his inordinate egotism and selfishness. The last qualities—as good an explanation as I can find for persons like Carlyle Harris—cause many a man, especially at his age, to look upon himself as an important lord of creation, from whose path to happiness all obstacles must simply be removed. Harris, in the course of his studies, had made some investigations of poisons; he had remarked to a classmate that by poison it ought not be difficult to remove any one. He saw a method by which to confuse the investigator who should attempt to discriminate between an innocent prescription, a fatal blunder and a felonious act.

Helen, otherwise in good health and spirits, had been subject to headaches, which were supposed to result from malaria. Carlyle Harris chose, for the compounding of his prescription, the old and reputable firm of Ewen McIntyre & Son, then as now at the corner of Sixth Avenue and Fifty-sixth Street.* It is a remarkable and unusual pharmacy, since it devotes itself, not to soda water, ice cream or quick luncheons, but to the business of a pharmacy. This firm compounded the capsules which have been described. Powdered morphine and quinine look alike, and one sixth grain of morphine is a harmless dose. Harris kept two of the capsules, with the idea of producing them and proving their innocence. Of the remaining four, he left three intact. As for the sixth and last capsule, there can be no doubt that he emptied it, and filled it with morphine. He had had opportunity to obtain this drug at the medical school, when, within a month, some of it had been passed around for inspection. Nor were there then the restrictions in the sale of narcotics which exist today. He then gave the box containing the four capsules, three innocent and one deadly, to his wife, and told her to take one each night before going to bed, and to talk to no one after taking them. Then he left the city for a few days.

The district attorney's office arranged for the exhumation of Helen's body and an autopsy. An account of this pathetic event may be found in the autobiography of the distinguished physician who performed the autopsy, Allan McLane Hamilton. The examination discovered morphine, but no quinine, and led to the theory that the sixth and fatal capsule had been prepared by Harris himself. His plans had begun to go to pieces, but he was always frank in demeanor and often bold. He appeared—like Mr. Molineux—before the authorities, and announced that he was at their disposal. His offer was soon accepted, and in the following winter, he was put upon his trial. We are a businesslike people, and often get around to the trial of a murder case within a year or more after the event.

The case was of sensational interest throughout the nation. One of

* In New York, city of perpetual change, it is always rash to assert that anything remains fixed for any length of time. Within one month of the date when this sentence was written, this pharmacy announced a change of location.

Harris' defenders was a brilliant young attorney named William Travers Jerome. The leading prosecutor was Francis L. Wellman. It is an interesting commentary upon the opinion of lawyers who hold criminal law and its practitioners in contempt that Mr. Wellman, after a long and distinguished career, chiefly in civil litigation, should return again and again in his published works to discussion of his part in the trial of Carlyle Harris, and realize that the most notable and interesting day he ever spent in court came at the climax of this extraordinary murder trial.

Public opinion was divided as to the guilt of the prisoner. He had his warm advocates, and his mother stood by him faithfully. In her terrible position, she must be judged leniently, but the fact remains that she filled the press and the public ear, not only with protestations of the innocence of her angel boy, but also, as time went on, with unjustified attacks upon the family of Helen, and even upon the dead girl herself.

The prosecution presented a closely reasoned case, in which the many items of circumstantial evidence fitted as beautifully as a well-reticulated suit of armor. It cut from under the defense almost every possible explanation of the death except that by morphine willfully and maliciously administered by the prisoner. It showed motive, in his desire to rid himself of his secret wife, of whom he had said, to a witness, that he would kill her and himself rather than have the marriage become public. It showed a cruel and callous disposition in his suggestion to another girl, with whom he was carrying on an intrigue, that she marry an old man with money, after which he would enrich her and himself by compassing the old man's death with a "pill" which he would give him. It disposed of the theory of the druggist's "awful mistake" by demonstrating, through the testimony of the two clerks who prepared the capsules, the care with which they were compounded. The analysis of the one remaining capsule which Harris was able to produce—he had lost the other—instead of working in his favor, proved the chemists to have been accurate. Suicide was shown to be an untenable theory; Helen was cheerful and in good spirits. The idea that she had some idiosyncrasy which could make one sixth grain of morphine fatal, or that she had an unrecognized kidney disease, which was aroused by that small amount of the drug, was disproved by the fact that she had already taken three capsules, each containing the one sixth grain of morphine named in the prescription.

The defense was reduced to suggesting that the death might have been due to kidney disease, and its expert witnesses—none of whom had ever seen Helen Potts, alive or dead—were produced to create a doubt in the minds of the jury. Against them the prosecution offered the unanimous and emphatic testimony of the doctors who for hours worked over the dying girl. They said it was an unmistakable and profound case of morphine poisoning. Dr. Hamilton testified that the autopsy showed no signs of kidney disease. The prosecuting attorney, Mr. Wellman, in a remarkable cross-examination, discredited the chief medical witness for the defense, and Mr. Jerome collapsed in court, from overwork and disappointment.

The jury, in about an hour, reported a verdict against the prisoner. The Court of Appeals unanimously sustained the verdict. Judge John C. Gray delivered the opinion of the Court. Discussing the remarkable combination of circumstances proved in evidence, he said:

Taking them in any combination, is there anything to help out the presumption of the defendant's innocence, and do not every incident and fact, with greater or less significance, form a chain of circumstantial evidence, which subjects and holds him to the consequences of an intentional destruction of the life of the woman, to rid himself of whom no other way seemed open? I can reach no other conclusion.

And Governor Flower, having access to still other and more convincing testimony than was permitted to the jury (including Helen's last statements to her friends), refused to commute the sentence. Harris continued to discuss the case, and coolly to protest his innocence.* His family, especially his mother, made every effort in his behalf. She was later to write a book called *The Judicial Murder of Carlyle Harris.*

In his last moment, he asked permission to speak, and said quite calmly:

"I have no further motive for concealment, and I desire to state that I am absolutely innocent of the crime for which I am to be executed." He then seated himself in the electric chair.

* Mr. Algernon Blackwood, the novelist, writes in his autobiography, *Episodes Before Thirty*, his recollections of a reporter assigned to the Tombs. He talked with murderers, and recalls ". . . the faces gazing at me through bars [which] would often haunt me for days. Carlyle Harris, calm, indifferent, cold as ice, I still see, as he peered past the iron in Murderers' Row, protesting his innocence with his steely blue eyes fixed on mine . . ." The belief that Mr. Blackwood wrote a story based on the Harris case probably arose from his tale, "Max Hensig" (in *The Listener*), which has, at the beginning, a few points of resemblance to Harris' crime.

How, it is asked by some persons, can a man make such a statement, unless it be true? I think that there are at least three reasons, any one of which, or all of which, may furnish the motive. One is that men have been saved at the last minute—while there is life there is hope. Governors are often softhearted and may relent. A confession may spoil everything. Next, there is the man's family to be considered; it may save them some measure of disgrace if they can say that the dying man protested his innocence to the end. The third reason is the wish to deny satisfaction to jury, judge and lawyers, who are responsible, in his estimation, for his plight. A man who could plot the murder and watch the death of a helpless and innocent girl who loved him would be capable of feeling some satisfaction in the thought that he might cause a few sleepless nights to the jurors who convicted him.

His mother had his coffin prepared a day or two in advance. The plate was engraved:

CARLYLE W. HARRIS
MURDERED, MAY 8, 1893.

FOOL'S MATE
By Stanley Ellin

The story of Mr. and Mrs. George Huneker
and an extraordinary chess match.

When George Huneker came home from the office that evening he was obviously fired by a strange excitement. His ordinarily sallow cheeks were flushed, his eyes shone behind his rimless spectacles and instead of carefully removing his rubbers and neatly placing them on the strip of mat laid for that purpose in a corner of the hallway, he pulled them off with reckless haste and tossed them aside. Then, still wearing his hat and overcoat, he undid the wrappings of the package he had brought with him and displayed a small, flat, leather case. When he opened the case Louise saw a bed of shabby green velvet in which rested the austere black and white forms of a set of chessmen.

"Aren't they beautiful?" George said. He ran a finger lovingly over one of the pieces. "Look at the work on this: nothing fancy to stick away in a glass case, you understand, but everything neat and clean and ready for action the way it ought to be. All genuine ivory and ebony, and all handmade, every one of them."

Louise's eyes narrowed. "And just how much did you pay out for this stuff?"

"I didn't," George said. "That is, I didn't buy it. Mr. Oelrichs gave it to me."

"Oelrichs?" said Louise. "You mean that old crank you brought home to dinner that time? The one who just sat and watched us like the cat that ate the canary, and wouldn't say a word unless you poked it out of him?"

14

"Oh, Louise!"

"Don't you 'Oh, Louise' me! I thought I made my feelings about him mighty clear to you long before this. And, may I ask, why should our fine Mr. Oelrichs suddenly decide to give you this thing?"

"Well," George said uneasily, "you know he's been pretty sick, and what with him needing only a few months more for retirement I was carrying most of his work for him. Today was his last day, and he gave me this as a kind of thank-you present. Said it was his favorite set, too, but he wanted to give me the best thing he could, and this was it."

"How generous of Mr. Oelrichs," Louise remarked frigidly. "Did it ever occur to him that if he wanted to pay you back for your time and trouble, something practical would be a lot more to the point?"

"Why, I was just doing him a favor, Louise. Even if he did offer me money or anything like that, I wouldn't take it."

"The more fool you." Louise sniffed. "All right, take off your things, put them away right and get ready for supper. It's just about ready."

She moved toward the kitchen, and George trailed after her placatingly. "You know, Louise, Mr. Oelrichs said something that was very interesting."

"I'm sure he did."

"Well, he said there were some people in the world who *needed* chess—that when they learned to play it real well they'd see for themselves how much they needed it. And what I thought was that there's no reason why you and I . . ."

She stopped short and faced him with her hands on her hips. "You mean that after I'm done taking care of the house, and shopping, and cooking your hot meals, and mending and darning, then I'm supposed to sit down and learn how to play games with you! For a man going on fifty, George Huneker, you get some peculiar ideas."

Pulling off his overcoat in the hallway, he reflected that there was small chance of his losing track of his age, at least not as long as Louise doted so much on reminding him. He had first heard about it a few months after his marriage when he was going on thirty and had been offered a chance to go into business for himself. He had heard about it every year since, on some occasion or other, although as he learned more and more about Louise he had fallen into fewer traps.

The only trouble was that Louise always managed to stay one

jump ahead of him, and while in time he came to understand that she would naturally put her foot down at such things as his leaving a good steady job, or at their having a baby when times were hard (and in Louise's opinion they always were), or at buying the house outright when they could rent it so cheap, it still came as a surprise that she so bitterly opposed the idea of having company to the house, or of reading some book he had just enjoyed, or of tuning in the radio to a symphony, or, as in this case, of taking up chess.

Company, she made it clear, was a bother and expense, small print hurt her eyes, symphonies gave her a splitting headache and chess, it seemed, was something for which she could not possibly find time. Before they had been married, George thought unhappily, it had all been different somehow. They were always in the midst of a crowd of his friends, and when books or music or anything like that were the topics of discussion, she followed the talk with bright and vivacious interest. Now she just wanted to sit with her knitting every night while she listened to comedians bellowing over the radio.

Not being well, of course, could be one reason for all this. She suffered from a host of aches and pains which she dwelt on in such vivid detail at times that George himself could feel sympathetic twinges go through him. Their medicine chest bulged with remedies, their diet had dwindled to a bland and tasteless series of concoctions and it was a rare month which did not find Louise running up a sizable doctor's bill for the treatment of what George vaguely came to think of as "women's troubles."

Still, George would have been the first to point out that despite the handicaps she worked under, Louise had been as good a wife as a man could ask for. His salary over the years had hardly been luxurious, but penny by penny she had managed to put aside fifteen thousand dollars in their bank account. This was a fact known only to the two of them, since Louise made it a point to dwell on their relative poverty in her conversations with anyone, and while George always felt some embarrassment when she did this, Louise pointed out that one of the best ways to save your money was not to let the world at large know you had any, and since a penny saved was a penny earned she was contributing as much to their income in her way as George was in his. This, while not reducing George's embarrassment, did succeed in glossing it with increased respect for Louise's wisdom and capability.

And when added to this was the knowledge that his home was

always neat as a pin, his clothing carefully mended and his health fanatically ministered to, it was easy to see why George chose to count his blessings rather than make an issue of anything so trivial as his wife's becoming his partner at chess. Which, as George himself might have admitted had you pinned him down to it, was a bit of a sacrifice, for in no time at all after receiving the set of chessmen he found himself a passionate devotee of the game. And chess, as he sometimes reflected while poring over his board of an evening with the radio booming in his ears and his wife's knitting needles flickering away contentedly, would seem to be a game greatly enhanced by the presence of an opponent. He did not reflect this ironically; there was no irony in George's nature.

Mr. Oelrichs, in giving him the set, had said he would be available for instruction at any time. But since Louise had already indicated that that gentleman would hardly be a welcome guest in her home, and since she had often expressed decided opinions on any man who would leave his hearth and home to go traipsing about for no reason, George did not even think the matter worth broaching. Instead, he turned to a little text aptly entitled *An Invitation to Chess*, was led by the invitation to essay other and more difficult texts and was thence led to a whole world of literature on chess, staggering in its magnitude and complexity.

He ate chess, drank chess and slept chess. He studied the masters and past masters until he could quote chapter and verse from even their minor triumphs. He learned the openings, the middle game and the end game. He learned to eschew the reckless foray which led nowhere in favor of the positional game where cunning strategy turned a side into a relentless force that inevitably broke and crushed the enemy before it. Strange names danced across his horizon: Alekhine, Capablanca, Lasker, Nimzovich, and he pursued them, drunk with the joy of discovery, through the ebony and ivory mazes of their universe.

But in all this there was still that one thing lacking: an opponent, a flesh-and-blood opponent against whom he could test himself. It was one thing, he sometimes thought disconsolately, to have a book at one's elbow while pondering a move; it would be quite another to ponder even the identical move with a man waiting across the board to turn it to his own advantage and destroy you with it. It became a growing hunger, that desire to make a move and see a hand reach across the table to answer it; it became a curious obsession so that at times, when Louise's shadow moved abruptly against the wall or a log settled in the fireplace, George would look up suddenly, half expecting to see the man seated in the empty chair opposite him.

He came to visualize the man quite clearly after a while. A quiet contemplative man much like himself, in fact, with graying hair and rimless spectacles that tended to slide a bit when he bent over the board. A man who played just a shade better than himself; not so well that he could not be beaten, but well enough to force George to his utmost to gain an occasional victory.

And there was one thing more he expected of this man: something a trifle unorthodox, perhaps, if one was a stickler for chess ritual. The man must prefer to play the white side all the time. It was the white side that moved first, that took the offensive until, perhaps, the tide could be turned against it. George himself infinitely preferred the black side, preferred to parry the thrusts and advances of white while he slowly built up a solid wall of defense against its climactic moves. *That* was the way to learn the game, George told himself: after a player learned how to make himself invulnerable on the defense, there was nothing he couldn't do on attack.

However, to practice one's defense still required a hand to set the offense into motion, and eventually George struck on a solution which, he felt with mild pride, was rather ingenious. He would set up the board, seat himself behind the black side, and then make the opening move for white. This he would counter with a black piece, after which he would move again for white, and so on until some decision was reached.

It was not long before the flaws in this system became distressingly obvious. Since he naturally favored the black side, and since he knew both plans of battle from their inception, black won game after game with ridiculous ease. And after the twentieth fiasco of this sort George sank back into his chair despairingly. If he could only put one side out of his mind completely while he was moving for the other, why, there would be no problem at all! Which, he realized cheerlessly, was a prospect about as logical as an ancient notion he had come across in his reading somewhere, the notion that if you cut a serpent in half, the separated halves would then turn on each other and fight themselves savagely to death.

He set up the board again after this glum reflection, and then walked around the table and seated himself in white's chair. Now, if he were playing the white side what would he do? A game depends not only on one's skill, he told himself, but also on one's knowledge of his opponent. And not only on the opponent's style of play, but also on his character, his personality, his whole nature. George solemnly looked across the table at black's now empty chair and brooded on this. Then slowly, deliberately, he made his opening move.

After that, he quickly walked around the table and sat down on black's side. The going, he found, was much easier here, and almost mechanically he answered white's move. With a thrill of excitement chasing inside him, he left his seat and moved around to the other side of the board again, already straining hard to put black and its affairs far out of his mind.

"For pity's sake, George, what *are* you doing!"

George started, and looked around dazedly. Louise was watching him, her lips compressed, her knitting dropped on her lap and her manner charged with such disapproval that the whole room seemed to frown at him. He opened his mouth to explain, and hastily thought better of it.

"Why, nothing," he said, "nothing at all."

"Nothing at all!" Louise declared tartly. "The way you're tramping around, somebody would think you can't find a comfortable chair in the house. You know I . . ."

Then her voice trailed off, her eyes became glassy, her body straightened and became rigid with devouring attention. The comedian on the radio had answered an insult with another evidently so devastating that the audience in the studio could do no more than roar in helpless laughter. Even Louise's lips turned up ever so slightly at the corners as she reached for her knitting again, and George gratefully seized this opportunity to drop into the chair behind black's side.

He had been on the verge of a great discovery, he knew that; but what exactly had it been? Was it that changing places physically had allowed him to project himself into the forms of two players, each separate and distinct from the other? If so, he was at the end of the line, George knew, because he would never be able to explain all that getting up and moving around to Louise.

But suppose the board itself were turned around after each move? Or, and George found himself charged with a growing excitement, since chess was completely a business of the mind anyhow—since, when one had mastered the game sufficiently it wasn't even necessary to use a board at all—wasn't the secret simply a matter of *turning oneself into the other player* when his move came?

It was white's move now, and George bent to his task. He was playing white's side, he must do what white would do—more than that, he must feel white's very emotions—but the harder he struggled and strained in his concentration, the more elusive became his goal. Again and again, at the instant he was about to reach his hand out, the thought of what black intended to do, of what black was surely *going* to do, slipped through his mind like a dot of quicksilver and made him writhe inwardly with a maddening sense of defeat.

This now became the obsession, and evening after evening he exercised himself at it. He lost weight, his face drew into haggard lines so that Louise was always at his heels during mealtimes trying to make him take an interest in her wholly uninteresting recipes. His interest in his job dwindled until it was barely perfunctory, and his superior, who at first had evinced no more than a mild surprise and irritation, started to shake his head ominously.

But with every game, every move, every effort he made, George felt with exultation he was coming nearer that goal. There would come a moment, he told himself with furious certainty, when he could view the side across the board with objectivity, with disinterest, with no more knowledge of its intentions and plans than he would have of any flesh-and-blood player who sat there; and when that day came, he would have achieved a triumph no other player before him could ever claim!

He was so sure of himself, so confident that the triumph lay beyond the next move each time he made a move, that when it came at last his immediate feeling was no more than a comfortable gratification and an expansive easing of all his nerves. Something like the feeling, he thought pleasurably, that a man gets after a hard day's work when he sinks into bed at night. Exactly that sort of feeling, in fact.

He had left the black position on the board perilously exposed through a bit of carelessness, and then in an effort to recover himself had moved the king's bishop in a neat defensive gesture that could cost white dear. When he looked up to study white's possible answer he saw White sitting there in the chair across the table, his fingertips gently touching each other, an ironic smile on his lips.

"Good," said White pleasantly. "Surprisingly good for you, George."

At this, George's sense of gratification vanished like a soap bubble flicked by a casual finger. It was not only the amiable insult conveyed by the words which nettled him; equally disturbing was the fact that White was utterly unlike the man that George had been prepared for.

He had not expected White to resemble him as one twin resembles another, yet feature for feature the resemblance was so marked that White could have been the image that stared back at him from his shaving mirror each morning. An image, however, which, unlike George's, seemed invested with a power and arrogance that were quite overwhelming. Here, George felt with a touch of resentment, was no man to hunch over a desk computing dreary rows of figures, but one who with dash and brilliance made great decisions at the head of a long committee table. A man who thought a little of tomorrow, but much more of today and the good things it offered. And one who would always find the price for those good things.

That much was evident in the matchless cut of White's clothing, in the grace and strength of the lean, well-manicured hands, in the merciless yet merry glint in the eyes that looked back into George's. It was when he looked into those eyes that George found himself fumbling for some thought that seemed to lie just beyond him. The image of himself was reflected so clearly in those eyes; perhaps it was not an image. Perhaps . . .

He was jarred from his train of thought by White's moving a piece. "Your move," said White carelessly, "that is, if you want to continue the game."

George looked at the board and found his position still secure. "Why shouldn't I want to continue the game? Our positions . . ."

"For the moment are equal," White interposed promptly. "What you fail to consider is the long view: I am playing to win; you are playing only to keep from losing."

"It seems very much the same thing," argued George.

"But it is not," said White, "and the proof of that lies in the fact that I shall win this game, and every other game we ever play."

The effrontery of this staggered George. "Maroczy was a master who relied a good deal on defensive strategy," he protested, "and if you are familiar with his games . . ."

"I am exactly as well acquainted with Maroczy's games as you are," White observed, "and I do not hesitate to say that had we ever played, I should have beaten him every game as well."

George reddened. "You think very well of yourself, don't you," he said, and was surprised to see that instead of taking offense White was regarding him with a look of infinite pity.

"No," White said at last, "it is you who think well of me," and then as if he had just managed to see and avoid a neatly baited trap, he shook his head and drew his lips into a faintly sardonic grimace. "Your move," he said.

With an effort George put aside the vaguely troubling thoughts that clustered in his mind, and made the move. He made only a few after that when he saw clearly that he was hopelessly and ignominiously beaten. He was beaten a second game, and then another after that, and then in the fourth game, he made a despairing effort to change his tactics. On his eleventh move he saw a devastating opportunity to go on the offensive, hesitated, refused it and was lost again. At that George grimly set about placing the pieces back in their case.

"You'll be back tomorrow?" he said, thoroughly put out at White's obvious amusement.

"If nothing prevents me."

George suddenly felt cold with fear. "What could prevent you?" he managed to say.

White picked up the white queen and revolved it slowly between his fingers. "Louise, perhaps. What if she decided not to let you indulge yourself in this fashion?"

"But why? Why should she? She's never minded up to now!"

"Louise, my good man, is an extremely stupid and petulant woman. . . ."

"Now, that's uncalled for!" George said, stung to the quick.

"And," White continued as if he had not been interrupted at all, "she is the master here. Such people now and then like to affirm their mastery seemingly for no reason at all. Actually, such gestures are a sop to their vanity—as necessary to them as the air they breathe."

George mustered up all the courage and indignation at his command. "If those are your honest opinions," he said bravely, "I don't think you have the right to come to this house ever again."

On the heels of his words Louise stirred in her armchair and turned toward him. "George," she said briskly, "that's quite enough of that game for the evening. Don't you have anything better to do with your time?"

"I'm putting everything away now," George answered hastily, but when he reached for the chessman still gripped between his opponent's fingers, he saw White studying Louise with a look that made him quail. White turned to him then, and his eyes were like pieces of dark glass through which one can see the almost unbearable light of a searing flame.

"Yes," White said slowly. "For what she is and what she has done to you I hate her with a consuming hate. Knowing that, do you wish me to return?"

The eyes were not unkind when they looked at him now, George saw, and the feel of the chessman which White thrust into his hand was warm and reassuring. He hesitated, cleared his throat, then, "I'll see you tomorrow," he said at last.

White's lips drew into that familiar sardonic grimace. "Tomorrow, the next day, any time you want me," he said. "But it will always be the same. You will never beat me."

Time proved that White had not underestimated himself. And time itself, as George learned, was something far better measured by an infinite series of chess games, by the moves within a chess game, than by any such device as a calendar or clock. The discovery was a delightful one; even more delightful was the realization that the world around him, when viewed clearly, had come to resemble nothing so much as an object seen through the wrong end of a binocular. All those people who pushed and prodded and poked and demanded countless explanations and apologies could be seen as sharp and clear as ever but nicely reduced in perspective, so that it was obvious that no matter how close they came, they could never really touch one.

There was a single exception to this: Louise. Every evening the world would close in around the chessboard and the figure of White lounging in the chair on the other side of it. But in a corner of the room sat Louise over her knitting, and the air around her was charged with a mounting resentment which would now and then eddy around George in the form of querulous complaints and demands from which there was no escape.

"How *can* you spend every minute at that idiotic game!" she demanded. "Don't you have anything to talk to me about?" And, in fact, he did not, any more than he had since the very first years of his marriage when he had been taught that he had neither voice nor vote in running his home, that she did not care to hear about the people he worked with in his office and that he could best keep to himself any reflections he had on some subject which was, by her own word, Highbrow.

"And how right she is," White had once taken pains to explain derisively. "If *you* had furnished your home it would be uncluttered and graceful, and Louise would feel awkward and out of place in it.

If she comes to know the people you work with too well, she might have to befriend them, entertain them, set her blatant ignorance before them for judgment. No, far better under the circumstances that she dwells in her vacuum, away from unhappy judgments."

As it always could, White's manner drove George to furious resentment. "For a set of opinions pulled out of a cocked hat that sounds very plausible," he burst out. "Tell me, how do you happen to know so much about Louise?"

White looked at him through veiled eyes. "I know only what you know," he said. "No more and no less."

Such passages left George sore and wounded, but for the sake of the game he endured them. When Louise was silent all the world retreated into unreality. Then the reality was the chessboard with White's hand hovering over it, mounting the attack, sweeping everything before it with a reckless brilliance that could only leave George admiring and dismayed.

In fact, if White had any weakness, George reflected mournfully, it was certainly not in his game, but rather in his deft and unpleasant way of turning each game into the occasion for a little discourse on the science of chess, a discourse which always wound up with some remarkably perverse and impudent reflections on George's personal affairs.

"You know that the way a man plays chess demonstrates that man's whole nature," White once remarked. "Knowing this, does it not strike you as significant that you always choose to play the defensive—and always lose?"

That sort of thing was bad enough, but White was at his most savage those times when Louise would intrude in a game: make some demand on George or openly insist that he put away the board. Then White's jaw would set, and his eyes would flare with that terrible hate that always seemed to be smoldering in them when he regarded the woman.

Once when Louise had gone so far as to actually pick up a piece from the board and bang it back into the case, White came to his feet so swiftly and menacingly that George leaped up to forestall some rash action. Louise glared at him for that.

"You don't have to jump like that," she snapped. "I didn't break anything. But I can tell you, George Huneker, if you don't stop this nonsense I'll do it for you. I'll break every one of these things to bits if that's what it takes to make you act like a human being again!"

"Answer her!" said White. "Go ahead, why don't you answer her!" And caught between these two fires George could do no more than stand there and shake his head helplessly.

It was this episode, however, which marked a new turn in White's manner: the entrance of a sinister purposefulness thinly concealed in each word and phrase.

"If she knew how to play the game," he said, "she might respect it, and you would have nothing to fear."

"It so happens," George replied defensively, "that Louise is too busy for chess."

White turned in his chair to look at her and then turned back with a grim smile. "She is knitting. And, it seems to me, she is always knitting. Would you call that being busy?"

"Wouldn't you?"

"No," said White, "I wouldn't. Penelope spent her years at the loom to keep off importunate suitors until her husband returned. Louise spends her years at knitting to keep off life until death comes. She takes no joy in what she does; one can see that with half an eye. But each stitch dropping off the end of those needles brings her one instant nearer death, and, although she does not know it, she rejoices in it."

"And you make all that out of the mere fact that she won't play at chess?" cried George incredulously.

"Not alone chess," said White. "Life."

"And what do you mean by that word 'life,' the way you use it?"

"Many things," said White. "The hunger to learn, the desire to create, the ability to feel vast emotions. Oh, many things."

"Many things, indeed," George scoffed. "Big words, that's all they are." But White only drew his lips into that sardonic grimace and said, "Very big. Far too big for Louise, I'm afraid," and then by moving a piece forced George to redirect his attention to the board.

It was as if White had discovered George's weak spot, and took a sadistic pleasure in returning to probe it again and again. And he played his conversational gambits as he made his moves at chess; cruelly, unerringly, always moving forward to the inescapable conclusion with a sort of flashing audacity. There were times when George, writhing helplessly, thought of asking him to drop the subject of Louise once and for all, but he could never bring himself to do so. Something in the recesses of George's mind warned him that these conversational fancies were as much a part of White as his capacity for chess, and that if George wanted him at all it would have to be on his own terms.

And George did want him, wanted him desperately, the more so on such an evening as that dreadful one when he came home to tell Louise that he would not be returning to his office for a while. He had not been discharged, of course, but there had been something about his taking a rest until he felt in shape again. Although, he hastily added in alarm as he saw Louise's face go slack and pale, he never felt better in his life.

In the scene that followed, with Louise standing before him and passionately telling him things about himself that left him sick and shaken, he found White's words pouring through his mind in a bitter torrent. It was only when Louise was sitting exhausted in her arm-chair, her eyes fixed blankly on the wall before her, her knitting in her lap to console her, and he was at his table setting up the pieces, that he could feel the brackish tide of his pain receding.

"And yet there is a solution for all this," White said softly, and turned his eyes toward Louise. "A remarkably simple solution when one comes to think of it."

George felt a chill run through him. "I don't care to hear about it," he said hoarsely.

"Have you ever noticed, George," White persisted, "that that piddling, hackneyed picture on the wall, set in that baroque monstrosity of a frame that Louise admires so much, is exactly like a pathetic little fife trying to make itself heard over an orchestra that is playing its loudest?"

George indicated the chessboard. "You have the first move," he said.

"Oh, the game," White said. "The game can wait, George. For the moment I'd much prefer to think what this room—this whole fine house, in fact—could be if it were all yours, George. Yours alone."

"I'd rather get on with the game," George pleaded.

"There's another thing, George," White said slowly, and when he leaned forward George saw his own image again staring at him strangely from those eyes, "another fine thing to think of. If you were all alone in this room, in this house, why, there wouldn't be anyone to tell you when to stop playing chess. You could play morning, noon and night, and all around to the next morning if you cared to!

"And that's not all, George. You can throw that picture out of the window and hang something respectable on the wall: a few good prints, perhaps—nothing extravagant, mind you—but a few good ones that stir you a bit the first time you come into the room each day and see them.

"And recordings! I understand they're doing marvelous things with recordings today, George. Think of a whole room filled with them: opera, symphony, concerto, quartet—just take your pick and play them to your heart's content!"

The sight of his image in those eyes always coming nearer, the jubilant flow of words, the terrible meaning of those words set George's head reeling. He clapped his hands over his ears and shook his head frantically.

"You're mad!" he cried. "Stop it!" And then he discovered to his horror that even with his hands covering his ears he could hear White's voice as clearly and distinctly as ever.

"Is it the loneliness you're afraid of, George? But that's foolish. There are so many people who would be glad to be your friends, to talk to you and, what's better, to listen to you. There are some who would even love you, if you chose."

"Loneliness?" George said unbelievingly. "Do you think it's loneliness I'm afraid of?"

"Then what is it?"

"You know as well as I," George said in a shaking voice, "what you're trying to lead me to. How could you expect me, expect any decent man, to be that cruel!"

White bared his teeth disdainfully. "Can you tell me anything more cruel than a weak and stupid woman whose only ambition in life was to marry a man infinitely superior to her and then cut him down to her level so that her weakness and stupidity could always be concealed?"

"You've got no right to talk about Louise like that!"

"I have every right," said White grimly, and somehow George knew in his heart that this was the dreadful truth. With a rising panic he clutched the edge of the table.

"I won't do it!" he said distractedly. "I'll never do it, do you understand!"

"But it will be done!" White said, and his voice was so naked with terrible decision that George looked up to see Louise coming toward the table with her sharp little footsteps. She stood over it, her mouth working angrily, and then through the confusion of his thoughts he heard her voice echoing the same words again and again. "You fool!" she was saying wildly. "It's this chess! I've had enough of it!" And suddenly she swept her hand over the board and dashed the pieces from it.

"No!" cried George, not at Louise's gesture, but at the sight of White standing before her, the heavy poker raised in his hand. "No!" George shouted again, and started up to block the fall of the poker, but knew even as he did so that it was too late.

Louise might have been dismayed at the untidy way her remains were deposited in the official basket; she would certainly have cried aloud (had she been in a condition to do so) at the unsightly scar on the polished woodwork made by the basket as it was dragged along the floor and borne out of the front door. Inspector Lund, however, merely closed the door casually behind the little cortege and turned back to the living room.

Obviously the Lieutenant had completed his interrogation of the quiet little man seated in the chair next to the chess table, and obviously the Lieutenant was not happy. He paced the center of the floor, studying his notes with a furrowed brow, while the little man watched him, silent and motionless.

"Well?" said Inspector Lund.

"Well," said the Lieutenant, "There's just one thing that doesn't tie in. From what I put together, here's a guy who's living his life all right, getting along fine, and all of a sudden he finds he's got another self, another personality. He's like a man split into two parts, you might say."

"Schizoid," remarked Inspector Lund. "That's not unusual."

"Maybe not," said the Lieutenant. "Anyhow, this other self is no good at all, and sure enough it winds up doing this killing."

"That all seems to tie in," said Inspector Lund. "What's the hitch?"

"Just one thing," the Lieutenant stated: "a matter of identity." He frowned at his notebook, and then turned to the little man in the chair next to the chess table. "What did you say your name was?" he demanded.

The little man drew his lips into a faintly sardonic grimace of rebuke. "Why, I've told you that so many times before, Lieutenant, surely you couldn't have forgotten it again." The little man smiled pleasantly. "My name is White."

THE AXEMAN WORE WINGS
By Robert Tallant

. . . .

*No one ever saw the Axeman who came in the night
and terrorized New Orleans.*

In 1918 New Orleans like all other American cities was busy thinking and reading about and devoting itself to the news and the duties
of World War I. In the spring of that year no one knew it would end
in November, although there was hope that it would not go on much
longer and a great deal of optimism that the Allies would win. Headlines in a New Orleans newspaper on May 3 read "Lull in Flanders;
Allied Lines Holding," yet by May 23 the same newspaper warned,
"Massed Germans Awaiting Orders Now to Open Drive," and Orleanians were instructed to "Kill the Germ in Germany—Liberty
Bonds Will Help!" On May 24 another headline announced, "Senate
Rejects Dry Amendment by 20 to 20 Vote." At New Orleans moving
picture theaters Charlie Chaplin was starring in *A Dog's Life* and
Theda Bara in *The Soul of Buddha*. Also on that day a woman was
arrested in New Orleans for wearing trousers on the street. But on
the same day there was another headline in all the papers in the city.
A couple named Maggio, who operated a small grocery at the corner
of Upperline and Magnolia streets, had been attacked during the
night before by an unknown assailant who was armed with an axe. It
had begun, although most Orleanians must have thought of it as a
shocking but isolated case, and they could hardly have dreamed of
what lay ahead.

On that morning of May 24, 1918, the *Times-Picayune* devoted a
good portion of its front page to the story, and in the center of the
page was a photograph of the room where the Maggios had been
sleeping, a room in their living quarters behind their store, with inset

pictures of the couple as they had looked at their wedding fifteen years before. According to the account, police thought it was just before dawn when someone had chiseled out a panel in a rear door of the apartment and entered. He had struck each of the sleepers once with an axe, then slit their throats with a razor. Mrs. Maggio lay on the floor, her head nearly severed from her body, Joseph Maggio was sprawled half out of bed. The razor lay on the floor in a pool of blood. The axe, as bloodstained as the razor, was found on the steps going out into the back yard; it had been Maggio's own property. There was a small safe in the room which was open and empty, yet a hundred dollars or more in cash was found beneath Maggio's blood-soaked pillow and on the dresser in a little pile was Mrs. Maggio's jewelry, including several diamond rings. The police were reported to have already stated that they did not believe robbery was a motive, but that the murderer had opened the safe to make it appear that it was.

In rooms on the other side of the house lived Joseph's brothers, Andrew and Jake. They had discovered the bodies. Jake told police that he awakened at about five o'clock and heard groaning and strange noises on the other side of the wall separating his bedroom from that of Joseph and his wife. He aroused Andrew and together they went into the room. Joseph was on the bed then, and still alive. He even tried to rise and fell half out of the bed. Andrew and Jake called the police at once. The police put them both under arrest, after a neighbor who rushed into the house along with them said he had seen Andrew come home some time between two and three in the morning. Later in the morning there was another curious discovery. Chalked on the sidewalk a block away were these words: MRS. MAG-GIO IS GOING TO SIT UP TONIGHT JUST LIKE MRS. TONEY.

The police went to work. In 1911 there had been three axe murders, similar to the Maggio case, all of Italian grocers and their wives. There had been a grocer named Cruti, then one named Rosetti, whose wife was murdered with him, finally a Tony Schiambra and his wife. Was the last the "Mrs. Toney" referred to in the sidewalk writing? People began talking of Mafia and of Black Hand. The Italian population was particularly worried and some of them demanded police protection.

In the meantime Andrew and Jake Maggio were in jail swearing their innocence. Andrew said it was true he had been out late the night before. He had been celebrating for he had just received his draft call. He had come home drunk and he would not have been able to notice anything strange if there had been anything to notice. Jake verified this and said he had had a hard time arousing Andrew. They were respectable, hard-working young men—Andrew was a barber, Jake a cobbler.

Jake was released the following day and Andrew on May 26. Andrew told a *Times-Picayune* reporter with "tear-filled eyes" that he would never get over this. "It's a terrible thing to be charged with the murder of your own brother when your heart is already broken by his death," he said. "When I'm about to go to war, too. I had been drinking heavily. I was too drunk even to have heard any noise next door." But he and Jake were free and were cleared of any suspicion.

The papers of May 26 announced that Detective Theodore Obitz had charge of the case and had "many theories." On the evening of May 26 Detective Obitz was shot through the heart by a Negro he had arrested for burglary. It had no connection with the Maggio murders.

Weeks passed and nothing more happened. The newspapers informed Orleanians that the Allies had been forced to retire on the Aisne and that the Russian Czar had been murdered. Many citizens probably almost forgot the Maggio case. They were rushing to the Strand Theatre to see James W. Gerard's *My Four Years in Germany* at road show prices and talking about putting New Orleans "over the top" in the new Red Cross drive.

Then on June 28 a baker, John Zanca, made his morning call to deliver bread and cakes to the grocery of Louis Besumer. It was after seven o'clock when he arrived, and as Besumer's store was still closed, Zanca went around to the living quarters in the rear to leave his bread there rather than risk having it stolen from the front of the store. When he reached the back door he stopped and stared in horror. A lower panel of the door was neatly chiseled out. Perhaps half-consciously Zanca knocked on the door. He said later, "There seemed nothing else to do."

And Louis Besumer opened the door. Blood streamed from a wound in his head. He said, "My God! My God!"

Zanca rushed past him and found the woman he had always thought Mrs. Besumer on the bed covered with a bloodstained sheet, unconscious and with a terrible head wound. He called the Charity Hospital and the police.

The newspapers announced the next day that "Mrs. Besumer" was in a serious condition, but still alive, and that Besumer had been released. Detectives believed the woman had been attacked on the gallery leading across one side of the living quarters, for there was much blood there, then had dragged herself or been carried back to the bed, possibly by Besumer. An axe, Besumer's property, was discovered in the bathroom, still bright, bright red with blood. Besumer, it was said, was Polish, and had lived in New Orleans only three months. He had come to the city from Jacksonville, Florida, and before that had operated a farm in South America.

On June 29 there were further developments. That morning the *Times-Picayune* carried a headline reading, "Spy Nest Suspected!" It was stated that letters to Besumer written in German, Russian and Yiddish had been found in a trunk in his apartment. The New Orleans *States* the same day asked the question, "Is Besumer a German Agent?" and "Was the Besumer Grocery a Front for a Spy Ring?" On June 30, a Sunday, a great deal of space was devoted to this, and it was hinted darkly that federal authorities were interested in the case. One reporter did note, however, that Besumer was not Italian and asked, "What of the Mafia theory in the axe killings?" It was also noted that Lewis Oubicon, a Negro employee of Besumer's, was being held for questioning.

Besumer's own statements were made public on July 1. The first thing he is reported to have said was "That woman is not my wife." He said the woman who had been attacked was named Mrs. Harriet Lowe and that she had come to New Orleans from Jacksonville with him, and that they had lived together ever since. His own wife was ill, he said, and with relatives in Cincinnati. He swore he did not know what had happened. Someone had struck him while he slept. When he regained consciousness he found Mrs. Lowe on the gallery and he had carried her to the bed. He had been about to summon an ambulance when Zanca knocked at the back door. He was not a German, but a Pole, and he had no use for the Germans. He spoke and received mail in a half-dozen languages. He was certainly no spy, he vowed. He offered the police his full cooperation.

But federal authorities did come into the case. Carrying a bathrobe for her, Besumer went to see Harriet Lowe at the hospital. He was refused admittance and the bathrobe was taken away from him and ripped open at the seams by government agents. The next day his grocery and living quarters were ransacked. Nothing was found.

Mrs. Lowe made her first statement on July 5, having by then regained consciousness. She said, "I've long suspected that Mr. Besumer was a German spy." Besumer was arrested at once.

On July 6 Mrs. Lowe was interviewed again. She said, "I am married to Mr. Besumer. If I am not I don't know what I'll do." Then she added, "I did not say Mr. Besumer is a German spy. That is perfectly ridiculous." A few days later Besumer was freed from government custody.

Mrs. Lowe at last talked of the attacks. She said that Besumer was working on his accounts about midnight, sitting at a table with a lot of money before him. She always worried about how careless he was with money, she said, and she warned him and asked him to put it in the safe. Then she smelled some prunes she was cooking in the kitchen and she went into the kitchen to look at them. There her memory left her. She supposed it was the blow on the head. She could not even remember going to bed. Her next memory was of awakening. "I don't even know what made me wake up," she told police, "but I opened my eyes and in the light from outside I saw a man standing over me, making some sort of motions with his hands. I saw the axe. I recall screaming, 'Go away! Don't push me that way!' He was a rather tall man, and heavy-set. He was a white man and he wore no hat or cap. I remember his hair was dark brown and almost stood on end. He wore a white shirt, opened at the neck. He just stood there, making motions with the axe, but not hitting me. The next thing I remember is lying out on the gallery with my face in a pool of blood."

The story changed on July 15. In another police interview that day Mrs. Lowe said she was not in bed when she was struck. She was on the gallery. Police thought this made more sense and again looked toward Besumer with suspicion. They questioned neighbors. Yes, the Besumers had had violent quarrels, they were told. Besumer was fifty-nine and Mrs. Lowe twenty-nine. He was jealous and they quarrelled over money, too. Police began asking one question: Could Besumer's own wound have been self-inflicted? A check with authorities in Jacksonville and in Cincinnati proved that Besumer and Mrs. Lowe had never been married and that Besumer had a living wife. That did not help matters, and they were far from convinced that Besumer was not a German agent. Neighbors gossiped about the foreigner who had odd ways and spoke German fluently, as well as other languages, who looked like a simple peasant and had the manners and airs of a cultured gentleman. People began saying that perhaps Besumer had attacked Mrs. Lowe, then wounded himself, all in imitation of the Axeman, perhaps because Mrs. Lowe knew too much of his activities as a spy.

Then on August 3 the doctors at Charity Hospital performed surgery upon Mrs. Lowe. Two days later she died, and, dying, mumbled that Besumer had struck her with the axe. He was arrested at once and charged with murder.

The Axeman chose that night, August 5, to strike again.

Edward Schneider, a young married man, was working late that night, and it was after midnight when he turned the key in the front door of his home in Elmira Street. When he reached his bedroom and turned on the light he was almost paralyzed with horror. His wife lay unconscious, her face and head covered with blood.

Mrs. Schneider, who was expecting a baby within a few days, was rushed to Charity Hospital. She regained consciousness and remembered awakening to see a dark form bending over her, an axe swung high. She recalled shrieking as the axe fell.

She recovered and a week later was delivered of a healthy baby girl. She was never able to tell more about what had occurred, however, and although the police searched diligently for clues none was found. To add to the general confusion were deviations from the Axeman's habits. No axe was about. The intruder seemed to have entered by a window, for no door panel was chiseled out. As usual, however, nothing was stolen.

The day after the attack upon Mrs. Schneider a newspaper for the first time put into a headline what Orleanians had been asking each other for months. The *Times-Picayune* asked, in large and dramatic type: IS AN AXEMAN AT LARGE IN NEW ORLEANS?

Pauline Bruno, aged eighteen, and Mary, her sister, aged thirteen, awoke shortly after three in the morning of August 10 when they heard strange noises coming from the next room, where their uncle, Joseph Romano, was sleeping. Pauline crawled out of bed, turned on her light and opened the door between the rooms. A man, whom she later described as "dark, tall, heavy-set, wearing a dark suit and a black slouch hat," was standing by her uncle's bed. Pauline screamed and then the man seemed to vanish. As if it were all a fantastic nightmare, her uncle rose from the bed, staggered through a door at the other side of the room and crashed to the floor there, which was the parlor. Pauline ran after him.

Later she told the following story to an *Item* reporter: "I've been nervous about the Axeman for weeks," she said, "and I haven't been sleeping much. I was dozing when I heard blows and scuffling in Uncle Joe's room. I sat up in bed and my sister woke up too. When I looked into my uncle's room this big heavy-set man was standing at the foot of his bed. I think he was a white man, but I couldn't swear to it. I screamed. My little sister screamed too. We were horribly scared. Then he vanished. It was almost as if he had wings!

"We rushed into the parlor, where my uncle had staggered. He had two big cuts on his head. We got him up and propped him in a chair. 'I've been hit,' he groaned. 'I don't know who did it. Call the Charity Hospital.' Then he fainted. Later he was able to walk to the ambulance with some help. I don't know that he had any enemies."

Romano died two days later in the hospital, without being able to make further statements. Police reported that this time there were all the Axeman's signatures. An axe was found in Romano's back yard, bloodstained and fearful. The panel of a rear door had been cut out. Nothing in the house was stolen, although Romano's room seemed to have been ransacked. The only thing that made it unlike some of the other cases was that Romano was a barber, not a grocer.

Now there was a new wave of hysteria among the Italians in New Orleans. Some of the families set up regular watches, taking turns standing guard over their sleeping relatives. A few were said to be leaving the city.

Police began to be flooded with reports about the Axeman after the Romano incident. Al Durand, a grocer, reported finding an axe and a chisel outside his back door on the morning of August 11. Joseph LeBeouf, a grocer at Gravier and Miro streets, only a block from the Romano home, came forward with the story that someone had chiseled out a panel of his back door on July 28, a day when he was not home. Still another grocer, Arthur Recknagel, told of finding a panel in one of his doors removed back in June, and of finding an axe in the grass of his rear yard. Recknagel lived only a half-dozen blocks from the Romano home. On August 15 several persons called to tell them the Axeman was wandering around in the neighborhood of Tulane Avenue and Broad Street disguised as a woman!

On August 21 a man was seen leaping a back fence at Gravier and South White streets. A woman reported she clearly saw an axe in this man's hand. Immediately the neighbors formed a kind of posse, as other people ran from their houses screaming that the Axeman had just jumped their fence! A young man named Joseph Garry vowed he had fired at the Axeman with his shotgun. Police arrived on the scene, but no one was apprehended, and the excitement quieted down about midnight, although it is doubtful if many people in the vicinity slept well that night or for several nights thereafter. The New Orleans *States* reported the next day:

Armed men are keeping watch over their sleeping families while the police are seeking to solve the mysteries of the axe attacks. Five victims have fallen under the dreadful blows of this weapon within the last few months. Extra police are being put to work daily.

At least four persons saw the Axeman this morning in the neighborhood of Iberville and Rendon. He was first seen in front of an Italian grocery. Twice he fled when citizens armed themselves and gave chase. There was something, agreed all, in the prowler's hand. Was it an axe? . . .

On August 30 a man named Nick Asunto called the police to tell them he had awakened and heard strange noises downstairs. He lived in a two-story house. He went to the head of his stairs and saw a dark, heavy-set man standing below, an axe in his hand. When Asunto yelled at him the Axeman ran out the front door. On August 31 Paul Lobella, a notions store proprietor at 7420 Zimple Street, found an axe in his alley. There were a dozen similar reports.

Now police made statements to the effect that they did not believe the Besumer case was of the now ordinary variety. They made public Mrs. Lowe's confession. Her memory cleared after the operation, they said, and she had told them that Besumer struck her with an axe after she had asked him for money. He chased her down the gallery, screaming, "I am going to make fire for you in the bottom of the ocean!" She had reiterated, too, that Besumer was a German spy. Therefore they were sure this was not the Axeman at work, although they believed all the other attacks, including that upon Mrs. Schneider, were the crimes of a single person, perhaps a homicidal maniac.

Joseph Dantonio, a retired detective, long an authority on Mafia activities, was questioned by a *States* reporter, and was quoted in that newspaper as saying, "The Axeman is a modern 'Dr. Jekyll and Mr. Hyde.' A criminal of this type may be a respectable, law-abiding citizen when his normal self. Compelled by an impulse to kill, he must obey this urge. Some years ago there were a number of similar cases, all bearing such strong resemblance to this outbreak that the same fiend may be responsible. Like Jack-the-Ripper, this sadist may go on with his periodic outbreaks until his death. For months, even for years, he may be normal, then go on another rampage. It is a mistake to blame the Mafia. Several of the victims have been other than Italians, and the Mafia never attacks women, as this murderer has done."

Then, as if he were exactly as Detective Dantonio had theorized, the Axeman did disappear. After the Romano killing and the other unauthenticated attacks and scares, nothing happened at all for a long time. Weeks and months passed, the fighting of World War I ended, Christmas came and then the New Year and no more attacks occurred. Orleanians, even the Italians, breathed freely again, and the police, still mystified, found nothing more to work with in solving the crimes. From time to time suspects were arrested, but all had to be released. Only Besumer remained in jail awaiting trial, the only real suspect they had in connection with any of the crimes.

Then, on March 10, 1919, Iorlando Jordano, a grocer in Gretna, just across the river from New Orleans, heard screams coming from the living quarters of another grocer across the street, a man named Charles Cortimiglia. He rushed over and into the Cortimiglia apartment. Mrs. Cortimiglia sat on the floor, still shrieking, blood gushing from her head and the body of her two-year-old daughter Mary clasped in her arms. Also bleeding frightfully, Charles Cortimiglia lay on the floor nearby.

Jordano tried to take Mary from her mother's arms, but she wouldn't let him, so he got wet towels from the bathroom and tried to bathe her face and that of her husband. Cortimiglia groaned, but did not regain full consciousness. Then Frank Jordano, young son of Iorlando, rushed in and began assisting his father. The father sent him to call an ambulance. Both the Cortimiglia parents had to be taken to the Charity Hospital with fractured skulls. Little Mary was dead.

When the police searched the property they found the familiar Axeman pattern—the back door panel chiseled, the bloody axe, Charles Cortimiglia's own, on the back steps, nothing stolen. Reading the newspapers the next morning Orleanians and the citizens of Gretna all knew the worst. The Axeman was back!

As soon as she could talk coherently Rosie Cortimiglia told of awakening to see her husband struggling with a large white man wearing dark clothes, who was armed with an axe. The man tore himself loose from Cortimiglia, sprang backward and struck once with the axe. When her husband fell to the floor and the Axeman swung around, Mrs. Cortimiglia seized Mary, who was asleep in her crib beside the parents' bed, clasped her to her and screamed, "Not my baby! Not my baby!" The Axeman struck twice more, then fled. Mary was killed instantly.

Both the Cortimiglias were badly injured, but Charles recovered first and left the hospital. A few days later Rosie made another statement, an accusation that amazed the police. "It was the Jordanos!" she said. "It was Frank Jordano and the old man helped him. It was those Jordanos!"

Charles Cortimiglia was questioned. He looked as astounded as the police. "It was not the Jordanos," he said. "I saw the man well and he was a stranger. No, it was not Frank Jordano."

Nevertheless, both Jordanos were arrested, charged with the murder of Mary Cortimiglia and placed in the Gretna jail.

Both protested their innocence fervently. Frank, who was only eighteen and about to be married, said at first he had been home all night, then admitted he had been to a dance with his girl and that he had lied because he did not want her name brought into the affair. The elder Jordano, sixty-nine and in poor health, told his story of finding the Cortimiglias over and over again.

Yet Rosie Cortimiglia told her story over and over, too. Frank and Iorlando had both been in the room. It was Frank who had struck them all, had murdered her baby. She said the Jordanos had hated her husband and herself a long time because both families were in the grocery business in the same block. It was jealousy, she said. She gave the police everything they needed—eyewitness identification and motive. Charles Cortimiglia continued to deny it all. "My wife must be out of her mind," he said. "It was a stranger." Rosie retaliated, "He is afraid for his own neck, that husband of mine. It was the Jordanos."

One thing seems to have bothered detectives working on the case more than anything else. For all his youth Frank Jordano was more than six feet tall and weighed over two hundred pounds. Making a test with a man of similar size, they admitted a man that size could not squeeze through the panel of a door. A giddy reporter on the

Times-Picayune wanted to know if it were possible the Axeman was really a midget.

When Rosie was released from the hospital she was taken to the Gretna jail. There she identified the Jordanos again. Pointing a finger at them she screamed, "You murdered my baby!" and fainted. It was announced that the Jordanos would go to trial for the murder in May.

But before that Louis Besumer went on trial. The trial opened on April 30. It was brief and few witnesses were called. District Attorney Chandler Luzenberg summoned Coroner Joseph O'Hara for the state, who described Mrs. Lowe's wounds and the cause of her death. Zanca, the baker, said that Besumer did not seem to know what he was doing that morning when he had opened the door or even to realize Mrs. Lowe was hurt. Federal officers admitted they had no evidence that Besumer had ever been a German agent. Besumer's attorney, George Rhodes, said it was a reflection on the United States Secret Service to say that Besumer had been a spy, and that Besumer was not being tried on that charge in any case and, besides, the war was over. The police to whom Mrs. Lowe had made her accusation of Besumer admitted that even then she had not been very coherent. Dr. H. W. Kostmayer said that only a very powerful man could have inflicted himself with the wound Besumer had received and he did not consider the accused strong enough to have accomplished it.

The next morning the jury debated but ten minutes and Besumer was found not guilty. Released, Besumer told reporters that he believed the same Axeman had attacked Mrs. Lowe and himself as had attacked the others and that his imprisonment had been due almost entirely to "war feeling," because he had been thought to be a German, although he was really a Pole and had never been a German sympathizer.

In the meantime the Cortimiglia case had brought on a new series of Axeman reports. Immediately after the attack upon the Gretna family, New Orleans police received numerous reports of chiseled panels, axes being found, dark, heavy-set men lurking in neighborhoods, particularly around grocery stores, and many Orleanians, particularly Italian grocers, appealed once more for police protection. The newspapers reviewed all the cases of 1918 and editorialized upon the mystery. It was announced that Police Superintendent Frank Mooney had again assigned special men to the task of uncovering the perpetrators of the crimes, despite the fact that the Jordanos were in the Gretna jail and that Superintendent Mooney had expressed the opinion that he ". . . was sure that all the crimes were committed by the same man, probably a bloodthirsty maniac, filled with a passion for human slaughter."

A *States* editor wrote, on March 11:

Who is the Axeman; what are his motives?

Is the fiend who butchered the Cortimiglias in Gretna Sunday the same man who committed the Maggio, Besumer and Romano crimes? Is he the same who has made all the attempts on other families?

If so, is he madman, robber, vendetta agent, sadist or some supernatural spirit of evil?

If a madman, why so cunning and careful in the execution of his crimes? If a robber, why the wanton shedding of blood and the fact that money and valuables have often been left in full view? If a vendetta of the Mafia, why include among victims persons of nationalities other than Italian?

The possibilities in searching for the motives in this extraordinary series of axe butcheries are unlimited. The records show no details of importance which vary. There is always the the door panel as a means of entrance, always the axe, always the frightful effusion of blood. In these three essentials the work of the Axeman is practically identical.

But the reaction of Orleanians to the 1919 outbreak of the Axeman was by no means all fearful and grim. Probably because the war was over and people were in a gayer mood than they had been the year before, there were some who joked about him and even found a kind of humor in the situation. There were reports of "Axeman parties" and a New Orleans composer wrote a song entitled "The Mysterious Axeman's Jazz" or "Don't Scare Me, Papa!" which Orleanians played on their pianos. Then, on March 14, a letter purporting to be from the Axeman appeared in a newspaper, which read as follows:

Hell, March 13, 1919

Editor of the *Times-Picayune*
New Orleans, Louisiana

Esteemed Mortal:

They have never caught me and they never will. They have never seen me, for I am invisible, even as the ether that surrounds your earth. I am not a human being, but a spirit and a fell demon from the hottest hell. I am what you Orleanians and your foolish police call the Axeman.

When I see fit, I shall come again and claim other victims. I alone know who they shall be. I shall leave no clue except my bloody axe, besmeared with the blood and brains of him whom I have sent below to keep me company.

If you wish you may tell the police not to rile me. Of course I am a reasonable spirit. I take no offense at the way they have conducted their investigations in the past. In fact, they have been so utterly stupid as to amuse not only me, but his Satanic Majesty, Francis Josef, etc. But tell them to beware. Let them not try to discover what I am, for it were better that they were never born than to incur the wrath of the Axeman. I don't think there is any need of such a warning, for I feel sure the police will always dodge me, as they have in the past. They are wise and know how to keep away from all harm.

Undoubtedly, you Orleanians think of me as a most horrible murderer, which I am, but I could be much worse if I wanted to. If I wished, I could pay a visit to your city every night. At will I could slay thousands of your best citizens, for I am in close relationship to the Angel of Death.

Now, to be exact, at 12:15 (earthly time) on next Tuesday night, I am going to visit New Orleans again. In my infinite mercy, I am going to make a proposition to you people. Here it is:

I am very fond of jazz music, and I swear by all the devils in the nether regions that every person shall be spared in whose home a jazz band is in full swing at the time I have mentioned. If everyone has a jazz band going, well, then, so much the better for you people. One thing is certain and that is that some of those people who do not jazz it on Tuesday night (if there be any) will get the axe.

Well, as I am cold and crave the warmth of my native Tartarus, and as it is about time that I leave your earthly home, I will cease my discourse. Hoping that thou wilt publish this, that it may go well with thee, I have been, am and will be the worst spirit that ever existed either in fact or realm of fancy.

THE AXEMAN

The Tuesday on which this "Axeman" promised to visit the city was March 19, St. Joseph's Night, a night when many Orleanians, and even more in 1919 than now, give parties and dances to celebrate a break in Lent.

That St. Joseph's Night in New Orleans seems to have been the loudest and most hilarious of any on record. All over the city Orleanians obeyed the instructions in the letter. Cabarets and clubs were jammed and friends and neighbors gathered in homes to "jazz it," according to the letter's edict. Bands and phonographs and inner-player pianos all over the city created bedlam, and every owner of a piano seemed to have on hand sheet music of "The Mysterious Axeman's Jazz" or "Don't Scare Me, Papa!"

Young men living in a fraternity house at 552 Lowerline Street even inserted an advertisement in the *Times-Picayune* inviting the Axeman to call. Appearing in the morning of Tuesday, March 19, the advertisement was signed by "Oscar Williams, William Schulze, A. M. La Fleur and William Simpson," and it informed the Axeman that a bathroom window would be left open for him, so that it would not be necessary for him to mar any doors; and that all doors would be left unlocked if he would stoop to making such a conventional entrance. He was told there would be, however, no jazz music, but only a rendering of "Nearer, My God, To Thee," which his hosts considered more suitable for the occasion. They concluded the advertisement by stating: "There is a sincere cordiality about this invitation that not even an Axeman can fail to recognize."

But the Axeman failed everybody that night and made no appearances. Apparently he was satisfied with the amount of jazz music being played all over the city.

Frank and Iorlando Jordano went to trial on May 21 for the murder of Mary Cortimiglia. The Gretna courtroom of Judge John H. Fleury was packed with friends and neighbors of both the victims and the accused.

The first witness was Coroner J. R. Fernandez, who went through the routine of describing the cause of Mary's death. In the front row sat Rosie Cortimiglia, dressed in black, tense and obviously near hysteria from the moment the proceedings began. Not far away sat her husband, but they did not look at each other or speak, for they had separated immediately after their disagreement over the identification of the Jordanos. Besumer was in the room, having been called because he was a survivor of a visitation of the Axeman. He was summoned to the stand early in the trial. He said he could not identify either Frank or Iorlando Jordano as the man who had attacked him and Mrs. Lowe. He could have identified no one, he concluded, because he had not seen the Axeman.

Rosie burst into tears when she took the stand, but she reiterated her identification, pointing to the men again. Some of the people in the courtroom hooted her and Judge Fleury had to ask for order and threaten to clear the room. Still, whispering and angry noises could be heard from friends of the Jordanos.

Charles Cortimiglia once again flatly denied the man with whom he had struggled was either of the Jordanos. He could not understand his wife's insistence on placing the blame on them, he said. He had seen the man. He had not been Frank; he had not been Iorlando Jordano. No! It was all wrong!

Defense Attorney William F. Byrnes summoned a stream of character witnesses for almost all of two days. All testified both the accused were respectable men of fine reputation in the town. Mrs. Iorlando Jordano took the stand. She was nervous and tense and she was kept only a moment. She said, "My old man was home all night and my boy was out with his girl."

During the second day Andrew Ojeda, a *States* reporter, was called by the defense. He testified that he had interviewed Mrs. Rosie Cortimiglia soon after she regained consciousness. At that time she had said, "I don't know who killed Mary. I believe my husband did it!"

This caused another commotion in the courtroom. A woman screamed in the rear. People who must have been friends of the Jordanos applauded; friends of the Cortimiglias hooted and hissed. Again the judge had to threaten to clear the room. Charles Cortimiglia sprang to his feet, then sat down again.

The defense summoned Dr. Jerome E. Landry, who had treated Mrs. Cortimiglia. Did Dr. Landry consider Rosie Cortimiglia's mental condition such that she would make a reliable witness? He stated that in his opinion it was. District Attorney Robert Rivarde summoned Dr. C. V. Unsworth. Did he consider Rosie Cortimiglia sane? He did. The defense then brought Dr. Joseph H. O'Hara to the stand and asked the same question. Dr. O'Hara stated that in his opinion she was suffering from paranoia.

As the trial went on more and more people fought their way inside, bringing small children, babies and box lunches. Several times a day Judge Fleury had to issue threats because of the bedlam in the room.

On the fourth day the defense issued new character witnesses for the Jordanos, one being another Gretna grocer, Santo Vicari, who testified that someone had tried to chisel through a panel in one of his doors only two nights before the attack upon the Cortimiglias and at a time when he knew the whereabouts of the Jordanos. When Iorlando Jordano took the stand he said that he thought Rosie Cortimiglia was not in her right mind. He had loved little Mary. She had called him "Grampa." Only a lunatic could imagine he would have harmed her. He had been as shocked and grieved by the cruel attack as if he had been the child's grandfather. He had run to the Cortimiglias' home in answer to Rosie's screams, then his son had come, later his wife. All they had tried to do was help. Now they were accused of the attack. His boy was a good boy.

Frank Jordano was on the stand two hours. He answered Mr. Byrnes's questions in a strong voice and he did not waver under the district attorney's cross-examination. He had been at a dance with his girl that night. He had lied about that, yes, but it had been to protect his sweetheart and to keep her out of this. He had been home in bed a little while when he heard Rosie Cortimiglia's shrieks. He had followed his father to the Cortimiglias'. His father had been trying to help. His mother had bathed Charles Cortimiglia's face.

Sheriff L. H. Marrero testified that Rosie Cortimiglia had accused the Jordanos at once. There had been no hesitation on her part to do so, he said, no doubt in her mind. She had been positive.

On the fifth day the jury had the case in their hands They were in consultation forty-five minutes. The Jordanos were found guilty. The courtroom resounded with angry shouts of protest.

A few days later sentence was passed. Frank Jordano was sentenced to be hanged. Iorlando Jordano was sentenced to life imprisonment.

The Axeman went back to work on August 10.

Early that morning a New Orleans grocer, Steve Boca, tottered out of his home in Elysian Fields Avenue and staggered down the alley next door to the entrance of the room where his friend Frank Genusa slept. When Genusa opened the door he caught Boca in his arms. The man's skull was split and he was drenched with blood. A Charity Hospital ambulance was called.

Boca recovered but he could tell nothing. He had awakened, seen the form over his bed and the blow coming. When he was conscious once more he had gone to Genusa for refuge. He could give no description of his attacker.

Police found all the usual signs of the Axeman's visit: the door panel was removed; the axe was in the kitchen; there had been no theft. Using a method that seemed usual with them, they then arrested Genusa. Boca himself defended him and he was released after a few days.

It was announced in the papers that William F. Byrnes was taking the Jordano case to the Supreme Court. It was said that most of the citizens of Gretna believed the father and son innocent, considered their conviction a miscarriage of justice. Rosie Cortimiglia was reported in hiding in New Orleans.

On September 2 William Carlson, a New Orleans druggist, heard a noise at his back door while he was reading late in the night. He got his revolver, called several times, then fired through the door. When he went outside no one was visible, but police rushing to the scene found what they believed were the marks of a chisel on one of the panels of the door.

On September 3, Sarah Laumann, a girl of nineteen, who lived alone, was found by neighbors who broke into her house when she failed to answer her bell. She was unconscious in her bed, several teeth knocked out, her head injured. A bloody axe was found beneath an open window. This time the Axeman had not used a door panel for entry. Was this another of his victims? It was thought so. Miss Laumann had a brain concussion, but recovered. She could recall nothing. Evidently the attack had taken place while she slept.

There were no more Axeman appearances until October 27. Early that morning Mrs. Mike Pepitone, wife of a grocer, awoke to hear sounds of a struggle in the room next to her own, where her husband slept. She reached the door between the rooms just in time to see a man disappear through another exit in her husband's room. Mike Pepitone lay on his bed covered with blood. Blood splattered the wall and a picture of the Virgin above the bed. Mrs. Pepitone shrieked and the six small children were awakened by their mother's screams. When the police arrived they found the signatures—the chiseled door panel was there and the axe lay on the back porch. Pepitone was dead. His wife could tell police little or nothing. She had seen the man, but her description was no less general than others they had received. It seemed as hopeless a case as the rest. By now they had a feeling that there was nothing to do but wait for the Axeman to strike again. Would it go on forever?

But it did not go on forever. No one knew it then, but it was over. Mike Pepitone was the last victim. Calls continued to reach the police from frightened citizens night after night, but all turned out to be scares and nothing more.

Throughout the months that passed and became a year, a number of arrests were made, but in vain. New Orleans began to relax again and discussion of the Axeman cases became infrequent. Only the

Jordanos languished in the Gretna jail, awaiting the new trial their attorney had promised them—or the hanging of Frank.

Then, on December 7, 1920, Rosie Cortimiglia appeared in the city room of the *Times-Picayune* and asked to speak to a reporter. Later accounts of her visit were highly dramatic. Rosie was utterly changed. Thin and ill, clothed in black, her face almost unrecognizable as that of the pretty young woman of a year before, she fell to her knees before the reporter assigned to interview her, screaming, "I lied! I lied! God forgive me, I lied!"

Everyone in the offices gathered about. This was it, great, sensational copy.

Rosie remained on her knees, tears streaming down her cheeks. "I lied," she said. "It was not the Jordanos who killed my baby. I did not know the man who attacked us."

Helped to her feet and then to a chair, Rosie leaned forward, her hands clutching her now scarred and pitted cheeks.

"Look at me!" she cried. "I have had smallpox. I have suffered for my lie. I hated the Jordanos, but they did not kill Mary. Saint Joseph told me I must tell the truth no matter what it cost me. You mustn't let them hang Frank!"

Rosie was taken to the Gretna jail at once. On the way she babbled incessantly of her suffering and that she had lied. She said Sheriff Marrero had forced the accusation on the Jordanos from her. Then she said she had made it simply out of hatred for the Jordanos.

In Frank Jordano's cell she threw herself on the floor and kissed his feet, crying, "Forgive me! Forgive me! You are innocent!"

Raising her head, she said, "God has punished me more than you. Look at my face! I have lost everything—my baby is dead, my husband has left me, I have had smallpox. God has punished me until I have suffered more than you!"

The Jordanos were soon free. There had been no real evidence against them but the testimony of Rosie Cortimiglia, and so there was no reason to hold them longer.

Frank Jordano visited the offices of the *Times-Picayune* on the day of his release. He said he would marry his sweetheart at once. He had always known God would not let him die for a crime of which he was innocent. He stood at a window of an office in the newspaper building and looked out into Lafayette Square just across the street, where the sun was bright on the greens. "Ain't it fine!" he said. "It all looks fine!"

But nothing had been solved about the Axeman crimes. It was almost as if the cruel attacks had been committed by a supernatural being, by a "fell demon from the hottest hell," as the letter purporting to be from the Axeman had put it. Many had been charged and all had been freed. No proof of the criminal's identity existed. With the freeing of the Jordanos the Axeman returned to the conversation of Orleanians and, briefly, to the editorial pages of the newspapers. Who was the Axeman? Had there been one Axeman or several—or many? Had each attack been the work of a different person? Or all of one?

Then, almost simultaneously with the confession of Rosie Cortimiglia, New Orleans police learned of a strange occurrence in Los Angeles. At first the news seemed almost unbelievable. Later they seem to have been anxious to believe it.

On December 2, 1920, an Orleanian named Joseph Mumfre was walking down a Los Angeles business street in the early afternoon. A "woman in black and heavily veiled" stepped from the doorway of a building, a revolver in her hand, and emptied the gun into Mumfre. He fell dead on the sunny sidewalk and the woman stood over him, making no attempt to escape or even to move.

Taken to the police station, the woman in black said at first that her name was Mrs. Esther Albano and refused to say why she had shot Mumfre. Days later she changed her mind and told Los Angeles detectives that she was Mrs. Mike Pepitone, the widow of the last victim of the New Orleans Axeman.

"He was the Axeman," she said. "I saw him running from my husband's room. I believe he killed all those people."

Immediately New Orleans police were drawn into the case. They knew a lot about Mumfre. He had a criminal record and had spent much time in prison. Dates were checked carefully. He had been released from a prison term in 1911, just before the slaughter of the Schiambras, of Cruti and of Rosetti. Then he had gone back to jail and had been freed only a few weeks before the Maggio attack began the latest series of such crimes. In the lull between the end of August, 1918, and March, 1919, he had once more been in jail on a burglary charge; this was the span of time between the attack on Mrs. Lowe and the others of that period and the next outbreak that began with the Cortimiglia family. It was known that Mumfre had left New Orleans just after the slaying of Mike Pepitone.

That much fitted. It was almost too perfect. Yet there was no proof that Mumfre was the Axeman. As the newspapers pointed out, the dates might be mere coincidence. It was thought he was the man who had attacked Mike Pepitone. All else remained a matter of conjecture.

Mrs. Pepitone was tried in a Los Angeles court in April. She pleaded guilty and the proceedings were brief. Her attorney's plea was justifiable homicide. This did not hold, but there was much sympathy in her favor. She received a sentence of ten years, but in little more than three she was freed, and subsequently vanished from sight.

Were the Axeman mysteries solved?

Most Orleanians did not think so and do not think so yet. Of course no one will ever know now if Mumfre was guilty of all the crimes, of some of them or only of the murder of Mike Pepitone. Probably the most general consensus of opinion in New Orleans, both among the police and the citizens, always remained that there was not one Axeman at all, but at least several.

Was the Mafia responsible?

Mumfre was not known to be a member of any such organization, but that in itself meant nothing. Membership was always secret. Yet, as Detective Dantonio said, the crimes never fitted the Mafia pattern. The Mafia did not attack anyone but Italians and they never murdered women. Besides it was thought the Mafia had passed from New Orleans forever with the apprehension of the kidnappers of little Walter Lamana.

If the Mafia did still exist and the Italians who were attacked were its victims, what of Mrs. Lowe, Mrs. Schneider, Sarah Laumann and the others who were not Italians yet had also been the Axeman's prey?

It is true that in all these cases the exact pattern of the Axeman's technique was not followed. Often one or more of his habits were omitted. He chose a different means of entry, for instance. Did this prove the assailant was not the same? Did it then mean that when the steps were followed carefully—when the door panel was chiseled out, the axe borrowed from the victim himself and left behind, and nothing was stolen—that the same murderer had called?

Was the following of the pattern indicative of the fact that the killer was a homicidal maniac, the "Dr. Jekyll and Mr. Hyde" of Detective Dantonio's theorizing? Adherence to such a pattern is thought to suggest the insane killer, who kills for pleasure and no other motive.

It must also be remembered that most of the victims were alike—Italian grocers. Did someone hate Italian grocers? Did someone want to kill all the Italian grocers in New Orleans—perhaps in the world? If that is so, we come full circle again. What of the others who were not Italian grocers?

Confusion did much harm in all cases. Then there were the false accusations—of Harriet Lowe against Besumer, of Rosie Cortimiglia against the Jordanos. There were lots of lies, without a doubt. There was fear. Probably some of the victims and their relatives did not tell all they knew, either for fear that the Mafia still existed and that they might be further punished, or because they knew the Mafia did exist and that one of its members would extort reprisals from someone in their family if they talked.

All we know now is that the Axeman did vanish from New Orleans about the time Joseph Mumfre left the city and that he never returned after Mumfre was killed. It is extremely doubtful that anyone will ever know more. The Axeman came and struck and went away. The citizens of New Orleans can only hope that they never hear the sound of the chisel at work on the door panel again.

STONE FROM THE STARS

By Valentina Zhuravleva

. . . .

*What was it about the meteorite that so frightened
the scientist Nikonov?*

Five hundred years ago a meteorite fell not far from the German town of Enzisheim on the Upper Rhine. The townsfolk chained it to the wall of their church so that the gift of heaven might not be withdrawn, and on it they engraved the inscription: MANY KNOW MUCH ABOUT THIS STONE, EVERYONE KNOWS SOMETHING, BUT NO ONE KNOWS QUITE ENOUGH.

Often as I think of the history of the Pamir meteorite I recall this old inscription. Yes, I know a great deal about it, more perhaps than anyone else, but by no means all. Yet the main facts about this remarkable phenomenon stand out all too clearly in my memory.

It was six months ago that the first news of the meteorite appeared in the papers—a brief item to the effect that a large meteorite had fallen in the Pamirs. My curiosity was aroused at once.

One would think that the falling of a meteorite would hardly be of interest to a biochemist. We biochemists, however, eagerly watch for every report of meteorites, for these fragments of "heavenly stones" can tell us a great deal about the origin of life on Earth. In short, we study the hydrocarbons found in meteorites.

The next newspaper report about the Pamir meteorite announced that an expedition had located it and had brought it down by helicopter from an altitude of four thousand meters. It was a huge chunk of stone about three meters long and weighing over four tons.

I had just finished reading the item, making a mental note to call up Nikonov about it in the morning, when the telephone rang. It was Nikonov.

Before I go any further let me say that Yevgeny Nikonov, whom I had known from my school days, was a man of extraordinary self-possession and restraint. I never remember seeing him rattled or upset. But now, as soon as he began speaking, I could tell that something out of the ordinary had happened. His voice was hoarse, his speech so incoherent that it took me some time to understand what he was saying.

All I could make out was that I must come at once, instantly and without delay, to the Institute of Astrophysics.

I called a car and in a few minutes was speeding through the quiet and deserted streets. A fine drizzle was falling and the colored lights of neon advertisements and signs were mirrored in the wet pavements. As I drove through the sleeping city I thought of all those who were not sleeping at this late hour, of those who at their microscopes, test tubes and notebooks filled with long rows of formulas, were intently searching for new knowledge. I thought of all the discoveries that were being made, changing the pattern of life and opening new vistas to the wondering gaze of man.

The tall building of the Institute of Astrophysics was ablaze with lights. It occurred to me that perhaps the Pamir meteorite might have something to do with all this activity, but I dismissed the thought. What could there be so unusual about a meteorite to cause such a flurry?

The institute hummed like a hornets' nest. People were rushing up and down the corridors with an air of suppressed excitement. Animated voices could be heard issuing from half-open doors.

I went straight to Nikonov's office. He met me in the doorway. I must admit that until that moment I had not attached much importance to this night summons. After all, we scientists are apt to exaggerate our successes and failures. I myself have often wanted to shout from the housetops when, after endless experiments, I have at last achieved some long-awaited result.

But Nikonov . . . One had to know the man as well as I did to realize how shaken he was.

He shook my hand in silence and with that quick, wordless handshake some of his excitement was communicated to me.

"The Pamir meteorite?" I asked.

"Yes," he replied.

He pulled out a heap of photographs and spread them out in front of me. They were photos of the meteorite. I examined them carefully, hardly knowing what to expect, although by now I was prepared for something extraordinary.

However, the meteorite looked exactly like dozens of others I had seen both in life and on photos: a spindle-shaped chunk of what appeared to be porous stone, with fused edges.

I handed the photos back to Nikonov. He shook his head and said in a strange, muffled voice: "This is not a meteorite. Under the stone covering is a metal cylinder. There is a living creature inside that cylinder."

Looking back at the events of that memorable night I am surprised that it took me so long to grasp the meaning of Nikonov's words. Yet it was simple enough, although the very simplicity of it made the whole thing seem so unreal, so fantastic.

The meteorite turned out to be a spaceship. The outer stone envelope, which was only about seven centimeters thick, served as a shield for a cylinder made of some heavy dark metal. Nikonov presumed (as was later confirmed) that the stone shield was designed to serve as protection against meteorites and to prevent overheating. What I had mistaken for porousness of the stone were indentations made by meteorites. Judging by the vast number of them the spaceship must have been many years on the way.

"If the cylinder were solid metal," said Nikonov, "it would weigh no less than twenty tons. As it is, it weighs a little more than two. There are some fine wires attached to it in three places. They are broken, which suggests that some apparatus outside the cylinder was torn off during the fall. A galvanometer connected to the broken ends of the wires registered weak electrical impulses."

"But why are you so certain that there is a living being inside the cylinder?" I objected. "Most likely it is some automatic device."

"No, it is alive," he answered quickly. "It knocks."

"Knocks?" I echoed, puzzled.

"Yes." Nikonov's voice was trembling. "When you approach the cylinder whoever is inside starts knocking. It seems to be able to see in some way. . . ."

The phone rang. Nikonov snatched up the receiver. I saw his face change.

"The cylinder has been subjected to ultrasonic tests," he said, laying the receiver down slowly. "The metal is less than twenty millimeters thick. There is no metal inside. . . ."

It struck me that there was something faulty in Nikonov's reasoning.

"Surely," I objected, "a cylinder less than three meters long and about sixty centimeters in diameter is hardly large enough to accommodate a living creature, let alone the water, food and diverse air-conditioning apparatus required."

"Wait," said Nikonov. "In about fifteen minutes we shall go and see for ourselves. I am waiting for someone else. The cylinder is being installed in a sealed chamber."

"But you must admit your assumption is a bit fantastic," I persisted. "There can't be any human beings inside."

"What exactly do you mean by human beings?"

"Well, thinking creatures."

"With arms and legs?" For the first time Nikonov smiled.

"Well, yes," I replied.

"No, of course, there are no beings like that in the spaceship," he said. "But there are thinking beings nevertheless. What they look like is hard to say."

I could not agree. I reminded him how Europeans, prior to the epoch of the great geographical discoveries, had imagined the inhabitants of unknown lands. They had pictured men with six arms, men with dogs' heads, dwarfs, giants. And they found that in Australia and in America and in New Zealand people were made exactly as in Europe. The same conditions of life and laws of development lead to identical results.

"Precisely," Nikonov said. "But what makes you think we are dealing here with conditions of life similar to ours?"

I explained that the existence and development of the higher forms of proteins is possible only within narrow margins of temperature, pressure and radiation. Hence the evolution of the organic world may be said to follow similar patterns everywhere.

"My dear friend," said Nikonov. "You are a leading biochemist, the biggest authority on biochemical synthesis." He made a mock bow, his calm, whimsical self again. "As far as the synthesis of proteins is concerned, I agree with you entirely. But you will forgive me if I say that one may know a great deal about making bricks without knowing much about architecture."

I did not take offense. Frankly speaking, I had never given much thought to the evolution of organic matter on other planets. After all, it was not my field.

"The medieval conception of men with dogs' heads living at the other end of the world did turn out to be nonsense," Nikonov went on. "But with the exception of climate, conditions on our Earth are everywhere more or less the same. And where they do differ, man differs as well. In the Peruvian Andes, at a height of three and a half kilometers, there lives a tribe of undersized Indians whose average weight is no more than fifty kilograms, but whose chest and lung expansion is one and a half times that of the average European. The process of adaptation to life in a rarefied mountain atmosphere has gradually changed the physical characteristics of the organism. Now just imagine how different from conditions on our Earth life on other planets may be. There is the force of gravity, to begin with. You seem to have forgotten about that. On Mercury, for example, the force of gravity is one-fourth that on Earth. If people existed on Mercury they would hardly need highly developed lower limbs. And on Jupiter the force of gravity is much greater than on Earth. For all we know under those conditions the evolution of vertebrates might not have led to a vertical posture of the body at all."

I saw an obvious flaw in that argument and I seized my opportunity.

"My dear friend," I said. "You are a prominent astrophysicist, the greatest living authority on spectral analysis of stellar atmospheres. So long as you stick to the planets I agree with you entirely. But one may know all about making bricks. . . . What I meant to say is that you have forgotten about hands—without hands there can be no labor and it is labor that created man, when it comes to that. But if the body is in a horizontal position all four limbs would be needed for support."

"Yes, but why should four be the limit?"

"Men with six arms?"

"Perhaps. On planets where the force of gravity is very great the vertebrates would most likely develop precisely in that direction. But there are other factors. The condition of the planet's surface, for instance. If the Earth had been permanently covered with oceans the evolution of the animal world would have taken an entirely different course."

"Mermaids?" I jokingly suggested.

"Possibly," Nikonov replied imperturbably. "Life in the ocean is constantly developing although much more slowly than on dry land. There are certain things essential to all rational beings, wherever they happen to live: a developed brain, a complex nervous system and organs enabling them to work and move. But this is hardly enough to give one any real idea of their general appearance."

"But surely," I persisted, unwilling to yield, "it is not altogether unlikely that thinking beings resembling ourselves may live on planets with conditions similar to our own, is it?"

"It is not impossible," he agreed. "But highly improbable. You disregard one very important factor—time. Man's appearance changes. Ten million years ago our ancestors had tails and no foreheads. How do we know what men will look like ten million years hence? It would be absurd to assume that man's appearance will never change. You talk about similar planets. True, there are planets with conditions similar to our own. But it is hardly likely that the evolution of rational beings on these planets would coincide in time as well. In a word, my dear friend, 'There are more things on heaven and earth . . .' "

I cannot remember all the details of that conversation. There were so many interruptions—the telephone rang constantly, people hurried in and out of the room, and Nikonov kept consulting his watch. Yet looking back at it now it seems to me that that conversation was in itself significant. For fantastic as our surmises might have seemed, the reality exceeded our wildest speculations.

It all seems simple enough to me now. If a ship from another planetary system reached us through boundless space, knowledge on that unknown planet had clearly advanced to a degree far beyond our earthly conception. That alone should have warned us not to jump to conclusions.

The arrival of Academician Astakhov, a specialist in astronautical medicine, cut short our conversation.

"What sort of an engine has it?" he demanded from the threshold.

He stood in the doorway, his ear cupped in his hand, waiting for an answer.

I felt annoyed with myself for not having asked that obvious question. The answer would have told us many things—the technical level of the newcomers, the distance they had flown, how much time they had journeyed in space, what rates of acceleration their bodies could endure. . . .

"There is no engine," said Nikonov. "The metallic cylinder underneath the stone envelope is absolutely smooth."

"No engine?" echoed Astakhov. He pondered this in silence for a few minutes, a look of profound amazement on his face. "But in that case . . . In that case they must have a gravitational engine."

"Yes," nodded Nikonov. "That's the answer, most likely."

"Can you power a ship by gravitation?" I asked.

"Theoretically you can," Nikonov replied. "There is no natural force which man will not eventually be able to understand and subdue. It is only a matter of time. True, so far we know very little about gravitation. We know Newton's law: every body in the Universe attracts every other body with a force that is directly proportional to the product of their masses, and inversely proportional to the square of the distance between their centers. We know, theoretically at least, that the only limit to gravitational acceleration is the speed of light. But that is about all. But the cause, the nature of gravitation—that we don't know."

The phone rang again. Nikonov picked up the receiver, answered briefly and hung up.

"Come," he said to us. "They are waiting for us."

We went out into the corridor.

"Some physicists believe that gravitation is a property of a specific type of particles called gravitons. I am not quite sure of that hypothesis. But if it is true, then the gravitons ought to be as much smaller than atomic nuclei as the atomic nuclei are smaller than ordinary bodies. The concentration of energy must be immeasurably greater in such minute dimensions than in the atomic nucleus."

We hurried down the steep winding staircase leading to the basement and along a narrow corridor. A group of institute personnel were waiting for us outside a massive metal door. Someone pressed a button and the door moved slowly aside.

There was the spaceship: a cylinder of some dark and very smooth metal, resting on two supports. The stone outer covering, cracked in several places, had been removed. Three fine wires hung from the base of the cylinder.

Nikonov who stood closer than the others to the cylinder took a step toward it and at once a muffled knocking sounded from within. It was not the rhythmic mechanical beat of a machine. It suggested the presence of some living creature. It occurred to me that it might be some animal—after all, had we not sent monkeys, dogs and rabbits up in our own space rockets?

Nikonov moved away and the knocking ceased. In the ensuing

silence someone's hoarse breathing could be distinctly heard.

Strangely enough, no thought of the new epoch that had dawned for science entered my mind at that moment. It was only afterward in recalling the scene that I found every detail of it stamped on my memory: the low-ceilinged room flooded with electric light, and in the middle—the dark, gleaming cylinder, and the tense, excited faces of the men gathered around it.

We set to work at once. It was the engineers' task to determine who was inside the cylinder; Astakhov's and mine to provide two-way biological protection—to protect the living creatures within from our earthly bacteria, and ourselves from any bacteria the space-ship might contain.

I do not know exactly how the engineers tackled their part of the job. I had no time to see what they were doing. I only remember that they subjected the cylinder to ultrasound and gamma radiation. Astakhov and I went to work on the biological end. After some discussion (Astakhov's being hard of hearing delayed things some-what), it was decided to open the cylinder with manipulators oper-ated from a distance. The sealed chamber in which the spaceship stood was to be treated with ultraviolet rays.

We worked at top speed, conscious of the living creature nearby awaiting our assistance. We did everything that was humanly possible to do.

The manipulators using a hydrogen burner carefully cut through the metal covering in which the spaceship's apparatus was encased. Through slit windows in the concrete wall of the room we watched the remarkable accuracy and precision with which the huge mechani-cal hands worked. Slowly, centimenter by centimeter, the flame of the burner cut through the strange, highly refractory metal, until at last the base of the cylinder could be removed.

What lay inside was living matter if not a living creature—a giant brain throbbing with life.

I use the word "brain" solely for want of any other word to describe what I saw. For a moment it looked to me like an exact replica, if magnified, of the human brain. On closer examination, however, I saw where I had been mistaken. It was only part of a brain. What was missing, we discovered later, were all those depart-ments, all those centers that govern the emotions and instincts. More-over, it had only a few of the innumerable "thinking" centers of the human brain, though these were enormously magnified.

To be more exact, it was a neutron-computing machine with artificial brain matter in place of the usual electronic diodes and triodes. I surmised this at once from a great number of minor indications, but my supposition later proved to be correct.

Somewhere, on some unknown planet, science had advanced far beyond our own. We on Earth have only begun to synthesize the simplest protein molecules. *They* had succeeded in synthesizing the highest forms of organic matter. We biochemists too are working toward that end, but we are still very far from our goal.

I must admit that the contents of the spaceship were a great surprise to all of us. All except Astakhov. He was the first to recover the power of speech.

"There you are!" he exclaimed. "Exactly what I predicted! You may remember what I wrote two years ago. . . . Interstellar distances are too great for man. Only spaceships that operate completely automatically can undertake journeys from one island universe to another. Automatically! Electronic machines, perhaps? No, too complicated. Out of the question. What is needed is the most perfect of all mechanisms—the brain. Two years ago I wrote about this. But some biochemists did not agree with me. I said that for interstellar travel we must have bio-automatons, capable of cellular regeneration. . . ."

Astakhov had indeed published an article two years before, advancing this idea. I confess it had sounded utterly fantastic to me. Yet he had been right after all. He had foreseen the possibility of synthesizing the highest form of matter—brain tissue—thus anticipating scientific progress by many centuries.

It must be admitted that we scientists who work in narrow fields show little imagination in predicting the future. We are far too engrossed in what we are doing in the present to foresee the shape of things to come. There are automobiles today, and in a hundred years there will be automobiles too, only with far greater speeds. Similarly we cannot imagine that the airplane of the future will differ greatly from the present except in the matter of speed. But alas, that only shows how limited our vision is. And that is why the shape of the Future is often more clearly envisioned by nonspecialists.

Sometimes that Future seems altogether incredible, altogether fantastic and unattainable. Nevertheless it comes to pass! Heinrich Hertz, who was the first to study electromagnetic vibrations, rejected the idea of wireless communication. Yet a few years later Alexander Popov invented the radio.

Yes, I had not believed in Astakhov's idea. In order to produce bio-automatons some extremely complex problems would have to be solved. We would have to synthesize the highest forms of proteins, learn to control bio-electronic processes, induce living and nonliving matter to work together. All this seemed to me to belong to the realm of sheer fantasy. Yet here right before our eyes was that distant Future. True, it was the fruit of the endeavors of men from another planet than ours, but nonetheless tangible confirmation of the great truth that there can be no limits to scientific knowledge, no idea too bold to be realized.

We did not know anything about the atmosphere inside the cylinder and how our own atmosphere would affect the artificial brain. Therefore, compressor units and gas containers were held in readiness to adjust the atmosphere inside the sealed chamber to that in the cylinder. When the cylinder was opened the atmosphere inside it was found to consist of one-fifth oxygen and four-fifths helium at a pressure one-tenth greater than that on Earth. The brain continued to pulsate, though perhaps a little faster than before.

There was a whining sound as the compressors went into action to raise the pressure. The first stage of the work was over.

I went upstairs to Nikonov's office. I moved his armchair over to the window and raised the blinds. Outside dusk was settling over the city. Night had come again, the second night since I had been summoned to the institute. Yet it seemed I had been there only a few hours.

So the atmosphere in the spaceship was 20 percent oxygen—the same as in the Earth's atmosphere. Was this fortuitous? No. This was exactly the concentration the human organism needs. Hence, there must be some sort of circulatory system in the spaceship. But if one part of the brain should die, circulation would be disrupted and hence the entire brain would perish.

This thought sent me hurrying downstairs again.

Even as I recall our efforts to save the artificial brain I am overwhelmed again by a feeling of impotence and bitterness.

What could we do? Nothing. Nothing but look on helplessly while the brain that had come to us from outer space, the brain created by the inhabitants of another planet, slowly expired.

The lower part dried up and turned black. Only the upper section remained throbbingly alive. When anyone approached it the throbbing became quick and feverish, as if the brain were calling frantically for help.

By now we knew how the brain was supplied with oxygen. As I

had presumed, it breathed with the help of a chemical compound resembling hemoglobin. We had also studied the devices that fed the brain, generated oxygen and removed the carbon dioxide from the atmosphere.

Yet we could do nothing to halt the destruction of the brain cells. Somewhere, on an unknown planet, thinking beings had been able to synthesize the most highly organized matter—brain matter. They had created an artificial brain and sent it out into space. There was no doubt that many of the secrets of the Universe were recorded in those brain cells. But we could not fathom them. The brain was dying before our eyes.

We tried everything, from antibiotics to surgery. Nothing helped.

In my capacity as chairman of the Special Commission of the Academy of Sciences I called a conference of my colleagues to ascertain whether there was anything else that could be done.

It was in the early hours before dawn. The scientists sat in the small conference hall in gloomy silence, their faces drawn with fatigue.

Nikonov passed a hand over his face as if to brush away his weariness.

"There is nothing more to be done," he said in a flat voice.

The others confirmed this tragic fact.

Throughout the next six days, while the few remaining cells of the artificial brain still lived, we kept up constant observations. It is hard to enumerate all that we learned in that time. But the most interesting was the discovery of the substance that protected the living tissue from radiation.

The outer shell of the spaceship was comparatively thin and could be easily penetrated by cosmic rays. This had prompted us from the very outset to search for some protective substance in the cells of the bio-automaton itself. And we found it. A minute concentration of this substance immunizes the body against the most powerful radiation. This discovery will enable us to simplify the design of our own spaceships. It obviates the need for heavy metal shields for the atomic reactor, and this brings the era of space travel in atom-powered ships much closer.

Extremely interesting too was the system for regeneration of oxygen. A colony of seaweed unknown to us and weighing less than a kilogram which absorbed carbon dioxide and exhaled oxygen had provided the ship with adequate "air conditioning" for many years.

But all these are purely biological discoveries. The knowledge gained in the sphere of engineering is perhaps even more important. As Astakhov had surmised, the spaceship was powered by a gravitation engine. Engineers have not yet grasped the principle of the mechanism. But it may be safely asserted that our physicists will have substantially to revise their ideas about the nature of gravitation. The epoch of atomic engineering will evidently be followed by an epoch of gravitational engineering, when men will have still greater sources of energy and speed at their disposal.

The outer covering of the spaceship consisted of an alloy of titanium and beryllium. As distinct from the usual alloys, the entire casing was made of a single-crystal metal. Our metals consist, roughly speaking, of myriads of crystals. And although each of them is strong enough, they do not cohere too well. The future belongs to the single-crystal metal, which will have properties we still have to discover. Moreover, by governing the systems of crystallization, man will be able to govern its optical properties, durability and heat conductivity at will.

Nevertheless, the most important discovery of all, though not as yet deciphered, is connected with the artificial brain. The three wires attached to the cylinder proved to be connected with the brain through a rather complicated amplifying system. For six days sensitive oscillographs registered the bio-automaton's currents. These currents were nothing like those of the human brain. And this is where the difference between the artificial and the human brain was manifested. After all, the brain of the spaceship was essentially nothing more than a cybernetic device, with living cells taking the place of electronic tubes. With all its complex structure this brain was immeasurably simpler and, as it were, more specialized than the human brain. Hence its electrical signals resembled a code more than the extremely complex pattern of biocurrents in the human brain.

Thousands of meters of oscillograms were recorded in those six days. Will it be possible to decipher them? What will they tell us? The story of a voyage through space perhaps?

It is hard to answer these questions. We are continuing to study the spaceship and each day brings some new discovery.

So far many know much about this stone, everyone knows something, but nobody knows enough. But the day is not far off when the last secrets of the star stone will be fathomed.

And then spaceships powered with gravitational engines will set out from the Earth for the boundless expanses of the universe. They will be manned not by human beings—for man's life is brief and the Universe is infinite. The interstellar ships will be manned by bio-automatons. After voyaging thousands of years in space, after reaching distant island universes, the ships will come back to Earth bearing the unfading torch of Knowledge.

THE QUEEN OF SPADES
By Alexander Pushkin

. . . .

The old countess had a fatal fascination
for the young officer, but he chose to approach her
through her young companion.

1

When bleak was the weather
They would meet together
For cards—God forgive them!
Some would win, others lost,
And they chalked up the cost
In bleak autumn weather
When they met together.

There was a card party in the rooms of Narumov, an officer of the Horse Guards. The long winter night had passed unnoticed and it was after four in the morning when the company sat down to supper. Those who had won enjoyed their food; the others sat absent-mindedly in front of empty plates. But when the champagne appeared conversation became more lively and general.

"How did you fare, Surin?" Narumov asked.

"Oh, I lost, as usual. I must confess, I have no luck: I stick to *mirandole*, never get excited, never lose my head and yet I never win."

"Do you mean to tell me you were not once tempted to back the red the whole evening? Your self-control amazes me."

"But look at Hermann," exclaimed one of the party, pointing to a young officer of the Engineers. "Never held a card in his hands, never made a bet in his life, and yet he sits up till five in the morning watching us play."

"Cards interest me very much," said Hermann, "but I am not in a position to risk the necessary in the hope of acquiring the superfluous."

"Hermann is a German: he's careful, that's what he is!" remarked Tomsky. "But if there is one person I can't understand it is my grandmother, Countess Anna Fedotovna."

"Why is that?" the guests cried.

"I cannot conceive how it is that my grandmother does not play."

"But surely there is nothing surprising in an old lady in the eighties not wanting to gamble?" said Narumov.

"Then you don't know about her?"

"No, nothing, absolutely nothing!"

"Well, listen then. I must tell you that some sixty years ago my grandmother went to Paris and was quite the rage there. People would run after her to catch a glimpse of *la Vénus moscovite*; Richelieu was at her beck and call, and Grandmamma maintains that he very nearly blew his brains out because of her cruelty to him. In those days ladies used to play faro. One evening at the Court she lost a very considerable sum to the Duke of Orleans. When she got home she told my grandfather of her loss while removing the beauty spots from her face and untying her farthingale, and commanded him to pay her debt. My grandfather, so far as I remember, acted as a sort of major-domo to my grandmother. He feared her like fire; however, when he heard of such a frightful gambling loss he almost went out of his mind, fetched the bills they owed and pointed out to her that in six months they had spent half a million rubles and that in Paris they had neither their Moscow nor their Saratov estates upon which to draw, and flatly refused to pay. Grandmamma gave him a box on the ear and retired to bed without him as a sign of her displeasure. The following morning she sent for her husband, hoping that the simple punishment had had its effect, but she found him as obdurate as ever. For the first time in her life she went so far as to reason with him and explain, thinking to rouse his conscience and arguing with condescension, that there were debts and debts, and that a prince was different from a coach builder. But it was not a bit of good— Grandfather just would not hear of it. 'Once and for all, no!' Grandmamma did not know what to do. Among her close acquaintances was a very remarkable man. You have heard of Count Saint-

Germain, about whom so many marvelous stories are told. You know that he posed as the Wandering Jew and claimed to have discovered the elixir of life and the philosopher's stone, and so on. People laughed at him as a charlatan, and Casanova in his *Memoirs* says that he was a spy. Be that as it may, Saint-Germain, in spite of the mystery that surrounded him, had a most dignified appearance and was a very amiable person in society. Grandmamma is still to this day quite devoted to his memory and gets angry if anyone speaks of him with disrespect. Grandmamma knew that Saint-Germain had plenty of money at his disposal. She decided to appeal to him, and wrote a note asking him to come and see her immediately. The eccentric old man came at once and found her in terrible distress. She described in the blackest colors her husband's inhumanity, and ended by declaring that she laid all her hopes on his friendship and kindness. Saint-Germain pondered. 'I could oblige you with the sum you want,' he said, 'but I know that you would not be easy until you had repaid me, and I should not like to involve you in fresh trouble. There is another way out—you could win it back.'

" 'But my dear count,' answered Grandmamma, 'I tell you I have no money at all.'

" 'That does not matter,' Saint-Germain replied. 'Listen now to what I am going to tell you.'

"And he revealed to her a secret which all of us would give a great deal to know. . . ."

The young gamblers redoubled their attention. Tomsky lit his pipe, puffed away for a moment and continued:

"That very evening Grandmamma appeared at Versailles, at the *jeu de la reine*. The Duke of Orleans kept the bank. Grandmamma lightly excused herself for not having brought the money to pay off her debt, inventing some little story by way of explanation, and began to play against him. She selected three cards and played them one after the other: all three won, and Grandmamma retrieved her loss completely."

"Luck!" said one of the party.

"A fairy tale!" remarked Hermann.

"Marked cards, perhaps," put in a third.

"I don't think so," replied Tomsky impressively.

"What!" said Narumov. "You have a grandmother who knows how to hit upon three lucky cards in succession, and you haven't learnt her secret yet?"

"That's the deuce of it!" Tomsky replied. "She had four sons, one of whom was my father; all four were desperate gamblers, and yet she did not reveal her secret to a single one of them, though it would not have been a bad thing for them, or for me either. But listen to what my uncle, Count Ivan Ilyich, used to say, assuring me on his word of honor that it was true. Tchaplitsky—you know him, he died a pauper after squandering millions—as a young man once lost three hundred thousand rubles, to Zorich, if I remember rightly. He was in despair. Grandmamma was always very severe on the follies of young men, but somehow she took pity on Tchaplitsky. She gave him three cards, which he was to play one after the other, at the same time exacting from him a promise that he would never afterward touch a card so long as he lived. Tchaplitsky went to Zorich's; they sat down to play. Tchaplitsky staked fifty thousand on his first card and won; doubled his stake and won; did the same again, won back his loss and ended up in pocket. . . .

"But I say, it's time to go to bed: it is a quarter to six already."

And indeed dawn was breaking. The young men emptied their glasses and went home.

2

> *"Il paraît que monsieur est décidément pour les suivantes."*
> *"Que voulez-vous, madame? Elles sont plus fraîches."*
> —FROM A SOCIETY CONVERSATION

The old Countess X was seated before the looking glass in her dressing room. Three maids were standing around her. One held a pot of rouge, another a box of hairpins and the third a tall cap with flame-colored ribbons. The countess had not the slightest pretensions to beauty—it had faded long ago—but she still preserved all the habits of her youth, followed strictly the fashion of the seventies and gave as much time and care to her toilette as she had sixty years before. A young girl whom she had brought up sat at an embroidery frame by the window.

"Good morning, *grand'maman!*" said a young officer, coming into the room. "*Bonjour, Mademoiselle Lise. Grand'maman*, I have a favor to ask of you."

"What is it, Paul?"

"I want you to let me introduce to you a friend of mine and bring him to your ball on Friday."

"Bring him straight to the ball and introduce him to me then. Were you at the princess's last night?"

"Of course I was! It was most enjoyable: we danced until five in the morning. Mademoiselle Yeletsky looked enchanting!"

"Come, my dear! What is there enchanting about her? She isn't a patch on her grandmother, Princess Daria Petrovna. By the way, I expect Princess Daria Petrovna must have aged considerably?"

"How do you mean, aged?" Tomsky replied absent-mindedly. "She's been dead for the last seven years."

The girl at the window raised her head and made a sign to the young man. He remembered that they concealed the deaths of her contemporaries from the old countess, and bit his lip. But the countess heard the news with the utmost indifference.

"Dead! I didn't know," she said. "We were maids of honor together, and as we were being presented the empress . . ."

And for the hundredth time the countess repeated the story to her grandson.

"Well, Paul," she said at the end, "now help me to my feet. *Lise*, where is my snuff box?"

And the countess went with her maids behind the screen to finish dressing. Tomsky was left *à deux* with the young girl.

"Who is it you want to introduce?" Lizaveta Ivanovna asked softly.

"Narumov. Do you know him?"

"No. Is he in the army?"

"Yes."

"In the Engineers?"

"No, Horse Guards. What made you think he was in the Engineers?"

The girl laughed and made no answer.

"Paul!" the countess called from behind the screen. "Send me a new novel to read, only pray not one of those modern ones."

"How do you mean, *Grand'maman?*"

"I want a book in which the hero does not strangle either his father or his mother, and where there are no drowned corpses. I have a horror of drowned persons."

"There aren't any novels of that sort nowadays. Wouldn't you like something in Russian?"

"Are there any Russian novels? . . . Send me something, my dear fellow, please send me something!"

"Excuse me, *Grand'maman*: I must hurry. . . . Good-bye, Liza-veta Ivanovna! I wonder, what made you think Narumov was in the Engineers?"

And Tomsky departed from the dressing room.

Lizaveta Ivanovna was left alone. She abandoned her work and began to look out of the window. Soon, round the corner of a house on the other side of the street, a young officer appeared. Color flooded her cheeks; she took up her work again, bending her head over her embroidery frame. At that moment the countess came in, having finished dressing.

"Order the carriage, *Lise*," she said, "and let us go for a drive."

Lizaveta Ivanovna rose from her embroidery frame and began putting away her work.

"What is the matter with you, my child, are you deaf?" the countess cried. "Be quick and order the carriage."

"I will go at once," the young girl answered quietly, and ran into the anteroom.

A servant came in and handed the countess a parcel of books from Prince Paul Alexandrovich.

"Good! Tell him I am much obliged," said the countess. "*Lise*, *Lise*, where are you off to?"

"To dress."

"There is plenty of time, my dear. Sit down here. Open the first volume and read to me."

The girl took the book and read a few lines.

"Louder!" said the countess. "What is the matter with you, my dear? Have you lost your voice, or what? Wait a minute. . . . Give me that footstool. A little closer. That will do!"

Lizaveta Ivanovna read two more pages. The countess yawned.

"Throw that book away," she said. "What nonsense it is! Send it back to Prince Paul with my thanks. . . . What about the carriage?"

"The carriage is ready," said Lizaveta Ivanovna, glancing out into the street.

"How is it you are not dressed?" the countess said. "You always keep people waiting. It really is intolerable!"

Liza ran to her room. Hardly two minutes passed before the countess started ringing with all her might. Three maids rushed in at one door and a footman at the other.

"Why is it you don't come when you are called?" the countess said to them. "Tell Lizaveta Ivanovna I am waiting."

Lizaveta Ivanovna returned, wearing a hat and a pelisse.

"At last, my dear!" said the countess. "Why the finery? What is it for? . . . For whose benefit? . . . And what is the weather like? Windy, isn't it?"

"No, your ladyship," the footman answered, "there is no wind at all."

"You say anything that comes into your head! Open the window. Just as I thought: there is a wind, and a very cold one too! Dismiss the carriage. *Lise*, my child, we won't go out—you need not have dressed up after all."

"And this is my life!" Lizaveta Ivanovna thought to herself.

Indeed, Lizaveta Ivanovna was a most unfortunate creature. "Another's bread is bitter to the taste," says Dante, "and his staircase hard to climb";* and who should know the bitterness of dependence better than a poor orphan brought up by an old lady of quality? The countess was certainly not badhearted but she had all the caprices of a woman spoiled by society; she was stingy and coldly selfish, like all old people who have done with love and are out of touch with life around them. She took part in all the vanities of the fashionable world, dragged herself to balls, where she sat in a corner, rouged and attired after some bygone mode, like a misshapen but indispensable ornament of the ballroom. On their arrival the guests all went up to her and bowed low, as though in accordance with an old-established rite, and after that no one took any more notice of her. She received the whole town at her house, observing the strictest etiquette and not recognizing the faces of any of her guests. Her numerous servants, grown fat and gray in her entrance hall and the maids' quarters, did what they liked and vied with each other in robbing the decrepit old woman. Lizaveta Ivanovna was the household martyr. She poured out tea and was reprimanded for using too much sugar; she read novels aloud to the countess and was blamed for all the author's mistakes; she accompanied the countess on her drives and was answerable for the weather and the state of the roads. She was supposed to receive a salary, which was never paid in full, and yet she was expected to be

* *La Divina Commedia, Il Paradiso,* canto xvii:
> Tu proverai si come sa di sale
> lo pane altrui, e com'è duro calle
> lo scendere e 'l salir per l'altrui scale.

as well dressed as everyone else—that is, as very few indeed. In society she played the most pitiable role. Everybody knew her and nobody gave her any thought. At balls she danced only when someone was short of a partner, and the ladies would take her by the arm each time they wanted to go the cloakroom to rearrange some detail of their toilette. She was sensitive and felt her position keenly, and looked about impatiently for a deliverer to come; but the young men, calculating in their empty-headed frivolity, honored her with scant attention though Lizaveta Ivanovna was a hundred times more charming than the cold, brazen-faced heiresses they ran after. Many a time she crept away from the tedious, glittering drawing room to go and weep in her humble little attic with its wallpaper screen, chest of drawers, small looking glass and painted wooden bedstead, and where a tallow candle burned dimly in a brass candlestick.

One morning, two days after the card party described at the beginning of this story and a week before the scene we have just witnessed —one morning Lizaveta Ivanovna, sitting at her embroidery frame by the window, happened to glance out into the street and see a young Engineers officer standing stock-still, gazing at her window. She lowered her head and went on with her work. Five minutes afterward she looked out again—the young officer was still on the same spot. Not being in the habit of coquetting with passing officers, she looked out no more and went on sewing for a couple of hours without raising her head. Luncheon was announced. She got up to put away her embroidery frame and, glancing casually into the street, saw the officer again. This seemed to her somewhat strange. After luncheon she went to the window with a certain feeling of uneasiness, but the officer was no longer there, and she forgot about him. . . .

A day or so later, just as she was stepping into the carriage with the countess, she saw him again. He was standing right by the front door, his face hidden by his beaver collar; his dark eyes sparkled beneath his fur cap. Lizaveta Ivanovna felt alarmed, though she did not know why, and seated herself in the carriage, inexplicably agitated.

On returning home she ran to the window—the officer was standing in his accustomed place, his eyes fixed on her. She drew back, consumed with curiosity and excited by a feeling quite new to her.

Since then not a day had passed without the young man appearing at a certain hour beneath the windows of their house, and between him and her a sort of mute acquaintance was established. Sitting at her work she would sense his approach, and lifting her head she looked at him longer and longer every day. The young man seemed to be grateful to her for looking out: with the keen eyes of youth she saw the quick flush of his pale cheeks every time their glances met. By the end of a week she had smiled at him. . . .

When Tomsky asked the countess' permission to introduce a friend of his the poor girl's heart beat violently. But hearing that Narumov was in the Horse Guards, not the Engineers, she regretted the indiscreet question by which she had betrayed her secret to the irresponsible Tomsky.

Hermann was the son of a German who had settled in Russia and who left him some small capital sum. Being firmly convinced that it was essential for him to make certain of his independence, Hermann did not touch even the interest on his income but lived on his pay, denying himself the slightest extravagance. But since he was reserved and ambitious his companions rarely had any opportunity for making fun of his extreme parsimony. He had strong passions and an ardent imagination, but strength of character preserved him from the customary mistakes of youth. Thus, for instance, though a gambler at heart he never touched cards, having decided that his means did not allow him (as he put it) "to risk the necessary in the hope of acquiring the superfluous." And yet he spent night after night at the card tables, watching with feverish anxiety the vicissitudes of the game.

The story of the three cards had made a powerful impression upon his imagination and it haunted his mind all night. Supposing, he thought to himself the following evening as he wandered about Petersburg, supposing the old countess were to reveal her secret to me? Or tell me the three winning cards! Why shouldn't I try my luck? . . . Get introduced to her, win her favor—become her lover, perhaps. But all that would take time, and she is eighty-seven. She might be dead next week, or the day after tomorrow even! . . . And the story itself? Is it likely? No, economy, moderation and hard work are my three winning cards. With them I can treble my capital—increase it sevenfold and obtain for myself leisure and independence! Musing thus, he found himself in one of the main streets of Petersburg, in front of a house of old-fashioned architecture. The street was lined with carriages which followed one another up to the lighted porch. Out of the carriages stepped now the shapely little foot of a young beauty, now a military boot with clinking spur, or a diplomat's striped stockings and buckled shoes. Fur coats and cloaks passed in rapid procession before the majestic-looking concierge. Hermann stopped.

"Whose house is that?" he asked a watchman in his box at the corner.

"The Countess X's," the man told him. It was Tomsky's grandmother.

Hermann started. The strange story of the three cards came into his mind again. He began walking up and down past the house, thinking of its owner and her wonderful secret. It was late when he returned to his humble lodgings; he could not get to sleep for a long time, and when sleep did come he dreamed of cards, a green baize table, stacks of bank notes and piles of gold. He played card after card, resolutely turning down the corners, winning all the time. He raked in the gold and stuffed his pockets with banknotes. Waking late in the morning, he sighed over the loss of his fantastic wealth, and then, sallying forth to wander about the town again, once more found himself outside the countess' house. It was as though some supernatural force drew him there. He stopped and looked up at the windows. In one of them he saw a dark head bent over a book or some needlework. The head was raised. Hermann caught sight of a rosy face and a pair of black eyes. That moment decided his fate.

3

Vous m'écrivez, mon ange, des lettres de quatre pages plus vite que je ne puis les lire. —FROM A CORRESPONDENCE

Lizaveta Ivanovna had scarcely taken off her hat and mantle before the countess sent for her and again ordered the carriage. They went out to take their seats. Just as the two footmen were lifting the old lady and helping her through the carriage door Lizaveta Ivanovna saw her Engineers officer standing by the wheel. He seized her hand; before she had recovered from her alarm the young man had disappeared, leaving a letter between her fingers. She hid it in her glove, and for the rest of the drive neither saw nor heard anything. It was the countess' habit when they were out in the carriage to ask a constant stream of questions: "Who was that we met?"—"What bridge is this?"—"What does that signboard say?" This time Liza-

veta Ivanovna returned such random and irrelevant answers that the
countess grew angry with her.

"What is the matter with you, my dear? Have you taken leave of
your senses? Don't you hear me or understand what I say? . . . I
speak distinctly enough, thank heaven, and am not in my dotage
yet!"

Lizaveta Ivanovna paid no attention to her. When they returned
home she ran up to her room and drew the letter out of her glove: it
was unsealed. She read it. The letter contained a declaration of love:
it was tender, respectful and had been copied word for word from a
German novel. But Lizaveta Ivanovna did not know any German
and she was delighted with it.

For all that, the letter troubled her greatly. For the first time in
her life she was embarking upon secret and intimate relations with a
young man. His boldness appalled her. She reproached herself for
her imprudent behavior, and did not know what to do: ought she to
give up sitting at the window and by a show of indifference damp the
young man's inclination to pursue her further? Should she return his
letter to him? Or answer it coldly and firmly? There was nobody to
whom she could turn for advice: she had neither female friend nor
preceptor. Lizaveta Ivanovna decided to reply to the letter.

She sat down at her little writing table, took pen and paper—and
began to ponder. Several times she made a start and then tore the
paper across: what she had written seemed to her either too indul-
gent or too harsh. At last she succeeded in composing a few lines
with which she felt satisfied. "I am sure," she wrote, "that your
intentions are honorable and that you had no wish to hurt me by
any thoughtless conduct; but our acquaintance ought not to have
begun in this manner. I return you your letter, and hope that in
future I shall have no cause to complain of being shown a lack of
respect which is undeserved."

Next day, as soon as she saw Hermann approaching, Lizaveta
Ivanovna got up from her embroidery frame, went into the drawing
room, opened the little ventilating window and threw the letter into
the street, trusting to the young officer's alertness. Hermann ran
forward, picked the letter up and went into a confectioner's shop.
Breaking the seal, he found his own letter and Lizaveta Ivanovna's
reply. It was just what he had expected and he returned home engrossed in his plot.

Three days after this a sharp-eyed young person brought Lizaveta

Ivanovna a note from a milliner's establishment. Lizaveta Ivanovna opened it uneasily, fearing it was a demand for money, and suddenly recognized Hermann's handwriting.

"You have made a mistake, my dear," she said. "This note is not for me."

"Oh yes it is for you!" retorted the girl boldly, not troubling to conceal a knowing smile. "Please read it."

Lizaveta Ivanovna glanced at the letter. In it Hermann wanted her to meet him.

"Impossible!" she cried, alarmed at the request, at its coming so soon, and at the means employed to transmit it. "I am sure this was not addressed to me." And she tore the letter into fragments.

"If the letter was not for you, why did you tear it up?" said the girl. "I would have returned it to the sender."

"Be good enough, my dear," said Lizaveta Ivanovna, flushing crimson at her remark, "not to bring me any more letters. And tell the person who sent you that he ought to be ashamed . . ."

But Hermann did not give in. Every day Lizaveta Ivanovna received a letter from him by one means or another. They were no longer translated from the German. Hermann wrote them inspired by passion and in a style which was his own: they reflected both his inexorable desire and the disorder of an unbridled imagination. Lizaveta Ivanovna no longer thought of returning them: she drank them in eagerly and took to answering—and the notes she sent grew longer and more affectionate every hour. At last she threw out of the window to him the following letter:

There is a ball tonight at the Embassy. The countess will be there. We shall stay until about two o'clock. Here is an opportunity for you to see me alone. As soon as the countess is away the servants are sure to go to their quarters, leaving the concierge in the hall but he usually retires to his lodge. Come at half-past eleven. Walk straight up the stairs. If you meet anyone in the anteroom, ask if the countess is at home. They will say "No," but there will be no help for it—you will have to go away. But probably you will not meet anyone. The maids all sit together in the one room. Turn to the left out of the anteroom and keep straight on until you reach the countess' bedroom. In the bedroom, behind a screen, you will find two small doors: the one on the right leads into the study where the countess never goes; and the other on the left opens into a passage with a narrow winding staircase up to my room.

Hermann waited for the appointed hour like a tiger trembling for its prey. By ten o'clock in the evening he was already standing outside the countess' house. It was a frightful night: the wind howled, wet snow fell in big flakes; the street lamps burned dimly; the streets were deserted. From time to time a sledge drawn by a sorry-looking hack passed by, the driver on the watch for a belated fare. Hermann stood there without his greatcoat, feeling neither the wind nor the snow. At last the countess' carriage was brought round. Hermann saw the old woman wrapped in sables being lifted into the vehicle by two footmen; then Liza in a light cloak, with natural flowers in her hair, flitted by. The carriage doors banged. The vehicle rolled heavily over the wet snow. The concierge closed the street-door. The lights in the windows went out. Hermann started to walk to and fro outside the deserted house; he went up to a street lamp and glanced at his watch: it was twenty minutes past eleven. He stood still by the lamppost, his eyes fixed on the hand of the watch. Precisely at half-past eleven Hermann walked up the steps of the house and entered the brightly lit vestibule. The concierge was not there. Hermann ran up the stairs, opened the door of the anteroom and saw a footman asleep in a soiled, old-fashioned armchair by the side of a lamp. With a light, firm tread Hermann passed quickly by him. The ballroom and drawing room were in darkness but the lamp in the anteroom shed a dim light into them. Hermann entered the bedroom. Ancient icons filled the icon-stand before which burned a golden lamp. Armchairs upholstered in faded damask and sofas with down cushions, the tassels of which had lost their gilt, were ranged with depressing symmetry round the walls hung with Chinese wallpaper. On one of the walls were two portraits painted in Paris by Madame Lebrun: the first of a stout, red-faced man of some forty years of age, in a light green uniform with a star on his breast; the other, a beautiful young woman with an aquiline nose and a rose in the powdered hair drawn back over her temples. Every corner was crowded with porcelain shepherdesses, clocks made by the celebrated Leroy, little boxes, roulettes, fans and all the thousand and one playthings invented for ladies of fashion at the end of the last century, together with Montgolfier's balloon and Mesmer's magnetism. Hermann stepped behind the screen. A small iron bedstead stood there; to the right was the door into the study—to the left, the other door into the passage. Hermann opened it and saw the narrow winding staircase leading to poor little Liza's room. But he turned about and went into the dark study.

The time passed slowly. Everything was quiet. The drawing-room clock struck twelve; the clocks in the other rooms chimed twelve, one after the other, and all was still again. Hermann stood leaning against the cold stove. He was quite calm: his heart beat evenly, like that of a man resolved upon a dangerous but inevitable undertaking. The clocks struck one, and then two, and he heard the distant rumble of a carriage. In spite of himself he was overcome with agitation. The carriage drove up to the house and stopped. He heard the clatter of the carriage-steps being lowered. In the house all was commotion. Servants ran to and fro, there was a confusion of voices, and the lights appeared everywhere. Three ancient lady's maids bustled into the bedroom, followed by the countess who, half dead with fatigue, sank into a Voltaire armchair. Hermann watched through a crack in the door. Lizaveta Ivanovna passed close by him and he heard her footsteps hurrying up the stairs to her room. For a moment something akin to remorse assailed him but he quickly hardened his heart again.

The countess began undressing before the looking glass. Her maids took off the cap trimmed with roses and lifted the powdered wig from her gray, closely cropped head. Pins showered about her. The silver-trimmed yellow dress fell at her puffy feet. Hermann witnessed the hideous mysteries of her toilet; at last the countess put on bed jacket and night cap, and in this attire, more suited to her age, she seemed less horrible and ugly.

Like most old people the countess suffered from sleeplessness. Having undressed, she sat down in a big armchair by the window and dismissed her maids. They took away the candles, leaving only the lamp before the icons to light the room. The countess sat there, her skin sallow with age, her flabby lips twitching, her body swaying to and fro. Her dim eyes were completely vacant and looking at her one might have imagined that the dreadful old woman was rocking her body not from choice but owing to some secret galvanic mechanism.

Suddenly an inexplicable change came over the deathlike face. The lips ceased to move, the eyes brightened: before the countess stood a strange young man.

"Do not be alarmed, for heaven's sake, do not be alarmed!" he said in a low, clear voice. "I have no intention of doing you any harm, I have come to beg a favor of you."

The old woman stared at him in silence, as if she had not heard. Hermann thought she must be deaf and bending down to her ear he repeated what he had just said. The old woman remained silent as before.

"You can ensure the happiness of my whole life," Hermann went on, "and at no cost to yourself. I know that you can name three cards in succession . . ."

Hermann stopped. The countess appeared to have grasped what he wanted and to be seeking words to frame her answer.

"It was a joke," she said at last. "I swear to you it was a joke."

"No, madam," Hermann retorted angrily. "Remember Tchaplit-sky, and how you enabled him to win back his loss."

The countess was plainly perturbed. Her face expressed profound agitation; but soon she relapsed into her former impassivity.

"Can you not tell me those three winning cards?" Hermann went on.

The countess said nothing. Hermann continued: "For whom would you keep your secret? For your grandsons? They are rich enough already: they don't appreciate the value of money. Your three cards would not help a spendthrift. A man who does not take care of his inheritance will die a beggar though all the demons of the world were at his command. I am not a spendthrift: I know the value of money. Your three cards would not be wasted on me. Well? . . ."

He paused, feverishly waiting for her reply. She was silent. Hermann fell on his knees.

"If your heart has ever known what it is to love, if you can remember the ecstasies of love, if you have ever smiled tenderly at the cry of your new-born son, if any human feeling has ever stirred in your breast, I appeal to you as wife, beloved one, mother—I implore you by all that is holy in life not to reject my prayer: tell me your secret. Of what use is it to you? Perhaps it is bound up with some terrible sin, with the loss of eternal salvation, with some bargain with the devil . . . Reflect—you are old: you have not much longer to live, and I am ready to take your sin upon my soul. Only tell me your secret. Remember that a man's happiness is in your hands; that not only I, but my children and my children's children will bless your memory and hold it sacred. . . ."

The old woman answered not a word.

Hermann rose to his feet.

"You old hag!" he said, grinding his teeth. "Then I will make you speak. . . ."

With these words he drew a pistol from his pocket. At the sight of the pistol the countess for the second time showed signs of agitation. Her head shook and she raised a hand as though to protect herself from the shot. . . . Then she fell back . . . and was still.

"Come, an end to this childish nonsense!" said Hermann, seizing her by the arm. "I ask you for the last time—will you tell me those three cards? Yes or no?"

The countess made no answer. Hermann saw that she was dead.

4

7 mai 18—
Homme sans mœurs et sans religion!
—FROM A CORRESPONDENCE

Lizaveta Ivanovna was sitting in her room, still in her ball dress, lost in thought. On returning home she had made haste to dismiss the sleepy maid who reluctantly offered to help her, saying that she would undress herself, and with trembling heart had gone to her own room, expecting to find Hermann and hoping that she would not find him. A glance convinced her he was not there, and she thanked fate for having prevented their meeting. She sat down without undressing and began to recall the circumstances that had led her so far in so short a time. It was not three weeks since she had first caught sight of the young man from the window—and yet she was carrying on a correspondence with him, and he had already succeeded in inducing her to agree to a nocturnal tryst! She knew his name only because he had signed some of his letters; she had never spoken to him, did not know the sound of his voice, had never heard him mentioned . . . until that evening. Strange to say, that very evening at the ball, Tomsky, piqued with the young Princess Pauline for flirting with somebody else instead of with him as she usually did, decided to revenge himself by a show of indifference. He asked Lizaveta Ivanovna to be his partner and danced the interminable mazurka with her. And all the time he kept teasing her about her partiality for officers of the Engineers, assuring her that he knew far more than she could suppose, and some of his sallies so found their mark that several times Lizaveta Ivanovna thought he must know her secret.

"Who told you all this?" she asked, laughing.

"A friend of someone you know," Tomsky answered, "a very remarkable person."

"And who is this remarkable man?"

"His name is Hermann."

Lizaveta Ivanovna said nothing; but her hands and feet turned to ice.

"This Hermann," continued Tomsky, "is a truly romantic figure: he has the profile of a Napoleon and the soul of a Mephistopheles. I think there must be at least three crimes on his conscience. How pale you look!"

"I have a bad headache. . . . Well, and what did this Hermann—or whatever his name is—tell you?"

"Hermann is very annoyed with his friend: he says that in his place he would act quite differently. . . . I suspect in fact that Hermann has designs upon you himself; at any rate he listens to his friend's ecstatic exclamations with anything but indifference."

"But where has he seen me?"

"In church, perhaps, or when you were out walking. . . . heaven only knows!—in your own room maybe, while you were asleep, for there is nothing he—"

Three ladies coming up to invite Tomsky to choose between *"oubli ou regret?"* interrupted the conversation which had become so painfully interesting to Lizaveta Ivanovna.

The lady chosen by Tomsky was the Princess Pauline herself. She succeeded in effecting a reconciliation with him while they danced an extra turn and spun round once more before she was conducted to her chair. When he returned to his place neither Hermann nor Lizaveta Ivanovna was in Tomsky's thoughts. Lizaveta Ivanovna longed to resume the interrupted conversation but the mazurka came to an end and shortly afterward the old countess took her departure.

Tomsky's words were nothing more than the usual small-talk of the ballroom, but they sank deep into the girl's romantic heart. The portrait sketched by Tomsky resembled the picture she had herself drawn, and thanks to the novels of the day the commonplace figure both terrified and fascinated her. She sat there with her bare arms crossed and with her head, still adorned with flowers, sunk upon her naked bosom. . . . Suddenly the door opened and Hermann came in. . . . She shuddered.

"Where were you?" she asked in a frightened whisper.

"In the old countess's bedroom," Hermann answered. "I have just left her. The countess is dead."

"Merciful heavens! . . . what are you saying?"

"And I think," added Hermann, "that I am the cause of her death."

Lizaveta darted a glance at him, and heard Tomsky's words echo in her soul: ". . . there must be at least three crimes on his conscience." Hermann sat down in the window beside her and related all that had happened.

Lizaveta Ivanovna listened to him aghast. So all those passionate letters, those ardent pleas, the bold, determined pursuit had not been inspired by love! Money!—that was what his soul craved! It was not she who could satisfy his desires and make him happy! Poor child, she had been nothing but the blind tool of a thief, of the murderer of her aged benefactress! . . . She wept bitterly in a vain agony of repentance. Hermann watched in silence: he too was suffering torment; but neither the poor girl's tears nor her indescribable charm in her grief touched his hardened soul. He felt no pricking of conscience at the thought of the dead old woman. One thing only horrified him: the irreparable loss of the secret which was to have brought him wealth.

"You are a monster!" said Lizaveta Ivanovna at last.

"I did not mean her to die," Hermann answered. "My pistol was not loaded."

Both were silent.

Morning came. Lizaveta Ivanovna blew out the candle which had burned down. A pale light illumined the room. She wiped her tear-stained eyes and looked up at Hermann: he was sitting on the window sill with his arms folded, a menacing frown on his face. In this attitude he bore a remarkable likeness to the portrait of Napoleon. The likeness struck even Lizaveta Ivanovna.

"How shall I get you out of the house?" she said at last. "I had thought of taking you down the secret staircase but that means going through the bedroom, and I am afraid."

"Tell me how to find this secret staircase—I will go alone."

Lizaveta rose, took a key from the chest of drawers and gave it to Hermann with precise instructions. Hermann pressed her cold, unresponsive hand, kissed her bowed head and left her.

He walked down the winding stairway and entered the countess' bedroom again. The dead woman sat as though turned to stone. Her face wore a look of profound tranquility. Hermann stood in front of her and gazed long and earnestly at her, as though trying to convince himself of the terrible truth. Then he went into the study, felt behind the tapestry for the door and began to descend the dark stairway, excited by strange emotions. Maybe some sixty years ago, at this very hour, he thought, some happy youth—long since turned to dust—was stealing up this staircase into that very bedroom, in an embroidered tunic, his hair dressed à l'oiseau royal, pressing his three-cornered hat to his breast; and today the heart of his aged mistress has ceased to beat. . . .

At the bottom of the stairs Hermann saw a door which he opened with the same key, and found himself in a passage leading to the street.

5

That night the dead Baroness von W. appeared before me. She was all in white and said: "How do you do, Mr Councillor?"   —SWEDENBORG

Three days after that fatal night, at nine o'clock in the morning Hermann repaired to the Convent of ——, where the last respects were to be paid to the mortal remains of the dead countess. Though he felt no remorse he could not altogether stifle the voice of conscience which kept repeating to him: "You are the old woman's murderer!" Having very little religious faith, he was exceedingly superstitious. Believing that the dead countess might exercise a malignant influence on his life, he decided to go to her funeral to beg and obtain her forgiveness.

The church was full. Hermann had difficulty in making his way through the crowd. The coffin rested on a rich catafalque beneath a canopy of velvet. The dead woman lay with her hands crossed on her breast, in a lace cap and a white satin robe. Around the bier stood the members of her household: servants in black clothes, with armorial ribbons on their shoulders and lighted candles in their hands; relatives in deep mourning—children, grandchildren and great-grandchildren. No one wept: tears would have been *une affectation.* The countess was so old that her death could not have taken anybody by surprise, and her family had long ceased to think of her as one of the living. A famous preacher delivered the funeral oration. In simple and touching phrases he described the peaceful passing of the saintly woman whose long life had been a quiet, touching preparation for a Christian end. "The angel of death," he declared, "found her vigilant in devout meditation, awaiting the midnight coming of the bridegroom." The service was concluded in melancholy decorum. First the relations went forward to bid farewell of the corpse. They were followed by a long procession of all those who had come to render their last homage to one who had for so many years been a participator in their frivolous amusements. After them came the members of the countess' household. The last of these was an old woman-retainer the same age as the deceased. Two young girls supported her by the arms. She had not strength to prostrate herself—and she was the only one to shed tears as she kissed her mistress' cold hand. Hermann decided to approach the coffin after her. He knelt down on the cold stone strewed with branches of spruce-fir, and remained in that position for some minutes; at last he rose to his feet and, pale as the deceased herself, walked up the steps of the catafalque and bent over the corpse. . . . At that moment it seemed to him that the dead woman darted a mocking look at him and winked her eye. Hermann drew back, missed his footing and crashed headlong to the floor. They picked him up. At the same time Lizaveta Ivanovna was carried out of the church in a swoon. This incident momentarily upset the solemnity of the mournful rite. There was a dull murmur among the congregation, and a tall thin man in the uniform of a court chamberlain, a close relative of the deceased, whispered in the ear of an Englishman who was standing near him that the young officer was the natural son of the countess, to which the Englishman coldly replied, "Oh?"

The whole of that day Hermann was strangely troubled. Repairing to a quiet little tavern to dine, he drank a great deal of wine, contrary to his habit, in the hope of stifling his inner agitation. But the wine only served to excite his imagination. Returning home, he threw himself on his bed without undressing, and fell heavily asleep.

It was night when he woke and the moon was shining into his room. He glanced at the time: it was a quarter to three. Sleep had left him; he sat on the bed and began thinking of the old countess' funeral.

Just then someone in the street looked in at him through the window and immediately walked on. Hermann paid no attention. A moment later he heard the door of his anteroom open. Hermann thought it was his orderly, drunk as usual, returning from some nocturnal excursion, but presently he heard an unfamiliar footstep: someone was softly shuffling along the floor in slippers. The door opened and a woman in white came in. Hermann mistook her for his old nurse and wondered what could have brought her at such an hour. But the woman in white glided across the room and stood before him—and Hermann recognized the countess!

"I have come to you against my will," she said in a firm voice, "but I am commanded to grant your request. The three, the seven and the ace will win for you if you play them in succession, provided that you do not stake more than one card in twenty-four hours and never play again as long as you live. I forgive you my death, on condition that you marry my ward, Lizaveta Ivanovna."

With these words she turned softly, rustled to the door in her slippers and disappeared. Hermann heard the street door click and again saw someone peeping in at him through the window.

It was a long time before he could pull himself together and go into the next room. His orderly was asleep on the floor; Hermann had difficulty in waking him. The man was drunk as usual; there was no getting any sense out of him. The street door was locked. Hermann returned to his room and, lighting a candle, wrote down all the details of his vision.

6

"Attendez!"
"*How dare you say* 'Attendez!' *to me?*"
"*Your Excellency, I said* 'Attendez,' *sir.*"

Two *idées fixes* cannot coexist in the moral world any more than two physical bodies can occupy one and the same space. "The three, the seven, the ace" soon drove all thought of the dead woman from Hermann's mind. "Three, seven, ace" were perpetually in his head and on his lips. If he saw a young girl he would say, "How graceful she is! A regular three of hearts!" Asked the time, he would reply, "Five minutes to seven." Every stout man reminded him of the ace. "Three, seven, ace" haunted his dreams, assuming all sorts of shapes.

The three blossomed before him like a luxuriant flower, the seven took the form of a Gothic portal, and aces became gigantic spiders. His whole attention was focused on one thought: how to make use of the secret which had cost him so dear. He began to consider resigning his commission in order to go and travel abroad. In the public gambling houses in Paris he would compel fortune to give him his magical treasure. Chance spared him the trouble.

A circle of wealthy gamblers existed in Moscow, presided over by the celebrated Tchekalinsky, who had spent his life at the card table and amassed millions, accepting promissory notes when he won and paying his losses in ready money. His long experience inspired the confidence of his fellow players, while his open house, his famous chef and his gay and friendly manner secured for him the general respect of the public. He came to Petersburg. The young men of the capital flocked to his rooms, forsaking balls for cards and preferring the excitement of gambling to the seductions of flirting. Narumov brought Hermann to him.

They passed through a succession of magnificent rooms full of attentive servants. The place was crowded. Several generals and privy councilors were playing whist; young men smoking long pipes lounged about on sofas upholstered in damask. In the drawing room some twenty gamblers jostled round a long table at which the master of the house was keeping bank. Tchekalinsky was a man of about sixty years of age and most dignified appearance; he had silvery-gray hair, a full, florid face with a kindly expression, and sparkling eyes which were always smiling. Narumov introduced Hermann. Shaking hands cordially, Tchekalinsky requested him not to stand on ceremony, and went on dealing.

The game continued for some while. On the table lay more than thirty cards. Tchekalinsky paused after each round to give the players time to arrange their cards and note their losses, listened courteously to their observations and more courteously still straightened the corner of a card that some careless hand had turned down. At last the game finished. Tchekalinsky shuffled the cards and prepared to deal again.

"Will you allow me to take a card?" said Hermann, stretching out his hand from behind a stout gentleman who was punting.

Tchekalinsky smiled and bowed graciously, in silent token of consent. Narumov laughingly congratulated Hermann on breaking his long abstention from cards and wished him a lucky start.

"There!" said Hermann, chalking some figures on the back of his card.

"How much?" asked the banker, screwing up his eyes. "Excuse me, I cannot see."

"Forty-seven thousand," Hermann answered.

At these words every head was turned in a flash, and all eyes were fixed on Hermann.

He has taken leave of his senses! thought Narumov.

"Allow me to point out to you," said Tchekalinsky with his unfailing smile, "that you are playing rather high: nobody here has ever staked more than two hundred and seventy-five at a time."

"Well?" returned Hermann. "Do you accept my card or not?"

Tchekalinsky bowed with the same air of humble acquiescence.

"I only wanted to observe," he said, "that, being honored with the confidence of my friends, I can only play against ready money. For my own part, of course, I am perfectly sure that your word is sufficient but for the sake of the rules of the game and our accounts I must request you to place the money on your card."

Hermann took a bank note from his pocket and handed it to Tchekalinsky, who after a cursory glance placed it on Hermann's card. He began to deal. On the right a nine turned up, and on the left a three.

"I win!" said Hermann, pointing to his card.

There was a murmur of astonishment among the company. Tchekalinsky frowned, but the smile quickly reappeared on his face.

"Would you like me to settle now?" he asked Hermann.

"If you please."

Tchekalinsky took a number of bank notes out of his pocket and paid there and then. Hermann picked up his money and left the table. Narumov could not believe his eyes. Hermann drank a glass of lemonade and departed home.

The following evening he appeared at Tchekalinsky's again. The host was dealing. Hermann walked up to the table; the players immediately made room for him. Tchekalinsky bowed graciously. Hermann waited for the next deal, took a card and placed on it his original forty-seven thousand together with his winnings of the day before. Tchekalinsky began to deal. A knave turned up on the right, a seven on the left.

Hermann showed his seven.

There was a general exclamation. Tchekalinsky was obviously disconcerted. He counted out ninety-four thousand and handed them to Hermann, who pocketed them in the coolest manner and instantly withdrew.

The next evening Hermann again made his appearance at the table. Every one was expecting him; the generals and privy councilors left their whist to watch such extraordinary play. The young officers leaped up from their sofas and all the waiters collected in the drawing room. Everyone pressed round Hermann. The other players left off punting, impatient to see what would happen. Hermann stood at the table, prepared to play alone against Tchekalinsky, who was pale but still smiling. Each broke the seal of a pack of cards. Tchekalinsky shuffled. Hermann took a card and covered it with a pile of bank notes. It was like a duel. Deep silence reigned in the room.

Tchekalinsky began dealing; his hands trembled. A queen fell on the right, an ace on the left.

"Ace wins!" said Hermann, and showed his card.

"Your queen has lost," said Tchekalinsky gently.

Hermann started: indeed, instead of an ace there lay before him the queen of spades. He could not believe his eyes or think how he could have made such a mistake.

At that moment it seemed to him that the queen of spades opened and closed her eye, and mocked him with a smile. He was struck by the extraordinary resemblance. . . .

"The old woman!" he cried in terror.

Tchekalinsky gathered up his winnings. Hermann stood rooted to the spot. When he left the table everyone began talking at once.

"A fine game, that!" said the players.

Tchekalinsky shuffled the cards afresh and the game resumed as usual.

CONCLUSION

Hermann went out of his mind. He is now in room number seventeen of the Obuhov Hospital. He returns no answer to questions put to him but mutters over and over again, with incredible rapidity: "Three, seven, ace! Three, seven, queen!"

Lizaveta Ivanovna has married a very pleasant young man; he is in the civil service somewhere and has a good income. He is the son of the old countess' former steward. Lizaveta Ivanovna in her turn is bringing up a poor relative.

And Tomsky, who has been promoted to the rank of captain, has married the Princess Pauline.

October-November 1833

BILLY: THE SEAL MISSION
By Stewart Alsop and Thomas Braden

．　．

Billy was good-looking, blond and gregarious,
and in November 1944 he dropped alone from a plane over Holland.
His last words to the pilot were:
"This is a hell of a way to be going home."

The word "spy" has a connotation of loneliness which frequently it does not deserve. In peacetime, most nations have the services of traveling businessmen who go about in foreign countries quite openly in search of customers and trade, and simply keep their eyes and ears open as they go. They are in fact spies, but their very stock in trade is their open congeniality.

In wartime, it is nearly always possible, as a later chapter will reveal, to get interesting facts about enemy countries by sending men into neutral countries. There is nothing lonely about the work of such men since they have a perfect right to be where they are, and can go about quite openly. Gregariousness for them is an admirable trait provided it is not accompanied by garrulousness.

In peace and in war, nations discover extremely important facts about each other by simply reading each other's newspapers and other publications. Movements in population, births and deaths, shipping statistics and labor trends, can all be compiled by the expert who sits comfortably at home and who knows what to look for in the newspapers. If such men are indeed spies, they are not lonely.

There is in fact no type of intelligence operation in which the spy depends solely upon himself. The very word intelligence in its synonymous sense of information calls to mind at least two people, one to impart and one to receive, and intelligence, as nations use the word, requires at least a third party, the one who uses it.

But there is one type of intelligence operation which depends more *heavily than any other upon the lone and secret agent. It is used in war-time, not only because it is one of the few types of operations which has a chance of success in wartime, but because a time of war is the only time when it is necessary to use it. It was used by both Germany and the Allies during the last war, and for the Allies at least, it was a highly suc-cessful type of intelligence operation. It consists of sending men alone into enemy territory. Naturally, they are given the names of certain friends with whom they can establish relations and seek shelter, but insofar as the word spy connotes the lonely, these men are lonely.*

Such a one-man operation was the Seal Mission, and such a spy was Billy. His is a typical story. It is also a true story. If it sounds fictional, that is typical too.

In the month of November, 1944, the country of Holland was a sea of hopelessness. To the south, British, Canadian and Polish troops, pushing north past Eindhoven, had bogged down in mud and over-flowing dikes. To the west, the Germans had blown the walls which let in the sea. British troops fought knee-deep in water.

To the north, there was mud and water too. Worse, there was famine. German soldiers, all but cut off from supply by the American push to the east, fighting bitterly in a last kind of trench warfare, knew by that time that their purpose in life was to stand and die. They took what food they could find from the Dutch. There seemed no longer any sense in paying.

The Resistance movement in Holland had slowed to a stand-still. In the occupied part of the country, packed deep with German troops, an uprising was out of the question. The nighttime vigils for the parachute supplies from England were likely to be interrupted disastrously at any moment by German troops on the move. More-over, the Resistance had been twice betrayed by a man they had accepted as their own.

He was called Bill of the Seaman's House and had once been a British agent, under another name, Bill Overveen. He had "turned." Now he traveled from one locality to another, met the local farmers and pretended to be an Allied courier from England. When the farmers had eagerly introduced him and taken him into their plans, he would suddenly disappear. A day later, everyone who had confided in him would be arrested. It was disheartening to the point of de-spair.

The Dutch people, even those who took no active part in the Resistance, were almost hopeless too. The work of industrious centuries spent in building out the sea had been destroyed. Many of the fields lay flooded. The Allies were never coming. All was dirt, water and mud.

Into that dismal bog, at eleven thirty on the night of November 10, a man dropped alone from the hole of a Liberator aircraft into a ditch a half mile north of Ulrum. His was the "Seal Mission," and he was known to the friends he left behind him as "Billy."

What it was that impelled Billy alone into the land of the enemy that night was not immediately apparent to the men who flew him there. To the pilot of the Liberator who asked about him afterward, to the other members of the crew and to all his casual friends in England, Billy was a gregarious, congenial fellow, twenty-seven years old, blond, good-looking except for that faint trace of coldness in the eyes which so often stamped the men whom OSS hired as agents.

There were two somewhat conflicting theories about Billy and his motives, and only one man, an OSS man whom we shall know as Peter Smith, was convinced that he knew the whole true history, and the true reason why, with apparently total nervelessness, Billy had joked with the pilot about "a hell of a way to be going home" up to the last minute before he disappeared into the darkness that night in November.

Smith believed—he "knew," he said—that years before, when the Germans had overrun his country in the spring of 1940, Billy had made up his mind about his own role in the war and had adhered to that role ever since with the kind of strength which permits of no second thoughts while waiting in an airplane, even for a man who has never jumped before.

The story which Peter Smith knew, which he believed and which he had heard from Billy's own lips when he had come to him in the spring of 1944 asking for a job, was as follows: He had been born, he said, in the Dutch East Indies, a Dutchman by nationality, and had become, at his parents' strong desires, a lawyer. His parents soon moved to Holland, and by 1937 his law degree had gained him a minor but promising post in the Dutch government. In 1938 his parents had died, and Billy tossed aside his future to become what he had always most wanted to be—an engineer. He was at the University of Utrecht when Germany swallowed the Lowlands.

Some of his friends at the university who were then tossed into jail were certain that Billy's intelligence was chained to his ambition. He left the university, secured a high position in the Netherlands Food

Distribution Office and kept his mouth closed. He said nothing against the new rulers, but within a year, according to Billy, he had established an underground network among food-distribution officials throughout Holland.

For two years the chain worked secretly and well. But as more and more German officials came carpetbagging into Holland, as more and more executive posts were turned over to aging German officers, the work became increasingly dangerous. In October 1943, Billy said, "My cover was blown." With three friends he escaped in a small boat to England, bringing with him files of intelligence which he had accumulated during two years of silent work.

He had then secured a post in the Dutch intelligence, working for the Dutch government-in-exile. He despised it, he said. He thought the exiled government had fascist tendencies, that it was bent on preserving itself and the *status quo*, that it was insensitive to the sufferings of the people in Holland across the sea. In April of 1944 he had resigned, and now he poured out his story to Smith, and begged to be sent on a mission to Holland.

There was another story—or rather another theory—about Billy. The Dutch government in London thought he was left-wing, perhaps Communist; not thoroughly suspicious; still, it refused what it considered the risk of sending him back to Holland on a mission of its own.

Smith, at first, was skeptical. Billy was suspected by his own government. His own government, for what might or might not be good reason, had refused to send him back to Holland. The man admitted that his cover had been blown once before in Holland, admitted therefore that the Germans knew of him. Yet he was asking to be sent back on what would certainly be, if he were what he pretended to be, an extremely dangerous mission.

Of course, Smith thought, if he were not what he pretended to be, it would not be dangerous. Across the mind of Smith there played the faint notion that in dealing with this man, he might possibly be dealing with what is known as a "double agent."

While the two men talked it out in Pall Mall restaurants, other OSS men investigated Billy's story. Everything checked. Yet there was that slight suspicion. Smith had made the final decision. Billy's open friendliness had won the day. "I am convinced," Smith said, "that Billy's politics are unimportant. He is motivated by a strong love of his country and his people." In October, 1944, Billy was assigned to

OSS, and given a mission to Holland.

He did not need much of a briefing, for he knew the country well. Peter Smith saw that he had the things he needed, and brought him up to date on the leaders of the Resistance. He looked over a map of Ulrum, and picked the spot where he thought the pilot could drop him with the least chance of danger. Smith told him what was known about the Germans in the area, and he warned him particularly just before he left about the activities of the German spy, Bill of the Seaman's House.

Billy was grateful for his chance. The last direct word which OSS had from him the night he went back to Holland was his thanks to Peter Smith and his promise of a safe return.

After that, for a while, nothing. On two occasions within the next ten days, an OSS-staffed plane flew high over the area where Billy had dropped, while Smith sent out the code signals to the ground, "Message for Billy; Smith to Billy, Smith calling Billy." There was no answer. There was no one on the air.

For Smith, the days became full of strain and worry. As always in the relations between an OSS agent in the field who did not report, and his friends back at base, suspicion would not down. It was strange that this should have been so. OSS men who had become firm friends would sit in a room together toasting each other's luck before one of them departed for enemy territory. Yet, when days passed and that man did not report by radio to headquarters, his friends would begin to remark to each other, "I wonder if he could have turned." Perhaps distrust is the inevitable result of nerves and tension. Perhaps no men who are forced to make a trade of deceit can ever fully trust each other.

But Smith and the others were worried for another reason. Whatever their opinions of his worthiness as an agent, everyone in OSS had liked Billy. It was impossible not to. On the eleventh night after his departure, on the night of November 21, Smith's faith seemed justified. It is still not possible to reveal completely what happened that night, but the essence of it is reportable in the messages which flowed out from an OSS plane over Holland to a field below. From the plane that night, Peter Smith sent out another signal for the agent on the ground:

"The time is now 2354, Pete calling Billy, Pete calling Billy, Pete to Billy, Pete to Billy." A pause. "The time is now 2358. This is Pete calling Billy, Pete to Billy, Hello Billy, Pete to Billy, Hello Billy."

There is a short silence, then a crackle of static, and in the airplane overhead Smith's voice can be heard over the noises of the engines saying simply, "Thank God, thank God."

"I am quite all right," the message spelled. "I am ready to receive my friends" (an acknowledgment of Billy's mission to set up landing points for more agents) "one mile north of the eleventh position."

"Is there anything you need?" Smith asked. And the reply: "I have landed in a big ditch, and lost part of my luggage. I have a car now. I need new maps, new batteries, five flashlights, two sets of automobile tires 16x25 and 17x50. I could not find my friend at first, and I had to stay near German posts. It is very dangerous. That is why I am so glad to contact you now."

When Smith made his report of the contact, OSS men who had worked with Billy heaved a collective sigh. When an agent asked for automobile tires, there was not any great need for immediate worry.

The first contact was renewed again and again. Billy soon began to pass intelligence. He did it in a careful, accurate style. He reported the movement of a panzer unit to Arnhem, naming the unit and the route taken. He reported that the Germans were making a water barrier between the Ems canal and the Wischoter Diep, and he gave the map reference. He reported the effectiveness of the Allied bombing of the docks at Gaarkeuken, and he proposed that the air forces bomb the railway bridge across the canal at Leeuwardem.

In later messages he said that it was difficult to keep warm in Holland, and asked for more clothes and for some cigarettes.

In the fourth contact with OSS, Billy made, for the first time, serious and definite proposals for the dropping of "friends" which had been promised him. And he ended, "Tell Pete I have a nice car now and I travel the country. It is very nice. We are always escorted by a German soldier. Now I must end. I must walk now, half an hour through muddy fields with the radio."

"Good night, Billy," came from the plane, "and good luck."

By the time the sixth message came from Billy, it was apparent that he was beginning to be worried about the arrival of his friends and of supplies. On January 10, and again on January 23, Billy reported that unless friends and packages came soon, his Dutch friends of the underground would begin to lose faith in him.

OSS men realized his predicament. They frequently received such messages from agents. They knew that the underground of Europe was of necessity a suspicious organization, and that if a man turned up among them, claiming to be an Allied agent, and could not show proof that he had the confidence of the Allies, he would soon be suspect with the underground.

But it was midwinter. The elements were waging a cosmic war of their own over the battlefields of Holland, and though OSS-stocked planes had several times tried to reach the pinpoints which Billy had described, they were unsuccessful. Billy reported that one plane had flown right over his reception field, but had not seen his group of friends on the ground. Perhaps, he said, he had not kept the lights lit long enough, but lights were very dangerous. He needed supplies, or friends, or both, he said, and he needed them immediately.

There was another contact on February 8. Again Billy asked for friends. Looking back later over the texts of his messages, OSS men noted that it was the last time he did so.

Beginning on February 15, there was something peculiar and suspect about Billy's messages. OSS realized it almost at once. On that date, he asked for packages and did not mention friends. Two days later, a successful drop of supplies was made, the first that OSS had been able to send him, throughout his time in the field. Smith then asked Billy specifically, if, now that the weather had broken, he was again ready for friends. He received the specific answer, "No friends."

On that same contact, Billy passed on some information. It was poor information, and Smith was surprised. Billy had passed a message about enemy units. "Be specific," Smith answered him. "What units?"

All these omissions seemed strange, and Smith again was worried. Still there was no real evidence that anything was wrong.

Then on February 28, the evidence came. At 2358 hours, a radioman in an OSS plane called to Billy: "I am hearing you O.K. tonight, Billy. Your signals are good. Billy, we are sorry we could not come over with packages. The weather was bad. Do you get that?"

From the ground came the answer, "I understand that the weather was poor, but it was damned bad standing there in the cold."

The radioman listening to the message signaled to Peter Smith. Together they continued to listen. The word came again, later in the message: "It is a damned good place for a drop." And just before he finished, once more in the very last line, "Don't wait till Saturday; it is damned dangerous unless you come on time."

There was no mistaking it. The word, "damned," had been agreed upon long before as the "danger signal." Smith gave no indication that he had heard it. "O.K., Billy," he said. "Good night." But he knew, as he flew back to London, that Billy was in the hands of the Gestapo. He was operating under duress.

When an agent is captured and is forced to send signals on his radio, the only way in which his headquarters can help him is to continue to send him messages, to keep up the pretense that all is well; to send him a little information or some supplies which will make the enemy believe that the agent is worth more to them alive than dead. Peter Smith and OSS did their best for Billy until a time came when it appeared that perhaps Billy was not doing his best for them.

Until March 31, OSS continued to send him messages. On that date, Billy asked that a plane fly over his area. In order to preserve the illusion for the Germans that they knew nothing of his capture, OSS complied.

The OSS man who rode in the plane reported that the moment he reached the target area, he began to hear the steady buzz of radar, the telltale sign that the German stations have picked up the presence of an airplane. It was unusual that it should have happened so quickly. Perhaps Billy had been used as a decoy so that the plane could be destroyed; perhaps the Germans were only following the plane's course in the hope that it would lead them to the areas of other Allied agents. The pilot didn't wait to find out, but headed immediately for home.

That was the last radio message OSS ever had from Billy. But more than two weeks later, on April 19, a cable was received from the Allied front lines by the British Intelligence Service which substantiated what some OSS men had been afraid of, and which cast doubt into the mind of even Peter Smith: "German courier captured morning 18 April," the cable read, "carried complete report Gestapo interrogation of Agent Billy. *He apparently told them all he knew....*"

Billy clambered out of the watery ditch in which he landed, unhooked the strap which connected him to the cumbersome British leg bag and folded his parachute, tying it neatly with the shroud lines in the way he had been taught at the school. He was feeling happy, exhilarated, as only a man can feel who has just jumped out of an airplane and is none the worse for it. For a moment, he sat still on the muddy bank, humming a tune to himself, and then he realized suddenly that around him the night was silent. He could no longer hear the noise of the plane; he was alone.

He remembered that the next thing was to bury the parachute. He began to dig with his hands, but the soil was ooze, and he made no headway. The night began to get on his nerves. The complete bliss which he had felt when he first landed departed as suddenly as it had come, and he thought of all the things he had to do, of his old friend, Johannes De Woelf, whom he must find in Ulrum, and of his danger. Perhaps someone had seen his parachute coming out of the plane. It was best to hurry; to ditch everything, and get away.

He untied the side of the leg bag, took from it the radio, the batteries, some clothes, medicine, his pistol and ammunition, and stuffed it all in his pockets and in the rucksack on his back. Then he tossed the neatly rolled parachute and the half-filled leg bag into the ditch, slapped a few handfuls of mud over them, and set off to the south, across the fields.

It was raining by the time he reached the outskirts of Ulrum, and his watch said one. De Woelf's house was about a mile away now, but there was always the chance he wasn't there. Billy had not heard from De Woelf since he himself had escaped from Holland two years ago, and De Woelf led a dangerous life as a member of the Resistance. He might have run away, or been taken away; it was even possible that his house was watched.

Billy decided to stay out all night, and try to see De Woelf in the morning. He sat down on the wet earth near a farmer's fence, and tried to light a cigarette. The rain came down in sheets now. It was no use. He huddled against the boards of the fence and tried to doze in the rain. When he woke with a start, it was three, and he was freezing cold.

There is no courage and no fear like the courage or fear born of discomfort. A man will leave his post in the lines, or attack the enemy single-handed, if by doing either he can get a little warmer, or get out of the rain. It was so with Billy. Before he had gone to sleep he had cautiously decided to avoid De Woelf's house that night. Now, when he woke from his doze, he ran down the length of the fence with but one purpose; to get warm and dry, and not until he was pounding on the door of the first farmhouse he saw did he think of what he would say, and how he would say it.

The farmer who lit a candle, clambered out of bed in his nightshirt and answered the frantic pounding on his front door that night was a sixty-two-year-old man named Gort. Billy blurted out a story about being in trouble with the Germans and running away. He was lucky. Gort offered to dry his clothes and to let him sleep in the barn. Billy took only one precaution. "Before I go out there, I'd like to use your telephone," he said, "to let my family know I'm safe."

"You'll have to wait till tomorrow," Gort grunted, "there's no telephone in this house." With that certain knowledge that even if he wanted to, Gort could not notify the police until morning, Billy slept in the barn.

At six he was awakened by Gort, and told to be off before the farmhands arrived and asked who he was. At six thirty, muddy and tired, Billy trudged up the steps to the home of his old friend, Johannes De Woelf.

The De Woelfs were already stirring. De Woelf's son, a full three inches taller than Billy remembered him, answered the door and called excitedly to his father. It was almost a party at breakfast that morning, the whole family amazed and pleased to see Billy, and Billy being very quiet and secretive about his work, and in spite of himself not quiet enough to prevent De Woelf's three sons from making him a hero.

As soon as he and De Woelf were alone, Billy told his friend everything. Together they made plans for the agents who were coming, the supplies which would be dropped and the intelligence service they would organize. De Woelf was eager to help, and he told Billy all about the underground service which already existed in the neighborhood, but which had no means of communicating directly with London. De Woelf knew a farmer, he said, who was on the right side and whose fields would be perfect for a dropping zone. Over the hot coffee which Mrs. De Woelf had provided from a scanty hoard in celebration of the arrival of a long lost friend, Billy and De Woelf talked until ten.

It was still raining when they got up from the table, and De Woelf urged Billy to go to bed and get some sleep. He could go back later for the parachute and the leg bag he had left in the ditch. Billy didn't argue for long. He climbed between fresh sheets and slept, which was fortunate, perhaps, for the next day, when he did go back to revisit the place where he landed, the parachute and the leg bag were gone.

Between November 11 and November 21, when he made his first

successful contact with London, Billy got acquainted with De Woelf's friends among the Resistance, and set up his own organization. De Woelf's farmer friend could be counted upon. His family was large and willing to work against the Germans. He had carts and horses and huge barns. Supplies could be hauled from the fields and hidden without anyone outside the family circle being any the wiser.

De Woelf's brother took him to Zwolle, where he met a leader in the Dutch underground who badly needed a direct contact with London. This man had developed a courier service between the principal towns of north Holland, passing and obtaining information from leading Dutch citizens, for transmission to the Dutch government in London. The couriers were guarded by German troops, and equipped with German passes to aid them in the work which the Germans believed they were doing. He offered Billy a car and a German soldier to guard it, and Billy accepted.

Billy also arranged with the leader in Zwolle an official cover for the two agents whom Billy expected from OSS. They were to work as government officials in the communal kitchens at Winschoden, where food, beds, a government car and a safe place for the radio could be easily arranged.

Quickly, much more quickly than he had any right to expect, even, perhaps, too quickly, Billy's underground organization was taking shape. Already he had a supply field, cover for himself, cover for the two friends he expected and a large organization to help him get information and pass it on.

Meanwhile, Billy tried several times without success to contact Pete in London, first from De Woelf's house, again from the home of De Woelf's farmer friend. Several times his aerial would not work; again he thought there was some interference. At last, on November 21, he was successful.

On this contact, arrangements were made for parachuting two more agents. If the weather held good, Billy had to work quickly. His friend in Zwolle was not yet ready to receive them at the communal kitchen. Papers and passes and documented stories had to be arranged before two men who had come from nowhere could be suddenly introduced into government jobs. Billy turned to De Woelf for help and De Woelf, in his haste to be of assistance, made the one fatal mistake of his underground career. He introduced Billy to a friend in the underground named Van Steele.

Van Steele was a thin little man with a narrow face, spindly legs and a physique born of life in the city. He was possessed by fear, and the fear Van Steele knew was sometimes the safeguard and more often the weakness of Resistance movements all over the world. Van Steele had joined the Resistance, he was able to persuade himself, because he hated Germans. In moments of deep privacy, he knew that he had joined it to hide from the eventual necessity of being sent off to forced labor in Germany.

From the moment of his joining, he lived in constant terror of being caught. Because he suspected his own loyalty, he was suspicious of everyone. He steered clear of the dangerous jobs, and covered his constant fear to his friends in the underground by posing as a sort of watchdog over their security, perpetually warning them to be careful of their speech and actions, and not to go too far. De Woelf could not really be blamed for believing that Van Steele was the one man to whom Billy could entrust his secret.

Billy told Van Steele his story, and told him that he expected the arrival of two friends. Would Van Steele hide the two friends until a permanent cover could be arranged?

At first Van Steele was wary. "If you have any doubts about me," Billy told him, "come night after tomorrow and I will show you that I am receiving supplies from London."

Van Steele was still uncertain. Billy clinched the argument by giving the man one of his pistols. Van Steele was the sort of person who fancied himself much safer if he were armed. The deal was closed. Van Steele was to hide the two agents.

Early on the morning of February 10, 1945, while the family of Johannes De Woelf was at breakfast, a Ford V-8 automobile stopped in front of the De Woelf house in Ulrum. Four men, wearing the shiny blue civilian suits of wartime, moved quickly and silently out of the car, and stationed themselves around the house. They were armed with Sten guns, hand grenades and revolvers. One of them knocked on the front door. De Woelf himself answered.

"Is Bill Van der Zeemanshuis here?"

De Woelf said, "No."

The man pulled a letter from his pocket, shoved it into De Woelf's hand and stood waiting, aggressively.

The letter was from the leader of the Dutch underground at Eindhoven. De Woelf knew the signature well. It was addressed to Van Steele.

"Permission to get rid of the man mentioned in your letter. Enclosed a revolver. Carry out the execution. If necessary inform local committee in Ulrum and ask for help. Arms and papers in Billy's possession must be captured, as presumably he once worked for British Intelligence. Give a very exact description. Make sure he is killed. Return revolver after execution."

De Woelf started with relieved surprise, and began a flow of explanation. He did not believe it for a moment, he said. He had known Billy for years. He had always been a member of the underground, and a loyal one. He, De Woelf, could prove it. Besides, he was never called "Bill of the Seaman's House." This Billy was a genuine Allied agent. Why, he would gladly show Van Steele the radio Billy used. But where was Van Steele?

The man at the door gestured impatiently. Van Steele had lost his nerve, he said. He and his three friends would carry out the execution instead. But the leader of the four men asked, "Where is the proof that this man is really an Allied agent?"

De Woelf hastened to the piano, lifted the cover on the top and from inside drew forth the radio which Billy used. He held it up triumphantly.

The man at the door looked at it, and with one hand behind his back, signaled through the open door to his three partners. In line, they planted themselves in front of De Woelf, leveling their weapons at his face, while his wife and three sons cowered behind him.

"You may as well know," the leader said, "since you've told us all we need to know." From his pocket he drew a black leather identification folder and held it out to De Woelf. Stamped clearly on the outside was the large white insignia of the skull and crossbones. De Woelf took one look at it and stepped backward. "The Gestapo."

If Billy had decided to escape at that moment it might have been possible for him to do so. From his upstairs room he had heard some of the conversation, though he was not sure how much De Woelf had told them, and of course, he did not know about the letter from the Resistance headquarters. When he heard De Woelf's last exclamation of astonishment, he knew that his work was finished. Still, he had a revolver, and by jumping through the upstairs window, while the Gestapo men were all down in the front room, there was just a chance, perhaps a good chance.

He stepped noiselessly around the room, quickly assembling his papers, notes and documents, his mind racing over the various courses which confronted him.

The mention of Bill of the Seaman's House did not puzzle him greatly. If the men downstairs were in truth the Gestapo, they certainly knew where Bill of the Seaman's House was, and they certainly knew he was not living with De Woelf. Obviously that was some kind of a trick. He thought again of the window.

On the other hand, there were the De Woelfs. What would happen to them with his radio discovered in their home, and the admission of his presence and his identity in their teeth? It was not difficult to imagine. No, it was better to go downstairs and deny everything until he could find out exactly how these men had found him, and how much they knew. Perhaps, if they didn't know everything, they would give him some kind of opening into which he could fit a story which would save himself and the De Woelfs. At least the De Woelfs. He burned his scraps of paper in the wastebasket, and opened the door of his room.

As he did so, two fists hit him in the face, and he fell down. They beat him unmercifully with fists and clubs. At intervals they paused. Staring then, at the patterns of blood on the floor an inch from his nose, Billy would wait for the order from the voice behind him: "Confess."

Again he would murmur, "There is nothing to confess." Then a jerk at his collar and for an instant he was on his feet again, facing them. Then fists slammed in his face and he would fall. Somewhere, far away, he could hear the sobs of Mrs. De Woelf.

It lasted for twenty minutes. At the end of that time, one of the men said, "Take him downstairs with the others, and we'll shoot them all."

Billy said, "No, I am ready to confess."

They led him downstairs. Three of his teeth were gone. He was bleeding from the ears. Laid out on the front table, he saw his radio equipment and his other weapons, saw how useless it had been to deny his work. He saw De Woelf and the oldest boy led out the door to the Ford. They let him sit down, and he waited, silently staring at the floor. After a while another car came, there was a gesture and he walked out the door.

Billy's arrest had been caused by a rare case of mistaken identity. There were three partners to it: Van Steele, the man who had promised safe lodgings for Billy's friends; the Dutch underground headquarters in Allied Territory in Eindhoven and the Gestapo.

Van Steele had made his promise to Billy early in December. He began to worry about it, and in this instance he had some superficial cause. Billy had told him that he would soon be receiving packages as well as friends. Van Steele had watched Billy warily, and had accompanied him sometimes to the farmer's field to wait for the parachutes from London. They never came. Day by day, Van Steele's suspicions grew. The obvious explanation, weather in England or weather in Holland, seemed too obvious for Van Steele. He reported his suspicions by courier to the Dutch underground headquarters across the German lines in liberated Eindhoven.

At the same time, Van Steele also reported that he suspected the presence in the neighborhood of Ulrum of the notorious Gestapo agent known as Bill of the Seaman's House, or Bill Overveen. Van Steele wondered if perhaps the Bill of the Seaman's House whom he had been warned about, and the Billy whom he had recently met, might not be the same man.

If Bill of the Seaman's House was really in the neighborhood of Ulrum, Van Steele was doing the Resistance good service in reporting it. Conceivably, he even had a right to question whether Billy, the American agent, might not be Bill of the Seaman's House. What he failed to do was to describe and identify Billy the American agent so carefully that there was no possibility of Resistance headquarters swallowing his suspicions and confusing the two men.

The men at headquarters in Eindhoven were remiss as well. If they had any doubts whatsoever about a possible confusion, they made no effort, at least inside Holland itself, to straighten out the matter. From Eindhoven headquarters went an order to Van Steele to liquidate Bill of the Seaman's House, and the order identified that man as living in Ulrum at the home of Johannes De Woelf.

Billy owed his life, for the time being at least, to the fact that Van Steele never got that letter. It fell into the hands of the Gestapo.

When Billy arrived at the prison in Groningen where he was taken after leaving the De Woelf home, he had as yet no plan, and no hope. The only question in his mind about his probable fate was why the Gestapo had asked De Woelf about Bill of the Seaman's House. He was not long in learning the answer.

Confronting him with proof of his guilt, the Gestapo showed him the letter from the Resistance headquarters to Van Steele. It referred, Billy and the Gestapo both knew, to his own movements, but called him by the Gestapo agent's name. But even while he glanced at the message, a plan of action raced to Billy's mind.

The Resistance had ordered him murdered. Very well. He would tell the Gestapo that he would work against the Resistance. It was his last and only hope.

When they gave him a chance to talk, Billy told the following story: He admitted that he was the man referred to in the letter to Van Steele. The name, he said, the "Bill of the Seaman's House," was wrong. He knew no such person. But it didn't matter. There was no doubt that he, Billy, was the man referred to, that he was an Allied agent.

Then he planted his story. He said that he hated the underground which had ordered him murdered. He blamed the whole thing on the Allied governments and particularly on the Americans, who had never been fair to him. He wanted nothing more than revenge against his betrayers. Then he made a proposal:

"I will work for the Gestapo as a double agent," he said, "if you will release the De Woelfs from prison, if you will punish the men who beat me and if you will give me the treatment in prison which is ordinarily due an Allied officer."

He made his statement with sincerity and vehemence and without the slightest show of fear. The Gestapo man made no comment. When he had finished, he was led back to his cell.

Two days later he was taken out again, bundled into a car and driven to Gestapo headquarters at Zwolle, where he was questioned again, this time more searchingly, the same questions being asked over and over.

The Gestapo was extremely polite. They always offered him a chair. They asked him about the organization of OSS, the organization of the British Secret Intelligence Service, the names of the men he had met, the places where he had trained, the organization of the Dutch Resistance, the manner of his dispatch into Holland, the code he used. Billy answered all the questions. He told them enough to write the long report which OSS was later to hear about in a telegram to London. When he had finished, he again proposed that he would be a useful agent for the Gestapo. His questioner merely grunted. He was taken to a new cell at the prison in Zwolle.

On the night of February 12, he was unlocked again, handed his radio, driven some miles to a lonely field and while four men stood over him with machine pistols, he was ordered to contact London.

It was his first operation under duress, and from the moment that

Billy realized that the Gestapo did not mean to shoot him immediately, he had prepared for it and decided what to do. That was the night on which Peter Smith in London first began to note something strange in Billy's messages. He asked for "packages only."

All this time Billy had been fairly well treated. At least he was not beaten up again, or starved. That fact gave him some hope that perhaps the one last chance he had been afforded through the case of mistaken identity would save his life. On February 16 his hopes were answered.

The Gestapo man who unlocked his cell door on that day remarked to him, "The drop was successful." Billy was afraid to speak. In his mind he could visualize the two "friends" who might have landed the night before. Down the long rows of cells and out into the office he went, in front of his guard, and as soon as he entered the room he knew he had been successful. Propped up against the wall was the huge tin container which had been dropped by parachute the night before. That was all. The Gestapo men were very pleased. Billy had proved himself to them, and they gave him cigarettes and chocolate out of the container, and told him that because of the successful drop, and to show the good faith of the Gestapo, the two De Woelfs, father and son, had been released from prison.

From that time on Billy was treated as a special prisoner. Food and cigarettes were his. On February 17 he contacted OSS again, and this time the Gestapo gave him some information to pass on. The information was general, but it was accurate, and Billy wondered about it. Walking through the field on the way back to prison, he chanced a question: "Why do you give them accurate information?" he asked.

"Wait till we get a reply," the Gestapo man answered. "They might ask you for a few more details, and we'd find out just what part of Holland they are interested in."

A few days later Billy was again taken out, this time to wait for a drop of packages. The weather was bad, and no plane arrived. All night they waited, and the Gestapo men were irritated. But the failure gave Billy the chance he had been waiting for.

On February 28, under the Gestapo eye, Billy tapped out the prearranged danger signal, the repeated word "damned." It did not go off as smoothly as he had hoped. The Gestapo asked him why he had used the word. He answered, half-jokingly, "I ought to have used something stronger after sitting out all night waiting for packages which never came." There was no answer. Evidently the Gestapo was satisfied.

On March 30, Billy contacted London for the last time. He did not know that it was for the last time, and he kept waiting for the usual order to come out of his cell and go to work with his radio. But the days passed and the Gestapo ignored him. The order never came again.

Alone in his cell, unable to plan, to argue or to act, he knew for the first time since his capture the loneliness of fear. Over and over he posed to himself the question of his chance for life. At first he had staked everything on his argument to the Gestapo that he would be willing to work for them as a double agent. But they hadn't answered that argument. Perhaps it was a useless hope.

Again he had experienced a quick mounting joy the night the Gestapo man had told him about the plan to get requests for specific information from OSS. Such a scheme might keep him alive until the war was over. But now he had sat and walked and tried to sleep in this small room of dirty whitewashed stone for days, and no one had come near him. Perhaps that was a useless hope too.

He passed the time in trying on, mentally, the logic of the Gestapo. He put himself in their place. If he were they, and they were he, would he think it worthwhile keeping them alive? Would he make them double agents? Would he use them to pass on information in the hope of getting some in return? Some days he thought the answer was yes. As the days went by, he was certain it was no. Two weeks passed, and Billy still did not know his fate. Then on April 17 the answer to his questions came.

He was led out of his cell and taken to the office of a Gestapo man whom Billy had met before and whom he knew as Shreieder. Shreieder greeted him in friendly fashion, asked him to sit down and then remarked: "We have decided to release you next week. What are you going to do then?"

The question was casual. Billy tried to be casual too. "I hope," he said, "that you will let me work for you."

It was agreed. During the next week, Shreieder and Billy worked out his mission behind the Allied lines.

It was in essence an attempt to put into practice the same plan to split the Allies which Germany had tried so frequently before. This time there was a new twist to it. Billy was to return to OSS with the following proposal from the Gestapo: that representatives of OSS and the Gestapo should meet in a round-table conference, at which the Gestapo would turn over to OSS all the valuable intelligence it possessed on Japan. In return for this information, OSS would attempt to persuade the Allied command to stall the war on the Western Front while Germany attempted to reach a decision with Russia. The United States would then be free to tackle Japan with the added advantage of the secrets about that country which the Gestapo would disclose.

The two men worked out a code also, by which Billy would keep in touch with Shreieder. There were to be four messages: the first to signify Billy's arrival, the second to report that he had delivered the Gestapo terms, the third to report whether or not the mission was successful, the fourth to let Shreieder know that Billy was returning through the lines.

Two more weeks were occupied in getting passports, pictures, a Gestapo pass and various other documents. Billy fretted at the delay; but he tried to seem particular about his documents and not too anxious to leave. Again and again, while he waited, he went over his cover story with Shreieder.

On May 3, near the town of Veenendaal, Billy shook hands with Shreieder, checked the documents he possessed as a German agent and set out through the mine fields in the company of an officer in the German SS. Halfway through, the SS officer pointed out the way. They stopped and chatted for a moment. Billy returned him his Gestapo pass, they shook hands and parted.

It was about this time, or a little before, that Pete Smith in London received a copy of the Gestapo interrogation of Billy which had been captured from a German courier some two weeks before.

The document is worth some attention because it completely and finally settled the question of Billy's allegiance, which had been under doubt from time to time, and which, when the document was first discovered, had stamped him definitely as a "turned" agent, a man who had gone over to the camp of the enemy.

The document began:

SECRET REICHS MATTER

To the Front Reconnaissance Commando 306
For the Attention of Major Von Feldmann

SUBJECT: The American Secret Service in the Netherlands
PRECEDENT: None

On February 10, 1945, the first of the American agents for Strategic Services of the United States Army was caught through the Special Command of the BDS in Ulrum Groningen. He has fully confessed.

The man to whom that document had first fallen, and who had sent the cable announcing that Billy "has apparently told them all he knew," had evidently read no further than this.

For there followed a piece of subterfuge as clever in planning and powerful in effect as a perfectly executed football play. Billy had completely fooled the Gestapo. He had told them nothing that they did not already know, and a great deal which, from that time on, they regarded as fact, and which was in reality sheer dream.

Billy had told them, the document proved, that he had been sent to Holland to get a job as a fisherman on a Rhine boat so as to carry out espionage in Germany. He told them that he had been forbidden to work with the Dutch Resistance, so that, therefore, he did not know any of their names. In this way he completely misled them as to his real mission.

Billy had told them that OSS was a part of the American State Department; that the Earl of Harewood, brother-in-law of the King, was the head of the British Secret Intelligence Service. He had invented fictitious addresses for OSS headquarters in London, and fictitious names for his friends in OSS. In this way he completely misled them as to the United States and British organizations.

Interspersed with all this information, he had given them a sprinkling of fact to make the whole story plausible. All of these facts the Germans already knew. He told them that General Donovan was the director of OSS, the location of the British parachute school (maps of which the Germans already had). He told them about the effect of V-2 bombings in London, and about British rationing systems. Both of these stories the Germans already knew.

But incredible as it may seem, these real facts were enough to make the Gestapo swallow whole everything else which Billy said. For most important of all, Billy's interrogation had led to one of the most mystifying German troop movements of the entire war:

The Germans had asked Billy about the possibilities of a further Allied invasion. He told them, quite frankly, that an invasion of north Holland was a part of the Allied plan, and that it would be made in the eastern area of Friesland, on the Dutch North Sea coast.

At a time when Germany's need was desperate, when every able-bodied man and many who were not were being rushed to stop the gaps in the West Wall, the Germans took that information so seriously that they moved thirty thousand of their finest troops, three parachute divisions, to the area Billy had pointed out on the map.

The German move was so bewildering that Allied headquarters suspected insanity in the enemy high command. Eisenhower had no more intention of invading Holland than the Germans then had of invading England. But Eisenhower did not know about Billy.

The final decision of OSS men after reading the captured report was set forth in a note from one of them: "It is clear that the underlined portion of the cable we received was absolutely false, and that Billy not only did not give the Germans any public knowledge or information which they did not already know, but that he prevented them from securing the names of his friends in OSS, and gave them other information which was completely incorrect."

Peter Smith, reading the report, summed it up too: "A damned good job."

In the late afternoon of May 3, a British soldier, lounging near his slit trench, looked up to see a tall thin man in civilian clothes coming toward him from the direction of the German lines. He was waving a white handkerchief above his head, and grinning from ear to ear.

Agent Billy had returned.

A WATCHER BY THE DEAD
By Ambrose Bierce

· ·

It wouldn't be so difficult to sit up all night
with only a dead man for company—
or so he thought.

I

In an upper room of an unoccupied dwelling in the part of San Francisco known as North Beach lay the body of a man, under a sheet. The hour was near nine in the evening; the room was dimly lighted by a single candle. Although the weather was warm, the two windows, contrary to the custom which gives the dead plenty of air, were closed and the blinds drawn down. The furniture of the room consisted of but three pieces—an armchair, a small reading stand supporting the candle, and a long kitchen table, supporting the body of the man. All these, as also the corpse, seemed to have been recently brought in, for an observer, had there been one, would have seen that all were free from dust, whereas everything else in the room was pretty thickly coated with it, and there were cobwebs in the angles of the walls.

Under the sheet the outlines of the body could be traced, even the features, these having that unnaturally sharp definition which seems to belong to faces of the dead, but is really characteristic of those only that have been wasted by disease. From the silence of the room one would rightly have inferred that it was not in the front of the house, facing a street. It really faced nothing but a high breast of rock, the rear of the building being set into a hill.

As a neighboring church clock was striking nine with an indolence which seemed to imply such an indifference to the flight of time that one could hardly help wondering why it took the trouble to strike at all, the single door of the room was opened and a man entered, advancing toward the body. As he did so the door closed, apparently of its own volition; there was a grating, as of a key turned with difficulty, and the snap of the lock bolt as it shot into its socket. A sound of retiring footsteps in the passage outside ensued, and the man was to all appearance a prisoner. Advancing to the table, he stood a moment looking down at the body; then with a slight shrug of the shoulders walked over to one of the windows and hoisted the blind. The darkness outside was absolute, the panes were covered with dust, but by wiping this away he could see that the window was fortified with strong iron bars crossing it within a few inches of the glass and imbedded in the masonry on each side. He examined the other window. It was the same. He manifested no great curiosity in the matter, did not even so much as raise the sash. If he was a prisoner he was apparently a tractable one. Having completed his examination of the room, he seated himself in the armchair, took a book from his pocket, drew the stand with its candle alongside and began to read.

The man was young—not more than thirty—dark in complexion, smooth-shaven, with brown hair. His face was thin and high-nosed, with a broad forehead and a "firmness" of the chin and jaw which is said by those having it to denote resolution. The eyes were gray and steadfast, not moving except with definitive purpose. They were now for the greater part of the time fixed upon his book, but he occasionally withdrew them and turned them to the body on the table, not, apparently, from any dismal fascination which under such circumstances it might be supposed to exercise upon even a courageous person, nor with a conscious rebellion against the contrary influence which might dominate a timid one. He looked at it as if in his reading he had come upon something recalling him to a sense of his surroundings. Clearly this watcher by the dead was discharging his trust with intelligence and composure, as became him.

After reading for perhaps a half hour he seemed to come to the end of a chapter and quietly laid away the book. He then rose and taking the reading stand from the floor carried it into a corner of the room near one of the windows, lifted the candle from it and returned to the empty fireplace before which he had been sitting.

A moment later he walked over to the body on the table, lifted the sheet and turned it back from the head, exposing a mass of dark hair and a thin face-cloth, beneath which the features showed with even sharper definition than before. Shading his eyes by interposing his free hand between them and the candle, he stood looking at his motionless companion with a serious and tranquil regard. Satisfied with his inspection, he pulled the sheet over the face again and returning to the chair, took some matches off the candlestick, put them in the side pocket of his sack coat and sat down. He then lifted the candle from its socket and looked at it critically, as if calculating how long it would last. It was barely two inches long; in another hour he would be in darkness. He replaced it in the candlestick and blew it out.

II

In a physician's office in Kearny Street three men sat about a table, drinking punch and smoking. It was late in the evening, almost midnight, indeed, and there had been no lack of punch. The gravest of the three, Dr. Helberson, was the host—it was in his rooms they sat. He was about thirty years of age; the others were even younger; all were physicians.

"The superstitious awe with which the living regard the dead," said Dr. Helberson, "is hereditary and incurable. One need no more be ashamed of it than of the fact that he inherits, for example, an incapacity for mathematics, or a tendency to lie."

The others laughed. "Oughtn't a man to be ashamed to lie?" asked the youngest of the three, who was in fact a medical student not yet graduated.

"My dear Harper, I said nothing about that. The tendency to lie is one thing; lying is another."

"But do you think," said the third man, "that this superstitious feeling, this fear of the dead, reasonless as we know it to be, is universal? I am myself not conscious of it."

"Oh, but it is 'in your system' for all that," replied Helberson. "It needs only the right conditions—what Shakespeare calls the 'confederate season'—to manifest itself in some very disagreeable way that will open your eyes. Physicians and soldiers are of course more nearly free from it than others."

"Physicians and soldiers!—why don't you add hangmen and headsmen? Let us have in all the assassin classes."

"No, my dear Mancher; the juries will not let the public executioners acquire sufficient familiarity with death to be altogether unmoved by it."

Young Harper, who had been helping himself to a fresh cigar at the sideboard, resumed his seat. "What would you consider conditions under which any man of woman born would become insupportably conscious of his share of our common weakness in this regard?" he asked, rather verbosely.

"Well, I should say that if a man were locked up all night with a corpse—alone—in a dark room—of a vacant house—with no bed covers to pull over his head—and lived through it without going altogether mad, he might justly boast himself not of woman born, nor yet, like Macduff, a product of Cæsarean section."

"I thought you never would finish piling up conditions," said Harper, "but I know a man who is neither a physician nor a soldier who will accept them all, for any stake you like to name."

"Who is he?"

"His name is Jarette—a stranger here; comes from my town in New York. I have no money to back him, but he will back himself with loads of it."

"How do you know that?"

"He would rather bet than eat. As for fear—I dare say he thinks it some cutaneous disorder, or possibly a particular kind of religious heresy."

"What does he look like?" Helberson was evidently becoming interested.

"Like Mancher, here—might be his twin brother."

"I accept the challenge," said Helberson, promptly.

"Awfully obliged to you for the compliment, I'm sure," drawled Mancher, who was growing sleepy. "Can't I get into this?"

"Not against me," Helberson said. "I don't want *your* money."

"All right," said Mancher, "I'll be the corpse."

The others laughed.

The outcome of this crazy conversation we have seen.

III

In extinguishing his meager allowance of candle Mr. Jarette's object was to preserve it against some unforeseen need. He may have thought, too, or half thought, that the darkness would be no worse at one time than another, and if the situation became insupportable it would be better to have a means of relief, or even release. At any rate it was wise to have a little reserve of light, even if only to enable him to look at his watch.

No sooner had he blown out the candle and set it on the floor at his side than he settled himself comfortably in the armchair, leaned back and closed his eyes, hoping and expecting to sleep. In this he was disappointed; he had never in his life felt less sleepy, and in a few minutes he gave up the attempt. But what could he do? He could not go groping about in absolute darkness at the risk of bruising himself —at the risk, too, of blundering against the table and rudely disturbing the dead. We all recognize their right to lie at rest, with immunity from all that is harsh and violent. Jarette almost succeeded in making himself believe that considerations of this kind restrained him from risking the collision and fixed him to the chair.

While thinking of this matter he fancied that he heard a faint sound in the direction of the table—what kind of sound he could hardly have explained. He did not turn his head. Why should he—in the darkness? But he listened—why should he not? And listening he grew giddy and grasped the arms of the chair for support. There was a strange ringing in his ears; his head seemed bursting; his chest was oppressed by the constriction of his clothing. He wondered why it was so, and whether these were symptoms of fear. Then, with a long and strong expiration, his chest appeared to collapse, and with the great gasp with which he refilled his exhausted lungs the vertigo left him and he knew that so intently had he listened that he had held his breath almost to suffocation. The revelation was vexatious; he arose, pushed away the chair with his foot and strode to the center of the room. But one does not stride far in darkness; he began to grope, and finding the wall followed it to an angle, turned, followed it past the two windows and there in another corner came into violent contact with the reading stand, overturning it. It made a clatter that startled him. He was annoyed. "How the devil could I have forgotten where it was?" he muttered, and groped his way along the third wall to the fireplace. "I must put things to rights," said he, feeling the floor for the candle.

Having recovered that, he lighted it and instantly turned his eyes to the table, where, naturally, nothing had undergone any change. The reading stand lay unobserved upon the floor: he had forgotten to "put it to rights." He looked all about the room, dispersing the deeper shadows by movements of the candle in his hand, and crossing over to the door tested it by turning and pulling the knob with all his strength. It did not yield and this seemed to afford him a certain satisfaction; indeed, he secured it more firmly by a bolt which he had not before observed. Returning to his chair, he looked at his watch; it was half-past nine. With a start of surprise he held the watch at his ear. It had not stopped. The candle was now visibly shorter. He again extinguished it, placing it on the floor at his side as before.

Mr. Jarette was not at his ease; he was distinctly dissatisfied with his surroundings, and with himself for being so. "What have I to fear?" he thought. "This is ridiculous and disgraceful; I will not be so great a fool." But courage does not come of saying, "I will be courageous," nor of recognizing its appropriateness to the occasion. The more Jarette condemned himself, the more reason he gave himself for condemnation; the greater the number of variations which he played upon the simple theme of the harmlessness of the dead, the more insupportable grew the discord of his emotions. "What!" he cried aloud in the anguish of his spirit. "What! Shall I, who have not a shade of superstition in my nature—I, who have no belief in immortality—I, who know (and never more clearly than now) that the after-life is the dream of a desire—shall I lose at once my bet, my honor and my self-respect, perhaps my reason, because certain savage ancestors dwelling in caves and burrows conceived the monstrous notion that the dead walk by night?—that——" Distinctly, unmistakably, Mr. Jarette heard behind him a light, soft sound of footfalls, deliberate, regular, successively nearer!

IV

Just before daybreak the next morning Dr. Helberson and his young friend Harper were driving slowly through the streets of North Beach in the doctor's coupé.

"Have you still the confidence of youth in the courage or stolidity of your friend?" said the elder man. "Do you believe that I have lost this wager?"

"I *know* you have," replied the other, with enfeebling emphasis.

"Well, upon my soul, I hope so."

It was spoken earnestly, almost solemnly. There was a silence for a few moments.

"Harper," the doctor resumed, looking very serious in the shifting half-lights that entered the carriage as they passed the street lamps, "I don't feel altogether comfortable about this business. If your friend had not irritated me by the contemptuous manner in which he treated my doubt of his endurance—a purely physical quality—and by the cool incivility of his suggestion that the corpse be that of a physician, I should not have gone on with it. If anything should happen we are ruined, as I fear we deserve to be."

"What can happen? Even if the matter should be taking a serious turn, of which I am not at all afraid, Mancher has only to 'resurrect' himself and explain matters. With a genuine 'subject' from the dissecting-room, or one of your late patients, it might be different."

Dr. Mancher, then, had been as good as his promise; he was the "corpse."

Dr. Helberson was silent for a long time, as the carriage, at a snail's pace, crept along the same street it had traveled two or three times already. Presently he spoke: "Well, let us hope that Mancher, if he has had to rise from the dead, has been discreet about it. A mistake in that might make matters worse instead of better."

"Yes," said Harper, "Jarette would kill him. But, Doctor"—looking at his watch as the carriage passed a gas lamp—"it is nearly four o'clock at last."

A moment later the two had quitted the vehicle and were walking briskly toward the long-unoccupied house belonging to the doctor in which they had immured Mr. Jarette in accordance with the terms of the mad wager. As they neared it they met a man running. "Can you tell me," he cried, suddenly checking his speed, "where I can find a doctor?"

"What's the matter?" Helberson asked, noncommittal.

"Go and see for yourself," said the man, resuming his running.

They hastened on. Arrived at the house, they saw several persons entering in haste and excitement. In some of the dwellings nearby and across the way the chamber windows were thrown up, showing a protrusion of heads. All heads were asking questions, none heeding the questions of the others. A few of the windows with closed blinds were illuminated; the inmates of those rooms were dressing to come down. Exactly opposite the door of the house that they sought a street lamp threw a yellow, insufficient light upon the scene, seeming to say that it could disclose a good deal more if it wished. Harper paused at the door and laid a hand upon his companion's arm. "It is all up with us, Doctor," he said in extreme agitation, which contrasted strangely with his free-and-easy words; "the game has gone against us all. Let's not go in there; I'm for lying low."

"I'm a physician," said Dr. Helberson, calmly. "There may be need of one."

They mounted the doorsteps and were about to enter. The door was open; the street lamp opposite lighted the passage into which it opened. It was full of men. Some had ascended the stairs at the farther end, and, denied admittance above, waited for better fortune. All were talking, none listening. Suddenly, on the upper landing there was a great commotion; a man had sprung out of a door and was breaking away from those endeavoring to detain him. Down through the mass of affrighted idlers he came, pushing them aside, flattening them against the wall on one side, or compelling them to cling to the rail on the other, clutching them by the throat, striking them savagely, thrusting them back down the stairs and walking over the fallen. His clothing was in disorder, he was without a hat. His eyes, wild and restless, had in them something more terrifying than his apparently superhuman strength. His face, smooth-shaven, was bloodless, his hair frost-white.

As the crowd at the foot of the stairs, having more freedom, fell away to let him pass Harper sprang forward. "Jarette! Jarette!" he cried.

Dr. Helberson seized Harper by the collar and dragged him back. The man looked into their faces without seeming to see them and sprang through the door, down the steps, into the street, and away. A stout policeman, who had had inferior success in conquering his way down the stairway, followed a moment later and started in pursuit, all the heads in the windows—those of women and children now—screaming in guidance.

The stairway being now partly cleared, most of the crowd having rushed down to the street to observe the flight and pursuit, Dr.

Helberson mounted to the landing, followed by Harper. At a door in the upper passage an officer denied them admittance. "We are physicians," said the doctor, and they passed in. The room was full of men, dimly seen, crowded about a table. The newcomers edged their way forward and looked over the shoulders of those in the front rank. Upon the table, the lower limbs covered with a sheet, lay the body of a man, brilliantly illuminated by the beam of a bull's-eye lantern held by a policeman standing at the feet. The others, excepting those near the head—the officer himself—all were in darkness. The face of the body showed yellow, repulsive, horrible! The eyes were partly open and upturned and the jaw fallen; traces of froth defiled the lips, the chin, the cheeks. A tall man, evidently a doctor, bent over the body with his hand thrust under the shirt front. He withdrew it and placed two fingers in the open mouth. "This man has been about six hours dead," said he. "It is a case for the coroner."

He drew a card from his pocket, handed it to the officer and made his way toward the door.

"Clear the room—out, all!" said the officer, sharply, and the body disappeared as if it had been snatched away, as shifting the lantern he flashed its beam of light here and there against the faces of the crowd. The effect was amazing! The men, blinded, confused, almost terrified, made a tumultuous rush for the door, pushing, crowding, and tumbling over one another as they fled, like the hosts of Night before the shafts of Apollo. Upon the struggling, trampling mass the officer poured his light without pity and without cessation. Caught in the current, Helberson and Harper were swept out of the room and cascaded down the stairs into the street.

"Good God, Doctor! did I not tell you that Jarette would kill him?" said Harper, as soon as they were clear of the crowd.

"I believe you did," replied the other, without apparent emotion.

They walked on in silence, block after block. Against the graying east the dwellings of the hill tribes showed in silhouette. The familiar milk wagon was already astir in the streets; the baker's man would soon come upon the scene; the newspaper carrier was abroad in the land.

"It strikes me, youngster," said Helberson, "that you and I have been having too much of the morning air lately. It is unwholesome; we need a change. What do you say to a tour in Europe?"

"When?"

"I'm not particular. I should suppose that four o'clock this afternoon would be early enough."

"I'll meet you at the boat," said Harper.

V

Seven years afterward these two men sat upon a bench in Madison Square, New York, in familiar conversation. Another man, who had been observing them for some time, himself unobserved, approached and, courteously lifting his hat from locks as white as frost, said: "I beg your pardon, gentlemen, but when you have killed a man by coming to life, it is best to change clothes with him, and at the first opportunity make a break for liberty."

Helberson and Harper exchanged significant glances. They were obviously amused. The former then looked the stranger kindly in the eye and replied:

"That has always been my plan. I entirely agree with you as to its advant——"

He stopped suddenly, rose and went white. He stared at the man, open-mouthed; he trembled visibly.

"Ah!" said the stranger, "I see that you are indisposed, Doctor. If you cannot treat yourself Dr. Harper can do something for you, I am sure."

"Who the devil are you?" said Harper, bluntly.

The stranger came nearer and, bending toward them, said in a whisper: "I call myself Jarette sometimes, but I don't mind telling you, for old friendship, that I am Dr. William Mancher."

The revelation brought Harper to his feet. "Mancher!" he cried; and Helberson added: "It is true, by God!"

"Yes," said the stranger, smiling vaguely, "it is true enough, no doubt."

He hesitated and seemed to be trying to recall something, then began humming a popular air. He had apparently forgotten their presence.

"Look here, Mancher," said the elder of the two, "tell us just what occurred that night—to Jarette, you know."

"Oh, yes, about Jarette," said the other. "It's odd I should have neglected to tell you—I tell it so often. You see I knew, by overhearing him talking to himself, that he was pretty badly frightened. So I couldn't resist the temptation to come to life and have a bit of fun out of him—I couldn't really. That was all right, though certainly I did not think he would take it so seriously; I did not, truly. And afterward—well, it was a tough job changing places with him, and then—damn you! you didn't let me out!"

Nothing could exceed the ferocity with which these last words were delivered. Both men stepped back in alarm.

"We?—why—why," Helberson stammered, losing his self-possession utterly, "we had nothing to do with it."

"Didn't I say you were Drs. Hell-born and Sharper?" inquired the man, laughing.

"My name is Helberson, yes; and this gentleman is Mr. Harper," replied the former, reassured by the laugh. "But we are not physicians now; we are—well, hang it, old man, we are gamblers."

And that was the truth.

"A very good profession—very good, indeed; and, by the way, I hope Sharper here paid over Jarette's money like an honest stakeholder. A very good and honorable profession," he repeated, thoughtfully, moving carelessly away, "but I stick to the old one. I am High Supreme Medical Officer of the Bloomingdale Asylum; it is my duty to cure the superintendent."

TEA PARTY
By Harold Pinter

. . . .

His eyes were worse.
He was pleased with his secretary.
His wife used to have fits of laughing.
He could see it all.

My eyes are worse. My physician is an inch under six feet. There is a gray strip in his hair, one, no more. He has a brown stain on his left cheek. His lamp shades are dark-blue drums. Each has a golden rim. They are identical. There is a deep black burn in his Indian carpet. His staff is bespectacled, to a woman. Through the blinds I hear the birds of his garden. Sometimes his wife appears, in white.

He is clearly skeptical on the subject of my eyes. According to him my eyes are normal, perhaps even better than normal. He finds no evidence that my sight is growing worse.

My eyes are worse. It is not that I do not see. I do see.

My job goes well. My family and I remain close friends. My two sons are my closest friends. My wife is closer. I am close friends with all my family, including my mother and my father. Often we sit and listen to Bach. When I go to Scotland I take them with me. My wife's brother came once and was useful on the trip.

I have my hobbies, one of which is using a hammer and nails, or a screwdriver and screws, or various saws, on wood, constructing things or making things useful, finding a use for an object that appears to have no value. But it is not so easy to do this when you see double, or when you are blinded by the object, or when you do not see at all, or when you are blinded by the object.

My wife is happy. I use my imagination in bed. We love with the light on. I watch her closely, she watches me. In the morning her eyes shine. I can see them shining through her spectacles.

All winter the skies were bright. Rain fell at night. In the morning the skies were bright. My backhand flip was my strongest weapon. Taking position to face my wife's brother, across the dear table, my paddle lightly clasped, my wrist flexing, I waited to loosen my flip to his forehand, watch him (shocked) dart and be beaten, flounder and sulk. My forehand was not so powerful, so swift. Predictably, he attacked my forehand. There was a ringing sound in the room, a rubber sound in the walls. Predictably, he attacked my forehand. But once far to the right on my forehand, and my weight genuinely disposed, I could employ my backhand flip, unanswerable, watch him flounder, skid and be beaten. They were close games. But it is not now so easy when you see the ping-pong ball double, or do not see it at all or when, hurling toward you at speed, the ball blinds you.

I am pleased with my secretary. She knows the business well and loves it. She is trustworthy. She makes calls to Newcastle and Birmingham on my behalf and is never fobbed off. She is respected on the telephone. Her voice is persuasive. My partner and I agree that she is of inestimable value to us. My partner and my wife often discuss her when the three of us meet for coffee or drinks. Neither of them, when discussing Wendy, can speak highly enough of her.

On bright days, of which there are many, I pull the blinds in my office in order to dictate. Often I touch her swelling body. She reads back, flips the page. She makes a telephone call to Birmingham. Even were I (while she speaks, holding the receiver lightly, her other hand poised for notes) to touch her swelling body, her call would still be followed to its conclusion. It is she who bandages my eyes, while I touch her swelling body.

I do not remember being like my sons in any way when I was a boy. Their reserve is remarkable. They seem stirred by no passion. They sit silent. An odd mutter passes between them. I can't hear you, what are you saying, speak up, I say. My wife says the same. I can't hear you, what are you saying, speak up. They are of an age. They work well at school, it appears. But at ping-pong both are duds. As a boy I was wide awake, of passionate interests, voluble, responsive, and my eyesight was excellent. They resemble me in no way. Their eyes are glazed and evasive behind their spectacles.

My brother-in-law was best man at our wedding. None of my own friends were at that time in the country. My closest friend, who was the natural choice, was called away suddenly on business. To his great regret he was therefore forced to opt out. He had prepared a superb speech in honor of the groom, to be delivered at the reception. My brother-in-law could not of course himself deliver it, since it referred to the long-standing friendship which existed between Atkins and myself, and my brother-in-law knew little of me. He was therefore confronted with a difficult problem. He solved it by making his sister his central point of reference. I still have the present he gave me, a carved pencil sharpener, from Bali.

The day I first interviewed Wendy she wore a tight tweed skirt. Her left thigh never ceased to caress her right, and vice versa. All this took place under her skirt. She seemed to me the perfect secretary. She listened to my counsel wide-eyed and attentive, her hands calmly clasped, trim, bulgy, plump, rosy, swelling. She was clearly the possessor of an active and inquiring intelligence. Three times she cleaned her spectacles with a silken kerchief.

After the wedding my brother-in-law asked my dear wife to remove her glasses. He peered deep into her eyes. You have married a good man, he said. He will make you happy. As he was doing nothing at the time, I invited him to join me in the business. Before long, he became my partner, so keen was his industry, so sharp his business acumen.

Wendy's common sense, her clarity, her discretion, are of inestimable value to our firm.

With my eye at the keyhole I hear goosing, the squeak of them. The slit is black, only the sliding gussle on my drum, the hiss and flap of their bliss. The room sits on my head, my skull creased on the brass and loathsome handle I dare not twist, for fear of seeing black screech and scrape of my secretary writhing golden and blind in my partner's paunch and jungle.

My wife reached down to me. Do you love me, she asked. I do love you, I spat into her eyeball. I shall prove it yet, I shall prove it yet, what proof yet, what proof remaining, what proof not yet given. All proof. (For my part, I decided on a more cunning, more allusive stratagem.) Do you love me, was my counter.

The ping-pong table streaked with slime. My hands pant to gain the ball. My sons watch. They cheer me on. They are loud in their loyalty. I am moved. I fall back on strokes, on gambits, long since gone, flip, cut, chop, shtip, bluff to my uttermost. I play the ball by nose. The twins hail my efforts gustily. But my brother-in-law is no chump. He slams again, he slams again, deep to my forehand. I skid, flounder, stare sightless into the crack of his bat.

Where are my hammers, my screws, my saws?

How are you, asked my partner. Bandage on straight? Knots tight?

The door slammed. Where was I? In the office or at home? Had someone come in as my partner went out? Had he gone out? Was it silence I heard, this scuffle, creak, squeal, scrape, gurgle and muff? Tea was being poured. Heavy thighs (Wendy's? my wife's? both? apart? together?) trembled in stilettos. I sipped the liquid. It was welcome. My physician greeted me warmly. In a minute, old chap, we'll take off those bandages. Have a rock cake. I declined. The birds are at the birdbath, called his white wife. They all rushed to look. My sons sent something flying. Some*one*? Surely not. I had never heard my sons in such good form. They chattered, chuckled, discussed their work eagerly with their uncle. My parents were silent. The room seemed very small, smaller than I had remembered it. I knew where everything was, every particular. But its smell had altered. Perhaps because the room was overcrowded. My wife broke gasping out of a fit of laughter, as she was wont to do in the early days of our marriage. Why was she laughing? Had someone told her a joke? Who? Her sons? Unlikely. My sons were discussing their work with my physician and his wife. Be with you in a minute, old chap, my physician called to me. Meanwhile my partner had the two women half stripped on a convenient rostrum. Whose body swelled most? I had forgotten. I picked up a ping-pong ball. It was hard. I wondered how far he had stripped the women. The top halves or the bottom halves? Or perhaps he was now raising his spectacles to view my wife's swelling buttocks, the swelling breasts of my secretary. How could I verify this? By movement, by touch. But that was out of the question. And could such a sight possibly take place under the eyes of my own children? Would they continue to chat and chuckle, as they still did, with my physician? Hardly. However, it was good to have the bandage on straight and the knots tight.

DEATH DRAWS A TRIANGLE
By Edward Hale Bierstadt

. . . .

The wife was sixteen years younger than
her husband, and her husband drank,
which resulted in the murder of a newspaperman
in mid-Victorian New York City.

A murder that involved the names of Horace Greeley, Whitelaw Reid, Henry Ward Beecher, Edwin Booth and Daniel Frohman; that resulted in stigmatizing the sovereign state of Indiana as "the Paradise of Adulterers," and in the characterization of most of the gentlemen named above as "notorious free lovers"; that rocked the city of New York from the Hudson to the East River—such a murder might fairly be called a *cause célèbre*.

This is the story of that murder and of its very curious consequences.

At about five o'clock on the afternoon of Thursday, November 25, 1869, a thickset man walked into what was known as the counting room of the New York *Tribune*. He came in from the Park Row entrance and waited quietly without attracting more than casual attention. He was seen and recognized, however, by a clerk as being one Daniel McFarland, an employee in the office of the City Assessor.

At about a quarter past five, Albert D. Richardson, a well-known journalist of the day, came briskly into the counting room, went up to one of the desks there and asked for his mail. Parenthetically, it may be remarked that the clerk at this desk was young Daniel Frohman, who is described in a contemporary account as being "a decidedly good-looking young gentleman of eighteen years, with black hair; and dressed in a fashionable black suit with a wide Byron collar."

Daniel Frohman turned to get Mr. Richardson his mail, and then jumped as a shot rang out behind him. Frohman about-faced in time to see Richardson stagger out of the door that led to the stairs going up to the editorial rooms, two floors above; and to observe McFarland slip out through the exit into Nassau Street.

There was only the crash of the shot and the sudden disappearance of the two men. No spoken word. No outcry. And it was some minutes before the startled occupants of the counting room realized what had happened. Then there was a stampede.

Richardson, mortally wounded as he was, managed to crawl up two—some accounts say four—flights of stairs to the editorial rooms, where he collapsed on a sofa, moaning with pain but quite conscious and coherent. He had been shot through the stomach.

Although by this time the entire *Tribune* building was in a panic of excitement—newspapers preferring their news a little less local—a doctor was immediately sent for, and within an hour Richardson had been moved to Room 115 of the Astor House, on Broadway, just across City Hall Park.

Meanwhile, according to his own account, Daniel McFarland walked calmly up Center Street, after leaving the *Tribune*, and, "feeling weak and hungry," stepped into a restaurant to partake of coffee and stew. He then walked on uptown, picking up his brother on the way, and, at about seven o'clock, checked in at the old Westmoreland Hotel at Seventeenth Street and Fourth Avenue (it has only just been demolished), where he was given Room 31.

But Daniel Frohman, the advertising clerk who had joined the *Tribune* three years before as office boy, and who was to become one of the great figures in the American theater, had not been the only witness to the murder. There had been a fellow clerk, George M. King, in the office, and King had actually seen the shot fired. Consequently, the police started looking for Daniel McFarland in a hurry.

At ten o'clock that evening, Captain Anthony J. Allaire of the Fourth Precinct arrested McFarland in his room at the Westmoreland.

It is at this point, at the very moment of arrest, that accounts begin to differ and, indeed, not only to differ, but to become completely opposed. As we shall see, there were excellent reasons for covering McFarland.

At the trial, McFarland's counsel stated in his opening speech for the defense that when Captain Allaire arrested him, McFarland exclaimed, "My God, it must have been me! No—it was not! Yes—it must have been me!" and continued with a description of the shooting in which McFarland is quoted as saying:

"I saw suddenly two eyes close upon me like those of a demon! I saw a flash; heard a report. I recollect nothing more."

Now the curious and interesting part of this is that nowhere in the actual testimony given at the trial is there the slightest basis for these quotations. They seem to have been sheer inventions, designed solely to support a plea of emotional insanity—beloved of the American killer!—and without any justification in fact.

What actually seems to have happened was that McFarland submitted quietly to arrest, was taken at once to Room 115 at the Astor House, where Richardson identified him, and was then lodged in Captain Allaire's own room at the Fourth Precinct Station House, where he sat "smoking and seemingly quite calm and unconcerned," according to the *Tribune* reporter who interviewed him there.

McFarland must be acquitted, McFarland must be whitewashed and to do this effectively it was necessary to blacken the other side. Precisely why all this was so essential to the political rulers of New York is the real reason for this story.

McFarland, Richardson and the woman who was the apex of the triangle were no more than the proverbial pawns who were to be used after the traditional manner. Their lives, their loves and hates, their personal tragedy, were destined to be lost sight of—or to be so distorted by malice as to bear no relation to reality—in the confusion of larger issues in which they became engulfed at five fifteen o'clock on that fatal Thursday afternoon.

The newspaper reports and the various pamphlets of the day that deal with this bloody drama are so violently partisan that it is only by checking and cross-checking, by exploring and examining, that the real truth can be known.

That truth, which throws so amazing a light upon mid-Victorian New York, is the essence of this tale.

Before going further into the almost incredible consequences of McFarland's act, it will be necessary to understand the events which led up to the murder.

Daniel McFarland was the son of an Irish immigrant who had come to this country in 1823 and had settled in New York. At fourteen Daniel was apprenticed to a tailor, but making clothes for other men had few charms for a boy who wanted to be well dressed himself, and the next few years were roving ones of which the account is fragmentary. Daniel McFarland went South for a time; came back and went into business with his brother, who was a harness maker in Newark; and, somewhere around 1840, gravitated to Boston, where his occupation was unknown. He must have had some ambition at this time, and he must have saved his money, for in 1848, when Daniel was twenty-eight years old, he entered Dartmouth College.

At Dartmouth, McFarland seems to have specialized in chemistry, and during his third year he was made a sort of informal assistant to the professor heading that department. But McFarland was restless —he was always restless—and his third college year was his last. At the suggestion of the professor of chemistry, he went to Europe to study, stayed there a year, came back and studied for the law! He was admitted to the bar in Massachusetts but never practiced. Then came another year as professor of logic and elocution—God knows how the two were coupled or even reconciled!—in Brandywine College down in Delaware; and at just about this time McFarland's further interest in any regular occupation seems to have ceased.

The man was a dreamer, but without the courage or stamina to carry out his dreams. He was born for failure because he hadn't the backbone for anything else. And when a man like that fails, he turns to crime.

During 1852, when McFarland was meandering through New England for no very special reason, he ran across a poor family of weavers who were living in Lowell, Massachusetts. Only one of the family interested McFarland, however, and that was Abby, the daughter, who was then about fourteen, an exceedingly pretty girl and one who gave the impression of having undiscovered potentialities. McFarland left Lowell, but he did not forget Abby Sage. Five years later, in 1857, he went back and married her.

They were married, this oddly assorted pair, on December 4, 1857, when Abby was nineteen and McFarland thirty-seven. Quite aside from any other drawback, the difference in years was too great. And there were other drawbacks, profound ones.

In the five years that had intervened between the meeting and the marriage, the little daughter of the weaver had grown in more than height. She had become the teacher of a little country school in Manchester, New Hampshire; and she had begun to write little pieces for the papers, pleasant, harmless little pieces about children and nature and what not. Abby Sage was on the way to becoming an author. But McFarland told her that he had a fine law business in Madison, Wisconsin—to which he had gravitated—with twenty or thirty thousand dollars in real money, and Abby was impressed. Not that she married him for that. There is every reason to believe that she really loved her Daniel, and doubtless she was touched by the fidelity of a man who had waited for her for five years. She was to learn, however, that whatever McFarland had been during those years he had certainly not been faithful, and she was to learn—other things. She had not long to wait after the wedding.

On their bridal journey, in New York, on their way to Madison, they stopped long enough to permit McFarland to borrow the remainder of their train fare. When they finally arrived at Madison, Abby discovered that the law practice, along with the twenty to thirty thousand dollars, was as mythical as buried treasure.

By February of '58, two months after their marriage, they were back in New York again. McFarland promptly and efficiently pawned the few small articles of value that Abby had, and then sent her home to her father to wait for better times. They never came.

The entire married life of the McFarlands is summarized by the first two months of their marriage. There was this difference, however: as Daniel went down, Abby went up. She refused to sink with him.

McFarland seems to have taken up drinking as a profession at about the time they moved to a cottage in Brooklyn, in the autumn of 1858. Before that he was no more than an earnest amateur. Now things went from bad to worse with an interesting rapidity.

If would be fruitless to follow these two through all the ups and downs—there were mighty few ups!—of the next ten years, but there are some events that stand out as being, not important in themselves, but as they bear on what was to follow. The red thread of destiny can be traced as it winds in and out through apparently unimportant happenings.

In 1860, the McFarlands were in Madison again, and in a desperate effort to get together enough money to keep them going Abby started giving "dramatic readings," a form of terrorism that is now fortunately almost extinct. The readings were definitely successful, however, and McFarland conceived the idea of returning to New York, fitting Abby for the stage, and, after her début, becoming himself an actor. This was apparently based on the not uncommon theory that if you fail at everything else you can always go on the stage. It was exactly the sort of idea that would seem like a stroke of genius to a man like McFarland, and he proceeded at once to act upon it.

In June, 1861, they returned to New York, took lodgings with Mrs. Oliver, at 58 Varick Street, and started in, living on what Abby had managed to save out in Wisconsin and on what little they had made from the sale of their few sticks of furniture.

Abby, her beauty more matured, her charm more engaging than ever, took what lessons she could afford from Mr. and Mrs. George Vandenhoff, who imparted the secrets of elocution to a few select pupils; and that fall and winter she managed to support the entire family—there were children by now—with her readings.

Just what she read and how she read it is lost to history, but at least she did sufficiently well so that she was able to make from one to two hundred dollars a recital, and was soon being "taken up by the right people."

The right people, in this instance, were Mrs. Cleveland, sister of Horace Greeley, the forthright editor of the *Tribune*; Mrs. Calhoun, who ran a popular column of gossip and chit-chat on the same paper and Mrs. Sinclair, wife of the *Tribune*'s publisher. And so it was that, purely by chance, Abby McFarland found herself projected, head, neck and heels, into a *Tribune* coterie, which was as placed, as marked, as definite, as final as was Tammany Hall, which it opposed. Abby's friends, her patrons, were all *Tribune* people. This was to prove, later, of tremendous importance. At the moment its only effect was to give her intellectual and sympathetic companionship, and to consolidate her readings at Steinway Hall, that Mecca of the mid-Victorian intelligentsia.

So matters went along for a while, Abby achieving her small triumphs on the platform, and McFarland gradually drinking himself into alcoholic insanity. By the winter of '62 he was threatening suicide half the time, and murder the other half. By the spring of the following year he had struck Abby in the face.

Abby told Mrs. Cleveland that she didn't think she could stand it much longer, and the Clevelands and Sinclairs, with their *Tribune* influence, got McFarland a job in the office of the provost marshal—

which should have had a salutary effect on him but didn't.

For nearly three years, until the autumn of 1866, affairs drifted along rather uneventfully, if by uneventfully one means the series of petty annoyances and minor disappointments that so often, imperceptibly but inevitably, bring life to a climax. True, during these three years the country was engulfed in the bloodiest war in its history, but for these people blood was still to shed.

It was in the autumn of '66 that Abby McFarland stepped from the recital platform to the dramatic stage, for it was at this time that she got a part at the Winter Garden at twenty dollars a week. It was Mrs. Calhoun, the *Tribune* columnist, who did that for her.

The Winter Garden, originally Tripler Hall, was on the west side of Broadway, nearly opposite Bond Street. Built in 1850 for the début of Jenny Lind in America, but completed too late for her to appear there, the Winter Garden was known as the largest music hall in the world, with a stage one hundred feet wide and everything else in proportion. Since 1850, it had passed through many hands and several changes of name, but in 1866 it was the Winter Garden, and under the management of no less a person than Edwin Booth, who was starring there with his own company.

Little Abby McFarland, née Sage, with her golden-brown hair and her sweetly careful voice, played Nerissa there to Booth's Shylock in 1866. Her first appearance was on the evening of November 28, and it is curious to observe how the last week of November dogged her footsteps. That week was always fatal to her. Nevertheless, the country schoolteacher was coming up in the world.

But even the theater didn't make Abby forget the little pieces she had once written about children and animals and flowers and whatnot, and so, while all this was going on, Abby was writing. Quite aside from any other consideration, she needed the money. Twenty dollars a week doesn't go very far toward keeping all of a family in food, and part of a family in liquor, and what McFarland did with the money he got from the provost marshal's office no one seemed to know. Certainly, Abby and the children never saw any of it. So Abby wrote.

She wrote for the *Riverside Magazine*, for the *Independent* and for several other publications, and these cultural activities brought into her life the man who was to give her the greatest happiness and the deepest sorrow she had ever known.

It was at either the Clevelands' or the Sinclairs'—accounts differ, and it is unimportant—that Abby McFarland met Albert D. Richardson. The evening she met him changed her life as definitely and as abruptly as the course of a stream changes when it has been dynamited.

Richardson, a man in his early thirties and a widower with three children, was a native of New England, and a brother of the editor and owner of a religious journal in Boston. He was the secret correspondent of the *Tribune* in the South while the acts of secession were being passed, and the army correspondent of the *Tribune* in the West during the war. He was captured by the Confederates and imprisoned in both Libby and Salisbury prisons. He escaped, crossed the country, reached the Union lines and soon afterward wrote a book called *Field, Dungeon and Escape*, which went to a sale of 96,000 copies. Later, he wrote a life of General Grant. When the Union Pacific Railroad was opened, the *Tribune* sent him on a trip over the line, during which he met and befriended Mark Twain, who was less well known than he, and that resulted in another book, *Beyond the Mississippi*, which sold over 70,000. Altogether, Albert D. Richardson, forgotten as he is today, was a highly successful journalist in the sixties. He was a fine-looking man too, with a blond beard, a high forehead, straight nose and sensitive mouth. His position, background and personality were all such as to attract a woman, just as Abby's beauty, talent and need for protection made their sure appeal.

How sudden, how violent the attraction of these two was for each other it is a little difficult to estimate. Two years later, there was so much mud-slinging that today one must dig for the truth. Abby was in trouble. Life at home was becoming rapidly and increasingly impossible. She had quite enough to think about and to worry over without a love affair to complicate matters. She liked and admired Richardson, but for the moment, that was all. On his part, it is probable that any emotion he may have felt was restrained by the fact that not only was Abby the wife of another man, but that she was sufficiently harassed to make any very marked attention from him unwelcome at that time. Whatever he felt, he seems to have realized that it was wiser to wait, and kinder to be a helpful friend rather than an importunate lover. Had he not had a madman to deal with, he would have been right.

Richardson's friendship for Abby manifested itself in a very practical way. He was a successful author. She was a needy beginner. He would help her to get her work published. There exists, in one of the many old pamphlets dealing with this curious case, a description that, while it is too long to quote in full, is too amusing to omit altogether. The scene takes place in the office of the American Publishing Company in Hartford, "on a snowy afternoon in the winter of 1867." The actors are Richardson, Abby McFarland, the editors of the publishing company and the staff artist.

Mr. Richardson said briefly, as he took a chair: "Mr. Bliss, this is Mrs. McFarland. She has some sheets of manuscript which she wants to have made into a book. I would like to have you examine them. I think they will sell among your customers."

Mrs. McFarland took a seat and unrolled a folio of manuscript.

"Is there any poetry in it?" said Bliss. "Poetry doesn't sell now. There's no market for it."

"I don't know. You will have to examine the manuscript," said Mr. Richardson.

"A good story will sell, I think," said Mr. Belknap, "if it is a good one. Let Mrs. McFarland read some of her composition."

"There ought to be plenty of woodcuts to sell a book," said Cox, the artist.

"Yes, pictures will sell a book when nothing else will," said Mr. Bliss with the black whiskers.

"The title that I think of taking for my book is *Pebbles and Pearls*," said Mrs. McFarland, in a low, womanly, musical voice.

"*Pebbles and Pearls?*" said Mr. Bliss with the sandy tuft, "hasn't that been done before?"

"I think not," said Mrs. McFarland. "It is at least original with me."

"Well, let Mrs. McFarland read some extracts from her manuscript, and then we shall be able to judge of its merit," said Mr. Belknap, who seemed to be the Chesterfield of the firm.

Mrs. McFarland then unrolled the manuscript, and in a tone which delighted so many audiences in Jersey, read the first extract on "Pat the News Boy."

"That wouldn't go bad with pictures," said Cox, the artist.

"Well, what do you think about your book? What is it worth?" said Mr. Bliss.

"Let me read further," said Mrs. McFarland. "I have a little poem which I would like you gentlemen to hear. Little Dan is my boy, and I have written this 'Little Dan.'"

Having read this poem, the artist interrupted. "I can make a nice picture of Little Dan, I think." [In this poem the lady lovingly described her child.]

"Have you any other nice, short sketches?" said Mr. Belknap to Mrs. McFarland.

The lady read a short fairy tale, with a singular charm in her voice.

It was about "The Voyagers." The reading of this manuscript being concluded, the different members of the firm began to look at each other inquiringly, not knowing exactly what to answer.

Mrs. McFarland waited awhile with the manuscript in her hands, for she had children to support, and bread must be earned for them somehow. Mr. Richardson sat quiet and collected, with sympathy for the fair authoress. Mr. Belknap finally said,

"Will you be kind enough to read some more, Mrs. McFarland?"

"Yes," said Mr. Bliss. "Be kind enough to read some more of the poems, if you please, and then we shall be better able to decide upon the matter."

Mrs. McFarland then read two poems, the first being a loving description of her two children, described only as a mother could describe them, and headed "In the Twilight." The second poem was calculated to interest those who had dear ones at sea and was entitled "The Sailor's Wife."

"I guess we'll take that book," said Mr. Bliss, "and we'll print it too. It's not bad."

Mrs. McFarland was satisfied and seemed much relieved at the decision of the American Publishing Company. The book sold well, and it is understood that the lady realized about $500 as her share of the profits.

As a picture of publishing in 1867, one doubts whether this has ever been equaled. Certainly, it has never been surpassed. As a matter of fact, Abby's literary output was neither better nor worse than the average run. Indeed, its sentimental mediocrity is common to the vaporings of the hack writer in every day and age.

There were other papers and more books, for by now Abby was writing not only for the *Riverside Magazine* and the *Independent*, but for the *Round Table* and even for the *Atlantic Monthly*. There were articles in the New York *Tribune* too, "Westward to the Indies" and "Eastward to the Indies," "Fairy Stories for Children," "Tales from Shakespeare and the Old English Poets," and "The Hamlets of the Stage," as was only fitting for one who had played with Booth. It was all very genteel, elegant even. And, withal, it is rather pathetic. Abby did her best, one may be sure; and was properly proud of her success as an "authoress." Richardson helped.

It was November of 1866 when Abby went on the Winter Garden stage, and the next month her landlady requested her to move, saying that she "could not possibly have an actress in the house." So Abby moved, husband and two children with her, to 86 Amity Street; and the next month, January, 1867, moved again to Number 72, in the same street. Here she took "the back parlor and extension room," and all four of them crowded in. Not much space for a tired actress and a working writer.

In February the train was fired that ultimately blew up the ship. Richardson decided to give up his rooms and move into the same house with the McFarlands. And not only into the same house, but into the next room to theirs. It was either unbelievably indiscreet or incredibly innocent. There is not the slightest evidence that they were having what is known as "an affair." If he loved her or she him, nothing had been said to indicate it. In all probability Richardson was in love with Abby by now, but he had not told her so. It was a mad thing to do—this move. It gave the gossips and scandalmongers of two years later just the chance they were looking for, and it gave McFarland, even at that moment, an opportunity to translate alcoholic insanity into jealous mania. True, he had no excuse, no real reason, but the jealous man or woman needs none.

One can follow, after a fumbling fashion, the devious involutions of McFarland's sick mind. He was a psychopathic case. The man was a drunken failure and knew it with all the maudlin self-pity of his kind. Undoubtedly, he interpreted Abby's small successes—her part at the Winter Garden, her writing, her friendship with the Clevelands and the Sinclairs, in whose drawing rooms he had no place—as a reflection on him. The man was eaten up with envy. He was totally unable to face the fact that he was a drunkard and a brute; that he was utterly dishonest, as he was; that he was looked upon with contemptuous dislike by people with whom he might have associated; and that all these things were entirely his own fault and that of no one else. All that he had was the realization of abject failure, and the imperative impulse to blame someone else for it. The type is by no means unusual.

With Richardson and the McFarlands in the same house, it was only natural that Abby and Albert should see something of one another. McFarland was out most of the day. He now had a job in the city assessor's office, where he was able to turn a dishonest penny by blackmailing tax dodgers. Abby ran in to consult Richardson about whatever manuscript she was working on, and he would knock at her door with whatever of interest he had to offer. No more than that. It is important to stress the fact because of later accusations, and if the point seems unduly labored it is only because the later smoke screen was so dense that it implied a conflagration that simply was not there.

McFarland did his best to drown his jealousy in drink, but that was like trying to put out a fire with oil. Scene followed scene, until finally, on the night of February 19, Richardson lay awake for hours listening to the drunken recriminations of McFarland in the next room, which at last rose to such a pitch that he wondered whether he ought not to interfere. At last, however, the house grew quiet.

That night marked the end for Abby McFarland. The next morning she left a brief note for McFarland and fled. From Amity Street she went straight to her friends the Sinclairs, but when she got there neither Mr. nor Mrs. Sinclair was at home. Instead, she found herself facing Miss Perry, Mrs. Sinclair's older sister, and Albert Richardson. He had guessed what her next step would be. There were few places left for her to go. Exhausted by ten years of struggle and humiliation, and worn out by the long scene of the night before, Abby broke down and cried like a tired child. She was through. Miss Perry and Richardson said little, but what they did say was to the point. Miss Perry told her briefly that she was a fool not to have left McFarland long before, and Richardson, with admirable restraint, said simply:

"This is a matter in which I cannot advise you, but whatever you make up your mind to do, I shall be glad to help you in."

Richardson had more than words to offer. He helped her make arrangements to send Percy, her oldest boy, home to her family in Massachusetts; sent word for her to several friends, including the invaluable Mrs. Calhoun; wired her father to come on at once; and, most of all, went himself to McFarland to tell him what had been done and to explain his own position as Abby's friend. This was on the twentieth of February, 1867.

On the twenty-third, Mr. Sage came on to New York, and the next day, in the presence of several friends, who had been called into the Sinclair house for the occasion, Abby told McFarland just why she had left him and that her decision was final. It was a fearful blow to the drunkard's pride. But McFarland was sober and, lacking the accustomed stimulus of liquor, humble. He accepted Abby's word without argument, and only said:

"I bow to your decision and submit to it."

Under the circumstances, there was nothing else for him to do. With all his calm, or perhaps even because of it, Abby urged her father to go home with McFarland and to stay the night with him "to see that he did nothing desperate." As she herself said afterward, she might easily have spared herself the trouble. If McFarland did anything desperate, it would not be to himself.

McFarland left the house with Mr. Sage, and Richardson prepared to go too. Abby went with him to the hall door and tried to thank him for what he had done. Richardson looked at her quietly.

"How do you feel about facing the world with two babies?" said he, and Abby replied:

"It looks bad for a woman, but then, I am sure I can get on better without that man than with him."

Richardson nodded, hesitated, and then said: "I wish you to remember, my child, that any responsibility you choose to give me in any possible future, I shall be very glad to take."

And that was all. It was a very guarded proposal.

Two days later, on February 26, Richardson called on Abby at the Sinclair house, where she had taken refuge, and renewed his proposal in more formal and explicit terms. He loved her, and he wanted her to divorce McFarland and marry him. It was reasonable. Any love she had ever had for McFarland had been killed long ago. But divorce was a very serious matter in those days, and while Abby admitted that she cared for him, she wanted to be sure that what he felt for her was more than pity. Also, she badly needed a period of calm, if she could get it, and, moreover, she was unwilling to divorce McFarland in New York, where the only ground was adultery. That was too messy, and there were the children to think of. So they decided to wait. It wouldn't have mattered. Nothing would have mattered. Their names were already written in red, but they didn't know that.

A day or so after this, Richardson went to Hartford to see his and Abby's publishers, and Abby went back to the rooms on Amity Street, where a friend came to stay with her. McFarland had cleared out.

On March 9, Richardson posted a letter to Abby from Hartford that was to be far-reaching in its effect. It was a love letter, flowery, after the fashion of the day, but harmless. Later, however, at the trial, each one of its quite innocent phrases was to be twisted about and deliberately misconstrued in the perfectly successful attempt to prove that white was black. Richardson addressed the letter to Abby in care of the *Tribune* office, no doubt because he thought that was safer. As it turned out, it was the most unsafe thing he could have done, for McFarland strolled into the office, saw the letter and appropriated it. It was not to be heard of again for almost two years.

(While this famous letter is far too long and not sufficiently interesting to quote here, it is worth remarking that to the unprejudiced reader it offers every assurance that the relationship between Abby and Richardson was perfectly innocent.)

On the twelfth, Richardson came back from Hartford, and on the evening of the next day called for Abby at the Winter Garden to take her home after the performance. They had not walked more than a few yards uptown from the theater when McFarland, who had evidently been waiting for them, came up behind and fired several shots at point-blank range. He must have been in his usual condition of drunkenness, however, because he missed Abby altogether, and only succeeded in giving Richardson a slight flesh wound in the side.

A policeman ran up, McFarland was arrested and the party adjourned to the station house, where Abby and Richardson refused to press the charge. If they had, it might have made a difference.

Abby took Richardson to the Sinclairs', where he was put to bed for a day or two. The wound was very slight. If anything had been needed to awaken Abby's love, this incident would have done it. Richardson had been wounded, had escaped death by chance, because of his love for her, and in the hours that she nursed him to recovery she knew that she loved him. Richardson was soon up and about, and Abby departed to stay with her father in Massachusetts.

On the night of the shooting, as soon as McFarland had been released by the police, he went to Abby's rooms on Amity Street and, after telling the landlady that he was a heartbroken man who had been betrayed by the wife of his bosom, proceeded to break open Abby's trunk and ransack her belongings. He was looking for compromising letters, and while he didn't find any—there being none to find—he did come across several from Mrs. Calhoun and Mrs. Sinclair that, in their warm expression of sympathy and affection, seemed to him to indicate a conspiracy on the part of these fine folk to alienate his wife from him for the express purpose of debauching her. And if this seems farfetched, it is at least no more than what McFarland's counsel stated at the trial.

On March 23, the famous Winter Garden burned to the ground, and Abby's theatrical career was interrupted for some time to come. She stayed on at Lowell with her father.

Even before this happened, however, McFarland made his next move in the campaign of persecution he had adopted. He instituted habeas corpus proceedings for the recovery of the two children, Percy and Dan, whom Abby had taken with her. He did more. By means of anonymous letters he tried to break Abby's nerve. In those days, a father's rights in his children, as in his wife, were rather of the Roman variety, and, after a short struggle, Abby agreed to compromise. Percy, the oldest boy, was to go to his father, while Danny, the infant of the family, stayed with her. She hated it, but it was the best she could do. This was in November, '67.

The next spring Abby went on to New York and tried to see Percy. She was met at the door of their lodgings by a violent storm of outrage and abuse from McFarland, and very little investigation sufficed to show that Percy had not been sent to school, but had been dragged from one roominghouse to another by his father, who entertained himself by trying to teach his son to drink. That finished it. Abby now had no other recourse but to sue for divorce and the custody of the children.

In 1868, Indiana appears to have been the most enlightened state in the Union, so far as marital relations were concerned, or at any rate, so Abby found it. Indiana allowed divorce for drunkenness, extreme cruelty and for failure to provide. Abby was manifestly entitled to her freedom on all three counts, and in June she started out on her adventure. No small feat in those days.

Particularly in view of the fact that McFarland's counsel was later to characterize Indiana as "that Paradise of Adulterers," and was to refer to Abby scathingly as "lurking in an obscure village in the Middle West," it is interesting to note that she went straight to Indianapolis and settled down there for the next sixteen months, making only one short visit home.

After the murder, when Abby's name was to provide a paraphrase for the Scarlet Woman, the Indianapolis correspondent of the Cincinnati *Commercial* was to write under the date of November 30, 1869—a very crucial date in the history of the case—that Mrs. McFarland was possessed of a "dignified and modest demeanor" and had "manifested neither anger nor vindictiveness toward her husband" during her stay in the West. New York papers were far less truthful, but there were reasons for that.

As soon as Abby got to Indianapolis, she presented letters to the Hon. Albert G. Porter, a distinguished local attorney who was to act for her in her divorce. She told Porter, among other things, that she was compiling a history of the United States for school use, and he introduced her, in turn, to the State librarian. (If this history was ever written and published, it seems to have escaped the record, which is a pity, for it would probably have been along strictly Weemsian lines.)

Abby settled down in the house of Mrs. Mathews, the mother of Vice President Colfax, who was an old friend. She opened a bank account with a Mr. Haughey, into which she paid such small sums as she got from her writings, usually from ten to twenty-five dollars. Out of this she had to support young Danny and herself and save enough for her attorney's fee. She went regularly to the Unitarian church, like a true daughter of New England, and otherwise went out very little. It is a record so clean that it is almost blank.

During this Indianapolis interlude, New York seems to have contributed only one incident of moment. McFarland brought civil suit against Albert Richardson, charging that he had alienated Abby's affections, and placing the somewhat high value of forty thousand dollars, with interest from the day Abby left him, on his wounded sensibilities. McFarland then published a notice of his suit in which he described himself as "a temperate, kindhearted, good man; and a kind, affectionate, and generous husband," going on to remark that Richardson had "seduced the affections of my wife from me, and had enticed her from her home." There was always that about McFarland. He could always be relied upon for a good forthright lie that would cover the entire situation. He was quite right, as events were to show. A half lie might have led him into trouble, but a good thumping falsehood was convincing—to the uninformed. Richardson replied in a brief, dignified statement which told the truth and was consequently uninteresting.

Abby's divorce case finally came up before Judge Woolen of Morgan County. Her witnesses were her father and Mrs. Calhoun, both of whom made the long journey out to testify for her. McFarland was painted as a drunken brute and loafer. In fact, in the words of one witness, "a most uncomfortable sort of a person; not fit to live and not prepared to die." The court apparently accepted this as accurate, as indeed it was, and the divorce was granted without delay. On the thirty-first of October, 1869, Abby came back to New York, as free as the courts of Indiana could make her.

For sixteen months Abby and Richardson had not seen each other, and while we may take it for granted that their reunion was a happy one, no actual record of it exists. Events now moved rapidly to their climax.

Now, if McFarland had been possessed of only a single one of the virtues with which he had so lavishly endowed himself, this story would have had another ending. But he was not. The man was bad all through, with the sick evil of a mind that had never been robust and that had been feeding for years on the dangerous dreams invoked by the Imp of the Bottle. It is one thing to drink and quite another to be a drunkard. McFarland was a drunkard of long standing, and for some years now he had been able to convince himself that somehow, somewhere and in some way he had been put upon and defrauded. Inevitably, Abby became the symbol of his defeat, and now to know that she was finally out of his power was more than he could endure. McFarland was not a nice man, but he was not an unusual one.

In 1869, the date of Thanksgiving had not been regularized as it has today. That year the holiday fell, not on the last Thursday of the month, but on the Thursday before that, the eighteenth of November. Abby was at Lowell with her family, and on Thanksgiving Eve Richardson came on from Medway, Massachusetts, where he had been staying with his mother and children, to spend Thanksgiving Day with the woman he was to marry. Abby met him at the railroad station, and they walked up to the house together. On the day following Thanksgiving Richardson went back to New York. Abby was not to see him again until he was on his deathbed.

How Daniel McFarland spent Thanksgiving is not known, but from the fact that he was drinking hard during all the week that followed, one may conjecture something of the day.

McFarland's mental condition during the week that intervened between the eighteenth and the twenty-fifth of November is probably most accurately described by saying that he was medically but not legally insane. For a good part of those seven days and nights he wandered through the streets, telling the story of his "wrongs" to anyone who would listen, and punctuating his story with hysterical and maudlin tears. He called on several doctors, complaining of his inability to sleep, and these ingenuous practitioners endeavored to alleviate his distress by the administration of morphia, Indian hemp, better known as hashish, hyosciamus and simple bromide of potassium. After these incredible doses, McFarland took the taste out of his mouth with more whisky. But—he knew what he was doing.

By the evening of Thursday, the twenty-fifth, all New York knew what he was doing, too, for at a quarter past five that afternoon he walked into the office of the *Tribune* and shot Albert Richardson through the body, in the startled presence of young Mr. Daniel

Frohman, who thereupon resolved to adopt a theatrical career.

Whatever he was before that hour, Daniel McFarland was perfectly calm after it. He was to remain so throughout the storm that followed. Newspapers were to grow hysterical in reports, headlines and editorials. Politicians were to become violent on the issue. Lawyers were to engage in fisticuffs because of the shooting; and the feeling of the public was to be keyed to an almost unbelievable tension over the affair. But Daniel McFarland remained calm through it all—only excepting the few times he was examined by alienists, when he did manage to put on a pretty good show. Who knows? Perhaps he was mad. Madness is debatable. Witness Hamlet!

And now, having left McFarland some time ago, sitting in the captain's room at the Fourth Precinct Station House, quietly smoking a cigar, we can take up our tale again at that very point. This recapitulation has been necessary because the story has never been plainly told before, and because without it one cannot appreciate the force of what followed.

The fact that Albert Richardson did not die at once, but lingered on in his room at the Astor House while doctors fought vainly for his life, gave New York just the opportunity it needed to take sides and prepare for battle.

Abby came on from Massachusetts at once, took up her quarters at the Astor House and stayed with Richardson until the end. That gave tongues a fine chance to wag, and they wagged freely.

There was no hope for Richardson from the first—McFarland had done his work too well—and as soon as this was realized, Richardson insisted that he and Abby be married, in order that she might have his name, along with what small property he had to leave, and that she might stand in a legal relationship to his children.

Divorce, in those days, was in a far worse state of confusion than it is now, and it is bad enough today. Legality and morality were hopelessly entangled, as they usually are, and Church and State looked at each other without trust. Abby's divorce had been obtained in Indiana. Was it binding in New York? McFarland was of the Roman Church, while Abby and Richardson were Protestants. How did that affect matters? Abby and Richardson had hoped that they would be able to straighten this out, quietly and at leisure, but there was no time for that now. They had to act at once, if they were to act at all. Albert Richardson was dying.

Accordingly, the kindly Mrs. Calhoun, armed with a letter of introduction from Horace Greeley, went to call on that powerful and popular divine, the Reverend Henry Ward Beecher. Mr. Beecher was a broad-minded man—some said too broad—and with him Mrs. Calhoun came to a rather curious agreement.

Abby and Richardson were to be married, and if Richardson died, the marriage was to be considered as entirely valid. If he did not die, the marriage was not to be consummated until all moot questions of law and morality had been settled to the satisfaction of both Church and State. Certainly, if there is any compromise possible between being married and being unmarried, these two hit upon it.

By Tuesday, November 30, it was clear that Richardson was sinking, and it was decided to perform the ceremony that same day. The officiating clergymen were Henry Ward Beecher, Mr. Frothingham, rector of the church that Richardson attended, and Mr. Henry M. Field of the *Evangelist*. Albert's brother, C. A. Richardson of Boston, was there with Albert's young son, and there were several friends of Abby's, always including Mrs. Calhoun. Obviously, every precaution was taken to conduct the affair in as circumspect a manner as possible. All the proprieties were rigidly observed. There was no room for criticism, but criticism has a way of making room for itself. The ceremony was brief and dignified, but the hullabaloo that followed was neither.

Two days later, on December 2, Albert Richardson died. On the day following, funeral services were held at the Astor House, and on the day after that at Franklin, Massachusetts, where Richardson was buried. The man had done his honest best to be decent and had been killed for it. This happens less infrequently than one might suppose. Richardson was thirty-six years old, though his pictures, consisting, as they do, chiefly of whiskers, make him look older.

The funeral at the Astor House was notable in that it testified to the fact that among Richardson's friends were such men as Horace Greeley, Whitelaw Reid and Edmund Clarence Stedman, who were all there along with many more. It was a conclave of such impeccable standing and respectability that one would have thought it above attack. In this, one would have been sadly mistaken.

The entire city was waiting eagerly to see whether Henry Ward Beecher, in his funeral sermon, would attempt to justify his outrageous behavior in marrying Albert Richardson to his "paramour."

It had gone as far as that already! The city needn't have worried. Mr. Beecher was ready with his answer.

Beecher's praise of Richardson was moderate in tone, rather astonishingly so under the circumstances, but he did manage to throw three bombs. In speaking of the dead man, he said:

"That he was imprudent, that his sympathy carried him into ways which a nicer prudence and a larger worldly wisdom would have eschewed is hardly to be doubted. But that he consciously violated any law of God, or any canon of morality which human society has thrown around the household, his most familiar friends utterly deny."

And again: "I believed that she [Abby] was both legally and morally justified in separation from a brutal husband, who, to excessive and outrageous personal abuse, had also furnished that one extreme ground of divorce which justifies it in the eyes of all Christendom."

And finally: "I vowed that they [defenders of the Union, of whom Richardson was one, during the recent Civil War] should be my brothers, and that as long as I lived, come what might, if they carried themselves faithfully toward my native land, then they should never lack a friend in me."

The first quotation says, in effect, that Richardson did not commit adultery. The second, that McFarland did. The third is a mere gesture.

Public opinion twisted these statements promptly, with this result.

Richardson and Abby were guilty of adultery. Therefore, they were adulterers, and Beecher was a defender of adultery. Second, nothing had been said about adultery when Abby got her divorce, and, therefore, in charging McFarland with adultery, Beecher was a liar and McFarland a martyr. Third, in his rhetorical promise to defenders of the Union, Beecher promised to defend all adulterers.

This may not seem quite sane. It was not sane! It was mad, and it foreshadowed very accurately what followed.

The only new point that Beecher raised was McFarland's infidelity. Abby had been quite frank in accusing him of it to her friends, though she had refused to divorce him on those grounds. Mrs. Calhoun had reported this to Beecher. Whether he was actually guilty or not, no one knows, though probably he was.

This was on December 3. The inquest had taken place the day

before at the coroner's office in City Hall. The proceedings were brief and formal. Proof of the shooting and of Richardson's death was given, and the jury returned a verdict against McFarland, who was remanded for trial. There were two points, however, that stand out as worthy of attention. McFarland was represented by counsel, the leader of which was the then famous John Graham, one of the best known trial lawyers in the city. Where did the money come from for this defense? By whom was McFarland being financed? A contemporary account of the inquest says that:

Many politicians crowded into the room, and most of them wore diamond cluster pins of large size and great value. The Coroner had one of these. So did one or two of his friends who conversed with him confidentially. While the testimony was being taken, some one of the politicians was imitating the crowing of a rooster in the hallway. This caused a momentary smile to overspread the countenances of the spectators and others. Almost immediately afterwards, it seemed as though the ceiling was coming down in consequence of a crowd of politicians rushing rudely out of a room overhead.

The juxtaposition of ideas in McFarland's mysterious defense fund and a gleeful crowd of politicians, is inescapable. Boss Tweed was in his heyday of power, and Tammany saw that McFarland was going to be useful. He was useful, very useful indeed.

Two newspaper editorials, published at this time, show which way the wind was blowing. The New York *Sun,* in speaking of Richardson's marriage to Abby, said in part:

The Astor House, in this city, was the scene, on Tuesday afternoon, of a ceremony which seems to us to set at defiance all those sentiments respecting the relation of marriage, which regard it as anything intrinsically superior to prostitution . . . and Mrs. McFarland, alias Miss Sage, whom Richardson, some time ago, seduced from allegiance to her lawful wedded husband. This husband had been guilty of a crime toward his wife—the crime of poverty . . . the Rev. Mr. Frothingham, who blasphemed in a prayer to God.

That was the general tone. McFarland was a martyr and a saint. Abby was a whore. Richardson, a seducer.

The *Tribune,* in commenting on Richardson's death, spoke well of the dead man, as was only to be expected, and ended its editorial with the assertion:

"In this coming trial it is not alone the State of New York against

Daniel McFarland: it is civilization against barbarism. It is the civil code against the code of the assassin.'"

The *Sun* against the *Tribune*. Dana against Greeley.

In his cell in the Tombs, Daniel McFarland smiled and said the *Sun* had done him no more than justice. He further remarked: "Since I have been in prison, I have received many visits from ladies and gentlemen, all of whom have expressed their sympathy in the warmest terms. I have today received hundreds of letters from married women, signifying their approval of my course."

The usual charity meted out to the "erring sister."

And the *Evening Republic* reported McFarland's brother as saying, in reply to the question: " 'How did this infatuation for Richardson come about?'

" 'It was all along of those Gilbert girls—one of them is a Calhoun now—and of the free-love tribe at Sam Sinclair's house. She [Abby] went reading just to get a chance to paint her face, pass for a beauty and get in with that free-love tribe at Sam Sinclair's.' "

We shall hear from the "free-love tribe" presently.

It is at this point in the story that we come upon that enterprising free-lance (not free-love) journalist, Isaac G. Reed, Junior. Reed rocked the boat. The man was a good reporter in a day when editors were important and reporters were not, in contradistinction to present times. Isaac G. Reed was to demonstrate, in advance of his journalistic age, just how dangerous good reporting can be.

First, Reed interviewed McFarland in the Tombs, but McFarland had already been worked for about all the copy he was good for. He could only retell the story he had already worn threadbare—that he was a kind, loving and generous husband, who had been driven to drink by the goings-on of his wife, and had finally, in a moment of righteous passion, shot down the man who had "broken up his home." It was a good story. It always is a good story. It's the same story Adam told about Eve and the Serpent, but Adam didn't get away with it. His many imitators have been far more fortunate. But in spite of being a good story, it wasn't exactly news. So Reed turned to the Rev. Mr. Beecher.

Henry Ward stuck to his guns, but there was one weakness in his position that Mr. Reed did not fail to spot. Reed forced Mr. Beecher to admit that the only grounds on which he recognized divorce were adultery, and then reminded him that adultery had not been formally charged. Mr. Beecher replied that he had been assured by his friends that McFarland had been guilty of it none the less, and that Abby McFarland was above all possible reproach. Still, it left him in a somewhat equivocal position. One remark of Beecher's is especially significant, in view of the "love scrape" that he was himself to go through in a few years. Reed asked him whether he didn't read the newspapers, to which Beecher replied:

"Very seldom, and never anything in them that is sensational or horrid. Anything about love scrapes or murders I strenuously avoid. They are not healthy."

He was even more right than he knew.

It was when Isaac G. Reed interviewed Horace Greeley that he really struck oil. Probably, in saving that interview for the last, he recognized that possibility. The interview with Beecher had appeared in the relatively unimportant *Sunday Mercury*, but the Greeley story was splashed across the pages of the *Sun*. While it is impossible to give the Greeley interview *in extenso*, there are portions of it that must be preserved to an admiring posterity. After a little preliminary licking of his chops, Mr. Reed continues:

Accordingly, we entered the *Tribune* office about five o'clock last Saturday afternoon, and after being suspiciously eyed by the various clerks and attachés of the establishment, and after having our ears shocked by an imprecation from Ottarson, who, like his illustrious chief, has forgotten all about the Third Commandment, we contrived to get our card laid before the eyes of the Hon. Horace Greeley, who immediately desired us to be admitted.

Ascending forthwith the winding, narrow, rickety stairs which led to the sanctum, we found Mr. Greeley in his den. "He sat like an editor taking his ease, with his Mss. all around him," and various specimens of his all but undecipherable penmanship lay on all sides of his desk, above which the lamp light shone full upon his venerable head and upturned spectacles.

The first point that Mr. Reed wanted to cover was whether or not Mr. Greeley had made a direct request of the Rev. Mr. Beecher to marry Abby and Richardson. Mr. Greeley denied emphatically that he had done so. He had simply given Mrs. Calhoun a letter to Mr. Beecher and had left the rest to her. And now let us follow the excellent Mr. Reed's example, and give a part of the interview in question and answer form.

GREELEY: I have not the slightest doubt that Mrs. Calhoun told Mr. Beecher the truth; that you may be sure of. You may depend what she said was true, every word of it; but I gave her no authority to represent me. Nobody *can* represent me!

REED: No one can adequately represent so wonderful a man.

[*Mutual bows.*]

GREELEY: But I tell you what it is, sir, there are plenty of people who can *mis*represent me, and they are doing it just about all the time!

REED: How?

GREELEY: In the newspapers, in the *Herald*, the *Sunday Mercury*—all the papers. They have all told lies about me, and the people believe them—because they want to or because they don't know any better. Why, they have all garbled the evidence in this matter regarding the Sinclairs!

REED: In what respect?

GREELEY: Why, they have suppressed in their published reports all the material facts in the testimony! What if Mr. Richardson and Mrs. McFarland did occupy the same room, or about the same room, as they call it? Don't they know well enough that Mr. Richardson was a wounded and feeble man? But no! It don't suit the papers to publish that! If all the testimony was published, the Sinclairs would be all right, but no—they must garble it to suit their damned petty malice! No, the Sinclairs and all the rest of us must be identified with this free-love crowd. By God [*bringing his venerable fist down upon the desk*], there's no such crowd—at least, not around the *Tribune* office. The whole thing has been got up by the enemies of the *Tribune!*

REED: I do not exactly understand.

GREELEY: There is the *World*, for instance, talking about the morality of the *Tribune*, when it hasn't any of its own! Why, if it hadn't been that the parties were in some way or another connected with the *Tribune*, there wouldn't have been a mother's son of the whole lot but would have thought it all right that Mrs. McFarland should be called Mrs. Richardson!

After which there was a wordy war between the two on the legality of the divorce and the consequent marriage. Greeley then made the statement, which should have been accorded more attention than it got, that McFarland had given up all rights in his wife of his own free will.

GREELEY: Yes, he told me so himself. You see, I didn't know about the case in any particular way until some time before the first shooting. Mac called upon me personally one day, and told me distinctly, "Mr. Greeley, I don't care about the woman. I don't want to get her back again. I wouldn't take her back. I do not want to live with her again. But that man has treated me badly!" Or some words meaning the same thing. I listened to him, and tried to comfort him; and then the villain—the dirty, deliberate, damned villain—

shot Richardson! And then he called on me again, and I told him I wouldn't have any more to do with him. "You're a bad man, Mac!" said I. Yes, I told him that he was a bad man, and so he is— a very bad man! And then, just look at that rascally recorder! What a damned pretty judge he is to talk in that style! He's a disgrace, by God! But the whole thing will be a nine-days' wonder, and then the people will forget all about it, or else they will learn the truth about it. And for my part, I hope the matter will be well ventilated, for I believe that the marriage of Albert D. Richardson and that woman was a just and true one, under the circumstances, and I think that the people, when they know all about it, will think so too.

Whereupon Mr. Reed gently rebuked Mr. Greeley for letting himself be used as a cat's-paw and took his hat and his departure.

Now, this is all very entertaining, if only because it is just about as typical a picture of Horace Greeley on the warpath as one could get. At the same time, however, that shrewd old fighter put his finger unerringly on the crux of the whole affair. The real issue was already lost sight of in the chance to attack the *Tribune*. There were other factors involved.

Adultery had sidetracked murder in the public mind, as it usually does in Anglo-Saxon communities which consider adultery much the more heinous crime of the two because it is so much more enjoyable. The point of view of the public on adultery is, generally, "I want to commit adultery, but I don't dare; and, by heaven, if I can't I'm not going to let you!" In other words—sour grapes. But all this quite aside, there was no actual issue of adultery here—unless it was Mc-Farland's—for there was not and never has been one jot or tittle of evidence indicating an improper relationship between Abby and Richardson. The thing was manufactured. There were three curious reasons why this was done.

First, there was the newspaper war, which was being fought with almost incredible violence in that day of bitter editorial enmities. Horace Greeley and his *Tribune* were on one side, and everybody else was on the other. Not that that bothered Greeley in the slightest, for a newspaper was nothing but a weapon to him, and a weapon that he well knew how to use. Dana had taken over the *Sun* in 1868, having quit Greeley in 1861, after fourteen years on the *Tribune*, and his parting from his old chief was not cordial. Bennett, of the *Herald*, had been at bitter odds with Greeley since before the Civil War, chiefly because Bennett felt that avoiding the war was more important than freeing the slaves, while Greeley was a red-hot Abolitionist.

The *World,* the only other paper of real consequence, was just coming into power and was more than willing to be a thorn in anybody's side. And Greeley was a violent man. He did not have opinions: he had passions. Either you were for him or you were against him, and if you were against him it was up to you to look out for your own skin. That type of man can exist only so long as he is able to defend himself. Once his guard is down—the pack is on him. These papers and their editors, along with the smaller fry, saw in the Richardson-McFarland affair the chance to push Greeley in a corner—to make him appear to be the defender of immorality, of free love and whatnot. They cared nothing for the facts they were distorting out of any reasonable shape and nothing for the justice they were perverting, or, if they cared about these matters at all, they cared about them far less than they did about the chance to knife Greeley and the *Tribune.* Use the tar brush. Blacken. Besmirch. No matter, so that Greeley was hit.

Second, there was the situation with Tammany. Boss Tweed was in his full flush of power; New York politics were as rotten as Tammany was able to make them, and every decent paper in the city was up in arms. (They put down their arms long enough to attack the *Tribune,* however. They didn't hate Tammany less, but Greeley more.) McFarland was a Romanist, which counted with Tammany. He was a ward heeler. And, most of all, he had shot a friend of Greeley's; his wife had divorced him for love of a *Tribune* correspondent. His enemies were friends of the *Tribune.* To defend him was to attack the *Tribune* and Greeley, Tammany's most feared and hated foe. The choice was not difficult.

McFarland thus had on his side Tammany, who would have defended him anyway, if it had bothered with him at all, which is very doubtful; and the entire press of New York, who were willing to forgo their fight with Tammany to hit the *Tribune.* But the third factor was the most important of all. That was public opinion.

The United States was, at this time, in the throes of one of those "moral blizzards" which now and again make havoc of its sanity. Whole libraries of books have been written to explain these phenomena, but most of the explanations differ unaccountably. It is a peculiarity of this country alone, and is probably what we mean when we refer to our "national institutions." The visible symbol of this outbreak was three words—Free Love and Fourierism.

Free love is always with us, more or less. We keep it in moth balls and drag it out when we lack other excitement. We had it not long ago when the alleged Soviet theory of the "communization of women" filled us with hope and alarm. An agitator and a soap box, with free love as the theme for the bedtime story, will always draw a crowd. In this instance, it remained only for Mr. Fourier to cast the first stone.

Fourier was a French philosopher who published his treatise in 1798, just when the French Revolution was gasping its life out, and whose work was promptly suppressed by Napoleon as soon as he was in a position to do any suppressing. Precisely what Fourierism was cannot be compassed in a few words, and a few words are all that it deserves. Enough, that it was one of the many Utopias of the period, faintly communistic, painfully logical, utterly impractical and slightly poetic. It was well calculated to appeal to the Penthouse Pink of that age, and could only have been feared by the type of mind that would see a phallic symbol in a lollipop.

Some time before this, Horace Greeley had permitted Alfred Brisbane, father of Mr. Hearst's famous editor, to write a series of articles on Fourierism for the *Tribune*. Mr. Brisbane was young and enthusiastic, and his articles had all the persuasive eloquence of a modern supersalesman—except that there were not many people willing to sign on the dotted line. To say that readers of the *Tribune* were shocked is to put it very mildly indeed. Outraged fathers of families seemed to see wives and daughters skittering off on the next train to disport themselves in Monsieur Fourier's experimental colony in a manner more advanced than becoming. An extract from a contemporary writer shows how they felt about it.

Free lovers are a class who should be shunned by any right-thinking person who wishes to preserve their purity and prevent the tongue of scandal being opened upon them. They should shun them as they would a serpent, whose venomous fangs would cause them instant death. What feeling can these people have for their wives, when they expose their portraits, taken in a state of nudity, and pass them from one to another, to pander to the vicious taste of such questionable company? And yet such scenes as this are said to have been enacted in the New York *Tribune* office!

It is difficult to believe that even the most ardent free lover could be much excited by a portrait of fat little Horace Greeley, with his fringe of white whiskers, in a state of nudity, but this sort of thing was taken seriously, none the less. One need not dwell on the curious English used by the writers of these diatribes. It would be too painful. But, astounding as it is, they were believed!

It must be clear by this that the Richardson-McFarland case had become a three-ringed circus, in which an infinite variety of clowns danced feverishly around the lonely figure of Abby Richardson and the dead body of the man she had loved. It is an elevating spectacle.

Richardson had died on December 2, and McFarland's trial was finally set for the fourth of the following April, 1870.

The fates chose the time well, for if the trial had come only a few months later public interest might have been diverted to the Franco-Prussian war, which broke out in July; to the still mysterious murder of that prominent citizen of New York, Benjamin Nathan, or to the building of the Brooklyn Bridge, which was got underway that summer. In April, however, there was nothing to distract attention from the question of whether or not Daniel McFarland should be hanged for murder.

The trial was held before Recorder Hackett, that same recorder of whom Horace Greeley had said, "What a damned pretty judge he is!"—a remark, by the way, which indicates that Mr. Hackett had made some extrajudicial statement soon after the killing, though what it may have been has been lost to history. Recorder Hackett was the son of Baron Hackett, the Shakespearean scholar and actor, and was well known as a baiter of the so-called free-love school. (One still wonders what on earth free love had to do with it!)

Chief of counsel for McFarland was John Graham, who had already appeared for the defense in the coroner's court. Graham had appeared as counsel in a number of *causes célèbres,* and was well known for his emotional outpourings. Put him in front of a jury, and John Graham could and would "throw fits" from dawn to dark. He was much esteemed. He had defended Daniel E. Sickles in 1859 on a charge of murdering his wife's lover, and had got him triumphantly acquitted. The sanctity-of-the-home was Graham's especial care.

Associated with John Graham was Charles S. Spencer, who made the opening address for the defense, an address which in the violence of its attack on Abby and Richardson piled lies on distortions, and of which Mr. Spencer was himself so thoroughly ashamed, when he had had time to sober up, that he published an apology and resigned from the case shortly after the trial opened. His defection was "much to the chagrin and astonishment of both the senior and junior counsel with whom he was connected, and on the strong expression of their personal and professional indignation." Mr. Spencer's associates were not ones to let a little thing like truth and justice stand in their way, and they naturally resented such squeamishness on the part of Mr. Spencer.

McFarland's junior counsel was none other than Elbridge T. Gerry, who was later to found the S.P.C.C., and who was then thirty-three years old. Mr. Gerry was "looked upon by the Bar of New York as one of its most promising, if not its ablest, young lawyers."

The defense was well represented by exceedingly able men. It was afterward known that the fee paid defense counsel was ten thousand dollars. Where did that money come from? The question has never been answered.

Judge Garvin and Judge Davis appeared for the state. They were both good lawyers, but of no special distinction. Too often counsel for the state are possessed of precisely these qualifications.

The case lasted more than a month, the jury returning their verdict on the tenth of May.

It would be a fruitless task, tedious alike to reader and writer, to deal in detail with McFarland's trial. In very truth it had already been held by a public opinion that had been whipped into flame by politicians and by conscienceless press. What remained could be little more than a formality.

The state presented its case against McFarland clearly and simply. He had deliberately killed Richardson, and he had known what he was doing when he fired the shot. There was no difficulty in proving this, and the testimony was presented without flourish. Perhaps that was its fault.

The defense opened on the second day. It admitted the shooting: there was no question as to that; but it advanced the claim that at the time of the murder McFarland was not responsible for his action *by reason of the fact that he had been driven insane through the conduct of his wife and Albert Richardson.* It was on this correlative clause that the entire emphasis was placed. It is entirely possible that McFarland might have been proven irresponsible without stressing this alleged reason. He was known as an habitual drunkard, given to ungovernable fits of temper, and physicians testified to his mental condition during the week before the shooting and to the many and varied drugs which they had given him. Undoubtedly, there was a proper legal defense in McFarland's mental state. But this was not enough. This would provide no mud which might be thrown on Greeley, Beecher, Sinclair and everyone else who was connected in any way with the *Tribune* interests. The only way in which these could be reached was to prove or to try to prove the immorality of Abby McFarland and of Richardson, for these two were friends of and had been defended by the group it was necessary to blacken. The matter of McFarland's sanity or insanity was almost passed over in the mad fury of the defense to show not simply that he was insane but why!

The actual defense then was that Abby and Richardson had maintained an adulterous relationship, and that Richardson had finally seduced Abby into leaving her home and husband, depriving him of his beloved children, and that this series of events had resulted in McFarland's mental downfall. In spite of the fact that Graham and Gerry worked for days in the effort to establish these alleged facts they were not able to adduce one iota of evidence to support their contention! And in spite of their utter failure, the "damned pretty judge" on the bench permitted and encouraged them to make statements and allegations in speech after speech to the jury which were vitally damaging to Abby and to Richardson, and which they were totally unable to prove. It was a sickening exhibition. When the state tried to offer rebutting testimony in disproof of these contentions, the court ruled that it was unnecessary to rebut mere statements of counsel. But the court permitted the statements to go on!

McFarland's crime was justified on the grounds that Richardson had robbed him of his wife, while, as a matter of fact, his wife had not lived with him for more than two years before the shooting, and at the time of the murder was not his legal wife at all!

When Judge Davis protested to the court and tried to show how outrageous this procedure was, Graham blustered to his feet, calling Davis a "damned coward" and shouting, "I'll have the clothes off your back! God damn you, I can lick you! I'll teach you what is due one gentleman to another!" Whereupon, McFarland, the supposedly insane man, put his hand on Graham's arm and said, "I hope you will not do anything to prejudice my case." Comment is superfluous.

Much was made of the letter from Richardson to Abby, which McFarland had intercepted. It has not been quoted here because it is neither interesting nor significant of anything beyond the fact that the two were in love with each other and, so far as the letter proves anything, in love in the most circumspect and proper manner. That it could have roused anyone to the point of murder is absurd, and yet defense counsel, *via* Mr. Spencer, were to say:

"I believe it is my best trait that I love my wife, and I believe she is as pure as an angel. But if ever I discovered a letter like that to her from any man, I would shoot him whether it made me mad or not!"

This was greeted with cheers. And yet we are annoyed when foreigners sneer at American justice!

This burlesque went on for a good five weeks, but the end finally came, it may well be through sheer exhaustion. At eight o'clock on the evening of May 10 the jury retired. It was an hour and fifty-five minutes before they were ready with their verdict.

A report had run through the still crowded courtroom that ten of the jury were for clear acquittal, only the foreman and one other holding out for conviction. They did not hold out long.

A contemporary report of the trial says that the words Not Guilty were ". . . drowned in a shout—not a cheer, not a hurrah—a simple emission of voice, in which, though it burst from over 300 persons, there was not a discordant note. It was one long, clear sound that seemed to proceed from one throat. It shook the windows, and seemed to vibrate back from the very walls. Cheer rose upon cheer. Hats were waved, and ladies, springing from their chairs, waved their handkerchiefs and joined their high notes to the deeper cheers of the men. Some ladies crowded around McFarland, shaking hands with him, and some kissing him."

Clearly, it was a very popular verdict.

Abby had, wisely, stayed away from the trial. A little later she issued her own statement, telling the whole story of her relationship with both McFarland and Richardson, and giving it all in a very simple and dignified way. This she put into the form of a deposition to which she took oath. Her own last paragraph may well be ours also.

"There is but one word more to say, and I will say it briefly. It is well known that I have been on trial before a New York court as much as Daniel McFarland, and for a crime more heinous and more bitterly punished in a woman than murder committed by a man. And it is clearly seen by all who see dispassionately that wherever a loophole was opened for any truth about my conduct or Mr. Richardson's it was immediately stopped. I have tasted to its dregs the cup of justice which, in the nineteenth century, men born of women mete out to one whose worst crime was the mistake of marrying a man who was half madman from natural inheritance, half brute from natural proclivity. Of the justice I have received, let those who read my story bear witness."

That witness is borne here.

THE NET

By Robert M. Coates

. . . .

Walter's wife had left him,
and Walter didn't like that—not at all!

Walter had just turned the corner of Charles Street into Seventh when he saw her. She was standing a little way up the block talking to a fellow in a black overcoat and a black felt hat, and just the way they were standing—the fellow leaning back against the wall of the building there and she crowded close against him, looking up at him —was enough to let Walter know the kind of talk they were having. Almost without thinking, he stopped and stepped back a pace down Charles, out of sight around the corner.

This was the way things went, then; this was what she had left him for. He had known it, but this was the first time he had ever had sight of it, and it sent a queer feeling through him, as if more air than he could breathe had been forced into him. He was a tall man, with a pale, solemn, heavy-jawed face and a slow, slightly awkward manner of movement. He placed himself against the railing of an areaway and stood there, looking down Seventh Avenue, waiting. He knew she would have to come around the corner when she started home, and whether she was alone or the fellow was still with her, he would have a right to speak to her then. Till then he would wait. He had time.

It was growing late and the evening had been cold; there were few people walking. Down by Christopher Street there was a cluster of bright signs and illuminated buildings, but up where he was the houses were mostly dark, and the only sound was the rough, shuffling whir of the tires on pavement as the cars went flying by. Then the traffic lights changed and the cars stopped, at Charles, at Tenth, at Christopher; at Charles, a black truck crawled out across the avenue and went slowly on down the street past Walter, toward Hudson.

That was all the cross traffic there was, but for a few seconds longer the avenue was still. Then the lights went green and the headlights moved forward, sifting past each other as the cars took up their varying speeds. A moment later, Walter heard the tap of her heels on the sidewalk, coming around the corner, and she passed him.

"Hello, Ann," he said softly.

She hadn't noticed him till then; he could tell that from the way her head snapped around and the look that came over her face. Then she turned her head away. She kept on walking. "Hello, Walter," she said wearily.

He was walking along beside her. "Where you been, Ann?" he asked. "I was at your people's house and they said you'd went to the movies."

"I did."

"Yeah. The movies."

She glanced up at him, and he could see her face pinching up in the way it did when she got angry. But she didn't say anything; she just turned her face forward again, tucked her chin down in the fur collar of her coat, and walked on. He kept pace with her. "I saw you talking to that fellow back there, Ann," he went on in his slow, insistent voice. "I saw you."

"Well," she said. "So you saw me. Can't a girl meet a friend on the street?"

"Yeah. But the movies."

He knew she didn't like to be prodded like that about things, even when she was telling the truth, and he half expected her to burst out with something then and there. He could feel his chest tightening already, in that mixture of fear and excitement and stubbornness that always came over him when they got into an argument. But she just kept on walking. After a few steps she turned to him again. "You was up to the folks'?" she asked, her voice very innocent and offhand. "Who'd you see? Was Ma there?"

"Yes, your mother was there," he said. "As you doubtless know. I know what you're thinking, Ann, but I didn't think it would give you pleasure. She didn't give me no nice reception. But that don't bother me, either; that I expected. I'm not blind, and I know who it was that turned you against me and broke up our marriage. But there's an old saying, Ann, that marriages are made in heaven, and I believe it, and I believe she will get her punishment, too, for what she's done—turning a man's wife against her lawful husband. If not now, then she'll surely get it in the hereafter. But it's not her I'm worried about; I leave her to her own devices. It's you, Ann. Listen," he said. "What you don't get is, I'd take you back tomorrow. Like that. I don't care who you been with, what you done—even that fellow back there, Ann, whoever he is. I don't ask. But a fellow you got to meet on street corners, can't even show to your folks—but even him, Ann; I'd forget everything. Just so long as you'd tell me, come clean about things. But this lying and hiding. Listen, Ann—" He had thought a good deal about this meeting and had planned for it, and this was one of the things he had figured on saying, so he found himself talking faster and faster. But just then a crazy thing happened.

They were passing a series of old-fashioned houses with high-stooped entrances, and the steps running down from them made the sidewalk narrow. And there was a couple, a man and a girl, walking up the street toward them; in his excitement, Walter didn't notice them until he was upon them, and then there wasn't room for them all to pass. The man bumped him, and Walter stumbled, trying to sidestep them, but all the time his eyes were on Ann. She had walked on, never varying her pace, as if she had nothing to do with him at all, and at the sight of her tan-stockinged legs flicking briskly away beneath her black coat a kind of panic took hold of him. "I'm your husband, Ann!" he yelled suddenly. He could see both the man's and the girl's faces turned toward him, but for the moment he didn't care. He shoved past them and ran after Ann, grabbing at her arm. "I'm your husband," he repeated, his voice still loud. "Don't that mean anything to you? For better or for worse." Then he saw that she was laughing, and he let go of her arm.

It was only a little way farther on to her family's apartment house. When they reached it, she ran up the three or four steps to the entrance. Walter followed her, letting the street door swing shut behind him. They were alone in the dim vestibule. She bent her head for a moment, fumbling in her bag for the key, then she glanced up. "Well, Walter," she said. She wasn't laughing now, but she might just as well have been; he could tell from the look on her face that she was only waiting to get on upstairs to start in again. "Well, it's been a enjoyable little walk."

He could feel the air crowding into his lungs again, so hard that it made his whole chest feel hot inside. "Maybe it ain't finished yet," he said.

"Well, it is for me. I'm going up."

"I'm coming up too."

"No you won't."

"Why won't I?" Without his meaning it to, he could hear his voice getting louder. "What you got to conceal up there?"

"Oh, Walter! It ain't that and you know it. But you know what'll happen. You and Ma." He hadn't realized that he had moved closer to her, but he must have, for suddenly she stepped back a pace and stared up at him. "Walter," she said. "You been drinking?"

"I have not been drinking," he said, and he let his voice go louder still when he said it. Let her scare a little, he was thinking; at least she wasn't laughing at him any more. She was paying attention to him now. "Well, then," she said, and she began talking faster. "Listen, Walter. This kind of chasing around ain't getting us anywhere, you hiding around corners and laying for me and all that. Why don't we get together some other way, sometime? I could come up to your place sometime, even. You still got the apartment, haven't you? We could talk."

"You come up there," he said, "and maybe you wouldn't never leave it again." He hadn't meant to put it like that; what he'd meant was that if she came up, it would have to be because she wanted to stay there and be with him again, but the way it came out it sounded threatening, even to him, and she must have thought so too, for she stared at him blankly a moment. Then, suddenly, she made a kind of a dive out of the corner where he had crowded her. "Then go home then! Get out of here!" he heard her cry, and she began pushing with both hands against his chest. He grabbed her wrists and she screamed. When she screamed, his hands went directly to her throat.

He had only intended to stop her screaming, but as soon as he touched her a strange kind of strength flowed into his hands, a strength that came from somewhere inside him and that once released could not be recalled, so that he couldn't have let go if he'd tried. For a while she struggled, jerking her body this way and that and pulling at his arms with her hands. It didn't bother him. He had shoved her back against the wall, so hard that her head bumped against it and her hat tipped over sidewise. He just stiffened his legs and stood there, his hands locked hard in the flesh of her throat; he was surprised at how strongly he stood there, meeting and conquering every move she made. "Laugh now," he said once, not loud, but almost gently.

Her knee worked up somehow between them until it was pressing against his thigh, but there was no strength in it; the strength was all in him, and soon the knee slipped harmlessly down again. Then her body lashed back and forth once or twice, fast and violently, and stopped, and her eyelids, which had been tight shut, opened so that he could see through her lashes the blue of her eyes, glittering in the dim light overhead. A kind of shudder ran through her. It was some time after that before he realized that she wasn't struggling any more.

It was the strain on his arms that told him of the change. Her body was just so much weight now, almost more than he could hold, and he let her slide slowly down along the wall until she was sitting on the floor, her back propped against the corner of the vestibule. Well, I did it, he thought, I did it; and for a moment he stood looking down at her uncertainly, not knowing what he ought to do next. One leg was crooked awkwardly sidewise, he noticed, so that the skirt was pulled up above the stocking top, and he bent down and pulled the hem over the knee. Then he turned and went out the door.

At the top of the steps he stopped and looked up and down the street. At first glance it seemed there was no one in sight at all, not a soul; then he noticed a couple of people standing in front of a house farther down the block—a man and a girl, he thought, though he couldn't be sure; about all he could see was their faces, and these were no more than pale spots in the shadows where they were standing. Farther still, down almost to Hudson, he sighted two others, two men, dark against the light from a shop window on the corner. And now there was a girl clipping quickly along on the opposite sidewalk; it was amazing how silently they all moved, and how easy it was not to notice them in the darkness. He stood where he was for a while, watching them, trying to determine if there was any sign of a concerted scheme in their actions. He had a feeling that they were only moving as they did in order to set a trap for him; at a signal they might all turn and begin running to surround him.

But none of them paid any attention to him. The couple down the block just stood there, the two men walked onward, the girl hurried around the corner and disappeared. Walter went down the steps and turned up toward Seventh Avenue. Well, I did it, he thought again, and as before, the thought carried no emotion with it except relief. It had to be done, it was coming to her; that was the way his thoughts ran, and what little guilt he had was submerged in a kind of careless irresponsibility, the feeling that a drunken man has when he knows he has done something wrong, admits it and doesn't care. The emotion was so close to that of drunkenness that even Walter recognized it. I could say I was drunk, he thought, his mind momentarily occupied with stratagems. But as soon as the idea came to him, he rejected it. I've got better reasons than that, he decided: her laughing at me, cheating on me, chasing at every corner. As he neared Fourth Street, another man, a new one, sprang up suddenly before him, a short, heavy-set fellow stepping out of the shadows and striding directly toward him.

The man passed without giving him a second glance, but after the man had gone by, Walter stopped and stepped back against a house wall, watching his progress down the street; suppose he was headed for *her* house, he was thinking, and the fear became so strong that he almost set out in pursuit of the stranger. I could ask him for a match, get him talking, lead him on past the door, he thought. As he hesitated, the man went by; he went three or four doors farther before he turned in.

Walter walked on. He didn't hurry, and when he reached the end of the block he even stopped for a moment, glancing, as if idly, up and down before crossing the street. The night was a net, he realized, with its streets and its people walking this way and that along them; what he had to do was to find his way out without disturbing anything or anyone. The thing that worried him most now was his breathing; he discovered that it had been bothering him for some time. He would find himself breathing fast and hard, so hard that it hurt his chest, and then he would take a deep breath, so long and so deep that when he let it out he could feel the flesh of his body shrinking away from his clothes, leaving the skin damp and prickly and cool. Then the hard, quick breathing would begin again.

Like a man that's been running, he thought. That was one thing he mustn't do; without even thinking about it, he knew he mustn't run. Or talk. For a while he had had the notion of going up to his brother-in-law's place. It was just a notion, or really it was more like a picture that had come into his mind; somehow, he didn't want to go home, and suddenly he had seen himself sitting with Frank and Ethel in their warm apartment, and then he had thought how pleasant it would be, it would rest him; they'd send out for some beer even, maybe. But he saw now that it wouldn't do. He'd get to talking, and there was no way of knowing how they'd take it. At the thought, the picture in his mind changed in a way that made him go cold all over; from seeing their faces smiling at him, friendly and companionable, he had seen them go white and staring, and hard with horror as they looked at him.

It was an awful thing he had done, all right, and the funny part was that he hadn't meant to. "God sakes!" he said. For the moment he was arguing with Frank and Ethel, and he found himself talking out loud. "If I'd meant to do it, wouldn't I have planned the thing different? Me here with no more than a couple bucks in my pocket." If it had been Friday, even, when his pay came through at the shop; then he'd have had a matter of thirty-five dollars in his hand, enough to start out with, anyway. But maybe Frank would lend him some money; he'd done as much for him on occasion.

"I swear, Frank, it's the first time I ever even laid hands on her. I never meant to harm a hair of her head." He had stopped talking out loud, but he was still arguing to himself when he remembered that Frank was Ann's brother; he had had an idea all along that his mind was running too fast for him, sort of, so that he was overlooking things. And maybe important things. This proved it. If Frank was Ann's brother, that left him out, of course; he was the last man to turn to now. It was late, too. His mind had been racing ahead, full of confidence, but now it was swarming with doubts and uncertainties: how could he expect to burst in on them now, at this hour, asking for money, without them asking questions? And even if he did get some money, where would he go? It would mean quitting his job, leaving everyone he knew, everything. Me a man that's near forty, he thought.

It was just that Frank was the only one in the family that had ever had a decent word for him.

And the thing was, he hadn't meant to do it. All the time back there in the vestibule it had seemed like all the dozen of times in the past when he and Ann would have arguments; and she'd slump down in a chair or a sofa, so mad that she couldn't keep from crying but still trying to hide it; and he'd shout something, slam the door and go out. And then, like as not, she'd get up, slam the door too, and go off to see one of her girl friends or something. But not now. Now she would lie where she was, in the dim hallway, until someone came in from the street or down from the apartments above, and stumbled over her.

It would happen any minute now, if it hadn't happened already, and at the thought a vast sorrow rose up slowly inside him and filled him—sorrow for himself and for Ann, but mostly for himself. What I've got myself in for, he kept thinking. A whole group of people, men and women all talking and laughing, were coming down the steps of a house ahead of him, and he slowed his pace so as not to get tangled up with them on the sidewalk. But they just stood there, and finally he had to brush past them. As he did so, he shoved one of the men and gave the whole group such a fierce look that they must have noticed it; he was sure he saw their faces change.

I could tell you something that would stop your giggling, he thought, and this time, when he thought of the terror he could bring to their faces, he felt an odd sort of satisfaction; it would serve them right, he thought. When he had gone a few paces farther on, he looked back. They were all trailing off down the street, and on an impulse he stopped and leaned against an areaway railing, watching them. It would happen any minute now, he thought.

How long he stood there he didn't know, but it couldn't have been long, and the thing that made him conscious of time again was a thin knife sound like a scream or a siren; then a car's headlights turned into the street from away down at Hudson. He watched them, and it was some seconds before he realized what was the matter with them: the car was heading up the wrong way, against traffic.

Only a police car would do that, he thought, and as if in confirmation he saw it swing in toward the curb and stop, just about where the entrance to Ann's house would be. Well, then, the police were coming, he thought; that was right, it was proper, and if the old woman—he realized that one of the things he had been worrying about was Ann's mother; he'd known she'd be mixed up in the scene down there some way. But if the police were there and she started her ranting and screaming—well, they'd know how to stop her. Slowly he pushed himself away from the railing.

He'd go on up to Frank's, he thought, but it was only when he started walking on up the street, toward Seventh, that he realized how tired he was. So maybe, after all, he'd go home. It's too much, he thought. It's too much to expect of a man. He was still arguing about this question of packing up and leaving town for good. But he was almost too tired, and too lonely to bother about it. Unexpectedly, as he walked, a picture came into his mind of the couple he had bumped into when Ann and he were walking home. Down this very block, it had been, and he could see them again, their faces turning in surprise as he shoved past them shouting; somehow, the recollection only added to his feeling of lonely helplessness.

If he could only talk to them, he thought, he could explain everything; they were the only people in the world, perhaps, who would understand. But they had gone, and the thought vanished too, almost as soon as it had come to him. He walked on up to Seventh and then turned north, toward the subway. Maybe he'd go up to Frank and Ethel's after all; if there had been a reason against going there, he had forgotten it, and anyway it wasn't worth bothering about now. Most of all, now, he felt tired.

PRISONER OF THE SAND
By Antoine de Saint-Exupéry

. . . .

*"I had been looking for a reason to hope and
had failed to find it. I had been looking for a sign of life,
and no sign of life had appeared."*

After three years of life in the desert, I was transferred out. The fortunes of the air service sent me wandering here and there until one day I decided to attempt a long-distance flight from Paris to Saigon. When, on December 29, 1935, I took off, I had no notion that the sands were preparing for me their ultimate and culminating ordeal. This is the story of the Paris-Saigon flight.

I paid my final visit to the weather bureau, where I found Monsieur Viaud stooped over his maps like a medieval alchemist over an alembic. Lucas had come with me, and we stared together at the curving lines marking the new-sprung winds. With their tiny flying arrows, they put me in mind of curving tendrils studded with thorns. All the atmospheric depressions of the world were charted on this enormous map, ochre-colored, like the earth of Asia.

"Here is a storm that we'll not hear from before Monday," Monsieur Viaud pointed out.

Over Russia and the Scandinavian peninsula the swirling lines took the form of a coiled demon. Out in Iraq, in the neighborhood of Basra, an imp was whirling.

"That fellow worries me a little," said Monsieur Viaud.

"Sandstorm, is it?"

I was not being idly curious. Day would not yet be breaking when I reached Basra and I was fearful of flying at night in one of those desert storms that turn the sky into a yellow furnace and wipe out hills, towns and riverbanks, drowning earth and sky in one great conflagration. It would be bad enough to fly in daylight through a chaos in which the very elements themselves were indistinguishable.

"Sandstorm? No, not exactly."

"So much the better," I said to myself, and I looked round the room. I liked this laboratory atmosphere. Viaud, I felt, was a man escaped from the world. When he came in here and hung up his hat and coat on the peg, he hung up with them all the confusion in which the rest of mankind lived. Family cares, thoughts of income, concerns of the heart—all that vanished on the threshold of this room as at the door of a hermit's cell, or an astronomer's tower, or a radio operator's shack. Here was one of those men who are able to lock themselves up in the secrecy of their retreat and hold discourse with the universe.

Gently, for he was reflecting, Monsieur Viaud rubbed the palms of his hands together.

"No, not a sandstorm. See here."

His finger traveled over the map and pointed out why.

At four in the morning Lucas shook me into consciousness.

"Wake up!"

And before I could so much as rub my eyes he was saying, "Look here, at this report. Look at the moon. You won't see much of her tonight. She's new, not very bright, and she'll set at ten o'clock. And here's something else for you: sunrise in Greenwich Meridian Time and in local time as well. And here: here are your maps, with your course all marked out. And here—"

"—is your bag packed for Saigon," my wife broke in.

A razor and a change of shirt. He who would travel happily must travel light.

We got into a car and motored out to Le Bourget while Fate spying in ambush put the finishing touches to her plan. Those favorable winds that were to wheel in the heavens, that moon that was to sink at ten o'clock, were so many strategic positions at which Fate was assembling her forces.

It was cold at the airport, and dark. The *Simoon* was wheeled out of her hangar. I walked round my ship, stroking her wings with the back of my hand in a caress that I believe was love. Eight thousand miles I had flown in her, and her engines had not skipped a beat; not a bolt in her had loosened. This was the marvel that was to save our lives the next night by refusing to be ground to powder on meeting the upsurging earth.

Friends had turned up. Every long flight starts in the same atmosphere, and nobody who has experienced it once would ever have it otherwise: the wind, the drizzle at daybreak, the engines purring quietly as they are warmed up; this instrument of conquest gleaming in her fresh coat of "dope"—all of it goes straight to the heart.

Already one has a foretaste of the treasures about to be garnered on the way—the green and brown and yellow lands promised by the maps; the rosary of resounding names that make up the pilot's beads; the hours to be picked up one by one on the eastward flight into the sun.

There is a particular flavor about the tiny cabin in which, still only half awake, you stow away your thermos flasks and odd parts and overnight bag; in the fuel tanks heavy with power; and best of all, forward, in the magical instruments set like jewels in their panel and glimmering like a constellation in the dark of night. The mineral glow of the artificial horizon, these stethoscopes designed to take the heartbeat of the heavens, are things a pilot loves. The cabin of a plane is a world unto itself, and to the pilot it is home.

I took off, and though the load of fuel was heavy, I got easily away. I avoided Paris with a jerk and up the Seine, at Melun, I found myself flying very low between showers of rain. I was heading for the valley of the Loire. Nevers lay below me, and then Lyon. Over the Rhône I was shaken up a bit. Mt. Ventoux was capped in snow. There lies Marignane and here comes Marseille.

The towns slipped past as in a dream. I was going so far—or thought I was going so far—that these wretched little distances were covered before I was aware of it. The minutes were flying. So much the better. There are times when, after a quarter hour of flight, you look at your watch and find that five minutes have gone by; other days when the hands turn a quarter of an hour in the wink of an eye. This was a day when time was flying. A good omen. I started out to sea.

Very odd, that little stream of vapor rising from the fuel gauge on my port wing! It might almost be a plume of smoke.

"Prévot!"

My mechanic leaned toward me.

"Look! Isn't that gas? Seems to me it's leaking pretty fast."

He had a look and shook his head.

"Better check our consumption," I said.

I wasn't turning back yet. My course was still set for Tunis. I looked round and could see Prévot at the gauge on the second fuel tank aft. He came forward and said: "You've used up about fifty gallons."

Nearly twenty had leaked away in the wind! That was serious. I put back to Marignane where I drank a cup of coffee while the time lost hurt like an open wound. Flyers in the Air France service wanted to know whether I was bound for Saigon or Madagascar and wished me luck. The tank was patched up and refilled, and I took off once more with a full load, again without mishap despite a bit of rough going over the soggy field.

As soon as I reached the sea I ran into low-hanging clouds that forced me down to sixty feet. The driving rain spattered against the windshield and the sea was churning and foaming. I strained to see ahead and keep from hooking the mast of some ship, while Prévot lit cigarettes for me.

"Coffee!"

He vanished into the stern of the cockpit and came back with the thermos flask. I drank. From time to time I flicked the throttle to keep the engines at exactly twenty-one hundred revolutions and ran my eye over the dials like a captain inspecting his troops. My company stood trim and erect: every needle was where it should be.

I glanced down at the sea and saw it bubbling under the steaming rain like a boiling cauldron. In a hydroplane this bumpy sea would have bothered me; but in this ship of mine, which could not possibly be set down here, I felt differently. It was silly, of course, but the thought gave me a sense of security. The sea was part of a world that I had nothing to do with. Engine trouble here was out of the question: there was not the least danger of such a thing. Why, I was not rigged for the sea!

After an hour and a half of this, the rain died down, and though the clouds still hung low a genial sun began to break through. I was immensely cheered by this promise of good weather. Overhead I could feel a thin layer of cotton wool and I swerved aside to avoid a downpour. I was past the point where I had to cut through the heart of squalls. Was not that the first rift in the cloud bank, there ahead of me?

I sensed it before I saw it, for straight ahead on the sea lay a long meadow-colored swath, a sort of oasis of deep and luminous green, reminding me of those barley fields in southern Morocco that would make me catch my breath each time I sighted them on coming up from Senegal across two thousand miles of sand. Here as at such times in Morocco I felt we had reached a place a man could live in, and it bucked me up. I flung a glance backward at Prévot and called out:

"We're over the worst of it. This is fine."

"Yes," he said, "fine."

This meant that I would not need to do any stunt flying when Sardinia hove unexpectedly into view. The island would not loom up suddenly like a mass of wreckage a hundred feet ahead of me: I should be able to see it rising on the horizon in the distant play of a thousand sparkling points of light.

I moved into this region bathed by the sun. No doubt about it, I was loafing along. Loafing at the rate of one hundred and seventy miles an hour, but loafing nevertheless. I smoked a few leisurely cigarettes. I lingered over my coffee. I kept a cautious fatherly eye on my brood of instruments. These clouds, this sun, this play of light, lent to my flight the relaxation of a Sunday afternoon stroll. The sea was as variegated as a country landscape broken into fields of green and violet and blue. Off in the distance, just where a squall was blowing, I could see the fermenting spray. Once again I recognized that the sea was of all things in the world the least monotonous, was formed of an ever-changing substance. A gust of wind mantles it with light or strips it bare. I turned back to Prévot.

"Look!" I said.

There in the distance lay the shores of Sardinia that we were about to skirt to the southward.

Prévot came forward and sat down beside me. He squinted with wrinkled forehead at the mountains struggling out of their shroud of mist. The clouds had been blown away and the island was coming into view in great slabs of field and woodland. I climbed to forty-five hundred feet and drifted along the coast of this island dotted with villages. After the flower-strewn but uninhabitable sea, this was a place where I could take things easily. For a little time I clung to our greathearted mother earth. Then, Sardinia behind me, I headed for Tunis.

I picked up the African continent at Bizerta and there I began to drop earthward. I was at home. Here was a place where I could dispense with altitude which, as every pilot knows, is our particular store of wealth. Not that we squander it when it is no longer needed: we swap it for another kind of treasure. When a flyer is within a quarter of an hour of port, he sets his controls for the down swing, throttling his motor a little—just enough to keep it from racing while the needle on his speedometer swings round from one hundred and seventy to two hundred miles an hour.

At that rate of speed the impalpable eddies of evening air drum softly on the wings and the plane seems to be drilling its way into a quivering crystal so delicate that the wake of a passing swallow would jar it to bits. I was already skirting the undulations of the hills and had given away almost the whole of my few hundred feet of altitude when I reached the airdrome, and there, shaving the roofs of the hangars, I set down my ship on the ground.

While the tanks were being refilled I signed some papers and shook hands with a few friends. And just as I was coming out of the administration building I heard a horrible grunt, one of those muffled impacts that tell their fatal story in a single sound; one of those echoless thuds complete in themselves, without appeal, in which fatality delivers its message. Instantly there came into my mind the memory of an identical sound—an explosion in a garage. Two men had died of that hoarse bark.

I looked now across to the road that ran alongside the airdrome: there in a puff of dust two high-powered cars had crashed head-on and stood frozen into motionlessness as if imprisoned in ice. Men were running toward the cars while others ran from them to the field office.

"Get a doctor.... Skull crushed...."

My heart sank. In the peace of the evening light Fate had taken a trick. A beauty, a mind, a life—something had been destroyed. It was as sudden as a raid in the desert. Marauding tribesmen creep up on silent feet in the night. The camp resounds briefly with the clashing tumult of a razzia. A moment later everything has sunk back into the golden silence. The same peace, the same stillness, followed this crash.

Nearby, someone spoke of a fractured skull. I had no mind to be told about that crushed and bloody cranium. Turning my back to the road, I went across to my ship, in my heart a foreboding of danger. I was to recognize that sound when I heard it again very soon. When the *Simoon* scraped the black plateau at a speed of one hundred and seventy miles an hour I should recognize that hoarse grunt, that same snarl of destiny keeping its appointment with us.

Off to Benghazi! We still have two hours of daylight. Before we crossed into Tripolitania I took off my glare glasses. The sands were golden under the slanting rays of the sun. How empty of life is this planet of ours! Once again it struck me that its rivers, its woods, its human habitations were the product of chance, of fortuitous conjunctions of circumstance. What a deal of the earth's surface is given over to rock and sand!

But all this was not my affair. My world was the world of flight. Already I could feel the oncoming night within which I should be enclosed as in the precincts of a temple—enclosed in the temple of night for the accomplishment of secret rites and absorption in inviolable contemplation.

Already this profane world was beginning to fade out: soon it would vanish altogether. This landscape was still laved in golden sunlight, but already something was evaporating out of it. I know nothing, nothing in the world, equal to the wonder of nightfall in the air.

Those who have been enthralled by the witchery of flying will know what I mean—and I do not speak of the men who, among other sports, enjoy taking a turn in a plane. I speak of those who fly professionally and have sacrificed much to their craft. Mermoz said once, "It's worth it, it's worth the final smash-up."

No question about it; but the reason is hard to formulate. A novice taking orders could appreciate this ascension toward the essence of things, since his profession too is one of renunciation: he renounces the world; he renounces riches; he renounces the love of woman. And by renunciation he discovers his hidden god.

I, too, in this flight, am renouncing things. I am giving up the broad golden surfaces that would befriend me if my engines were to fail. I am giving up the landmarks by which I might be taking my bearings. I am giving up the profiles of mountains against the sky that would warn me of pitfalls. I am plunging into the night. I am navigating. I have on my side only the stars.

The diurnal death of the world is a slow death. It is only little by little that the divine beacon of daylight recedes from me. Earth and sky begin to merge into each other. The earth rises and seems to spread like a mist. The first stars tremble as if shimmering in green water. Hours must pass before their glimmer hardens into the frozen glitter of diamonds. I shall have a long wait before I witness the soundless frolic of the shooting stars. In the profound darkness of certain nights I have seen the sky streaked with so many trailing sparks that it seemed to me a great gale must be blowing through the outer heavens.

Prévot was testing the lamps in their sockets and the emergency torches. Round the bulbs he was wrapping red paper.

"Another layer."

He added another wrapping of paper and touched a switch. The dim light within the plane was still too bright. As in a photographer's darkroom, it veiled the pale picture of the external world. It hid that glowing phosphorescence which sometimes, at night, clings to the surface of things. Now night has fallen, but it is not yet true night. A crescent moon persists.

Prévot dove aft and came back with a sandwich. I nibbled a bunch of grapes. I was not hungry. I was neither hungry nor thirsty. I felt no weariness. It seemed to me that I could go on like this at the controls for ten years. I was happy.

The moon had set. It was pitch dark when we came in sight of Benghazi. The town lay at the bottom of an obscurity so dense that it was without a halo. I saw the place only when I was over it. As I was hunting for the airdrome the red obstruction lights were switched on. They cut out a black rectangle in the earth.

I banked, and at that moment the rays of the floodlight rose into the sky like a jet from a firehose. It pivoted and traced a golden lane over the landing field. I circled again to get a clear view of what might be in my way. The port was equipped with everything to make a night landing easy. I throttled down my engine and dropped like a diver into black water.

It was eleven o'clock local time when I landed and taxied across to the beacon. The most helpful ground crew in the world wove in and out of the blinding ray of a searchlight, alternately visible and invisible. They took my papers and began promptly to fill my tanks. Twenty minutes of my time was all they asked for, and I was touched by their great readiness to help. As I was taking off, one of them said:

"Better circle round and fly over us; otherwise we shan't be sure you got off all right."

I rolled down the golden lane toward an unimpeded opening. My *Simoon* lifted her overload clear of the ground well before I reached the end of the runway. The searchlight following me made it hard for me to wheel. Soon it let me go: the men on the ground had guessed that it was dazzling me. I turned right about and banked vertically, and at that moment the searchlight caught me between the eyes again; but scarcely had it touched me when it fled and sent elsewhere its long golden flute. I knew that the ground crew were being most thoughtful and I was grateful. And now I was off to the desert.

All along the line, at Paris, at Tunis and at Benghazi, I had been told that I should have a following wind of up to twenty-five miles an hour. I was counting on a speed of 190 m.p.h. as I set my course on the middle of the stretch between Alexandria and Cairo. On this course I should avoid the danger zones along the coast, and despite any drifting I might do without knowing it, I should pick up either to port or to starboard the lights of one of those two cities. Failing them I should certainly not miss the lights of the Nile valley. With a steady wind I should reach the Nile in three hours and twenty minutes; if the wind fell, three hours and three quarters. Calculating thus I began to eat up the six hundred and fifty miles of desert ahead of me.

There was no moon. The world was a bubble of pitch that had dilated until it reached the very stars in the heavens. I should not see a single gleam of light, should not profit by the faintest landmark. Carrying no wireless, I should receive no message from the earth until I reached the Nile. It was useless to try to look at anything other than the compass and the artificial horizon. I might blot the world out of my mind and concentrate my attention upon the slow pulsation of the narrow thread of radium paint that ran along the dark background of the dials.

Whenever Prévot stirred I brought the plane smoothly back to plumb. I went up to six thousand feet where I had been told the winds would be favorable. At long intervals I switched on a lamp to glance at the engine dials, not all of which were phosphorescent; but most of the time I wrapped myself closely round in darkness among my miniature constellations which gave off the same mineral glow as the stars, the same mysterious and unwearied light, and spoke the same language.

Like the astronomers, I too was reading in the book of celestial mechanics. I too seemed to myself studious and uncorrupted. Everything in the world that might have lured me from my studies had gone out. The external world had ceased to exist.

There was Prévot, who, after a vain resistance, had fallen asleep and left me to the greater enjoyment of my solitude. There was the gentle purr of my beautiful little motor, and before me, on the instrument panel, there were all those tranquil stars. I was most decidedly not sleepy. If this state of quiet well-being persisted until tomorrow night, I intended to push on without a stop to Saigon.

Now the flight was beginning to seem to me short. Benghazi, the only troublesome night landing on the route, had banked its fires and settled down behind the horizon in that dark shuttering in which cities take their slumber.

Meanwhile I was turning things over in my mind. We were without the moon's help and we had no wireless. No slightest tenuous tie was to bind us to earth until the Nile showed its thread of light directly ahead of us. We were truly alone in the universe—a thought that caused me not the least worry. If my motor were to cough, that sound would startle me more than if my heart should skip a beat.

Into my mind came the image of Sabathier, the white-haired engineer with the clear eye. I was thinking that, from one point of view, it would be hard to draw a distinction in the matter of human values between a profession like his and that of the painter, the composer or the poet. I could see in the mind's eye those watchmaker's hands of his that had brought into being this clockwork I was piloting. Men who have given their lives to labors of love go straight to my heart.

"Couldn't I change this?" I had asked him.

"I shouldn't advise it," he had answered.

I was remembering our last conversation. He had thought it inadvisable, and of course that had settled it. A physician, that's it! Exactly the way one puts oneself into the hands of one's doctor—when he has that look in his eye. It was by his motor that we hung suspended in air and were able to go on living with the ticking of time in this penetrable pitch. We were crossing the great dark valley of a fairy tale, the Valley of Ordeal. Like the prince in the tale, we must meet the test without succor. Failure here would not be forgiven. We were in the lap of the inexorable gods.

A ray of light was filtering through a joint in the lamp shaft. I woke up Prévot and told him to put it out. Prévot stirred in the darkness like a bear, snorted and came forward. He fumbled for a bit with handkerchiefs and black paper, and the ray of light vanished. That light had bothered me because it was not of my world. It swore at the pale and distant gleam of the phosphorescence and was like a night-club spotlight compared to the gleam of a star. Besides, it had dazzled me and had outshone all else that gleamed.

We had been flying for three hours. A brightness that seemed to me a glare spurted on the starboard side. I stared. A streamer of light which I had hitherto not noticed was fluttering from a lamp at the tip of the wing. It was an intermittent glow, now brilliant, now dim. It told me that I had flown into a cloud, and it was on the cloud that the lamp was reflected.

I was nearing the landmarks upon which I had counted; a clear sky would have helped a lot. The wing shone bright under the halo. The light steadied itself, became fixed and then began to radiate in the form of a bouquet of pink blossoms. Great eddies of air were swinging me to and fro. I was navigating somewhere in the belly of a cumulus whose thickness I could not guess. I rose to seventy-five hundred feet and was still in it. Down again to three thousand, and the bouquet of flowers was still with me, motionless and growing brighter.

Well, there it was and there was nothing to do about it. I would think of something else, and wait to get clear of it. Just the same, I did not like this sinister glitter of a one-eyed grog shop.

Let me think, I said to myself. I am bouncing round a bit, but there's nothing abnormal about that. I've been bumped all the way, despite a clear sky and plenty of ceiling. The wind has not died down, and I must be doing better than the 190 m.p.h. I counted on. This was about as far as I could get. Oh, well, when I got through the cloud bank I would try to take my bearings.

Out of it we flew. The bouquet suddenly vanished, letting me know I was in the clear again. I stared ahead and saw, if one can speak of "seeing" space, a narrow valley of sky and the wall of the next cumulus. Already the bouquet was coming to life again. I was free of that viscous mess from time to time but only for a few seconds each time. After three and a half hours of flying it began to get on my nerves. If I had made the time I imagined, we were certainly approaching the Nile. With a little luck I might be able to spot the river through the rifts, but they were getting rare. I dared not come down, for if I was actually slower than I thought, I was still over high-lying country.

Thus far I was entirely without anxiety; my only fear was that I might presently be wasting time. I decided that I would take things easy until I had flown four and a quarter hours: after that, even in a dead calm (which was highly unlikely) I should have crossed the Nile. When I reached the fringes of the cloud bank the bouquet winked on and off more and more swiftly and then suddenly went out. Decidedly, I did not like these dot-and-dash messages from the demons of the night.

A green star appeared ahead of me, flashing like a lighthouse. Was it a lighthouse? or really a star? I took no pleasure from this supernatural gleam, this star the Magi might have seen, this dangerous decoy.

Prévot, meanwhile, had waked up and turned his electric torch on the engine dials. I waved him off, him and his torch. We had just sailed into the clear between two clouds and I was busy staring below. Prévot went back to sleep. The gap in the clouds was no help: there was nothing below.

Four hours and five minutes in the air. Prévot awoke and sat down beside me.

"I'll bet we're near Cairo," he said.

"We must be."

"What's that? A star? or is it a lighthouse?"

I had throttled the engine down a little. This, probably, was what had awakened Prévot. He is sensitive to all the variations of sound in flight.

I began a slow descent, intending to slip under the mass of clouds. Meanwhile I had had a look at my map. One thing was sure—the land below me lay at sea level, and there was no risk of conking against a hill. Down I went, flying due north so that the lights of the cities would strike square into my windows. I must have overflown them, and should therefore see them on my left.

Now I was flying below the cumulus. But alongside was another cloud hanging lower down on the left. I swerved so as not to be caught in its net, and headed north-northeast. This second cloud bank certainly went down a long way, for it blocked my view of the horizon. I dared not give up any more altitude. My altimeter registered twelve hundred feet, but I had no notion of the atmospheric pressure here. Prévot leaned toward me and I shouted to him, "I'm going out to sea. I'd rather come down on it than risk a crash here."

As a matter of fact, there was nothing to prove that we had not drifted over the sea already. Below that cloud bank visibility was exactly nil. I hugged my window, trying to read below me, to discover flares, signs of life. I was a man raking dead ashes, trying in vain to retrieve the flame of life in a hearth.

"A lighthouse!"

Both of us spied it at the same moment, that winking decoy! What madness! Where was that phantom light, that invention of the night? For at the very second when Prévot and I leaned forward to pick it out of the air where it had glittered nine hundred feet below our wings, suddenly, at that very instant . . .

"Oh!"

I am quite sure that this was all I said. I am quite sure that all I felt was a terrific crash that rocked our world to its foundations. We had crashed against the earth at a hundred and seventy miles an hour. I am quite sure that in the split second that followed all I expected was the great flash of ruddy light of the explosion in which Prévot and I were to be blown up together. Neither he nor I had felt the least emotion of any kind. All I could observe in myself was an extraordinary tense feeling of expectancy, the expectancy of that resplendent star in which we were to vanish within the second.

But there was no ruddy star. Instead there was a sort of earthquake that splintered our cabin, ripped away the windows, blew sheets of metal hurtling though space a hundred yards away and filled our very entrails with its roar. The ship quivered like a knife blade thrown from a distance into a block of oak, and its anger mashed us as if we were so much pulp.

One second, two seconds passed, and the plane still quivered while I waited with a grotesque impatience for the forces within it to burst it like a bomb. But the subterranean quakings went on without a climax of eruption while I marveled uncomprehendingly at its invisible travail. I was baffled by the quaking, the anger, the interminable postponement. Five seconds passed; six seconds. And suddenly we were seized by a spinning motion, a shock that jerked our cigarettes out of the window, pulverized the starboard wing—and then nothing, nothing but a frozen immobility. I shouted to Prévot:

"Jump!"

And in that instant he cried out: "Fire!"

We dove together through the wrecked window and found ourselves standing side by side, sixty feet from the plane. I said: "Are you hurt?"

He answered: "Not a bit."

But he was rubbing his knee.

"Better run your hands over yourself," I said; "move about a bit. Sure no bones are broken?"

He answered: "I'm all right. It's that emergency pump."

Emergency pump! I was sure he was going to keel over any minute and split open from head to navel there before my eyes. But he kept repeating with a glassy stare: "That pump, that emergency pump."

He's out of his head, I thought. He'll start dancing in a minute.

Finally he stopped staring at the plane—which had not gone up in flames—and stared at me instead. And he said again: "I'm all right. It's that emergency pump. It got me in the knee."

Why we were not blown up, I do not know. I switched on my electric torch and went back over the furrow in the ground traced by the plane. Two hundred and fifty yards from where we stopped the ship had begun to shed the twisted iron and sheet metal that spattered the sand the length of her traces. We were to see, when day came, that we had run almost tangentially into a gentle slope at the top of a barren plateau. At the point of impact there was a hole in the sand that looked as if it had been made by a plough. Maintaining an even keel, the plane had run its course with the fury and the tail lashings of a reptile gliding on its belly at the rate of a hundred and seventy miles an hour. We owed our lives to the fact that this desert was surfaced with round black pebbles which had rolled over and over like ball bearings beneath us. They must have rained upward to the heavens as we shot through them.

Prévot disconnected the batteries for fear of fire by short circuit. I leaned against the motor and turned the situation over in my mind. I had been flying high for four hours and a quarter, possibly with a thirty-mile following wind. I had been jolted a good deal. If the wind had changed since the weather people forecast it, I was unable to say into what quarter it had veered. All I could make out was that we had crashed in an empty square two hundred and fifty miles on each side.

Prévot came up and sat down beside me.

"I can't believe that we're alive," he said.

I said nothing. Even that thought could not cheer me. A germ of an idea was at work in my mind and was already bothering me. Telling Prévot to switch on his torch as a landmark, I walked straight out, scrutinizing the ground in the light of my own torch as I went.

I went forward slowly, swung round in a wide arc, and changed

direction a number of times. I kept my eyes fixed on the ground like
a man hunting a lost ring.

Only a little while before I had been straining just as hard to see a
gleam of light from the air. Through the darkness I went, bowed over
the traveling disk of white light. Just as I thought, I said to myself,
and I went slowly back to the plane. I sat down beside the cabin and
ruminated. I had been looking for a reason to hope and had failed to
find it. I had been looking for a sign of life, and no sign of life had
appeared.

"Prévot, I couldn't find a single blade of grass."

Prévot said nothing, and I was not sure he had understood. Well,
we could talk about it again when the curtain rose at dawn. Meanwhile I was dead tired and all I could think was, Two hundred and
fifty miles more or less in the desert.

Suddenly I jumped to my feet. "Water!" I said.

Gas tanks and oil tanks were smashed in. So was our supply of
drinking water. The sand had drunk everything. We found a pint of
coffee in a battered thermos flask and half a pint of white wine in
another. We filtered both, and poured them into one flask. There
were some grapes, too, and a single orange. Meanwhile I was computing: "All this will last us five hours of tramping in the sun."

We crawled into the cabin and waited for dawn. I stretched out,
and as I settled down to sleep I took stock of our situation. We didn't
know where we were; we had less than a quart of liquid between us;
if we were not too far off the Benghazi-Cairo lane we should be found
in a week, and that would be too late. Yet it was the best we could
hope for. If, on the other hand, we had drifted off our course, we
shouldn't be found in six months. One thing was sure—we could not
count on being picked up by a plane; the men who came out for us
would have two thousand miles to cover.

"You know, it's a shame," Prévot said suddenly.

"What's a shame?"

"That we didn't crash properly and have it over with."

It seemed pretty early to be throwing in one's hand. Prévot and I
pulled ourselves together. There was still a chance, slender as it was,
that we might be saved miraculously by a plane. On the other hand,
we couldn't stay here and perhaps miss a nearby oasis. We would
walk all day and come back to the plane before dark. And before
going off we would write our plan in huge letters in the sand.

With this I curled up and settled down to sleep. I was happy to go to sleep. My weariness wrapped me round like a multiple presence. I was not alone in the desert: my drowsiness was peopled with voices and memories and whispered confidences. I was not yet thirsty; I felt strong and I surrendered myself to sleep as to an aimless journey. Reality lost ground before the advance of dreams.

Ah, but things were different when I awoke!

In times past I have loved the Sahara. I have spent nights alone in the path of marauding tribes and have waked up with untroubled mind in the golden emptiness of the desert where the wind like a sea had raised sand-waves upon its surface. Asleep under the wing of my plane I have looked forward with confidence to being rescued next day. But this was not the Sahara!

Prévot and I walked along the slopes of rolling mounds. The ground was sand covered over with a single layer of shining black pebbles. They gleamed like metal scales and all the domes about us shone like coats of mail. We had dropped down into a mineral world and were hemmed in by iron hills.

When we reached the top of the first crest we saw in the distance another just like it, black and gleaming. As we walked we scraped the ground with our boots, marking a trail over which to return to the plane. We went forward with the sun in our eyes. It was not logical to go due east like this, for everything—the weather reports, the duration of the flight—had made it plain that we had crossed the Nile. But I had started tentatively toward the west and had felt a vague foreboding I could not explain to myself. So I had put off the west till tomorrow. In the same way, provisionally, I had given up going north, though that led to the sea.

Three days later, when scourged by thirst into abandoning the plane and walking straight on until we dropped in our tracks, it was still eastward that we tramped. More precisely, we walked east-northeast. And this too was in defiance of all reason and even of all hope. Yet after we had been rescued we discovered that if we had gone in any other direction we should have been lost.

Northward, we should never have had the endurance to reach the sea. And absurd as it may appear, it seems to me now, since I had no other motive, that I must have chosen the east simply because it was by going eastward that Guillaumet had been saved in the Andes, after I had hunted for him everywhere. In a confused way the east had become for me the direction of life.

We walked on for five hours and then the landscape changed. A river of sand seemed to be running through a valley, and we followed this river bed, taking long strides in order to cover as much ground as possible and get back to the plane before night fell, if our march was in vain. Suddenly I stopped.

"Prévot!"

"What's up?"

"Our tracks!"

How long was it since we had forgotten to leave a wake behind us? We had to find it or die.

We went back, bearing to the right. When we had gone back far enough we would make a right angle to the left and eventually intersect our tracks where we had still remembered to mark them.

This we did and were off again. The heat rose and with it came the mirages. But these were still the commonplace kind—sheets of water that materialized and then vanished as we neared them. We decided to cross the valley of sand and climb the highest dome in order to look round the horizon. This was after six hours of march in which, striding along, we must have covered twenty miles.

When we had struggled up to the top of the black hump we sat down and looked at each other. At our feet lay our valley of sand, opening into a desert of sand whose dazzling brightness seared our eyes. As far as the eye could see lay empty space. But in that space the play of light created mirages which, this time, were of a disturbing kind, fortresses and minarets, angular geometric hulks. I could see also a black mass that pretended to be vegetation, overhung by the last of those clouds that dissolve during the day only to return at night. This mass of vegetation was the shadow of a cumulus.

It was no good going on. The experiment was a failure. We would have to go back to our plane, to that red and white beacon which, perhaps, would be picked out by a flyer. I was not staking great hopes on a rescue party, but it did seem to me our last chance of salvation. In any case, we had to get back to our few drops of liquid, for our throats were parched. We were imprisoned in this iron circle, captives of the curt dictatorship of thirst.

And yet, how hard it was to turn back when there was a chance that we might be on the road to life! Beyond the mirages the horizon was perhaps rich in veritable treasures, in meadows and runnels of sweet water. I knew I was doing the right thing by returning to the plane, and yet as I swung round and started back I was filled with portents of disaster.

We were resting on the ground beside the plane. Nearly forty miles of wandering this day. The last drop of liquid had been drained. No sign of life had appeared to the east. No plane had soared overhead. How long should we be able to hold out? Already our thirst was terrible.

We had built up a great pyre out of bits of the splintered wing. Our gasoline was ready, and we had flung on the heap sheets of metal whose magnesium coating would burn with a hard white flame. We were waiting now for night to come down before we lighted our conflagration. But where were there men to see it?

Night fell and the flames rose. Prayerfully we watched our mute and radiant fanion mount resplendent into the night. As I looked I said to myself that this message was not only a cry for help, it was fraught also with a great deal of love. We were begging water, but we were also begging the communion of human society. Only man can create fire: let another flame light up the night; let man answer man!

I was haunted by a vision of my wife's eyes under the halo of her hat. Of her face I could see only the eyes, questioning me, looking at me yearningly. I am answering, answering with all my strength! What flame could leap higher than this that darts up into the night from my heart?

What I could do, I have done. What we could do, we have done. Nearly forty miles, almost without a drop to drink. Now there was no water left. Was it our fault that we could wait no longer? Suppose we had sat quietly by the plane, taking suck at the mouths of our water bottles? But from the moment I breathed in the moist bottom of the tin cup, a clock had started up in me. From the second when I had sucked up the last drop, I had begun to slip downhill. Could I help it if time like a river was carrying me away? Prévot was weeping. I tapped him on the shoulder and said, to console him:

"If we're done for we're done for, and that's all there is to it."

He said: "Do you think it's me I'm bawling about?"

I might have known it. It was evident enough. Nothing is unbearable. Tomorrow, and the day after, I should learn that nothing was really unbearable. I had never really believed in torture. Reading Poe as a kid, I had already said as much to myself. Once, jammed in the cabin of a plane, I thought I was going to drown; and I had not suffered much. Several times it had seemed to me that the final smash-up was coming, and I don't remember that I thought of it as a cosmic event. And I didn't believe this was going to be agonizing either. There will be time tomorrow to find out stranger things about it. Meanwhile, God knows that despite the bonfire I had decidedly given up hope that our cries would be heard by the world.

"Do you think it's me? . . ." There you have what is truly unbearable! Every time I saw those yearning eyes it was as if a flame were searing me. They were like a scream for help, like the flares of a sinking ship. I felt that I should not sit idly by: I should jump up and run—anywhere! straight ahead of me!

What a strange reversal of roles! But I have always thought it would be like this. Still, I needed Prévot beside me to be quite sure of it. Prévot was a level-headed fellow. He loved life. And yet Prévot no more than I was wringing his hands at the sight of death the way we are told men do. But there did exist something that he could not bear any more than I could. I was perfectly ready to fall asleep, whether for a night or for eternity. If I did fall asleep, I could not even know whether it was for the one or for the other. And the peace of sleep! But that cry that would be sent up at home, that great wail of desolation—that was what I could not bear. I could not stand idly by and look on at that disaster. Each second of silence drove the knife deeper into someone loved. At the thought, a blind rage surged up in me. Why do these chains bind me and prevent me from rescuing those who are drowning? Why does our conflagration not carry our cry to the ends of the world? Hear me, you out here! Patience. We are coming to save you.

The magnesium had been licked off and the metal was glowing red. There was left only a heap of embers round which we crouched to warm ourselves. Our flaming call had spent itself. Had it set anything in the world in motion? I knew well enough that it hadn't. Here was a prayer that had of necessity gone unheard.

That was that.

I ought to get some sleep.

At daybreak I took a rag and mopped up a little dew on the wings. The mixture of water and paint and oil yielded a spoonful of nauseating liquid which we sipped because it would at least moisten our lips. After this banquet Prévot said: "Thank God we've got a gun."

Instantly I became furious and turned on him with an aggressiveness which I regretted directly I felt it. There was nothing I should have loathed more at that moment than a gush of sentimentality. I am so made that I have to believe that everything is simple. Birth is simple. Growing up is simple. And dying of thirst is simple. I watched Prévot out of the corner of my eye, ready to wound his feelings, if that was necessary to shut him up.

But Prévot had spoken without emotion. He had been discussing a matter of hygiene, and might have said in the same tone, "We ought to wash our hands." That being so, we were agreed. Indeed already yesterday, my eye falling by chance on the leather holster, the same thought had crossed my mind, and with me too it had been a reasonable reflex, not an emotional one. Pathos resides in social man, not in the individual; what was pathetic was our powerlessness to reassure those for whom we were responsible, not what we might do with the gun.

There was still no sign that we were being sought; or rather they were doubtless hunting for us elsewhere, probably in Arabia. We were to hear no sound of a plane until the day after we had abandoned our own. And if ships did pass overhead, what could that mean to us? What could they see in us except two black dots among the thousand shadowy dots in the desert? Absurd to think of being distinguishable from them. None of the reflections that might be attributed to me on the score of this torture would be true. I should not feel in the least tortured. The aerial rescue party would seem to me, each time I sighted one, to be moving through a universe that was not mine. When searchers have to cover two thousand miles of territory, it takes them a good two weeks to spot a plane in the desert from the sky.

They were probably looking for us all along the line from Tripoli to Persia. And still, with all this, I clung to the slim chance that they might pick us out. Was that not our only chance of being saved? I changed my tactics, determining to go reconnoitering by myself. Prévot would get another bonfire together and kindle it in the event that visitors showed up. But we were to have no callers that day.

So off I went without knowing whether or not I should have the stamina to come back. I remembered what I knew about this Libyan desert. When, in the Sahara, humidity is still at forty percent of saturation, it is only eighteen here in Libya. Life here evaporates like a vapor. Bedouins, explorers and colonial officers all tell us that a man may go nineteen hours without water. Thereafter his eyes fill with light, and that marks the beginning of the end. The progress made by thirst is swift and terrible. But this northeast wind, this abnormal wind that had blown us out off our course and had marooned us on this plateau, was now prolonging our lives. What was the length of the reprieve it would grant us before our eyes began to fill with light? I went forward with the feeling of a man canoeing in mid-ocean.

I will admit that at daybreak this landscape seemed to me less infernal, and that I began my walk with my hands in my pockets, like a tramp on a highroad. The evening before we had set snares at the mouths of certain mysterious burrows in the ground, and the poacher in me was on the alert. I went first to have a look at our traps. They were empty.

Well, this meant that I should not be drinking blood today; and indeed I hadn't expected to. But though I was not disappointed, my curiosity was aroused. What was there in the desert for these animals to live on? These were certainly the holes of fennecs, a long-eared carnivorous sand fox the size of a rabbit. I spotted the tracks made by one of them, and gave way to the impulse to follow them. They led to a narrow stream of sand where each footprint was plainly outlined and where I marveled at the pretty palm formed by the three toes spread fanwise on the sand.

I could imagine my little friend trotting blithely along at dawn and licking the dew off the rocks. Here the tracks were wider apart: my fennec had broken into a run. And now I see that a companion has joined him and they have trotted on side by side. These signs of a morning stroll gave me a strange thrill. They were signs of life, and I loved them for that. I almost forgot that I was thirsty.

Finally I came to the pasture ground of my foxes. Here, every hundred yards or so, I saw sticking up out of the sand a small dry shrub, its twigs heavy with little golden snails. The fennec came here at dawn to do his marketing. And here I was able to observe another of nature's mysteries.

My fennec did not stop at all the shrubs. There were some weighed down with snails which he disdained. Obviously he avoided them with some wariness. Others he stopped at but did not strip of all they bore. He must have picked out two or three shells and then gone on to another restaurant. What was he up to? Was he nurseryman to the snails, encouraging their reproduction by refraining from exhausting the stock on a given shrub, or a given twig? Or was he amusing himself by delaying repletion, putting off satiety in order to enhance the pleasure he took from his morning stroll?

The tracks led me back to the hole in which he lived. Doubtless my fennec crouched below, listening to me and startled by the crunching of my footsteps. I said to him:

"Fox, my little fox, I'm done for; but somehow that doesn't prevent me from taking an interest in your mood."

And there I stayed a bit, ruminating and telling myself that a man was able to adapt himself to anything. The notion that he is to die in thirty years has probably never spoiled any man's fun. Thirty years . . . or thirty days: it's all a matter of perspective.

Only, you have to be able to put certain visions out of your mind.

I went on, finally, and the time came when, along with my weariness, something in me began to change. If those were not mirages, I was inventing them.

"Hi! Hi, there!"

I shouted and waved my arms, but the man I had seen waving at me turned out to be a black rock. Everything in the desert had grown animate. I stooped to waken a sleeping Bedouin and he turned into the trunk of a black tree. A tree trunk? Here in the desert? I was amazed and bent over to lift a broken bough. It was solid marble.

Straightening up I looked round and saw more black marble. An antediluvian forest littered the ground with its broken treetops. How many thousand years ago, under what hurricane of the time of Genesis, had this cathedral of wood crumbled in this spot? Countless centuries had rolled these fragments of giant pillars at my feet, polished them like steel, petrified and vitrified them and indued them with the color of jet.

I could distinguish the knots in their branches, the twisting of their once-living boughs, could count the rings of life in them. This forest had rustled with birds and been filled with music that now was struck by doom and frozen into salt. And all this was hostile to me. Blacker than the chain mail of the hummocks, these solemn derelicts rejected me. What had I, a living man, to do with this incorruptible stone? Perishable as I was, I whose body was to crumble into dust, what place had I in this eternity?

Since yesterday I had walked nearly fifty miles. This dizziness that

I felt came doubtless from my thirst. Or from the sun. It glittered on these hulks until they shone as if smeared with oil. It blazed down on this universal carapace. Sand and fox had no life here. This world was a gigantic anvil upon which the sun beat down. I strode across this anvil and at my temples I could feel the hammer strokes of the sun.

"Hi! Hi, there!" I called out.

"There is nothing there," I told myself. "Take it easy. You are delirious."

I had to talk to myself aloud, had to bring myself to reason. It was hard for me to reject what I was seeing, hard not to run toward that caravan plodding on the horizon. "There! Do you see it?"

"Fool! You know very well that you are inventing it."

"You mean that nothing in the world is real?"

Nothing in the world is real if that cross which I see ten miles off on the top of a hill is not real. Or is it a lighthouse? No, the sea does not lie in that direction. Then it must be a cross.

I had spent the night studying my map—but uselessly, since I did not know my position. Still, I had scrutinized all the signs that marked the marvelous presence of man. And somewhere on the map I had seen a little circle surmounted by just such a cross. I had glanced down at the legend to get an explanation of the symbol and had read: "Religious institution."

Close to the cross there had been a black dot. Again I had run my finger down the legend and had read: "Permanent well." My heart had jumped and I had repeated the legend aloud: "Permanent well, permanent well." What were all of Ali Baba's treasures compared with a permanent well? A little farther on were two white circles. "Temporary wells," the legend said. Not quite so exciting. And round about them was nothing . . . unless it was the blankness of despair. But this must be my "religious institution"! The monks must certainly have planted a great cross on the hill expressly for men in our plight! All I had to do was to walk across to them. I should be taken in by those Dominicans. . . .

"But there are only Coptic monasteries in Libya!" I told myself.

. . . by those learned Dominicans. They have a great cool kitchen with red tiles, and out in the courtyard a marvelous rusted pump. Beneath the rusted pump; beneath the rusted pump . . . you've guessed it! . . . beneath the rusted pump is dug the permanent well! Ah, what rejoicing when I ring at their gate, when I get my hands on the rope of the great bell.

"Madman! You are describing a house in Provence; and what's more the house has no bell!"

. . . on the rope of the great bell. The porter will raise his arms to Heaven and cry out, "You are the messenger of the Lord!" and he will call aloud to all the monks. They will pour out of the monastery. They will welcome me with a great feast, as if I were the Prodigal Son. They will lead me to the kitchen and will say to me, "One moment, my son, one moment. We'll just be off to the permanent well." And I shall be trembling with happiness.

No, no! I will *not* weep just because there happens to be no cross on the hill.

The treasures of the west turned out to be mere illusion. I have veered due north. At least the north is filled with the sound of the sea.

Over the hilltop. Look there, at the horizon! The most beautiful city in the world!

"You know perfectly well that is a mirage."

Of course I know it is a mirage! Am I the sort of man who can be fooled? But what if I *want* to go after that mirage? Suppose I enjoy indulging my hope? Suppose it suits me to love that crenelated town all beflagged with sunlight? What if I choose to walk straight ahead on light feet—for you must know that I have dropped my weariness behind me, I am happy now. . . . Prévot and his gun! Don't make me laugh! I prefer my drunkenness. I am drunk. I am dying of thirst.

It took the twilight to sober me. Suddenly I stopped, appalled to think how far I was from our base. In the twilight the mirage was dying. The horizon had stripped itself of its pomp, its palaces, its priestly vestments. It was the old desert horizon again.

"A fine day's work you've done! Night will overtake you. You won't be able to go on before daybreak, and by that time your tracks will have been blown away and you'll be properly nowhere."

In that case I may as well walk straight on. Why turn back? Why should I bring my ship round when I may find the sea straight ahead of me?

"When did you catch a glimpse of the sea? What makes you think you could walk that far? Meanwhile there's Prévot watching for you beside the *Simoon*. He may have been picked up by a caravan, for all you know."

Very good. I'll go back. But first I want to call out for help.

"Hi! Hi!"

By God! You can't tell me this planet is not inhabited. Where are its men?

"Hi! Hi!"

I was hoarse. My voice was gone. I knew it was ridiculous to croak like this, but—one more try:

"Hi! Hi!"

And I turned back.

I had been walking two hours when I saw the flames of the bonfire that Prévot, frightened by my long absence, had sent up. They mattered very little to me now.

Another hour of trudging. Five hundred yards away. A hundred yards. Fifty yards.

"Good Lord!"

Amazement stopped me in my tracks. Joy surged up and filled my heart with its violence. In the firelight stood Prévot, talking to two Arabs who were leaning against the motor. He had not noticed me, for he was too full of his own joy. If only I had sat still and waited with him! I should have been saved already. Exultantly I called out:

"Hi! Hi!"

The two Bedouins gave a start and stared at me. Prévot left them standing and came forward to meet me. I opened my arms to him. He caught me by the elbow. Did he think I was keeling over? I said:

"At last, eh?"

"What do you mean?"

"The Arabs!"

"What Arabs?"

"Those Arabs there, with you."

Prévot looked at me queerly, and when he spoke I felt as if he was very reluctantly confiding a great secret to me: "There are no Arabs here."

This time I know I am going to cry.

A man can go nineteen hours without water, and what have we drunk since last night? A few drops of dew at dawn. But the northeast wind is still blowing, still slowing up the process of our evaporation. To it, also, we owe the continued accumulation of high clouds. If only they would drift straight overhead and break into rain! But it never rains in the desert.

"Look here, Prévot. Let's rip up one of the parachutes and spread the sections out on the ground, weighed down with stones. If the wind stays in the same quarter till morning, they'll catch the dew and we can wring them out into one of the tanks."

We spread six triangular sections of parachute under the stars, and Prévot unhooked a fuel tank. This was as much as we could do for ourselves till dawn. But, miracle of miracles! Prévot had come upon an orange while working over the tank. We shared it, and though it was little enough to men who could have used a few gallons of sweet water, still I was overcome with relief.

Stretched out beside the fire I looked at the glowing fruit and said to myself that men did not know what an orange was. "Here we are, condemned to death," I said to myself, "and still the certainty of dying cannot compare with the pleasure I am feeling. The joy I take from this half of an orange which I am holding in my hand is one of the greatest joys I have ever known."

I lay flat on my back, sucking my orange and counting the shooting stars. Here I was, for one minute infinitely happy. "Nobody can know anything of the world in which the individual moves and has his being," I reflected. "There is no guessing it. Only the man locked up in it can know what it is."

For the first time I understood the cigarette and glass of rum that are handed to the criminal about to be executed. I used to think that for a man to accept these wretched gifts at the foot of the gallows was beneath human dignity. Now I was learning that he took pleasure from them. People thought him courageous when he smiled as he smoked or drank. I knew now that he smiled because the taste gave him pleasure. People could not see that his perspective had changed, and that for him the last hour of his life was a life in itself.

We collected an enormous quantity of water—perhaps as much as two quarts. Never again would we be thirsty! We were saved; we had a liquid to drink!

I dipped my tin cup into the tank and brought up a beautifully yellow-green liquid the first mouthful of which nauseated me so that despite my thirst I had to catch my breath before swallowing it. I would have swallowed mud, I swear; but this taste of poisonous metal cut keener than thirst.

I glanced at Prévot and saw him going round and round with his eyes fixed to the ground as if looking for something. Suddenly he leaned forward and began to vomit without interrupting his spinning. Half a minute later it was my turn. I was seized by such convulsions that I went down on my knees and dug my fingers into the sand while I puked. Neither of us spoke, and for a quarter of an hour we remained thus shaken, bringing up nothing but a little bile.

After a time it passed and all I felt was a vague, distant nausea. But our last hope had fled. Whether our bad luck was due to a sizing on the parachute or to the magnesium lining of the tank, I never found out. Certain it was that we needed either another set of clothes or another receptacle.

Well, it was broad daylight and time we were on our way. This time we should strike out as fast as we could, leave this cursed plateau and tramp till we dropped in our tracks. That was what Guillaumet had done in the Andes. I had been thinking of him all the day before and had determined to follow his example. I should do violence to the pilot's unwritten law, which is to stick by the ship; but I was sure no one would be along to look for us here.

Once again we discovered that it was not we who were ship-wrecked, not we but those who were waiting for news of us, those who were alarmed by our silence, were already torn with grief by some atrocious and fantastic report. We could not but strive toward them. Guillaumet had done it, had scrambled toward his lost ones. To do so is a universal impulse.

"If I were alone in the world," Prévot said, "I'd lie down right here. Damned if I wouldn't."

East-northeast we tramped. If we had in fact crossed the Nile, each step was leading us deeper and deeper into the desert.

I don't remember anything about that day. I remember only my haste. I was hurrying desperately toward something—toward some finality. I remember also that I walked with my eyes to the ground, for the mirages were more than I could bear. From time to time we would correct our course by the compass, and now and again we would lie down to catch our breath. I remember having flung away my waterproof, which I had held on to as covering for the night. That is as much as I recall about the day. Of what happened when the chill of evening came, I remember more. But during the day I had simply turned to sand and was a being without mind.

When the sun set we decided to make camp. Oh, I knew as well as anybody that we should push on, that this one waterless night would finish us off. But we had brought along the bits of parachute, and if the poison was not in the sizing, we might get a sip of water next morning. Once again we spread our trap for the dew under the stars.

But the sky in the north was cloudless. The wind no longer had the same taste on the lip. It had moved into another quarter. Something was rustling against us, but this time it seemed to be the desert itself. The wild beast was stalking us, had us in its power. I could feel its breath in my face, could feel it lick my face and hands. Suppose I walked on: at the best I could do five or six miles more. Remember that in three days I had covered one hundred miles, practically without water.

And then, just as we stopped, Prévot said: "I swear to you I see a lake!"

"You're crazy."

"Have you ever heard of a mirage after sunset?" he challenged.

I didn't seem able to answer him. I had long ago given up believing my own eyes. Perhaps it was not a mirage; but in that case it was a hallucination. How could Prévot go on believing? But he was stubborn about it.

"It's only twenty minutes off. I'll go have a look."

His mulishness got on my nerves.

"Go ahead!" I shouted. "Take your little constitutional. Nothing better for a man. But let me tell you, if your lake exists it is salt. And whether it's salt or not, it's a devil of a way off. And besides, there is no damned lake!"

Prévot was already on his way, his eyes glassy. I knew the strength of these irresistible obsessions. I was thinking: "There are somnambulists who walk straight into locomotives." And I knew that Prévot would not come back. He would be seized by the vertigo of empty space and would be unable to turn back. And then he would keel over. He somewhere, and I somewhere else. Not that it was important.

Thinking thus, it struck me that this mood of resignation was doing me no good. Once when I was half drowned I had let myself go like this. Lying now flat on my face on the stony ground, I took this occasion to write a letter for posthumous delivery. It gave me a chance, also, to take stock of myself again. I tried to bring up a little saliva: how long was it since I had spit? No saliva. If I kept my mouth closed, a kind of glue sealed my lips together. It dried on the outside of the lips and formed a hard crust. However, I found I was still able to swallow, and I bethought me that I was still not seeing a blinding light in my eyes. Once I was treated to that radiant spectacle I might know that the end was a couple of hours away.

Night fell. The moon had swollen since I last saw it. Prévot was still not back. I stretched out on my back and turned these few data over in my mind. A familiar impression came over me, and I tried to seize it. I was . . . I was . . . I was at sea. I was on a ship going to South America and was stretched out, exactly like this, on the boat deck. The tip of the mast was swaying to and fro, very slowly, among the stars. That mast was missing tonight, but again I was at sea, bound for a port I was to make without raising a finger. Slave traders had flung me on this ship.

I thought of Prévot, who was still not back. Not once had I heard him complain. That was a good thing. To hear him whine would have been unbearable. Prévot was a man.

What was that! Five hundred yards ahead of me I could see the light of his lamp. He has lost his way. I had no lamp with which to signal back. I stood up and shouted, but he could not hear me.

A second lamp, and then a third! God in Heaven! It was a search party and it was me they were hunting!

"Hi! Hi!" I shouted.

But they had not heard me. The three lamps were still signaling me.

"Tonight I am sane," I said to myself. "I am relaxed. I am not out of my head. Those are certainly three lamps and they are about five hundred yards off." I stared at them and shouted again, and again I gathered that they could not hear me.

Then, for the first and only time, I was really seized with panic. I could still run, I thought. "Wait! Wait!" I screamed. They seemed to be turning away from me, going off, hunting me elsewhere! And I stood tottering, tottering on the brink of life when there were arms out there ready to catch me! I shouted and screamed again and again.

They had heard me! An answering shout had come. I was strangling, suffocating, but I ran on, shouting as I ran, until I saw Prévot and keeled over.

When I could speak again I said: "Whew! When I saw all those lights . . ."

"What lights?"

God in Heaven, it was true! He was alone!

This time I was beyond despair. I was filled with a sort of dumb fury.

"What about your lake?" I rasped.

"As fast as I moved toward it, it moved back. I walked after it for about half an hour. Then it seemed still too far away, so I came back. But I am positive, now, that it is a lake."

"You're crazy. Absolutely crazy. Why did you do it? Tell me. Why?"

What had he done? Why had he done it? I was ready to weep with indignation, yet I scarcely knew why I was so indignant. Prévot mumbled his excuse:

"I felt I had to find some water. You . . . your lips were awfully pale."

Well! My anger died within me. I passed my hand over my forehead as if I were waking out of sleep. I was suddenly sad. I said:

"There was no mistake about it. I saw them as clearly as I see you now. Three lights there were. I tell you, Prévot, I saw them!"

Prévot made no comment.

"Well," he said finally, "I guess we're in a bad way."

In this air devoid of moisture the soil is swift to give off its temperature. It was already very cold. I stood up and stamped about. But soon a violent fit of trembling came over me. My dehydrated blood was moving sluggishly and I was pierced by a freezing chill which was not merely the chill of night. My teeth were chattering and my whole body had begun to twitch. My hand shook so that I could not hold an electric torch. I who had never been sensitive to cold was about to die of cold. What a strange effect thirst can have!

Somewhere, tired of carrying it in the sun, I had let my waterproof drop. Now the wind was growing bitter and I was learning that in the desert there is no place of refuge. The desert is as smooth as marble. By day it throws no shadow; by night it hands you over naked to the wind. Not a tree, not a hedge, not a rock behind which I could seek shelter. The wind was charging me like a troop of cavalry across open country. I turned and twisted to escape it: I lay down, stood up, lay down again, and still I was exposed to its freezing lash. I had no strength to run from the assassin and under the saber stroke I tumbled to my knees, my head between my hands.

A little later I pieced these bits together and remembered that I had struggled to my feet and had started to walk on, shivering as I went. I had started forward wondering where I was and then I had heard Prévot. His shouting had jolted me into consciousness.

I went back toward him, still trembling from head to foot—quivering with the attack of hiccups that was convulsing my whole body. To myself I said: "It isn't the cold. It's something else. It's the end." The simple fact was that I hadn't enough water in me. I had tramped too far yesterday and the day before when I was off by myself, and I was dehydrated.

The thought of dying of the cold hurt me. I preferred the phantoms of my mind, the cross, the trees, the lamps. At least they would have killed me by enchantment. But to be whipped to death like a slave! . . .

Confound it! Down on my knees again! We had with us a little store of medicines—a hundred grams of 90 per cent alcohol, the same of pure ether and a small bottle of iodine. I tried to swallow a little of the ether: it was like swallowing a knife. Then I tried the alcohol: it contracted my gullet. I dug a pit in the sand, lay down in it and flung handfuls of sand over me until all but my face was buried in it.

Prévot was able to collect a few twigs, and he lit a fire which soon burnt itself out. He wouldn't bury himself in the sand, but preferred to stamp round and round in a circle. That was foolish.

My throat stayed shut, and though I knew that was a bad sign, I felt better. I felt calm. I felt a peace that was beyond all hope. Once more, despite myself, I was journeying, trussed up on the deck of my slave ship under the stars. It seemed to me that I was perhaps not in such a bad pass after all.

So long as I lay absolutely motionless, I no longer felt the cold. This allowed me to forget my body buried in the sand. I said to myself that I would not budge an inch, and would therefore never suffer again. As a matter of fact, we really suffer very little. Back of all these torments there is the orchestration of fatigue or of delirium, and we live on in a kind of picture book, a slightly cruel fairy tale.

A little while ago the wind had been after me with whip and spur, and I was running in circles like a frightened fox. After that came a time when I couldn't breathe. A great knee was crushing in my chest.

A knee. I was writhing in vain to free myself from the weight of the angel who had overthrown me. There had not been a moment when I was alone in this desert. But now I have ceased to believe in my surroundings; I have withdrawn into myself, have shut my eyes, have not so much as batted an eyelid. I have the feeling that this torrent of visions is sweeping me away to a tranquil dream: so rivers cease their turbulence in the embrace of the sea.

Farewell, eyes that I loved! Do not blame me if the human body cannot go three days without water. I should never have believed that man was so truly the prisoner of the springs and freshets. I had no notion that our self-sufficiency was so circumscribed. We take it for granted that a man is able to stride straight out into the world. We believe that man is free. We never see the cord that binds him to wells and fountains, that umbilical cord by which he is tied to the womb of the world. Let man take but one step too many . . . and the cord snaps.

Apart from your suffering, I have no regrets. All in all, it has been a good life. If I got free of this I should start right in again. A man cannot live a decent life in cities, and I need to feel myself live. I am not thinking of aviation. The airplane is a means, not an end. One doesn't risk one's life for a plane any more than a farmer ploughs for the sake of the plough. But the airplane is a means of getting away from towns and their bookkeeping and coming to grips with reality.

Flying is a man's job and its worries are a man's worries. A pilot's business is with the wind, with the stars, with night, with sand, with the sea. He strives to outwit the forces of nature. He stares in expectancy for the coming of dawn the way a gardener awaits the coming of spring. He looks forward to port as to a promised land, and truth for him is what lives in the stars.

I have nothing to complain of. For three days I have tramped the desert, have known the pangs of thirst, have followed false scents in the sand, have pinned my faith on the dew. I have struggled to rejoin my kind, whose very existence on earth I had forgotten. These are the cares of men alive in every fiber, and I cannot help thinking them more important than the fretful choosing of a night club in which to spend the evening. Compare the one life with the other, and all things considered this is luxury! I have no regrets. I have gambled and lost. It was all in the day's work. At least I have had the unforgettable taste of the sea on my lips.

I am not talking about living dangerously. Such words are meaningless to me. The toreador does not stir me to enthusiasm. It is not danger I love. I know what I love. It is life.

The sky seemed to me faintly bright. I drew up one arm through the sand. There was a bit of the torn parachute within reach, and I ran my hand over it. It was bone dry. Let's see. Dew falls at dawn. Here was dawn risen and no moisture on the cloth. My mind was befuddled and I heard myself say: "There is a dry heart here, a dry heart that cannot know the relief of tears."

I scrambled to my feet. "We're off, Prévot," I said. "Our throats are still open. Get along, man!"

The wind that shrivels up a man in nineteen hours was now blowing out of the west. My gullet was not yet shut, but it was hard and painful and I could feel that there was a rasp in it. Soon that cough would begin that I had been told about and was now expecting. My tongue was becoming a nuisance. But most serious of all, I was beginning to see shining spots before my eyes. When those spots changed into flames, I should simply lie down.

The first morning hours were cool and we took advantage of them to get on at a good pace. We knew that once the sun was high there would be no more walking for us. We no longer had the right to sweat. Certainly not to stop and catch our breath. The coolness was merely the coolness of low humidity. The prevailing wind was coming from the desert, and under its soft and treacherous caress the blood was being dried out of us.

Our first day's nourishment had been a few grapes. In the next three days each of us ate half an orange and a bit of cake. If we had had anything left now, we couldn't have eaten it because we had no saliva with which to masticate it. But I had stopped being hungry. Thirsty I was, yes, and it seemed to me that I was suffering less from thirst itself than from the effects of thirst. Gullet hard. Tongue like plaster-of-Paris. A rasping in the throat. A horrible taste in the mouth.

All these sensations were new to me, and though I believed water could rid me of them, nothing in my memory associated them with water. Thirst had become more and more a disease and less and less a craving. I began to realize that the thought of water and fruit was now less agonizing than it had been. I was forgetting the radiance of the orange, just as I was forgetting the eyes under the hat brim.

Perhaps I was forgetting everything.

We had sat down after all, but it could not be for long. Nevertheless, it was impossible to go five hundred yards without our legs giving way. To stretch out on the sand would be marvelous—but it could not be.

The landscape had begun to change. Rocky places grew rarer and the sand was now firm beneath out feet. A mile ahead stood dunes and on those dunes we could see a scrubby vegetation. At least this sand was preferable to the steely surface over which we had been trudging. This was the golden desert. This might have been the Sahara. It was in a sense my country.

Two hundred yards had now become our limit, but we had determined to carry on until we reached the vegetation. Better than that we could not hope to do. A week later, when we went back over our traces in a car to have a look at the *Simoon*, I measured this last lap and found that it was just short of fifty miles. All told we had done one hundred and twenty-four miles.

The previous day I had tramped without hope. Today the word "hope" had grown meaningless. Today we were tramping simply because we were tramping. Probably oxen work for the same reason. Yesterday I had dreamed of a paradise of orange trees. Today I would not give a button for paradise; I did not believe oranges existed. When I thought about myself I found in me nothing but a heart squeezed dry. I was tottering but emotionless. I felt no distress whatever, and in a way I regretted it: misery would have seemed to me as sweet as water. I might then have felt sorry for myself and commiserated with myself as with a friend. But I had not a friend left on earth.

Later, when we were rescued, seeing our burnt-out eyes men thought we must have called aloud and wept and suffered. But cries of despair, misery, sobbing grief are a kind of wealth, and we possessed no wealth. When a young girl is disappointed in love she weeps and knows sorrow. Sorrow is one of the vibrations that prove the fact of living. I felt no sorrow. I was the desert. I could no longer bring up a little saliva; neither could I any longer summon those moving visions toward which I should have loved to stretch forth arms. The sun had dried up the springs of tears in me.

And yet, what was that? A ripple of hope went through me like a faint breeze over a lake. What was this sign that had awakened my instinct before knocking on the door of my consciousness? Nothing had changed, and yet everything was changed. This sheet of sand, these low hummocks and sparse tufts of verdure that had been a landscape, were now become a stage setting. Thus far the stage was empty, but the scene was set. I looked at Prévot. The same astonishing thing had happened to him as to me, but he was as far from guessing its significance as I was.

I swear to you that something is about to happen. I swear that life has sprung in this desert. I swear that this emptiness, this stillness, has suddenly become more stirring than a tumult on a public square.

"Prévot! Footprints! We are saved!"

We had wandered from the trail of the human species; we had cast ourselves forth from the tribe; we had found ourselves alone on earth and forgotten by the universal migration; and here, imprinted in the sand, were the divine and naked feet of man!

"Look, Prévot, here two men stood together and then separated."

"Here a camel knelt."

"Here . . ."

But it was not true that we were already saved. It was not enough to squat down and wait. Before long we should be past saving. Once the cough has begun, the progress made by thirst is swift.

Still, I believed in that caravan swaying somewhere in the desert, heavy with its cargo of treasure.

We went on. Suddenly I heard a cock crow. I remembered what Guillaumet had told me: "Toward the end I heard cocks crowing in the Andes. And I heard the railway train." The instant the cock crowed I thought of Guillaumet and I said to myself: "First it was my eyes that played tricks on me. I suppose this is another of the effects of thirst. Probably my ears have merely held out longer than my eyes." But Prévot grabbed my arm:

"Did you hear that?"

"What?"

"The cock."

"Why . . . why, yes, I did."

To myself I said: "Fool! Get it through your head! This means life!"

I had one last hallucination—three dogs chasing one another. Prévot looked, but could not see them. However, both of us waved our arms at a Bedouin. Both of us shouted with all the breath in our bodies, and laughed for happiness.

But our voices could not carry thirty yards. The Bedouin on his slow-moving camel had come into view from behind a dune and now he was moving slowly out of sight. The man was probably the only Arab in this desert, sent by a demon to materialize and vanish before the eyes of us who could not run.

We saw in profile on the dune another Arab. We shouted, but our shouts were whispers. We waved our arms and it seemed to us that they must fill the sky with monstrous signals. Still the Bedouin stared with averted face away from us.

At last, slowly, slowly, he began a right angle turn in our direction. At the very second when he came face to face with us, I thought, the curtain would come down. At the very second when his eyes met ours, thirst would vanish and by this man would death and the mirages be wiped out. Let this man but make a quarter-turn left and the world is changed. Let him but bring his torso round, but sweep the scene with a glance, and like a god he can create life.

The miracle had come to pass. He was walking toward us over the sand like a god over the waves.

The Arab looked at us without a word. He placed his hands upon our shoulders and we obeyed him: we stretched out upon the sand. Race, language, religion were forgotten. There was only this humble nomad with the hands of an archangel on our shoulders.

Face to the sand, we waited. And when the water came, we drank like calves with our faces in the basin, and with a greediness which alarmed the Bedouin so that from time to time he pulled us back. But as soon as his hand fell away from us we plunged our faces anew into the water.

Water, thou hast no taste, no color, no odor; canst not be defined, art relished while ever mysterious. Not necessary to life, but rather life itself, thou fillest us with a gratification that exceeds the delight of the senses. By thy might, there return into us treasures that we had abandoned. By thy grace, there are released in us all the dried-up runnels of our heart. Of the riches that exist in the world, thou art the rarest and also the most delicate—thou so pure within the bowels of the earth! A man may die of thirst lying beside a magnesian spring. He may die within reach of a salt lake. He may die though he hold in his hand a jug of dew, if it be inhabited by evil salts. For thou, water, art a proud divinity, allowing no alteration, no foreignness in thy being. And the joy that thou spreadest is an infinitely simple joy.

You, Bedouin of Libya who saved our lives, though you will dwell forever in my memory yet I shall never be able to recapture your features. You are Humanity and your face comes into my mind simply as man incarnate. You, our beloved fellowman, did not know who we might be, and yet you recognized us without fail. And I, in my turn, shall recognize you in the faces of all mankind. You came toward me in an aureole of charity and magnanimity bearing the gift of water. All my friends and all my enemies marched toward me in your person. It did not seem to me that you were rescuing me: rather did it seem that you were forgiving me. And I felt I had no enemy left in all the world.

This is the end of my story. Lifted onto a camel, we went on for three hours. Then, broken with weariness, we asked to be set down at a camp while the cameleers went on ahead for help. Toward six in the evening a car manned by armed Bedouins came to fetch us. A half hour later we were set down at the house of a Swiss engineer named Raccaud who was operating a soda factory beside saline deposits in the desert. He was unforgettably kind to us. By midnight we were in Cairo.

I awoke between white sheets. Through the curtains came the rays of a sun that was no longer an enemy. I spread butter and honey on my bread. I smiled. I recaptured the savor of my childhood and all its marvels. And I read and reread the telegram from those dearest to me in all the world whose three words had shattered me:

"So terribly happy!"

THE END OF THE PARTY
By Graham Greene

* *

Terror and twins, brought together most poignantly.

Peter Morton woke with a start to face the first light. Through the window he could see a bare bough dropping across a frame of silver. Rain tapped against the glass. It was January the fifth.

He looked across a table, on which a night light had guttered into a pool of water, at the other bed. Francis Morton was still asleep, and Peter lay down again with his eyes on his brother. It amused him to imagine that it was himself whom he watched, the same hair, the same eyes, the same lips and line of cheek. But the thought soon palled, and the mind went back to the fact which lent the day importance. It was the fifth of January. He could hardly believe that a year had passed since Mrs. Henne-Falcon had given her last children's party.

Francis turned suddenly upon his back and threw an arm across his face, blocking his mouth. Peter's heart began to beat fast, not with pleasure now but with uneasiness. He sat up and called across the table, "Wake up." Francis' shoulders shook and he waved a clenched fist in the air, but his eyes remained closed. To Peter Morton the whole room seemed suddenly to darken, and he had the impression of a great bird swooping. He cried again, "Wake up," and once more there was silver light and the touch of rain on the windows. Francis rubbed his eyes. "Did you call out?" he asked.

"You are having a bad dream," Peter said with confidence. Already experience had taught him how far their minds reflected each other. But he was the elder, by a matter of minutes, and that brief extra interval of light, while his brother still struggled in pain and darkness, had given him self-reliance and an instinct of protection toward the other who was afraid of so many things.

"I dreamed that I was dead," Francis said.

"What was it like?" Peter asked with curiosity.

"I can't remember," Francis said, and his eyes turned with relief to the silver of day, as he allowed the fragmentary memories to fade.

"You dreamed of a big bird."

"Did I?" Francis accepted his brother's knowledge without question, and for a little the two lay silent in bed facing each other, the same green eyes, the same nose tilting at the tip, the same firm lips parted and the same premature modeling of the chin. The fifth of January, Peter thought again, his mind drifting idly from the image of cakes to the prizes which might be won. Egg-and-spoon races, spearing apples in basins of water, blindman's buff.

"I don't want to go," Francis said suddenly. "I suppose Joyce will be there . . . Mabel Warren." Hateful to him, the thought of a party shared with those two. They were older than he. Joyce was eleven and Mabel Warren thirteen. Their long pigtails swung superciliously to a masculine stride. Their sex humiliated him, as they watched him fumble with his egg, from under lowered scornful lids. And last year . . . he turned his face away from Peter, his cheeks scarlet.

"What's the matter?" Peter asked.

"Oh, nothing. I don't think I'm well. I've got a cold. I oughtn't to go to the party." Peter was puzzled. "But Francis, is it a bad cold?"

"It will be a bad cold if I go to the party. Perhaps I shall die."

"Then you mustn't go," Peter said with decision, prepared to solve all difficulties with one plain sentence, and Francis let his nerves relax in a delicious relief, ready to leave everything to Peter. But though he was grateful he did not turn his face toward his brother. His cheeks still bore the badge of a shameful memory, of the game of hide and seek last year in the darkened house, and of how he had screamed when Mabel Warren put her hand suddenly upon his arm. He had not heard her coming. Girls were like that. Their shoes never squeaked. No boards whined under their tread. They slunk like cats on padded claws.

When the nurse came in with hot water Francis lay tranquil, leaving everything to Peter. Peter said: "Nurse, Francis has got a cold."

The tall starched woman laid the towels across the cans and said, without turning: "The washing won't be back till tomorrow. You must lend him some of your handkerchiefs."

"But Nurse," Peter asked, "hadn't he better stay in bed?"

"We'll take him for a good walk this morning," the nurse said. "Wind'll blow away the germs. Get up now, both of you," and she closed the door behind her.

"I'm sorry," Peter said, and then, worried at the sight of a face creased again by misery and foreboding, "Why don't you just stay in bed? I'll tell Mother you felt too ill to get up." But such a rebellion against destiny was not in Francis' power. Besides, if he stayed in bed they would come up and tap his chest and put a thermometer in his mouth and look at his tongue, and they would discover that he was malingering. It was true that he felt ill, a sick empty sensation in his stomach and a rapidly beating heart, but he knew that the cause was only fear, fear of the party, fear of being made to hide by himself in the dark, uncompanioned by Peter and with no night light to make a blessed breach.

"No, I'll get up," he said, and then with sudden desperation: "But I won't go to Mrs. Henne-Falcon's party. I swear on the Bible I won't." Now surely all would be well, he thought. God would not allow him to break so solemn an oath. He would show him a way. There was all the morning before him and all the afternoon until four o'clock. No need to worry now when the grass was still crisp with the early frost. Anything might happen. He might cut himself or break his leg or really catch a bad cold. God would manage somehow.

He had such confidence in God that when at breakfast his mother said, "I hear you have a cold, Francis," he made light of it. "We should have heard more about it," his mother said with irony, "if there was not a party this evening," and Francis smiled uneasily, amazed and daunted by her ignorance of him. His happiness would have lasted longer if, out for a walk that morning, he had not met Joyce. He was alone with his nurse, for Peter had leave to finish a rabbit hutch in the woodshed. If Peter had been there he would have cared less; the nurse was Peter's nurse also, but now it was as though she were employed only for his sake, because he could not be trusted to go for a walk alone. Joyce was only two years older and she was by herself.

She came striding toward them, pigtails flapping. She glanced scornfully at Francis and spoke with ostentation to the nurse. "Hello, Nurse. Are you bringing Francis to the party this evening? Mabel and

I are coming." And she was off again down the street in the direction of Mabel Warren's home, consciously alone and self-sufficient in the long empty road. "Such a nice girl," the nurse said. But Francis was silent, feeling again the jump-jump of his heart, realizing how soon the hour of the party would arrive. God had done nothing for him, and the minutes flew.

They flew too quickly to plan any evasion, or even to prepare his heart for the coming ordeal. Panic nearly overcame him when, all unready, he found himself standing on the doorstep, with coat collar turned up against a cold wind, and the nurse's electric torch making a short luminous trail through the darkness. Behind him were the lights of the hall and the sound of a servant laying the table for dinner, which his mother and father would eat alone. He was nearly overcome by a desire to run back into the house and call out to his mother that he would not go to the party, that he dared not go. They could not make him go. He could almost hear himself saying those final words, breaking down forever, as he knew instinctively, the barrier of ignorance that saved his mind from his parents' knowledge. "I'm afraid of going. I won't go. I daren't go. They'll make me hide in the dark, and I'm afraid of the dark. I'll scream and scream and scream." He could see the expression of amazement on his mother's face, and then the cold confidence of a grownup's retort.

"Don't be silly. You must go. We've accepted Mrs. Henne-Falcon's invitation." But they couldn't make him go; hesitating on the doorstep while the nurse's feet crunched across the frost-covered grass to the gate, he knew that. He would answer: "You can say I'm ill. I won't go. I'm afraid of the dark." And his mother: "Don't be silly. You know there's nothing to be afraid of in the dark." But he knew the falsity of that reasoning; he knew how they taught also that there was nothing to fear in death, and how fearfully they avoided the idea of it. But they couldn't make him go to the party. "I'll scream. I'll scream."

"Francis, come along." He heard the nurse's voice across the dimly phosphorescent lawn and saw the small yellow circle of her torch wheel from tree to shrub and back to tree again. "I'm coming," he called with despair, leaving the lighted doorway of the house; he couldn't bring himself to lay bare his last secrets and end reserve between his mother and himself, for there was still in the last resort a further appeal possible to Mrs. Henne-Falcon. He comforted himself with that, as he advanced steadily across the hall, very small, toward her enormous bulk. His heart beat unevenly, but he had control now over his voice, as he said with meticulous accent, "Good evening, Mrs. Henne-Falcon. It was very good of you to ask me to your party." With his strained face lifted toward the curve of her breasts, and his polite set speech, he was like an old withered man. For Francis mixed very little with other children. As a twin he was in many ways an only child. To address Peter was to speak to his own image in a mirror, an image a little altered by a flaw in the glass, so as to throw back less a likeness of what he was than of what he wished to be, what he would be without his unreasoning fear of darkness, footsteps of strangers, the flight of bats in dusk-filled gardens.

"Sweet child," said Mrs. Henne-Falcon absent-mindedly, before, with a wave of her arms, as though the children were a flock of chickens, she whirled them into her set program of entertainments: egg-and-spoon races, three-legged races, the spearing of apples, games which held for Francis nothing worse than humiliation. And in the frequent intervals when nothing was required of him and he could stand alone in corners as far removed as possible from Mabel Warren's scornful gaze, he was able to plan how he might avoid the approaching terror of the dark. He knew there was nothing to fear until after tea, and not until he was sitting down in a pool of yellow radiance cast by the ten candles on Colin Henne-Falcon's birthday cake did he become fully conscious of the imminence of what he feared. Through the confusion of his brain, now assailed suddenly by a dozen contradictory plans he heard Joyce's high voice down the table. "After tea we are going to play hide and seek in the dark."

"Oh, no," Peter said, watching Francis' troubled face with pity and an imperfect understanding, "don't let's. We play that every year."

"But it's in the program," cried Mabel Warren. "I saw it myself. I looked over Mrs. Henne-Falcon's shoulder. Five o'clock, tea. A quarter to six to half-past, hide and seek in the dark. It's all written down in the program."

Peter did not argue, for if hide and seek had been inserted in Mrs. Henne-Falcon's program, nothing which he could say could avert it. He asked for another piece of birthday cake and sipped his tea slowly. Perhaps it might be possible to delay the game for a quarter of an hour, allow Francis at least a few extra minutes to form a plan, but even in that Peter failed, for children were already leaving the table in twos and threes. It was his third failure, and again, the reflection of an image in another's mind, he saw a great bird darken his brother's face with its wings. But he upbraided himself silently for his folly, and finished his cake encouraged by the memory of that adult refrain, "There's nothing to fear in the dark." The last to leave the table, the brothers came together to the hall to meet the mustering and impatient eyes of Mrs. Henne-Falcon.

"And now," she said, "we will play hide and seek in the dark."

Peter watched his brother and saw, as he had expected, the lips tighten. Francis, he knew, had feared this moment from the beginning of the party, had tried to meet it with courage and had abandoned the attempt. He must have prayed desperately for cunning to evade the game, which was now welcomed with cries of excitement by all the other children. "Oh, do let's." "We must pick sides." "Is any of the house out of bounds?" "Where shall home be?"

"I think," said Francis Morton, approaching Mrs. Henne-Falcon, his eyes focused unwaveringly on her cxubcrant breasts, "it will be no use my playing. My nurse will be calling for me very soon."

"Oh, but your nurse can wait, Francis," said Mrs. Henne-Falcon absent-mindedly, while she clapped her hands together to summon to her side a few children who were already straying up the wide staircase to upper floors. "Your mother will never mind."

That had been the limit of Francis' cunning. He had refused to believe that so well-prepared an excuse could fail. All that he could say now, still in the precise tone which other children hated, thinking it a symbol of conceit, was, "I think I had better not play." He stood motionless, retaining, though afraid, unmoved features. But the knowledge of his terror, or the reflection of the terror itself, reached his brother's brain. For the moment Peter Morton could have cried aloud with the fear of bright lights going out, leaving him alone in an island of dark surrounded by the gentle lapping of strange footsteps. Then he remembered that the fear was not his own, but his brother's. He said impulsively to Mrs. Henne-Falcon: "Please. I don't think Francis should play. The dark makes him jump so." They were the wrong words. Six children began to sing, "Cowardy, cowardy custard," turning torturing faces with the vacancy of wide sunflowers toward Francis Morton.

Without looking at his brother, Francis said, "Of course I will play. I am not afraid. I only thought . . ." But he was already forgotten by his human tormentors and was able in loneliness to contemplate the approach of the spiritual, the more unbounded torture. The children scrambled round Mrs. Henne-Falcon, their shrill voices pecking at her with questions and suggestions. "Yes, anywhere in the house. We will turn out all the lights. Yes, you can hide in the cupboards. You must stay hidden as long as you can. There will be no home."

Peter, too, stood apart, ashamed of the clumsy manner in which he had tried to help his brother. Now he could feel, creeping in at the corners of his brain, all Francis' resentment of his championing. Several children ran upstairs, and the lights on the top floor went out. Then darkness came down like the wings of a bat and settled on the landing. Others began to put out the lights at the edge of the hall, till the children were all gathered in the central radiance of the chandelier, while the bats squatted round on hooded wings and waited for that, too, to be extinguished.

"You and Francis are on the hiding side," a tall girl said, and then the light was gone, and the carpet wavered under his feet with the sibilance of footfalls, like small cold draughts, creeping away into corners.

Where's Francis? he wondered. If I join him he'll be less frightened of all these sounds. "These sounds" were the casing of silence. The squeak of a loose board, the cautious closing of a cupboard door, the whine of a finger drawn along polished wood.

Peter stood in the center of the dark deserted floor, not listening but waiting for the idea of his brother's whereabouts to enter his brain. But Francis crouched with fingers on his ears, eyes uselessly closed, mind numbed against impressions, and only a sense of strain could cross the gap of dark. Then a voice called "Coming," and as though his brother's self-possession had been shattered by the sudden cry, Peter Morton jumped with his fear. But it was not his own fear. What in his brother was a burning panic, admitting no ideas except those which added to the flame, was in him an altruistic emotion that left the reason unimpaired. Where, if I were Francis, should I hide? Such, roughly, was his thought. And because he was, if not Francis himself, at least a mirror to him, the answer was immediate. Between the oak bookcase on the left of the study door, and the leather settee. Peter Morton was unsurprised by the swiftness of the response. Between the twins there could be no jargon of telepathy. They had been together in the womb, and they could not be parted.

Peter Morton tiptoed toward Francis' hiding place. Occasionally a board rattled, and because he feared to be caught by one of the soft questers through the dark, he bent and untied his laces. A tag struck the floor and the metallic sound set a host of cautious feet moving in his direction. But by that time he was in his stockings and would have laughed inwardly at the pursuit had not the noise of someone stumbling on his abandoned shoes made his heart trip in the reflection of another's surprise. No more boards revealed Peter Morton's progress. On stockinged feet he moved silently and unerringly toward his object. Instinct told him that he was near the wall, and, extending a hand, he laid the fingers across his brother's face.

Francis did not cry out, but the leap of his own heart revealed to Peter a proportion of Francis' terror. "It's all right," he whispered, feeling down the squatting figure until he captured a clenched hand. "It's only me. I'll stay with you." And grasping the other tightly, he listened to the cascade of whispers his utterance had caused to fall. A hand touched the bookcase close to Peter's head and he was aware of how Francis' fear continued in spite of his presence. It was less intense, more bearable, he hoped, but it remained. He knew that it was his brother's fear and not his own that he experienced. The dark to him was only an absence of light; the groping hand that of a familiar child. Patiently he waited to be found.

He did not speak again, for between Francis and himself touch was the most intimate communion. By way of joined hands thought could flow more swiftly than lips could shape themselves round words. He could experience the whole progress of his brother's emotion, from the leap of panic at the unexpected contact to the steady pulse of fear, which now went on and on with the regularity of a heartbeat. Peter Morton thought with intensity, I am here. You needn't be afraid. The lights will go on again soon. That rustle, that movement is nothing to fear. Only Joyce, only Mabel Warren. He bombarded the drooping form with thoughts of safety, but he was conscious that the fear continued. They are beginning to whisper together. They are tired of looking for us. The lights will go on soon. We shall have won. Don't be afraid. That was only someone on the stairs. I believe it's Mrs. Henne-Falcon. Listen. They are feeling for the lights. Feet moving on a carpet, hands brushing a wall, a curtain pulled apart, a clicking handle, the opening of a cupboard door. In the case above their heads a loose book shifted under a touch. Only Joyce, only Mabel Warren, only Mrs. Henne-Falcon, a crescendo of reassuring thought before the chandelier burst, like a fruit tree, into bloom.

The voices of the children rose shrilly into the radiance. "Where's

Peter?" "Have you looked upstairs?" "Where's Francis?" but they were silenced again by Mrs. Henne-Falcon's scream. But she was not the first to notice Francis Morton's stillness, where he had collapsed against the wall at the touch of his brother's hand. Peter continued to hold the clenched fingers in an arid and puzzled grief. It was not merely that his brother was dead. His brain, too young to realize the full paradox, yet wondered with an obscure self-pity why it was that the pulse of his brother's fear went on and on, when Francis was now where he had been always told there was no more terror and no more darkness.

THE LAST INHABITANT OF THE TUILERIES

By André Castelot

． ．

An empress flees Paris, and the angry crowds are unaware.

In that tragic summer of 1870 a frail woman, almost pitiful in her little black cashmere dress adorned with linen, would wander through the château of the Tuileries, in which the armchairs and sofas, as they were every summer when the court was at Compiègne or Saint-Cloud, were covered with dust sheets printed with large bouquets of mauve iris. At mealtimes the frail woman was brought a few dishes on a tray, which she barely touched.

That woman was the Empress Eugénie, the Regent of the Empire while her husband was following his retreating soldiers across the plains of Champagne. He had become a miserable wreck relegated to the baggage wagons, undermined by sickness, no longer able even to sit a horse. The unhappy, vanquished man was now proceeding in a berlin, whose jolting gave him terrible stabbing pains in his kidneys and bladder, toward the stage where his surgeon was waiting to sound him, toward the stage that took him nearer every day to Sedan.

Sedan. The Empress heard of it for the first time in the evening of September 2. "Our communications with Sedan are cut. Our army may be blockaded at that place."

That was all she knew at the end of the afternoon of September 3. She was unaware of the magnitude of the disaster. That evening the Empress was alone. Henri Chevreau, Minister of the Interior, was announced. He was ghastly pale. In silence he handed his sovereign a telegram, the telegram from Sedan:

"The army is defeated. Having been unable to be killed among my soldiers, I have had to constitute myself prisoner to save the army. Napoleon."

A minute later Eugénie's two secretaries, Conti and Filon, saw their mistress appear at the head of a little spiral staircase linking the Emperor's apartments with those of the Empress on the first floor overlooking the gardens. The unhappy woman was "pale, her hard eyes blazing with anger." She cried out to them, panting:

"Do you know what they say? That the Emperor has given himself up, that he has capitulated! Do you not believe this infamy?"

Horrified by this apparition, Conti and Filon did not dare utter a word. In a hoarse voice she resumed, almost menacingly: "You do not believe it?"

Conti gathered up his courage.

"Madame, there are circumstances in which the bravest . . ."

Eugénie, her features convulsed, interrupted him, shouting: "No, the Emperor has not capitulated! A Napoleon does not capitulate. He is dead. . . . You hear me, he is dead and they want to keep it from me."

Then, when she was forced to admit the facts, raising her arms, "her eyes haggard like those of a Fury," she almost yelled: "Why did he *not* let himself be killed? Did he not feel he was dishonoring himself? What kind of name will he leave his son!"

The terrible news had run through Paris. Already the faces of 1830 or 1848 were appearing in the suburbs. Insurrection was in the air. Would the Tuileries be defended?

"Whatever happens," the Empress decided, "the soldiers must not fire on the people."

The Empress could still have tried to save the regime by giving executive power to the Chamber. She did not decide to do so.

Night fell on the city. In her bedroom Eugénie could hear dull rumblings. Soon she saw filing down the Rue de Rivoli men bearing torches and crepe-hung flags. Through the confused noise she heard cries of "Long live the Republic!"

The governor of Paris, General Trochu—that "past participle of the verb *trop choir* [to sink excessively]"—did not interfere.

At one o'clock in the morning Jules Favre mounted the tribune in the Chamber demanding the deposition of the imperial family. But the deputies took no decision and separated, adjourning the session until noon the following day. At dawn on the next day, September 4, at dawn on that fine, warm summer Sunday, the uprising began. It was the third revolution in forty years, without counting upheavals and insurrections. But this time a few hours would suffice for the street to be master of the Tuileries. It is true that Paris was fighting a woman.

Very early the city was awakened by cries of paper sellers: "The Emperor a prisoner!"

At eight in the morning a great murmuring came to the windows of the Tuileries. "On all sides," wrote the Goncourts, "a movement was growing that bore toward the center of Paris the inhabitants of the outer districts. The Rue de Rivoli and the Place du Carrousel were black with people. The weather was wonderful and everyone knows that the Parisians are always in a flutter on Sundays. Some walked peacefully round the arcades and along the pavements; others hurried feverishly to the Palais-Bourbon, where they foresaw work to be done. Others again massed at the crossroads, on the top of the pavements, waited, watched, drinking in the warm air of a real summer's day."

Soon demonstrators invaded the Chamber of Deputies and tore down the imperial eagles.

"This time," the workers cried, "we must have the Republic! No republic that allows a king to return when the bed is well warmed, and no republic of deputies either!"

The Place de la Concorde appeared like a stormy sea beating against the gates of the swing bridge. Troops raised the butts of their rifles. What was to be done? Shouts came from the street, shouts insulting the woman whom the Parisians considered responsible for the war and the defeat: "Down with the Spaniard!"

"You do not want to abdicate, madame," faithful Conti said to her. "Very well, in an hour you will be in the hands of people who will make you abdicate by force. If you escape, wherever you go you will take your rights with you."

"Remember the Princesse de Lamballe," Henri Chevreau murmured quietly.

To bring the Empress to the decision to flee required the immense clamor of the crowd which, forcing the gates in the Place de la Concorde, rushed into the garden, an immense clamor that was like a blow to the Regent. For the fifth time in eighty years the Tuileries was to experience the dreaded invasion.

"Madame," implored Nigra, the Italian ambassador, who had hurried to the château with Metternich, his Austrian colleague. "Madame, do not delay any longer."

Distracted, the Empress threw a glance of distress on everything about her. Would she have to leave all that? Was it really the end of the fairy tale that had made of Eugénie de Montijo the empress of the French?

It was a quarter past one.

Eugénie put on a hat and a thin coat and left the room, followed by the two ambassadors, her reader, Mme. Lebreton and a few faithfuls. The little group went down to the ground floor by the Empress' staircase and reached the stairs which were a private exit from the Prince Imperial's apartments, on the very site of the former entrance to M. de Villequier's apartments by which, formerly, Louis XVI and his family left the château for Varennes. The Empress' coupé was waiting for her as usual. On the door were painted the arms of the French Empire and the coachman was wearing imperial livery. How could they cross Paris in such a carriage when, behind the Carrousel gates, the crowd was already calling for death? There was only one solution: to attempt to leave by the Louvre museum. Eugénie took the narrow corridor that ran the whole length of the château; it was lit by gas both day and night. Through the great gallery, the Carré room, the gallery of Apollo, the little group reached the Hall of the Seven Chimneys. There, in front of Géricault's painting of "The Raft of the Méduse," the Empress stopped. She gave her hand to her faithful companions to kiss. After the last bow, in company with Mme. Lebreton and the two diplomats she hastened toward the staircase. Before going down she looked for the last time, through the window of the small Salle Henri II, at the long façade of the château. At that moment the flag floating on top of the central pavilion of the Tuileries came slowly down its pole. This happened every time the sovereigns left the château for another residence. But today, when the victorious revolution surrounded the Tuileries and the Louvre, where was Eugénie to go? Mme. Lebreton had five hundred francs on her. The regent's only luggage was two handkerchiefs, and she had a very bad cold.

Through the Egyptian section the fugitives reached the vault that opens onto the Place Saint-Germain-l'Auxerrois, under Perrault's colonnade. The crowd was too busy shouting, "Long live the Republic!" to pay attention to those two women in black and those two bourgeois in their tall hats. Nigra hailed a cab that was jolting by.

How is one to explain the fact that the two ambassadors, who had been the Empress' friends for years, left her, on the pavement, after entrusting her to a passing cab? The fact is there, completely incomprehensible. Eugénie gave the two ambassadors her hand to kiss and entered the carriage. Mme. Lebreton followed her, giving the coachman the first address that came into her head, that of State Councilor Besson, in the Boulevard Haussmann. Not without difficulty the cab went up the Rue de Rivoli through the yelling mob. Eugénie could see the rioters, who were already breaking the stone eagles adorning the façades.

"Long live the nation!" cried a workman, sticking his head through the window.

At Mme. Lebreton's request, the coachman left the Rue de Rivoli and soon arrived in the Boulevard Haussmann. Calm succeeded the storm. The district was deserted. M. Besson was not at home and no one opened the door. There was the same failure at the house of M. de Piennes, the Empress' chamberlain, who lived in the Avenue de Wagram. Eugénie then thought of her American dentist, Dr. Evans. She gave the coachman the address: "Avenue Malakoff, at the corner of . . . Avenue de l'Impératrice."

The dentist was out as well.

The visitors, who refused to give their names, asked the valet if they could wait for the dentist and the servant showed the two women into the library.

Dr. Thomas W. Evans, who had been living in France since the end of Louis-Philippe's reign, was a man of forty-six, with an open, attractive countenance. He had spent the day watching Paris live through its first republican hours. Jules Favre had managed to get the crowd out of the Palais Bourbon by crying: "No day of blood! It is not here that you must proclaim the Republic, it is at the Hôtel de Ville!"

And the crowd, suddenly docile, had followed Jules Favre and Jules Ferry along the right bank, while another column of Parisians marched behind Gambetta and Pelletan along the left bank. At the Hôtel de Ville they found the leaders of the extremist parties—Blanqui, Delescluze, Flourens, Pyat—who were preparing to form a government. The competition was serious. How was it to be neutralized? Ferry proposed:

"The Paris deputies, to the government!"

The proposal was accepted. Trochu became president of the government, Jules Favre vice-president. Rochefort, just freed, entered the Government of National Defense with Arago, Gambetta, Jules Ferry, Garnier-Pagès, Pelletan, Crémieux and Simon.

The Third Republic had taken power without one drop of blood being shed.

Dr. Evans has left a picturesque account of his walk through Paris, in which one sees the children in the Champs-Elysées "disporting themselves in the care of their nurses, riding on the roundabouts or gathering round the puppet shows," while a short distance away, in the Place de la Concorde and around the Palais Bourbon, was "A black, stormy, tumultuous mass," shouting for the downfall of the imperial regime.

The doctor returned home at the end of the afternoon. He was accompanied by his compatriot and friend Dr. Crane. One can imagine Evans' stupefaction when he pushed open the door of his library. The Empress was there, tragically pale, sunk in a large armchair near the window. She was dressed in a black cashmere dress and wore a "Derby" hat to which was attached a dark veil. She blew her nose continuously; tears filled her eyes.

"You see, I am no longer happy. The bad days have come."

Without hesitation the two doctors agreed to help the Empress. Mrs. Evans was at the moment in the Hôtel du Casino at Deauville. Would not the best plan be to try to join her by road, first taking the doctor's carriage, then trying to find post horses? From Trouville the fugitives would perhaps be fortunate enough to find a boat to take them across the Channel.

It was ten o'clock in the evening and the Empress wished to leave at once. Evans calmed her. She had had hardly any rest for three days. It was settled that they would leave the following morning at half-past five. While Eugénie and Mme. Lebreton tried in vain to sleep the two doctors went to take the pulse of the town. Everything was calm at the Porte Maillot, through which in a few hours the fugitives would try to leave Paris. Around the Tuileries there was great animation, but the château was not occupied by the people—they would make up for it later. The sentries were on duty as usual. The words "National Property" had simply been written on the walls in chalk. The N's had disappeared from the pediments of all the public monuments. The Rue du Dix-Décembre had become the Rue du Quatre-Septembre. The crowd moved happily about. It sang, laughed and acclaimed the National Guards, whose rifles were now carrying bouquets. The café terraces were full of customers. The regime had crumbled with an almost miraculous rapidity. The "Third" was indeed mistress of Paris.

On their return from their expedition Crane and Evans did not go to bed. They feared at each instant to learn that the order had been given to close the city gates.

The sun had not yet risen when the dentist's landau left his house and drove down the Avenue Malakoff. The road sweepers were already at work and the shopkeepers were taking down their shutters. In those days Paris rose early. At the gate of the Porte Maillot the soldier in charge signed to the carriage to stop. Evans, who was sitting on the bench in front, opened a window and leaned out so as to mask the opening almost completely. So that the N.C.O. could not see anything inside the landau the dentist held an open newspaper in his left hand, on the side of the Empress.

"I am an American. I am known to everyone in the neighborhood. I am going to the country with some friends."

The soldier took a step backward.

"Go on!"

A second later the carriage was rumbling over the bridge across the moat of the fortifications.

The last French sovereign had left Paris.

JESTING PILOT

By Lewis Padgett

. . . .

They were in the City, behind the Barrier.
They had been specially conditioned from birth.
None of them had ever known normal existence.
A frightening story—of a world to come?

The city screamed. It had been screaming for six hundred years. And as long as that unendurable scream continued, the city was an efficient unit.

"You're getting special treatment," Nehral said, looking across the big, bare, silent room to where young Fleming sat on the cushioned seat. "Normally you wouldn't have graduated to Control for another six months, but something's come up. The others think a fresh viewpoint might help. And you're elected, since you're the oldest acolyte."

"Britton's older than I am," Fleming said. He was a short, heavy, red-haired boy with an unusual sensitivity conditioned into his blunt features. Utterly relaxed, he sat waiting.

"Physiological age doesn't mean anything. The civilization index is more important. And the empathy level. You're seventeen, but you're emotionally mature. On the other hand, you're not—set. You haven't been a Controller for years. We think you may have some fresh angles that can help us."

"Aren't fresh angles undesirable?"

Nehral's thin, tired face twisted into a faint smile. "There's been debate about that. A culture is a living organism and it can't exist in its own waste products. Not indefinitely. But we don't intend to remain isolated indefinitely."

"I didn't know that," Fleming said.

Nehral studied his finger tips. "Don't get the idea that we're the masters. We're servants, far more so than the citizens. We've got to follow the plan. And we don't know all the details of the plan. That was arranged purposely. Someday the Barrier will lift. Then the city won't be isolated any longer."

"But—outside!" Fleming said, a little nervously. "Suppose—"

Nehral said, "Six hundred years ago the city was built and the Barrier created. The Barrier's quite impassable. There's a switch—I'll show it to you sometime—that's useless at present. Its purpose is to bring the Barrier into existence. But no one knows how to destroy the Barrier. One theory is that it can't be destroyed until its half-life is run, and the energy's reached a sufficiently low level. Then it blinks out automatically."

"When?"

Nehral shrugged. "Nobody knows that either. Tomorrow, or a thousand years from now. Here's the idea. The city was isolated for protection. That meant—complete isolation. Nothing—*nothing at all* —can pass the Barrier. So we're safe. When the Barrier goes, we can see what's happened to the rest of the world. If the danger's gone, we can colonize. If it hasn't, we pull the switch again, and we're safe behind the Barrier for another indefinite period."

Danger. The earth had been too big, and too full of people. Archaic mores had prevailed. The new science had plunged on, but civilization had lagged fatally. In those days many plans had been proposed. Only one had proved practicable. Rigid control—thorough utilization of the new power—and unbreakable armor. So the city was built and isolated by the Barrier, at a time when all other cities were falling. . . .

Nehral said, "We know the danger of *status quo*. New theories, new experiments aren't forbidden. Far from it. Some of them can't be studied now, a great many of them. But records are kept. That reference library will be available when the Barrier's lifted. Meanwhile, the city's a lifeboat. This part of the human race has to survive. That's the main concern. You don't study physics in a lifeboat. You try to survive. After you've reached land, you can go to work again. But now . . ."

The other cities fell, and the terror roared across the earth, six hundred years ago. It was an age of genius and viciousness. The weapons of the gods were at last available. The foundations of mat-

ter ripped screaming apart as the weapons were used. The lifeboat rode a typhoon. The Ark breasted a deluge.

In other words, one thing led to another—until the planet shook.

"First the builders thought the Barrier alone would be enough. The city, of course, had to be a self-contained unit. That was difficult. A human being isn't. He has to get food, fuel—from the air, from plants and animals. The solution lay in creating all the necessities within the city. But then matters got worse. There were germ warfare and germ mutations. There were the chain reactions. The atmosphere itself, under the constant bombardment . . ."

More and more complicated grew the Ark.

"So they built the city as it had to be built, and then they found that it would be—uninhabitable."

Fleming tilted back his head. Nehral said, "Oh, we're shielded. We're specialized. For we're the Controllers."

"Yes, I know. But I've wondered. Why can't the citizens—"

"Be shielded as we are? Because they're to be the survivors. We're important only till the Barrier lifts. After that, we'll be useless, away from the lifeboat. In a normal world, we have no place. But now and here, as Controllers of the city, we *are* important. We serve."

Fleming stirred uneasily.

Nehral said, "It will be difficult for you to conceive this. You have been specially conditioned since before your birth. You never knew—none of us ever knew—normal existence. You are deaf, dumb and blind."

The boy caught a little of the meaning. "That means—"

"Certain senses the citizens have, because they'll be needed when the Barrier lifts. We can't afford to have them, under the circumstances. The telepathic sense is substituted. I'll tell you more about that later. Right now I want you to concentrate on the problem of Bill Norman. He's a citizen."

Nehral paused. He could feel the immense weight of the city above him, and it seemed to him that the foundations were beginning to crumble. . . .

"He's getting out of control," Nehral said flatly.

"But I'm not important," Bill Norman said.

They were dancing. Flickering, quiet lights beat out from the Seventh Monument, towering even above the roof garden where they were. Far overhead was the gray emptiness of the Barrier. The music was exciting. Mia's hand crept up and ruffled the back of his neck.

"You are to me," she said. "Still, I'm prejudiced."

She was a tall, slim, dark girl, sharp contrast to Norman's blond hugeness. His faintly puzzled blue eyes studied her.

"I'm lucky. I'm not so sure you are, Mia."

The orchestra reached a rhythmic climax; brass hit a low, nostalgic note, throbbingly sustained. Norman moved his big shoulders uneasily and turned toward the parapet, towing Mia beside him. They walked in silence through the crowd, to a walled embrasure where they were alone, in a tiny vantage point overlooking the city.

Mia stole occasional glances at the man's troubled face. He was looking at the Seventh Monument, crowned with light, and beyond it to the Sixth, and, smaller in the distance, the Fifth—each a memorial to one of the great eras of man's history.

But the city—

There had never been a city like it in all the world. For no city before had ever been built for man. Memphis was a towered colossus for the memory of kings; Bagdad was a sultan's jewel; they were stately pleasure domes by decree. New York and London, Paris and Moscow—they were less functional, less efficient for their citizens than the caves of the troglodytes. In cities man had always tried to sow on arid ground.

But this was a city for men.

It was not merely a matter of parks and roads, of rolling ramps and paragravity currents for levitation, not simply a question of design and architecture. The city was planned according to rules of human psychology. The people fitted into it as into a foam mattress. It was quiet. It was beautiful and functional. It was perfect for its purpose.

"I saw that psychologist again today," Norman said.

Mia folded her arms and leaned on the parapet. She didn't look at her companion.

"And?"

"Generalizations."

"But they always know the answers," Mia said. "They always know the *right* answers."

"This one didn't."

"It may take time. Really, Bill, you know, no one's—frustrated."

"I don't know what it is," Norman said. "Heredity, perhaps. All I know is I get these—these flashes. Which the psychologists can't explain."

"But there has to be an explanation."

"That's what the psychologist said. Still, he couldn't tell me what it was."

"Can't you analyze it at all?" she asked, sliding her hand into his. His fingers tightened. He looked at the Seventh Monument and beyond it.

"No," he said. "It's just that I feel there isn't any answer."

"To what?"

"I don't know. I—I wish I could get out of the city."

Her hand relaxed suddenly. "Bill. You know—"

He laughed softly. "I know. There's no way out. Not through the Barrier. Maybe that isn't what I want, after all. But this—this—" He stared at the Monument. "It seems all wrong sometimes. I just can't explain it. It's the whole city. It makes me feel haywire. Then I get these flashes—"

She felt his hand stiffen. It was jerked away abruptly. Bill Norman covered his eyes and screamed.

"Flashes of realization," Nehral said to Fleming. "They don't last long. If they did, he'd go insane or die. Of course the citizen psychologists can't help him; it's outside their scope by definition."

Fleming, sensitive to telepathic emotion, said, "You're worried."

"Naturally. We Controllers have our own conditioning. An ordinary citizen couldn't hold our power; it wouldn't be safe. The builders worked out a good many plans before they decided to create us. They'd thought of making androids and robots to control, but the human factor was needed. Emotion's needed, to react to the conditioning. From birth, by hypnosis, we're conditioned to protect and serve the citizens. We couldn't do anything else if we tried. It's ingrained."

"Every citizen?" Fleming asked, and Nehral sighed.

"That's the trouble. *Every* citizen. The whole is equal to the sum total of the parts. One citizen, to us, represents the entire group. I'm not certain that this wasn't a mistake of the builders. For when one citizen threatens the group—as Norman does—"

"But we've got to solve Norman's problem."

"Yes. It's our problem. Every citizen must have physical and mental balance—*must*. I was wondering—"

"Well?"

"For the good of the whole, it would be better if Norman could be eliminated. On purely logical grounds, he should be allowed to go mad or die. I can't countenance that, though. I'm too firmly conditioned against it."

"So am I," Fleming said, and Nehral nodded.

"Exactly. We *must* cure him. We've got to get him back to a sane psychological balance. Or we may crack up ourselves—because we're not conditioned to react to failure. Now. You're the youngest of us available; you have more in common with the citizens than any of us. So you may find an answer where we can't."

"Norman should have been a Controller," Fleming said.

"Yes. But it's too late for that now. He's mature. His heredity— bad, from our viewpoint. Mathematicians and theologians. The problems of every citizen in the city can be solved with the Monuments. We can give them answers that are right for them. But Norman's hunting an abstraction. That's the trouble. *We can't give him a satisfactory answer!*"

"Haven't there ever been parallel psychoses?"

"It's not a psychosis, that's the difficulty. Except by the arbitrary standards of the city. Oh, there've been plenty of human problems—a woman who wants children, for example, and can't have them. If medicine fails to help her, the Monuments will. By creating diversion—arousing her maternal instinct for something else, or channeling it elsewhere. By substitution. Making her believe she has a mission of some sort. Or creating an emotional attachment of another kind, not maternal. The idea is to trace the problems back to their psychological roots, and then get rid of the frustration somehow. It's the frustration that's fatal."

"Diversion, perhaps?"

"I don't think it's possible. Norman's problem is an abstraction. And if we answered it—he would go insane."

"I don't know what my problem is," Norman said desperately. "I don't have any. I'm young, healthy, doing work I like, I'm engaged—"

The psychologist scratched his jaw. "It we knew what your problem was, we could do something about it," he said. "The most suggestive point here—" He rustled through the papers before him. "Let's see. Do I seem real to you now?"

"Very," Norman said.

"But there are times—the syndrome's familiar. Sometimes you doubt reality. Most people have that feeling occasionally." He leaned back and made thoughtful noises. Through the transparent wall, the Fifth Monument was visible, pulsating with soft beats of light. It was very quiet here.

"You mean you don't know what's wrong with me," Norman said.

"I don't know yet. But I will. First we must find out what your problem is."

"How long will that take? Ten years?"

"I had a problem myself once," the psychologist said. "At the time I didn't know what it was. I've found out since. I was heading for megalomania; I wanted to change people. So I took up this work. I turned my energy into a useful channel. That solved my problem for me. It's the right way for you, once we get at what's bothering you."

"All I want is to get rid of these hallucinations," Norman said.

"Auditory, visual and olfactory—mostly. And without external basis in fact. They're not illusions, they're hallucinations. I wish you could give me more details about them."

"I can't." Norman seemed to shrink. "It's like being dropped into boiling metal. It's simply indescribable. An impression of noise, lights—it comes and goes in a flash. But it's a flash of hell."

"Tomorrow we'll try narcosynthesis again. I want to correlate my ideas in the meantime. It's just possible . . ."

Norman stepped into a levitating current and was borne upward. At the level of the Fifth Monument's upper balcony he stepped off. There were a few people here, not many, and they were busy with their own affairs—love-making and sight-seeing. Norman rested his arms on the rail and stared down. He had come up here because of a vague, unlikely hope that it would be quieter on the high balcony far above the city.

It was quiet, but no more so than the city had been. The rolling ways curved and slid smoothly beneath him. They were silent. Above him the Barrier was a gray, silent dome. He thought that gigantic claps of thunder were pounding at the Barrier from outside, that the impregnable hemisphere was beginning to crack, to buckle—to admit chaos in a roaring flood.

He gripped the cool plastic rail hard. Its solidity wasn't reassuring.

In a moment the Barrier would split wide open. . . .

There was no relief on the Monument. He glanced behind him at the base of the softly shining globe, with its rippling patterns of light, but that looked ready to shatter too. He stumbled as he jumped back into the drop-current. In fact, he missed it entirely. There was a heart-stopping instant when he was in free fall; then a safety-paragravity locked tight on his body and slid him easily into the current. He fell slowly.

But he had a new thought now. Suicide.

There were two questions involved. Did he want to commit suicide? And would suicide be possible? He studied the second point.

Without noticing, automatically he stepped on a moving way and dropped into one of the cushioned seats. No one died of violence in the city. No one ever had, as far as he knew. But had people tried to kill themselves?

It was a new, strange concept. There were so many safeties. No danger had been overlooked. There were no accidents.

The road curved. Forty feet away, across a lawn and a low wall, was the Barrier. Norman stood up and walked toward it. He was conscious of both attraction and repulsion.

Beyond the Barrier . . .

He stopped. There it was, directly before him, a smooth gray substance without any mark or pattern. It wasn't matter. It was something the builders had made, in the old days.

What was it like outside? Six hundred years had passed since the Barrier was created. In that time, the rest of the world could have changed considerably. An odd idea struck him: suppose the planet had been destroyed? Suppose a chain reaction had finally volatilized it? Would the city have been affected? Or was the city, within that fantastic barrier, not merely shielded but actually shifted into another plane of existence?

He struck his fist hard against the grayness; it was like striking rubber. Without warning the terror engulfed him. He could not hear himself screaming.

Afterward, he wondered how an eternity could be compressed into one instant. His thoughts swung back to suicide.

"Suicide?" Fleming said.

Nehral's mind was troubled. "Ecology fails," he remarked. "I suppose the trouble is that the city's a closed unit. We're doing artificially what was a natural law six hundred years ago. But nature didn't play favorites, as we're doing. And nature used variables. Mutations, I mean. There weren't any rules about introducing new pieces into the game—in fact, there weren't any rules about not introducing new rules. But here in the city we've got to stick by the original rules and the original pieces. If Bill Norman kills himself, I don't know what may happen."

"To us?"

"To us, and, through us, to the citizens. Norman's psychologist can't help him; he's a citizen, too. He doesn't know—"

"What was his problem, by the way? The psychologist's, I mean. He told Norman he'd solved it by taking up psychology."

"Sadism. We took care of that easily enough. We aroused his interest in the study of psychology. His mental index was so high we couldn't give him surgery; he needed a subtler intellectual release. But he's thoroughly social and well balanced now. The practice of psychology is the sublimation he needed, and he's very competent. However, he'll never get at the root of Norman's trouble. Ecology fails," he repeated. "The relationship between an organism and its environment—irreconcilable, in this case. Hallucinations! Norman doesn't have hallucinations. Or even illusions. He simply has rational periods—luckily brief."

"It's an abnormal ecology anyway."

"It had to be. The city is uninhabitable."

The city screamed!

It was a microcosm, and it had to battle unimaginable stresses to maintain its efficiency. It was an outboard motor on a lifeboat. The storm raged. The motor strained, shrilled, sparked—screamed. The environment was so completely artificial that no normal technology could have kept the balance.

Six hundred years ago the builders had studied and discarded plan after plan. The maximum diameter of a Barrier was five miles. The vulnerability increased according to the square of the diameter. And invulnerability was the main factor.

The city had to be built and maintained as a self-sufficient unit within an impossibly small radius.

Consider the problems. *Self-sufficient.* There were no pipe lines to the outside. A civilization had to exist for an indefinite period in its own waste products. Steamships, spaceships, are not parallels. They have to make port and take in fresh supplies.

This lifeboat would be at sea for much longer than six hundred years. And the citizens—the survivors—must be kept not only alive but healthy physically and mentally.

The smaller the area, the higher the concentration. The builders could make the necessary machines. They knew how to do that. But such machines had never been constructed before on the planet. Not in such concentration!

Civilization is an artificial environment. With the machines that were necessary, the city became so artificial that nobody could live in it. The builders got their efficiency; they made the city so that it could exist indefinitely, supplying all the air, water, food and power required. The machines took care of that.

But such machines!

The energy required and released was slightly inconceivable. It had to be released, of course. And it was. In light and sound and radiation—within the five-mile area under the Barrier.

Anyone living in the city would have developed a neurosis in two minutes, a psychosis in ten and would have lived a little while longer than that. Thus the builders had an efficient city, but nobody could use it.

There was one answer.

Hypnosis.

Everyone in the city was under hypnosis. It was selective telepathic hypnosis, with the so-called Monuments—powerful hypnopedic machines—as the control devices. The survivors in the lifeboat didn't know there was a storm. They saw only placid water on which the boat drifted smoothly.

The city screamed to deaf ears. No one had heard it for six hundred years. No one had felt the radiation or seen the blinding, shocking light that flashed through the city. The citizens could not, and the Controllers could not either, because they were blind and deaf and dumb, and lacking in certain other senses. They had their telepathy, their ESP, which enabled them to accomplish their task of steering the lifeboat. As for the citizens, their job was to survive.

No one had heard the city screaming for six hundred years— except Bill Norman.

"He has an inquiring mind," Nehral said dryly. "Too inquiring. His problem's an abstraction, as I've mentioned, and if he gets the right answer it'll kill him. If he doesn't, he'll go insane. In either case, we'll suffer, because we're not conditioned to failure. The main hypnotic maxim implanted in our minds is that every citizen must survive. All right. You've got the facts now, Fleming. Does anything suggest itself?"

"I don't have all the facts. What's Norman's problem?"

"He comes of dangerous stock," Nehral answered indirectly. "Theologians and mathematicians. His mind is—a little too rational. As for his problem—well, Pilate asked the same question three thousand years ago, and I don't recall his ever getting an answer. It's a question that's lain behind every bit of research since research first started. But the answer has never been fatal till now. Norman's question is simply this—*what is truth?*"

There was a pause. Nehral went on.

"He hasn't expressed it even to himself. He doesn't know he's asking that question. But we know; we have entrée to his mind. That's the question that he's finding insoluble, and the problem that's bringing him gradually out of control, out of his hypnosis. So far there've been only flashes of realization. Split-second rational periods. Those are bad enough, for him. He's heard and seen the city as it is."

Another pause. Fleming's thoughts stilled. Nehral said:

"It's the only problem we can't solve by hypnotic suggestion. We've tried. But it's useless. Norman's that remarkably rare person, someone who is looking for the truth."

Fleming said slowly, "He's looking for the truth. But—does he have—to find it?"

His thoughts raced into Nehral's brain, flint against steel, and struck fire there.

Three weeks later the psychologist pronounced Norman cured and he instantly married Mia. They went up to the Fifth Monument and held hands.

"As long as you understand—" Norman said.

"I'll go with you," she told him. "Anywhere."

"Well, it won't be tomorrow. I was going at it the wrong way. Imagine trying to tunnel out through the Barrier! No. I'll have to fight fire with fire. The Barrier's the result of natural physical laws.

There's no secret about how it was created. But how to destroy it—that's another thing entirely."

"They say it can't be destroyed. Someday it'll disappear, Bill."

"When? I'm not going to wait for that. It may take me years, because I'll have to learn how to use my weapons. Years of study and practice and research. But I've got a purpose."

"You can't become an expert nuclear physicist overnight."

He laughed and put his arm around her shoulders. "I don't expect to. First things come first. First I'll have to learn to be a good physicist. Ehrlich and Pasteur and Curie—they had a drive, a motivation. So have I, now. I know what I want. I want out."

"Bill, if you should fail—"

"I expect to, at first. But in the end I won't fail. I know what I want. *Out!*"

She moved closer to him, and they were silent, looking down at the quiet, familiar friendliness of the city. I can stand it for a while, Norman thought. Especially with Mia. Now that the psychologist's got rid of my trouble, I can settle down to work.

Above them the rippling, soft light beat out from the great globe atop the Monument.

"Mia—"

"Yes?"

"I know what I want now."

"But he doesn't know," Fleming said.

"That's all right," Nehral said cheerfully. "He never really knew what his problem was. You found the answer. Not the one he wanted, but the best one. Displacement, diversion, sublimation—the name doesn't matter. It was the same treatment, basically, as turning sadistic tendencies into channels of beneficial surgery. We've given Norman his compromise. He still doesn't know what he's looking for, but he's been hypnotized into believing that he can find it outside the city. Put food on top of a wall, out of reach of a starving man, and you'll get a neurosis. But if you give the man materials for building a ladder, his energy will be deflected into a productive channel. Norman will spend all his life in research, and probably make some valuable discoveries. He's sane again. He's under the preventive hypnosis. And he'll die thinking there's a way out."

"Through the Barrier? There isn't."

"Of course there isn't. But Norman could accept the hypnotic suggestion that there *was* a way, if only he could find it. We've given him the materials to build his ladder. He'll fail and fail, but he'll never really get discouraged. He's looking for truth. We've told him he can find truth outside the Barrier, and that he can find a way out. He's happy now. He's stopped rocking the lifeboat."

"Truth . . ." Fleming said, and then, "Nehral—I've been wondering."

"What?"

"Is there a Barrier?"

Nehral said, "But the city's survived! Nothing from outside has ever come through the Barrier—"

"Suppose there isn't a Barrier," Fleming said. "How would the city look from outside? Like a—a furnace, perhaps. It's uninhabitable. We can't conceive of the real city, any more than the hypnotized citizens can. Would you walk into a furnace? Nehral, perhaps the city's its own Barrier."

"But we sense the Barrier. The citizens see the Barrier—"

"Do they? Do—we? Or is that part of the hypnosis too, a part we don't know about? Nehral—I don't know. There may be a Barrier, and it may disappear when its half-time is run. But suppose we just *think* there's a Barrier."

"But—" Nehral said, and stopped. "That would mean—Norman might find a way out!"

"I wonder if that was what the builders planned," Fleming said.

SHATTERING THE MYTH OF JOHN WILKES BOOTH'S ESCAPE

By William G. Shepherd

. . . .

He was indescribably handsome,
strangely out of place in the wild western country.
He said he was John Wilkes Booth. Who was he?

(The legend has long been current in the Southwest that the man who was shot by Boston Corbett at Garrett's farm and identified as the assassin of Abraham Lincoln was not John Wilkes Booth but that Booth escaped to Texas and Oklahoma. Evidence in support of the story has recently appeared in one of the state historical journals in the West, and a prominent churchman has for years lectured on the subject to thousands of people. This legend has proved so strangely persistent that *Harper's Magazine* asked Mr. Shepherd to probe the evidence to a conclusive issue. The story which Mr. Shepherd has brought back after an extended investigation, involving two trips to Texas and Oklahoma, is a timely, interesting narrative of a remarkable adventure in journalism.
—EDITOR'S NOTE, *Harper's Monthly Magazine*, November, 1924.)

In twenty years of investigating and writing for newspapers and magazines I have never encountered a more absorbing story than the Enid legend of John Wilkes Booth. To meet the believers of this legend in the Oklahoma country, where it arose; to hear them explain their firm belief that John Wilkes Booth escaped and was never punished for the assassination of Lincoln, but lived and died among them; and to discover proofs that they were wrong—has been one of my most interesting experiences.

This legend is no mild rumor. It has penetrated the office of *Har-*

per's Magazine, as well as others, many times during the past twenty years. It still finds its way occasionally into the columns of the daily newspapers. When H. H. Kohlsaat recently published in a magazine an account of how the family of John Wilkes Booth secured his body from the government at Washington and buried it in the family cemetery lot in Baltimore, he received many letters from various parts of the country announcing that John Wilkes Booth had never been captured. He received a front-page article in a prominent Western newspaper which in 1924 carried the story of Booth's escape and of his death at Enid, Oklahoma. An officer in the American army sent him a book relating the Enid legend. Mr. Kohlsaat was called to account for not knowing that John Wilkes Booth was never punished. The Enid legend came to the front from everywhere. Therefore I was asked by the editors of *Harper's Magazine* to put the Enid legend, if I could, through the sieve of fact and history.

Perhaps the most extraordinary feature of the whole legend is that to this day, unless it has been recently disposed of, the body of a man who claimed to be John Wilkes Booth lies mummified and unburied in the city of Memphis, Tennessee.

My sifting of the legend imposed upon me within the past year the unpleasant task of viewing this body. It was in a coffinlike pine box, lying in a garage in the rear of a home on a fine Memphis residential street. For twenty-one years it had been preserved by Finis L. Bates, an eminent citizen of Memphis, a lawyer well known throughout the South. Up to the day of his death, Thanksgiving Day of 1923, Mr. Bates believed that he was holding the body of John Wilkes Booth; and that in time, for the "correction of history" he could prove to the United States government that John Wilkes Booth had escaped punishment.

It was in the evening after dinner and after the unsuspecting colored servants had retired to their quarters that I was escorted to the garage to see the mummy. There was the body of an old man, with bushy white hair, parted low, as young Booth parted his. If this were Booth's body, then Booth must have lived to be sixty-five years old. My hostess, the widow of Mr. Bates, and her son pointed out to me the raised eyebrow. Booth's right eyebrow had been scarred in a stage duel. They called attention to the right thumb, which closely hugged the index finger. The lower joint of Booth's right thumb had been crushed in a stage curtain and he always carried his cane in such a manner that the handle would hide this injury.

Could I see a slight irregularity on the bone of the right ankle?

Booth broke his ankle when, in jumping from the President's box at Ford's Theater that April evening, his foot caught in the draping of an American flag.

It was difficult for me to see these distinctive marks. The skin of the mummy was like wrinkled parchment. But there was enough of a suggestion of such marks to prevent anyone from then and there declaring that this was not the body of John Wilkes Booth.

John Wilkes Booth had been a handsome man and the despair of lovely women. Could this long gray hair, still curling and plenteous, have been the adornment of that young man who mastered the stage of his day with his talent and his physical beauty? This poor old man, unburied yet after twenty-one years of death!—could he have been John Wilkes Booth? And if he could, what a fate it would be—more ghastly than any punishing judge could impose—that his body should not be laid to rest. Strange thoughts to try to think out on a cold garage floor in the heart of the residence district of one of our fine cities, under the light of electric lamps, with a neighborhood radio concert beating in your ears and with two smiling, amiable hosts studying your bewilderment.

I was glad enough to go back into the warmth and light of the big house.

And from this house I went out through the South to different cities and towns to trail down, as best I could, the legend that John Wilkes Booth was never captured and did not pay the penalty of his crime, but that he died a suicide in the city of Enid, Oklahoma, in January, 1903.

At the outset I must say there would have been no legend of Enid if the records of the War Department concerning the capture and burial of John Wilkes Booth had not been prepared in secrecy and if many of the facts about it had not been shrouded in wartime mystery. In haste, without public notice, without civilian identification, with few onlookers, the body officially described as that of John Wilkes Booth was disposed of. In 1914, before the Great War, it would have been difficult to understand the haste and mystery which surrounded the burial of Booth's body; with the Great War fresh in our minds and with a lively appreciation of what little chance civilians have to know of official wartime doings, it is easier to comprehend the secret military methods which were followed in disposing of the remains of Lincoln's assassin. The secret service department of the army had charge of the Booth affair. Colonel L. C. Baker, a detective, was given sole responsibility for the capture of Booth by Secretary of War Stanton. Colonel Baker put his cousin, Lieutenant L. B. Baker, in charge of the field search. The two Bakers controlled subsequent events—one in Washington and the other along the highways of Maryland and Virginia. They held themselves accountable to no one except the Secretary of War. They even acted as their own censors in telling their story of the capture and death of Booth. A reporter for the New York *World*, at that time writing of the capture of Booth as it was related to him by the officials, practically told his readers that his story was being censored. He began, "A hard and grizzly face overlooks me as I write. This is the face of Lafayette Baker. I tell you the story of the capture of Booth as he told it to me." And he ends his story by throwing doubt on it all, by saying, in effect, "When Herrold, Booth's companion, came out of the burning barn, he said to the soldiers, 'Who is that man that was with me in there? He told me his name was Boyd.'"

Even at the time there were those who doubted that the Bakers had captured John Wilkes Booth. And the two Bakers made no attempt to prove conclusively to the public that the body in their possession—that of the man shot in the Garrett barn ten days after Lincoln's assassination—was that of John Wilkes Booth. This body was brought to Washington on the steamer *John I. Ide*. A group of military men viewed it on a monitor two days after the news had been flashed out to the world that Booth had been captured. A diary written by Booth had been found on the body. There were thousands of citizens in Washington who knew John Wilkes Booth by sight, but not one of them—not even one of his stage associates—was asked to identify the remains. The identification was entirely an official affair. The only civilian who was asked to view the remains was Dr. J. Frederick May, of Washington, who had once performed an operation on Booth's neck. Dr. May, on seeing the body, said, "I don't recognize that as Booth." In later years, however, Dr. May explained in a booklet entitled *The Mark of the Scalpel* that Colonel Baker, there on the boat in the presence of the body, explained to him that Booth had been a fugitive for almost two weeks and that he had suffered for want of food and drink and sleep; whereupon Dr. May reluctantly identified what seemed to be a scar on Booth's neck which might have been the mark of the operation, and expressed his amazement at the astonishing change which suffering had produced in the person of Booth.

Then suddenly one night the body disappeared from the boat. History is befuddled as to what was done with it. The story of the

Bakers is that they placed it in a rowboat, having removed it from the deck in a blanket. They carried weights in the boat to give the impression that they intended to sink the body in the Potomac. Instead, they rowed through the darkness to where the penitentiary bordered the river, and through a hole which had been made in the penitentiary walls they thrust the body into a penitentiary cell and there buried it, by lantern light, under flagstones. Dr. George L. Porter, high in the medical service of the Union army, had charge of the Lincoln murderers and suspects. He says that he and four soldiers buried it one afternoon in a cell in the old arsenal where the War College now stands. For four years—indeed, not until the body was removed because of building operations and turned back to the Booth family—the public did not know what disposition had been made of the assassin's body.

In short, there was mystery enough about the capture and burial of Booth—due to justified caution, perhaps, in view of the wartime conditions and the fear that the Confederates would find the body and treat it as a hero's—to render it not unreasonable to entertain the Enid legend. Booth *might* have got away. There was a loophole for him. It is this one loophole that made the Enid legend not entirely incredible.

With these facts in mind I sat through several long drowsy summer afternoons in a home in Memphis, listening to a sturdy, white-haired Southern lawyer telling the strange story of what had befallen him in his very early days when he went to Texas to get his start in life. His name was Finis L. Bates. His forebears and relatives had been eminent in civilian and in governmental life; he himself had been a state's attorney general. When he was a cub attorney of twenty-one in Texas he had had an amazing experience which shadowed and to a great extent molded his entire life. He became acquainted with a man whom he believed to be John Wilkes Booth, *eight years after* Booth had assassinated Abraham Lincoln. I could not doubt this man's sincerity or his utter sanity. I listened enthralled as he spun me his yarn, in soft Southern dialect, of those days in 1872 in Texas and of the years of time and thousands of dollars he had since expended in trying to establish in the public mind, "for the correction of history, sir," his belief that John Wilkes Booth had escaped punishment. The gist of his long story, which sent me trailing through the South and West, was this:

"When I was a young lawyer, in the early seventies, I went to the town of Grandberry, Texas, to seek my fortune. It was a small, wild town, with wild ways. One day a client of mine came to me and told me a story of trouble. In those days and in those parts of the country, grocery keepers and keepers of general stores used to sell whisky and other alcoholic drinks. They were required to take out government licenses. Bars were sometimes attached to the stores. Well, my client had recently sold his store at Glen Rose Mills nearby to a stranger named John St. Helen, a man who came up from somewhere in Mexico. This John St. Helen had failed to take out a license for selling liquor, and my client had been indicted and summoned to court for this failure. Of course, a mistake had been made. It was John St. Helen who should have been arrested. The federal authorities, in a town two days distant from us by horse, did not know of the sale of the store.

"I sent word to this John St. Helen that I wanted to see him, and he came to my office within a day or two. I never in all my subsequent years and experiences saw such a man as this stranger. He was indescribably handsome. He had a poise and a carriage that commanded instant attention. His voice and his speech fascinated me as they fascinated all with whom he came in contact. He was strangely out of place in this wild Western country. But in those days you did not ask a man in Texas about his past—you took him at his face value.

"When I told him that a warrant had been wrongly issued for the former owner of the store for selling whisky without a license, St. Helen admitted that whisky had been sold in his store since he had purchased the place. But he had not known that it was necessary to secure a license; he showed an unfamiliarity with storekeeping which did not surprise me. He was no storekeeper.

"He asked me if he might retain me as his lawyer. When I agreed to this he said, 'I don't dare to go to a federal court. It's a matter of life and death with me. Can't you persuade the man who sold me the store to go to court and plead guilty? I will pay the fine and all expenses.'"

The upshot of this negotiation was that the former storekeeper went on a two days' journey in a buggy with the young lawyer, Bates, and pleaded guilty. From a pocketbook containing a liberal supply of money which John St. Helen had given him, the boy lawyer paid the fine and all the expenses of the trip.

"John St. Helen met us when we drove into the main street of Grandberry and was delighted with the news. I returned him his pocketbook, not emptied by any means, and he put it into his pocket without counting the bills, and thanked both of us profusely."

Not long after that, as the Fourth of July of the year 1872 approached, John St. Helen invited the young lawyer of Grandberry to come to Glen Rose Mills to deliver the Independence Day oration. Ranchers and cowboys came from many miles to the great barbecue. But on that day the leader of the occasion was not the promising young lawyer from Grandberry. It was John St. Helen—slender, flashing-eyed, golden-voiced, and eloquent—who carried off the honors.

"As soon as he rose to introduce me," my white-haired host told me, "I knew that the oratorical honors were not to be mine. I knew I could never stir such emotions in that rough audience as he commanded. The crowd cheered and cheered, and demanded, later in the day, that he speak again. His fame as an orator was fixed that day.

"But after a time he sold his store at Glen Rose Mills and moved to Grandberry, where he set up another store. I noted that he did little actual storekeeping. He had a very able Mexican who did most of the work. He lived in a comfortably furnished little room in the store building. He and I used to spend many hours together every day.

"He turned me to Shakespeare and to Roman history. He gave me innumerable lessons in oratory. He taught me what to do with my hands and feet before an audience. He taught me gestures and voice inflection. His imitations of public speakers who made errors in platform manners were excruciatingly funny. Whenever a play came to town he was sure to see it. More than once he took young men who came to town as actors and gave them hours of lessons in the dramatic art. They always knew instinctively that this strange man was a master worth listening to.

"He drank heavily. His drinking spells were followed, very often, by spells of illness.

"Once he became very ill; the doctor thought he could not live. St. Helen sent for me and I hurried to his little room at the store. I found him exceedingly weak. And he seemed very uncomfortable mentally. When the doctor had left he sent the boy out of the room and motioned to me to come to his bedside.

" 'I don't believe I shall live,' he told me. 'Reach under my pillow and take out a picture you'll find there,' he said.

"I found a tintype under the pillow, a picture of him.

" 'If I don't live,' he told me, 'I want you, as my lawyer, to send that picture to Edwin Booth, in New York City, and tell him the man in that picture is dead. Tell him how I died.'

"I promised him and then I called in the Mexican boy and told him to get some brandy. He and I turned in where the doctor had left off. We rubbed St. Helen with brandy from head to foot until we were almost exhausted. And we pulled him through. Though he was very weak the next day, the doctor found him better. Within a few weeks he was up and around again.

"At last, one day, he mentioned to me his strange request. 'Take a walk into the country,' he said. 'I want to tell you something.' "

Along the road leading from the little town, John St. Helen told the story which affected Finis L. Bates's entire life.

" 'I am John Wilkes Booth,' he said to me," continued Bates. " 'I am the man who killed the best man that ever lived, Abraham Lincoln.' "

Here was a client speaking to his attorney. For hours, Bates told me, he tried to disprove to St. Helen his own amazing claim; he thought he saw madness in his friend. Why, Booth had been killed at the Garrett home, in Virginia! Boston Corbett, a sergeant, had shot him in a burning corncrib. Booth's body had been taken to Washington and had been sunk in the Potomac thirteen years before. Booth's diary had been found on the body. Everybody in that plot against Lincoln and the government had been executed; they were all dead.

" 'Not I,' said St. Helen. 'I am John Wilkes Booth and I escaped.' "

They had other talks on the subject and then one day St. Helen (rather impatiently, I judged from Bates's tale) said, in substance:

" 'Look here! I'm going to tell you as a lawyer some things that only John Wilkes Booth himself and no other man on earth could know.' "

In the story that followed, John St. Helen put Finis L. Bates on the trail of historical or official facts that kept Bates busy all his life, that caused him to write a book entitled *The Escape and Suicide of John Wilkes Booth*, full of the mystery of what happened in the city of Washington on that indescribable night of April 14, 1865, and that caused him, years afterward, to keep unburied a body which he believed to be that of John Wilkes Booth.

" 'How do you suppose Herrold and I got away from Washington that night without the help of men high in the government?' demanded St. Helen. 'I rode into Washington on the morning of that day, intending to take part in a plot to abduct President Lincoln and carry him to Richmond, Virginia. But at the bridge Herrold and I were told that Richmond had fallen. Then I knew the abduction plot had failed. The sentries had held us at the bridge because we had refused to give our names. But when I saw that with the fall of Richmond there could be no abduction, I told the sentries that I was John Wilkes Booth, the actor, and that Herrold was my friend, and they let us pass into the city.' "

In what follows I am not going to name a very high official who was designated to me by Bates. It is part of the Enid legend that a certain government official of great power and position planned the killing of Lincoln and helped Booth to escape. Let his name be Blank.

" 'That afternoon,' " Bates quoted St. Helen, " 'I met Mr. Blank.' " According to St. Helen's story Blank had been in the abduction plot, and he was greatly disappointed because it had failed.

" 'Are you too fainthearted to kill him?' St. Helen said Mr. Blank asked him, over a glass of brandy. 'And then,' St. Helen said, 'Blank told me how Lincoln was preparing to ruin and devastate the South. "I can arrange matters so that you can escape," he told me. "Lincoln is going to Ford's Theater this evening."

" 'Mr. Blank showed me that he could give Herrold and me the password at the bridge. He made it appear to me that I would be committing not assassination but an act of war. And so I yielded. He gave me the password late in the day, and that night Herrold and I gave the password to two sentries at the bridge and the sentries permitted us to go through.' "

This story did not convince Bates, he told me.

"What kept General Grant and his wife from going to the theater with Lincoln that night?" Bates told me that John St. Helen asked him. "If I were not John Wilkes Booth how could I know what I'm going to tell you now? I told Mr. Blank, who was urging me to kill Lincoln, that it would be certain death for me to go into Lincoln's box with General Grant present. It had been announced in the afternoon papers that Grant would be there. Mr. Blank told me that he would arrange matters so that Grant would not be there. And Grant wasn't there. Blank had only a few hours in which to act. I don't know how he arranged it but he kept his word. Grant was not there. Up to a late hour in the afternoon, Grant intended appearing in the box with Lincoln—his first public appearance as the hero of the war. But a few hours later he was on a train leaving Washington. I don't know what happened. But Mr. Blank kept his word to me."

Mr. Bates dug out from among his papers a letter which he had received years later from General Grant's secretary. It said that something had happened at the White House that afternoon to disturb Mrs. Grant: a rumor, something she had heard, some intuition of trouble. And she had persuaded General Grant to leave the city with her, foregoing the gala presentation with the President at Ford's Theater.

"How could any man but Booth have known that?" Bates asked me.

"Well, then, if this John St. Helen told the truth, who was the man who was shot in the corncrib at the Garrett Farm?" I asked Bates. And Bates told me he had asked the same question of John St. Helen.

"It must have been a soldier named Ruddy," St. Helen told Bates. "After the escape from Washington I had ridden in a Negro's wagon under a pile of furniture to a ferry. After I had crossed the ferry I discovered that my diary and some other papers had fallen out of my pocket. I asked this Confederate soldier to go back on the ferry and catch up with the wagon and get my papers. When he returned he could find out where I should be hiding.

"I slept in a room of the Garrett house that night, with Herrold. The next day Herrold went off to Bowling Green to get me a pair of shoes. On the afternoon of that day, while I was lying out on the Garrett lawn, I saw some Union soldiers riding past. I knew they were looking for me. I dropped my field glasses on the lawn and, without saying anything to the Garretts, I went out into the woods back of the house and got away. It must have been Ruddy, bringing back my papers, who was caught in the corncrib. Look up the records and see if my field glasses were not found on the lawn."

Finis Bates, in after years, did look up the records; the glasses *had* been found on the lawn.

Bates looked up many records; looking up records became part of his life work.

There *were* strange doings in Washington that day. It is a fact of record that all the sentries were removed from all the approaches to Washington on the afternoon and evening of the day of the assassination; all of the sentries except those at one bridge. And these sentries permitted Booth and Herrold to pass and held back an honest citizen —John Fletcher, a liveryman—who was trying to recover from Herrold his stolen horse.

Quietly and without ceremony or farewells, John St. Helen departed from Grandberry, Texas, as if sorry he had spoken to Bates, even in confidence. Twenty-five years went by. The tintype remained in Bates's possession, but John St. Helen dropped from Bates's ken.

Finis L. Bates, however, challenged by St. Helen's story, began to delve into history. In a great mass of material which he accumulated during his lifetime were letters from one of the sentries who permitted Booth to cross the bridge; from Lieutenant D. D. Dana, aide to the provost marshal of Washington at the time of the assassination; from Grant's secretary; from members of the Garrett family and from many others who took part in the strange events of that time. Bates, as a lawyer, received in time enough confirmation of the story of John St. Helen to cause him to believe it. But John St. Helen had disappeared.

At last, by a stroke of luck, Bates found F. A. Demond, of Cavendish, Vermont, who had been one of the sentries at the bridge the night Booth escaped.

All of the mystery that John St. Helen put into his story was in the story of this sentry. Demond was eighteen years old in 1865; he was sixty-nine years old when he made his statement for Finis L. Bates. But through all the years Demond himself had been puzzled by the strange orders he and his fellow sentries received at the bridge that night: they were orders that gave freedom to the murderers of Lincoln and held back all others.

As Bates compared the story of the strange John St. Helen with the story told by Sentry Demond, is it amazing that he began to believe that John St. Helen must have been John Wilkes Booth?

"I was sent down to guard the end of the bridge from Washington to Uniontown, Maryland," Demond told Bates. "On the morning of April 14, as Private Drake and myself were sitting on a timber by the side of the road, two men came along. I asked them where they were going. They said, 'Only looking around.'"

They refused to give their names. John St. Helen had told Bates that he did not give his name until he heard that Richmond had fallen and had decided that the kidnaping plot had failed.

"While talking with them a captain came along on horseback; he was one of the aides of General Augur, the provost marshal. He wanted to know what the trouble was. Booth took him aside and talked with him. Then the captain said they were all right. But Drake and I said that we took orders only from Lieutenant Dana, and the captain rode off.

"About two o'clock an orderly came from headquarters and told us to let the men go. We did so. We thought it was funny but we had to obey orders."

An hour later Booth, according to history, was at the Kirkwood hotel in Washington, trying to get in contact with the same official whom John St. Helen had named in his talk with Bates. Booth left a note for this official, which was later found by military detectives.

The sentry's story of what happened that black night on the bridge strengthened more than ever the belief of Bates that no one but Booth could have known what St. Helen knew.

"At nine o'clock that night we shut the gate and Drake went on guard," Demond told Bates.

"Just as we were getting ready for guard duty, a little after ten o'clock, Lieutenant Dana came to us and told us not to let anyone through without a password—'T.B.' with the countersign 'T.B. Road.'

"*We thought that strange, for it was the first time that we ever had a password to use since we were on that bridge.*"

Almost at the very hour that Lincoln was to be slain the sentries were given orders which forced them to assist the assassin to escape!

It was a day of mystery in Washington, that fourteenth day of April. John St. Helen had told Bates that during the afternoon of that day a government official had promised to assist and protect him if he would kill Lincoln. And here, in the evening, these sentries at the bridge are puzzled by the order that they are to permit no one to pass who does not know that double watchword—"T.B." and then "T.B. Road." John St. Helen told Bates he was given these passwords by Mr. Blank late in the afternoon; now Bates has the story of the sentry who was amazed at receiving them.

Booth and Herrold, riding five minutes apart, gave the proper passwords and passed through into the South.

"But we were puzzled by what had happened," Demond told Bates. "I said, 'It's funny what's going on here tonight.'"

At that very moment Washington, two miles away, was horror-stricken by the shooting of Lincoln and the attack on Secretary Seward.

The story of Private Demond convinced Bates that John St. Helen's story was true. The fact that he was unable to disprove the story of St. Helen preyed on his mind. Finally, twenty years after St. Helen had told him the story, Bates wrote a letter to the War Department in Washington suggesting that Booth had not been captured and that it might be possible to find him still alive. He received a reply, coldly official, which said merely that the War Department would not be interested in the project.

The date of this letter to the War Department (1898) is of the utmost importance in proving the sincerity of Finis L. Bates, for this letter was sent *five* years before the Enid legend arose. On the story of John St. Helen alone, Bates, after years of investigation, was willing to rest his case; was willing to declare that Booth had escaped punishment.

And then came the Enid legend.

While Finis L. Bates, in the city of Memphis, was carrying on his law practice and was from time to time journeying about the country to talk with those who might know something of the Booth case, or was trying by means of correspondence to discover the whereabouts of John St. Helen, there appeared in the little town of El Reno, in the spring of 1901, an elderly man who gave his name at the Anstien hotel, where he registered, as David E. George.

Oklahoma was then a territory. The federal government was preparing to give the land to the public and, though the land distribution was still many months away, thousands of land-buying citizens were thronging to El Reno, Enid and other Oklahoma towns to select land which they hoped later to receive as gifts from the government. It was into this turbulent and exciting atmosphere that this dignified man of mystery came.

I talked recently with Mrs. N. J. Anstien, whose husband was the proprietor of the hotel at El Reno where this strange man first appeared. There is no doubt in her mind, she told me, that David E. George was John Wilkes Booth.

"There were several little cottages in the yard behind the hotel and Mr. George took a room in one of these. He was a striking man. His hair was curly and jet black. He dyed it, of course. I imagined he was about sixty years old.

"He was a fascinating talker when he wanted to talk. He never spoke to us about his family. One day he told my husband that his trade was that of a house painter. My husband wouldn't believe him.

His hands were not calloused or stained; his fingers were long and slender, like a woman's. I could not imagine that he had done a day's work in his life. Just for fun my husband gave him an order to paint the little cottage in which he lived. Mr. George puttered around for several days and made a terrible botch of things.

" 'I told you he was not a painter,' my husband said to me.

"He used to get very sick from overdrinking," Mrs. Anstien continued. "He would get up out of bed and go out into the yard and pump a pitcher of water and take it back into his room to drink. I took care of him many times, carrying food to him. He was always extremely grateful. It was pleasant in those wild days to meet such a gentleman as he was. I was not surprised to hear afterward that he was John Wilkes Booth.

"I remember one day while he was sick in his cottage room, a father and mother brought their daughter to him. They insisted that he should marry her. They said the girl had fallen in love with him and that it was not her fault. They did not claim that he had wronged her, except mentally. They thought he had a great deal of money and that he was a fine gentleman. I was out in the yard when he sent them away. He went into a tremendous fury and I heard him shout, 'Madame, I have not wronged your daughter. She does not say I have wronged her. Out! Out! All of you. Begone!' He talked like an actor in a tragedy. When they had left I went into his room.

" 'Me! Me!' he was saying. 'They challenge me!' And then he said to me, 'Why, they don't know who I am. Why, I killed the best man that ever lived.' I thought his talk was all part of his spell of fury and I did not know, until a year later when he was dead, what he meant."

This strange old man made an impression on men and women wherever he went. It was easy for me to trace his twenty-two-year-old trail through the town affairs of El Reno and Enid. He was a proud old man, vain of his appearance.

He was very careful about dyeing his hair and mustache; he purchased his dye of a druggist who remembers this customer.

"But I never thought he was John Wilkes Booth," the druggist tells you—(every elderly person in El Reno and in Enid, three hours away, either believes or does not believe that David E. George was John Wilkes Booth)—"he bought house paint from me and when he died he owed me forty dollars."

He read theatrical journals, sitting in a rocking chair in the little lobby of the Anstien hotel. He talked occasionally with guests of the hotel who seemed worth while, but not every Tom, Dick or Harry could find him willing to converse.

Then one day he announced that he would buy himself a house in El Reno. He told his host that he was no longer a young man and that it was time he settled down. The house he bought is standing in El Reno today. He bought it from a man named Vanness.

In everything that David E. George does, from now on, you will see a wandering, friendless, proud old man trying to protect himself from a friendless end; trying to make sure that there will be help and comfort and peace and friendliness about his bed when he dies.

He must have used all but his last dollar to make a payment of three hundred and fifty dollars for the simple little four-roomed house which he bought in El Reno. He found a man and his wife, Mr. and Mrs. J. W. Simmons, who were willing to live in the house, rent free, and give him care, board and lodging.

He drank in the town saloons, but even in his cups he seemed to be able to command the respect of his fellow drinkers. He recited poetry and he was sentimental. Even among those who did not believe that David E. George was John Wilkes Booth I found a man who could remember George's barroom poetry. He was W. H. Ryan, who in recent years has been mayor of Enid.

"I never thought he was Booth and I don't think so today," Mr. Ryan told me. "But he could recite. I can easily remember a verse I used to hear him repeat." And then Mr. Ryan quoted:

> Come not when I am dead
> To shed thy tears around my head.
> Let the winds weep and the plover cry,
> But, thou, oh foolish man, go by!

"But did he quote Shakespeare?" I asked.

"It may have sounded like Shakespeare to the men in the saloons who heard it," he answered, laughing. "But we didn't know much of Shakespeare in Oklahoma territory in those days. He could recite very well, very impressively."

He made other friends, outside of barrooms. Guests in the home where he lived found him interesting; he entertained them with his conversation; to them he was fascinating, a man of mystery.

But in following his trail you discover that this strange person, even in this household, was carefully selecting those persons who might aid and be kind to an old man who might soon be dying.

One of these was Mrs. Anna Smith. In the courthouse at Enid,

Oklahoma, I found a will which David E. George had made in favor of Anna K. Smith; it was dated June 17, 1902, a few months after he came to El Reno. He became acquainted with Mr. and Mrs. George E. Smith and impressed them with the fact that he had considerable property. They befriended him—and he made a will which would leave to Mrs. Smith "all his property." He named her husband as the executor.

Another person to whom the old man tried to cling was Mrs. Ida Harper, wife of the Methodist clergyman of El Reno. She was among the visitors who called on the family with which he lived. A month after he had established himself in the little house, and three months before he had made his will, he came into the house one afternoon, greeted Mrs. Simmons, Mrs. Harper and another lady who was calling, and passed to his own room through the one where they were sitting. Within a short time the women heard him calling for help. They ran into the room and found him ill, lying on his bed. His eyes were dilated as though he had taken a drug.

"I'm very ill," he said. While the other two women ran out of the room to make strong coffee, George called Mrs. Harper to his bedside.

"I believe I'm going to die," he said. "I'm not an ordinary painter. I killed the best man that ever lived."

I give her story as she made oath to it when George was dead, almost a year later, and as it appeared in Bates's book.

"I asked him who it was he killed, and he said, 'Abraham Lincoln.' I could not believe it and thought he was out of his head, so I asked 'Who was Abraham Lincoln?' 'Is it possible you are so ignorant as not to know?' he answered. Then he took a pencil and paper and wrote, in a peculiar but legible hand, the name, *Abraham Lincoln*. 'Don't doubt me,' he said. 'I am John Wilkes Booth. I am dying now.'

"He told me he was well off; and he seemed to be perfectly rational. I really thought he was dying. He made me promise that I would keep his secret until he was dead. He said that if anyone should find out he was John Wilkes Booth, they would take him out and hang him and the people who loved him would despise him. He told me that people high in official life hated Lincoln and were implicated in his assassination. He said that Mrs. Surratt was innocent, and the thought that he was responsible for her death as well as of others stalked before him like a ghost. He said he was devoted to acting but that he had to give it up because of his rash deed, and the thought that he had to run away from the stage when he loved so well the life of an actor made him restless and ill-tempered. He said he had plenty of money but had to play the role of workman to keep his mind occupied."

A doctor came in while George was talking to Mrs. Harper, and he drew the old man back to life. Mrs. Harper kept her secret for a time.

Just as St. Helen had disappeared from the knowledge of Finis L. Bates after telling his strange story, so David E. George, thirty years later, was suddenly lost to his acquaintance in El Reno. His over-drinking proved his undoing with the Simmons family; Mrs. Simmons told her husband she could not endure hearing the old man talk and rave to himself. So the Simmons family took over the house, giving a note to George for three hundred and fifty dollars, and the old man went away.

I could not find that he had said good-bye to anyone, even to Mrs. Harper to whom he had told his strange story.

And now the old man is coming to the end of his trail. We pick it up at Enid, a few hours' train ride from El Reno. He registered at the Grand Avenue Hotel. It was a good hotel as hotels went in Enid in those days. The office was on the second floor; on the first floor was a store. Guests slept in cubbyholes separated by partitions that did not reach to the ceiling. One took no comfort in his room except while in bed. In the lobby were rocking chairs where guests did their reading, talking and smoking. It was in early December that George registered here; the hotel is gone now and so is the register.

Drinking made up the few weeks of life that were left to the old man; drinking and days spent in bed in his miserable little room under the depression of alcoholism. I could not piece together exactly what happened to him in the Grand Avenue Hotel. But I found in the courthouse at Enid a will which he made. On the face of it, it is an ordinary will. But as I delved into the facts, this piece of paper told of tragedy; a story of a weak, tired, helpless man at the end of his days, too hard pressed by the world.

First, in this will, he gave a seven-hundred-acre tract of land— which he did not possess—to a nephew, Willy George, who was never found.

Next, he bequeathed to "my friend," Isaac Bernstein, the money from a life-insurance policy for three thousand dollars, his watch, trunk and all his wearing apparel. There was no such policy. Isaac Bernstein kept the saloon where George drank; when he made this will George had known him for less than a month.

Next, he bequeathed life insurance amounting to twenty-five hundred dollars "to my friend, George E. Smith, after he shall pay all the expenses of my illness and all funeral expenses." There was no last illness and though David E. George has been dead twenty-two years, there has been, at this writing, no funeral. And there was no life-insurance policy for twenty-five hundred dollars.

He left one hundred dollars to "my friend, S. S. Dumont." Mr. Dumont was the hotel proprietor, to whom the sad, helpless old man was indebted for food and lodging. He left another hundred dollars to "my friend, L. S. Houston," together with the Simmons note for three hundred and fifty dollars. The will does not say who Houston was, but I discovered that he was the lawyer who drew up the will. It is hardly possible that George, who had been in town only a few weeks, even knew him. But an aged man, penniless, must find some way (even if it be by bequest) to pay a lawyer who draws up his will. And then he gave the remainder of his property, though there was none, to the Roman Catholic church of El Reno. He made Lawyer Houston his executor.

He made this will on the last day of the year 1902.

There is a man living, and I have talked with him, who signed this will as a witness. He is Charles S. Evans, one of the leading druggists of the lively Enid of today.

"I remember signing the will," he told me. "I lived at the Grand Avenue Hotel then. I was a drug clerk. I knew the old man and used to talk with him in the hotel lobby. I've always sort of thought he might have been John Wilkes Booth. That forenoon the clerk of the hotel, R. B. Brown, came running in through the back door of the drugstore, which was near the hotel, and told me that Mr. George was dying and that he was making his will; they wanted me to be a witness to it. I hurried over to the hotel. Dumont, the hotel proprietor, Charlie Wood, another drug clerk, and Lawyer Houston were in the room. George was lying in bed, looking very weak, with his eyes closed. There were three witnesses—Brown, Wood and myself. They asked old man George to sign the will, and he opened his eyes and sat up. He took the pen in his hand, and I was surprised to see how strong he was. He put down his signature and then lay back on the bed again and closed his eyes while we put down our names."

These were creditors of the old man—Dumont and Houston and Bernstein the saloonkeeper; and the old man had no money; he was at the end of his rope. In that sad will he promised to pay after he was dead. Did they ask him to make the will? Or did he call them in to make it? There is no way of knowing. But the harried old man got up from his sick bed, after a day or two, and opened the new year of 1903 with more drinking at Bernstein's. He had new credit there now; and he had new credit at the Grand Avenue Hotel. He would pay, if not sooner, at least when he was dead; and the payment he would make after death would be far greater than any debts his hotel keeper or his saloonkeeper would permit him to assume; they had their hands on the old man's affairs; and Lawyer Houston, their friend, was the executor of the will.

Two weeks of drinking and illness, drinking and illness—and then what happened? Did his credit again run low? And did his creditors again press him? An old man who cannot work, who is very proud and cannot beg, must still have his whisky if he has used it through long years; he must have his tobacco and his food and his bed.

Then he played a trick on everybody in Enid. He wrote a note and thrust it into his coat pocket. He went to the drugstore where he knew the clerks and complained about a dog which had howled during the night. They too had heard the dog.

"Give me some poison and I'll kill him," he said.

A clerk gave him the poison, and in the forenoon of January 13, 1903, he took the poison and died. They had heard groans coming from over the partition of his cubicle. The clerk and guests had run to his "room." Dr. Field, who happened to be passing, had been called in. A clerk had climbed over the partition and had opened the door. Dr. Field had rushed in, but it had been too late. The poison bottle stood there, empty.

Dr. Field is an old man now. I found him the other day in Enid, sitting in the room of the leading undertaker, W. H. Ryan. He remembered the incident clearly. So did Mr. Ryan. Mr. Ryan was an undertaker's assistant then, working for W. B. Penniman, the furniture man, at fifty-five dollars a month. Since then he has become wealthy and one of the city's leading businessmen. He has been mayor. Mr. Ryan remembered that he went for the body of the old man who had poisoned himself in the Grand Avenue Hotel and took it to a back room in the furniture store. They have remembered that day and its happenings.

The local newspapers told the story; a well-dressed man had killed himself with poison in the Grand Avenue Hotel; his name was David E. George. Mrs. Ida Harper heard the news.

"While I was fixing up the body," Mr. Ryan told me, "the Reverend Mr. Harper came into the room and looked at the corpse.

"He gave sort of a cry and then he said to me, 'Do you know who that is?' I said, 'Why, his name is George.' 'No, sir, it isn't,' said the Reverend Mr. Harper. 'You are embalming the body of John Wilkes Booth—the man who killed Abraham Lincoln.' And then he told me the story that George had told Mrs. Harper. 'Of course I took special pains with the body after that; I did the best job of embalming I've ever done. If it was Booth's body, I wanted to preserve it for the Washington officials when they came. But they never came,' he added. 'At least, not so far as I ever knew.' "

The newspapers printed Mrs. Harper's story and it reached Finis L. Bates in faraway Memphis—Bates who had known John St. Helen and had been floundering for twenty-five years with his unsolvable puzzle. Bates hurried to Enid. The town was in excitement. There was talk of burning the body if Mrs. Harper's story proved true; a pyre in the town square was suggested. Penniman, the furniture man who was also the undertaker, didn't want trouble. He knew that Bates was coming from Memphis to look at the body and he met the visitor at the train and advised him to keep silent.

"Don't let folks know who you are," he said. "If you identify that body as Booth's and the public hears about it, we'll have trouble."

It was two o'clock in the morning when Finis L. Bates was escorted into the rear room of the furniture store. Twenty-five years had passed since he had seen John St. Helen.

"My old friend! My old friend St. Helen!" Bates said, and then began to weep.

"I was watching his face," Mr. Penniman told me. "I've seen hundreds of identifications in my time and Bates's identification was genuine. He was sure that George was St. Helen."

Mr. Ryan, too, remembers the identification. Mr. Ryan does not believe that David E. George was John Wilkes Booth.

"Bates didn't persuade me that night that it was John Wilkes Booth's body. I never have thought it was. Booth had black eyes, they say. Well, a hundred times in that back room I went to the corpse and raised the lids and looked at those eyes and they were dark blue. I pointed out the blue eyes to my friends. I've always said the eyes were blue; and Booth's eyes were black."

Excitement came thick and fast in Enid that January twenty-one years ago. When Bates's story became public knowledge there was no doubt in the public mind that here was the corpse of John Wilkes Booth. Men, women and children thronged by the thousands to look at the body in the rear of the furniture store. Newspaper reporters *proved* in ingenious ways that the body was Booth's; the editors of both local newspapers said they believed that George was Booth. Newspapers in St. Louis and Kansas City carried stories to this effect, sent to them by the Enid correspondents. All comers were permitted to see the corpse. Any visitor could get his name into the paper by merely saying, "Why, I once saw Booth on the stage, and this man looks like Booth." The Booth they might have seen could not have been more than twenty-five years old; this old man had reached the sixties; but no one doubted such identifications.

"That back room was a queer place," Mr. Ryan told me. "Almost every day some visitor would find something new, and some new story would go out." It was in the midst of this atmosphere of excitement and rumor that Bates was trying to solve his life problem. For more than a quarter of a century he had been puzzling over John St. Helen's story; and now he was sure he had found St. Helen dead. He went about hearing the stories of all those who had known George. He was a lawyer and took depositions; people gave oath to the stories he wanted to put down. It was these depositions that form the backbone of Bates's legend of Enid.

Bates carried into the back room the photograph which he had taken from under the pillow of John St. Helen. A number of people insisted that it was a picture of the dead man, though the dead man was in the sixties and the man of the photograph in the thirties.

There was no funeral, no burial. Penniman the undertaker could not see his way clear to put the body away if it was that of John Wilkes Booth—the government officials might want it. And there was still a standing reward (unpaid by the government, he was told) for the assassin of Lincoln. None of the local officials wanted to take the responsibility of insisting on burial; the government men might come someday and claim the body.

Days, weeks, months passed, and then the years went by. Enid became accustomed to having the mummy on display in the rear room of the furniture store; it was one of the sights of Enid. Townsfolk brought visitors into the store and said, "We'd like to see the body of John Wilkes Booth." "Go right on back," the proprietor or a clerk would say.

No one claimed the body. So Finis L. Bates, with the permission of W. B. Penniman, the undertaker—who had been appointed administrator of the old man's effects and affairs—took the body back to his home in Memphis.

"There was a mystery about the old man, all right," the undertaker, W. B. Penniman, told me in his present home in Columbus, Ohio, a few days before I sat down to write this strange tale. "We handled hundreds of bodies taken from all sorts of places in those days; from haystacks and box cars, from fields and roads and hotel rooms. We never found a body that wasn't identified and claimed in due time and buried at the expense of relatives or friends—except one: that was the body of poor old George."

And there you have the Enid legend of John Wilkes Booth. To prove it or disprove it had been my task.

Two pennies were in the old man's pockets when he died, and that was all, except a note. It was dated the day he died; it knocked into a cocked hat whatever financial hopes may have been entertained by Jack Bernstein, the saloonkeeper, and the men who were in the gruesome gathering at the bedside of the old man that day in his hotel room. It read:

I am informed that I made a will a few days ago and I am indistinct of having done it. I hereby recall every letter, syllable and word of that will that I may have signed at Enid. I owe Jack Bernstein about ten dollars, but he has my watch in pawn for that amount. D. E. George.

What he left belonged to Anna K. Smith, one of the ladies who had been kind to him the time he had tried to settle down peacefully in the little house in El Reno. But what he left was nothing.

No one had claimed the effects of David E. George. Mr. Penniman, the undertaker, had taken charge of the few papers which were found in his room—so an old-time clerk in the office of the probate court at Enid told me. And so I went to the home of Mr. Penniman in Columbus, Ohio. From the basement he brought a musty old grip full of papers.

"I haven't looked at them for years," he told me.

Among them we found a canceled check. That check brought me to the end of *my* trail. There it had lain for years, unseen by Bates and unexamined by any of the leading believers and supporters of the Enid legend. It was in the handwriting of David E. George. It was the check for three hundred and fifty dollars he had made in payment for the little house in El Reno.

Within two days I held that check in my hand in an attic room in the War Department in Washington where are stored the dusty relics, archives and exhibits in the case of John Wilkes Booth. With permission of the War Department and in the presence of two guards, I had access to all the documents in the Booth case. In the other hand I held a little book, covered with red leather and lined with decaying silk—the diary of John Wilkes Booth, found on the body taken from the Garrett corncrib. It is such an important historical document that it is not kept with the rest of the papers but has special protection in a safe. In one of the pockets of the book were the photographs, carried by Booth through his flight, of four exquisitely beautiful women.

Putting the check and the diary side by side, I had my proof. Different hands wrote that check and that diary. One was the hand of a man who wrote laboriously: a man so unaccustomed to check-writing that he spelled out the number of his check, "One," instead of using the numeral, as if this were the first check he had ever made out in all his long life. The other was the hand of John Wilkes Booth. That afternoon in the War Department attic in Washington I ended, to my own satisfaction, the Enid legend. George was not John Wilkes Booth.

No mystery remains in my mind about the end of John Wilkes Booth. The signature on David E. George's check backs up evidence from another source which might perhaps be disputed, but now need not be. There is in the Booth family plot in a cemetery in Baltimore, an unmarked grave. In that grave, four years after the assassination of Abraham Lincoln, was placed a body which had been turned over to Edwin Booth and the Booth family by the government at Washington on the order of President Andrew Johnson. The rough casket bore the name of John Wilkes Booth.

In that casket, according to contemporary accounts, was the body of a man dressed in the uniform of a Confederate soldier. It is said that a member of the Booth family identified it as that of John Wilkes Booth. On one foot, when the casket was opened at the time of the transfer, was found a riding boot. On the other foot was a soldier's heavy brogan. It had been slashed with a knife across the instep to ease a broken foot.

John St. Helen's messenger who, St. Helen said, was killed instead of Booth, would not have been lame as Booth was with a broken bone. John St. Helen's messenger, "Ruddy," who he said had been sent away by Booth to buy a pair of shoes for the fugitive, brought no shoes to the Garrett place. No new shoes were found there, but a crutch was found in the barn—the crutch on which Booth had hobbled away from the home of Dr. Mudd, who had dressed his broken shin.

The evidence against the Enid legend is overwhelming. But what a strange story it is! And into what times and places its trail leads! If John St. Helen and David E. George were one and the same man, what kind of man was he? The very name "John St. Helen," was one that John Wilkes Booth, with his delusions of grandeur, might have chosen. This man told a story which fitted so plausibly into the true and inner account of the movements and experiences of the assassin of Abraham Lincoln that, to this day, it throws into high relief the very elements of the official records which are mysterious and unprovable.

To my mind there is little wonder that Finis L. Bates, with the facts at his disposal, believed in the story of John St. Helen; there is little wonder that there are still those who, being only half-informed, still credit the strange Enid legend of John Wilkes Booth.

A PIECE OF STEAK
By Jack London

. . . .

He had the face of a man to be afraid of in a dark alley,
but he was a professional and fighting was a business with him—
and all he really wanted was a piece of steak.

With the last morsel of bread Tom King wiped his plate clean of the last particle of flour gravy and chewed the resulting mouthful in a slow and meditative way. When he arose from the table, he was oppressed by the feeling that he was distinctly hungry. Yet he alone had eaten. The two children in the other room had been sent early to bed in order that in sleep they might forget they had gone supperless. His wife had touched nothing, and had sat silently and watched him with solicitous eyes. She was a thin, worn woman of the working class, though signs of an earlier prettiness were not wanting in her face. The flour for the gravy she had borrowed from the neighbor across the hall. The last two ha'pennies had gone to buy the bread.

He sat down by the window on a rickety chair that protested under his weight, and quite mechanically he put his pipe in his mouth and dipped into the side pocket of his coat. The absence of any tobacco made him aware of his action, and with a scowl for his forgetfulness he put the pipe away. His movements were slow, almost hulking, as though he were burdened by the heavy weight of his muscles. He was a solid-bodied, stolid-looking man, and his appearance did not suffer from being overprepossessing. His rough clothes were old and slouchy. The uppers of his shoes were too weak to carry the heavy resoling that was itself of no recent date. And his cotton shirt, a cheap, two-shilling affair, showed a frayed collar and ineradicable paint stains.

But it was Tom King's face that advertised him unmistakably for what he was. It was the face of a typical prize fighter; of one who had put in long years of service in the squared ring and, by that means, developed and emphasized all the marks of the fighting beast. It was distinctly a lowering countenance, and, that no feature of it might escape notice, it was clean-shaven. The lips were shapeless and constituted a mouth harsh to excess, that was like a gash in his face. The jaw was aggressive, brutal, heavy. The eyes, slow of movement and heavy-lidded, were almost expressionless under the shaggy, indrawn brows. Sheer animal that he was, the eyes were the most animal-like feature about him. They were sleepy, lionlike—the eyes of a fighting animal. The forehead slanted quickly back to the hair, which, clipped close, showed every bump of a villainous-looking head. A nose, twice broken and molded variously by countless blows, and a cauliflower ear, permanently swollen and distorted to twice its size, completed his adornment, while the beard, fresh-shaven as it was, sprouted in the skin and gave the face a blue-black stain.

Altogether, it was the face of a man to be afraid of in a dark alley or lonely place. And yet Tom King was not a criminal, nor had he ever done anything criminal. Outside of brawls, common to his walk in life, he had harmed no one. Nor had he ever been known to pick a quarrel. He was a professional, and all the fighting brutishness of him was reserved for his professional appearances. Outside the ring he was slow-going, easy-natured and, in his younger days, when money was flush, too openhanded for his own good. He bore no grudges and had few enemies. Fighting was a business with him. In the ring he struck to hurt, struck to maim, struck to destroy; but there was no animus in it. It was a plain business proposition. Audiences assembled and paid for the spectacle of men knocking each other out. The winner took the big end of the purse. When Tom King faced the Woolloomoolloo Gouger, twenty years before, he knew that the Gouger's jaw was only four months healed after having been broken in a Newcastle bout. And he had played for that jaw and broken it again in the ninth round, not because he bore the Gouger any ill will, but because that was the surest way to put the Gouger out and win the big end of the purse. Nor had the Gouger borne him any ill will for it. It was the game, and both knew the game and played it.

Tom King had never been a talker, and he sat by the window, morosely silent, staring at his hands. The veins stood out on the backs of the hands, large and swollen; and the knuckles, smashed and battered and malformed, testified to the use to which they had been put. He had never heard that a man's life was the life of his arteries, but well he knew the meaning of those big, upstanding veins. His heart had pumped too much blood through them at top pressure. They no longer did the work. He had stretched the elasticity out of them, and with their distention had passed his endurance. He tired easily now. No longer could he do a fast twenty rounds, hammer and tongs, fight, fight, fight, from gong to gong, with fierce rally on top of fierce rally, beaten to the ropes and in turn beating his opponent to the ropes, and rallying fiercest and fastest of all in that last, twentieth round, with the house on its feet and yelling, himself rushing, striking, ducking, raining showers of blows upon showers of blows and receiving showers of blows in return, and all the time the heart faithfully pumping the surging blood through the adequate veins. The veins, swollen at the time, had always shrunk down again, though not quite—each time, imperceptibly at first, remaining just a trifle larger than before. He stared at them and at his battered knuckles, and, for the moment, caught a vision of the youthful excellence of those hands before the first knuckle had been smashed on the head of Benny Jones, otherwise known as the Welsh Terror.

The impression of his hunger came back on him.

"Blimey, but couldn't I go a piece of steak!" he muttered aloud, clenching his huge fists and spitting out a smothered oath.

"I tried both Burke's an' Sawley's," his wife said half apologetically.

"An' they wouldn't?" he demanded.

"Not a ha'penny. Burke said—" She faltered.

"G'wan! Wot'd he say?"

"As how 'e was thinkin' Sandel 'ud do ye tonight, an' as how yer score was comfortable big as it was."

Tom King grunted but did not reply. He was busy thinking of the bull terrier he had kept in his younger days to which he had fed steaks without end. Burke would have given him credit for a thousand steaks—then. But times had changed. Tom King was getting old; and old men, fighting before second-rate clubs, couldn't expect to run bills of any size with the tradesmen.

He had got up in the morning with a longing for a piece of steak, and the longing had not abated. He had not had a fair training for this fight. It was a drought year in Australia, times were hard, and even the most irregular work was difficult to find. He had had no sparring partner, and his food had not been of the best nor always sufficient. He had done a few days' navvy work when he could get it, and he had run around the Domain in the early mornings to get his legs in shape. But it was hard, training without a partner and with a wife and two kiddies that must be fed. Credit with the tradesmen had undergone very slight expansion when he was matched with Sandel. The secretary of the Gayety Club had advanced him three pounds—the loser's end of the purse—and beyond that had refused to go. Now and again he had managed to borrow a few shillings from old pals, who would have lent more only that it was a drought year and they were hard put themselves. No—and there was no use in disguising the fact—his training had not been satisfactory. He should have had better food and no worries. Besides, when a man is forty, it is harder to get into condition than when he is twenty.

"What time is it, Lizzie?" he asked.

His wife went across the hall to inquire, and came back.

"Quarter before eight."

"They'll be startin' the first bout in a few minutes," he said. "Only a tryout. Then there's a four-round spar 'tween Dealer Wells an' Gridley, an' a ten-round go 'tween Starlight an' some sailor bloke. I don't come on for over an hour."

At the end of another silent ten minutes he rose to his feet.

"Truth is, Lizzie, I ain't had proper trainin'."

He reached for his hat and started for the door. He did not offer to kiss her—he never did on going out—but on this night she dared to kiss him, throwing her arms around him and compelling him to bend down to her face. She looked quite small against the massive bulk of the man.

"Good luck, Tom," she said. "You gotter do 'im."

"Ay, I gotter do 'im," he repeated. "That's all there is to it. I jus' gotter do 'im."

He laughed with an attempt at heartiness, while she pressed more closely against him. Across her shoulders he looked around the bare room. It was all he had in the world, with the rent overdue, and her and the kiddies. And he was leaving it to go out into the night to get meat for his mate and cubs—not like a modern workingman going to his machine grind, but in the old, primitive, royal, animal way, by fighting for it.

"I gotter do 'im," he repeated, this time a hint of desperation in his voice. "If it's a win, it's thirty quid—an' I can pay all that's owin', with a lump o' money left over. If it's a lose, I get naught—not even a penny for me to ride home on the tram. The secretary's give all that's comin' from a loser's end. Good-bye, old woman. I'll come straight home if it's a win."

"An' I'll be waitin' up," she called to him along the hall. It was full two miles to the Gayety, and as he walked along he remembered how in his palmy days—he had once been the heavyweight champion of New South Wales—he would have ridden in a cab to the fight, and how, most likely, some heavy backer would have paid for the cab and ridden with him. There were Tommy Burns and that Yankee, Jack Johnson—they rode about in motorcars. And he walked! And, as any man knew, a hard two miles was not the best preliminary to a fight. He was an old un, and the world did not wag well with old uns. He was good for nothing now except navvy work, and his broken nose and swollen ear were against him even in that. He found himself wishing that he had learned a trade. It would have been better in the long run. But no one had told him, and he knew, deep down in his heart, that he would not have listened if they had. It had been so easy. Big money—sharp, glorious fights—periods of rest and loafing in between—a following of eager flatterers, the slaps on the back, the shakes of the hand, the toffs glad to buy him a drink for the privilege of five minutes' talk—and the glory of it, the yelling houses, the whirlwind finish, the referee's "King wins!" and his name in the sporting columns next day.

Those had been times! But he realized now, in his slow, ruminating way, that it was the old uns he had been putting away. He was Youth, rising; and they were Age, sinking. No wonder it had been easy—they with their swollen veins and battered knuckles and weary in the bones of them from the long battles they had already fought. He remembered the time he put out old Stowsher Bill, at Rush-Cutters Bay, in the eighteenth round, and how old Bill had cried afterward in the dressing room like a baby. Perhaps old Bill's rent had been overdue. Perhaps he'd had at home a missus an' a couple of kiddies. And perhaps Bill, that very day of the fight, had had a hungering for a piece of steak. Bill had fought game and taken incredible punishment. He could see now, after he had gone through the mill himself, that Stowsher Bill had fought for a bigger stake, that night twenty years ago, than had young Tom King, who had fought for glory and easy money. No wonder Stowsher Bill had cried afterward in the dressing room.

Well, a man had only so many fights in him, to begin with. It was the iron law of the game. One man might have a hundred hard fights in him, another man only twenty; each, according to the make of him and the quality of his fiber, had a definite number, and when he had fought them he was done. Yes, he had had more fights in him than most of them, and he had had far more than his share of the hard, grueling fights—the kind that worked the heart and lungs to bursting, that took the elastic out of the arteries and made hard knots of muscle out of youth's sleek suppleness, that wore out nerve and stamina and made brain and bones weary from excess of effort and endurance overwrought. Yes, he had done better than all of them. There were none of his old fighting partners left. He was the last of the old guard. He had seen them all finished, and he had had a hand in finishing some of them.

They had tried him out against the old uns, and one after another he had put them away—laughing when, like old Stowsher Bill, they cried in the dressing room. And now he was an old un, and they tried out the youngsters on him. There was that bloke Sandel. He had come over from New Zealand with a record behind him. But nobody in Australia knew anything about him, so they put him up against old Tom King. If Sandel made a showing, he would be given better men to fight, with bigger purses to win; so it was to be depended upon that he would put up a fierce battle. He had everything to win by it— money and glory and career; and Tom King was the grizzled old chopping block that guarded the highway to fame and fortune. And he had nothing to win except thirty quid, to pay to the landlord and the tradesmen. And as Tom King thus ruminated, there came to his stolid vision the form of youth, glorious youth, rising exultant and invincible, supple of muscle and silken of skin, with heart and lungs that had never been tired and torn and that laughed at limitation of effort. Yes, youth was the nemesis. It destroyed the old uns and recked not that, in so doing, it destroyed itself. It enlarged its arteries and smashed its knuckles, and was in turn destroyed by youth. For youth was ever youthful. It was only age that grew old.

At Castlereagh Street he turned to the left, and three blocks along came to the Gayety. A crowd of young larrikins hanging outside the door made respectful way for him, and he heard one say to another: "That's 'im! That's Tom King!"

Inside, on the way to his dressing room, he encountered the secretary, a keen-eyed, shrewd-faced young man, who shook his hand.

"How are you feelin', Tom?" he asked.

"Fit as a fiddle," King answered, though he knew that he lied, and that if he had a quid he would give it right there for a good piece of steak.

When he emerged from the dressing room, his seconds behind him, and came down the aisle to the squared ring in the center of the hall, a burst of greeting and applause went up from the waiting crowd. He acknowledged salutations right and left, though few of the faces did he know. Most of them were the faces of kiddies unborn when he was winning his first laurels in the squared ring. He leaped lightly to the raised platform and ducked through the ropes to his corner, where he sat down on a folding stool. Jack Ball, the referee, came over and shook his hand. Ball was a broken-down pugilist who for over ten years had not entered the ring as a principal. King was glad that he had him for referee. They were both old uns. If he should rough it with Sandel a bit beyond the rules, he knew Ball could be depended upon to pass it by.

Aspiring young heavyweights, one after another, were climbing into the ring and being presented to the audience by the referee. Also he issued their challenges for them.

"Young Pronto," Bill announced, "from North Sydney, challenges the winner for fifty pounds side bet."

The audience applauded, and applauded again as Sandel himself sprang through the ropes and sat down in his corner. Tom King looked across the ring at him curiously, for in a few minutes they would be locked together in merciless combat, each trying with all the force of him to knock the other into unconsciousness. But little could he see, for Sandel, like himself, had trousers and sweater on over his ring costume. His face was strongly handsome, crowned with a curly mop of yellow hair, while his thick, muscular neck hinted at bodily magnificence.

Young Pronto went to one corner and then the other, shaking hands with the principals and dropping down out of the ring. The challenges went on. Ever youth climbed through the ropes—youth unknown but insatiable, crying out to mankind that with strength and skill it would match issues with the winner. A few years before, in his own heyday of invincibleness, Tom King would have been amused and bored by these preliminaries. But now he sat fascinated, unable to shake the vision of youth from his eyes. Always were these youngsters rising up in the boxing game, springing through the ropes and shouting their defiance; and always were the old uns going down before them. They climbed to success over the bodies of the old uns. And ever they came, more and more youngsters—youth unquenchable and irresistible—and ever they put the old uns away, themselves becoming old uns and traveling the same downward path, while behind them, ever pressing on them, was youth eternal—the new babies, grown lusty and dragging their elders down, with behind them more babies to the end of time—youth that must have its will and that will never die.

King glanced over to the press box and nodded to Morgan, of the *Sportsman*, and Corbett, of the *Referee*. Then he held out his hands, while Sid Sullivan and Charley Bates, his seconds, slipped on his gloves and laced them tight, closely watched by one of Sandel's seconds, who first examined critically the tapes on King's knuckles. A second of his own was in Sandel's corner, performing a like office. Sandel's trousers were pulled off, and as he stood up his sweater was skinned off over his head. And Tom King, looking, saw youth incarnate, deep-chested, heavy-thewed, with muscles that slipped and slid like live things under the white satin skin. The whole body was acrawl with life, and Tom King knew that it was a life that had never oozed its freshness out through the aching pores during the long fights wherein youth paid its toll and departed not quite so young as when it entered.

The two men advanced to meet each other, and as the gong sounded and the seconds clattered out of the ring with the folding stools, they shook hands and instantly took their fighting attitudes; and instantly, like a mechanism of steel and springs balanced on a hair trigger, Sandel was in and out and in again, landing a left to the eyes, a right to the ribs, ducking a counter, dancing lightly away and dancing menacingly back again. He was swift and clever. It was a dazzling exhibition. The house yelled its approbation. But King was not dazzled. He had fought too many fights and too many youngsters. He knew the blows for what they were—too quick and too deft to be dangerous. Evidently Sandel was going to rush things from the start. It was to be expected. It was the way of youth, expending its splendor and excellence in wild insurgence and furious onslaught, overwhelming opposition with its own unlimited glory of strength and desire.

Sandel was in and out, here, there and everywhere, light-footed and eager hearted, a living wonder of white flesh and stinging muscle that wove itself into a dazzling fabric of attack, slipping and leaping like a flying shuttle from action to action through a thousand actions, all of them centered upon the destruction of Tom King, who stood between him and fortune. And Tom King patiently endured. He knew his business, and he knew youth now that youth was no longer his. There was nothing to do till the other lost some of his steam, was his thought, and he grinned to himself as he deliberately ducked so as to receive a heavy blow on the top of his head. It was a wicked thing to do, yet eminently fair according to the rules of the boxing game. A man was supposed to take care of his own knuckles, and if he insisted on hitting an opponent on the top of the head he did so at his own peril. King could have ducked lower and let the blow whiz harmlessly past, but he remembered his own early fights and how he smashed his first knuckle on the head of the Welsh Terror. He was but playing the game. That duck had accounted for one of Sandel's knuckles. Not that Sandel would mind it now. He would go on, superbly regardless, hitting as hard as ever throughout the fight. But later on, when the long ring battles had begun to tell, he would regret that knuckle and look back and remember how he smashed it on Tom King's head.

The first round was all Sandel's and he had the house yelling with the rapidity of his whirlwind rushes. He overwhelmed King with avalanches of punches, and King did nothing. He never struck once, contenting himself with covering up, blocking and ducking and clinching to avoid punishment. He occasionally feinted, shook his head when the weight of a punch landed, and moved stolidly about, never leaping or springing or wasting an ounce of strength. Sandel must foam the froth of youth away before discreet age could dare to retaliate. All King's movements were slow and methodical, and his heavy-lidded, slow-moving eyes gave him the appearance of being half asleep or dazed. Yet they were eyes that saw everything, that had been trained to see everything through all his twenty years and odd in the ring. They were eyes that did not blink or waver before an impending blow, but that coolly saw and measured distance.

Seated in his corner for the minute's rest at the end of the round, he lay back with outstretched legs, his arms resting on the right angle of the ropes, his chest and abdomen heaving frankly and deeply as he gulped down the air driven by the towels of his seconds. He listened with closed eyes to the voices of the house. "Why don't yeh fight, Tom?" many were crying. "Yeh ain't afraid of 'im, are yeh?"

"Muscle-bound," he heard a man on a front seat comment. "He can't move quicker. Two to one on Sandel, in quids."

The gong struck and the two men advanced from their corners. Sandel came forward fully three quarters of the distance, eager to begin again; but King was content to advance the shorter distance. It was in line with his policy of economy. He had not been well trained, and he had not had enough to eat, and every step counted. Besides, he had already walked two miles to the ringside. It was a repetition of the first round, with Sandel attacking like a whirlwind and with the audience indignantly demanding why King did not fight. Beyond feinting and several slowly delivered and ineffectual blows he did nothing save block and stall and clinch. Sandel wanted to make the pace fast, while King, out of his wisdom, refused to accommodate him. He grinned with a certain wistful pathos in his ring-battered countenance, and went on cherishing his strength with the jealousy of which only age is capable. Sandel was youth, and he threw his strength away with the munificent abandon of youth. To King belonged the ring generalship, the wisdom bred of long, aching fights. He watched with cool eyes and head, moving slowly and waiting for Sandel's froth to foam away. To the majority of the onlookers it seemed as though King was hopelessly outclassed, and they voiced their opinions in offers of three to one on Sandel. But there were wise ones, a few, who knew King of old time, and who covered what they considered easy money.

The third round began as usual, one-sided, with Sandel doing all the leading and delivering all the punishment. A half minute had passed when Sandel, overconfident, left an opening. King's eyes and right arm flashed in the same instant. It was his first real blow—a hook, with the twisted arch of the arm to make it rigid, and with all the weight of the half-pivoted body behind it. It was like a sleepy-seeming lion suddenly thrusting out a lightning paw. Sandel, caught on the side of the jaw, was felled like a bullock. The audience gasped and murmured awestricken applause. The man was not muscle-bound, after all, and he could drive a blow like a trip hammer.

Sandel was shaken. He rolled over and attempted to rise, but the sharp yells from his seconds to take the count restrained him. He knelt on one knee, ready to rise, and waited, while the referee stood over him, counting the seconds loudly in his ear. At the ninth he rose in fighting attitude, and Tom King, facing him, knew regret that the blow had not been an inch nearer the point of the jaw. That would have been a knockout, and he could have carried the thirty quid home to the missus and the kiddies.

The round continued to the end of its three minutes, Sandel for the first time respectful of his opponent and King slow of movement and sleepy-eyed as ever. As the round neared its close, King, warned of the fact by sight of the seconds crouching outside ready for the spring in through the ropes, worked the fight around to his own corner. And when the gong struck, he sat down immediately on the waiting stool, while Sandel had to walk all the way across the diagonal of the square to his own corner. It was a little thing, but it was the sum of little things that counted. Sandel was compelled to walk that many more steps, to give up that much energy, and to lose a part of the precious minute of rest. At the beginning of every round King loafed slowly out from his corner, forcing his opponent to advance the greater distance. The end of every round found the fight maneuvered by King into his own corner so that he could immediately sit down.

Two more rounds went by, in which King was parsimonious of effort and Sandel prodigal. The latter's attempt to force a fast pace made King uncomfortable, for a fair percentage of the multitudinous blows showered upon him went home. Yet King persisted in his dogged slowness, despite the crying of the young hotheads for him to go in and fight. Again, in the sixth round, Sandel was careless, again Tom King's fearful right flashed out to the jaw, and again Sandel took the nine seconds' count.

By the seventh round Sandel's pink of condition was gone, and he settled down to what he knew was to be the hardest fight in his experience. Tom King was an old un, but a better old un than he had ever encountered—an old un who never lost his head, who was remarkably able at defense, whose blows had the impact of a knotted club and who had a knockout in either hand. Nevertheless, Tom King dared not hit often. He never forgot his battered knuckles, and knew that every hit must count if the knuckles were to last out the fight. As he sat in his corner, glancing across at his opponent, the thought came to him that the sum of his wisdom and Sandel's youth would constitute a world's champion heavyweight. But that was the trouble. Sandel would never become a world champion. He lacked the wisdom, and the only way for him to get it was to buy it with youth; and when wisdom was his, youth would have been spent in buying it.

King took every advantage he knew. He never missed an opportunity to clinch, and in effecting most of the clinches his shoulder drove stiffly into the other's ribs. In the philosophy of the ring a shoulder was as good as a punch so far as damage was concerned, and a great deal better so far as concerned expenditure of effort. Also in the clinches King rested his weight on his opponent, and was loath to let go. This compelled the interference of the referee, who tore them apart, always assisted by Sandel, who had not yet learned to rest. He could not refrain from using those glorious flying arms and writhing muscles of his, and when the other rushed into a clinch, striking shoulder against ribs, and with head resting under Sandel's left arm, Sandel almost invariably swung his right behind his own back and into the projecting face. It was a clever stroke, much admired by the audience, but it was not dangerous, and was, therefore, just that much wasted strength. But Sandel was tireless and unaware of limitations, and King grinned and doggedly endured.

Sandel developed a fierce right to the body, which made it appear that King was taking an enormous amount of punishment, and it was only the old ringsters who appreciated the deft touch of King's left glove to the other's biceps just before the impact of the blow. It was true, the blow landed each time; but each time it was robbed of its power by that touch on the biceps. In the ninth round, three times inside a minute, King's right hooked its twisted arch to the jaw; and three times Sandel's body, heavy as it was, was leveled to the mat. Each time he took the nine seconds allowed him and rose to his feet, shaken and jarred, but still strong. He had lost much of his speed, and he wasted less effort. He was fighting grimly; but he continued to draw upon his chief asset, which was youth. King's chief asset was experience. As his vitality had dimmed and his vigor abated, he had replaced them with cunning, with wisdom born of the long fights and with a careful shepherding of strength. Not alone had he learned never to make a superfluous movement, but he had learned how to seduce an opponent into throwing his strength away. Again and again, by feint of foot and hand and body, he continued to inveigle Sandel into leaping back, ducking or countering. King rested, but he never permitted Sandel to rest. It was the strategy of age.

Early in the tenth round King began stopping the other's rushes with straight lefts to the face, and Sandel, grown wary, responded by drawing the left, then by ducking it and delivering his right in a swinging hook to the side of the head. It was too high up to be vitally effective; but when first it landed King knew the old, familiar descent of the black veil of unconsciousness across his mind. For the instant, or for the slightest fraction of an instant, rather, he ceased. In the one moment he saw his opponent ducking out of his field of vision and the background of white, watching faces; in the next moment he again saw his opponent and the background of faces. It was as if he had slept for a time and just opened his eyes again, and yet the interval of unconsciousness was so microscopically short that there had been no time for him to fall. The audience saw him totter and his knees give, and then saw him recover and tuck his chin deeper into the shelter of his left shoulder.

Several times Sandel repeated the blow, keeping King partially dazed, and then the latter worked out of his defense, which was also a counter. Feinting with his left, he took a half step backward, at the same time uppercutting with the whole strength of his right. So accurately was it timed that it landed squarely on Sandel's face in the full, downward sweep of the duck, and Sandel lifted in the air and curled backward, striking the mat on his head and shoulders. Twice King achieved this, then turned loose and hammered his opponent to the ropes. He gave Sandel no chance to rest or to set himself, but smashed blow in upon blow till the house rose to its feet and the air was filled with an unbroken roar of applause. But Sandel's strength and endurance were superb, and he continued to stay on his feet. A knockout seemed certain, and a captain of police, appalled at the dreadful punishment, arose by the ringside to stop the fight. The gong struck for the end of the round and Sandel staggered to his corner, protesting to the captain that he was sound and strong. To prove it, he threw two back air springs, and the police captain gave in.

Tom King, leaning back in his corner and breathing hard, was disappointed. If the fight had been stopped, the referee, perforce, would have rendered him the decision and the purse would have been his. Unlike Sandel, he was not fighting for glory or career, but for thirty quid. And now Sandel would recuperate in the minute of rest.

Youth will be served—this saying flashed into King's mind, and he remembered the first time he had heard it, the night when he had put away Stowsher Bill. The toff who had bought him a drink after the fight and patted him on the shoulder had used those words. Youth will be served! The toff was right. And on that night in the long ago he had been youth. Tonight youth sat in the opposite corner. As for himself, he had been fighting for half an hour now, and he was an old man. Had he fought like Sandel, he would not have lasted fifteen minutes. But the point was that he did not recuperate. Those up-standing arteries and that sorely tried heart would not enable him to gather strength in the intervals between the rounds. And he had not had sufficient strength in him to begin with. His legs were heavy under him and beginning to cramp. He should not have walked those two miles to the fight. And there was the steak which he had got up longing for that morning. A great and terrible hatred rose up in him for the butchers who had refused him credit. It was hard for an old man to go into a fight without enough to eat. And a piece of steak was such a little thing, a few pennies at best; yet it meant thirty quid to him.

With the gong that opened the eleventh round Sandel rushed, mak-ing a show of freshness which he did not really possess. King knew it for what it was—a bluff as old as the game itself. He clinched to save himself, then, going free, allowed Sandel to get set. This was what King desired. He feinted with his left, drew the answering duck and swinging upward hook, then made the half step backward, delivered the uppercut full to the face and crumpled Sandel over to the mat. After that he never let him rest, receiving punishment himself, but inflicting far more, smashing Sandel to the ropes, hooking and driv-ing all manner of blows into him, tearing away from his clinches or punching him out of attempted clinches, and even when Sandel would have fallen, catching him with one uplifting hand and with the other immediately smashing him into the ropes where he could not fall.

The house by this time had gone mad, and it was his house, nearly every voice yelling: "Go it, Tom!" "Get 'im! Get 'im!" "You've got 'im, Tom! You've got 'im!" It was to be a whirlwind finish, and that was what a ringside audience paid to see.

And Tom King, who for half an hour had conserved his strength, now expended it prodigally in the one great effort he knew he had in him. It was his one chance—now or not at all. His strength was waning fast, and his hope was that before the last of it ebbed out of him he would have beaten his opponent down for the count. And as he continued to strike and force, coolly estimating the weight of his blows and the quality of the damage wrought, he realized how hard a man Sandel was to knock out. Stamina and endurance were his to an extreme degree, and they were the virgin stamina and endurance of youth. Sandel was certainly a coming man. He had it in him. Only out of such rugged fiber were successful fighters fashioned.

Sandel was reeling and staggering, but Tom King's legs were cramping and his knuckles going back on him. Yet he steeled himself to strike the fierce blows, every one of which brought anguish to his tortured hands. Though now he was receiving practically no punishment, he was weakening as rapidly as the other. His blows went home, but there was no longer the weight behind them, and each blow was the result of a severe effort of will. His legs were like lead, and they dragged visibly under him; while Sandel's backers, cheered by this symptom, began calling encouragement to their man.

King was spurred to a burst of effort. He delivered two blows in succession—a left, a trifle too high, to the solar plexus, and a right cross to the jaw. They were not heavy blows, yet so weak and dazed was Sandel that he went down and lay quivering. The referee stood over him, shouting the count of the fatal seconds in his ear. If before the tenth second was called he did not rise, the fight was lost. The house stood in hushed silence. King rested on trembling legs. A mortal dizziness was upon him, and before his eyes the sea of faces sagged and swayed, while to his ears, as from a remote distance, came the count of the referee. Yet he looked upon the fight as his. It was impossible that a man so punished could rise.

Only youth could rise, and Sandel rose. At the fourth second he rolled over on his face and groped blindly for the ropes. By the seventh second he had dragged himself to his knee, where he rested, his head rolling groggily on his shoulders. As the referee cried "Nine!" Sandel stood upright, in proper stalling position, his left arm wrapped about his face, his right wrapped about his stomach. Thus were his vital points guarded, while he lurched forward toward King in the hope of effecting a clinch and gaining more time.

At the instant Sandel arose, King was at him, but the two blows he delivered were muffled on the stalled arms. The next moment Sandel was in the clinch and holding on desperately while the referee strove to drag the two men apart. King helped to force himself free. He knew the rapidity with which youth recovered, and he knew that Sandel was his if he could prevent that recovery. One stiff punch would do it. Sandel was his, indubitably his. He had outgeneraled him, outfought him, outpointed him. Sandel reeled out of the clinch, balanced on the hair line between defeat or survival. One good blow would topple him over and down and out. And Tom King, in a flash of bitterness, remembered the piece of steak and wished that he had it then behind that necessary punch he must deliver. He nerved himself for the blow, but it was not heavy enough nor swift enough. Sandel swayed but did not fall, staggering back to the ropes and holding on. King staggered after him, and, with a pang like that of dissolution, delivered another blow. But his body had deserted him. All that was left of him was a fighting intelligence that was dimmed and clouded from exhaustion. The blow that was aimed for the jaw struck no higher than the shoulder. He had willed the blow higher, but the tired muscles had not been able to obey. And, from the impact of the blow, Tom King himself reeled back and nearly fell. Once again he strove. This time his punch missed altogether, and from absolute weakness he fell against Sandel and clinched, holding on to him to save himself from sinking to the floor.

King did not attempt to free himself. He had shot his bolt. He was gone. And youth had been served. Even in the clinch he could feel Sandel growing stronger against him. When the referee thrust them apart, there, before his eyes, he saw youth recuperate. From instant to instant Sandel grew stronger. His punches, weak and futile, at first, became stiff and accurate. Tom King's bleared eyes saw the gloved fist driving at his jaw, and he willed to guard it by interposing his arm. He saw the danger, willed the act; but the arm was too heavy. It seemed burdened with a hundredweight of lead. It would not lift itself, and he strove to lift it with his soul. Then the gloved fist landed home. He experienced a sharp snap that was like an electric spark, and simultaneously the veil of blackness enveloped him.

When he opened his eyes again he was in his corner, and he heard the yelling of the audience like the roar of the surf at Bondi Beach. A wet sponge was being pressed against the base of his brain, and Sid Sullivan was blowing cold water in a refreshing spray over his face and chest. His gloves had already been removed, and Sandel, bending over him, was shaking his hand. He bore no ill will toward the man who had put him out, and he returned the grip with a heartiness that made his battered knuckles protest. Then Sandel stepped to the center of the ring and the audience hushed its pandemonium to hear him accept young Pronto's challenge and offer to increase the side bet to one hundred pounds. King looked on apathetically while his seconds mopped the streaming water from him, dried his face and prepared him to leave the ring. He felt hungry. It was not the ordinary, gnawing kind, but a great faintness, a palpitation at the pit of the stomach that communicated itself to all his body. He remembered back into the fight to the moment when he had Sandel swaying and tottering on the hairline balance of defeat. Ah, that piece of steak would have done it! He had lacked just that for the decisive blow, and he had lost. It was all because of the piece of steak.

His seconds were half supporting him as they helped him through the ropes. He tore free from them, ducked through the ropes unaided and leaped heavily to the floor, following on their heels as they forced a passage for him down the crowded center aisle. Leaving the dressing room for the street, in the entrance to the hall, some young fellow spoke to him.

"W'y didn't yuh go in an' get 'im when yuh 'ad 'im!" the young fellow asked.

"Aw, go to hell!" said Tom King, and passed down the steps to the sidewalk.

The doors of the public house at the corner were swinging wide, and he saw the lights and the smiling barmaids, heard the many voices discussing the fight and the prosperous chink of money on the bar. Somebody called to him to have a drink. He hesitated perceptibly, then refused and went on his way.

He had not a copper in his pocket, and the two-mile walk home seemed very long. He was certainly getting old. Crossing the Domain he sat down suddenly on a bench, unnerved by the thought of the missus sitting up for him, waiting to learn the outcome of the fight. That was harder than any knockout, and it seemed almost impossible to face.

He felt weak and sore, and the pain of his smashed knuckles warned him that, even if he could find a job at navvy work, it would be a week before he could grip a pick handle or a shovel. The hunger palpitation at the pit of the stomach was sickening. His wretchedness overwhelmed him, and into his eyes came an unwonted moisture. He covered his face with his hands, and, as he cried, he remembered Stowsher Bill and how he had served him that night in the long ago. Poor old Stowsher Bill! He could understand now why Bill had cried in the dressing room.

THE GAME OF MURDER
By Gerd Gaiser

. . . .

*Sometimes Murder is just a game, and sometimes
one never wants to play that game again.*

Presumably you all know the game, which may well acquire a ticklish, somewhat dubious character when adults take it up. Pieces of paper are thrown together, each person draws one, sees what is on it for him and puts it away. Somebody will have picked the murderer's part, somebody else the detective's, all the other pieces of paper are empty, anyone can be the victim. Nobody may know who the murderer is, he must conceal his identity; the party decides whether the detective is to remain unknown as well. Now the company can follow their inclination, disperse throughout the house right up to the attics and even include the cellars; they can pretend that they are on board ship and declare a terrace to be a deck where people can promenade, or they can scatter among the garden shrubs. Night, perhaps an artificial night, helps the game along, some darkness at least is required. He who wishes to can make himself safe by looking for a hiding place, while someone else will mingle with the others: but in doing so he may easily come up against his murderer. Nobody knows when the attack will take place or who will be set upon. While it is happening a game of cards may be started, or some hurried caresses may be exchanged. In the meantime death walks through the library; in the shape of a lady, whispering, it suddenly raises its arm from a cloud of tulle. In normal circumstances it is agreed to banish evil; but now for an hour it has the right to steal through the door, and there is a sense of horror as when children play at hanging. Breathless and twisted; nobody knows whether the victim will slump down quietly, or whether he will emit a murmur, a scream or a shout as he plays the game out, nobody knows himself what sounds will accompany his sudden exit, the ear has to be prepared for anything. Not until the wicked deed has happened may noise break out, a disturbance that is both artificial and real, and then the detective hunts for the criminal.

I played the game for the last time—for I would rather not play it again, I have lost all taste for the game—for the last time, then, in Valea Calugareasca, that luxurious and desirable area where the rich people from the city had their country houses. It was one of those long-drawn-out parties where people who are wearied with distractions keep on inventing new excuses for refusing to let the party break up; a good many unusual people, and many ordinary ones too, with three or four different languages flowing in and through one another like the disks in a kaleidoscope, and three kinds of uniform as well as civilian pin stripe, and plenty of tulle and silk, and the whole affair not a little forced. For it was wartime, and the war was past its prime; in all the splendor the worm was already gnawing and the fuse to the gunpowder was set.

Everybody had been drinking. Nobody had had too much, but they had all drunk a lot of the heavy, narcotic wine which was made on the estates nearby and which had the color of moonlight. The pieces of paper had been drawn, and now somebody was twisting at the fuses so that the lights went out all at once. Then we saw that day was waiting outside, but as yet it remained beneath the threshold.

I say that I had been drinking like everyone else, not excessively, but so much that any idea could distract me and my mind had its own adventures; I let myself drift, without concentrating on the game as I should have done. I forgot to mention that my paper had picked me as the detective, but it was all the same to me, I wasn't going to make hard work of it; in any case, when the disaster came, I intended to be in the mood for jokes. I watched people who were on their own, I kept on the track of couples, I paid attention to people's movements, for these had so much reality when everything was so artificial.

As in boyar houses, a gallery extended on all four sides around the top story beneath the roof; it was open and cool there, there was a draft. The wind moved keenly before dawn, and the foothills of the Carpathians stood with etched outlines beneath the sky.

As I stepped out, a female figure disappeared in front of me like a shadow. The victim hiding herself, I thought. She takes you for her murderer. I went after her. She fled. I followed her round three sides of the house, saw her head more clearly, the forehead and knot of hair, her thin neck, a scarf fluttering against the semi-brightness, then she had slipped away. I stepped after her, then I stood still by the upper balustrade, looked a few times behind me for reasons of safety. Being the detective, I didn't want to be killed myself. Then I forgot myself again and looked down into the expanse of hall through which pale light was creeping; there people were moving by restlessly in twos and threes amid subdued sounds. Once or twice I caught sight of the person with the scarf again as she made her way upright and yet softly moving. Then I caught my foot on something solid, and what was solid at once gave way.

I had been going to walk down the steps, but now I at once bent down, made a grasp and felt with my hand that somebody was lying stretched out on his face. I sounded the alarm on the spot, for I remembered that we were in the midst of a game and my own part in the game came back to me; I sounded the alarm then, and called for help in the way that could be expected of me. Light; people rushed together from above and below. A little group gathered on the steps; high-pitched voices; they pressed forward and resisted, leaned on each other's shoulders. Those in front bent down, pulled the victim's nose, tickled him or blew into his ear in order to try his powers of dissimulation, they tried to lift him up, they shook him amid terrifying jests. He was a heavy person. I had seen him that evening for the first time, but I well remembered his movements, his shortness of breath, his little feet that pointed outward; a prosperous man in a short gray sack suit made to fit him loosely by an expensive tailor. Now who would have expected him to act the dead man? He did it well, this funny man, a devil of a fellow, not moving a muscle; everybody enjoyed it, they were grateful to him for making such good fun out of it and holding out for such a long time, until suddenly several people called in a strange tone: "Stop! No, do stop it!" Then all at once you could hear everybody breathing, it would have been like being under water if you had not heard the many drawings of breath. Only those at the back still pressed against those in front, and you could still hear isolated queries like, "What is it?" or "What did he mean?"

What sort of reply is to be given here? Many a one, whose turn happens to have come, must die between three and four o'clock in the morning. Strangely enough, outside the sun was obviously rising, the half-light was disappearing, drained from all the faces, and the faces didn't look well. They were ashamed perhaps; we were ashamed perhaps, I should have said. And meanwhile the Rumanian staff doctor who had been making an examination stood up from the dead man and pushed down his shirt sleeves; he looked from one to another and presumably wanted to say something, only he could not find the right words. Then someone let out a scream of empty, bewildered terror that a woman would let out, and then there was something else in the dying fall of this scream, something uninterpretable, that is if a scream can be interpreted. I saw too that the scream came from the person I had encountered on the gallery. I had heard of her. She was a pianist who came and went in the house. There was something else I had heard about her: she had had an Armenian mother, the family had come to grief, the father was said to have been rich, until some political episode finished him. There she stood now, the woman with the knot of hair, her hand pressed against her mouth, her knuckles between her teeth, her fist stifling the scream.

"Ladies and gentlemen," the Rumanian doctor said. "We have been playing a game. The game has punished us, and so nobody should know what the parts were any more. As if it had never taken place. All of you come with me to the fire; each is to burn his piece of paper there without anyone else seeing it."

Everybody did so, in silence too, including myself. I joined in, although it did not concern me so closely, and also I did not understand what the Rumanian was trying to say, but then he came from another country, and perhaps they saw everything differently there, or better. That was how the party ended. The cars dispersed quickly, going in different directions, this way and that. When we came to the suburbs, the streets were still quiet, and the first trams were screeching along. The pianist had come to sit by me and up to now had been wholly silent, but all at once she said without pausing, as if she were talking to herself and were out of her mind: "I did it, I did it."

And then she went on: "I did it, and that's why it had to be me. I did the murder."

As you can imagine, I did not answer, for her words did not seem meant for me, or to need any answer. But then she turned toward me, and her eyes terrified me in my state of weariness, and the thought went through my head: But why, why does she tell me?

"Murder?" I said, terrified and sleepy. We talked in low voices, and I looked toward the front in case they could hear us there, but they were singing and calling to one another to prevent themselves dozing off and to make sure the driver stayed awake, and I believe they were pushing one another and had begun to tell jokes. Nobody bothered about us.

"Murder?" I said, then: "You mean the accident, madam. That was an accident, nothing more. Nobody is responsible for it."

"You are wrong. We called, then it happened that way. Everybody had a part."

When I heard this, I thought: Oh, yes, she too belongs to the other country.

I replied: "Maybe, but remember, the roles have all been wiped out."

Then she held up her hand. The piece of paper which she had drawn and then kept lay in her hand. The word MURDERER stood on it in large, rather clumsy letters.

"You see," she said.

I thought again: Why ever does she talk like this to me? and then said aloud: "A tactless coincidence. You shouldn't pay any attention to it." And then I was shocked by the gesture with which she answered me.

She said: "Not pay any attention to it? Oh! There speaks a man who cannot weep."

"A death has a right to be mourned," I said. "But apart from that I can't possibly take a coincidence like that seriously."

"Coincidence? Seriously? Hate is not a matter of chance. Hate is serious. Did you perhaps hate the man who was suddenly lying there?"

"He did not seem particularly pleasant to me. To be precise, I was indifferent about him."

"Oh, yes. And that was why you had a blank paper."

"But I didn't have a blank paper," I almost replied, until it suddenly occurred to me that I should not let her know what my role had been. I should not tell her yet that I was the detective, for she was talking as in a dream, and she was capable of giving a start and falling over the edge if someone called to her, and I thought quickly again: "Of course, that is why she must talk with me; after all, I am the detective," and "The game is punishing us, these people know." But I did not say a single word aloud.

Then she added: "As for me, I hated. I hated this man so much that I began to sob with laughter as he lay there. Then I was aware that it was me."

I turned my head. A few moments earlier I should still have thought we could not understand each other. Now I began to understand; I understood something that we here, ladies and gentlemen, have scarcely any inkling of, but I couldn't talk about it. I didn't say any more. She could forget that she had been talking, and that she had talked to me; perhaps it was preferable for her, if we ever met again and she had to believe that she had spoken to somebody who did not understand anything about it. Soon she spoke again in a different tone of voice: "Please stop now. Let me get out. We're there."

I was surprised to think that we were there, for I thought I recalled where she lived, and this was not the district. It was indeed no sort of district to live in. Here there were only poor nameless people, low, higgledy-piggledy roofs and a church standing against the light and casting a shadow.

"Can't I go with you?" I asked, and held the door.

"Certainly not. Go on, go on quickly."

"But you've got a long way home."

We looked at one another, shivering, although the sun was now beginning to be warm, but we were weary and, like everyone else, had been drinking. We had never met before, and now I had to remember what she had said. Who wanted something from us?

"Home?" she whispered, exhausted. "Not there, where I meet myself."

I could think of nothing to say. In front the others turned round and waited.

"Do go on, please," she said once more. "Go quickly."

I watched her walk away across the wretched pavement on her high-heeled shoes, unlovely and alone. The car went on, and it was not until we were a street farther on that it occurred to me to ask what she had meant with her "We're there." Now I got out as well, stood still until the car had disappeared and then walked back. The sun was still not high in the sky, and between the miserable houses the church cast its cool shadow over the square where a dog was stretching and shivering. I waited at the porch until somebody from inside should come out and I could take the door latch from his hand in order to slip in unseen. Then I saw her: she was lying on the ground. We don't do that in our country. She was lying on the ground looking toward the golden wall veiling the secret, and she was praying.

ON THE KILLING OF
ERATOSTHENES THE SEDUCER

By Kathleen Freeman

. . . .

*Dr. Freeman was a Greek scholar, and, under a pseudonym,
a mystery writer. She knew that in 400 B.C. adultery was
very seriously regarded in Athens.*

Speech written for the defendant, by Lysias. Exact date unknown:
some time between 400 and 380 B.C.

The defendant's name is Euphiletus. The dead man's name is
Eratosthenes. Eratosthenes had seduced the wife of Euphiletus, and
Euphiletus had finally caught them together. Euphiletus had availed
himself of his legal right to kill the adulterer; his act was justifiable
homicide, and not punishable unless it could be proved that he had
some other motive for the slaughter. However, the relatives of the
dead man brought the killer to trial on the ground that the whole
situation leading to the slaughter had been planned by Euphiletus;
they therefore charged him with murder. Euphiletus denied the
charge and affirmed that his sole motive was to exact vengeance on
the adulterer, as was allowed by law.

The case came before a court sitting at the Delphinion. The
penalty was death, or if the accused felt that the case was going
against him, he could leave after the first day: he would then suffer
exile and confiscation of his property. After the prosecution have
stated their case, Euphiletus speaks:

THE PROEM

I would give a great deal, members of the jury, to find you, as
judges of this case, taking the same attitude toward me as you would

adopt toward your own behavior in similar circumstances. I am sure that if you felt about others in the same way as you did about yourselves, not one of you would fail to be angered by these deeds, and all of you would consider the punishment a small one for those guilty of such conduct.

Moreover, the same opinion would be found prevailing not only among you, but everywhere throughout Greece. This is the one crime for which, under any government, democratic or exclusive, equal satisfaction is granted to the meanest against the mightiest, so that the least of them receives the same justice as the most exalted. Such is the detestation, members of the jury, in which this outrage is held by all mankind.

Concerning the severity of the penalty, therefore, you are, I imagine, all of the same opinion: not one of you is so easygoing as to believe that those guilty of such great offenses should obtain pardon, or are deserving of a light penalty. What I have to prove, I take it, is just this: that Eratosthenes seduced my wife, and that in corrupting her he brought shame upon my children and outrage upon me, by entering my home; that there was no other enmity between him and me except this and that I did not commit this act for the sake of money, in order to rise from poverty to wealth, nor for any other advantage except the satisfaction allowed by law.

I shall expound my case to you in full from the beginning, omitting nothing and telling the truth. In this alone lies my salvation, I imagine—if I can explain to you everything that happened.

THE NARRATIVE

Members of the jury: when I decided to marry and had brought a wife home, at first my attitude toward her was this: I did not wish to annoy her, but neither was she to have too much of her own way. I watched her as well as I could, and kept an eye on her as was proper. But later, after my child had been born, I came to trust her, and I handed all my possessions over to her, believing that this was the greatest possible proof of affection.

Well, members of the jury, in the beginning she was the best of women. She was a clever housewife, economical and exact in her management of everything. But then my mother died; and her death has proved to be the source of all my troubles, because it was when my wife went to the funeral that this man Eratosthenes saw her; and as time went on, he was able to seduce her. He kept a lookout for our maid who goes to market; and approaching her with his suggestions, he succeeded in corrupting her mistress.

Now first of all, gentlemen, I must explain that I have a small house which is divided into two—the men's quarters and the women's —each having the same space, the women's upstairs and the men's downstairs.

After the birth of my child, his mother nursed him; but I did not want her to run the risk of going downstairs every time she had to give him a bath, so I myself took over the upper story, and let the women have the ground floor. And so it came about that by this time it was quite customary for my wife often to go downstairs and sleep with the child, so that she could give him the breast and stop him from crying.

This went on for a long while, and I had not the slightest suspicion. On the contrary, I was in such a fool's paradise that I believed my wife to be the chastest woman in all the city.

Time passed, gentlemen. One day, when I had come home unexpectedly from the country, after dinner, the child began crying and complaining. Actually it was the maid who was pinching him on purpose to make him behave so, because—as I found out later—this man was in the house.

Well, I told my wife to go and feed the child, to stop his crying. But at first she refused, pretending that she was so glad to see me back after my long absence. At last I began to get annoyed, and I insisted on her going.

"Oh, yes!" she said. "To leave *you* alone with the maid up here! You mauled her about before, when you were drunk!"

I laughed. She got up, went out, closed the door—pretending that it was a joke—and locked it. As for me, I thought no harm of all this, and I had not the slightest suspicion. I went to sleep, glad to do so after my journey from the country.

Toward morning, she returned and unlocked the door.

I asked her why the doors had been creaking during the night. She explained that the lamp beside the baby had gone out, and that she had then gone to get a light from the neighbors.

I said no more. I thought it really was so. But it did seem to me, members of the jury, that she had done up her face with cosmetics, in spite of the fact that her brother had died only a month before. Still, even so, I said nothing about it. I just went off, without a word.

After this, members of the jury, an interval elapsed, during which my injuries had progressed, leaving me far behind. Then, one day, I was approached by an old hag. She had been sent by a woman—Eratosthenes' previous mistress, as I found out later. This woman, furious because he no longer came to see her as before, had been on the lookout until she had discovered the reason. The old crone, therefore, had come and was lying in wait for me near my house.

"Euphiletus," she said, "please don't think that my approaching you is in any way due to a wish to interfere. The fact is, the man who is wronging your wife is an enemy of ours. Now if you catch the woman who does your shopping and works for you, and put her through an examination, you will discover all. The culprit," she added, "is Eratosthenes from Oea. Your wife is not the only one he has seduced—there are plenty of others. It's his profession."

With these words, members of the jury, she went off.

At once I was overwhelmed. Everything rushed into my mind, and I was filled with suspicion. I reflected how I had been locked into the bedroom. I remembered how on that night the middle and outer doors had creaked, a thing that had never happened before; and how I had had the idea that my wife's face was rouged. All these things rushed into my mind, and I was filled with suspicion.

I went back home, and told the servant to come with me to market. I took her instead to the house of one of my friends; and there I informed her that I had discovered all that was going on in my house.

"As for you," I said, "two courses are open to you: either to be flogged and sent to the treadmill, and never be released from a life of utter misery; or to confess the whole truth and suffer no punishment, but win pardon from me for your wrongdoing. Tell me no lies. Speak the whole truth."

At first she tried denial, and told me that I could do as I pleased—she knew nothing. But when I named Eratosthenes to her face, and said that he was the man who had been visiting my wife, she was dumfounded, thinking that I had found out everything exactly. And then at last, falling at my feet and exacting a promise from me that no harm should be done to her, she denounced the villain. She described how he had first approached her after the funeral, and then how in the end she had passed the message on, and in the course of time my wife had been overpersuaded. She explained the way in which he had contrived to get into the house, and how when I was in the country my wife had gone to a religious service with this man's mother, and everything else that had happened. She recounted it all exactly.

When she had told all, I said: "See to it that nobody gets to know of this; otherwise the promise I made you will not hold good. And furthermore, I expect you to show me this actually happening. I have no use for words. I want the *fact* to be exhibited, if it really is so."

She agreed to do this.

Four or five days then elapsed, as I shall prove to you by important evidence. But before I do so, I wish to narrate the events of the last day.

I had a friend and relative named Sôstratus. He was coming home from the country after sunset when I met him. I knew that as he had got back so late, he would not find any of his own people at home; so I asked him to dine with me. We went home to my place, and going upstairs to the upper story, we had dinner there. When he felt restored, he went off; and I went to bed.

Then, members of the jury, Eratosthenes made his entry; and the maid wakened me and told me that he was in the house.

I told her to watch the door; and going downstairs, I slipped out noiselessly.

I went to the houses of one man after another. Some I found at home; others, I was told, were out of town. So, collecting as many as I could of those who were there, I went back. We procured torches from the shop nearby, and entered my house. The door had been left open by arrangement with the maid.

We forced the bedroom door. The first of us to enter saw him still lying beside my wife. Those who followed saw him standing naked on the bed.

I knocked him down, members of the jury, with one blow. I then twisted his hands behind his back and tied them. And then I asked him why he was committing this crime against me, of breaking into my house.

He answered that he admitted his guilt; but he begged and besought me not to kill him—to accept a money payment instead.

But I replied: "It is not I who shall be killing you, but the law of the State, which you, in transgressing, have valued less highly than your own pleasures. You have preferred to commit this great crime against my wife and my children, rather than to obey the law and be of decent behavior."

Thus, members of the jury, this man met the fate which the laws prescribe for wrongdoers of his kind.

THE ARGUMENTS

Eratosthenes was not seized in the street and carried off, nor had he taken refuge at the altar, as the prosecution alleges. The facts do not admit of it: he was struck in the bedroom, he fell at once and I bound his hands behind his back. There were so many present that he could not possibly escape through their midst, since he had neither steel nor wood nor any other weapon with which he could have defended himself against all those who had entered the room.

No, members of the jury: you know as well as I do how wrongdoers will not admit that their adversaries are speaking the truth, and attempt by lies and trickery of other kinds to excite the anger of the hearers against those whose acts are in accordance with Justice.

(To the Clerk of the Court):

Read the Law.

(The Law of Solon is read, that an adulterer may be put to death by the man who catches him.)

He made no denial, members of the jury. He admitted his guilt, and begged and implored that he should not be put to death, offering to pay compensation. But I would not accept his estimate. I preferred to accord a higher authority to the law of the State, and I took that satisfaction which you, because you thought it the most just, have decreed for those who commit such offenses.

Witnesses to the preceding, kindly step up.

(The witnesses come to the front of the Court, and the Clerk reads their depositions. When the Clerk has finished reading, and the witnesses have agreed that the depositions are correct, the defendant again addresses the Clerk.)

Now please read this further law from the pillar of the Court of the Areopagus:

(The Clerk reads another version of Solon's law, as recorded on the pillar of the Areopagus Court.)

You hear, members of the jury, how it is expressly decreed by the Court of the Areopagus itself, which both traditionally and in your own day has been granted the right to try cases of murder, that no person shall be found guilty of murder who catches an adulterer with his wife and inflicts this punishment. The Lawgiver was so strongly convinced of the justice of these provisions in the case of married women, that he applied them also to concubines, who are of less importance. Yet obviously, if he had known of any greater punishment than this for cases where married women are concerned, he would have provided it. But in fact, as it was impossible for him to invent any more severe penalty for corruption of wives, he decided to provide the same punishment as in the case of concubines.

(To the Clerk of the Court):

Please read me this Law also.

(The Clerk reads out further clauses from Solon's laws on rape.)

You hear, members of the jury, how the Lawgiver ordains that if anyone debauch by force a free man or boy, the fine shall be double that decreed in the case of a slave. If anyone debauch a woman—in which case it is *permitted* to kill him—he shall be liable to the same fine. Thus, members of the jury, the Lawgiver considered violators deserving of a lesser penalty than seducers: for the latter he provided the death penalty; for the former, the doubled fine. His idea was that those who use force are loathed by the persons violated, whereas those who have got their way by persuasion corrupt women's minds, in such a way as to make other men's wives more attached to themselves than to their husbands, so that the whole house is in their power, and it is uncertain who is the children's father, the husband or the lover. These considerations caused the Lawgiver to affix death as the penalty for seduction.

And so, members of the jury, in my case the laws not only hold me innocent, but actually order me to take this satisfaction; but it depends on you whether they are to be effective or of no moment. The reason, in my opinion, why all States lay down laws is in order that, whenever we are in doubt on any point, we can refer to these laws and find out our duty. And therefore it is the laws which in such cases enjoin upon the injured party to exact this penalty. I exhort you to show yourselves in agreement with them; otherwise you will be granting such impunity to adulterers that you will encourage even burglars to declare themselves adulterers, in the knowledge that if they allege this reason for their action and plead that this was their purpose in entering other men's houses, no one will lay a finger on them. They will all realize that they need not bother about the law on adultery, but need only fear your verdict, since this is the supreme authority in the State.

Consider, members of the jury, their accusation that it was I who on that day told the maid to fetch the young man. In my opinion, gentlemen, I should have been justified in using any means to catch the seducer of my wife. If there had been only words spoken and no actual offense, I should have been doing wrong; but when by that time they had gone to all lengths and he had often gained entry into my house, I consider that I should have been within my rights whatever means I employ to catch him. But observe that this allegation of the prosecution is also false. You can easily convince yourselves by considering the following:

I have already told you how Sôstratus, an intimate friend of mine, met me coming in from the country around sunset, and dined with me, and when he felt refreshed, went off. Now in the first place, gentlemen, ask yourselves whether, if on that night I had had designs on Eratosthenes, it would have been better for me that Sôstratus should dine elsewhere, or that I should take a guest home with me to dinner. Surely in the latter circumstances Eratosthenes would have been less inclined to venture into the house. Further, does it seem to you probable that I would have let my guest go, and been left alone, without company? Would I not rather have urged him to stay, so that he could help me to punish the adulterer?

Again, gentlemen, does it not seem to you probable that I would have passed the word round among my friends during the daytime, and told them to assemble at the house of one of my friends who lived nearest, rather than have started to run round at night, as soon as I found out, without knowing whom I should find at home and whom away? Actually, I called for Harmodius and certain others who were out of town—I did not know it—and others, I found, were not at home, so I went along taking with me whomever I could. But if I had known beforehand, does it not seem to you probable that I would have arranged for servants and passed the word round to my friends, so that I myself could go in with the maximum of safety—for how did I know whether he too might not have had a dagger or something?—and also in order that I might exact the penalty in the presence of the greatest number of witnesses? But in fact, since I knew nothing of what was going to happen on that night, I took with me whomever I could get.

Witnesses to the preceding, please step up.

(Further witnesses come forward, and confirm their evidence as read out by the Clerk.)

You have heard the witnesses, members of the jury. Now consider the case further in your own minds, inquiring whether there had ever existed between Eratosthenes and myself any other enmity but this. You will find none. He never brought any malicious charge against me, nor tried to secure my banishment, nor prosecuted me in any private suit. Neither had he knowledge of any crime of which I feared the revelation, so that I desired to kill him; nor by carrying out this act did I hope to gain money. So far from ever having had any dispute with him, or drunken brawl, or any other quarrel, I had never even set eyes on the man before that night. What possible object could I have had, therefore, in running so great a risk, except that I had suffered the greatest of all injuries at his hands? Again, would I myself have called in witnesses to my crime, when it was possible for me, if I desired to murder him without justification, to have had no confidants?

THE EPILOGUE

It is my belief, members of the jury, that this punishment was inflicted not in my own interests, but in those of the whole community. Such villains, seeing the rewards which await their crimes, will be less ready to commit offenses against others if they see that you too hold the same opinion of them. Otherwise it would be far better to wipe out the existing laws and make different ones, which will penalize those who keep guard over their own wives, and grant full immunity to those who criminally pursue them. This would be a far more just procedure than to set a trap for citizens by means of the laws, which urge the man who catches an adulterer to do with him whatever he will, and yet allow the injured party to undergo a trial far more perilous than that which faces the law breaker who seduces other men's wives. Of this, I am an example—I, who now stand in danger of losing life, property, everything, because I have obeyed the laws of the State.

This speech is an excellent example of advocacy and of Lysias' particular skill. The defense rests confidently on the law of Solon permitting the slaughter of an adulterer caught in the act, and on the inability of the prosecution to prove a different motive. The advocate feels in a sufficiently strong position to let his client say that he was not merely acting in accordance with the laws, but obeying their definite instructions in slaying the adulterer. This of course is untrue: the law allowed, but did not insist upon this revenge; and it is clear that a money payment could be offered and accepted. As no other case of the slaughter of an adulterer is recorded, we can assume that the money compensation was usual.

The real skill of the advocate, however, is devoted to building up a character and a situation. The Proem is brief, and sketches the general detestation in which adultery is held. The Narrative is long, vivid and detailed: its purpose is to show a normal husband, kindly, trusting but not foolish, grossly deceived in his own home over a long period by a habitual seducer, so that by the time the defendant reaches the actual deed of blood, the jury will be in sympathy with him and will not be disgusted at the thought of a helpless unarmed man butchered in the presence of so many other men in spite of his plea for mercy.

The Argumentation, based mostly on probability, aims at showing that the deed was a direct punishment for the offense, and not premeditated and prearranged. The Epilogue, also short, suggests to the jury that in acquitting the defendant they will be acting in the public interest, and striking a blow for the sanctity of the home.

An outstanding feature is the passivity of the wife, or rather, the unimportance of her attitude. She was "approached" through her maid, on one of the few occasions when an Athenian woman could appear in public—at a funeral. She is described as having been "corrupted" and "seduced," though it is clear that she was an active conspirator. Her husband does not refer to her guilt, which is ascribed to the persuasion of the seducer. The religious festival which she attended with the mother of her lover was called the Thesmophoria, and was a yearly celebration in honor of the goddess Demeter, attended by women only. Her adultery having been proved, she would be automatically divorced; but beyond that, we cannot guess at her fate.

The maid cannot be very much blamed for her betrayal of her mistress. Her fate was in the hands of her master, and the "examination" suggested by the aged crone included, if he wished, physical torture. Short of putting her to death, he could do anything he liked with her.

The Narrative contains the best existing description of an ordinary Athenian house. The stairs to which the husband refers were a mere ladder: hence the danger in going up and down them, especially for a woman carrying a baby.

Though the verdict is not known, it is fairly safe to assume that the defendant was successful. Adultery was very seriously regarded in Athens, because of the importance of the blood tie in determining inheritance, and the duty of the sons to look after the ancestral tombs and perform the rites to the dead. Every possible means were taken to ensure the chastity of free-born women, hence the haremlike seclusion of their wives. The breaking-through of the barriers round the home would arouse the strongest resentment in the jury; and though they might not fully approve of Euphiletus' savage act, they would probably feel him to be justified, and give him their votes.

THE ADVENTURE
OF THE CLAPHAM COOK
By Agatha Christie

. . . .

When the cook disappeared mysteriously,
Hercule Poirot involved himself in the case, even though
the cook's mistress tried to dismiss him.

At the time that I was sharing rooms with my friend Hercule Poirot, it was my custom to read aloud to him the headlines in the morning newspaper, *The Daily Blare.*

The Daily Blare was a paper that made the most of any opportunity for sensationalism. Robberies and murders did not lurk obscurely in its back pages. Instead they hit you in the eye in large type on the front page.

> *Absconding Bank Clerk Disappears with Fifty Thousand Pounds Worth of Negotiable Securities* [I read].
> *Husband Puts His Head in Gas Oven. Unhappy Home Life. Missing Typist. Pretty Girl of Twenty-one. Where is Edna Field?*

"There you are, Poirot, plenty to choose from. An absconding bank clerk, a mysterious suicide, a missing typist—which will you have?"

My friend was in a placid mood. He quietly shook his head.

"I am not greatly attracted to any of them, *mon ami.* Today I feel inclined for the life of ease. It would have to be a very interesting problem to tempt me from my chair. See you, I have affairs of importance of my own to attend to."

"Such as?"

"My wardrobe, Hastings. If I mistake not, there is on my new gray suit the spot of grease—only the unique spot, but it is sufficient to trouble me. Then there is my winter overcoat—I must lay him aside in the powder of Keatings. And I think—yes, I think—the moment is ripe for the trimmings of my mustaches—and afterward I must apply the *pomade*."

"Well," I said, strolling to the window, "I doubt if you'll be able to carry out this delirious program. That was a ring at the bell. You have a client."

"Unless the affair is one of national importance, I touch it not," declared Poirot with dignity.

A moment later our privacy was invaded by a stout, red-faced lady who panted audibly as a result of her rapid ascent of the stairs.

"You're Monsieur Poirot?" she demanded, as she sank into a chair.

"I am Hercule Poirot, yes, Madame."

"You're not a bit like what I thought you'd be," said the lady, eyeing him with some disfavor. "Did you pay for the bit in the paper saying what a clever detective you were, or did they put it in themselves?"

"Madame!" said Poirot, drawing himself up.

"I'm sorry, I'm sure, but you know what these papers are nowadays. You begin reading a nice article 'What a bride said to her plain unmarried friend,' and it's all about a simple thing you buy at the chemist's and shampoo your hair with. Nothing but puff. But no offense taken, I hope? I'll tell you what I want you to do for me. I want you to find my cook."

Poirot stared at her; for once his ready tongue failed him. I turned aside to hide the broadening smile I could not control.

"It's all this wicked dole," continued the lady. "Putting ideas into servants' heads, wanting to be typists and whatnots. Stop the dole, that's what I say. I'd like to know what *my* servants have to complain of—afternoon and evening off a week, alternate Sundays, washing put out, same food as we have—and never a bit of margarine in the house, nothing but the very best butter."

She paused for want of breath and Poirot seized his opportunity. He spoke in his haughtiest manner, rising to his feet as he did so.

"I fear you are making a mistake, Madame. I am not holding an inquiry into the conditions of domestic service. I am a private detective."

"I know that," said our visitor. "Didn't I tell you I wanted you to find my cook for me? Walked out of the house on Wednesday, without so much as a word to me, and never came back."

"I am sorry, Madame, but I do not touch this particular kind of business. I wish you good morning."

Our visitor snorted with indignation.

"That's it, is it, my fine fellow? Too proud, eh? Only deal with Government secrets and countesses' jewels? Let me tell you a servant's every bit as important as a tiara to a woman in my position. We can't all be fine ladies going out in our motors with our diamonds and our pearls. A good cook's a good cook—and when you lose her, it's as much to you as her pearls are to some fine lady."

For a moment or two it appeared to be a tossup between Poirot's dignity and his sense of humor. Finally he laughed and sat down again.

"Madame, you are in the right, and I am in the wrong. Your remarks are just and intelligent. This case will be a novelty. Never yet have I hunted a missing domestic. Truly here is the problem of national importance that I was demanding of fate just before your arrival. *En avant!* You say this jewel of a cook went out on Wednesday and did not return. That is the day before yesterday."

"Yes, it was her day out."

"But probably, Madame, she has met with some accident. Have you inquired at any of the hospitals?"

"That's exactly what I thought yesterday, but this morning, if you please, she sent for her box. And not so much as a line to me! If I'd been at home, I'd not have let it go—treating me like that! But I'd just stepped out to the butcher."

"Will you describe her to me?"

"She was middle-aged, stout, black hair turning gray—most respectable. She'd been ten years in her last place. Eliza Dunn, her name was."

"And you had had—no disagreement with her on the Wednesday?"

"None whatever. That's what makes it all so queer."

"How many servants do you keep, Madame?"

"Two. The house parlormaid, Annie, is a very nice girl. A bit forgetful and her head full of young men, but a good servant if you keep her up to her work."

"Did she and the cook get on well together?"

"They had their ups and downs, of course—but on the whole, very well."

"And the girl can throw no light on the mystery?"

"She says not—but you know what servants are—they all hang together."

"Well, well, we must look into this. Where did you say you resided, Madame?"

"At Clapham; eighty-eight Prince Albert Road."

"*Bien*, Madame, I will wish you good morning, and you may count upon seeing me at your residence during the course of the day."

Mrs. Todd, for such was our new friend's name, then took her departure. Poirot looked at me somewhat ruefully.

"Well, well, Hastings, this is a novel affair that we have here. The Disappearance of the Clapham Cook! Never, *never*, must our friend Inspector Japp get to hear of this!"

He then proceeded to heat an iron and carefully removed the grease spot from his gray suit by means of a piece of blotting paper. His mustaches he regretfully postponed to another day, and we set out for Clapham.

Prince Albert Road proved to be a street of small prim houses, all exactly alike, with neat lace curtains veiling the windows, and well-polished brass knockers on the doors.

We rang the bell at No. 88, and the door was opened by a neat maid with a pretty face. Mrs. Todd came out in the hall to greet us.

"Don't go, Annie," she cried. "This gentleman's a detective and he'll want to ask you some questions."

Annie's face displayed a struggle between alarm and a pleasurable excitement.

"I thank you, Madame," said Poirot, bowing. "I would like to question your maid now—and to see her alone, if I may."

We were shown into a small drawing room, and when Mrs. Todd, with obvious reluctance, had left the room, Poirot commenced his cross-examination.

"*Voyons*, Mademoiselle Annie, all that you shall tell us will be of the greatest importance. You alone can shed any light on the case. Without your assistance I can do nothing."

The alarm vanished from the girl's face and the pleasurable excitement became more strongly marked.

"I'm sure, sir," she said, "I'll tell you anything I can."

"That is good." Poirot beamed approval on her. "Now, first of all what is your own idea? You are a girl of remarkable intelligence. That can be seen at once! What is your own explanation of Eliza's disappearance?"

Thus encouraged, Annie fairly flowed into excited speech.

"White slavers, sir, I've said so all along! Cook was always warning me against them. *'Don't you sniff no scent, or eat any sweets—no matter how gentlemanly the fellow!'* Those were her words to me. And now they've got her! I'm sure of it. As likely as not, she's been shipped to Turkey or one of them Eastern places where I've heard they like them fat!"

Poirot preserved an admirable gravity.

"But in that case—and it is indeed an idea—would she have sent for her trunk?"

"Well, I don't know, sir. She'd want her things—even in those foreign places."

"Who came for the trunk—a man?"

"It was Carter Paterson, sir."

"Did you pack it?"

"No, sir, it was already packed and corded."

"Ah! that is interesting. That shows that when she left the house on Wednesday, she had already determined not to return. You see that, do you not?"

"Yes, sir." Annie looked slightly taken aback. "I hadn't thought of that. But it might still have been White Slavers, mightn't it, sir?" she added wistfully.

"Undoubtedly!" said Poirot gravely. He went on: "Did you both occupy the same bedroom?"

"No, sir, we had separate rooms."

"And had Eliza expressed any dissatisfaction with her present post to you at all? Were you both happy here?"

"She'd never mentioned leaving. The place is all right—" The girl hesitated.

"Speak freely," said Poirot kindly. "I shall not tell your mistress."

"Well, of course, sir, she's a caution, Missus is. But the food's good. Plenty of it, and no stinting. Something hot for supper, good outings and as much frying fat as you like. And anyway, if Eliza did want to make a change, she'd never have gone off this way, I'm sure. She'd have stayed her month. Why, Missus could have a month's wages out of her for doing this!"

"And the work, it is not too hard?"

"Well, she's particular—always poking round in corners and looking for dust. And then there's the lodger, or paying guest as he's always called. But that's only breakfast and dinner, same as Master. They're out all day in the city."

"You like your master?"

"He's all right—very quiet and a bit on the stingy side."

"You can't remember, I suppose, the last thing Eliza said before she went out?"

"Yes, I can. 'If there's any stewed peaches over from the dining room,' she says, 'we'll have them for supper, and a bit of bacon and some fried potatoes.' Mad over stewed peaches, she was. I shouldn't wonder if they didn't get her that way."

"Was Wednesday her regular day out?"

"Yes, she had Wednesdays and I had Thursdays."

Poirot asked a few more questions, then declared himself satisfied. Annie departed, and Mrs. Todd hurried in, her face alight with curiosity. She had, I felt certain, bitterly resented her exclusion from the room during our conversation with Annie. Poirot, however, was careful to soothe her feelings tactfully.

"It is difficult," he explained, "for a woman of exceptional intelligence such as yourself, Madame, to bear patiently the roundabout methods we poor detectives are forced to use. To have patience with stupidity is difficult for the quick-witted."

Having thus charmed away any little resentment on Mrs. Todd's part, he brought the conversation round to her husband and elicited the information that he worked with a firm in the City and would not be home until after six.

"Doubtless he is very disturbed and worried by this unaccountable business, eh? Is it not so?"

"He's never worried," declared Mrs. Todd. " 'Well, well, get another, my dear.' That's all he said! He's so calm that it drives me to distraction sometimes. 'An ungrateful woman,' he said. 'We are well rid of her.' "

"What about the other inmates of the house, Madame?"

"You mean Mr. Simpson, our paying guest? Well, as long as he gets his breakfast and his evening meal all right, he doesn't worry."

"What is his profession, Madame?"

"He works in a bank." She mentioned its name, and I started slightly, remembering my perusal of The Daily Blare.

"A young man?"

"Twenty-eight, I believe. Nice quiet young fellow."

"I should like to have a few words with him, and also with your husband, if I may. I will return for that purpose this evening. I venture to suggest that you should repose yourself a little, Madame, you looked fatigued."

"I should just think I am! First the worry about Eliza, and then I was at the Sales practically all yesterday, and you know what *that* is, Mr. Poirot, and what with one thing and another and a lot to do in the house, because of course Annie can't do it all—and very likely she'll give notice anyway, being unsettled in this way—well, what with it all, I'm tired out!"

Poirot murmured sympathetically, and we took our leave.

"It's a curious coincidence," I said, "but that absconding clerk, Davis, was from the same bank as Simpson. Can there be any connection, do you think?"

Poirot smiled.

"At the one end, a defaulting clerk, at the other a vanishing cook. It is hard to see any relation between the two, unless possibly Davis visited Simpson, fell in love with the cook and persuaded her to accompany him on his flight!"

I laughed. But Poirot remained grave.

"He might have done worse," he said reprovingly. "Remember, Hastings, if you are going into exile, a good cook may be of more comfort than a pretty face!" He paused for a moment and then went on. "It is a curious case, full of contradictory features. I am interested—yes, I am distinctly interested."

That evening we returned to 88 Prince Albert Road and interviewed both Todd and Simpson. The former was a melancholy, lantern-jawed man of forty-odd.

"Oh! yes, yes," he said vaguely. "Eliza. Yes. A good cook, I believe. And economical. I make a strong point of economy."

"Can you imagine any reason for her leaving you so suddenly?"

"Oh, well," said Mr. Todd vaguely. "Servants, you know. My wife worries too much. Worn out from always worrying. The whole problem's quite simple really. 'Get another, my dear,' I say. 'Get another.' That's all there is to it. No good crying over spilt milk."

Mr. Simpson was equally unhelpful. He was a quiet, inconspicuous young man with spectacles.

"I must have seen her, I suppose," he said. "Elderly woman, wasn't she? Of course, it's the other one I see always, Annie. Nice girl. Very obliging."

"Were those two on good terms with each other?"

Mr. Simpson said he couldn't say, he was sure. He supposed so.

"Well, we got nothing of interest there, *mon ami*," said Poirot as we left the house. Our departure had been delayed by a burst of vociferous repetition from Mrs. Todd, who repeated everything she had said that morning at rather greater length.

"Are you disappointed?" I asked. "Did you expect to hear something?"

Poirot shook his head.

"There was a possibility, of course," he said. "But I hardly thought it likely."

The next development was a letter which Poirot received on the following morning. He read it, turned purple with indignation and handed it to me.

> *Mrs. Todd regrets that after all she will not avail herself of Mr. Poirot's services. After talking the matter over with her husband she sees that it is foolish to call in a detective about a purely domestic affair. Mrs. Todd encloses a guinea for consultation fee.*

"Aha!" cried Poirot angrily. "And they think to get rid of Hercule Poirot like that! As a favor—a great favor—I consent to investigate their miserable little twopenny halfpenny affair—and they dismiss me *comme ça!* Here, I mistake not, is the hand of Mr. Todd. But I say— No!—thirty-six times no! I will spend my own guineas, thirty-six hundred of them if need be, but I will get to the bottom of this matter!"

"Yes," I said. "But how?"

Poirot calmed down a little.

"*D'abord*," he said, "we will advertise in the papers. Let me see— yes—something like this: 'If Eliza Dunn will communicate with this address, she will hear of something to her advantage.' Put it in all the papers you can think of, Hastings. Then I will make some little inquiries of my own. Go, go—all must be done as quickly as possible!"

I did not see him again until the evening, when he condescended to tell me what he had been doing.

"I have made inquiries at the firm of Mr. Todd. He was not absent on Wednesday, and he bears a good character—so much for him.

Then Simpson, on Thursday he was ill and did not come to the bank, but he was there on Wednesday. He was moderately friendly with Davis. Nothing out of the common. There does not seem to be anything there. No. We must place our reliance on the advertisement."

The advertisement duly appeared in all the principal daily papers. By Poirot's orders it was to be continued every day for a week. His eagerness over this uninteresting matter of a defaulting cook was extraordinary, but I realized that he considered it a point of honor to persevere until he finally succeeded. Several extremely interesting cases were brought to him about this time, but he declined them all. Every morning he would rush at his letters, scrutinize them earnestly and then lay them down with a sigh.

But our patience was rewarded at last. On the Wednesday following Mrs. Todd's visit, our landlady informed us that a person of the name of Eliza Dunn had called.

"*Enfin!*" cried Poirot. "But make her mount then! At once. Immediately."

Thus admonished, our landlady hurried out and returned a moment or two later, ushering in Miss Dunn. Our quarry was much as described: tall, stout and eminently respectable.

"I came in answer to the advertisement," she explained. "I thought there must be some muddle or other, and that perhaps you didn't know I'd already got my legacy."

Poirot was studying her attentively. He drew forward a chair with a flourish.

"The truth of the matter is," he explained, "that your late mistress, Mrs. Todd, was much concerned about you. She feared some accident might have befallen you."

Eliza Dunn seemed very much surprised.

"Didn't she get my letter then?"

"She got no word of any kind." He paused, and then said persuasively: "Recount to me the whole story, will you not?"

Eliza Dunn needed no encouragement. She plunged at once into a lengthy narrative.

"I was just coming home on Wednesday night and had nearly got to the house, when a gentleman stopped me. A tall gentleman he was, with a beard and a big hat. 'Miss Eliza Dunn?' he said. 'Yes,' I said. 'I've been inquiring for you at Number Eighty-eight,' he said. 'They told me I might meet you coming along here. Miss Dunn, I have come from Australia specially to find you. Do you happen to know the maiden name of your maternal grandmother?' 'Jane Emmott,' I said. 'Exactly,' he said. 'Now, Miss Dunn, although you may never have heard of the fact, your grandmother had a great friend, Eliza Leech. This friend went to Australia where she married a very wealthy settler. Her two children died in infancy, and she inherited all her husband's property. She died a few months ago, and by her will you inherit a house in this country and a considerable sum of money.'

"You could have knocked me down with a feather," continued Miss Dunn. "For a minute, I was suspicious, and he must have seen it, for he smiled. 'Quite right to be on your guard, Miss Dunn,' he said. 'Here are my credentials.' He handed me a letter from some lawyers in Melbourne, Hurst and Crotchet, and a card. He was Mr. Crochet. 'There are one or two conditions,' he said. 'Our client was a little eccentric, you know. The bequest is conditional on your taking possession of the house (it is in Cumberland) before twelve o'clock tomorrow. The other condition is of no importance—it is merely a stipulation that you should not be in domestic service.' My face fell. 'Oh! Mr. Crochet,' I said. 'I'm a cook. Didn't they tell you at the house?' 'Dear, dear,' he said. 'I had no idea of such a thing. I thought you might possibly be a companion or governess there. This is very unfortunate—very unfortunate indeed.'

" 'Shall I have to lose all the money?' I said anxious like. He thought for a minute or two. 'There are always ways of getting round the law, Miss Dunn,' he said at last. 'We lawyers know that. The way out here is for you to have left your employment this afternoon.' 'But my month?' I said. 'My dear Miss Dunn,' he said, with a smile, 'you can leave an employer any minute by forfeiting a month's wages. Your mistress will understand in view of the circumstances. The difficulty is *time!* It is imperative that you should catch the eleven-five from King's Cross to the North. I can advance you ten pounds or so for the fare, and you can write a note at the station to your employer. I will take it to her myself and explain the whole circumstances.' I agreed, of course, and an hour later I was in the train, so flustered that I didn't know whether I was on my head or my heels. Indeed by the time I got to Carlisle, I was half inclined to think the whole thing was one of those confidence tricks you read about. But I went to the address he had given me—solicitors they were, and it was all right. A nice little house, and an income of three hundred a year. These lawyers knew very little, they'd just got a letter from a gentleman in London instructing them to hand over the house to me and a hundred and fifty pounds for the first six months. Mr. Crotchet sent up my things to me, but there was no word from Missus. I supposed she was angry and grudged me my bit of luck. She kept back my box too, and sent my clothes in paper parcels. But there, of course if she never had my letter, she might think it a bit cool of me."

Poirot had listened attentively to this long history. Now he nodded his head as though completely satisfied.

"Thank you, Mademoiselle. There had been, as you say, a little muddle. Permit me to recompense you for your trouble." He handed her an envelope. "You return to Cumberland immediately? A little word in your ear. *Do not forget how to cook*. It is always useful to have something to fall back upon in case things go wrong."

"Credulous," he murmured, as our visitor departed, "but perhaps not more than most of her class." His face grew grave. "Come, Hastings, there is no time to be lost. Get a taxi while I write a note to Japp."

Poirot was waiting on the doorstep when I returned with the taxi.

"Where are we going?" I asked anxiously.

"First, to despatch this note by special messenger."

This was done and re-entering the taxi Poirot gave the address to the driver.

"Eighty-eight Prince Albert Road, Clapham."

"So we are going there?"

"*Mais oui*. Though frankly I fear we shall be too late. Our bird will have flown, Hastings."

"Who is our bird?"

Poirot smiled. "The inconspicuous Mr. Simpson."

"What?" I exclaimed.

"Oh, come now, Hastings, do not tell me that all is not clear to you now?"

"The cook was got out of the way, I realize that," I said, slightly piqued. "But why? *Why* should Simpson wish to get her out of the house? Did she know something about him?"

"Nothing whatever."

"Well, then—"

"But he wanted something that she had."

"Money? The Australian legacy?"

"No, my friend—something quite different." He paused a moment and then said gravely: "A *battered tin trunk* . . ."

I looked sideways at him. His statement seemed so fantastic that I suspected him of pulling my leg, but he was perfectly grave and serious.

"Seriously he could buy a trunk if he wanted one," I cried.

"He did not want a new trunk. He wanted a trunk of pedigree. A trunk of assured respectability."

"Look here, Poirot," I cried, "this really is a bit thick. You're pulling my leg."

He looked at me.

"You lack the brains and the imagination of Mr. Simpson, Hastings. See here: On Wednesday evening, Simpson decoys away the cook. A printed card and a printed sheet of notepaper are simple matters to obtain, and he is willing to pay a hundred and fifty pounds and a year's house rent to assure the success of his plan. Miss Dunn does not recognize him—the beard and the hat and the slight colonial accent completely deceive her. That is the end of Wednesday—except for the trifling fact that Simpson has helped himself to fifty thousand pounds worth of negotiable securities."

"*Simpson*—but it was *Davis*—"

"If you will kindly permit me to continue, Hastings! Simpson knows that the theft will be discovered on Thursday afternoon. He does not go to the bank on Thursday, but he lies in wait for Davis when he comes out to lunch. Perhaps he admits the theft and tells Davis he will return the securities to him—anyhow he succeeds in getting Davis to come to Clapham with him. It is the maid's day out, and Mrs. Todd was at the Sales, so there is no one in the house. When the theft is discovered and Davis is missing, the implication will be overwhelming. Davis is the thief! Mr. Simpson will be perfectly safe, and can return to work on the morrow like the honest clerk they think him."

"And Davis?"

Poirot made an expressive gesture, and slowly shook his head.

"It seems too cold-blooded to be believed, and yet what other explanation can there be, *mon ami*. The one difficulty for a murderer is the disposal of the body—and Simpson had planned that out beforehand. I was struck at once by the fact that although Eliza Dunn obviously meant to return that night when she went out (witness her remark about the stewed peaches) *yet her trunk was already packed when they came for it.* It was Simpson who sent word to Carter Paterson to call on Friday and it was Simpson who corded up the box on Thursday afternoon. What suspicion could possibly arise? A maid leaves and sends for her box, it is labeled and addressed ready in her name, probably to a railroad station within easy reach of London. On Saturday afternoon, Simpson, in his Australian disguise, claims it, he affixes a new label and address and re-despatches it somewhere else, again 'to be left till called for.' When the authorities get suspicious, for excellent reasons, and open it, all that can be elicited will be that a bearded colonial despatched it from some junction near London. There will be nothing to connect it with Eighty-eight Prince Albert Road. Ah! here we are."

Poirot's prognostications had been correct. Simpson had left two days previously. But he was not to escape the consequences of his crime. By the aid of wireless, he was discovered on the *Olympia*, en route to America.

A tin trunk, addressed to Mr. Henry Wintergreen, attracted the attention of the railroad officials at Glasgow. It was opened and found to contain the body of the unfortunate Davis.

Mrs. Todd's check for a guinea was never cashed. Instead Poirot had it framed and hung on the wall of our sitting room.

"It is to me a little reminder, Hastings: Never to despise the trivial —the undignified. A disappearing domestic at one end—a cold-blooded murder at the other. To me, one of the most interesting of my cases."

THE LAST NIGHT OF THE WORLD
By Ray Bradbury

. . . .

October 19, 1969. Remember that date!
For, though it was a pretty ordinary day, everyone everywhere
had dreamed what was going to happen that night.

"What would you do if you knew that this was the last night of the world?"

"What would I do? You mean seriously?"

"Yes, seriously."

"I don't know. I hadn't thought."

He poured some coffee. In the background the two girls were playing blocks on the parlor rug in the light of the green hurricane lamps. There was an easy, clean aroma of the brewed coffee in the evening air.

"Well, better start thinking about it," he said.

"You don't mean it!"

He nodded.

"A war?"

He shook his head.

"Not the hydrogen or atom bomb?"

"No."

"Or germ warfare?"

"None of those at all," he said, stirring his coffee slowly. "But just, let's say, the closing of a book."

"I don't think I understand."

"No, nor do I, really; it's just a feeling. Sometimes it frightens me, sometimes I'm not frightened at all but at peace." He glanced in at the girls and their yellow hair shining in the lamplight. "I didn't say

302

anything to you. It first happened about four nights ago."

"What?"

"A dream I had. I dreamed that it was all going to be over, and a voice said it was; not any kind of voice I can remember, but a voice anyway, and it said things would stop here on Earth. I didn't think too much about it the next day, but then I went to the office and caught Stan Willis looking out the window in the middle of the afternoon, and I said a penny for your thoughts, Stan, and he said, I had a dream last night, and before he even told me the dream I knew what it was. I could have told him, but he told me and I listened to him."

"It was the same dream?"

"The same. I told Stan I had dreamed it too. He didn't seem surprised. He relaxed, in fact. Then we started walking through the office, for the hell of it. It wasn't planned. We didn't say, 'Let's walk around.' We just walked on our own, and everywhere we saw people looking at their desks or their hands or out windows. I talked to a few. So did Stan."

"And they all had dreamed?"

"All of them. The same dream, with no difference."

"Do you believe in it?"

"Yes. I've never been more certain."

"And when will it stop? The world, I mean."

"Sometime during the night for us, and then as the night goes on around the world, that'll go too. It'll take twenty-four hours for it all to go."

They sat awhile not touching their coffee. Then they lifted it slowly and drank, looking at each other.

"Do we deserve this?" she said.

"It's not a matter of deserving; it's just that things didn't work out. I notice you didn't even argue about this. Why not?"

"I guess I've a reason," she said.

"The same one everyone at the office had?"

She nodded slowly. "I didn't want to say anything. It happened last night. And the women on the block talked about it, among themselves, today. They dreamed. I thought it was only a coincidence." She picked up the evening paper. "There's nothing in the paper about it."

"Everyone knows, so there's no need."

He sat back in his chair, watching her. "Are you afraid?"

"No. I always thought I would be, but I'm not."

"Where's that spirit called self-preservation they talk so much about?"

"I don't know. You don't get too excited when you feel things are logical. This is logical. Nothing else but this could have happened from the way we've lived."

"We haven't been too bad, have we?"

"No, nor enormously good. I suppose that's the trouble—we haven't been very much of anything except us, while a big part of the world was busy being lots of quite awful things."

The girls were laughing in the parlor.

"I always thought people would be screaming in the streets at a time like this."

"I guess not. You don't scream about the real thing."

"Do you know, I won't miss anything but you and the girls. I never liked cities or my work or anything except you three. I won't miss a thing except perhaps the change in the weather, and a glass of ice water when it's hot, and I might miss sleeping. How can we sit here and talk this way?"

"Because there's nothing else to do."

"That's it, of course; for if there were, we'd be doing it. I suppose this is the first time in the history of the world that everyone has known just what they were going to do during the night."

"I wonder what everyone else will do now, this evening, for the next few hours."

"Go to a show, listen to the radio, watch television, play cards, put the children to bed, go to bed themselves, like always."

"In a way that's something to be proud of—like always."

They sat a moment and then he poured himself another coffee. "Why do you suppose it's tonight?"

"Because."

"Why not some other night in the last century, or five centuries ago, or ten?"

"Maybe it's because it was never October 19, 1969, ever before in history, and now it is and that's it; because this date means more than any other date ever meant; because it's the year when things are as they are all over the world and that's why it's the end."

"There are bombers on their schedules both ways across the ocean tonight that'll never see land."

"That's part of the reason why."

"Well," he said, getting up, "what shall it be? Wash the dishes?"

They washed the dishes and stacked them away with special neatness. At eight thirty the girls were put to bed and kissed good night and the little lights by their beds turned on and the door left open just a trifle.

"I wonder," said the husband, coming from the bedroom and glancing back, standing there with his pipe for a moment.

"What?"

"If the door will be shut all the way, or if it'll be left just a little ajar so some light comes in."

"I wonder if the children know."

"No, of course not."

They sat and read the papers and talked and listened to some radio music and then sat together by the fireplace watching the charcoal embers as the clock struck ten thirty and eleven and eleven thirty. They thought of all the other people in the world who had spent their evening, each in his own special way.

"Well," he said at last.

He kissed his wife for a long time.

"We've been good for each other, anyway."

"Do you want to cry?" he asked.

"I don't think so."

They moved through the house and turned out the lights and went into the bedroom and stood in the night cool darkness undressing and pushing back the covers. "The sheets are so clean and nice."

"I'm tired."

"We're *all* tired."

They got into bed and lay back.

"Just a moment," she said.

He heard her get out of bed and go into the kitchen. A moment later, she returned. "I left the water running in the sink," she said.

Something about this was so very funny that he had to laugh.

She laughed with him, not knowing what it was that she had done that was funny. They stopped laughing at last and lay in their cool night bed, their hands clasped, their heads together.

"Good night," he said, after a moment.

"Good night," she said.

"THEY"

By Rudyard Kipling

. . . .

A soft kiss on the palm of the hand reveals
the nature of the children playing in the gardens of the great
English house. A tale by a writer who was an expert
on the sorrows of childhood.

One view called me to another; one hilltop to its fellow, half across the county, and since I could answer at no more trouble than the snapping forward of a lever, I let the country flow under my wheels. The orchid-studded flats of the East gave way to the thyme, ilex and gray grass of the Downs; these again to the rich cornland and fig trees of the lower coast, where you carry the beat of the tide on your left hand for fifteen level miles; and when at last I turned inland through a huddle of rounded hills and woods I had run myself clean out of my known marks. Beyond that precise hamlet which stands god-mother to the capital of the United States, I found hidden villages where bees, the only things awake, boomed in eighty-foot lindens that overhung gray Norman churches; miraculous brooks diving under stone bridges built for heavier traffic than would ever vex them again; tithe barns larger than their churches and an old smithy that cried out aloud how it had once been a hall of the Knights of the Temple. Gipsies I found on a common where the gorse, bracken and heath fought it out together up a mile of Roman road; and a little farther on I disturbed a red fox rolling dog-fashion in the naked sunlight.

As the wooded hills closed about me I stood up in the car to take the bearings of that great Down whose ringed head is a landmark for fifty miles across the low countries. I judged that the lie of the

country would bring me across some westward running road that
went to his feet, but I did not allow for the confusing veils of the
woods. A quick turn plunged me first into a green cutting brimful of
liquid sunshine, next into a gloomy tunnel where last year's dead
leaves whispered and scuffled about my tires. The strong hazel stuff
meeting overhead had not been cut for a couple of generations at
least, nor had any axe helped the moss-cankered oak and beech to
spring above them. Here the road changed frankly into a carpeted
ride on whose brown velvet spent primrose-clumps showed like jade,
and a few sickly, white-stalked bluebells nodded together. As the
slope favored I shut off the power and slid over the whirled leaves,
expecting every moment to meet a keeper; but I only heard a jay, far
off, arguing against the silence under the twilight of the trees.

Still the track descended. I was on the point of reversing and
working my way back on the second speed ere I ended in some
swamp, when I saw sunshine through the tangle ahead and lifted the
brake.

It was down again at once. As the light beat across my face my
forewheels took the turf of a great still lawn from which sprang
horsemen ten feet high with leveled lances, monstrous peacocks and
sleek round-headed maids of honor—blue, black and glistening—all
of clipped yew. Across the lawn—the marshaled woods besieged it
on three sides—stood an ancient house of lichened and weather-
worn stone, with mullioned windows and roofs of rose-red tile. It was
flanked by semicircular walls, also rose-red, that closed the lawn on
the fourth side, and at their feet a box hedge grew man-high. There
were doves on the roof about the slim brick chimneys, and I caught
a glimpse of an octagonal dove house behind the screening wall.

Here, then, I stayed; a horseman's green spear laid at my breast;
held by the exceeding beauty of that jewel in that setting.

If I am not packed off for a trespasser, or if this knight does not
ride a wallop at me, thought I, Shakespeare and Queen Elizabeth at
least must come out of that half-open garden door and ask me to
tea.

A child appeared at an upper window, and I thought the little
thing waved a friendly hand. But it was to call a companion, for
presently another bright head showed. Then I heard a laugh among
the yew-peacocks, and turning to make sure (till then I had been
watching the house only), I saw the silver of a fountain behind a
hedge thrown up against the sun. The doves on the roof cooed to the

cooing water; but between the two notes I caught the utterly happy chuckle of a child absorbed in some light mischief.

The garden door—heavy oak sunk deep in the thickness of the wall—opened further: a woman in a big garden hat set her foot slowly on the time-hollowed stone step and as slowly walked across the turf. I was forming some apology when she lifted up her head and I saw that she was blind.

"I heard you," she said. "Isn't that a motor car?"

"I'm afraid I've made a mistake in my road. I should have turned off up above—I never dreamed"—I began.

"But I'm very glad. Fancy a motor car coming into the garden! It will be such a treat—" She turned and made as though looking about her. "You—you haven't seen any one have you—perhaps?"

"No one to speak to, but the children seemed interested at a distance."

"Which?"

"I saw a couple up at the window just now, and I think I heard a little chap in the grounds."

"Oh, lucky you!" she cried, and her face brightened. "I hear them, of course, but that's all. You've seen them and heard them?"

"Yes," I answered. "And if I know anything of children one of them's having a beautiful time by the fountain yonder. Escaped, I should imagine."

"You're fond of children?"

I gave her one or two reasons why I did not altogether hate them.

"Of course, of course," she said. "Then you understand. Then you won't think it foolish if I ask you to take your car through the gardens, once or twice—quite slowly. I'm sure they'd like to see it. They see so little, poor things. One tries to make their life pleasant, but—" she threw out her hands toward the woods. "We're so out of the world here."

"That will be splendid," I said. "But I can't cut up your grass."

She faced to the right. "Wait a minute," she said. "We're at the south gate, aren't we? Behind those peacocks there's a flagged path. We call it the Peacock's Walk. You can't see it from here, they tell me, but if you squeeze along by the edge of the wood you can turn at the first peacock and get onto the flags."

It was a sacrilege to wake that dreaming house front with the clatter of machinery, but I swung the car to clear the turf, brushed

along the edge of the wood and turned in on the broad stone path
where the fountain basin lay like one star sapphire.

"May I come too?" she cried. "No, please, don't help me. They'll
like it better if they see me."

She felt her way lightly to the front of the car, and with one foot
on the step she called: "Children, oh, children! Look and see what's
going to happen!"

The voice would have drawn lost souls from the Pit, for the
yearning that underlay its sweetness, and I was not surprised to hear
an answering shout behind the yews. It must have been the child by
the fountain, but he fled at our approach, leaving a little toy boat in
the water. I saw the glint of his blue blouse among the still horsemen.

Very disposedly we paraded the length of the walk and at her
request backed again. This time the child had got the better of his
panic, but stood far off and doubting.

"The little fellow's watching us," I said. "I wonder if he'd like a
ride."

"They're very shy still. Very shy. But oh, lucky you to be able to
see them! Let's listen."

I stopped the machine at once, and the humid stillness, heavy with
the scent of box, cloaked us deep. Shears I could hear where some
gardener was clipping; a mumble of bees and broken voices that might
have been the doves.

"Oh, unkind!" she said wearily.

"Perhaps they're only shy of the motor. The little maid at the
window looks tremendously interested."

"Yes?" She raised her head. "It was wrong of me to say that. They
are really fond of me. It's the only thing that makes life worth
living—when they're fond of you, isn't it? I daren't think what the
place would be without them. By the way, is it beautiful?"

"I think it is the most beautiful place I have ever seen."

"So they all tell me. I can feel it, of course, but that isn't quite the
same thing."

"Then have you never—?" I began, but stopped abashed.

"Not since I can remember. It happened when I was only a few
months old, they tell me. And yet I must remember something, else
how could I dream about colors. I see light in my dreams, and
colors, but I never see *them*. I only hear them just as I do when I'm
awake."

"It's difficult to see faces in dreams. Some people can, but most of us haven't the gift," I went on, looking up at the window where the child stood all but hidden.

"I've heard that too," she said. "And they tell me that one never sees a dead person's face in a dream. Is that true?"

"I believe it is—now I come to think of it."

"But how is it with yourself—yourself?" The blind eyes turned toward me.

"I have never seen the faces of my dead in any dream," I answered.

"Then it must be as bad as being blind."

The sun had dipped behind the woods and the long shades were possessing the insolent horsemen one by one. I saw the light die from off the top of a glossy-leaved lance and all the brave hard green turn to soft black. The house, accepting another day at end, as it had accepted a hundred thousand gone, seemed to settle deeper into its rest among the shadows.

"Have you ever wanted to?" she said after the silence.

"Very much sometimes," I replied. The child had left the window as the shadows closed upon it.

"Ah! So've I, but I don't suppose it's allowed. . . . Where d'you live?"

"Quite the other side of the county—sixty miles and more, and I must be going back. I've come without my big lamp."

"But it's not dark yet. I can feel it."

"I'm afraid it will be by the time I get home. Could you lend me someone to set me on my road at first? I've utterly lost myself."

"I'll send Madden with you to the crossroads. We are so out of the world, I don't wonder you were lost! I'll guide you round to the front of the house; but you will go slowly, won't you, till you're out of the grounds? It isn't foolish, do you think?"

"I promise you I'll go like this," I said, and let the car start herself down the flagged path.

We skirted the left wing of the house, whose elaborately cast lead guttering alone was worth a day's journey; passed under a great rose-grown gate in the red wall, and so round to the high front of the house which in beauty and stateliness as much excelled the back as that of all others I had seen.

"Is it so very beautiful?" she said wistfully, when she heard my raptures. "And you like the lead figures too? There's the old azalea garden behind. They say that this place must have been made for children. Will you help me out, please? I should like to come with you as far as the crossroads, but I mustn't leave them. Is that you, Madden? I want you to show this gentleman the way to the crossroads. He has lost his way but—he has seen them."

A butler appeared noiselessly at the miracle of old oak that must be called the front door, and slipped aside to put on his hat. She stood looking at me with open blue eyes in which no sight lay, and I saw for the first time that she was beautiful.

"Remember," she said quietly, "if you are fond of them you will come again," and disappeared within the house.

The butler in the car said nothing till we were nearly at the lodge gates, where catching a glimpse of a blue blouse in a shrubbery I swerved amply lest the devil that leads little boys to play should drag me into child murder.

"Excuse me," he asked of a sudden, "but why did you do that, sir?"

"The child yonder."

"Our young gentleman in blue?"

"Of course."

"He runs about a good deal. Did you see him by the fountain, sir?"

"Oh, yes, several times. Do we turn here?"

"Yes, sir. And did you 'appen to see them upstairs too?"

"At the upper window? Yes."

"Was that before the mistress come out to speak to you, sir?"

"A little before that. Why d'you want to know?"

He paused a little. "Only to make sure that—that they had seen the car, sir, because with children running about, though I'm sure you're driving particularly careful, there might be an accident. That was all, sir. Here are the crossroads. You can't miss your way from now on. Thank you, sir, but that isn't *our* custom, not with—"

"I beg your pardon," I said, and thrust away the British silver.

"Oh, it's quite all right with the rest of 'em as a rule. Good-bye, sir."

He retired into the armor-plated conning tower of his caste and walked away. Evidently a butler solicitous for the honor of his house, and interested, probably through a maid, in the nursery.

Once beyond the signposts at the crossroads I looked back, but the crumpled hills interlaced so jealously that I could not see where the house had lain. When I asked its name at a cottage along the road, the fat woman who sold sweetmeats there gave me to understand that people with motor cars had small right to live—much less to "go about talking like carriage folk." They were not a pleasant-mannered community.

When I retraced my route on the map that evening I was little wiser. Hawkin's Old Farm appeared to be the survey title of the place, and the old County Gazeteer, generally so ample, did not allude to it. The big house of those parts was Hodnington Hall, Georgian with early Victorian embellishments, as an atrocious steel engraving attested. I carried my difficulty to a neighbor—a deep-rooted tree of that soil—and he gave me a name of a family which conveyed no meaning.

A month or so later—I went again, or it may have been that my car took the road of her own volition. She over-ran the fruitless Downs, threaded every turn of the maze of lanes below the hills, drew through the high-walled woods, impenetrable in their full leaf, came out at the crossroads where the butler had left me and a little further on developed an internal trouble which forced me to turn her in on a grass way-waste that cut into a summer-silent hazel wood. So far as I could make sure by the sun and a six-inch Ordinance map, this should be the road flank of that wood which I had first explored from the heights above. I made a mighty serious business of my repairs and a glittering shop of my repair kit, spanners, pump and the like, which I spread out orderly upon a rug. It was a trap to catch all childhood, for on such a day, I argued, the children would not be far off. When I paused in my work I listened, but the wood was so full of the noises of summer (though the birds had mated) that I could not at first distinguish these from the tread of small cautious feet stealing across the dead leaves. I rang my bell in an alluring manner, but the feet fled, and I repented, for to a child a sudden noise is very real terror. I must have been at work half an hour when I heard in the wood the voice of the blind woman crying: "Children, oh, children, where are you?" and the stillness made slow to close on the perfection of that cry. She came toward me, half feeling her way between the tree boles, and though a child it seemed clung to her skirt, it swerved into the leafage like a rabbit as she drew nearer.

"Is that you?" she said, "from the other side of the county?"

"Yes, it's me from the other side of the county."

"Then why didn't you come through the upper woods? They were there just now."

"They were here a few minutes ago. I expect they knew my car had broken down, and came to see the fun."

"Nothing serious, I hope? How do cars break down?"

"In fifty different ways. Only mine has chosen the fifty-first."

She laughed merrily at the tiny joke, cooed with delicious laughter and pushed her hat back.

"Let me hear," she said.

"Wait a moment," I cried, "and I'll get you a cushion."

She set her foot on the rug all covered with spare parts, and stooped above it eagerly. "What delightful things!" The hands through which she saw glanced in the checkered sunlight. "A box here—another box! Why you've arranged them like playing shop!"

"I confess now that I put it out to attract them. I don't need half those things really."

"How nice of you! I heard your bell in the upper wood. You say they were here before that?"

"I'm sure of it. Why are they so shy? That little fellow in blue who was with you just now ought to have got over his fright. He's been watching me like a Red Indian."

"It must have been your bell," she said. "I heard one of them go past me in trouble when I was coming down. They're shy—so shy even with me." She turned her face over her shoulder and cried again: "Children! Oh, children! Look and see!"

"They must have gone off together on their own affairs," I suggested, for there was a murmur behind us of lowered voices broken by the sudden squeaking giggles of childhood. I returned to my tinkerings and she leaned forward, her chin on her hand, listening interestedly.

"How many are they?" I said at last. The work was finished, but I saw no reason to go.

Her forehead puckered a little in thought. "I don't quite know," she said simply. "Sometimes more—sometimes less. They come and stay with me because I love them, you see."

"That must be very jolly," I said, replacing a drawer, and as I spoke I heard the inanity of my answer.

"You—you aren't laughing at me," she cried. "I—I haven't any of my own. I never married. People laugh at me sometimes about them because—because—"

"Because they're savages," I returned. "It's nothing to fret for. That sort laugh at everything that isn't in their own fat lives."

"I don't know. How should I? I only don't like being laughed at about *them*. It hurts; and when one can't see . . . I don't want to seem silly," her chin quivered like a child's as she spoke, "but we blindies have only one skin, I think. Everything outside hits straight at our souls. It's different with you. You've such good defenses in your eyes—looking out—before anyone can really pain you in your soul. People forget that with us."

I was silent reviewing that inexhaustible matter—the more than inherited (since it is also carefully taught) brutality of the Christian peoples, beside which the mere heathendom of the West Coast nigger is clean and restrained. It led me a long distance into myself.

"Don't do that!" she said of a sudden, putting her hands before her eyes.

"What?"

She made a gesture with her hand.

"That! It's—it's all purple and black. Don't! That color hurts."

"But how in the world do you know about colors?" I exclaimed, for here was a revelation indeed.

"Colors as colors?" she asked.

"No. *Those* colors which you saw just now."

"You know as well as I do." She laughed. "Else you wouldn't have asked that question. They aren't in the world at all. They're in *you*—when you went so angry."

"D'you mean a dull purplish patch, like port wine mixed with ink?" I said.

"I've never seen ink or port wine, but the colors aren't mixed. They are separate—all separate."

"Do you mean black streaks and jags across the purple?"

She nodded. "Yes—if they are like this," and zigzagged her finger again, "but it's more red than purple—that bad color."

"And what are the colors at the top of the—whatever you see?"

Slowly she leaned forward and traced on the rug the figure of the Egg itself.

"I see them so," she said, pointing with a grass stem, "white, green, yellow, red, purple, and when people are angry or bad, black across the red—as you were just now."

"Who told you anything about it—in the beginning?" I demanded.

"About the colors? No one. I used to ask what colors were when I was little—in table covers and curtains and carpets, you see—

because some colors hurt me and some made me happy. People told me; and when I got older that was how I saw people." Again she traced the outline of the Egg, which it is given to very few of us to see.

"All by yourself?" I repeated.

"All by myself. There wasn't anyone else. I only found out afterward that other people did not see the colors."

She leaned against the tree bole plaiting and unplaiting chance-plucked grass stems. The children in the wood had drawn nearer. I could see them with the tail of my eye frolicking like squirrels.

"Now I am sure you will never laugh at me," she went on after a long silence. "Nor at *them*."

"Goodness! No!" I cried, jolted out of my train of thought. "A man who laughs at a child—unless the child is laughing too—is a heathen!"

"I didn't mean that of course. You'd never laugh *at* children, but I thought—I used to think—that perhaps you might laugh about *them*. So now I beg your pardon. . . . What are you going to laugh at?"

I had made no sound, but she knew.

"At the notion of your begging my pardon. If you had done your duty as a pillar of the state and a landed proprietress you ought to have summoned me for trespass when I barged through your woods the other day. It was disgraceful of me—inexcusable."

She looked at me, her head against the tree trunk—long and stead-fastly—this woman who could see the naked soul.

"How curious," she half whispered. "How very curious."

"Why, what have I done?"

"You don't understand . . . and yet you understood about the colors. Don't you understand?"

She spoke with a passion that nothing had justified, and I faced her bewilderedly as she rose. The children had gathered themselves in a roundel behind a bramble bush. One sleek head bent over something smaller, and the set of the little shoulders told me that fingers were on lips. They, too, had some child's tremendous secret. I alone was hopelessly astray there in the broad sunlight.

"No," I said, and shook my head as though the dead eyes could note. "Whatever it is, I don't understand yet. Perhaps I shall later—if you'll let me come again."

"You will come again," she answered. "You will surely come again and walk in the wood."

"Perhaps the children will know me well enough by that time to let me play with them—as a favor. You know what children are like."

"It isn't a matter of favor but of right," she replied, and while I wondered what she meant, a disheveled woman plunged round the bend of the road, loose-haired, purple, almost lowing with agony as she ran. It was my rude fat friend of the sweetmeat shop. The blind woman heard and stepped forward. "What is it, Mrs. Madehurst?" she asked.

The woman flung her apron over her head and literally groveled in the dust, crying that her grandchild was sick to death, that the local doctor was away fishing, that Jenny the mother was at her wit's end and so forth, with repetitions and bellowings.

"Where's the next nearest doctor?" I asked between paroxysms.

"Madden will tell you. Go round to the house and take him with you. I'll attend to this. Be quick!" She half supported the fat woman into the shade. In two minutes I was blowing all the horns of Jericho under the front of the House Beautiful, and Madden, in the pantry, rose to the crisis like a butler and a man.

A quarter of an hour at illegal speeds caught us a doctor five miles away. Within the half-hour we had decanted him, much interested in motors, at the door of the sweetmeat shop, and drew up the road to await the verdict.

"Useful things cars," said Madden, all man and no butler. "If I'd had one when mine took sick she wouldn't have died."

"How was it?" I asked.

"Croup. Mrs. Madden was away. No one knew what to do. I drove eight miles in a tax cart for the doctor. She was choked when we came back. This car'd ha' saved her. She'd have been close on ten now."

"I'm sorry," I said. "I thought you were rather fond of children from what you told me going to the crossroads the other day."

"Have you seen 'em again, sir—this mornin'?"

"Yes, but they're well broke to cars. I couldn't get any of them within twenty yards of it."

He looked at me carefully as a scout considers a stranger—not as a menial should lift his eyes to his divinely appointed superior.

"I wonder why," he said just above the breath that he drew.

We waited on. A light wind from the sea wandered up and down the long lines of the woods, and the wayside grasses, whitened already with summer dust, rose and bowed in sallow waves.

A woman, wiping the suds off her arms, came out of the cottage next the sweetmeat shop.

"I've be'n listenin' in de back yard," she said cheerily. "He says Arthur's unaccountable bad. Did ye hear him shruck just now? Unaccountable bad. I reckon t'will come Jenny's turn to walk in de wood nex' week along Mr. Madden."

"Excuse me, sir, but your lap robe is slipping," said Madden deferentially. The woman started, dropped curtsey and hurried away.

"What does she mean by 'walking in the wood'?" I asked.

"It must be some saying they use hereabouts. I'm from Norfolk myself," said Madden. "They're an independent lot in this county. She took you for a chauffeur, sir."

I saw the doctor come out of the cottage followed by a draggle-tailed wench who clung to his arm as though he could make treaty for her with Death. "Dat sort," she wailed—"dey're just as much to us dat has 'em as if dey was lawful born. Just as much—just as much! An' God he'd be just as pleased if you saved 'un, Doctor. Don't take it from me. Miss Florence will tell ye de very same. Don't leave 'im, Doctor!"

"I know. I know," said the man, "but he'll be quiet for a while now. We'll get the nurse and the medicine as fast as we can." He signaled me to come forward with the car, and I strove not to be privy to what followed; but I saw the girl's face, blotched and frozen with grief, and I felt the hand without a ring clutching at my knees when we moved away.

The doctor was a man of some humor, for I remember he claimed my car under the Oath of Æsculapius, and used it and me without mercy. First we convoyed Mrs. Madehurst and the blind woman to wait by the sick bed till the nurse should come. Next we invaded a neat county town for prescriptions (the doctor said the trouble was cerebrospinal meningitis), and when the County Institute, banked and flanked with scared market cattle, reported itself out of nurses for the moment we literally flung ourselves loose upon the county. We conferred with the owners of great houses—magnates at the ends of overarching avenues whose big-boned womenfolk strode away from their tea tables to listen to the imperious doctor. At last a white-haired lady sitting under a cedar of Lebanon and surrounded by a court of magnificent Borzois—all hostile to motors—gave the doctor, who received them as from a princess, written orders which we bore many miles at top speed, through a park, to a French nunnery, where we took over in exchange a pallid-faced and trembling Sister. She knelt at the bottom of the tonneau telling her beads without pause till, by short cuts of the doctor's invention, we had her to the sweetmeat shop once more. It was a long afternoon crowded with mad episodes that rose and dissolved like the dust of our wheels; cross-sections of remote and incomprehensible lives through which we raced at right angles; and I went home in the dusk, wearied out, to dream of the clashing horns of cattle; round-eyed nuns walking in a garden of graves; pleasant tea parties beneath shaded trees; the carbolic-scented, gray-painted corridors of the County Institute; the steps of shy children in the wood and the hands that clung to my knees as the motor began to move.

I had intended to return in a day or two, but it pleased fate to hold me from that side of the county, on many pretexts, till the elder and the wild rose had fruited. There came at last a brilliant day, swept clear from the southwest, that brought the hills within hand's reach —a day of unstable airs and high filmy clouds. Through no merit of my own I was free, and set the car for the third time on that known road. As I reached the crest of the Downs I felt the soft air change, saw it glaze under the sun; and, looking down at the sea, in that instant beheld the blue of the Channel turn through polished silver and dulled steel to dingy pewter. A laden collier hugging the coast steered outward for deeper water and, across copper-colored haze, I saw sails rise one by one on the anchored fishing fleet. In a deep dene behind me an eddy of sudden wind drummed through sheltered oaks, and spun aloft the first day sample of autumn leaves. When I reached the beach road the sea fog fumed over the brickfields, and the side was telling all the groins of the gale beyond Ushant. In less than an hour summer England vanished in chill gray. We were again the shut island of the North, all the ships of the world bellowing at our perilous gates; and between their outcries ran the piping of bewildered gulls. My cap dripped moisture, the folds of the rug held it in pools or sluiced it away in runnels, and the salt rime stuck to my lips.

Inland the smell of autumn loaded the thickened fog among the trees, and the drip became a continuous shower. Yet the late flowers —mallow of the wayside, scabious of the field, and dahlia of the garden—showed gay in the midst, and beyond the sea's breath there was little sign of decay in the leaf. Yet in the villages the house doors were all open, and bare-legged, bare-headed children sat at ease on the damp doorsteps to shout "pip-pip" at the stranger.

I made bold to call at the sweetmeat shop, where Mrs. Madehurst met me with a fat woman's hospitable tears. Jenny's child, she said had died two days after the nun had come. It was, she felt, best out of the way, even though insurance offices, for reasons which she did not pretend to follow, would not willingly insure such stray lives. "Not but what Jenny didn't tend to Arthur as though he'd come all proper at de end of de first year—like Jenny herself." Thanks to Miss Florence, the child had been buried with a pomp which, in Mrs. Madehurst's opinion, more than covered the small irregularity of its birth. She described the coffin, within and without, the glass hearse and the evergreen lining of the grave.

"But how's the mother?" I asked.

"Jenny? Oh, she'll get over it. I've felt dat way with one or two o' my own. She'll get over. She's walkin' in de wood now."

"In this weather?"

Mrs. Madehurst looked at me with narrowed eyes across the counter.

"I dunno but it opens de 'eart like. Yes, it opens de 'eart. Dat's where losin' and bearin' comes so alike in de long run, we do say."

Now the wisdom of the old wives is greater than that of all the Fathers, and this last oracle sent me thinking so extendedly as I went up the road, that I nearly ran over a woman and a child at the wooded corner by the lodge gates of the House Beautiful.

"Awful weather!" I cried, as I slowed dead for the turn.

"Not so bad," she answered placidly out of the fog. "Mine's used to 'un. You'll find yours indoors, I reckon."

Indoors, Madden received me with professional courtesy, and kind inquiries for the health of the motor, which he would put under cover.

I waited in a still, nut-brown hall, pleasant with late flowers and warmed with a delicious wood fire—a place of good influence and great peace. (Men and women may sometimes, after great effort, achieve a creditable lie; but the house, which is their temple, cannot say anything save the truth of those who have lived in it.) A child's cart and a doll lay on the black-and-white floor, where a rug had been kicked back. I felt that the children had only just hurried away —to hide themselves, most like—in the many turns of the great adzed staircase that climbed statelily out of the hall, or to crouch at gaze behind the lions and roses of the carven gallery above. Then I heard her voice above me, singing as the blind sing—from the soul:

In the pleasant orchard-closes.

And all my early summer came back at the call.

    In the pleasant orchard-closes,
      God bless all our gains say we—
    But may God bless all our losses,
      Better suits with our degree.

She dropped the marring fifth line, and repeated—

    Better suits with our degree!

I saw her lean over the gallery, her linked hands white as pearl against the oak.

"Is that you—from the other side of the county?" she called.

"Yes, me—from the other side of the county," I answered, laughing.

"What a long time before you had to come here again."

She ran down the stairs, one hand lightly touching the broad rail. "It's two months and four days. Summer's gone!"

"I meant to come before, but fate prevented."

"I knew it. Please do something to that fire. They won't let me play with it, but I can feel it's behaving badly. Hit it!"

I looked on either side of the deep fireplace, and found but a half-charred hedge stake with which I punched a black log into flame.

"It never goes out, day or night," she said, as though explaining. "In case anyone comes in with cold toes, you see."

"It's even lovelier inside than it was out," I murmured. The red light poured itself along the age-polished dusky panels till the Tudor roses and lions of the gallery took color and motion. An old eagle-topped convex mirror gathered the picture into its mysterious heart, distorting afresh the distorted shadows, and curving the gallery lines into the curves of a ship. The day was shutting down in half a gale as the fog turned to stringy scud. Through the uncurtained mullions of the broad window I could see valiant horsemen of the lawn rear and recover against the wind that taunted them with legions of dead leaves.

"Yes, it must be beautiful," she said. "Would you like to go over it? There's still light enough upstairs."

I followed her up the unflinching, wagon-wide staircase to the gallery whence opened the thin fluted Elizabethan doors.

"Feel how they put the latch low down for the sake of the children." She swung a light door inward.

"By the way, where are they?" I asked. "I haven't even heard them today."

She did not answer at once. Then, "I can only hear them," she replied softly. "This is one of their rooms—everything ready, you see."

She pointed into a heavily timbered room. There were little low gate tables and children's chairs. A doll's house, its hooked front half open, faced a great dappled rocking horse, from whose padded saddle it was but a child's scramble to the broad window seat overlooking the lawn. A toy gun lay in a corner beside a gilt wooden cannon.

"Surely they've only just gone," I whispered. In the falling light a door creaked cautiously. I heard the rustle of a frock and the patter of feet—quick feet through a room beyond.

"I heard that," she cried triumphantly. "Did you? Children, O children, where are you?"

The voice filled the walls that held it lovingly to the last perfect note, but there came no answering shout such as I had heard in the garden. We hurried on from room to oak-floored room; up a step here, down three steps there; among a maze of passages; always mocked by our quarry. One might as well have tried to work an unstopped warren with a single ferret. There were bolt holes innumerable—recesses in walls, embrasures of deep slitted windows now darkened, whence they could start up behind us; and abandoned fireplaces, six feet deep in the masonry, as well as the tangle of communicating doors. Above all, they had the twilight for their helper in our game. I had caught one or two joyous chuckles of evasion, and once or twice had seen the silhouette of a child's frock against some darkening window at the end of a passage; but we returned empty-handed to the gallery, just as a middle-aged woman was setting a lamp in its niche.

"No, I haven't seen her either this evening, Miss Florence," I heard her say, "but that Turpin he says he wants to see you about his shed."

"Oh, Mr. Turpin must want to see me very badly. Tell him to come to the hall, Mrs. Madden."

I looked down into the hall whose only light was the dulled fire, and deep in the shadow I saw them at last. They must have slipped down while we were in the passages, and now thought themselves perfectly hidden behind an old gilt leather screen. By child's law, my fruitless chase was as good as an introduction, but since I had taken so much trouble I resolved to force them to come forward later by the simple trick, which children detest, of pretending not to notice them. They lay close, in a little huddle, no more than shadows except when a quick flame betrayed an outline.

"And now we'll have some tea," she said. "I believe I ought to have offered it you at first, but one doesn't arrive at manners somehow when one lives alone and is considered—h'm—peculiar." Then with very pretty scorn, "Would you like a lamp to see to eat by?"

"The firelight's much pleasanter, I think." We descended into that delicious gloom and Madden brought tea.

I took my chair in the direction of the screen ready to surprise or be surprised as the game should go, and at her permission, since a hearth is always sacred, bent forward to play with the fire.

"Where do you get these beautiful short faggots from?" I asked idly. "Why, they are tallies!"

"Of course," she said. "As I can't read or write I'm driven back on the early English tally for my accounts. Give me one and I'll tell you what it meant."

I passed her an unburned hazel tally, about a foot long, and she ran her thumb down the nicks.

"This is the milk record for the home farm for the month of April last year, in gallons," said she. "I don't know what I should have done without tallies. An old forester of mine taught me the system. It's out of date now for everyone else; but my tenants respect it. One of them's coming now to see me. Oh, it doesn't matter. He has no business here out of office hours. He's a greedy, ignorant man—very greedy or—he wouldn't come here after dark."

"Have you much land then?"

"Only a couple of hundred acres in hand, thank goodness. The other six hundred are nearly all let to folk who knew my folk before me, but this Turpin is quite a new man—and a highway robber."

"But are you sure I shan't be—?"

"Certainly not. You have the right. He hasn't any children."

"Ah, the children!" I said, and slid my low chair back till it nearly touched the screen that hid them. "I wonder whether they'll come out for me."

There was a murmur of voices—Madden's and a deeper note—at the low, dark side door, and a ginger-headed, canvas-gaitered giant of the unmistakable tenant-farmer type stumbled or was pushed in.

"Come to the fire, Mr. Turpin," she said.

"If—if you please, miss, I'll—I'll be quite as well by the door." He clung to the latch as he spoke like a frightened child. Of a sudden I realized that he was in the grip of some almost overpowering fear.

"Well?"

"About that new shed for the young stock—that was all. These first autumn storms settin' in . . . but I'll come back again, miss." His teeth did not chatter much more than the door latch.

"I think not," she answered levelly. "The new shed—m'm. What did my agent write you on the fifteenth?"

"I—fancied p'raps that if I came to see you—ma—man to man like, miss. But—"

His eyes rolled into every corner of the room wide with horror. He half-opened the door through which he had entered, but I noticed it shut again—from without and firmly.

"He wrote what I told him," she went on. "You are overstocked already. Dunnett's Farm never carried more than fifty bullocks—even in Mr. Wright's time. And *he* used cake. You've sixty-seven and you don't cake. You've broken the lease in that respect. You're dragging the heart out of the farm."

"I'm—I'm getting some minerals—superphosphates—next week. I've as good as ordered a truckload already. I'll go down to the station tomorrow about 'em. Then I can come and see you man to man like, miss, in the daylight. . . . That gentleman's not going away, is he?" He almost shrieked.

I had only slid the chair a little further back, reaching behind me to tap on the leather of the screen, but he jumped like a rat.

"No. Please attend to me, Mr. Turpin." She turned in her chair and faced him with his back to the door. It was an old and sordid little piece of scheming that she forced from him—his plea for the new cowshed at his landlady's expense, that he might with the covered manure pay his next year's rent out of the valuation after, as she made clear, he had bled the enriched pastures to the bone. I could not but admire the intensity of his greed, when I saw him outfacing for its sake whatever terror it was that ran wet on his forehead.

I ceased to tap the leather—was, indeed, calculating the cost of the shed—when I felt my relaxed hand taken and turned softly between the soft hands of a child. So at last I had triumphed. In a moment I would turn and acquaint myself with those quick-footed wanderers. . . .

The little brushing kiss fell in the center of my palm—as a gift on which the fingers were, once, expected to close: as the all faithful, half-reproachful signal of a waiting child not used to neglect even when grownups were busiest—a fragment of the mute code devised very long ago.

Then I knew. And it was as though I had known from the first day when I looked across the lawn at the high window.

I heard the door shut. The woman turned to me in silence, and I felt that she knew.

What time passed after this I cannot say. I was roused by the fall of a log, and mechanically rose to put it back. Then I returned to my place in the chair very close to the screen.

"Now you understand," she whispered, across the packed shadows.

"Yes, I understand—now. Thank you."

"I—I only hear them." She bowed her head in her hands. "I have no right, you know—no other right. I have neither borne nor lost—neither borne nor lost!"

"Be very glad then," said I, for my soul was torn open within me.

"Forgive me!"

She was still, and I went back to my sorrow and my joy.

"It was because I loved them so," she said at last, brokenly. "*That* was why it was, even from the first—even before I knew that they—they were all I should ever have. And I loved them so!"

She stretched out her arms to the shadows and the shadows within the shadow.

"They came because I loved them—because I needed them. I—I must have made them come. Was that wrong, think you?"

"No—no."

"I—I grant you that the toys and—and all that sort of thing were nonsense, but—but I used to so hate empty rooms myself when I was little." She pointed to the gallery. "And the passages all empty . . . And how could I ever bear the garden door shut? Suppose—"

"Don't! For pity's sake, don't!" I cried. The twilight had brought a cold rain with gusty squalls that plucked at the leaded windows.

"And the same thing with keeping the fire in all night. I don't think it so foolish—do you?"

I looked at the broad brick hearth, saw, through tears I believe, that there was no unpassable iron on or near it, and bowed my head.

"I did all that and lots of other things—just to make believe. Then they came. I heard them, but I didn't know that they were not mine by right till Mrs. Madden told me—"

"The butler's wife? What?"

"One of them—I heard—she saw. And knew. Hers! *Not* for me. I didn't know at first. Perhaps I was jealous. Afterward, I began to understand that it was only because I loved them, not because—Oh, you *must* bear or lose," she said piteously. "There is no other way—and yet they love me. They must! Don't they?"

There was no sound in the room except the lapping voices of the fire, but we two listened intently, and she at least took comfort from what she heard. She recovered herself and half rose. I sat still in my chair by the screen.

"Don't think me a wretch to whine about myself like this, but—but I'm in the dark, you know, and *you* can see."

In truth I could see, and my vision confirmed me in my resolve, though that was like the very parting of spirit and flesh. Yet a little longer I would stay since it was the last time.

"You think it is wrong, then?" she cried sharply, though I had said nothing.

"Not for you. A thousand times no. For you it is right. . . . I am grateful to you beyond words. For me it would be wrong. For me only . . ."

"Why?" she said, but passed her hand before her face as she had done at our second meeting in the wood. "Oh, I see," she went on simply as a child. "For you it would be wrong." Then with a little indrawn laugh, "And, d'you remember I called you lucky—once—at first. You who must never come here again!"

She left me to sit a little longer by the screen, and I heard the sound of her feet die out along the gallery above.

THE CHAIR
By John Bartlow Martin

. . . .

His mother encouraged him to read the Bible,
his father taught him carpentry, but when he was thirteen
he got into trouble because of a girl,
and when he was twenty-four he and a friend butchered
the Niebel family of Mansfield, Ohio.

"I am not going to say any more, you got enough on me to electrocute me."
—Murl Daniels to a policeman, as quoted by the policeman.

In closing the week-long trial the lawyer for the accused asked mercy and the prosecutor asked death—"evil, vicious and merciless crime . . . stripped and murdered in cold blood"—and the three judges left the bench to deliberate. They walked out of the county courthouse—across the street, in the town square, people dozed on benches beneath the shade trees near the bandstand—and walked a few blocks to a cafeteria and ate lunch, then returned to the office of the presiding local judge to write their verdict and sentence. Their deliberations and lunch having consumed only an hour and a half, they reconvened court and the presiding judge asked the defendant if he had anything to say as to why sentence should not be pronounced. He said a good deal, but it made no difference. The presiding judge, a careful youngish man with a calm, incisive voice, began to read:

"It is the sentence, order and judgment of this Court, that the defendant, Robert Murl Daniels, on the third day of January, A.D. 1949, within the walls of the Ohio Penitentiary, Columbus, Ohio, be executed by causing a current of electricity, of sufficient intensity to cause death, to pass through the body of the said Robert Murl Daniels, and the application of such current continued until the said Robert Murl Daniels is dead. . . ."

(The law provides that a man can be executed 100 days after he is sentenced, but 100 days from that day would have been Christmas Day. So they made it January 3, that is, 109 days.)

The courtroom, oak-paneled and dim-lit, with sunlight slanting in through Venetian blinds behind the judges' bench, was small and crowded, and people who couldn't get in stood in the corridor outside. The defendant Daniels was slender, blond, of medium height, with a handsome oval face and a long, thin neck. He was twenty-four years old. He had been expecting this a long time. They led him out and next day drove him sixty-five miles over rolling Ohio farmland, fresh and rich with harvest, to the city where he had grown up, Columbus. They put him in Cell No. 1 of Death Row. He had 109 days to wait. No, 108 now.

Murl Daniels was born April 8, 1924, at Nelsonville in the Hocking Valley near the Ohio River, a once booming coal town now grown sleepy in the clay hills of southern Ohio. His parents both were from the hill country. His father, Robert Lee Daniels, a rather small, wiry man, was born in the mountains of West Virginia, one of ten sons of a Welsh ferryman. Robert Lee Daniels is proud of his lineage—"My mother was the daughter of Captain Morgan Day of General Lee's army"—and gives the impression that only ill chance and trickery deprived him of a considerable inheritance. His father died in 1898, when Robert Lee was seven, and the mother took the family to Athens County, Ohio, where the boys mined coal in the Hocking Valley hills. After grade school he went to night school two years, studying to be a drug clerk, but quit at the age of twenty to marry a river-town girl and go to Columbus. He found a job as a drop forger. Two children, a boy and a girl, were born. After ten years he tired of strikes and shutdowns and night work and in 1921 took his family back to the Hocking Valley "to build mine cars and blacksmith." There a second daughter was born and so was the last child, our subject, Murl Robert Daniels (though subsequently sentenced to death as "Robert Murl Daniels," his name was Murl Robert Daniels). When Murl was less than a year old the family moved back to Columbus, this time permanently. But the hill country stamp is powerful.

They lived in the Goodale section of Columbus behind the Union Station. The once fine homes there have become rooming houses, hemmed in by factories and truck-loading docks, and High Street is lined with second-hand car lots and second-run movie houses, chili parlors and flashy night clubs. Only a couple of blocks away rise the gray walls of the Ohio State Penitentiary. In the Goodale section Murl Daniels spent his boyhood.

His parents tried hard to raise him right. They were hard-working, God-fearing, honest people who paid their bills and never got in trouble. They knew few people socially, seldom went out together or entertained callers. His mother, a stooped woman with a soft, kind, unhappy face, a woman of poor health and almost no education, has said, "I've never worked out, always been to home and took good care of my children. I'm a woman who never drank or smoked a cigarette in my life, I'm what you call a home woman. My whole life was in my home and my children." She was very religious: "We had family prayer. I'd gather the children all around and all of them pray and I'd pray with them, evenings and sometimes during the day too." She also placed cleanliness high among the virtues. On her knees she scrubbed her house ceaselessly. Of Murl she has said, "He was just as clean and neat as a pin, took a bath every night."

His father, after settling permanently in Columbus, had become a plasterer and carpenter. He had a hard time during the depression and took in roomers. He has said, "It's just been a life of work, a life of struggle, what everybody has in this world. We've fared well, ups and downs like everyone has. We've always been awful independent. A man's not happy unless he's workin'—that's what man was made out fer." He too was very religious. He was active in the Salvation Army, rising to the position of sergeant major, preaching on street corners for five years. "I taught the young people to play in the band. I don't play myself, can't keep time, can't beat the drum. But I know the scales." Looking back upon his life after Murl got into serious trouble, he said, "I think I was happiest when I was sitting at the Salvation Army in the circle with my boys, telling them Bible stories." At the Salvation Army he found a homeless delinquent of fourteen on parole from the Boys Industrial School; he taught him to play the cornet in the Salvation Army band, and took him home and reared him.

Murl was the youngest of four children, the baby. His parents and his next older sister, Esther, watched him carefully. They made him play close to home, in the alley, not the street. He had to be in before dark. When he was six, in June of 1930, he was sitting in his wagon in an alley near his home when a truck ran over him. It bruised and lacerated his head and body. He was in the hospital a few days. His parents say that thereafter he seemed nervous and disobedient, but his doctor recalls that he recovered "fairly well" and exhibited no more nervousness than might have been expected.

He got along all right in school. He always had to come straight home from school and report to his mother before going out to play. Even when he was eleven years old and went to a motion picture at night, his father met him and walked home with him. When he was seven he began selling newspapers. He gave some of his earnings to his mother. His father taught him carpentering and plastering. His mother encouraged him to read the Bible.

On June 22, 1937, when Murl was thirteen, he was nearly killed when another truck hit him while he was riding his bicycle. His left leg was deeply cut, his left arm fractured, his face and body bruised and cut. X rays showed no skull fracture. But he was semiconscious for several days and re-examination disclosed that he had received not only a mild cerebral concussion, but also, probably, a brain laceration and hemorrhage. He was in the hospital over a month. His broken arm and external injuries healed satisfactorily. But his parents noted that he was nervous, irritable, stubborn, irrational and had severe headaches. The family doctor agreed that Murl had not recovered satisfactorily from the head injury. His parents took him to a psychiatrist, an expense of forty dollars they could ill afford, and he told them, the father recalls, that "when this boy grows up he's got a chance to outgrow his injury, but if he don't and if someone says throw a brick through the window he'll throw it, if he's feeling like it."

He went back to school that fall, 1937, but did poorly. In December he got in trouble for the first time. He was then thirteen. Some girls took candy from a store and, caught, admitted they'd had sexual relations with several youths, including Murl. His parents took him to the State Bureau of Juvenile Research, which merely referred the case back to Murl's own physician, Dr. William P. Smith. He reported, "There is no doubt in my mind that this brain injury has resulted in definite mental disturbance in the form of irritability and a marked tendency to stubbornness, together with a dislike of authority. Just how much improvement we can hope for in a case of this type is problematical. . . ."

Murl had finished the sixth grade of school and entered junior high. He fell behind in his work, and the superintendent thought he might do better in a school where he could learn a trade. His parents sent him to one. But he went only a few months, and intermittently. In June of 1938 he broke into a store with some other boys and stole some fireworks. A few months later he burglarized a peanut machine in a restaurant. His father later recalled, "He seemed to get acquainted with a bunch of boys and he got into trouble, one trouble right after the other," and his attorney: "Most of the cases were dismissed. He had a pleasant nature, a pleasant appearance, and he always said he was led into these things by older boys." In 1939, Murl later recalled, "Eight or ten of us, we got into a brewery, stole a bunch of beer." The Court of Domestic Relations put him on probation. Except for a few months, the rest of his life he was either on probation, on parole or locked up.

By now he was adrift, wasn't going to school and wasn't working regularly either. His father bought him a truck, and he collected junk and hauled baggage. He was sixteen and not earning money enough to buy the clothes and car he wanted. In October of 1940 he was arrested for stealing an automobile. He claimed that he was just standing on a street corner when a friend of his drove past and offered him a ride; they picked up some girls and, driving eighty miles an hour, wrecked the car. Murl was sent to the Bureau of Juvenile Research, located on the spacious grounds of the State Hospital for the Insane. He was under observation for about three months. One interviewer noted: "Prognosis—very poor" and another: ". . . the boy is a potential menace in a community where there are adverse companions. On the other hand . . . if he was placed in a neighborhood where he would meet nondelinquent boys, he would soon be led into normal habits. . . ."

The Bureau psychologists found that Murl had an intelligence quotient of 106, about average. They thought him "very slow and deliberate," lazy—he wouldn't even do his best at the tests they gave him, and he exerted himself only when playing ping-pong. He talked about his troubles in a "lackadaisical" manner and volunteered "that he just wasn't able to resist the suggestion of other boys." He respected authority and was "classed generally among the better boys," but he did only what was required of him and was "very secretive and reserved." The other boys regarded him as a leader, and he assumed over them "a somewhat superior air." The attendants considered him "sneaking," perhaps because they couldn't keep him from trading food for cigarettes, from finding secluded places to smoke.

His parents blamed everything on his accident and evil companions. The Bureau psychologists, however, reported that his parents and sisters were "extremely overprotective" of him. They suggested his parents move to a more desirable neighborhood; his mother agreed, but his father, the psychologists reported, "stated that he did not choose to move at the present time." The father suggested that Murl live temporarily with a brother in another part of Columbus, but the psychologists thought this useless—he'd soon be back in his own home, and anyway he'd just "help his sister-in-law in the little chores about the home and spend the rest of his time amusing himself with his little nephew or playing at the Salvation Army Recreational Hall." The psychologists reported, "We have been able to observe no indications that he will present a better adjustment in the future than he has in the past. He seems to believe that since he had been able to get out of all former difficulties without any great discomfort, that he can continue to do so." The psychologists thought he needed "strict and fairly constant supervision, and a job," but since "we see no hope of making a change in the attitude of the parents or his sister," they recommended that Murl be committed to some correctional institution. The Court, however, upon recommendation of its referee, in February of 1941, gave him a suspended reformatory sentence and put him on probation for a year with relatives at Chauncey, Ohio, in the Hocking Valley hills where he was born.

His father took Murl's old truck down to him, and he worked a little, junking. He helped with his relatives' spring planting. He had nosebleeds and headaches, which his relatives treated with "a family remedy, a penny on his teeth." They testified later, when he pleaded insanity to a murder charge, that he played with their six-year-old daughter's dolls and played with their ten-year-old son at digging coal mines under the porch. One of them testified, "Murl would carry on his own private conversation himself . . . he would pretend to be an intoxicated man, he would fold his fingers, and talk like his tongue was thick; he would say, 'Officer I am looking for a parking place.' He would answer his own question, 'What do you want with a parking place, you haven't a car?' and he would say, 'That is why I want the parking space, my car is in it.'" At the time he was with them they told the probation supervisor that Murl "is getting along splendidly," and they said nothing about irrationality.

One evening early in June he said he was going to the village and he kept going, he went to Columbus "to see Mom." He came back, but in a couple of weeks he again ran off to Columbus and this time he stole a 1941 Ford coupe, picked up a girl and drove to Michigan, where he was arrested. He was sent to the Boys Industrial School at Lancaster, an institution for boy lawbreakers up to sixteen. The boys live in dormitories and, according to one, are punished for breaking the rules by being whipped with a leather paddle or being made to toe the line or duck-walk. Murl was there about a year and, apparently, was punished only once.

When he got out his family had moved to a better section near the University, of big old houses, some the homes of workingmen, some rooming houses for students. Murl got a job at a Curtiss-Wright war plant, working nights on the assembly line. But he wanted to go into the army. His father recalls, "He complained about all the boys being gone and him home, it didn't look right. He said, 'When I go out on the street I don't see any boys, nothing but girls.'" He took his physical examination and was rejected. He came home and said, "Mom, do you think I am nuts?" His mother remembers, "He was mad, he said he was going to find out why they turned him down. I said, 'Don't, you're all right.'" Murl said, "Well, they the same thing as told me I was nuts—they said I had too many head injuries." His father told him, "You're as smart as anybody." He tried to volunteer twice again, and the last time his father went with him, but he was rejected.

He was nineteen, handsome, smiling often. He was five feet, eight inches tall and well built, his complexion was good, he had silky blond-brown hair and blue eyes, and though his face was the least bit lopsided this only enhanced his charm when he tilted his head a bit and let a smile spread slowly across his face. He had a long neck. His teeth were bad. He moved slowly and usually gave the impression of being easygoing. He spoke in a slow drawl. His sister taught him to play the guitar, "folk songs," she said, not saying "hillbilly songs." When he was talking, he had a habit of picking his teeth absently, of leaning forward as though tired, of flicking the ashes off a cigarette deliberately, of looking closely at his fingernails. He was likable. He only moved when he had to. He walked with a saunter. He chewed gum. He was free with money and drank a good deal. He hated dirt and labor, liked cleanliness and sport clothes and fun. His mother recalls that he'd get dressed to go out in the evening, then "he'd stop and say, 'Mom, do I look all right?' and he'd come back and change his clothes to look better."

His parents were losing contact with him. He was away a lot, working days now, going out nights. He settled into a pattern—changing his clothes and bathing after work, then going out on the town, to the drab honky-tonks on High Street near his old home neighborhood, to a "club" upstairs over a burlesque show. He went to pick up girls. Girls were crazy about him. And he knew it. He had no close boy friends. His father remembers, "I only knew the girls' first names, not their last. They'd call him, fifteen a night." His father used to ask him if he thought he'd ever get married. He'd laugh and say, "Pop, all the girls wants to get married. When I think of getting married, Pop, my toes turn up and chills come all over me." His father says, "Whenever they got too strong he'd give 'em the shake." His sister recalls, "He liked all the girls he seen and everyone he met he was going to marry her the next morning." Some of the girls that he abandoned came to see his parents or telephoned them. His father remembers: "They said, 'Murl left me with my suitcase standing,' said, 'I can't figure that boy out.'" Nobody could.

On September 22, 1943, he and two other fellows and three girls —one of the couples was married—drove downstate in a stolen car for what they termed an "elopement" weekend. When, just as their money and gasoline were running low, one of the girls mentioned a storekeeper in Waverly who had a good deal of money, they got some guns, held the grocer up, tied him in a back room and got about fifty miles away before they came to a sheriff's roadblock and were arrested. The charge was robbery, and Murl Daniels was no boy. He was sentenced to serve one to twenty-five years in the Ohio State Reformatory at Mansfield. He was delivered there on January 28, 1944.

The Mansfield Reformatory is an ancient, gloomy, forbidding place, constructed some sixty years ago of massive stone. Its gray towers and ramparts rise like a feudal castle's amid rolling green lawns and ponds on the edge of Mansfield, a pleasant farm-industrial town of 45,000. To the Mansfield Reformatory are sent all male first offenders between sixteen and thirty years old who have been convicted of any crime except murder. This means that Mansfield receives everything from sixteen-year-old tire thieves to twenty-nine-year-old rapists. Though the older criminals are officially listed as "first offenders," they actually may have committed dozens of crimes before they were caught. Some men have spent fifteen years at Mansfield. Futhermore, a recent census of the 1,871 inmates revealed that less than half—879 or 47 percent—were of normal intelligence (33 percent normal and 14 percent low normal or dullard). Throwing out 1.5 percent not classified, this meant that 964, about 51.5 percent, were abnormal in some respect, as follows: 8 percent of the total were homosexuals, 21 percent psychopathic personalities, 12 percent psychopathic delinquents, 10 percent mental defectives, .5 percent borderline insane. Nor is this all. The Mansfield Reformatory is overcrowded—it has 960 cells intended for single occupancy, but by doubling up all except homosexuals and lunatics the warden has been able to cram 1,400 into them. With so mixed and dangerous a population, it is not surprising that Mansfield, though called a "reformatory," is a "maximum security institution." Escapes are rare, discipline strict. The wall is from thirty to thirty-five feet high, with five towers manned by guards with shotguns and rifles—"You're asking for it when you start over that wall," says a guard—and when the railroad gate is opened to bring in supplies, two machine-gunners stand guard. The prisoners are housed in two cell blocks. The "big block" rises fifty feet, bars all the way up from the concrete floor to the concrete ceiling, light slanting in gray from high windows in the outside wall as in a cathedral; and the cells open off the block in six tiers, one hundred cells side by side and back to back in each tier, six hundred cells compressed together like a bee's honeycomb, a thousand criminals packed into them. (Prisoners yearn for transfer to the second cell block, smaller and less crowded, quieter, with no pervert range or detention cells.) Each cell is about six by nine feet, maybe four steps from door to wall. On one side, hanging by chains, is a pair of double-deck bunks, on the other side a little table, at the rear a washbowl and a toilet, and the walls are steel. In each cell ventilator is a radio to which the prisoners may listen till 10 P.M. (the last hour in the dark) or 11 P.M. if a championship fight or other special event is broadcast. The prisoners are counted in their cells five times a day—6:30 A.M., 11:30 A.M., 5 P.M., 7:30 P.M. and midnight—and each prisoner is rechecked almost constantly at his work during the day. They are roused by a bugle at 7 A.M., they march in formation (silence enforced) to the mess hall at 7:30, and at 8:00 they go (silently in formation) to their jobs in the shops—print shop, machine shop, garage, tailorshop, furniture factory, and the maintenance places: powerhouse, laundry, library, hospital, kitchen, for this is like an independent city, with its own power plant and water system, a walled city. The walls enclose some dozen acres, concrete and dirt, the tiny grass plot for convalescents the only green in sight. In their blue shirts and gray pants and jackets, the prisoners march at 11:30 to the mess hall, then back to work; at 4:15 the whistle blows, at 4:30 they eat and at 5:00 when the count is verified they are locked in their cells till the next day. All prisoners work, even the perverts and psychopaths, except a few in school and a few too violently demented and those being punished. These last are kept in detention cells in the cell block or in The Hole, that is, solitary confinement cells underground where the fare is bread and water (plus a full meal every three days), where there is no light, no radio, no furniture, no exercise, where prisoners have no clothes but pajamas and sleep on the steel floor.

On Sundays there are shows and chapel, on Saturdays baseball games and other sports. For some prisoners it is a chance to learn a trade, for others an endless round of lathes and tools, assembly line and labor. They are paid from one to five cents an hour. Most of them depart with twenty-five dollars and a railroad ticket and a cheap suit of clothes. About six hundred inmates are assigned to the five honor farms, one just outside the walls and the others scattered about the state. At these are no walls, and the prisoners live in dormitories, not cells, and enjoy little freedoms. Nonetheless, not all long for the honor farms—farm labor is hard, especially for city boys.

Many men who have served time at Mansfield complain that the guards are brutal. The then superintendent, Arthur L. Glattke, an efficient, intelligent former high-school coach who gives the impression of being firm but fair, denies this. "I won't say guards never hit a boy," he has said. "That's why the boys are sent here—they don't conform. But the guards aren't brutal. Every time they use force they have to report it." Former inmates, however, tell stories about boys beaten mercilessly with clubs or forced to drink large quantities of castor oil or put into The Hole while sick; about "pets" of the guards given special privileges. One has said, "If the guard tells you to salute him or say 'sir' to him, you do. I had a guard kick me for telling him I didn't salute even my own dad." More than one prisoner has threatened to "get" a guard after he gets out. One former inmate has said, "I'll bet you there ain't a boy comes out of there ain't mad enough to kill somebody, they beat you like an animal so long," and another: "Any person if they're not a little bit crazy when they go in Mansfield they're a little crazy when they come out." And: "If they send you over there to reform you why they all the time knockin' you in the head? They send little kids in and put 'em with old-timers. They learn more over there about crime in a year than they'd learn all their life outside." A few men view guard work as school-teachers view teaching, but only a few. To most, it is just a job, ill paid. To the worst, it is a license to use a club. Top pay is $211.17 a month. During the war, when the pay was even lower, it was almost impossible to hire guards; today it isn't much easier. On the whole Mansfield probably is neither better nor worse than most similar institutions that have been set up to accommodate wrong-doers.

When Murl Daniels arrived at Mansfield he was nineteen years old. His I.Q. was rated at 101, average, but it was noted that he had a psychopathic personality. He had syphilis. Cured, he was put to work in the shoe shop. In general, his record at Mansfield was good. He broke a few minor rules. A guard recalls, "He wasn't hard to handle —maybe a little surly but that's all." After eighteen months, on August 1, 1945, he was transferred to the Grafton honor farm. In two months he ran away and hitchhiked home to see his mother, who, ill in the hospital, had been unable to visit him. His father told him to telephone the warden and surrender. He did. A guard took him back to Mansfield, first visiting the hospital (and taking care not to let Murl's mother know he'd escaped). He had been gone seven days. He was deprived of his recreational privileges and given six months' extra time. The warden has said since, "We knew he was a psychopathic personality, didn't foresee the consequences of his acts, so we weren't too surprised that he escaped." A little later Murl gave an inmate some parts of a broken band saw which could have been used in an attempt to escape, and for this he got two months more extra time. He committed no more offenses and was given another chance: on June 3, 1947, he was assigned to the honor farm just outside the walls. And here he first met John Coulter West.

Now, West too was a boy from the river towns and hills. He had been reared near Parkersburg, West Virginia, had left school at sixteen because he was "backward," had worked briefly in a factory at

Meadville, Pennsylvania, and in 1946 had gone to Cleveland, where his parents were working. He had driven trucks for several factories, then had bought his own truck and done long-distance hauling. He had burglarized a store in April of 1946 and got probation. He had jacked up a truck in Akron and stolen the tires and been sentenced to one to seven years at Mansfield. West was about twenty-one years old, small, fox-faced, with big ears, rimless glasses, a big nose, a pointed chin, a tiny mouth and pursed lips. His face was crooked— his right ear stuck out farther than his left, his glasses sat crookedly on the bridge of his nose, hair was heavy on the right side and thin on the left, and the lower part of his face inclined to the left. A probation officer later remembered him as "neurotic, unstable, nervous and evasive, but docile and a good listener." He had an I.Q. of 60—a moron. West arrived at Mansfield Reformatory January 16, 1947. He broke no rules and June 30 was transferred to the hog farm, where Murl Daniels had just been put to work. They were together all that summer.

The head farmer there, the man in charge, was John Elmer Niebel, a six-foot man weighing about 230 pounds, a Reformatory employee since 1928, and although Niebel later played an important role in Murl Daniels' life at the hog farm they had nothing directly to do with each other. But Daniels did establish some sort of relationship, at least in his own mind, with one of the guards under Niebel, a man named Willis Harris. Harris had been first appointed a guard in 1923. He resigned in 1941 to manage a private farm. A reformatory inmate was paroled to him. One day the parolee quarreled with Harris and told him he was going to leave, and Harris, being bedfast with a broken back and so unable to halt him with bodily force, shot him. On April 2, 1942, Harris pleaded guilty to a charge of maliciously shooting him with intent to wound him and was sentenced to one to twenty years in the Ohio State Penitentiary. Harris served almost two years. On March 5, 1944, about four days after he was paroled, he was hired again as a guard at Mansfield Reformatory, even though he himself still was on parole. Superintendent Glattke, who hired him, has said, "He is not criminally inclined. He had a very good record here. I needed a man."

Harris and Superintendent Glattke deny that Harris ever knew Daniels or West while they were at Mansfield. The records show that they were assigned to the hog farm, Harris to the horse barn. People familiar with the Reformatory point out, however, that overseers like

Harris, in charge of a single department of the farm, sometimes "borrow" inmates from one another without altering the official records. (Superintendent Glattke denies this is common.) At any rate, Daniels later testified flatly that he was in Harris' direct charge at the horse barn, and he testified that Harris hit him: ". . . it was over a harness or a bridle that I couldn't find. . . . I told Harris about it and he said, 'Do you want me to find it for you, huh?' or something on the order of that. . . . He was always, I don't know, kind of had a chip on his shoulder for me or something like that. He was always hollering at me, among all the other teamsters it was me that he picked out for to do the dirty jobs, to have someone to pick on and I was standing there with my team just outside the horse barn and he come out with his bridle in his hand and he hit me with it. . . . [The bit] was metal and he hit me in the face with it, I remember now and almost knocked me down and then he hit me again . . . about three or four times . . . he cussed me, he called me about everything he could think of and he kicked me but I got away. . . ." Daniels testified to another episode: ". . . I went out there to get the wagon and there was only three or four spokes in one of the wheels; I come back and told him . . . and he throwed a club at me." And what impression, Daniels' attorney asked, did this create on him? Daniels testified: "I wanted to get him, I wanted to get even with him, because all the time I was out there when that man would come around me I felt just like I was a little pup, I was scared to death of him and I wanted to go home and I was trying to keep my conduct good and I knew if I ever hit him back for hitting me I would get a year's added time and I just more or less put up with it so that I could go home." He said he told Harris he was doing his best in order to get out soon and asked Harris to transfer him if Harris was not pleased with his work. But, Daniels testified, Harris "said, 'No . . . I don't like you . . . I never did since you have come out here.'" Daniels had heard a rumor that Harris had been in the Penitentiary; Harris now corroborated it: ". . . he said, 'Yes, I suppose you know that I pulled time in the Penitentiary,' he said, 'I am going to tell you about it,' he said, 'You know while I was down there I had a hard way to go . . . they used to stick sticks in me and throw things at me and they kept me locked up all the time that I was there,' he said, 'I had a tough way to go down there and,' he said, 'you son of a bitch, I am going to give you just as tough a way as I had.' He lived up to his word, too, he gave me a tough way to go." Once, Daniels testified, he threatened Harris. "I told Mr. Harris that I would see him on the outside. . . . He said, 'I have been told that before.' I said, 'Well I'll keep my word.' "

Daniels told the police: "I wanted to take this Harris out. I'd like to took him out, I'd like to fought him and I'd like to have somebody there with me to see that he fought me fair and I'd like to have fought him with bare fists. I'd like to have beat him down to a pulp and I'd like to have stumped his face right in the ground, just give him a beating he would never forget. But I didn't want to do that until I got off parole. . . . A fellow that would pick on somebody when he's in jail, he's not much of a man." Daniels told the police: "When you're in a place like that, pulling time, it's hard, it's hard as hell to do. When you've got somebody over you and they're riding you all the time, like he did, everything you do is wrong, and he's hollering at you from daylight to dark and gives you all the rotten jobs and things like that, it really makes it tough on you, see, when a guy's riding you on top of all this environment."

John Coulter West hated the guards too. Daniels said, ". . . we'd talk about it, 'Before we get out, what do you say, West, let's come up and just beat that s.o.b. Now watch him, we're laying here in the grass and he'll come over here and have something to say,' and sure enough he would. A lot of guys laying around on the grass, they were allowed to, and [Harris or another guard] would come over and say 'What are you doing here, put your shirt tail in, roll your shirt sleeves down,' only two they would pick on, just me and him, see." One day West said, "You know I would like to team up with you. You're the type of guy I would like to run around with." And Daniels said, "Well, maybe we will, West."

Daniels was paroled first, on September 25, 1947. He had served a little less than four years. He went to Columbus, where his parents, now prosperous, had moved again, had bought a comfortable, old, low, rambling house near the University. To them Murl seemed nervous, unpredictably depressed or enraged, extravagantly affectionate toward his dog, absent-minded. For a time, he worked with his father, plastering. He puttered around the house, spading the back yard. In February he got a job at General Motors, where his sister and brother also worked. He worked nights, operating a bending machine. He earned about sixty dollars a week, and did his work well. He had enough money to make the down payment on a 1936 Chevrolet coupe. He had plenty of girls again. He went out almost every night.

On March 12, 1948, John Coulter West was paroled. On his way home to West Virginia, he telephoned Murl Daniels' home. Daniels wasn't there. Daniels' mother asked, "Where did you know him?" West replied, "At Mansfield." That night Mrs. Daniels told her husband about it, and he said, "Forget it, don't tell Murl nothing concerning nobody at Mansfield." They didn't.

The factory laid Murl off in April. He worked with his father. West wrote to him, inviting him to visit. His father recalls: "I told Murl, I said, 'Keep away from that boy, Murl.' Murl drawed his fist up like that and hit it down on the bed and said, 'Pop, he is a smart son of a bitch . . . the smartest man I ever saw.' I said, 'Keep away from him, Murl,' I said, 'He is too smart for you.' Murl never mentioned West to me no more."

About June 18 Murl left home and two days later, his mother recalls, "He come in and went into a bedroom and I followed him in and I said, 'Murl where have you been?' and he didn't seem to want to tell me where he had been. . . . He started to roll things over in his dresser drawer and I said, 'Murl what are you going to do?' I said, 'You are not going away again, are you?' He just looked at me with such staring eyes, he said, 'Yes, I am going away.' I said, 'You better stay here and not go away, you don't look good,' I said, 'there is something wrong with you.' He said, 'I'll be all right, I'll be all right.' He went to the basement. I followed him down to the basement where we had some old clothes stored away and he picked up an old shirt that was ragged, he hadn't wore for I don't know how long and I said, 'Murl what are you putting that shirt on for?' and he said. 'Well I might go fishing,' I said 'Go fishing,' he jerked it off, just a mad temper like and he came back upstairs to his bedroom and I saw him pack up; still I was crying, begging him not to go away because I knew he didn't act right, then he went into the dresser drawer and started rolling things over again and another old pair of overalls, he got them, he rolled them up in a newspaper. I said, 'Murl what are you taking them old overalls for?' He said, 'Well I might get a job,' and I said, 'Why you don't need no job, you have a job with your father.' So he started out through the kitchen, the back door, and I followed him clear to the door crying, begging him not to go away and so then he went outside, just outside the kitchen door and then he came back inside and he says, 'Mom, what do you want to act like that for, what is the matter with you, what is the matter with you?' He kept saying that I don't know how many times over and over. I said, 'There is something wrong with you,' he said, 'No,' I said 'Murl, do you want to go away because you are not acting right?' His eyes looked large and starey looking and shaking all over like, from the time he came in, just nervous like and that was the last I seen of him." He was gone for good.

West was waiting for him down the street in a car they had just stolen from a parking lot, a 1947 two-tone gray Pontiac. Daniels had been visiting him in Parkersburg during the preceding two days. Since being paroled West had worked in a foundry and on his family's farm. By the time Daniels visited him he "wanted to start on a spree to get money," Daniels remembered. They went back to Columbus together. Daniels had sold his own car. Daniels got his own license plates to put on the Pontiac they had stolen and then, "I bought me a gun and he had a gun and we started robbing and drinking."

"John Coulter West was green," Daniels later told the police, "so we took on some filling station jobs." West was nothing but a burglar, and in truth Daniels himself was little more. That first night they held up two filling stations in Columbus. At the first one, as Daniels was taking the attendant down the steps, John West blackjacked him needlessly. "I didn't know he hit him until he fell; it happened so quick, I didn't see Johnny come behind him." Then West jumped on the attendant and beat him on the head. En route to the next filling station, Daniels told West, "We're not going to hit this guy, we're going to stop all that stuff, we mess around and hit a guy and kill him and they will have the heat on us." Daniels reported: "He said, 'Murl, I'm green at this, you've been around a lot more than I have, and I want . . . to prove to you I've got guts.' So I told him it's all right to have guts, but have a little brains, too." They simply took the next attendant's money, "and we got away just as easy."

They slept in a tourist cabin. Next night they advanced another step: to tavern robbery. They went into Ryan's Grill, drank some beer and waited till only a few patrons remained at the tables; then Daniels called the bartender to him and said quietly, "I've got a gun right at your head, now don't move, put your hand on the bar." West was nervous. Daniels had told him to keep his guns hidden. But he pulled two guns. Daniels later recalled, "Johnny wasn't very good at talking, he would rather shoot them than talk and he talked to this guy, he told him, 'If you don't start smiling and act like you are happy I am going to blow your brains out,' so this bartender got happy; while Johnny was taking care of this bartender, keeping him on the end of the bar, I got the money [about $1,600]." They headed for St. Louis for a vacation. Just outside Columbus they encountered a State Highway Patrol roadblock, but the officers simply waved them on. Next day at Indianapolis Daniels stopped at a bank to get the money changed and found himself locked in, but it wasn't a trap, it was simply closing time; and when they got to St. Louis everything was fine. And what did they do in St. Louis? "We did about everything," Daniels testified. "We went to a park . . . and met some girls." Daniels had brought his guitar along and he played it at a night club in East St. Louis, Illinois, the tough town across the Mississippi.

They considered they had done well. They had girls, money, liquor, a car, clothes, guns, no nagging job, no parents, no guards, they were free. For the next month, from June 23 to July 23, they lived freely, driving all day over the hot Midwest roads, usually sleeping in tourist cabins, now and then in the car, occasionally stopping for a few days in some town because of girls, but usually keeping on the move, pulling a stickup, then lying low. They operated without plan. "We don't case a joint because they never go right anyway." Their stolen gray Pontiac was their home. They lived out of the luggage trunk. Each had two suitcases. And they also had a little black suitcase, in this they kept their guns, loaded. Daniels started with a .32 and West with a .38 but they kept stealing and buying more—a .22 rifle, a .30 rifle, a pair of .25 automatics, a .380 Beretta, a .45 automatic.

West did the driving. Daniels remembered: "He said he had never drove a car like that before with a gear shift on the steering wheel and he liked to drive it, so I let him drive and he used to take those curves wide open; I know I couldn't have done it." They made an effective team. West was nervous, "jumpy"—"he always told me he didn't like to monkey around, get it over with and get away. . . . Johnny liked a lot of excitement, gun play. . . ." Daniels was cool. Once in St. Louis while he was waiting on a street corner for West, three policemen drove up "and got out . . . and walked toward me, when they got almost to me they turned and went in the store," and he hadn't moved, he'd just watched them while pretending to read a newspaper, his .25 automatic ready.

West admired Daniels inordinately. West started out with only one change of clothes besides the suit the Reformatory had given him. He bought sport shirts, neckties, suits, all exactly like Daniels'. Daniels had a paisley dressing gown, and West hunted all over the Midwest for one like it. They saw eye to eye. Daniels remembered that, before they started out together, "We talked it over and it always seemed like that West wanted the same things out of life that I did and we'd never get them working for them, so—"

Q. (by a policeman) What were those things, Murl?
A. I don't know, nice clothes, an automobile.
Q. Good times?
A. Well, you might put it that way.

From St. Louis they went to Nashville, Tennessee, to attend a studio production of a radio program they admired, "Grand Ole Opry." They missed it, though—got drunk instead. They stayed about a week, celebrating the Fourth of July with whisky-and-root beer, firecrackers and girls. They headed back toward Columbus, and in Kentucky they got two more girls, "hillbillies," Daniels said. They saw the first one walking along the road. They picked her up and she led them to some whisky and another girl. ". . . they wanted to go to Columbus, they had never been there." In a tourist cabin en route Daniels telephoned home; his girl was "hollering and messing around," but he heard his mother say that if he didn't come home she'd notify his parole officer. It was his last call home.

They took the girls to Columbus. They told the girls they were stickup men, and the girls wanted to go along. But the girls embarrassed them: "we couldn't get them to wear dresses, they wanted to wear bluejeans all the time, and you know you can't take them nowhere in overalls. We bought them dresses, but they wouldn't put them on." So they ditched the girls. And then went out and bought more guns and that night pulled another stickup, at Joe's Grill on West Broad Street. Joe's was crowded and some of the customers, seeing the guns, ran out the back door and Daniels ran after them, and the bartender took his hands off the bar, and West fired a shot with his .45, perhaps unintentionally ("It's a squeeze action, you know"). He didn't hit anybody, and it calmed things down. Daniels came back and finished emptying the cash register and made the proprietor open the safe, and they got away.

They drove around awhile and chanced to pass a tavern on Fifth

Avenue, Earl Ambrose's. West didn't like its looks, but Daniels did, so they stopped. They went through the rear entrance and stepped to the bar and ordered beer. The place was almost empty—a couple of men at the bar, a few more in booths and at tables. At one table sat the proprietor, Ambrose; but Daniels and West didn't know it as, drawing their guns, they said it was a stickup and Daniels went behind the bar, West, as always, guarded the patrons. While at the cash register Daniels heard West say something like "Get your hand out of your pocket," but "I didn't pay no attention to it, I thought it was probably just a drunk and then I heard some shooting. I had my gun in my hand of course so without looking I just put my gun over my left shoulder and fired." The man who had moved was Ambrose. The bartender, first to see the guns, had warned him, and Ambrose had started for a phone booth. West shot him three times. "He got him every time, too," Daniels said. "He's a crack shot. . . . I guess it appealed to him." Ambrose stumbled, took a few more steps and dropped, dead. West and Daniels let the safe alone. They left Columbus with about $8,000, heading back to St. Louis. "We knew we were hot [they had seen a bystander take note of their license number, L4190]."

This happened on July 10, 1948. The Homicide Squad identified Daniels immediately through his license number, checked his previous record, began watching his home, his hangouts, his friends. Within five days they had identified West. They declared them parole violators and put out an alarm via teletype and circulars—WANTED FOR MURDER.

But West and Daniels were safe in St. Louis again, buying clothes, buying new tires for the car ("We was all the time getting the car fixed . . . getting it washed and waxed and the oil changed"), putting the car's own plates, D4351, back on it, drinking and playing the guitar at a roadhouse, getting girls. They picked up a couple of girls, telephone operators, and took them to Arkansas: "I don't know how I met this girl, but I sobered up in Arkansas . . . and I had spent five or six hundred dollars on a set of rings and a wrist watch for this girl that I didn't even know . . . and we are already to get married, I mean Johnny was, I wasn't. . . . I was scared . . . she said I proposed to her." West, Daniels thought, really intended to marry the girl he had: "He said it was the only girl he ever loved," and previous girls had spurned West. But West's girl was only seventeen, and she telephoned her mother. West "was too backward" to talk to the mother, so Daniels talked to her and "she cussed me out left and right, and told me the police was hunting me, so I said I had better get rid of these girls because, with murder on our tail, you can't be messing around with some girls." They took the girls to "some little old town down there somewhere, we let them out, they caught a bus and went on home or something, then we picked up a couple more." These were waitresses; they took them to East St. Louis and "stayed out there a couple of nights, and hit a few hot spots, threw some money around, played these one-arm bandits, you know. . . ." In a little town they went to the Eagle's Hall or the Moose Lodge where the girls were known, and "I got drunk there and when I come to and knew what I was doing we were on our way to Michigan. . . . I was in the back seat, this girl was choking me and then I hit the bottle again and I was, yeah I drove the car, almost wrecked it so Johnny tells me, and we pulled over to the road and slept on our way to Michigan . . . some place up there, it is a vacation land." It was Benton Harbor.

They rented a double tourist cabin. But next morning "Johnny was getting kind of fed up with these girls" and, breakfasting early in a restaurant, Daniels and West remembered the guards at Mansfield Reformatory, especially Willis Harris. "And so we agreed that we would ditch these girls and come to Mansfield" to get even with Harris and another guard who once had "busted Johnny's head with a club." They left about 7 A.M.—it was Tuesday, July 20, 1948—and during the all-day drive they did not waver in their resolve.

They arrived at Mansfield about 6 P.M. West said Harris hung out at the Ringside, a tavern near the town square. On the first floor was a big tile-floored barroom, upstairs a dark, low-ceilinged dance hall. They asked a waitress if she'd seen Harris. She hadn't. They went out and rode around town, looking for him on the quiet streets, where cars were parked slantwise around the square and window-shoppers strolled along. They didn't see him, but they did see another guard from Mansfield, "and Johnny wanted to get him because he had said he could whip any ten guys that ever walked. . . . Johnny didn't like that. . . . It seemed like anybody, I don't know how to put it, anybody that could do anything better than Johnny like play a game or something . . . he didn't like it and he wouldn't participate. . . ." But the guard, who was with his wife, went into a motion-picture show. Daniels asked the ticket seller when the show would be over.

They drove around some more, and "we almost killed some niggers . . . some niggers went past in a car and they hollered something. . . . Johnny told me what they said and I am not going to say what they said in court, but he said, 'Let's go get them' so we went after them . . . caught them. . . . Johnny pulled his guns out and I pulled mine out and these niggers really got down, they apologized. . . ." They wanted nothing further from the Negroes.

Trying to find out where Harris lived, West began telephoning all the Harrises in the phone book. Daniels looked up the numbers. Once a fifteen-year-old girl answered and said that Walter, not Willis, Harris lived there, and West asked if she was sure, and she said, "I ought to know, he's my daddy." Daniels thought this hopeless. They cruised around town some more. Finally, they went back to the Ringside. Harris still wasn't there. "Johnny wanted to kill these two girls in the floor show." They had not even talked to the girls. "I told him that he better not. . . . Anything that was beautiful he wanted to kill it. . . ." They hit upon the idea of getting Harris' address from Harris' superior, John Elmer Niebel, the head farmer at the Reformatory. They knew where Niebel lived. So in their stolen gray Pontiac they drove to the Niebel home.

John Niebel had worked at the Reformatory twenty years, had been head farmer ten. As head farmer he did not boss the prisoners directly; sixteen men under him, including Harris, did. Niebel was fifty, big, with a full fleshy face, a family man, active in the Masonic order, his wife active in the Eastern Star. His two sons had married and moved away. His daughter, Phyllis, a heavy blonde girl of twenty, who did clerical work at a local factory, lived with her parents in their white frame home on the North Main Street Road outside Mansfield, "the first house on the left past the Reformatory horse barns" (where Daniels claimed Harris had beaten him).

The Niebel house was dark when, a little past midnight, Daniels and West went to the front door. (In reconstructing what ensued, we have only Daniels' various statements and testimony.) Soon Niebel, dressed in pants, undershirt and slippers, opened the door. Daniels told him their car had broken down and he wanted to call a garage. Niebel pointed to the phone. Daniels, stalling, looked up the numbers of some garages and dialed a couple; neither answered. Niebel still was standing by the door across the room; Daniels wanted to get Niebel between himself and West, so Daniels asked Niebel to call a garage, saying, "I'm a stranger around these parts and I don't know much about this telephone system." Niebel, Daniels recalled later, "looked at Johnny and he says, 'This fellow here don't look like he's a stranger around these parts. What's your name?'"

West lied: "John Le Vond." It was a name he had used before.

Niebel went upstairs to get his eyeglasses. When he came back Daniels put a gun on him, told him not to move and asked where he kept his guns. (He at first merely wanted to make sure Niebel didn't try to use them, but then decided he might as well take them.) Daniels asked who else was in the house. Niebel said his wife and daughter were upstairs. Daniels asked if they were asleep. Niebel didn't know. Daniels told him to call to them, and Niebel did, and they answered; and so the three men went upstairs. West took Niebel into Phyllis' bedroom. Daniels waited in the hall for Mrs. Niebel, a heavy, soft-faced woman, and took her into Phyllis' room too. Daniels and West were smoking and mashing the butts out on the floor. Niebel sat on a chair. His wife stood by the dresser, wearing a bathrobe. His daughter Phyllis sat up in bed, clad in a nightgown, pulling the covers up around her. Daniels sat down on the edge of her bed to talk to Niebel about Harris. Daniels later recalled, "Johnny threw his gun at Mr. Niebel's feet and . . . wanted Mr. Niebel to reach for it. . . ." Niebel wouldn't. Daniels asked for Harris' address and Niebel wrote it down on Reformatory stationery, adding that Harris lived in the next house up the road. They talked about Harris for a quarter of an hour. Once Phyllis started to say something; her father told her to be quiet, to say nothing and to do exactly what the gunmen ordered and nothing more, "and he would take care of everything." After Daniels and West had ransacked drawers, they told the Niebels to come with them. Phyllis "slipped in a kimono or a house dress . . . and we took all three downstairs."

If they were to carry out their plan of getting Harris, they had to make sure the Niebels wouldn't interfere. But how? "Johnny he is forever snooping, he finds a door that leads down the basement and he said, 'Let's take them down and tie them up, then we'll get Harris.'" But in the basement they found no rope. "Johnny said he had some rope in the car . . . he said, 'We will take them out along the road and tie them up.'" So they put them in the car, West driving, Daniels beside him, the three Niebels in the back seat together for the last time alive.

They drove into Mansfield, dark now and quiet, and several times they circled the deserted courthouse square, hunting the right road out, till West spotted a sign: CLEVELAND 74 MILES and they headed north on Route 42, crossing the factory flats and climbing the hill and driving out the broad highway past scattered dwellings and tourist cabins and into the countryside. They came to a gravel side road and turned right. The road wound past an old farmhouse and pasture, moonlight bright on the sycamore trees, and dropped down into the broad fertile valley of the Rocky Fork, corn land. They drove a mile across the valley, came to a T, turned around, drove back a few hundred feet the way they'd come and stopped by the side of the road.

The night was hot and sultry, the moon bright. They marched the Niebels across the shallow ditch and sixty feet through the corn and lined them up about three feet apart in one corn row, Phyllis between her parents. "I looked at them for a while and I said, 'Take your clothes off.'" He thought they could not readily give an alarm naked. They disrobed. West gathered the clothes into a bundle. Daniels told him to take the clothes to the car and bring back a rope. Daniels faced them with his gun while West was gone. West returned. "He said, 'There ain't no rope.' So I said, 'Well, there's only one thing left to do and that's hit them in the head or something.'" Phyllis protested that "Daddy can't help it because he works for the State." Daniels told her, "Yes, but he doesn't have to be such a —— about it." Her father again cautioned her to be quiet. Daniels later recalled, "I wanted to hit them in the back of the head with this blackjack, I didn't want to kill them. . . . I didn't have any grudge against his wife and daughter, but they were there and were unfortunate in being there. So I told them, I said, 'Tip your head forward just a little bit. . . . This won't hurt you, otherwise it might kill you.' So they tipped their heads forward and I thought about it for a long while. I don't know, it seemed like a long time, it might have been a minute, two minutes, something like that. If I hit them and they come to they'd start screaming. I remembered that house . . . not so far away." West made up his mind for him: "Johnny pulled the trigger on one of his guns, on his .25 automatic. It never went off, but it jammed on him, so he cocks it and he tries it again." It jammed again. He was aiming at Mrs. Niebel. Why? Had she cried out for help? "No," Daniels said, "he just wanted to kill her. So I watched him there for a while, and I said, 'That damned gun.' So I'm thinking do I want to kill them or not. So just right on the spur of the moment I opened up and let them have it. . . . I just walked right down the line. . . . I started from the right and worked left." He shot them all in the tops of their heads, which were bowed. He shot the father first, two shots fast with his automatic, standing six feet away ("I didn't want to get no blood on me so I stood back quite a ways.") He shot the daughter second; she looked up a little. He shot the mother last, and as she fell, West, who had got his gun working, "put a shot in her for good measure." It hit her in the abdomen. Daniels and West went back to the car and drove to Cleveland.

And now the world they fought bestirred itself. About noon some Boy Scouts, led by a minister, happened upon the naked bodies in the corn. Daniels and West were identified as the killers by nightfall. By next morning rewards had been posted, a nationwide alarm was out, roads were blocked in six states, city and county and state police headquarters were stripped of men, and newspapers were calling it the "greatest manhunt in Ohio history."

En route to Cleveland after the murders, West had got sleepy and Daniels had driven. They tarried in Cleveland only long enough to shave, wash and buy some shirts. They drove to Akron, bought a .30 caliber rifle and slept. Thursday they started out for Findlay. They reached Tiffin at 1:00 P.M. and went to a tourist home, parked their car in the rear, rented a room (telling the landlady they were on vacation), slept till 5:30 P.M., went out, came back at 9:00 P.M. and left immediately, taking their luggage. They had no time now for girls or night clubs. They were just running. They were hot and they knew it. And they knew their car was hot too, the stolen car that the newspapers were calling "the dread two-tone gray Pontiac."

They had to get another car. They "went out looking for a Buick," any Buick. In a park they spotted one at a root-beer stand, a woman and her little boy in it; they somehow lost it in traffic, but almost immediately saw another. In it were a man and his wife, a young farmer named James J. Smith. They pulled alongside, forced them to stop. Daniels flashed a light in Smith's eyes, got out and walked around to the door beside the woman. "I just got the door open and heard a shot." West had asked Smith for his driver's license and, while Smith was getting it out, had shot him dead. Daniels told Mrs. Smith to get in the back seat. She jumped and ran, screaming, to a nearby house. Daniels and West, frightened, got into their gray Pontiac and drove away. Daniels recalled, "I didn't like it and I told him so. We had a little argument after he shot this farmer, but that soon died down."

They still needed a car, any car. They drove aimlessly. At a roadside park a few miles outside town they saw a truck parked. It was a "haulaway," a big trailer that carried five new Studebaker automobiles. They stopped and Daniels walked quietly to the haulaway. In the cab, the driver was asleep. "Johnny said: 'I'll take care of him,'" and walked him away. Daniels transferred their luggage to the truck. He heard shots, and West, coming back, said: "Let's go." They drove off in the haulaway, leaving their gray Pontiac near the body of the trucker, Orville Taylor, a young man with a wife and four small children at home.

It was now about 11 P.M. They halted at a truck stop and crawled into the front car atop their haulaway and slept. In the morning they drank some whisky from a gallon jug that Daniels had transferred from the Pontiac, then went to the truck-stop restaurant for breakfast. They "got something, which we didn't eat, and I told the lady that pie wasn't worth twenty cents." They got into their haulaway and headed for St. Louis. And as they started out, West remarked that he didn't think he'd live through the day.

West, once a trucker, was driving. The day was hot already, the sun bright on the road across the flat farmland. Daniels was in the front car atop the haulaway. Before long they came to a police roadblock. The police waved them through. Who would suspect a haulaway? (Orville Taylor's body was not yet identified.) They got through another roadblock, a couple more. But as they lumbered up to a roadblock at the intersection of Routes 637 and 224, a few miles from Van Wert near the Ohio line, Sheriff Roy Shaffer stepped from his car and flagged the truck. West stopped. The sheriff asked where he was from. From Tiffin, said West. Was he alone? He was. The sheriff walked alongside the haulaway. He became suspicious: these were new Studebaker cars, but they were heading in the wrong direction, back toward the factory. Telling Sergeant Leonard Conn to stand guard with a submachine gun, the sheriff climbed onto the top deck of the haulaway and walked forward along the catwalk. The new cars were covered with canvas. The canvas on the front car was slit. The sheriff pulled it aside. There sat Daniels, a rifle in his lap and a revolver in each hand (Daniels maintained he was asleep). "I ordered him to drop his guns and ordered him to come out," the sheriff later testified. "He dropped his guns and did as I told him. He said, 'You have got me, don't kill me, I'll do anything you tell me.'" The sheriff searched him, took a .25 automatic from his hip pocket, threw it down into the roadside ditch. And down below the shooting started. West, using the truck door as a shield, shot Sergeant Conn in the abdomen. Conn sprayed the cab of the truck with machine-gun slugs. West tumbled to the pavement, dying.

A game warden, who, happening along, had been wounded slightly, helped the sheriff get Daniels down off the haulaway. The sheriff radioed for help. The date was July 23, one month after Daniels and West had stolen the Pontiac. They had perpetrated five holdups and six murders.

Daniels was a national headline desperado. For a time he seemed to enjoy it, even bragged a little, as though trying to play his role well. Dozens of assorted police officials questioned him, and, sitting on a davenport in the sheriff's parlor at the Van Wert jail, he talked freely, so fast that a policeman writing down his words had to ask him to slow down. The sheriff took him out on the steps to face a crowd of newspapermen and photographers and a larger crowd of townsfolk, and he said, "Give me credit for the Niebels." The crowd yelled, "Kill him, lynch him," and the authorities removed him to Celina "for safekeeping." Before long he had stopped bragging, he was regretting an early statement that he had told the Niebels, "I'll give you three minutes to get right with the Lord"; "Lieutenant, I don't want that in there, the Lord's name is in vain there, I would like to have you take that out."

Several counties wanted him. Richland County got him and he was taken to the jail at Mansfield and indicted for the first degree murders of Phyllis, Nolana and John Elmer Niebel. The Mansfield *News-Journal* paid its reward to Mrs. Smith, the farmer's widow, and she gave it to Mrs. Orville Taylor, the trucker's widow, who was left with four children under eight, no home but a room in a boardinghouse, no insurance, no savings and forty dollars cash. Nearly everyone thought Daniels should be electrocuted and townsfolk of Mansfield stopped Prosecutor Theodore Lutz on the streets to say so. The Niebels had been a part of the community; many had known them. Daniels himself had told police they had enough on him to send him to the chair, although, awaiting trial, he seemed more hopeful. In jail he ate well, slept soundly, read magazines and comic books. His family visited him. They had no money for attorneys. Judge G. E. Kalbfleisch of Common Pleas Court appointed attorney Lydon Beam to defend him. Attorney Beam entered a plea of not guilty by reason of insanity at the time of the murders. Judge Kalbfleisch ordered two psychiatrists from state institutions, Dr. J. F. Bateman and Dr. R. E.

Bushong, to examine Daniels. Daniels waived a jury, so the Ohio Supreme Court appointed two other judges to hear the evidence with Judge Kalbfleisch, Judges Chester Pendleton and H. E. Culbertson.

On September 13, 1948, the trial began, and the three judges crowded the small bench before the American flag, and spectators crowded the small space beyond the oaken railing. Bobby-soxers came. Daniels would wink at them as he sauntered out at recess. At the counsel table he would slump with his cheek on his hand, as though a little bored. His father and his two sisters sat near him, behind the lawyers.

The key testimony, of course, dealt with his sanity. In Ohio a man cannot be held accountable for a crime unless at the time of the crime he was able to distinguish between right and wrong and, further, unless he also possessed the will power to refrain from doing the wrong. Daniels' parents testified that he had not been fully sane since the truck ran over him when he was thirteen and that his condition had been aggravated at Mansfield Reformatory. His father said, "We have always felt that he was mentally ill. . . . He wasn't able to control himself, he was easily persuaded and pushed, if told to do anything he would do it regardless of the cost." His sister testified: ". . . at times my brother is very sane, other times, I would say he is crazy. . . . He just didn't act right." His mother: "Well, he would take awful crazy spells, I would say; he would sit and stare; he maybe would be sitting at the table eating and he would just set his eyes on something and he would just stare ever so long . . . I would say, 'Murl, what is the matter?' He wouldn't give no answer at all, he would sit there ever so long." They testified he "acted queer" and "heard voices"; they recounted several incidents, but in one of these Murl merely talked to his typewriter and in another he merely beat a train recklessly to the crossing and some of the incidents showed little more than willfulness or ill temper. His father testified that his own mother (that is, Murl's grandmother) had been confined to an asylum for eighteen months and that two of his mother's nieces had been placed in an institution for the feeble-minded; but no documentary corroboration was produced and cross-examination indicated that the mother's condition resulted from an accident. The testimony of Dr. Smith, Murl Daniels' own physician from long ago, was more impressive. He blamed Murl's accident. "I feel that he had more than a concussion . . . he probably had some brain laceration and contusion or hemorrhage inside the brain." He quoted an outstanding surgeon who "went so far as to say he would prefer not to wake up after a severe head injury because of the mental changes which might ensue." Some persons injured as Daniels was, Dr. Smith said, have difficulty adjusting themselves to their surroundings. "You can call it psychopathy, which means something that is abnormal."

The two court-appointed psychiatrists had interviewed Daniels twice in the sheriff's parlor at the jail (once for four and a half hours, once for two and a half hours), had reviewed pertinent records and had obtained a spinal fluid analysis and an electroencephalographic study (the electroencephalograph is a machine that records the brain's activity; in its operation several electrodes are fastened to the subject's skull, a practice that must call the electric chair to the mind of a man facing it). The doctors testified that Daniels was not insane at either the time of the examination or the crime and that he was able to distinguish between right and wrong; and Dr. Bushong testified he thought Daniels could control his impulses. Dr. Bateman acknowledged that as a result of the childhood accident Daniels "could well have had brain damage and undoubtedly he did," and that such an injury may manifest itself spasmodically and is often induced to do so by alcohol. Dr. Bushong testified that a head injury is "quite liable to change a person's characteristics." Symptoms of change, he said, include headaches, dizziness, sleep disturbance, ringing in the ears, restlessness, moodiness, excitability and sometimes anxiety and lack of concentration. Daniels' counsel said Daniels exhibited those symptoms, but Dr. Bushong said he had not found all of them and even if he had he would not alter his opinion of Daniels' sanity.

Daniels himself, testifying, burst out: ". . . my sister used to . . . say, 'Ain't he nuts?' but I am not nuts, I am not and I know I am not." He testified for a day and a half (once he interrupted to say, "If I don't get a drink of water before very long, I'm going to dry up and blow away."). At first he seemed to be under the impression that a faulty memory was his greatest asset, and therefore much of his testimony was vague and useless, but his memory improved the longer he talked. Once he said: "I am not going to gain anything by lying, because I was caught and I guess that is all that matters." He did insist he couldn't remember killing the Niebels, that he only knew that West had told him he had. Sometimes Daniels seemed to be trying to be helpful, to comport himself properly.

The trial began on a Monday, September 13, 1948, and ended on

Friday, September 17, 1948. Reconvening court after lunch, Judge Kalbfleisch asked Daniels if he had anything to say. Daniels said: "Yeah, I got a lot to say if I may have a few minutes, I would like to be unhandcuffed, I got a few notes in my pocket—it is not going to do me any good." The handcuffs were removed. Daniels spoke 369 words, including these: "I know how I would feel if my mother, my father and my sister was killed all at one time; I think that is awful cruel, a great injustice to society. If I knew in my mind for sure that I actually killed them, I would think I deserved the electric chair, but until I am convinced in my own mind that I pulled the trigger and killed those people and I get the death penalty, which I know I am going to get, I know I feel I will not be justified."

He was a young blond man in a neat plaid suit. He had asked his parents to go home that day; only his uncle was there. Judge Kalbfleisch read the sentence: Death by electrocution. The handcuffs were locked again and he was led away. Attorneys agreed it had been "a nice smooth trial." Many people seemed to think that although Daniels might have been "a little off," his death would be all for the best.

Surely no one could maintain seriously that a man who would do the things Murl Daniels did was wholly normal. Not only his crimes, but little things he did bespeak a carelessness of the consequences of his acts. He committed the first murder in his hometown in a stolen car bearing his own license plates. He made no attempt to conceal himself at Mansfield while hunting Harris. But he was not insane; that is, he suffered from no recognized mental disease, such as dementia praecox. What was wrong with him? We are told he was a psychopath. A pyschopath may have a high I.Q. yet his *character* is deficient; that is, his morals and emotions deviate from those of most of us (and laymen consider him hostile, not sick). That Daniels was psychopathic seems clear. But what made him psychopathic? We do not know.

The state was criticized for paroling Daniels. State officials replied that if Daniels was not parolable nobody was. The State was criticized for not supervising Daniels' parole closely enough. It was replied that parole officers are underpaid and overworked. But the State's responsibility goes back much further. When the State's attention first was directed to Daniels, the State paid little heed to Dr. Smith's warning that Daniels' accident had damaged his mind. The Bureau of Juvenile Research psychologists later recommended he be locked up, not treated; the Court sent him to Chauncey, where he was no more likely to get help than in a Columbus slum. Yet what else could be done? The State had no proper place to put him, no place where he would receive treatment as well as discipline. At Mansfield the State's responsibility stands out most clearly. West, a moron, and Daniels, an unstable psychopath, certainly should not have been brought together by the State of Ohio. Yet they were, since Ohio has no prisoner classification system. Again, one questions the State's wisdom in rehiring the guard Harris. This has been defended on the ground that if the State is to ask private business to hire ex-convicts, it cannot refuse to do so itself. But simply because an ex-convict can be safely hired, say, to help build a road is no reason to assume he can be safely hired to guard prisoners.

The Ohio State Penitentiary, more than one hundred years old, with high stone and brick walls and turrets, stands three-blocks-square on Spring Street in downtown Columbus. When Murl Daniels first arrived at Death Row, a row of cells adjoining a cell block, he threw a fit of panic. Some fifteen other condemned men yelled at him to shut up. Guards subdued him forcibly, and the psychiatrist said he was faking, and thereafter he caused no trouble at all. He settled into a routine—pace from the wall to the barred cell door, read, eat, sleep. He had a chair and a bunk and a toilet and on the door a placard:

87057
DANIELS

Outside Death Row was a narrow passageway walled with heavy screening; beyond this was a bare room; and on the far wall of the bare room were high, dirty windows, screened and barred, through which gray daylight filtered dimly. His visitors sat on stools in the bare room and Daniels was let out of his cell to face them through the heavy screen. His parents, his sisters, his brother visited him often. He was permitted unlimited visitors. No one else came, not his old girl friends, nobody. He had no boy friends. He listened to the radio, read a good deal. Early in December he embraced the Catholic faith, receiving counsel from Father C. V. Lucein, a prison chaplain. He was taken out daily for exercise in the prison yard until he told another prisoner that the next time he was going to run for the wall, apparently in the hope a guard would kill him.

One evening several weeks before the execution day his father said, "He don't fear the chair. He cheers 'em all up. The jailer there told me, you got a mighty fine boy there, Mr. Daniels." His sister said, "It'll be a sin to put anybody in that electric chair in that condition—if people stop and consider if they were in that condition. Just strap him in like that." His mother said: "Even if he'd a done what they said he did they'd be a doin' a whole lot worse sin to put him in that chair. And I'll never believe he done it." And she said: "He should of been doctored 'stead of throwin' him in jails, it only made his mind worse."

His father, sitting barefoot in the kitchen while his wife scrubbed the floor which was already clean, said, "The way I been done by society I'm pret' near soured, I don't think I've had justice in no way shape or form. I'm a fellow always done right, I give my overcoat away one time, don't hurt no man's feelings, don't be a grouch, don't be rash, but now I'm pret' near soured." Mrs. Daniels said, "Don't talk that way, Lee." He went on, "Society raised him and now they'll kill him. I'm soured on society. I worked hard all my life, I raised my family, I don't owe nobody a dime, but I ain't got nothin' to fight a case with. He ain't got a chance. Don't get me wrong—I'm not give up. Not yet. Not while my boy's still living. I wouldn't be much of a father if I did." And he and his wife took a final appeal to the State Pardon and Parole Commission on December 21, thirteen days before the execution date. Hopefully they presented a letter from a woman who said that she had picked up two hitchhikers she was sure were Daniels and West and that West had told her he had killed the Niebels. The Commission considered the letter of little significance. The Commission asked if they had any physicians' statements. Daniels' father said these had been filed years ago. The Danielses went home. Their last hope died December 30—the governor refused to intervene.

Daniels heard this news over the radio, listening in his cell. The next day was Friday, the next Saturday, the next Sunday and the next his last—Monday, January 3, 1949. On the last day his two sisters and his brother, not his parents, came to visit him at 12:30 P.M. They stayed until 3:30 P.M., when they had to leave. He gave his sister what little money he had. At 5:05 P.M. guards unlocked his cell in Death Row and led him through the low doorway and across the prison yard to the Death House, a small rectangular building with two rooms—a cell for him and a room for the electric chair. In the cell he ate his last meal—he had ordered grape juice, orange juice, fried chicken, fried oysters, chili, potatoes, Limburger cheese, bread, butter, coffee, vanilla ice cream with chocolate syrup, chocolate cake —and he had as his guest another prisoner, a man he had known at Mansfield Reformatory. Sometime that evening, precisely when he did not know, he would die.

The witnesses gathered in the warden's carpeted office at 7:30 P.M., guards, reporters, the police sergeant who had killed West, other officers, about two dozen in all. A woman telephoned to ask what time he would die ("No, ma'am, we don't give that out"), a politician called asking admittance (refused). A reporter asked how many volts were used (the warden would not say); somebody said it was 20-40-10, that is, 20,000 volts, then increased to 40,000, then back down to 10,000; somebody asked if the current dimmed lights all over the prison (it doesn't, anymore). The warden, Ralph W. Alvis, a husky, ruddy-faced man with short-cropped sandy hair, arranged to keep his telephone line clear so he could notify the Governor. Somebody said, "Who's got the correct time?" and the warden said, "Seven forty-five," and then, "Let's get started," and led the way out through barred, thick-walled doorways. The night was warm for January but wet and drizzling, and the lights scattered about the prison yard had shimmering yellow haloes. Red lights blinked atop a water tower, and floodlights were bright on the wall. High alongside the walk rose a cell house, heavy bars on the windows, and from inside came the sound of whistling and yelling, and in a window of the fourth and topmost floor of another building four human figures appeared, heads and shoulders of uneven height pressed together and leaning sideways, men looking down upon the strung-out party of witnesses walking to the Death House.

The door to the Death House opened silently and the witnesses filed in and ranged themselves along one wall, standing in front of big picture frames holding small oval photographs of the scores of men who had died there. The warden, head bowed and hands clasped behind, stood two paces in front of the others. They faced the electric chair, brown wood and black leather, tipped slightly backward, a rather small machine. It stood on a low dais. The room was bright-lit and small, the chair only a few feet across the concrete floor from the witnesses. Over it glowed a small naked blue light bulb. The outside door closed. A guard in the far corner rapped on a door in the wall behind the chair. In a moment, it opened. Daniels came in. He was leaning heavily on the chaplain's arm, and they both were praying aloud, "Our Father who art in Heaven . . ." and Daniels' eyes were shut tight. Two guards helped guide him. He moved rapidly, though clumsily since his eyes were shut, and one felt he was trying hard to do the right thing. He sat in the chair and he was still praying and the black-clad priest with him. The guards were fastening the straps, a gray strap across his chest—"Give us this day"—and they bent over his wrists and fastened them, then knelt beside his ankles—"as we forgive"—and he winced as a strap jerked tight. He wore brown pants with the right leg slit for the electrode, and his leg was white and thin. He wore a white shirt open at the throat revealing a scapular chain, and in his right hand on the arm of the chair he clutched a crucifix and in the left a rosary. His head was tilted back a little, his neck very long and very white, his Adam's apple large and white. His eyebrows looked white. "Hail Mary full of grace"—the other electrode was on his head, and now the mask over his face, black leather, heavy and black above his throat, covering the eyes, the nose, the mouth, only a small flap for breathing. The guards were finished. They stepped aside. The priest stepped back, a short slow step at a time, staying directly in front of the chair but stepping back, finishing the "Hail Mary" and another prayer, "Sacred Heart of Jesus," and beginning again "Our Father who art . . ." his voice low and rapid, Daniels' voice coming thin and muffled and anxious through the mask. The blue light went off, the red one below it on, a dynamo hummed, his body jerked once, hard, and lay strained forward against the heavy straps. At 8:02 the red light went out and the blue one on again and a wisp of blue smoke curled up from his bare right leg. He was wearing blue socks and brown shoes. His body relaxed, but it was held too tight to slump much. One minute's silence, and the priest stepped forward and loosened his shirt and listened for the heart beneath the hairy chest, then spoke some words almost inaudibly and stepped aside. Swinging a stethoscope, a doctor stepped onto the dais and placed the stethoscope on Daniels' chest. Daniels' ears and his long throat and his chest had turned a bright scarlet. Only his Adam's apple still was white. The doctor stepped back, a second stepped up. A guard watched, his face lean, his mouth a hard line. At 8:09 the doctor said, "I think he is dead," and the other doctor turned to the warden and said, "Warden Alvis, sufficient electricity has passed through the body of Robert Murl Daniels, 87057, to have caused death at 8:01 P.M.'' The warden turned to the witnesses, said, "That's all, gentlemen," and they filed out. Daniels' body was left alone in the chair except for the guards.

Outside the penitentiary walls traffic flowed quietly along the damp street, and in the fog and shadow beside a darkened factory figures were huddled, the curious, staring at the prison walls, not knowing yet it all was over. An ambulance waited for his body, soon received it and drove rapidly away. His parents buried him in secret.

OLD FAGS

By Stacy Aumonier

. . . .

He was called Old Fags because he picked cigarette butts
out of the gutters in London to support himself.
Work was scarce in London in those days but Mrs. Bastien-Melland
could still afford to have a groom to walk her ten dear
little dogs—until one day . . .

The boys called him "Old Fags," and the reason was not hard to
seek. He occupied a room in a block of tenements off Lisson Grove,
bearing the somewhat grandiloquent title of Bolingbroke Buildings,
and conspicuous among the many doubtful callings that occupied his
time was one in which he issued forth with a deplorable old canvas
sack, which, after a day's peregrination along the gutters, he would
manage to partly fill with cigar and cigarette ends. The exact means
by which he managed to convert this patiently gathered garbage into
the wherewithal to support his disreputable body, nobody took the
trouble to inquire; nor was there any further interest aroused by the
disposal of the contents of the same sack when he returned with the
gleanings of dustbins, distributed thoughtfully at intervals along certain thoroughfares by a maternal Borough Council.

No one had ever penetrated to the inside of his room, but the
general opinion in Bolingbroke Buildings was that he managed to
live in a state of comfortable filth. And Mrs. Read, who lived in the
room opposite Number 477 with her four children, was of the opinion that "Old Fags 'ad 'oarded up a bit." He certainly was never
behind with the payment of the weekly three and sixpence that entitled him to the sole enjoyment of Number 475; and when the door
was opened, among the curious blend of odors that issued forth, that
of onions and other luxuries of this sort was undeniable. Neverthe-

less, he was not a popular figure in the Buildings; many, in fact, looked upon him as a social blot on the Bolingbroke escutcheon. The inhabitants were mostly laborers and their wives, charwomen and lady helps, dressmakers' assistants and mechanics. There was a vague, tentative effort among a great body of them to be a little respectable, and among some, even to be clean. No such uncomfortable considerations hampered the movements of Old Fags. He was frankly and ostentatiously a social derelict. He had no pride and no shame. He shuffled out in the morning, his blotchy face covered with dirt and black hair, his threadbare green clothes tattered and in rags, the toes all too visible through his forlorn-looking boots. He was rather a large man with a fat, flabby person, and a shiny face that was overaffable and bleary through a too constant attention to the gin bottle.

He had a habit of ceaseless talk. He talked and chuckled to himself all the time; he talked to everyone he met in an undercurrent of jeering affability. Sometimes he would retire to his room with a gin bottle for days together and then—the walls at Bolingbroke Buildings are not very thick—he would be heard to talk and chuckle and snore alternately, until the percolating atmosphere of stewed onions heralded the fact that Old Fags was shortly on the warpath again.

He would meet Mrs. Read with her children on the stairs and would mutter: "Oh! here we are again! All these dear little children. Been out for a walk, eh? Oh! these dear little children!" and he would pat one of them gaily on the head. And Mrs. Read would say: "'Ere, you, keep your filthy 'ands off my kids, you dirty old swine, or I'll catch you a swipe over the mouth!" and Old Fags would shuffle off muttering: "Oh, dear; oh, dear; these dear little children! Oh, dear; oh, dear." And the boys would call after him and even throw orange peel and other things at him, but nothing seemed to disturb the serenity of Old Fags. Even when young Charlie Good threw a dead mouse, that hit him on the chin, he only said: "Oh, these Boys! These BOYS!"

Quarrels, noise and bad odors were the prevailing characteristics of Bolingbroke Buildings, and Old Fags, though contributing in some degree to the latter quality, rode serenely through the other two in spite of multiform aggression. The penetrating intensity of his onion stew had driven two lodgers already from Number 476, and was again a source of aggravation to the present holders, old Mrs. Birdle and her daughter, Minnie.

Minnie Birdle was what was known as a "tweeny" at a house in

Hyde Park Square, but she lived at home. Her mistress—to whom she had never spoken, being engaged by the housekeeper—was Mrs. Bastien-Melland, a lady who owned a valuable collection of little dogs. These little dogs somehow gave Minnie an unfathomable sense of respectability. She loved to talk about them. She told Mrs. Read that her mistress paid "'undreds and 'undreds of pahnds for each of them." They were taken out every day by a groom on two leads of five—ten highly groomed, bustling, yapping, snapping, vicious little luxuries. Some had won prizes at dog shows, and two men were engaged for the sole purpose of ministering to their creature comforts.

The consciousness of working in a house which furnished such an exhibition of festive cultivation brought into sharp relief the degrading social condition of her next-room neighbor. Minnie hated Old Fags with a bitter hatred. She even wrote to a firm of lawyers, who represented some remote landlord, and complained of the dirty habits of the old drunken wretch next door. But she never received any answer to her complaint. It was known that Old Fags had lived there for seven years and paid his rent regularly. Moreover, on one critical occasion, Mrs. Read, who had periods of rheumatic gout and could not work, had got into hopeless financial straits, having reached the very limit of her borrowing capacity, and being three weeks in arrears with her rent, Old Fags had come over and had insisted on lending her fifteen shillings! Mrs. Read eventually paid it back, and the knowledge of the transaction further accentuated her animosity toward him.

One day Old Fags was returning from his dubious round and was passing through Hyde Park Square with his canvas bag slung over his back, when he ran into the cortege of little dogs under the control of Meads, the groom.

"Oh, dear! Oh, dear!" muttered Old Fags to himself. "What dear little dogs! H'm! What dear little dogs!"

A minute later Minnie Birdle ran up the area steps and gave Meads a bright smile. "Good night, Mr. Meads," she said.

Mr. Meads looked at her and said: "'Ullo! you off?"

"Yes!" she answered.

"Oh, well," he said, "good night! Be good!" They both sniggered, and Minnie hurried down the street. Before she reached Lisson Grove, Old Fags had caught her up.

"I say," he said, getting into her stride, "what dear little dogs those are! Oh, dear! what dear little dogs!"

Minnie turned, and when she saw him her face flushed, and she said: "Oh, you go to Hell!" with which unladylike expression she darted across the road and was lost to sight.

"Oh, these women!" said Old Fags to himself, "these WOMEN!"

It often happened, thereafter, that Old Fags's business carried him in the neighborhood of Hyde Park Square, and he ran into the little dogs. One day he even ventured to address Meads and to congratulate him on the beauty of his canine protégés, an attention that elicited a very unsympathetic response; a response, in fact, that amounted to being told "to clear off."

The incident of Old Fags running into this society was entirely accidental. It was due, in part, to the fact that the way lay through there to a tract of land in Paddington that Old Fags seemed to find peculiarly attractive. It was a neglected strip of ground by the railway, that butted at one end onto a canal. It would have made quite a good siding, but that it seemed somehow to have been overlooked by the railway company, and to have become a dumping ground for tins and old refuse from the houses in the neighborhood of Harrow Road. Old Fags would spend hours there alone with his canvas bag.

When the winter came on there was a great wave of what the papers would call economic unrest. There were strikes in three great industries, a political upheaval and a severe tightening of the money market. All of these misfortunes reacted on Bolingbroke Buildings. The dwellers became even more impecunious, and consequently more quarrelsome, more noisy and more malodorous. Rents were all in arrears, ejections were the order of the day and borrowing became a tradition rather than an actuality. Want and hunger brooded over the dejected Buildings. But still Old Fags came and went, carrying his shameless gin and permeating the passages with his onion stews.

Old Mrs. Birdle became bedridden and the support of Room Number 476 fell on the shoulders of Minnie. The wages of a "tweeny" are not excessive, and the way in which she managed to support herself and her invalid mother must have excited the wonder of the other dwellers in the building, if they had not had more pressing affairs of their own to wonder about. Minnie was a short, sallow little thing with a rather full figure, and heavy gray eyes that somehow conveyed a sense of sleeping passion. She had a certain instinct for dress, a knack of putting some trinket in the right place and of always being neat. Mrs. Bastien-Melland had one day asked who she was. On being informed, her curiosity did not prompt her to push the matter further, and she did not speak to her; but the incident gave Minnie a better standing in the domestic household at Hyde Park Square. It was probably this attention that caused Meads, the head dog groom, to cast an eye in her direction. It is certain that he did so, and, moreover, on a certain Thursday evening had taken her to a cinema performance in the Edgware Road. Such attention naturally gave rise to discussion; and, alas, to jealousy; for there was an under housemaid, and even a lady's maid, who were not impervious to the attentions of the good-looking groom.

When Mrs. Bastien-Melland went to Egypt in January, she took only three of the small dogs with her, for she could not be bothered with the society of a groom, and three dogs were as many as her two maids could spare time for, after devoting their energies to Mrs. Bastien-Melland's toilette. Consequently, Meads was left behind, and was held directly responsible for seven—five Chows and two Pekinese, or, as he expressed it, over a thousand pounds' worth of dogs. It was a position of enormous responsibility. They had to be fed on the very best food, all carefully prepared and cooked, and in small quantities. They had to be taken for regular exercise, and washed in specially prepared condiments. Moreover, at the slightest symptom of indisposition he was to telephone to Sir Andrew Fossiter, the great veterinary specialist in Hanover Square. It is not to be wondered at that Meads became a person of considerable standing and envy, and that little Minnie Birdle was intensely flattered when he occasionally condescended to look in her direction. She had been in Mrs. Bastien-Melland's service now for seven months, and the attentions of the dog groom had not only been a matter of general observation, for some time past, but had become a subject of reckless mirth and innuendo among the other servants.

One night she was hurrying home. Her mother had been rather worse than usual of late, and she was carrying a few scraps that the cook had given her. It was a wretched night and she was not feeling well herself: a mood of tired dejection possessed her. She crossed a drab street off Lisson Grove and, as she reached the curb, her eye lighted on Old Fags. He did not see her. He was walking along the gutter, patting the road occasionally with his stick. She had not spoken to him since the occasion we have mentioned. For once he was not talking—his eyes were fixed in listless apathy on the road.

As he passed, she caught the angle of his chin silhouetted against the window of a shop. For the rest of her walk the haunting vision of that chin beneath the drawn cheeks, and the brooding hopelessness of those sunken eyes, kept recurring to her. Perhaps, in some remote past, he had been as good to look upon as Meads, the groom! Perhaps someone had cared for him! She tried to push this thought from her, but some chord in her nature seemed to have been awakened and to vibrate with an unaccountable sympathy toward this undesirable fellow lodger.

She hurried home, and in the night was ill. She could not go to Mrs. Melland's for three days and she wanted the money badly. When she got about again she was subject to fainting fits and sickness. On one such occasion, as she was going upstairs at the Buildings, she felt faint and leaned against the wall just as Old Fags was going up.

He stopped and said: "Hullo, now what are we doing? Oh, dear! Oh, dear!" And she said: "It's all right, old 'un." These were the kindest words she had ever spoken to Old Fags.

During the next month there were strange symptoms about Minnie Birdle that caused considerable comment, and there were occasions when old Mrs. Birdle pulled herself together, and became the active partner and waited on Minnie. On one such occasion, Old Fags came home late and, after drawing a cork, varied his usual program of talking and snoring by singing in a maudlin key, and old Mrs. Birdle came banging at his door and shrieked out: "Stop your row, you old ——. My daughter is ill. Can't you hear?"

And Old Fags came to his door and blinked at her and said: "Ill, is she? Oh, dear! oh, dear! Would she like some stew, eh?"

And old Mrs. Birdle said: "No, she don't want any of your muck," and bundled back. But they did not hear any more of Old Fags that night, or any other night when Minnie came home queer.

Early in March Minnie got the sack from Hyde Park Square. Mrs. Melland was still away—having decided to winter in Rome—but the housekeeper assumed the responsibility of this action, and in writing to Mrs. Melland, justified the course she had taken by saying that "she could not expect the other maids to work in the same house with an unmarried girl in that condition." Mrs. Melland—whose letter in reply was full of the serious illness of poor little Annisette, one of the Chows, that had suffered in Egypt on account of a maid giving it too much rice with its boned chicken; and how much better it had been in Rome under the treatment of Dr. Lascati—made no special reference to the question of Minnie Birdle, only saying that "she was *so* sorry if Mrs. Bellingham was having trouble with these tiresome servants."

The spring came, and the summer, and the two inhabitants of Room 476 eked out their miserable existence. One day Minnie would pull herself together and get a day's charring and occasionally Mrs. Birdle would struggle along to a laundry in Maida Vale, where a benevolent proprietress would pay her one shilling and threepence to do a day's ironing; for the old lady was rather neat with her hands. And once, when things were very desperate, the brother of a nephew from Walthamstow turned up. He was a small cabinetmaker by trade, and he agreed to allow them three shillings a week, "till things righted themselves a bit." But nothing was seen of Meads, the groom. One night Minnie was rather worse and the idea occurred to her that she would like to send a message to him. It was right that he should know. He had made no attempt to see her since she had left Mrs. Melland's service. She lay awake thinking of him and wondering how she could send a message, when she suddenly thought of Old Fags. He had been quiet of late; whether the demand for cigarette ends was abating and he could not afford the luxuries that their disposal seemed to supply, or whether he was keeping quiet for any ulterior reason, she was not able to determine. In the morning she sent her mother across to ask him if he would "oblige by calling at Hyde Park Square and asking Mr. Meads if he would oblige by calling at four seventy-six Bolingbroke Buildings, to see Miss Birdle."

There is no record of how Old Fags delivered this message, but it is known that that same afternoon Mr. Meads did call. He left about three thirty in a great state of perturbation and in a very bad temper. He passed Old Fags on the stairs, and the only comment he made was: "I never have any luck! God help me!" And he did not return, although he had apparently promised to do so.

In a few weeks' time the position of the occupants of Room 476 became desperate. It was, in fact, a desperate time all round. Work was scarce and money scarcer. Waves of ill temper and depression swept Bolingbroke Buildings. Mrs. Read had gone—Heaven knows where. Even Old Fags seemed at the end of his tether. True, he still managed to secure his inevitable bottle, but the stews became scarcer and less potent. All Mrs. Birdle's time and energy were taken up in nursing Minnie, and the two somehow existed on the money—now increased to four shillings a week—which the sympathetic cabinet-maker from Walthamstow allowed them. The question of rent was shelved. Four shillings a week for two people means ceaseless, gnawing hunger. The widow and her daughter lost pride and hope, and further messages to Mr. Meads failed to elicit any response. The widow became so desperate that she even asked Old Fags one night if he could spare a little stew for her daughter who was starving. The pungent odor of the hot food was too much for her.

Old Fags came to the door: "Oh, dear! Oh, dear!" he said, "what trouble there is! Let's see what we can do!" He messed about for some time and then took it across to them. It was a strange concoction. Meat that it would have been difficult to know what to ask for at a butcher's, and many bones, but the onions seemed to pull it together. To anyone starving it was good. After that it became a sort of established thing: whenever Old Fags *had* a stew, he sent some over to the widow and daughter. But apparently things were not going too well in the cigarette-end trade, for the stews became more and more intermittent, and sometimes were desperately "boney."

And then one night a climax was reached. Old Fags was awakened in the night by fearful screams. There was a district nurse in the next room, and also a student from a great hospital. No one knows how it all affected Old Fags. He went out at a very unusual hour in the early morning, and seemed more garrulous and meandering in his speech. He stopped the widow in the passage and mumbled incomprehensible solicitude.

Minnie was very ill for three days, but she recovered, faced by the insoluble proposition of feeding three mouths, instead of two, and two of them requiring enormous quantities of milk. This terrible crisis brought out many good qualities in various people. The cabinet-maker sent ten shillings extra, and others came forward as though driven by some race instinct. Old Fags disappeared for ten days after that. It was owing to an unfortunate incident in Hyde Park, when he insisted on sleeping on a flower bed with a gin bottle under his left arm, and on account of the unreasonable attitude that he took up toward a policeman in the matter. When he returned things were assuming their normal course. Mrs. Birdle's greeting was: " 'Ullo, old 'un, we've missed your stoos."

Old Fags had undoubtedly secured a more stable position in the eyes of the Birdles, and one day he was even allowed to see the baby. He talked to it from the door.

"Oh, dear! oh, dear!" he said. "What a beautiful little baby! What a dear little baby! Oh, dear! oh, dear!" The baby shrieked with unrestrained terror at sight of him, but that night some more stew was sent in.

Then the autumn came on. People, whose romantic instincts had been touched at the arrival of the child, gradually lost interest and fell away. The cabinetmaker from Walthamstow wrote a long letter, saying that after next week the payment of the four shillings would have to stop, he hoped he had been of some help in their trouble, but that things were going on all right now; of course he had to think of his own family first, and so on.

The lawyers of the remote landlord, who was assiduously killing stags in Scotland, regretted that their client could not see his way to allow any further delay in the matter of the payment of rent due. The position of the Birdle family became once more desperate. Old Mrs. Birdle had become frailer, and though Minnie could now get about, she found work difficult to obtain, owing to people's demand for a character from the last place. Their thoughts once more reverted to Meads, and Minnie lay in wait for him one morning as he was taking the dogs out. There was a very trying scene ending in a very vulgar quarrel, and Minnie came home and cried all the rest of the day and through half the night.

Old Fags's stews became scarcer and less palatable. He, too, seemed in dire straits.

We now come to an incident that, we are ashamed to say, owes its inception to the effect of alcohol. It was a wretched morning in late October, bleak and foggy. The blue-gray corridors of Bolingbroke Buildings seemed to exude damp. The strident voices of the unkempt children, quarreling in the courtyard below, permeated the whole Buildings. The strange odor, that was its characteristic, lay upon it like the foul breath of some evil god. All its inhabitants seemed hungry, wretched and vile. Their lives of constant protest seemed, for the moment, lulled to a sullen indifference, whilst they huddled behind their gloomy doors and listened to the raucous railings of their offspring.

The widow Birdle and her daughter sat silently in their room. The child was asleep. It had had its milk, and it would have to have its milk, whatever happened. The crumbs from the bread the women had had at breakfast lay ungathered on the bare table. They were both hungry and very desperate. There was a knock at the door. Minnie went to it, and there stood Old Fags. He leered at them meekly and under his arm carried a gin bottle, three parts full.

"Oh, dear! Oh, dear!" he said. "What a dreadful day! What a dreadful day! Will you have a little drop of gin to comfort you? Now! What do you say?"

Minnie looked at her mother—in other days the door would have been slammed in his face, but Old Fags had certainly been kind in the matter of stews. They asked him to sit down. Then old Mrs. Birdle did accept just a tiny drop of gin, and they both persuaded Minnie to have a little. Now neither of the women had had food of any worth for days, and the gin went straight to their heads. It was already in Old Fags's head, firmly established. The three immediately became garrulous. They all talked volubly and intimately. The women railed Old Fags about his dirt, but allowed that he had "a good 'eart." They talked longingly and lovingly about "his stoos" and Old Fags said: "Well, my dears, you shall have the finest stoo you've ever had in your lives tonight."

He repeated this nine times, only each time the whole sentence sounded like one word.

Then the conversation drifted to the child, and the hard lot of parents, and by a natural sequence to Meads, its father. Meads was discussed with considerable bitterness, and the constant reiteration of the threat by the women that they meant to 'ave the Lor on 'im all right, mingled with the jeering sophistries of Old Fags on the genalman's behavior, and the impossibility of expecting a dog groom to be a sportsman, lasted a considerable time. Old Fags talked expansively about leaving it to him, and somehow as he stood there with his large, puffy figure looming up in the dimly lighted room, and waving his long arms, he appeared to the women a figure of portentous significance. In the eyes of the women he typified powers they had not dreamt of. Under the veneer of his hidebound depravity Minnie seemed to detect some slow-moving force trying to assert itself.

He meandered on in a vague monologue, using terms and expressions they did not know the meaning of. He gave the impression of some fettered animal, launching a fierce indictment against the fact of its life. At last he took up the gin bottle and moved to the door and then leered round the room.

"You shall have the finest stoo you've ever had in your life tonight, my dears."

He repeated this seven times again and then went heavily out.

That afternoon a very amazing fact was observed by several inhabitants of Bolingbroke Buildings. Old Fags washed his face! He went out about three o'clock without his sack. His face had certainly been cleaned up and his clothes seemed in some mysterious fashion to hold together. He went across Lisson Grove and made for Hyde Park Square. He hung about for nearly an hour at the corner, and then he saw a man come up the area steps of a house on the south side and walk rapidly away. Old Fags followed him. He took a turning sharp to the left through a mews, and entered a narrow street at the end. There he entered a deserted-looking pub, kept by an ex-butler and his wife. He passed right through to a room at the back and called for some beer. Before it was brought, Old Fags was seated at the next table ordering gin.

"Dear, oh, dear! what a wretched day!" said Old Fags.

The groom grunted assent. But Old Fags was not to be put off by mere indifference. He broke ground on one or two subjects that interested the groom, one subject in particular being Dog. He seemed to have a profound knowledge of Dog, and before Mr. Meads quite realized what was happening he was trying gin in his beer at Old Fags's expense.

The groom was feeling particularly morose that afternoon. His luck seemed out. Bookmakers had appropriated several half crowns that he sorely begrudged, and he had other expenses. The beer-gin mixture comforted him, and the rambling eloquence of the old fool, who seemed disposed to be content paying for the drinks and talking, fitted in with his mood. They drank and talked for a full hour, and at length got to a subject that all men get to sooner or later if they drink and talk long enough—the subject of Woman.

Mr. Meads became confiding and philosophic. He talked of women in general and what triumphs and adventures he had had among them in particular. But what a trial and tribulation they had been to him in spite of all! Old Fags winked knowingly and was splendidly comprehensive and tolerant of Meads's peccadillos.

"It's all a game," said Meads. "You've got to manage 'em. There ain't much I don't know, old bird!" Then suddenly Old Fags leaned forward in the dark room and said: "No, Mr. Meads, but you ought to play the game, you know. Oh, dear, yes!"

"What do you mean, *Mister Meads?*" said that gentleman sharply.

"Minnie Birdle, eh, you haven't mentioned Minnie Birdle yet!" said Old Fags.

"What the Devil are you talking about?" said Meads drunkenly.

"She's starving," said Old Fags, "starving, wretched, alone with her old mother and your child. Oh, dear! yes, it's terrible!"

Meads's eyes flashed with a sullen frenzy, but fear was gnawing at his heart, and he felt more disposed to placate this mysterious old man than to quarrel with him.

"I tell you I have no luck," he said after a pause. Old Fags looked at him gloomily and ordered some more gin. When it was brought he said: "You ought to play the game, you know, Mr. Meads. After all—luck? Oh, dear! Would you rather be the woman? Five shillings a week, you know, would—"

"No, I'm damned if I do!" cried Meads fiercely. "It's all right for all these women—Gawd! How do I know if it's true? Look here, old bird, do you know I'm already done in for two five bobs a week, eh! One up in Norfolk and the other at Enfield. Ten shillings a week of my —— money goes to these blasted women. No fear, no more, I'm through with it!"

"Oh, dear! oh, dear!" said Old Fags, and he moved a little further into the shadow of the room and watched the groom out of the depths of his sunken eyes.

But Meads's courage was now fortified by the fumes of a large quantity of fiery alcohol, and he spoke witheringly of women in general and seemed disposed to quarrel if Old Fags disputed his right to place them in the position that Meads considered their right and natural position. But Old Fags gave no evidence of taking up the challenge—on the contrary he seemed to suddenly shift his ground. He grinned and leered and nodded at Meads's string of coarse sophistry, and suddenly he touched him on the arm and looked around the room and said very confidentially:

"Oh, dear! yes, Mr. Meads. Don't take too much to heart what I said," and then he sniffed and whispered: "I could put you on to a very nice thing, Mr. Meads. I could introduce you to a lady I know would take a fancy to you, and you to her. Oh, dear, yes!"

Meads pricked up his ears like a fox terrier and his small eyes glittered.

"Oh!" he said. "Are you one of those, eh, old bird? Who is she?"

Old Fags took out a piece of paper and fumbled with a pencil. He then wrote down a name and address somewhere at Shepherds Bush.

"What's a good time to call?" said Meads.

"Between six and seven," answered Old Fags.

"Oh, hell!" said Meads. "I can't do it. I've got to get back and take the dogs out at half-past five, old bird. From half-past five to half-past six. The missus is back, she'll kick up a hell of a row."

"Oh, dear! oh, dear!" said Old Fags. "What a pity! The young lady is going away, too!" He thought for a moment and then an idea seemed to strike him. "Look here, would you like me to meet you and take the dogs round the park till you return?"

"What!" said Meads, "trust you with a thousand pounds' worth of dogs! Not much."

"No, no, of course not, I hadn't thought of that!" said Old Fags humbly.

Meads looked at him, and it is very difficult to tell what it was about the old man that gave him a sudden feeling of complete trust. The ingenuity of his speech, the ingratiating confidence that a mixture of beer-gin gives, tempered by the knowledge that famous pedigree Pekinese would be almost impossible to dispose of, perhaps it was a combination of these motives. In any case a riotous impulse drove him to fall in with Old Fags's suggestion, and he made the appointment for half-past five.

Evening had fallen early, and a fine rain was driving in fitful gusts when the two met at the corner of Hyde Park. There were the ten little dogs on their lead, and Meads with a cap pulled close over his eyes.

"Oh, dear! oh, dear!" cried Old Fags as he approached. "What dear little dogs! What dear little dogs!"

Meads handed the lead over to Old Fags and asked more precise instructions of the way to get to the address.

"What are you wearing that canvas sack inside your coat for, old bird, eh?" asked Meads when these instructions had been given.

"Oh, my dear sir," said Old Fags, "if you had the asthma like I get it! and no underclothes on these damp days! Oh, dear! Oh, dear!" He wheezed drearily.

Meads gave him one or two more exhortations about the extreme care and tact he was to observe.

"Be very careful with that little Chow on the left lead. 'E's got his coat on, see? 'E's 'ad a chill and you must keep 'im on the move. Gently, see?"

"Oh, dear! oh, dear! poor little chap! What's his name?" said Old Fags.

"Pelleas," answered Mr. Meads.

"Oh, poor little Pelleas! Poor little Pelleas! Come along, you won't be too long, Mr. Meads, will you?"

"You bet I won't," said the groom, and nodding he crossed the road rapidly and mounting a Shepherds Bush motor bus, he set out on his journey to an address that didn't exist.

Old Fags ambled slowly round the park, snuffling and talking to the dogs. He gauged the time when Meads would be somewhere about Queens Road, then he ambled slowly back to the point from which he had started. With extreme care he piloted the small army across the High Road and led them in the direction of Paddington. He drifted with leisurely confidence through a maze of small streets. Several people stopped and looked at the dogs and the boys barked and mimicked them, but nobody took the trouble to look at Old Fags. At length he came to a district where their presence seemed more conspicuous. Rows of squalid houses and advertisement hoardings. He slightly increased his pace, and a very stout policeman standing outside a funeral furnisher's glanced at him with a vague suspicion. In strict accordance, however, with an ingrained officialism that hates to act "without instructions" he let the cortege pass.

Old Fags wandered through a wretched street that seemed entirely peopled by children. Several of them came up and followed the dogs.

"Dear little dogs, aren't they? Oh my, yes, dear little dogs!" he said to the children.

At last he reached a broad, gloomy thoroughfare with low, irregular buildings on one side, and an interminable length of hoardings on the other, that screened a strip of land by the railway land that harbored a wilderness of tins and garbage. Old Fags led the dogs along by the hoarding. It was very dark. Three children who had been following tired of the pastime and drifted away. He went along once more. There was a gap in a hoarding on which was notified that "Program's Landaulettes could be hired for the evening at an inclusive fee of two guineas. Telephone 47901 Mayfair." The meager light from a street lamp thirty yards away revealed a colossal colored picture of a very beautiful young man and woman stepping out of a car and entering a gorgeous restaurant, having evidently just enjoyed the advantage of this peerless luxury.

Old Fags went on another forty yards and then returned. There was no one in sight.

"Oh, dear little dogs!" he said. "Oh, dear! oh, dear! what dear little dogs! Just through here, my pretty pets. Gently, Pelleas! gently, very gently! There, there, there! Oh, what dear little dogs!"

He stumbled forward through the quagmire of desolation, picking his way as though familiar with every inch of ground, to the further corner where it was even darker, and where the noise of shunting freight trains drowned every other murmur of the night.

It was eight o'clock when Old Fags reached his room in Bolingbroke Buildings, carrying his heavily laden sack across his shoulders. The child in Room 476 had been peevish and fretful all the afternoon, and the two women were lying down, exhausted. They heard Old Fags come in. He seemed very busy, banging about with bottles and tins and alternately coughing and wheezing. But soon the potent aroma of onions reached their nostrils and they knew he was preparing to keep his word.

At nine o'clock he staggered across with a steaming saucepan of hot stew. In contrast to the morning's conversation, which though devoid of self-consciousness had taken on at times an air of moribund analysis, making little stabs at fundamental things, the evening passed off on a note of almost joyous levity. The stew was extremely good to the starving women, and Old Fags developed a vein of fantastic pleasantry. He talked unceasingly, sometimes on things they understood, sometimes on matters of which they were entirely ignorant; and sometimes he appeared to them obtuse, maudlin and incoherent. Nevertheless, he brought to their room a certain lighthearted raillery that had never visited it before. No mention was made of Meads.

The only blemish to the serenity of this bizarre supper party was that Old Fags developed intervals of violent coughing, intervals when he had to walk around the room and beat his chest. These fits had the unfortunate result of waking the baby.

When this undesirable result had occurred for the fourth time, Old Fags said: "Oh, dear! oh, dear! this won't do. Oh, no, this won't do. I must go back to my hotel!" A remark that caused paroxysms of mirth to old Mrs. Birdle. Nevertheless, Old Fags retired, and it was then just on eleven o'clock.

The women went to bed, and all through the night Minnie heard the old man coughing.

Meads jumped off the bus at Shepherds Bush and hurried in the direction that Old Fags had instructed him. He asked three people for the Pomeranian Road before an errand boy told him that he believed it was somewhere off Giles Avenue; but at Giles Avenue no one seemed to know it. He retraced his steps in a very bad temper and inquired again. Five other people had never heard of it. So he went to a post office, and a young lady in charge informed him that there was no such road in the neighborhood. He tried other roads whose names vaguely resembled it, then he came to the conclusion that "that blamed old fool had made some silly mistake."

He took a bus back with a curious gnawing fear at the pit of his stomach, a fear that he kept thrusting back, he dare not allow himself to contemplate it. It was nearly seven thirty when he got back to Hyde Park, and his eye quickly scanned the length of railing near which Old Fags was to be. Immediately that he saw no sign of him or the little dogs, a horrible feeling of physical sickness assailed him. The whole truth flashed through his mind. He saw the fabric of his life crumble to dust. He was conscious of visions of past acts and misdeeds tumbling over each other in a furious kaleidoscope. The groom was terribly frightened. Mrs. Bastien-Melland would be in at eight o'clock to dinner, and the first thing she would ask for would be the little dogs. They were never supposed to go out after dark, but he had been busy that afternoon and arranged to take them out later. How was he to account for himself and their loss? He visualized himself in a dock, and all sorts of other horrid things coming up—a forged character, an affair in Norfolk, and another at Enfield, and a little trouble with a bookmaker seven years ago. For he felt convinced that the little dogs had gone forever, and Old Fags with them.

He cursed blindly in his soul at his foul luck and the wretched inclination that had lured him to drink "beer-gin" with the old thief. Forms of terrific vengeance passed through his mind, if he should meet the old devil again. In the meantime what should he do? He had never even thought of making Old Fags give him any sort of address. He dared not go back to Hyde Park Square without the dogs. He ran breathlessly up and down, peering in every direction. Eight o'clock came and there was still no sign. Suddenly he remembered Minnie Birdle. He remembered that the old ruffian had mentioned, and seemed to know, Minnie Birdle. It was a connection that he had hoped to have wiped out of his life, but the case was desperate.

Curiously enough, during his desultory courtship of Minnie, he had never been to her home; the only occasion when he *had* visited it was before the birth of the child. He had done so under the influence of three pints of beer, and he hadn't the faintest recollection now of the number or the block. He hurried there, however, in feverish trepidation.

Now Bolingbroke Buildings harbor some eight hundred people; and it is a remarkable fact that, although the Birdles had lived there about a year, of the eleven people that Meads asked, not one happened to know the name. People develop a profound sense of self-concentration in Bolingbroke Buildings.

Meads wandered up all the stairs and through the slate-tile passages. Twice he passed their door without knowing it—on the first occasion, only five minutes after Old Fags had carried a saucepan of steaming stew from Number 475 to Number 476. At ten o'clock he gave it up. He had four shillings on him, and he adjourned to a small "pub" hard by, and ordered a tankard of ale, and as an afterthought three pennyworth of gin which he mixed in it. Probably he thought that this mixture, which was so directly responsible for the train of tragic circumstance that encompassed him, might continue to act in some manner toward a more desirable conclusion.

It did, indeed, drive him to action of a sort, for he sat there drinking and smoking Navy Cut cigarettes, and by degrees he evolved a most engaging, but impossible, story, of being lured to the river by three men and chloroformed; and when he came to, finding that the dogs and the men had gone. He drank a further quantity of beer-gin, and rehearsed his role in detail, and at length brought himself to the point of facing Mrs. Melland. . . .

It was the most terrifying ordeal of his life. The servants frightened him for a start. They almost shrieked when they saw him and drew back. Mrs. Bastien-Melland had left word that he was to go to a small breakfast room in the basement directly he came in, and she would come and see him. There was a small dinner party on that evening and an agitated game of bridge. Meads had not stood on the hearth rug of the breakfast room two minutes before he heard the foreboding swish of skirts, the door burst open and Mrs. Bastien-Melland stood before him, a thing of penetrating perfumes, highlights and trepidation.

She just said, "Well!" and fixed her hard, bright eyes on him.

Meads launched forth into his impossible story, but he dared not look at her. He tried to gather together the pieces of the tale he had so carefully rehearsed in the pub, but he felt like some helpless bark at the mercy of a hostile battle fleet; the searchlight of Mrs. Melland's cruel eyes was concentrated on him; while a flotilla of small diamonds on her heaving bosom winked and glittered with a dangerous insolence.

He was stumbling over a phrase about the effects of chloroform when he became aware that Mrs. Melland was not listening to the matter of his story, she was only concerned with the manner. Her lips were set and her straining eyes insisted on catching his. He looked full at her and caught his breath and stopped.

Mrs. Melland, still staring at him, was moving slowly to the door. A moment of panic seized him. He mumbled something, and also moved toward the door. Mrs. Melland was first to grip the handle. Meads made a wild dive and seized her wrist. But Mrs. Bastien-Melland came of a hard-riding Yorkshire family. She did not lose her head. She struck him across the mouth with her flat hand, and as he reeled back she opened the door and called to the servants.

Suddenly Meads remembered that the room had a French window onto the garden. He pushed her clumsily against the door and sprang across the room. He clutched wildly at the bolts while Mrs. Melland's voice was ringing out:

"Catch that man! Hold him! Catch thief!"

But before the other servants had had time to arrive he managed to get through the door and to pull it after him. His hand was bleeding with cuts from broken glass, but he leaped the wall and got into the shadow of some shrubs three gardens away.

He heard whistles blowing and the dominant voice of Mrs. Melland, directing a hue-and-cry. He rested some moments, then panic seized him and he labored over another wall and found the passage of a semidetached house. A servant opened a door and looked out and screamed. He struck her wildly and unreasonably on the shoulder, and rushed up some steps and got into a front garden. There was no one there, and he darted into the street and across the road.

In a few minutes he was lost in a labyrinth of back streets and laughing hysterically to himself.

He had two shillings and eightpence on him. He spent fourpence of this on whisky, and then another fourpence just before the pubs closed. He struggled vainly to formulate some definite plan of campaign. The only point that seemed terribly clear to him was that he must get away. He knew Mrs. Melland only too well. She would spare no trouble in hunting him down. She would exact the uttermost farthing. It meant jail and ruin. The obvious impediment to getting away was that he had no money and no friends. He had not sufficient strength of character to face a tramp life. He had lived too long in the society of the pampered Pekinese. He loved comfort.

Out of the simmering tumult of his soul grew a very definite passion—the passion of hate. He developed a vast, bitter, scorching hatred for the person who had caused this ghastly climax to his unfortunate career—Old Fags. He went over the whole incident of the day again, rapidly recalling every phase of Old Fags's conversation and manner. What a blind fool he was not to have seen through the filthy old swine's game! But what had he done with the dogs? Sold the lot for a pound, perhaps! The idea made Meads shiver. He slouched through the streets harboring his pariahlike lust.

We will not attempt to record the psychologic changes that harassed the soul of Mr. Meads during the next two days and nights; the ugly passions that stirred him and beat their wings against the night; the tentative intuitions urging toward some vague new start; the various compromises he made with himself, his weakness and inconsistency that found him bereft of any quality other than the somber shadow of some ill-conceived revenge. We will only note that on the evening of the day we mention, he turned up at Bolingbroke Buildings. His face was haggard and drawn, his eyes bloodshot and his clothes tattered and muddy. His appearance and demeanor were, unfortunately, not so alien to the general character of Bolingbroke Buildings as to attract any particular attention, and he slunk like a wolf through the dreary passages, and watched the people come and go.

It was at about a quarter to ten, when he was going along a passage in Block F, that he suddenly saw Minnie Birdle come out of one door and go into another. His small eyes glittered and he went on tiptoe. He waited till Minnie was quite silent in her room and then he went stealthily to Room 475. He tried the handle and it gave. He opened the door and peered in. There was a cheap tin lamp guttering on a box, that dimly revealed a room of repulsive wretchedness. The furniture seemed to mostly consist of bottles and rags. But in one corner on a mattress he beheld the grinning face of his enemy—Old Fags.

Meads shut the door silently and stood with his back to it.

"Oh," he said, "so here we are at last, old bird, eh!"

This move was apparently a supremely successful dramatic coup; for Old Fags lay still, paralyzed with fear, no doubt.

"So this is our little 'ome, eh?" Meads continued, "where we bring little dogs and sell 'em. What have you got to say, you old ——"

The groom's face blazed into a sudden accumulated fury. He thrust his chin forward and let forth a volley of frightful and blasting oaths. But Old Fags didn't answer, his shiny face seemed to be intensely amused with this outburst.

"We got to settle our little account, old bird, see?" and the suppressed fury of Meads's voice denoted some physical climax. "Why the hell don't you answer?" he suddenly shrieked; and springing forward he lashed Old Fags across the cheek.

A terrible horror came over him. The cheek he had struck was as cold as marble and the head fell a little impotently to one side.

Trembling as though struck with an ague the groom picked up the guttering lamp and held it close to the face of Old Fags. It was set in an impenetrable repose, the significance of which even the groom could not misunderstand. The features were calm and childlike, lit by a half-smile of splendid tolerance, that seemed to have over-ridden the temporary buffets of a queer world.

Meads had no idea how long he stood there gazing horror-struck at the face of his enemy. He only knew that he was presently conscious that Minnie Birdle was standing by his side; and as he looked at her, her gaze was fixed on Old Fags, and a tear was trickling down either cheek.

" 'E's dead," she said. "Old Fags is dead. 'E died this morning of noomonyer."

She said this quite simply, as though it was a statement that explained the wonder of her presence. She did not look at Meads, or seem aware of him.

He watched the flickering light from the lamp illumining the underside of her chin and nostrils and her quivering brows.

" 'E's dead," she said again, and the statement seemed to come as an edict of dismissal, as though love and hatred and revenge had no place in these fundamental things.

Meads looked from her to the tousled head, leaning slightly to one side on the mattress, and he felt himself in the presence of forces he could not comprehend. He put the lamp back quietly on the box and tiptoed from the room.

". . . DEAD MEN WORKING IN THE CANE FIELDS"

By William Seabrook

. . . .

They were zombies, and they toiled in the sun,
dumbly, day after day; and their food was tasteless and unseasoned,
for everyone knew that zombies must never
be permitted to taste salt or meat.

Pretty mulatto Julie had taken baby Marianne to bed. Constant Polynice and I sat late before the doorway of his *caille*, talking of fire-hags, demons, werewolves and vampires, while a full moon, rising slowly, flooded his sloping cotton fields and the dark rolling hills beyond.

Polynice was a Haitian farmer, but he was no common jungle peasant. He lived on the island of La Gonave, where I shall return to him later on. He seldom went over to the Haitian mainland, but he knew what was going on in Port-au-Prince, and spoke sometimes of installing a radio.

A countryman, half peasant born and bred, he was familiar with every superstition of the mountains and the plain, yet too intelligent to believe them literally true—or at least so I gathered from his talk.

He was interested in helping me toward an understanding of the tangled Haitian folklore. It was only by chance that we came presently to a subject which—though I refused for a long time to admit it—lies in a baffling category on the ragged edge of things which are beyond either superstition or reason. He had been telling me of fire-hags who left their skins at home and set the cane fields blazing; of the vampire, a woman sometimes living, sometimes dead, who sucked the blood of children and who could be distinguished because her hair always turned an ugly red; of the werewolf—*chauché*, in creole—a man or woman who took the form of some animal, usually a dog, and went killing lambs, young goats, sometimes babies.

All this, I gathered, he considered to be pure superstition, as he told me with tolerant scorn how his friend and neighbor Osmann had one night seen a gray dog slinking with bloody jaws from his sheep pen, and who, after having shot and exorcized and buried it, was so convinced he had killed a certain girl named Liane who was generally reputed to be a *chauché* that when he met her two days later on the path to Grande Source, he believed she was a ghost come back for vengeance, and fled howling.

As Polynice talked on, I reflected that these tales ran closely parallel not only with those of the Negroes in Georgia and the Carolinas, but with the medieval folklore of white Europe. Werewolves, vampires and demons were certainly no novelty. But I recalled one creature I had been hearing about in Haiti, which sounded exclusively local—the *zombie*.

It seemed (or so I had been assured by Negroes more credulous than Polynice) that while the zombie came from the grave, it was neither a ghost, nor yet a person who had been raised like Lazarus from the dead. The zombie, they say, is a soulless human corpse, still dead, but taken from the grave and endowed by sorcery with a mechanical semblance of life—it is a dead body which is made to walk and act and move as if it were alive. People who have the power to do this go to a fresh grave, dig up the body before it has had time to rot, galvanize it into movement and then make of it a servant or slave, occasionally for the commission of some crime, more often simply as a drudge around the habitation or the farm, setting it dull heavy tasks, and beating it like a dumb beast if it slackens.

As this was revolving in my mind, I said to Polynice: "It seems to me that these werewolves and vampires are first cousins to those we have at home, but I have never, except in Haiti, heard of anything like zombies. Let us talk of them for a little while. I wonder if you can tell me something of this zombie superstition. I should like to get at some idea of how it originated."

My rational friend Polynice was deeply astonished. He leaned over and put his hand in protest on my knee.

"Superstition? But I assure you that this of which you now speak is not a matter of superstition. Alas, these things—and other evil practices connected with the dead—exist. They exist to an extent that you whites do not dream of, though evidences are everywhere under your eyes.

"Why do you suppose that even the poorest peasants, when they can, bury their dead beneath solid tombs of masonry?

"Why do they bury them so often in their own yards, close to the doorway?

"Why, so often, do you see a tomb or grave set close beside a busy road or footpath where people are always passing?

"It is to assure the poor unhappy dead such protection as we can.

"I will take you in the morning to see the grave of my brother, who was killed in the way you know. It is over there on the little ridge which you can see clearly now in the moonlight, open space all round it, close beside the trail which everybody passes going to and from Grande Source. Through four nights we watched yonder, in the peristyle, Osmann and I, with shotguns—for at that time both my dead brother and I had bitter enemies—until we were sure the body had begun to rot.

"No, my friend, no, no. There are only too many true cases. At this very moment, in the moonlight, there are zombies working on this island, less than two hours' ride from my own habitation. We know about them, but we do not dare to interfere so long as our own dead are left unmolested. If you will ride with me tomorrow night, yes, I will show you dead men working in the cane fields. Close even to the cities, there are sometimes zombies. Perhaps you have already heard of those that were at Hasco. . . ."

"What about Hasco?" I interrupted him, for in the whole of Haiti, Hasco is perhaps the last name anybody would think of connecting with either sorcery or superstition.

The word is American-commercial-synthetic, like Nabisco, Delco, Socony. It stands for the Haitian-American Sugar Company—an immense factory plant, dominated by a huge chimney, with clanging machinery, steam whistles, freight cars. It is like a chunk of Hoboken. It lies in the eastern suburbs of Port-au-Prince, and beyond it stretch the cane fields of the Cul-de-Sac. Hasco makes rum when the sugar market is off, pays low wages, twenty or thirty cents a day, and gives steady work. It is modern big business, and it sounds it, looks it, smells it.

Such, then, was the incongruous background for the weird tale Constant Polynice now told me.

The spring of 1918 was a big cane season, and the factory, which had its own plantations, offered a bonus on the wages of new workers. Soon heads of families and villages from the mountain and the plain came trailing their ragtag little armies, men, women, children, trooping to the registration bureau and thence into the fields.

One morning an old black headman, Ti Joseph of Colombier, appeared leading a band of ragged creatures who shuffled along behind him, staring dumbly, like people walking in a daze. As Joseph lined them up for registration, they still stared, vacant-eyed like cattle, and made no reply when asked to give their names.

Joseph said they were ignorant people from the slopes of Morne-au-Diable, a roadless mountain district near the Dominican border, and that they did not understand the creole of the plains. They were frightened, he said, by the din and smoke of the great factory, but under his direction they would work hard in the fields. The farther they were sent away from the factory, from the noise and bustle of the railroad yards, the better it would be.

Better indeed, for these were not living men and women but poor unhappy zombies whom Joseph and his wife Croyance had dragged from their peaceful graves to slave for him in the sun—and if by chance a brother or father of the dead should see and recognize them, Joseph knew that it would be a very bad affair for him.

So they were assigned to distant fields beyond the crossroads, and camped there, keeping to themselves like any proper family or village group; but in the evening when other little companies, encamped apart as they were, gathered each around its one big common pot of savory millet or plantains, generously seasoned with dried fish and garlic, Croyance would tend *two* pots upon the fire, for as everyone knows, the zombies must never be permitted to taste salt or meat. So the food prepared for them was tasteless and unseasoned.

As the zombies toiled day after day dumbly in the sun, Joseph sometimes beat them to make them move faster, but Croyance began to pity the poor dead creatures who should be at rest—and pitied them in the evenings when she dished out their flat, tasteless *bouillie*.

Each Saturday afternoon, Joseph went to collect the wages for them all, and what divison he made was no concern of Hasco, so long as the work went forward. Sometimes Joseph alone, and sometimes Croyance alone, went to Croix de Bouquet for the Saturday night *bamboche* or the Sunday cockfight, but always one of them remained with the zombies to prepare their food and see that they did not stray away.

Through February this continued, until Fête Dieu approached, with a Saturday-Sunday-Monday holiday for all the workers. Joseph, with his pockets full of money, went to Port-au-Prince and left Croyance behind, cautioning her as usual; and she agreed to remain and tend the zombies, for he promised her that at the Mardi Gras she should visit the city.

But when Sunday morning dawned, it was lonely in the fields, and her kind old woman's heart was filled with pity for the zombies, and she thought, "Perhaps it will cheer them a little to see the gay crowds and the processions at Croix de Bouquet, and since all the Morne-au-Diable people will have gone back to the mountain to celebrate Fête Dieu at home, no one will recognize them, and no harm can come of it." And it is the truth that Croyance also wished to see the gay procession.

So she tied a new bright-colored handkerchief around her head, aroused the zombies from the sleep that was scarcely different from their waking, gave them their morning bowl of cold, unsalted plantains boiled in water, which they ate dumbly uncomplaining, and set out with them for the town, single file, as the country people always walk. Croyance, in her bright kerchief, leading the nine dead men and women behind her, past the railroad crossing, where she murmured a prayer to Legba, past the great white-painted wooden Christ, who hung life-sized in the glaring sun, where she stopped to kneel and cross herself—but the poor zombies prayed neither to Papa Legba nor to Brother Jesus, for they were dead bodies walking, without souls or minds.

They followed her to the market square, before the church where hundreds of little thatched, open shelters, used on weekdays for buying and selling, were empty of trade, but crowded here and there by gossiping groups in the grateful shade.

To the shade of one of these market booths, which was still unoccupied, she led the zombies, and they sat like people asleep with their eyes open, staring, but seeing nothing, as the bells in the church began to ring, and the procession came from the priest's house—red-purple robes, golden crucifix held aloft, tinkling bells and swinging incense pots, followed by little black boys in white lace robes, little black girls in starched white dresses, with shoes and stockings, from the parish school, with colored ribbons in their kinky hair, a nun beneath a big umbrella leading them.

Croyance knelt with the throng as the procession passed, and wished she might follow it across the square to the church steps, but the zombies just sat and stared, seeing nothing.

When noontime came, women with baskets passed to and fro in the crowd, or sat selling bonbons (which were not candy but little sweet cakes), figs (which were not figs but sweet bananas), oranges, dried herring, biscuit, casava bread, and *clairin* poured from a bottle at a penny a glass.

As Croyance sat with her savory dried herring and biscuit baked with salt and soda, and provision of *clairin* in the tin cup by her side, she pitied the zombies who had worked so faithfully for Joseph in the cane fields, and who now had nothing, while all the other groups around were feasting, and as she pitied them, a woman passed, crying,

"*Tablettes! Tablettes pistaches! T'ois pour dix cobs!*"

Tablettes are a sort of candy, in shape and size like cookies, made of brown cane sugar (*rapadou*); sometimes with *pistaches*, which in Haiti are peanuts, or with coriander seed.

And Croyance thought, "These *tablettes* are not salted or seasoned, they are sweet, and can do no harm to the zombies just this once."

So she untied the corner of her kerchief, took out a coin, a *gourdon*, the quarter of a *gourde*, and bought some of the *tablettes*, which she broke in halves and divided among the zombies, who began sucking and mumbling them in their mouths.

But the baker of the *tablettes* had salted the *pistache* nuts before stirring them into the *rapadou*, and as the zombies tasted the salt, they knew that they were dead and made a dreadful outcry and arose and turned their faces toward the mountain.

No one dared stop them, for they were corpses walking in the sunlight, and they themselves and all the people knew that they were corpses. And they disappeared toward the mountain.

When later they drew near their own village on the slopes of Morne-au-Diable, these dead men and women walking single file in the twilight, with no soul leading them or daring to follow, the people of their village, who were also holding *bamboche* in the market place, saw them drawing closer, recognized among them fathers, brothers, wives and daughters whom they had buried months before.

Most of them knew at once the truth, that these were zombies who had been dragged dead from their graves, but others hoped that a blessed miracle had taken place on this Fête Dieu, and rushed forward to take them in their arms and welcome them.

But the zombies shuffled through the marketplace, recognizing neither father nor wife nor mother, and as they turned leftward up the path leading to the graveyard, a woman whose daughter was in the procession of the dead threw herself screaming before the girl's shuffling feet and begged her to stay; but the grave-cold feet of the daughter and the feet of the other dead shuffled over her and onward; and as they approached the graveyard, they began to shuffle faster and rushed among the graves, and each before his own empty grave began clawing at the stones and earth to enter it again; and as their cold hands touched the earth of their own graves, they fell and lay there, rotting carrion.

That night the fathers, sons and brothers of the zombies, after restoring the bodies to their graves, sent a messenger on muleback down the mountain, who returned next day with the name of Ti Joseph and with a stolen shirt of Ti Joseph's which had been worn next his skin and was steeped in the grease-sweat of his body.

They collected silver in the village and went with the name of Ti Joseph and the shirt of Ti Joseph to a *bocor* beyond Trou Caiman, who made a deadly needle *ouanga*, a black bag *ouanga*, pierced all through with pins and needles, filled with dry goat dung, circled with cock's feathers dipped in blood.

And lest the needle *ouanga* be slow in working or be rendered weak by Joseph's counter magic, they sent men down to the plain, who lay in wait patiently for Joseph, and one night hacked off his head with a machete. . . .

When Polynice had finished this recital, I said to him, after a moment of silence, "You are not a peasant like those of the Cul-de-Sac; you are a reasonable man, or at least it seems to me you are. Now how much of that story, honestly, do you believe?"

He replied earnestly: "I did not see these special things, but there were many witnesses, and why should I not believe them when I myself have also seen zombies? When you also have seen them, with their faces and their eyes in which there is no life, you will not only believe in these zombies who should be resting in their graves, you will pity them from the bottom of your heart."

Before finally taking leave of La Gonave, I did see these "walking dead men," and I did, in a sense, believe in them and pitied them, indeed, from the bottom of my heart. It was not the next night, though Polynice, true to his promise, rode with me across the Plaine Mapou to the deserted, silent cane fields where he had hoped to show me zombies laboring. It was not on any night. It was in broad daylight one afternoon, when we passed that way again, on the lower trail to Picmy. Polynice reined in his horse and pointed to a rough, stony, terraced slope—on which four laborers, three men and a woman, were chopping the earth with machetes, among straggling cotton stalks, a hundred yards distant from the trail.

"Wait while I go up there," he said, excited because a chance had come to fulfill his promise. "I think it is Lamercie with the zombies. If I wave to you, leave your horse and come." Starting up the slope, he shouted to the woman, "It is I, Polynice," and when he waved later, I followed.

As I clambered up, Polynice was talking to the woman. She had stopped work—a big-boned, hard-faced black girl, who regarded us with surly unfriendliness. My first impression of the three supposed zombies, who continued dumbly at work, was that there was something about them unnatural and strange. They were plodding like brutes, like automatons. Without stooping down, I could not fully see their faces, which were bent expressionless over their work. Polynice touched one of them on the shoulder, motioned him to get up. Obediently, like an animal, he slowly stood erect—and what I saw then, coupled with what I had heard previously, or despite it, came as a rather sickening shock. The eyes were the worst. It was not my imagination. They were in truth like the eyes of a dead man, not blind, but staring, unfocused, unseeing. The whole face, for that matter, was bad enough. It was vacant, as if there was nothing behind it. It seemed not only expressionless, but incapable of expression. I had seen so much previously in Haiti that was outside ordinary normal experience that for the flash of a second I had a sickening, almost panicky lapse in which I thought, or rather felt, Great God, maybe this stuff is really true, and if it is true, it is rather awful, for it upsets everything. By "everything" I meant the natural fixed laws and processes on which all modern human thought and actions are based. Then suddenly I remembered—and my mind seized the memory as a man sinking in water clutches a solid plank—the face of a dog I had once seen in the histological laboratory at Columbia. Its entire front brain had been removed in an experimental operation weeks before;

it moved about, it was alive, but its eyes were like the eyes I now saw staring.

I recovered from my mental panic. I reached out and grasped one of the dangling hands. It was calloused, solid, human. Holding it, I said, *"Bonjour, compère."* The zombie stared without responding. The black wench, Lamercie, who was their keeper, now more sullen than ever, pushed me away—*"Z'affai' nèg' pas z'affai' blanc"* (Negroes' affairs are not for whites). But I had seen enough. "Keeper" was the key to it. "Keeper" was the word that had leapt naturally into my mind as she protested, and just as naturally the zombies were nothing but poor, ordinary demented human beings, idiots, forced to toil in the fields.

It was a good rational explanation, but it is far from being the end of this story. It satisfied me then, and I said as much to Polynice as we went down the slope. At first he did not contradict me, even said doubtfully, "Perhaps"; but as we reached the horses, before mounting, he stopped and said, "Look here, I respect your distrust of what you call superstition and your desire to find out the truth, but if what you were saying now were the whole truth, how could it be that over and over again, people who have stood by and seen their own relatives buried have, sometimes soon, sometimes months or years afterward, found those relatives working as zombies, and have sometimes killed the man who held them in servitude?"

"Polynice," I said, "that's just the part of it that I can't believe. The zombies in such cases may have resembled the dead persons, or even been 'doubles'—you know what doubles are, how two people resemble each other to a startling degree. But it is a fixed rule of reasoning in America that we will never accept the possibility of a thing's being 'supernatural' so long as any natural explanation, even farfetched, seems adequate."

"Well," said he, "if you spent many years in Haiti, you would have a very hard time to fit this American reasoning into some of the things you encountered here."

As I have said, there is more to this story—and I think it is best to tell it very simply.

In all Haiti, there is no clearer scientifically trained mind, no sounder pragmatic rationalist, than Dr. Antoine Villiers. When I sat later with him in his study, surrounded by hundreds of scientific books in French, German and English, and told him of what I had seen and of my conversations with Polynice, he said:

"My dear sir, I do not believe in miracles nor in supernatural events, and I do not want to shock your Anglo-Saxon intelligence, but this Polynice of yours, with all his superstition, may have been closer to the partial truth than you were. Understand me clearly. I do not believe that anyone has ever been raised literally from the dead —neither Lazarus, nor the daughter of Jairus, nor Jesus Christ himself—yet I am not sure, paradoxical as it may sound, that there is not something frightful, something in the nature of criminal sorcery if you like, in some cases at least, in this matter of zombies. I am by no means sure that some of them who now toil in the fields were not dragged from the actual graves in which they lay in their coffins, buried by their mourning families!"

"It is then something like suspended animation?" I asked.

"I will show you," he replied, "a thing which may supply the key to what you are seeking," and standing on a chair, he pulled down a paperbound book from a top shelf. It was nothing mysterious or esoteric. It was the current official *Code Pénal* (Criminal Code) of the Republic of Haiti. He thumbed through it and pointed to a paragraph which read:

"*Article* 249. Also shall be qualified as attempted murder the employment which may be made against any person of substances which, without causing actual death, produce a lethargic coma more or less prolonged. If, after the administering of such substances, the person has been buried, the act shall be considered murder no matter what result follows."

HOW THE BRIGADIER
LOST HIS EAR

By Sir Arthur Conan Doyle

. . . .

You all know Sherlock Holmes. Now meet Etienne Gerard,
who had his sword, his horse, his mother,
his emperor, his career—and Lucia, for whose love
he embarked on a terrible adventure.

It was the old brigadier who was talking in the café.

I have seen a great many cities, my friends. I would not dare to tell you how many I have entered as a conqueror with eight hundred of my little fighting devils clanking and jingling behind me.

The cavalry were in front of the Grande Armée, and the Hussars of Conflans were in front of the cavalry, and I was in front of the Hussars. But of all the cities which we visited Venice is the most ill-built and ridiculous. I cannot imagine how the people who laid it out thought that the cavalry could maneuver. It would puzzle Murat or Lasalle to bring a squadron into that square of theirs. For this reason we left Kellermann's heavy brigade and also my own Hussars at Padua on the mainland. But Suchet with the infantry held the town, and he had chosen me as his aide-de-camp for that winter, because he was pleased about the affair of the Italian fencing master at Milan. The fellow was a good swordsman, and it was fortunate for the credit of French arms that it was I who was opposed to him. Besides, he deserved a lesson, for if one does not like a prima donna's singing one can always be silent, but it is intolerable that a public affront should be put upon a pretty woman. So the sympathy was all with me, and after the affair had blown over, and the man's widow had been pensioned, Suchet chose me as his own galloper, and I followed him to Venice, where I had the strange adventure which I am about to tell you.

You have not been to Venice? No, for it is seldom that the French travel. We were great travelers in those days. From Moscow to Cairo we have traveled everywhere, but we went in larger parties than were convenient to those whom we visited, and we carried our passports in our limbers. It will be a bad day for Europe when the French start traveling again, for they are slow to leave their homes; but when they have done so no one can say how far they will go if they have a guide like our little man to point out the way. But the great days are gone, and the great men are dead, and here am I, the last of them, drinking wine of Suresnes and telling old tales in a café.

But it is of Venice that I would speak. The folks there live like water rats upon a mud bank; but the houses are very fine, and the churches, especially that of St. Mark, are as great as any I have seen. But above all, they are all proud of their statues and their pictures, which are the most famous in Europe. There are many soldiers who think that because one's trade is to make war one should never have a thought above fighting and plunder. There was old Bouvet, for example—the one who was killed by the Prussians on the day that I won the Emperor's medal; if you took him away from the camp and the canteen, and spoke to him of books or of art, he would sit and stare at you. But the highest soldier is a man like myself who can understand the things of the mind and the soul. It is true that I was very young when I joined the army, and that the quartermaster was my only teacher; but if you go about the world with your eyes open you cannot help learning a great deal.

Thus I was able to admire the pictures in Venice, and to know the names of the great men, Michael, Titiens and Angelus, and the others, who had painted them. No one can say that Napoleon did not admire them also, for the very first thing which he did when he captured the town was to send the best of them to Paris. We all took what we could get, and I had two pictures for my share. One of them, called "Nymphs Surprised," I kept for myself, and the other, "Saint Barbara," I sent as a present for my mother.

It must be confessed, however, that some of our men behaved very badly in this matter of the statues and the pictures. The people at Venice were very much attached to them, and as to the four bronze horses which stood over the gate of their great church, they loved them as dearly as if they had been their children. I have always been a judge of a horse, and I had a good look at these ones, but I could not see that there was much to be said for them. They were too coarse-limbed for light cavalry chargers, and they had not the weight for the gun teams. However, they were the only four horses, alive or dead, in the whole town, so it was not to be expected that the people would know any better. They wept bitterly when they were sent away, and ten French soldiers were found floating in the canals that night. As a punishment for these murders a great many more of their pictures were sent away, and the soldiers took to breaking the statues and firing their muskets at the stained-glass windows. This made the people furious, and there was very bad feeling in the town. Many officers and men disappeared during that winter, and even their bodies were never found.

For myself I had plenty to do, and I never found the time heavy on my hands. In every country it has been my custom to try to learn the language. For this reason I always look round for some lady who will be kind enough to teach it to me, and then we practice it together. This is the most interesting way of picking it up, and before I was thirty I could speak nearly every tongue in Europe; but it must be confessed that what you learn is not of much use for the ordinary purpose of life. My business, for example, has usually been with soldiers and peasants, and what advantage is it to be able to say to them that I love only them, and that I will come back when the wars are over?

Never have I had so sweet a teacher as in Venice. Lucia was her first name, and her second—but a gentleman forgets second names. I can say this with all discretion, that she was of one of the senatorial families of Venice, and that her grandfather had been Doge of the town. She was of an exquisite beauty—and when I, Etienne Gerard, use such a word as "exquisite," my friends, it has a meaning. I have judgment, I have memories, I have the means of comparison. Of all the women who have loved me there are not twenty to whom I could apply such a term as that. But I say again that Lucia was exquisite. Of the dark type I do not recall her equal unless it were Dolores of Toledo. There was a little brunette whom I loved at Santarem when I was soldiering under Massena in Portugal—her name has escaped me. She was of a perfect beauty, but she had not the figure nor the grace of Lucia. There was Agnes also. I could not put one before the other, but I do none an injustice when I say that Lucia was the equal of the best.

It was over this matter of pictures that I had first met her, for her father owned a palace on the farther side of the Rialto Bridge upon the Grand Canal, and it was so packed with wall paintings that Suchet sent a party of sappers to cut some of them out and send them to Paris. I had gone down with them, and after I had seen Lucia in tears it appeared to me that the plaster would crack if it were taken from the support of the wall. I said so, and the sappers were withdrawn. After that I was the friend of the family, and many a flask of Chianti have I cracked with the father and many a sweet lesson have I had from the daughter. Some of our French officers married in Venice that winter, and I might have done the same, for I loved her with all my heart; but Etienne Gerard had his sword, his horse, his regiment, his mother, his Emperor and his career. A debonair Hussar has room in his heart for love, but none for a wife. So I thought then, my friends, but I did not see the lonely days when I should long to clasp those vanished hands, and turn my head away when I saw old comrades with their tall children standing round their chairs. This love which I had thought was a joke and a plaything—it is only now that I understand that it is the molder of one's life, the most solemn and sacred of all things. . . . Thank you, my friend, thank you! It is a good wine, and a second bottle cannot hurt.

And now I will tell you how my love for Lucia was the cause of one of the most terrible of all the wonderful adventures which have ever befallen me, and how it was that I came to lose the top of my right ear. You have often asked me why it was missing. Tonight for the first time I will tell you.

Suchet's headquarters at that time was the old palace of the Doge Dandolo, which stands on the lagoon not far from the place of San Marco. It was near the end of the winter, and I had returned one night from the Theatre Goldini, when I found a note from Lucia and a gondola waiting. She prayed me to come to her at once as she was in trouble. To a Frenchman and a soldier there was but one answer to such a note. In an instant I was in the boat, and the gondolier was pushing out into the dark lagoon. I remember that as I took my seat in the boat I was struck by the man's great size. He was not tall, but he was one of the broadest men that I have ever seen in my life. But the gondoliers of Venice are a strong breed, and powerful men are common enough among them. The fellow took his place behind me and began to row.

A good soldier in an enemy's country should everywhere and at all times be on the alert. It has been one of the rules of my life, and if I have lived to wear gray hairs it is because I have observed it. And yet upon that night I was as careless as a foolish young recruit who fears lest he should be thought to be afraid. My pistols I had left behind in my hurry. My sword was at my belt, but it is not always the most convenient of weapons. I lay back in my seat in the gondola, lulled by the gentle swish of the water and the steady creaking of the oar. Our way lay through a network of narrow canals with high houses towering on either side and a thin slit of star-spangled sky above us. Here and there, on the bridges which spanned the canal, there was the dim glimmer of an oil lamp, and sometimes there came a gleam from some niche, where a candle burned before the image of a saint. But save for this it was all black, and one could only see the water by the white fringe which curled round the long black nose of our boat. It was a place and a time for dreaming. I thought of my own past life, of all the great deeds in which I had been concerned, of the horses that I had handled, and of the women that I had loved. Then I thought also of my dear mother, and I fancied her joy when she heard the folk in the village talking about the fame of her son. Of the Emperor also I thought, and of France, the dear fatherland, the sunny France, mother of beautiful daughters and of gallant sons. My heart glowed within me as I thought of how we had brought her colors so many hundred leagues beyond her borders. To her greatness I would dedicate my life. I placed my hand upon my heart as I swore it, and at that instant the gondolier fell upon me from behind.

When I say that he fell upon me I do not mean merely that he attacked me, but that he really did tumble upon me with all his weight. The fellow stands behind you and above you as he rows, so that you can neither see him nor can you in any way guard against such an assault. One moment I had sat with my mind filled with sublime resolutions, the next I was flattened out upon the bottom of the boat, the breath dashed out of my body, and this monster pinning me down. I felt the fierce pants of his hot breath upon the back of my neck. In an instant he had torn away my sword, had slipped a sack over my head and had tied a rope firmly round the outside of it. There I was at the bottom of the gondola as helpless as a trussed fowl. I could not shout, I could not move; I was a mere bundle. An instant later I heard once more the swishing of the water and the creaking of the oar. This fellow had done his work and had resumed his journey as quietly and unconcernedly as if he were accustomed to clap a sack over a colonel of Hussars every day of the week.

I cannot tell you the humiliation and also the fury which filled my mind as I lay there like a helpless sheep being carried to the butcher's. I, Etienne Gerard, the champion of the six brigades of light cavalry, and the first swordsman of the Grand Army, to be overpowered by a single unarmed man in such a fashion! Yet I lay quiet, for there is a time to resist and there is a time to save one's strength. I had felt the fellow's grip upon my arms, and I knew that I would be a child in his hands. I waited quietly, therefore, with a heart that burned with rage, until my opportunity should come.

How long I lay there at the bottom of the boat I cannot tell; but it seemed to me to be a long time, and always there were the hiss of the waters and the steady creaking of the oars. Several times we turned corners, for I heard the long, sad cry which these gondoliers give when they wish to warn their fellows that they are coming. At last, after a considerable journey, I felt the side of the boat scrape up against a landing place. The fellow knocked three times with his oar upon wood, and in answer to his summons I heard the rasping of bars and the turning of keys. A great door creaked back upon its hinges.

"Have you got him?" asked a voice in Italian.

My monster gave a laugh and kicked the sack in which I lay.

"Here he is," said he.

"They are waiting." He added something which I could not understand.

"Take him, then," said my captor. He raised me in his arms, ascended some steps, and I was thrown down upon a hard floor. A moment later the bars creaked and the key whined once more. I was a prisoner inside a house.

From the voices and the steps there seemed now to be several people round me. I understand Italian a great deal better than I speak it, and I could make out very well what they were saying.

"You have not killed him, Matteo?"

"What matter if I have?"

"My faith, you will have to answer for it to the tribunal."

"They will kill him, will they not?"

"Yes, but it is not for you or me to take it out of their hands."

"Tut! I have not killed him. Dead men do not bite, and his cursed teeth met in my thumb as I pulled the sack over his head."

"He lies very quiet."

"Tumble him out and you will find he is lively enough."

The cord which bound me was undone and the sack drawn from over my head. With my eyes closed I lay motionless upon the floor.

"By the saints, Matteo, I tell you that you have broken his neck."

"Not I. He has only fainted. The better for him if he never came out of it again."

I felt a hand within my tunic.

"Matteo is right," said a voice. "His heart beats like a hammer. Let him lie, and he will soon find his senses."

I waited for a minute or so, and then I ventured to take a stealthy peep from between my lashes. At first I could see nothing, for I had been so long in darkness and it was but a dim light in which I found myself. Soon, however, I made out that a high and vaulted ceiling covered with painted gods and goddesses was arching over my head. This was no mean den of cutthroats into which I had been carried, but it must be the hall of some Venetian palace. Then, without movement, very slowly and stealthily I had a peep at the men who surrounded me. There was the gondolier, a swart, hard-face, murderous ruffian, and beside him were three other men, one of them a little twisted fellow with an air of authority and several keys in his hand, the other two tall young servants in a smart livery. As I listened to their talk I saw that the small man was the steward of the house, and that the others were under his orders.

There were four of them, then, but the little steward might be left out of the reckoning. Had I a weapon I should have smiled at such odds as those. But, hand to hand, I was no match for the one even without three others to aid him. Cunning, then, not force, must be my aid. I wished to look round for some mode of escape, and in doing so I made an almost imperceptible movement of my head. Slight as it was it did not escape my guardians.

"Come, wake up, wake up!" cried the steward.

"Get on your feet, little Frenchman," growled the gondolier. "Get up, I say!" and for the second time he spurned me with his foot.

Never in the world was a command obeyed so promptly as that one. In an instant I had bounded to my feet and rushed as hard as I could run to the back of the hall. They were after me as I have seen the English hounds follow a fox, but there was a long passage down which I tore. It turned to the left and again to the left, and then I found myself back in the hall once more. They were almost within touch of me, and there was no time for thought. I turned toward the staircase, but two men were coming down it. I dodged back and tried the door through which I had been brought, but it was fastened with great bars and I could not loosen them. The gondolier was on me with his knife, but I met him with a kick on the body which stretched him on his back. His dagger flew with a clatter across the marble floor. I had no time to seize it, for there were half a dozen of them now clutching at me. As I rushed through them the little steward thrust his leg before me and I fell with a crash, but I was up in an instant, and breaking from their grasp I burst through the very middle of them and made for a door at the other end of the hall. I reached it well in front of them, and I gave a shout of triumph as the handle turned freely in my hand, for I could see that it led to the outside and that all was clear for my escape. But I had forgotten the strange city in which I was. Every house is an island. As I flung open the door, ready to bound out into the street, the light of the hall shone upon the deep, still, black water which lay flush with the topmost step. I shrank back, and in an instant my pursuers were on me. But I am not taken so easily.

Again I kicked and fought my way through them, although one of them tore a handful of hair from my head in his effort to hold me. The little steward struck me with a key and I was battered and bruised, but once more I cleared a way in front of me. Up the grand staircase I rushed, burst open the pair of huge folding doors which faced me and learned at last that my efforts were in vain.

The room into which I had broken was brilliantly lighted. With its gold cornices, its massive pillars and its painted walls and ceilings, it was evidently the grand hall of some famous Venetian palace. There are many hundred such in this strange city, any one of which has rooms which would grace the Louvre or Versailles. In the center of this great hall there was a raised dais, and upon it in a half circle there sat twelve men all clad in black gowns, like those of a Franciscan monk, and each with a mask over the upper part of his face.

A group of armed men—rough-looking rascals—were standing round the door, and amid them facing the dais was a young fellow in the uniform of the light infantry. As he turned his head I recognized him. It was Captain Auret, of the Seventh, a young Basque with whom I had drunk many a glass during the winter. He was deadly white, poor wretch, but he held himself manfully amid the assassins who surrounded him. Never shall I forget the sudden flash of hope which shone in his dark eyes when he saw a comrade burst into the room, or the look of despair which followed as he understood that I had come not to change his fate but to share it.

You can think how amazed these people were when I hurled myself into their presence. My pursuers had crowded in behind me and choked the doorway, so that all further flight was out of the question. It is at such instants that my nature asserts itself. With dignity I advanced toward the tribunal. My jacket was torn, my hair was disheveled, my head was bleeding, but there was that in my eyes and in my carriage which made them realize that no common man was before them. Not a hand was raised to arrest me until I halted in front of a formidable old man whose long gray beard and masterful manner told me that both by years and by character he was the man in authority.

"Sir," said I, "you will perhaps tell me why I have been forcibly arrested and brought to this place. I am an honorable soldier, as is this other gentleman here, and I demand that you will instantly set us both at liberty."

There was an appalling silence to my appeal. It is not pleasant to have twelve masked faces turned upon you, and to see twelve pairs of vindictive Italian eyes fixed with fierce intentness upon your face. But I stood as a debonair soldier should, and I could not but reflect how much credit I was bringing upon the Hussars of Conflans by the dignity of my bearing. I do not think that anyone could have carried himself better under such difficult circumstances. I looked with a fearless face from one assassin to another, and I waited for some reply.

It was the graybeard who at last broke the silence.

"Who is this man?" he asked.

"His name is Gerard," said the little steward at the door.

"Colonel Gerard," said I. "I will not deceive you. I am Etienne Gerard, *the* Colonel Gerard, five times mentioned in despatches and recommended for the sword of honor. I am aide-de-camp to General Suchet, and I demand my instant release, together with that of my comrade in arms."

The same terrible silence fell upon the assembly and the same twelve pairs of merciless eyes were bent upon my face. Again it was the graybeard who spoke.

"He is out of his order. There are two names upon our list before his."

"He escaped from our hands and burst into the room."

"Let him await his turn. Take him down to the wooden cell."

"If he resists us, your excellency?"

"Bury your knives in his body. The tribunal will uphold you. Remove him until we have dealt with the others."

They advanced upon me, and for an instant I thought of resistance. It would have been a heroic death, but who was there to see it or to chronicle it? I might be only postponing my fate, and yet I had been in so many bad places and come out unhurt that I had learned always to hope and to trust my star. I allowed these rascals to seize me, and I was led from the room, the gondolier walking at my side with a long naked knife in his hand. I could see in his brutal eyes the satisfaction which it would give him if he could find some excuse for plunging it into my body.

They are wonderful places, these great Venetian houses, palaces and fortresses and prisons all in one. I was led along a passage and down a bare stone stair until we came to a short corridor from which three doors opened. Through one of these I was thrust, and the spring lock closed behind me. The only light came dimly through a small grating which opened on the passage. Peering and feeling, I carefully examined the chamber in which I had been placed. I understood from what I had heard that I should soon have to leave it again in order to appear before this tribunal, but still it is not my nature to throw away any possible chances.

The stone floor of the cell was so damp and the walls for some feet high were so slimy and foul that it was evident they were beneath the level of the water. A single slanting hole high up near the ceiling was the only aperture for light or air. Through it I saw one bright star shining down upon me, and the sight filled me with comfort and with hope. I have never been a man of religion, though I have always had a respect for those who were, but I remember that night that the star shining down the shaft seemed to be an all-seeing eye which was upon me, and I felt as a young and frightened recruit might feel in battle when he saw the calm gaze of his colonel turned upon him.

Three of the sides of my prison were formed of stone, but the fourth was of wood, and I could see that it had only recently been erected. Evidently a partition had been thrown up to divide a single large cell into two smaller ones. There was no hope for me in the old walls, in the tiny window, or in the massive door. It was only in this one direction of the wooden screen that there was any possibility of exploring. My reason told me that if I should pierce it—which did not seem very difficult—it would only be to find myself in another cell as strong as that in which I then was. Yet I had always rather be doing something than doing nothing, so I bent all my attention and all my energies upon the wooden wall. Two planks were badly jointed, and so loose that I was certain I could easily detach them. I searched about for some tool, and I found one in the leg of a small bed which stood in the corner. I forced the end of this into the chink of the planks, and I was about to twist them outwards when the sound of rapid footsteps caused me to pause and to listen.

I wish I could forget what I heard. Many a hundred men have I seen die in battle, and I have slain more myself than I care to think of, but all that was fair fight and the duty of a soldier. It was a very different matter to listen to a murder in this den of assassins. They were pushing someone along the passage, someone who resisted and who clung to my door as he passed. They must have taken him into the third cell, the one which was farthest from me. "Help! help!" cried a voice, and then I heard a blow and a scream. "Help! help!" cried the voice again, and then, "Gerard! Colonel Gerard!" It was my poor captain of infantry whom they were slaughtering.

"Murderers! Murderers!" I yelled, and I kicked at my door, but again I heard him shout, and then everything was silent. A minute later there was a heavy splash, and I knew that no human eye would ever see Auret again. He had gone as a hundred others had gone whose names were missing from the roll calls of their regiments during that winter in Venice.

The steps returned along the passage, and I thought that they were coming for me. Instead of that they opened the door of the cell next to mine, and they took someone out of it. I heard the steps die away up the stair. At once I renewed my work upon the planks, and within a very few minutes I had loosened them in such a way that I could remove and replace them at pleasure. Passing through the aperture I found myself in the farther cell, which, as I expected, was the other half of the one in which I had been confined. I was not any nearer to escape than I had been before, for there was no other wooden wall which I could penetrate, and the spring lock of the door had been closed. There were no traces to show who was my companion in misfortune. Closing the two loose planks behind me, I returned to my own cell, and waited there with all the courage which I could command for the summons which would probably be my death knell.

It was a long time in coming, but at last I heard the sound of feet once more in the passage, and I nerved myself to listen to some other odious deed and to hear the cries of the poor victim. Nothing of the kind occurred, however, and the prisoner was placed in the cell without violence. I had no time to peep through my hole of communication, for next moment my own door was flung open and my rascally gondolier, with the other assassins, came into the cell.

"Come, Frenchman," said he. He held his bloodstained knife in his great hairy hand, and I read in his fierce eyes that he only looked for some excuse in order to plunge it into my heart. Resistance was useless. I followed without a word. I was led up the stone stair and back into that gorgeous chamber in which I had left the secret tribunal. I was ushered in, but to my surprise it was not on me that their attention was fixed. One of their own number, a tall, dark young man, was standing before them and was pleading with them in low, earnest tones. His voice quivered with anxiety, and his hands darted in and out or writhed together in an agony of entreaty. "You cannot do it! You cannot do it!" he cried. "I implore the tribunal to reconsider this decision."

"Stand aside, brother," said the old man who presided. "The case is decided, and another is up for judgment."

"For Heaven's sake, be merciful!" cried the young man.

"We have already been merciful," the other answered. "Death would have been a small penalty for such an offense. Be silent and let judgment take its course."

I saw the young man throw himself in an agony of grief into his chair. I had no time, however, to speculate as to what it was which was troubling him, for his eleven colleagues had already fixed their stern eyes upon me. The moment of fate had arrived.

"You are Colonel Gerard?" said the terrible old man.

"I am."

"Aide-de-camp to the robber who calls himself General Suchet, who in turn represents that arch-robber Buonaparte?"

It was on my lips to tell him that he was a liar, but there is a time to argue and a time to be silent.

"I am an honorable soldier," said I. "I have obeyed my orders and done my duty."

The blood flushed into the old man's face, and his eyes blazed through his mask.

"You are thieves and murderers, every man of you," he cried.

"What are you doing here? You are Frenchmen. Why are you not in France? Did we invite you to Venice? By what right are you here? Where are our pictures? Where are the horses of St. Mark? Who are you that you should pilfer those treasures which our fathers through so many centuries have collected? We were a great city when France was a desert. Your drunken, brawling, ignorant soldiers have undone the work of saints and heroes. What have you to say to it?"

He was, indeed, a formidable old man, for his white beard bristled with fury, and he barked out the little sentences like a savage hound. For my part I could have told him that his pictures would be safe in Paris, that his horses were really not worth making a fuss about and that he could see heroes—I say nothing of saints—without going back to his ancestors or even moving out of his chair. All this I could have pointed out, but one might as well argue with a mameluke about religion. I shrugged my shoulders and said nothing.

"The prisoner has no defense," said one of my masked judges.

"Has anyone any observation to make before judgment is passed?" The old man glared round him at the others.

"There is one matter, your excellency," said another. "It can scarce be referred to without reopening a brother's wounds, but I would remind you that there is a very particular reason why an exemplary punishment should be inflicted in the case of this officer."

"I had not forgotten it," the old man answered. "Brother, if the tribunal has injured you in one direction, it will give you ample satisfaction in another."

The young man who had been pleading when I entered the room staggered to his feet.

"I cannot endure it," he cried. "Your excellency must forgive me. The tribunal can act without me. I am ill! I am mad!" He flung his hands up with a furious gesture and rushed from the room.

"Let him go! Let him go!" said the president. "It is, indeed, more than can be asked of flesh and blood that he should remain under this roof. But he is a true Venetian, and when the first agony is over he will understand that it could not be otherwise."

I had been forgotten during this episode, and though I am not a man who is accustomed to being overlooked, I should have been all the happier had they continued to neglect me. But now the old president glared at me again like a tiger who comes back to his victim.

"You shall pay for it all, and it is but justice that you should," said he. "You, an upstart adventurer and foreigner, have dared to raise your eyes in love to the granddaughter of a Doge of Venice who was already betrothed to the heir of the Loredans. He who enjoys such privileges must pay a price for them."

"It cannot be higher than they are worth," said I.

"You will tell us that when you have made a part payment," he said. "Perhaps your spirit may not be so proud by that time. Matteo, you will lead this prisoner to the wooden cell. Tonight is Monday. Let him have no food or water, and let him be led before the tribunal again on Wednesday night. We shall then decide upon the death which he is to die."

It was not a pleasant prospect, and yet it was a reprieve. One is thankful for small mercies when a hairy savage with a bloodstained knife is standing at one's elbow. He dragged me from the room, and I was thrust down the stairs and back into my cell. The door was locked and I was left to my reflections.

My first thought was to establish connection with my neighbor in misfortune. I waited until the steps had died away, and then I cautiously drew aside the two boards and peeped through. The light was very dim, so dim that I could only just discern a figure huddled in the corner, and I could hear the low whisper of a voice which prayed as one prays who is in deadly fear. The boards must have made a creaking. There was a sharp exclamation of surprise.

"Courage, friend, courage!" I cried. "All is not lost. Keep a stout heart, for Etienne Gerard is by your side."

"Etienne!" It was a woman's voice which spoke—a voice which was always music to my ears. I sprang through the gap and I flung my arms round her. "Lucia! Lucia!" I cried.

It was "Etienne!" and "Lucia!" for some minutes, for one does not make speeches at moments like that. It was she who came to her senses first.

"Oh, Etienne, they will kill you. How came you into their hands?"

"In answer to your letter."

"I wrote no letter."

"The cunning demons! But you?"

"I came also in answer to your letter."

"Lucia, I wrote no letter."

"They have trapped us both with the same bait."

"I care nothing about myself, Lucia. Besides, there is no pressing danger with me. They have simply returned me to my cell."

"Oh, Etienne, Etienne, they will kill you. Lorenzo is there."

"The old graybeard?"

"No, no, a young dark man. He loved me, and I thought I loved him until—until I learned what love is, Etienne. He will never forgive you. He has a heart of stone."

"Let them do what they like. They cannot rob me of the past, Lucia. But you—what about you?"

"It will be nothing, Etienne. Only a pang for an instant and then all over. They mean it as a badge of infamy, dear, but I will carry it like a crown of honor since it was through you that I gained it."

Her words froze my blood with horror. All my adventures were insignificant compared to this terrible shadow which was creeping over my soul.

"Lucia! Lucia!" I cried. "For pity's sake, tell me what these butchers are about to do. Tell me, Lucia! Tell me!"

"I will not tell you, Etienne, for it would hurt you far more than it would me. Well, well, I will tell you lest you should fear it was something worse. The president has ordered that my ear be cut off, that I may be marked forever as having loved a Frenchman."

Her ear! The dear little ear which I had kissed so often. I put my hand to each little velvet shell to make certain that this sacrilege had not yet been committed. Only over my dead body should they reach them. I swore it to her between my clenched teeth.

"You must not care, Etienne. And yet I love that you should care all the same."

"They shall not hurt you—the fiends!"

"I have hopes, Etienne. Lorenzo is there. He was silent while I was judged, but he may have pleaded for me after I was gone."

"He did. I heard him."

"Then he may have softened their hearts."

I knew that it was not so, but how could I bring myself to tell her? I might as well have done so, for with the quick instinct of woman my silence was speech to her.

"They would not listen to him! You need not fear to tell me, dear, for you will find that I am worthy to be loved by such a soldier. Where is Lorenzo now?"

"He left the hall."

"Then he may have left the house as well."

"I believe that he did."

"He has abandoned me to my fate. Etienne, Etienne, they are coming!"

Afar off I heard those fateful steps and the jingle of distant keys. What were they coming for now, since there were no other prisoners to drag to judgment? It could only be to carry out the sentence upon my darling. I stood between her and the door with the strength of a lion in my limbs. I would tear the house down before they should touch her.

"Go back! Go back!" she cried. "They will murder you, Etienne. My life, at least, is safe. For the love you bear me, Etienne, go back. It is nothing. I will make no sound. You will not hear that it is done."

She wrestled with me, this delicate creature, and by main force she dragged me to the opening between the cells. But a sudden thought had crossed my mind.

"We may yet be saved!" I whispered. "Do what I tell you at once and without argument. Go into my cell. Quick!"

I pushed her through the gap and helped her to replace the planks. I had retained her cloak in my hands, and with this wrapped round me I crept into the darkest corner of her cell. There I lay when the door was opened and several men came in. I had reckoned that they would bring no lantern, for they had none with them before. To their eyes I was only a black blur in the corner.

"Bring a light," said one of them.

"No, no; curse it!" cried a rough voice, which I knew to be that of the ruffian Matteo. "It is not a job that I like, and the more I saw it the less I should like it. I am sorry, signora, but the order of the tribunal has to be obeyed."

My impulse was to spring to my feet and to rush through them all and out by the open door. But how would that help Lucia? Suppose that I got clear away, she would be in their hands until I could come back with help, for single-handed I could not hope to clear a way for her. All this flashed through my mind in an instant, and I saw that the only course for me was to lie still, take what came and wait my chance. The fellow's coarse hand felt about among my curls—those curls in which only a woman's fingers had ever wandered. The next instant he gripped my ear, and a pain shot through me as if I had been touched with a hot iron. I bit my lip to stifle a cry, and I felt the blood run warm down my neck and back.

"There, thank Heaven that's over," said the fellow, giving me a friendly pat on the head. "You're a brave girl, signora, I'll say that for you, and I only wish you'd have better taste than to love a Frenchman. You can blame him and not me for what I have done."

What could I do save to lie still and grind my teeth at my own helplessness? At the same time my pain and my rage were always soothed by the reflection that I had suffered for the woman whom I loved. It is the custom of men to say to ladies that they would willingly endure any pain for their sake, but it was my privilege to show that I had said no more than I meant. I thought also how nobly I would seem to have acted if ever the story came to be told, and how proud the regiment of Conflans might well be of their colonel. These thoughts helped me to suffer in silence while the blood still trickled over my neck and dripped upon the stone floor. It was that sound which nearly led to my destruction.

"She's bleeding fast," said one of the valets. "You had best fetch a surgeon or you will find her dead in the morning."

"She lies very still and she has never opened her mouth," said another. "The shock has killed her."

"Nonsense; a young woman does not die so easily." It was Matteo who spoke. "Besides, I did but snip off enough to leave the tribunal's mark upon her. Rouse up, signora, rouse up!"

He shook me by the shoulder, and my heart stood still for fear he should feel the epaulette under the mantle.

"How is it with you now?" he asked.

I made no answer.

"Curse it! I wish I had to do with a man instead of a woman, and the fairest woman in Venice," said the gondolier. "Here, Nicholas, lend me your handkerchief and bring a light."

It was all over. The worst had happened. Nothing could save me. I still crouched in the corner, but I was tense in every muscle, like a wildcat about to spring. If I had to die I was determined that my end should be worthy of my life.

One of them had gone for a lamp, and Matteo was stooping over me with a handkerchief. In another instant my secret would be discovered. But he suddenly drew himself straight and stood motionless. At the same instant there came a confused murmuring sound through the little window far above my head. It was the rattle of oars and the buzz of many voices. Then there was a crash upon the door upstairs, and a terrible voice roared: "Open! Open in the name of the Emperor!"

The Emperor! It was like the mention of some saint, which, by its very sound, can frighten the demons. Away they ran with cries of terror—Matteo, the valets, the steward, all of the murderous gang. Another shout and then the crash of a hatchet and the splintering of planks. There were the rattle of arms and the cries of French soldiers in the hall. Next instant feet came flying down the stair and a man burst frantically into my cell.

"Lucia!" he cried, "Lucia!" He stood in the dim light, panting and unable to find his words. Then he broke out again. "Have I not shown you how I love you, Lucia? What more could I do to prove it? I have betrayed my country, I have broken my vow, I have ruined my friends and I have given my life in order to save you."

It was young Lorenzo Loredan, the lover whom I had superseded. My heart was heavy for him at the time, but after all it is every man for himself in love, and if one fails in the game it is some consolation to lose to one who can be a graceful and considerate winner. I was about to point this out to him, but at the first word I uttered he gave a shout of astonishment, and, rushing out, he seized the lamp which hung in the corridor and flashed it in my face.

"It is you, you villain!" he cried. "You French coxcomb! You shall pay me for the wrong which you have done me."

But the next instant he saw the pallor of my face and the blood which was still pouring from my head.

"What is this?" he asked. "How come you to have lost your ear?"

I shook off my weakness, and, pressing my handkerchief to my wound, I rose from my couch, the debonair colonel of Hussars.

"My injury, sir, is nothing. With your permission we will not allude to a matter so trifling and so personal."

But Lucia had burst through from her cell, and was pouring out the whole story while she clasped Lorenzo's arm.

"This noble gentleman—he has taken my place, Lorenzo! He has borne it for me. He has suffered that I might be saved."

I could sympathize with the struggle which I could see in the Italian's face. At last he held out his hand to me.

"Colonel Gerard," he said, "you are worthy of a great love. I forgive you, for if you have wronged me you have made a noble atonement. But I wonder to see you alive. I left the tribunal before you were judged, but I understood that no mercy would be shown to any Frenchman since the destruction of the ornaments of Venice."

"He did not destroy them," cried Lucia. "He has helped to

preserve those in our palace."

"One of them, at any rate," said I, as I stooped and kissed her hand.

This was the way, my friends, in which I lost my ear. Lorenzo was found stabbed to the heart in the Piazza of St. Mark within two days of the night of my adventure. Of the tribunal and its ruffians, Matteo and three others were shot, the rest banished from the town. Lucia, my lovely Lucia, retired into a convent at Murano after the French had left the city, and there she still may be, some gentle lady abbess who has perhaps long forgotten the days when our hearts throbbed together, and when the whole great world seemed so small a thing beside the love which burned in our veins. Or perhaps it may not be so. Perhaps she has not forgotten. There may still be times when the peace of the cloister is broken by the memory of the old soldier who loved her in those distant days. Youth is past and passion is gone, but the soul of the gentleman can never change, and still Etienne Gerard would bow his gray head before her, and would very gladly lose this other ear if he might do her a service.

DRY SEPTEMBER
By William Faulkner

. . . .

"I dont believe Will Mayes did it," the barber said . . .
"You mean to tell me," McLendon said, "that you'd take a nigger's
word before a white woman's?" William Faulkner describes
the quiet heat of terror.

I

Through the bloody September twilight, aftermath of sixty-two rain-
less days, it had gone like a fire in dry grass—the rumor, the story,
whatever it was. Something about Miss Minnie Cooper and a Negro.
Attacked, insulted, frightened: none of them, gathered in the barber
shop on that Saturday evening where the ceiling fan stirred, without
freshening it, the vitiated air, sending back upon them, in recurrent
surges of stale pomade and lotion, their own stale breath and odors,
knew exactly what had happened.

"Except it wasn't Will Mayes," a barber said. He was a man of
middle age; a thin, sand-colored man with a mild face, who was
shaving a client. "I know Will Mayes. He's a good nigger. And I
know Miss Minnie Cooper, too."

"What do you know about her?" a second barber said.

"Who is she?" the client said. "A young girl?"

"No," the barber said. "She's about forty, I reckon. She aint married. That's why I dont believe—"

"Believe, hell!" a hulking youth in a sweat-stained silk shirt said.
"Wont you take a white woman's word before a nigger's?"

"I dont believe Will Mayes did it," the barber said. "I know Will
Mayes."

"Maybe you know who did it, then. Maybe you already got him out of town, you damn niggerlover."

"I dont believe anybody did anything. I dont believe anything happened. I leave it to you fellows if them ladies that get old without getting married dont have notions that a man cant—"

"Then you are a hell of a white man," the client said. He moved under the cloth. The youth had sprung to his feet.

"You dont?" he said. "Do you accuse a white woman of lying?"

The barber held the razor poised above the half-risen client. He did not look around.

"It's this durn weather," another said. "It's enough to make a man do anything. Even to her."

Nobody laughed. The barber said in his mild, stubborn tone: "I aint accusing nobody of nothing. I just know and you fellows know how a woman that never—"

"You damn niggerlover!" the youth said.

"Shut up, Butch," another said. "We'll get the facts in plenty of time to act."

"Who is? Who's getting them?" the youth said. "Facts, hell! I—"

"You're a fine white man," the client said. "Aint you?" In his frothy beard he looked like a desert rat in the moving pictures. "You tell them, Jack," he said to the youth. "If there aint any white men in this town, you can count on me, even if I aint only a drummer and a stranger."

"That's right, boys," the barber said. "Find out the truth first. I know Will Mayes."

"Well, by God!" the youth shouted. "To think that a white man in this town—"

"Shut up, Butch," the second speaker said. "We got plenty of time."

The client sat up. He looked at the speaker. "Do you claim that anything excuses a nigger attacking a white woman? Do you mean to tell me you are a white man and you'll stand for it? You better go back North where you came from. The South dont want your kind here."

"North what?" the second said. "I was born and raised in this town."

"Well, by God!" the youth said. He looked about with a strained, baffled gaze, as if he was trying to remember what it was he wanted to say or to do. He drew his sleeve across his sweating face. "Damn if I'm going to let a white woman—"

"You tell them, Jack," the drummer said. "By God, if they—"

The screen door crashed open. A man stood in the floor, his feet apart and his heavy-set body poised easily. His white shirt was open at the throat; he wore a felt hat. His hot, bold glance swept the group. His name was McLendon. He had commanded troops at the front in France and had been decorated for valor.

"Well," he said, "are you going to sit there and let a black son rape a white woman on the streets of Jefferson?"

Butch sprang up again. The silk of his shirt clung flat to his heavy shoulders. At each armpit was a dark halfmoon. "That's what I been telling them! That's what I—"

"Did it really happen?" a third said. "This aint the first man scare she ever had, like Hawkshaw says. Wasn't there something about a man on the kitchen roof, watching her undress, about a year ago?"

"What?" the client said. "What's that?" The barber had been slowly forcing him back into the chair; he arrested himself reclining, his head lifted, the barber still pressing him down.

McLendon whirled on the third speaker. "Happen? What the hell difference does it make? Are you going to let the black sons get away with it until one really does it?"

"That's what I'm telling them!" Butch shouted. He cursed, long and steady, pointless.

"Here, here," a fourth said. "Not so loud. Dont talk so loud."

"Sure," McLendon said; "no talking necessary at all. I've done my talking. Who's with me?" He poised on the balls of his feet, roving his gaze.

The barber held the drummer's face down, the razor poised. "Find out the facts first, boys. I know Willy Mayes. It wasn't him. Let's get the sheriff and do this thing right."

McLendon whirled upon him his furious, rigid face. The barber did not look away. They looked like men of different races. The other barbers had ceased also above their prone clients. "You mean to tell me," McLendon said, "that you'd take a nigger's word before a white woman's? Why, you damn niggerloving—"

The third speaker rose and grasped McLendon's arm; he too had been a soldier. "Now, now. Let's figure this thing out. Who knows anything about what really happened?"

"Figure out hell!" McLendon jerked his arm free. "All that're with me get up from there. The ones that aint—" He roved his gaze, dragging his sleeve across his face.

Three men rose. The drummer in the chair sat up. "Here," he said, jerking at the cloth about his neck; "get this rag off me. I'm with him. I dont live here, but by God, if our mothers and wives and sisters—" He smeared the cloth over his face and flung it to the floor. McLendon stood in the floor and cursed the others. Another rose and moved toward him. The remainder sat uncomfortable, not looking at one another, then one by one they rose and joined him.

The barber picked the cloth from the floor. He began to fold it neatly. "Boys, dont do that. Will Mayes never done it. I know."

"Come on," McLendon said. He whirled. From his hip pocket protruded the butt of a heavy automatic pistol. They went out. The screen door crashed behind them reverberant in the dead air.

The barber wiped the razor carefully and swiftly, and put it away, and ran to the rear, and took his hat from the wall. "I'll be back as soon as I can," he said to the other barbers. "I cant let—" He went out, running. The two other barbers followed him to the door and caught it on the rebound, leaning out and looking up the street after him. The air was flat and dead. It had a metallic taste at the base of the tongue.

"What can he do?" the first said. The second one was saying "Jees Christ, Jees Christ" under his breath. "I'd just as lief be Will Mayes as Hawk, if he gets McLendon riled."

"Jees Christ, Jees Christ," the second whispered.

"You reckon he really done it to her?" the first said.

II

She was thirty-eight or thirty-nine. She lived in a small frame house with her invalid mother and a thin, sallow, unflagging aunt, where each morning between ten and eleven she would appear on the porch in a lace-trimmed boudoir cap, to sit swinging in the porch swing until noon. After dinner she lay down for a while, until the afternoon began to cool. Then, in one of the three or four new voile dresses which she had each summer, she would go downtown to spend the afternoon in the stores with the other ladies, where they would handle the goods and haggle over the prices in cold, immediate voices, without any intention of buying.

She was of comfortable people—not the best in Jefferson, but good people enough—and she was still on the slender side of ordinary looking, with a bright, faintly haggard manner and dress. When she was young she had had a slender, nervous body and a sort of hard vivacity which had enabled her for a time to ride upon the crest of the town's social life as exemplified by the high school party and church social period of her contemporaries while still children enough to be unclassconscious.

She was the last to realize that she was losing ground; that those among whom she had been a little brighter and louder flame than any other were beginning to learn the pleasure of snobbery—male—and retaliation—female. That was when her face began to wear that bright, haggard look. She still carried it to parties on shadowy porticoes and summer lawns, like a mask or a flag, with that bafflement of furious repudiation of truth in her eyes. One evening at a party she heard a boy and two girls, all schoolmates, talking. She never accepted another invitation.

She watched the girls with whom she had grown up as they married and got homes and children, but no man ever called on her steadily until the children of the other girls had been calling her "aunty" for several years, the while their mothers told them in bright voices about how popular Aunt Minnie had been as a girl. Then the town began to see her driving on Sunday afternoons with the cashier in the bank. He was a widower of about forty—a high-colored man, smelling always faintly of the barber shop or of whisky. He owned the first automobile in town, a red runabout; Minnie had the first motoring bonnet and veil the town ever saw. Then the town began to say: "Poor Minnie." "But she is old enough to take care of herself," others said. That was when she began to ask her old schoolmates that their children call her "cousin" instead of "aunty."

It was twelve years now since she had been relegated into adultery by public opinion, and eight years since the cashier had gone to a Memphis bank, returning for one day each Christmas, which he spent at an annual bachelors' party at a hunting club on the river. From behind their curtains the neighbors would see the party pass, and during the over-the-way Christmas day visiting they would tell her about him, about how well he looked, and how they heard that he was prospering in the city, watching with bright, secret eyes her haggard, bright face. Usually by that hour there would be the scent of whisky on her breath. It was supplied her by a youth, a clerk at the soda fountain: "Sure; I buy it for the old gal. I reckon she's entitled to a little fun."

Her mother kept to her room altogether now; the gaunt aunt ran the house. Against that background Minnie's bright dresses, her idle and empty days, had a quality of furious unreality. She went out in the evenings only with women now, neighbors, to the moving pictures. Each afternoon she dressed in one of the new dresses and went downtown alone, where her young "cousins" were already strolling in the late afternoons with their delicate, silken heads and thin, awkward arms and conscious hips, clinging to one another or shrieking and giggling with paired boys in the soda fountain when she passed and went on along the serried store fronts, in the doors of which the sitting and lounging men did not even follow her with their eyes any more.

III

The barber went swiftly up the street where the sparse lights, insect-swirled, glared in rigid and violent suspension in the lifeless air. The day had died in a pall of dust; above the darkened square, shrouded by the spent dust, the sky was as clear as the inside of a brass bell. Below the east was a rumor of the twice-waxed moon.

When he overtook them McLendon and three others were getting into a car parked in an alley. McLendon stooped his thick head, peering out beneath the top. "Changed your mind, did you?" he said. "Damn good thing; by God, tomorrow when this town hears about how you talked tonight—"

"Now, now," the other ex-soldier said. "Hawkshaw's all right. Come on, Hawk; jump in."

"Will Mayes never done it, boys," the barber said. "If anybody done it. Why, you all know well as I do there aint any town where they got better niggers than us. And you know how a lady will kind of think things about men when there aint any reason to, and Miss Minnie anyway—"

"Sure, sure," the soldier said. "We're just going to talk to him a little; that's all."

"Talk hell!" Butch said. "When we're through with the—"

"Shut up, for God's sake!" the soldier said. "Do you want everybody in town—"

"Tell them, by God!" McLendon said. "Tell every one of the sons that'll let a white woman—"

"Let's go; let's go: here's the other car." The second car slid squealing out of a cloud of dust at the alley mouth. McLendon started his car and took the lead. Dust lay like fog in the street. The street lights hung nimbused as in water. They drove on out of town.

A rutted lane turned at right angles. Dust hung above it too, and above all the land. The dark bulk of the ice plant, where the Negro Mayes was night watchman, rose against the sky. "Better stop here, hadn't we?" the soldier said. McLendon did not reply. He hurled the car up and slammed to a stop, the headlights glaring on the blank wall.

"Listen here, boys," the barber said, "if he's here, dont that prove he never done it? Dont it? If it was him, he would run. Dont you see he would?" The second car came up and stopped. McLendon got down; Butch sprang down beside him. "Listen, boys," the barber said.

"Cut the lights off!" McLendon said. The breathless dark rushed down. There was no sound in it save their lungs as they sought air in the parched dust in which for two months they had lived; then the diminishing crunch of McLendon's and Butch's feet, and a moment later McLendon's voice:

"Will! . . . Will!"

Below the east the wan hemorrhage of the moon increased. It heaved above the ridge, silvering the air, the dust, so that they seemed to breathe, live, in a bowl of molten lead. There was no sound of nightbird nor insect, no sound save their breathing and a faint ticking of contracting metal about the cars. Where their bodies touched one another they seemed to sweat dryly, for no more moisture came. "Christ!" a voice said. "Let's get out of here."

But they didn't move until vague noises began to grow out of the darkness ahead; then they got out and waited tensely in the breathless dark. There was another sound: a blow, a hissing expulsion of breath and McLendon cursing in undertone. They stood a moment longer, then they ran forward. They ran in a stumbling clump, as though they were fleeing something. "Kill him, kill the son," a voice whispered. McLendon flung them back.

"Not here," he said. "Get him into the car." "Kill him, kill the black son!" the voice murmured. They dragged the Negro to the car. The barber had waited beside the car. He could feel himself sweating and he knew he was going to be sick at the stomach.

"What is it, captains?" the Negro said. "I aint done nothing. 'Fore God, Mr John." Someone produced handcuffs. They worked busily about the Negro as though he were a post, quiet, intent, getting in one another's way. He submitted to the handcuffs, looking swiftly and constantly from dim face to dim face. "Who's here, captains?" he said, leaning to peer into the faces until they could feel his breath and smell his sweaty reek. He spoke a name or two. "What you all say I done, Mr John?"

McLendon jerked the car door open. "Get in!" he said.

The Negro did not move. "What you all going to do with me, Mr John? I aint done nothing. White folks, captains, I aint done nothing: I swear 'fore God." He called another name.

"Get in!" McLendon said. He struck the Negro. The others expelled their breath in a dry hissing and struck him with random blows and he whirled and cursed them, and swept his manacled hands across their faces and slashed the barber upon the mouth, and the barber struck him also. "Get him in there," McLendon said. They pushed at him. He ceased struggling and got in and sat quietly as the others took their places. He sat between the barber and the soldier, drawing his limbs in so as not to touch them, his eyes going swiftly and constantly from face to face. Butch clung to the running board. The car moved on. The barber nursed his mouth with his handkerchief.

"What's the matter, Hawk?" the soldier said.

"Nothing," the barber said. They regained the highroad and turned away from town. The second car dropped back out of the dust. They went on, gaining speed; the final fringe of houses dropped behind.

"Goddamn, he stinks!" the soldier said.

"We'll fix that," the drummer in front beside McLendon said. On the running board Butch cursed into the hot rush of air. The barber leaned suddenly forward and touched McLendon's arm.

"Let me out, John," he said.

"Jump out, niggerlover," McLendon said without turning his head. He drove swiftly. Behind them the sourceless lights of the second car glared in the dust. Presently McLendon turned into a narrow road. It was rutted with disuse. It led back to an abandoned brick kiln—a series of reddish mounds and weed- and vine-choked vats without bottom. It had been used for pasture once, until one day the owner missed one of his mules. Although he prodded carefully in the vats with a long pole, he could not even find the bottom of them.

"John," the barber said.

"Jump out, then," McLendon said, hurling the car along the ruts. Beside the barber the Negro spoke:

"Mr Henry."

The barber sat forward. The narrow tunnel of the road rushed up and past. Their motion was like an extinct furnace blast: cooler, but utterly dead. The car bounded from rut to rut.

"Mr Henry," the Negro said.

The barber began to tug furiously at the door. "Look out, there!" the soldier said, but the barber had already kicked the door open and swung onto the running board. The soldier leaned across the Negro and grasped at him, but he had already jumped. The car went on without checking speed.

The impetus hurled him crashing through dust-sheathed weeds, into the ditch. Dust puffed about him, and in a thin, vicious crackling of sapless stems he lay choking and retching until the second car passed and died away. Then he rose and limped on until he reached the highroad and turned toward town, brushing at his clothes with his hands. The moon was higher, riding high and clear of the dust at last, and after a while the town began to glare beneath the dust. He went on, limping. Presently he heard cars and the glow of them grew in the dust behind him and he left the road and crouched again in the weeds until they passed. McLendon's car came last now. There were four people in it and Butch was not on the running board.

They went on; the dust swallowed them; the glare and the sound died away. The dust of them hung for a while, but soon the eternal dust absorbed it again. The barber climbed back onto the road and limped on toward town.

IV

As she dressed for supper on that Saturday evening, her own flesh felt like fever. Her hands trembled among the hooks and eyes, and her eyes had a feverish look, and her hair swirled crisp and crackling under the comb. While she was still dressing the friends called for her and sat while she donned her sheerest underthings and stockings and a new voile dress. "Do you feel strong enough to go out?" they said, their eyes bright too, with a dark glitter. "When you have had time to get over the shock, you must tell us what happened. What he said and did; everything."

In the leafed darkness, as they walked toward the square, she began to breathe deeply, something like a swimmer preparing to dive, until she ceased trembling, the four of them walking slowly because of the terrible heat and out of solicitude for her. But as they neared the square she began to tremble again, walking with her head up, her hands clenched at her sides, their voices about her murmurous, also with that feverish, glittering quality of their eyes.

They entered the square, she in the center of the group, fragile in her fresh dress. She was trembling worse. She walked slower and slower, as children eat ice cream, her head up and her eyes bright in the haggard banner of her face, passing the hotel and the coatless drummers in chairs along the curb looking around at her: "That's the one: see? The one in pink in the middle." "Is that her? What did they do with the nigger? Did they—?" "Sure. He's all right." "All right, is he?" "Sure. He went on a little trip." Then the drugstore, where even the young men lounging in the doorway tipped their hats and followed with their eyes the motion of her hips and legs when she passed.

They went on, passing the lifted hats of the gentlemen, the suddenly ceased voices, deferent, protective. "Do you see?" the friends said. Their voices sounded like long, hovering sighs of hissing exultation. "There's not a Negro on the square. Not one."

They reached the picture show. It was like a miniature fairyland with its lighted lobby and colored lithographs of life caught in its terrible and beautiful mutations. Her lips began to tingle. In the dark, when the picture began, it would be all right; she could hold back the laughing so it would not waste away so fast and so soon. So she hurried on before the turning faces, the undertones of low astonishment, and they took their accustomed places where she could see the aisle against the silver glare and the young men and girls coming in two and two against it.

The lights flicked away; the screen glowed silver and soon life began to unfold, beautiful and passionate and sad, while still the young men and girls entered, scented and sibilant in the half dark, their paired backs in silhouette delicate and sleek, their slim, quick bodies awkward, divinely young, while beyond them the silver dream accumulated, inevitably on and on. She began to laugh. In trying to suppress it, it made more noise than ever; heads began to turn. Still laughing, her friends raised her and led her out, and she stood at the curb, laughing on a high, sustained note, until the taxi came up and they helped her in.

They removed the pink voile and the sheer underthings and the stockings, and put her to bed, and cracked ice for her temples, and sent for the doctor. He was hard to locate, so they ministered to her with hushed ejaculations, renewing the ice and fanning her. While the ice was fresh and cold she stopped laughing and lay still for a time, moaning only a little. But soon the laughing welled again and her voice rose screaming.

"Shhhhhhhhhh! Shhhhhhhhhhhhhh!" they said, freshening the icepack, smoothing her hair, examining it for gray; "poor girl!" Then to one another: "Do you suppose anything really happened?" their eyes darkly aglitter, secret and passionate. "Shhhhhhhhhh! Poor girl! Poor Minnie!"

V

It was midnight when McLendon drove up to his neat new house. It was trim and fresh as a birdcage and almost as small, with its clean, green-and-white paint. He locked the car and mounted the porch and entered. His wife rose from a chair beside the reading lamp. McLendon stopped in the floor and stared at her until she looked down.

"Look at that clock," he said, lifting his arm, pointing. She stood before him, her face lowered, a magazine in her hands. Her face was pale, strained and weary-looking. "Haven't I told you about sitting up like this, waiting to see when I come in?"

"John," she said. She laid the magazine down. Poised on the balls of his feet, he glared at her with his hot eyes, his sweating face.

"Didn't I tell you?" He went toward her. She looked up then. He caught her shoulder. She stood passive, looking at him.

"Dont, John. I couldn't sleep . . . The heat; something. Please, John. You're hurting me."

"Didn't I tell you?" He released her and half struck, half flung her across the chair, and she lay there and watched him quietly as he left the room.

He went on through the house, ripping off his shirt, and on the dark, screened porch at the rear he stood and mopped his head and shoulders with the shirt and flung it away. He took the pistol from his hip and laid it on the table beside the bed, and sat on the bed and removed his shoes, and rose and slipped his trousers off. He was sweating again already, and he stooped and hunted furiously for the shirt. At last he found it and wiped his body again, and, with his body pressed against the dusty screen, he stood panting. There was no movement, no sound, not even an insect. The dark world seemed to lie stricken beneath the cold moon and the lidless stars.

RATTENBURY AND STONER
By F. Tennyson Jesse

· · · · · · · · · · · · · · · · · · ·

*Mrs. Rattenbury was thirty-eight years old
and Stoner, her chauffeur-handyman, was eighteen.
F. Tennyson Jesse has chronicled brilliantly the story of their trial
for the murder of Francis Mawson Rattenbury.*

On 25 September 1934, the following advertisement appeared in the *Bournemouth Daily Echo:* "Daily willing lad, 14–18, for housework. Scout-trained preferred."

This advertisement had been inserted by a Mrs. Rattenbury, of Villa Madeira, Manor Park Road, and was answered by a youth called George Percy Stoner. Since he was of an age to drive a car, and his previous employment had been in a garage, he was engaged as chauffeur-handyman.

On Monday, 27 May 1935, Alma Victoria Rattenbury and George Percy Stoner were charged at the Central Criminal Court with the murder of the woman's husband, Francis Mawson Rattenbury. Both the accused pleaded not guilty: Mrs. Rattenbury was thirty-eight years old, and Stone had attained the age of eighteen in November of 1934. Mrs. Rattenbury and Stoner had become lovers soon after Stoner was taken into Mr. Rattenbury's employ.

Both Mr. and Mrs. Rattenbury had been previously married; he once and she twice. Mr. Rattenbury had a grown-up son; and Mrs. Rattenbury, a little boy called Christopher, born in 1922. The marriage of Francis Rattenbury and Alma Victoria took place about 1928, and a boy, John, was born a year after. Since the birth of this child Mr. and Mrs. Rattenbury had not lived together as husband

and wife. Mr. Rattenbury was sixty-seven years old and not a young man for his age. He was an architect of distinction, and had lived most of his working life in Canada, but when he retired in 1928, he and his wife came to live in Bournemouth. Eventually they took a little white house called Villa Madeira in a pleasant suburban road near the sea, shaded by pines. A companion-help, Miss Irene Riggs, came to live with them. Little John went to school, but came home every weekend, and Christopher, the child of Mrs. Rattenbury's second marriage, spent his holidays at Villa Madeira.

When Stoner was first employed at Villa Madeira, he lived at home and went to his work by day, but in November he took up his residence in the house. He had become Mrs. Rattenbury's lover before that.

On the night of Sunday, 24 March 1935, Mr. Rattenbury was attacked from behind as he sat sleeping in an armchair in the drawing room. It was never in dispute that the weapon employed was a carpenter's mallet, which Stoner had fetched from his grandfather's house that afternoon.

The events that night, as they first were made known in the newspapers, were as follows:

Mrs. Rattenbury declared that at about ten thirty, after she had gone to bed, she heard a groan from the room below, that she went downstairs, and found her husband in the easy-chair, unconscious, with blood flowing from his head. She called Irene Riggs, her companion-maid, and told her to telephone for Dr. O'Donnell, who was her doctor. Dr. O'Donnell arrived and found Mrs. Rattenbury very drunk, and Mr. Rattenbury unconscious with blood flowing from his head. Mrs. Rattenbury said: "Look at him—look at the blood—someone has finished him."

Dr. O'Donnell telephoned for Mr. Rooke, a well-known surgeon. Mr. Rooke arrived and found it impossible to examine the patient as Mrs. Rattenbury was very drunk and excitable, and kept getting in his way. The ambulance was sent for, and the patient removed to Strathallen Nursing Home. After his head had been shaved in the operating theater, Mr. Rooke and Dr. O'Donnell saw three serious wounds on the head, that could not have been self-inflicted, and, accordingly, they communicated with the police.

Mr. Rooke operated on Mr. Rattenbury, and Dr. O'Donnell between three thirty and four A.M. returned to Villa Madeira. He found Mrs. Rattenbury running about extremely intoxicated, four or five police officers in the house (some of whom she was trying to kiss), the radio-gramophone playing and all the lights on. He gave Mrs. Rattenbury half a grain of morphia, and put her to bed. During the hours of progressive drunkenness Mrs. Rattenbury had kept on making statements to the effect that she had killed her husband. The next morning she repeated her assertions in a slightly varied form and she was taken to the Bournemouth Police Station and charged with doing grievous bodily harm with intent to murder. When she was charged Mrs. Rattenbury said: "That is right—I did it deliberately, and would do it again."

Such was the terrible case for the prosecution against Alma Victoria Rattenbury, and the picture that had inevitably formed itself before the public mind was revolting.

There was probably no one in England, and no one in Court when the trial opened, save Mrs. Rattenbury, her solicitor and counsel, Stoner and his solicitor and counsel, and Irene Riggs, who did not think Mrs. Rattenbury was guilty of the crime of murder. In everyone's mind, including that of this writer, there was a picture of Mrs. Rattenbury as a coarse, brawling, drunken and callous woman. But life is not as simple as that, and very often an accurate report fails to convey truth, because only certain things have been reported. The form of the English oath has been very wisely thought out—"the truth, the whole truth and nothing but the truth." It is possible to give an erroneous impression by merely telling the truth and nothing but the truth. The "whole truth" is a very important factor. The whole truth about Mrs. Rattenbury came out during the trial, and the woman, who at first seemed so guilty, was seen to be undoubtedly innocent. This was not merely because there proved to be no evidence beyond her own drunken utterances, but because of her own attitude in the witness box. For there is no test of truth so relentless as the witness box—it is deadly to the guilty, and it may save the innocent.

In most criminal trials the pattern is set at the beginning and merely strengthens as the trial progresses. In the Rattenbury case the evidence—which seemed so damning on the first day—completely altered in character; what had seemed to be undoubted fact proved to be an airy nothing and the whole complex pattern shifted and changed much as the pattern of sand changes when it is shaken, and, like sand, it slipped away between the fingers, leaving a residue of grains of truth very different from the pile that the prosecution had originally built up. Even at the end of the trial, so rigid is the English fashion of thinking—or rather feeling, for it is not as careful or accurate a process as thought—on sexual matters, that many people still considered Mrs. Rattenbury morally damned. That worst of all Anglo-Saxon attitudes, a contemptuous condemnation of the man and woman, but more particularly the woman, unfortunate enough to be found out in sexual delinquency, never had finer scope than was provided by the Rattenbury case.

Mrs. Rattenbury was born Alma Victoria Clark, in Victoria, British Columbia, and was the daughter of a printer in quite humble circumstances. She was extremely talented musically. The cheap strain in her came out in the words of her lyrics, but she was a really fine pianist. She grew up to young womanhood just before the First World War, already well known in western Canada as a musician, and, although not strictly speaking pretty, very attractive to men. In the witness box she still showed as a very elegant woman. She was well and quietly dressed in dark blue. She had a pale face, with a beautiful egglike line of the jaw, dark gray eyes and a mouth with a very full lower lip. She was, undoubtedly, and always must have been a *femme aux hommes*. That is to say, that although she had women friends, and was a generous, easy, kindly, sentimental creature, she was first and foremost a woman to attract men and be attracted by them. She first married a young Englishman called Caledon Dolly, who joined the Canadian forces on the outbreak of war, and was transferred to England. She followed him and obtained employment in Whitehall. She was very devoted to her husband, but he was killed in action. This was the only completely happy relationship with a man which Mrs. Rattenbury was ever to know. She joined a Scottish nursing unit, and then became a transport driver, and worked hard throughout the war. After the Armistice she married, for the second time, a man whose wife divorced him, citing Alma Victoria Dolly. She married this second husband in 1921, and the child of that union was born the following year. The marriage was unhappy, and she returned to the house of an aunt in Victoria, and there she met Mr. Rattenbury. Mr. Rattenbury was married himself at the time, but fell very much in love with Alma Victoria, and his wife divorced him, citing her. At this time Mr. Rattenbury was about sixty years of age, and Mrs. Rattenbury thirty-one. Life was not too easy for Mr. Rattenbury and his new wife in a country where everyone knew of the scandal of the divorce, and this was the chief reason why the Rattenburys came to England to settle in Bournemouth.

Mrs. Rattenbury was a highly sexed woman, and six years of being deprived of sexual satisfaction had combined with the tuberculosis from which she suffered to bring her to the verge of nymphomania. Now nymphomania is not admirable, but neither is it blameworthy. It is a disease. In spite of the urgency of her desires, which must have tormented her, Mrs. Rattenbury had not, as far as is known, had a lover since the birth of little John. She certainly had had none the four years she had lived in Bournemouth, and she had no abnormal tendencies. She was fond of her husband in a friendly fashion, and he was devoted to her, very interested in her song writing and anxious for her to succeed. He would often talk to Irene Riggs about his wife, and dwell on the unhappy life she had led, and he never in these conversations said anything against her. Miss Riggs, one of my informants as to these matters, also said that Mrs. Rattenbury was very kind to her husband, that she was, indeed, kind to everyone. The household was not an unhappy one, but neither was it happy. For one thing, Mrs. Rattenbury was a gregarious creature, and her husband was of an unsociable frame of mind. He knew hardly anyone of his own station in life, except Dr. O'Donnell and Mr. Jenks, a retired barrister who had an estate at Bridport. But Mrs. Rattenbury was very different from her husband; she had that lavish, easy friendliness which one associates with music-hall artists, and she could not live without affection. When she made a friend of Irene Riggs, she did so because it was her nature to be friendly with the people who surrounded her. She was fond of Irene Riggs, who, on her side, was devoted to her employer, in spite of the latter's impatient temper. Any little outing to London, any treat, such as a theater, Mrs. Rattenbury shared with Irene Riggs, and the girl remained attached to the memory of the kindest person she ever met, who helped anyone in need that she came across. But the chief devotion of Mrs. Rattenbury's life was for her children. No one denies that she was a good and loving mother. Dr. O'Donnell and Miss Riggs both say that Mrs. Rattenbury thought nothing too good for her children, and that there was nothing she would not have done for them. She was forever thinking and talking about them, and occupying herself in practical ways for their welfare.

The Rattenburys lived peaceably as a rule, but sometimes they had quarrels—these were about money. Mr. Rattenbury, like a great many men, was generous in big matters, but difficult in small ones. He allowed his wife £1,000 a year, and many newspapers reported this fact in such a manner that the reading public might easily have imagined that this sum was hers for herself alone. As a matter of fact, out of it she paid for the food for herself, her husband, the domestics and the children when at home, and for one of the boys' schooling. She also paid for Mr. Rattenbury's clothes and for her own, and she paid the servants' wages. Mr. Rattenbury was a heavy drinker of whisky, and every few weeks Mrs. Rattenbury would drink more cocktails than would be good for her, so that the bill for drinks alone must have amounted to a good deal. It will be seen that £1,000 a year, even then, was not too large a sum out of which to support and clothe a household and educate a child. Mrs. Rattenbury herself had very little money sense, and her husband had every reason to fear her lavish spending. About twice a year Mrs. Rattenbury would coax an extra sum out of him; a large sum, over £100, but this he parted with much more easily than he would have parted with small sums more often. Mrs. Rattenbury did not pretend that she told her husband true stories to induce him to give her this extra money. She admitted she invented whatever story would be the most likely to achieve the desired result. Mr. Rattenbury was frequently very depressed about financial matters; like everyone else he had suffered in the slump, and he was apt, during his moods of depression, to threaten to commit suicide. One day in July, 1934, he harped on this threat at greater length than usual, and his wife lost her temper, and told him it was a pity that he did not do it instead of always talking about it. Mr. Rattenbury in his turn then lost his temper and hit his wife, giving her a black eye. She sent for Dr. O'Donnell, who found her very agitated and upset. Her husband had left the house, and she feared that he really had gone to kill himself. Mr. Rattenbury did not, in fact, return till about two in the morning, by which time Dr. O'Donnell also was extremely anxious. Mrs. Rattenbury was by then so ill that he injected a quarter of a grain of morphia, and she slept for twelve hours. After that, life went on as usual with the Rattenburys. She bore him no grudge for having struck her. She was a person of quick temper herself, but generous in what children call "making it up." This was the only serious quarrel between the Rattenburys that Dr. O'Donnell or Irene Riggs knew of in four years. In the box, Mrs. Rattenbury was asked whether her married life was happy, and she answered: "Like that . . . !" with a gesture of her hand. A gesture that sketched the married life of the larger part of muddled humanity.

Life might have gone on in the usual pedestrian fashion at Villa

Madeira forever, but George Percy Stoner joined the household, and Mrs. Rattenbury fell in love with him.

The expression "falling in love" is an attempt to define something which escapes definition. Mankind has a natural weakness for labels, for they simplify life, and though this particular label is one of the most pernicious which have been evolved, it must be remembered that it covers not only a multitude of sins, but of virtues. Perhaps no two people would give quite the same definition of its meaning. Very few people trouble to try. Mrs. Rattenbury herself was a woman who dealt in labels, and she accepted the expression "falling in love." She wrote cheap little lyrics of the more obvious variety, and she herself would never have questioned what "in love" meant. She was "in love" with Stoner, who, except for his virility, was not a particularly interesting or attractive person. Indeed, lack of taste is one of the chief charges against Mrs. Rattenbury, both in her work and in her life. She was very uncontrolled emotionally. Her lyrics were appalling. She was subject to drinking bouts, which added to her natural excitability. She had not scrupled, twice, to take other women's husbands away from them and she seems to have been, to use a slang phrase, a natural-born bad picker. When she took Stoner as her lover, she said to Dr. O'Donnell: "There is something I want to tell you. I am afraid you will be shocked and never want to speak to me again." Dr. O'Donnell replied that there were very few things he had not been told in the course of his life, and that he was not easily shocked. She then told him the step she had taken, and he spoke to her seriously, warning her that she was probably being very unwise. But she was too far gone in love by then to heed any advice he gave her. She merely reiterated that she was in love with Stoner.

The obvious solution to the question as to what love meant for her is that it meant physical satisfaction. Yet, if it had meant only this, it would have deserted her when she stood in peril of her life. It did not do so, and neither did Stoner's love for her. Stoner refused to go into the box, and told his counsel he did not deny having attacked Mr. Rattenbury. The woman for weeks insisted, to her solicitor and counsel, that she wished to take the blame, so as to save Stoner. Mr. Lewis-Manning, her solicitor, made it clear to her that, if she lied, her story would not stand the test of the witness box, and that she would only hang herself without saving Stoner. But not till Christopher, the little boy of her second marriage, was sent to her in prison to plead with her to tell the truth, did she give way. And, afterward, in the witness box, she said as little against her lover as possible, making light of certain alleged attacks of violence toward herself, attacks which had frightened her so much that, long before the murder, she consulted Dr. O'Donnell about them. Indeed, one of the most interesting points in this case is that it is the only one, as far as I am aware, where two people have been charged together on the capital indictment when neither of the accused has abandoned the other in a scramble for safety. Milson and Fowler, Field and Gray, Gabrielle Bompard and Eyrand, Mr. and Mrs. Manning, Ruth Snyder and Judd Gray, to remember only a few at random, all tried to throw the blame on the partner in crime. Mrs. Thompson, terrified and conscious of her own innocence of murder, never gave a thought to the safety of her lover, Bywaters. Mrs. Rattenbury was willing and anxious to take the whole blame if by so doing she could save her lover. It is Mr. Lewis-Manning's considered opinion that Mrs. Rattenbury was not merely in a condition of exaltation that would have failed her at the last pass, but that she would have hanged without a tremor if by so doing she could have saved Stoner.

The story of Mrs. Rattenbury's life is a mingling of tragedy and futility. It is easy to be sentimental and see only the tragedy. It is easy to be stupid and see only the futility. The truth is, that it is always easy to label people, but because a thing is easy, it is not necessarily accurate. No human being is simple. Stoner may have seemed simple enough to his family; he had always been a quiet boy who did not make friends, but his quiet appearance concealed stormy adolescent yearnings. He had the dramatic instincts natural to the young, and, unfortunately, circumstances thrust him into real drama before he could tell the difference between what was real and what was make-believe. Physically, he was very passionate, and nothing in his mental training had equipped him to cope with the extraordinary life to which it had pleased Mrs. Rattenbury to call him.

Francis Rattenbury, that outwardly quiet man, is a pathetic figure in retrospect. Mr. Justice Humphreys referred to him as being "that very unpleasant character for which, I think, we have no suitable expression, but which the French call a *mari complaisant*. A man who knew that his wife was committing adultery, and had no objection to it." Mrs. Rattenbury said, in the box, that she thought her husband knew because she had told him she was living her own life. But she may well have told him that without his taking in the meaning of her words. He was completely incurious, and he lived not in the present, but in regrets for the past and anxieties for the future.

Irene Riggs, Dr. O'Donnell and, indeed, everyone acquainted with the household to whom the writer has spoken, was of the opinion that Mr. Rattenbury was not aware that his wife and his chauffeur were lovers. But when I saw Villa Madeira, I thought this difficult to credit. It is so small as to be remarkable, small as the witch's cottage in *Hansel and Gretel*. On the ground floor are the kitchen, drawing room, dining room and a room that Mr. Rattenbury used as a bedroom, and which opened off the drawing room. Is it possible that a man, in a house as small as Villa Madeira, would not hear the footsteps over his head whenever Stoner came into Mrs. Rattenbury's room, and that he would not hear the occasionally loud quarrels which took place between them? Looking at Villa Madeira, the answer would seem to be that it would be quite impossible. And yet Mr. Rattenbury's known character and habits supply a different answer. Every night Mr. Rattenbury drank the best part of a bottle of whisky. He was a man brilliant in his profession, with many excellent qualities, and he was not a drunkard, but he was not a young man, and he was very deaf. The alcohol which he consumed every night explains why he no longer lived with his wife, why he was completely incurious as to her doings and why he heard nothing of what was going on over his head. He was not, in the opinion of all who knew him, the doctor, his own relations and Irene Riggs, who lived in the house, the character stigmatized by Mr. Justice Humphreys as a *"mari complaisant*, not a nice character." He was a quiet, pleasant man whose finances worried him, and whose emotional relationships had disappointed him.

A man in Mr. Rattenbury's condition, and of his age, is apt to forget the power that the natural inclinations of the flesh had over him in youth and middle age, and he may fail to realize that it is still a factor in the life of anyone else. As far as Mr. Rattenbury knew, he was a good husband to his wife. He admired her, was genuinely fond of her. There was nothing within his power that he would not have done for her, and Mrs. Rattenbury was astute enough to take advantage of this whenever possible. In regard to his wife, his chief anxieties were financial, and after he had started to take his prolonged nightcap each evening, the rest of the world existed very little for him. The passions, the jealousies of a decade earlier, had ceased, not only in the present, but even as a memory of the past. The chief tragedy in life is not what we are but what we have ceased to be, and Mr. Rattenbury was an example of this truth. It is easy to say that a man who knows his wife is committing adultery and has no objection is not a nice character. But it is not necessarily the truth. It is possible that a man who no longer leads a normal life with his wife, yet thinks of her, not as his property, but as a human being who belongs to herself, and has a right to a normal life. I do not say that this was Mr. Rattenbury's attitude (although Mrs. Rattenbury said that it was), I merely say that it would not necessarily have been a despicable attitude. But, of course, the judgment of the man in the street is the same as that of Mr. Justice Humphreys. It is an Anglo-Saxon attitude. Another Anglo-Saxon attitude, accepted by the learned Judge, by counsel on both sides and by the British public, was that, because of her greater age, Mrs. Rattenbury dominated her young lover. It was this same assumption which hanged Mrs. Thompson. There has been a growing consensus of public opinion ever since the Bywaters-Thompson trial, that the female prisoner was wrongly convicted; and the memory of the earlier trial haunted the courtroom like a ghost. The Rattenbury case seemed like an echo of that tragedy, and it is not fanciful to say that Mrs. Thompson's fate did much to save Mrs. Rattenbury. A judge who knew how to point out firmly and clearly to the jury that a woman must not, because of her moral character, be convicted of murder, and a jury who were determined that no confusion of thought or prejudice should lead them into giving a wrong verdict were two great safeguards for Mrs. Rattenbury, and the uneasy memory of Edith Thompson was yet a third. Nevertheless, the assumption of the Bywaters-Thompson case, that an elderly woman dominates her young lover, still obtained at the Rattenbury trial. The actual truth is that there is no woman so under the dominion of her lover as the elderly mistress of a very much younger man. The great Benjamin Franklin knew this, and there is extant a letter of advice written by him to a young man, which is a model of clear thinking. The original belongs to the U.S. Government, and is in the custody of the Librarian of Congress at Washington, D.C.

June 25th, 1745

My Dear Friend,

   I know of no medicine fit to diminish the violent nocturnal inclinations you mention, and if I did, I think I should not communicate it to you. Marriage is the proper remedy.

   It is the most natural state of man, and therefore the state in which you are most likely to find solid happiness. Your reasons against entering it at present appear to me not well founded. The circumstantial advantages you have in view of postponing it are not only uncertain, but they are small in comparison with that of the thing itself—the being married and settled.

It is the man and woman united that make the complete human being. Separate, she wants his force of body and strength of reason; he, her softness, sensibility and acute discernment. Together they are most likely to succeed in the world. A single man has not nearly the value he would have in a state of union. He is an incomplete animal; he resembles the odd half of a pair of scissors. If you get a prudent healthy wife, your industry in your profession, with her good economy, will be a fortune sufficient.

But if you will not take this counsel, and persist in thinking a commerce with the sex inevitable, then I repeat my former advice, that in your amours you should prefer OLD WOMEN to YOUNG ONES. You call this a paradox, and demand reasons. They are these:

First. Because they have more knowledge of the World, and their minds are better stored with observations; their conversation is more improving and more lastingly agreeable.

Second. Because when women cease to be handsome, they study to be good. To maintain their influence over men they supply the diminution of beauty by an augmentation of utility. They learn to do a thousand services, small and great, and are the most tender and useful of all friends when you are sick. Thus they continue amiable, and hence there is scarcely such a thing to be found as an old woman who is not a good woman.

Third. Because there is no hazard of children, which irregularly produced, may be attended with much inconvenience.

Fourth. Because, through more experience, they are more prudent and discreet in conducting an intrigue to prevent suspicion. The commerce with them is therefore safe with regard to your reputation, and with regard to theirs. If the affair should happen to be known, considerate people might be rather inclined to excuse an old woman who would kindly take care of a young man, form his manners by her good counsels, and prevent his ruining his health and fortune among mercenary prostitutes.

Fifth. Because in every animal that walks upright the deficiency of the fluid that fills the muscles appears but on the highest part. The face first grows lank and wrinkled, then the neck, then the breast and arms—the lower parts continuing to the last as plump as ever; so that, covering all above with a basket, and regarding only what is below the girdle, it is impossible of two women, to known an old from a young one. And as in the dark all cats are grey, the pleasure of corporal enjoyment with an old woman is at least equal and frequently superior; every knack being, by practice, capable of improvement.

Sixth. Because the sin is less. The debauching a virgin may be her ruin and make her life unhappy.

Seventh. Because the compunction is less. The having made a young girl miserable may give you frequent bitter reflections, none of which can attend the making an Old woman Happy.

Eighth and Lastly. They are so grateful.

This much for my paradox, but still I advise you to marry immediately, being sincerely,

Your affectionate friend,
(Signed) B. Franklin.

"Eighth and Lastly" is worthy of the consideration of English lawyers and the English public when a Thompson-Bywaters or Rattenbury-Stoner case is under consideration. Once Stoner had become Mrs. Rattenbury's lover, she worshiped him. It was before the consummation of her desire that she was the dominating character, and to that extent she was responsible for the whole tragedy, but to that extent only. She felt this responsibility deeply, and it was remorse as well as love that made her eager and willing to save Stoner even at the cost of her own life. It was, indeed, a terrible responsibility in view of the events. She could not know that Stoner would be wild with jealousy, but she must have known, had she paused to think, that a lad of Stoner's age and antecedents would lose all sense of values when he became the lover of his social superior, who dazzled him with a whole new mode of life. If Stoner's first love affair had been with a girl of his own class, no ill need have come of it. Nevertheless, another strange assumption was made—that it is somehow harmful for a young man of eighteen to have sexual connexion. Dr. Gillespie, physician for psycho-medicine at Guy's Hospital, a witness for the defense, was asked in cross-examination by Mr. Croom-Johnson, whether "regular sexual intercourse with a member of the opposite sex by a boy of eighteen or onward, would be likely to do him good or harm?" Dr. Gillespie replied that it would not do him good "if a moral point of view were meant." Mr. Croom-Johnson said that he was not talking from a moral point of view, that he was asking him as a doctor. Still Dr. Gillespie wisely refused to commit himself. "Do you think it would likely be good for his constitution— a boy of eighteen—just think what you are saying, Doctor?" "I am not saying that it is good for his constitution, but I am saying that if it were occurring with such frequency as my lord had said, namely such as nature would permit, it would not necessarily show the effects in his external appearance." "Take the ordinary case—the ordinary boy, not somebody very strong, talking about the ordinary English youth of eighteen—do you really find yourself in any difficulty in answering the question?" "I find difficulty," replied the doctor, "in answering the question as I believe you expect it to be answered." Doctors, as a rule, make excellent witnesses, and in this little cross-examination, Dr. Gillespie was no exception to the rule, but with what frank, Homeric laughter the question would have been greeted in a Latin country! In England it is apparently impossible to admit the simple truth that a young man of eighteen is an adult who would normally take a mate, were it not that economic conditions render it impossible.

Mrs. Rattenbury was a good witness, and in nothing more notably so than in her simple acceptance of the values of life as she knew it. "You have told us that on the Sunday night Stoner came into your bedroom and got into bed with you. Was that something that happened frequently?" asked Mr. Croom-Johnson. "Oh, yes," replied Mrs. Rattenbury simply. And later on: "Did it occur to you that if you went to Bridport, Mr. Rattenbury might want to treat you as his wife?"—"No, if I had thought it was going to happen like that I would never have suggested going." "It never occurred to you?"—"No." "You know what I mean by saying 'treat you as his wife'?"—"Yes, exactly," replied Mrs. Rattenbury, as though mildly surprised that there could be any mistake about it.

Mrs. Rattenbury's vagueness about money matters and her lavish spending came out as clearly in the witness box as her attitude toward sensual matters. In answering a question as to her habit of giving away cigarette holders, she said, "That is nothing for me. If anyone sees a cigarette holder and likes it, I always say 'take it.' It is my disposition"; and later: "I am very vague about money." This was certainly true. Mr. Croom-Johnson asked her in cross-examination how much money her husband let her have in the course of a year, to which she replied she "really couldn't say." "Hundreds?" "I suppose so," said Mrs. Rattenbury. "About how much a year did he let you have?" "He used to give me regularly £50 a month, and I was regularly overdrawn." "£50 a month would be £600 a year?" "I see," said Mrs. Rattenbury; and one received the impression she had not worked out this fairly simple sum for herself ever before. "In addition to that," went on Mr. Croom-Johnson, "about £150 on each of two occasions?"—"Yes, I daresay." Later, cross-examining her about the clothes she had lavished on Stoner in London, Mr. Croom-Johnson said: "You used the words that he 'required clothes'?"—"Yes, I considered so." "Silk pajamas at 60s a suit?"—

"That might seem absurd, but that is my disposition." And certainly it was her disposition.

So, as we have seen, Mr. Rattenbury was reserved, kindly, but rather mean in money matters. Mrs. Rattenbury was unreserved, also kindly, but in a more indiscriminate fashion than her husband, and her generosity was indiscriminating also. Irene Riggs liked both of them, but her loyalty was naturally for the mistress who had been kinder to her than any human being she had ever met.

Irene Riggs was not as happy after Stoner's arrival as she had been before. Mrs. Rattenbury told her about the liaison, and Irene was too fond of her to blame her, but nevertheless she felt uneasy about the affair, and sorry that Mrs. Rattenbury could not have found happiness with someone more of her own age and class. Though Miss Riggs and Stoner did not like each other, they got on together well enough. He was a very quiet boy; she also was quiet, self-effacing and efficient. She was shocked when Mrs. Rattenbury first told her the truth, but human nature quickly adapts itself to knowledge, and Miss Riggs very rightly felt that it was not for her to praise or to blame. She stayed behind when, on 19 March, Mrs. Rattenbury arranged to take Stoner with her on a trip to London, because Stoner was very jealous of any third person, and the charm of the little friendly expeditions that had been the highlights in Irene Riggs's life before the coming of Stoner was gone. In London Mrs. Rattenbury and Stoner stayed at the Royal Palace Hotel, Kensington, and spent their days in shopping and going about London. Mrs. Rattenbury explained the trip to her husband by saying she was going to have an operation (she had had several minor operations in the preceding years), and he gave her the generous sum of £250 for this purpose. Mrs. Rattenbury used a large part of this sum to pay outstanding housekeeping bills, and the rest she spent wildly upon the London trip and presents for Stoner. The importance of the expedition to London lies in the fact that, for four or five days, Stoner was accepted by the little world about him as Mrs. Rattenbury's social equal. He did not go to the Royal Palace Hotel as her chauffeur, but as her brother. They had two rooms opposite each other, and he had free access to his mistress. He was called "Sir" by the servants, and every day Mrs. Rattenbury bought him presents which to his simple mind must have appeared equivalent to Danae's golden shower. Crêpe-de-chine pajamas at three guineas a pair and a made-to-measure suit must have seemed to the young man, who was a laborer's son, most exciting luxuries.

The learned Judge referred to the "orgy in London." It is difficult to imagine an orgy at the Royal Palace Hotel at Kensington, and, indeed, I have never been able to discover of what an "orgy" consists. It is associated, more or less vaguely, in the popular mind with the "historical" productions of Mr. C. de Mille: glasses of wine, dancing girls, tiger skins and cushions are some of its component parts. The private coming together of a pair of lovers and their normal physical ecstasies, however reprehensible these may be morally, do not seem well described by the word "orgy." Even shopping at Harrods does not quite come under this heading. However, in this trial, as in all others of the same nature, the stock phrases were used of which most people are heartily tired. "Adulterous intercourse," "illicit union," "this wretched woman" and the like, all have a very familiar ring. They are clichés, and come to the lips of those concerned in the administration of the law as inevitably as the adjective "fashionably dressed" is attached to the noun "woman" in any reporter's account of the female spectators at a murder trial. Leaving these clichés, the fact, nevertheless, remains that Stoner's trip to London must have thoroughly unsettled him. He was happy enough at Villa Madeira, where the social régime was easy and pleasant for such as he.

Mrs. Rattenbury affected no superiority with anyone in humbler circumstances of life than her own, and Mr. Rattenbury had lived for years of his life in the democratic country where Mrs. Rattenbury was born. Stoner often played cards with him in the evening, and Mr. Rattenbury, Stoner and Miss Riggs took their meals together. Therefore, merely to have returned to Villa Madeira, to continue its pleasant, easy life, would not necessarily have upset Stoner. But this was not exactly what happened. The lovers arrived back late on Friday evening. Mr. Rattenbury, already having imbibed his nightcap, asked no questions; even next day, according to Mrs. Rattenbury, and as far as Irene Riggs's knowledge went, he never inquired about the operation his wife had ostensibly been to London to undergo. The Saturday found him in one of his worst fits of depression. A scheme for building some flats, of which he was to have been the architect, was hanging fire, owing to the financial depression, and Mrs. Rattenbury tried to cheer him up in vain.

On the Sunday, Mr. Rattenbury was still more depressed. In the morning Mrs. Rattenbury took him for a drive. After lunch Mr. Rattenbury slept. They had tea together, little John with them. Mr. Rattenbury had been reading a book, a novel in which there was a perfect holocaust of suicides, and, according to Mrs. Rattenbury, he expressed his admiration for anyone who had the courage to make an end of himself. Mrs. Rattenbury suggested that she should ring up their friend Mr. Jenks, at Bridport, and ask whether they could go over on the Monday. She did indeed telephone, and Mr. Jenks said he would be pleased to see them, and asked them to spend the night, an invitation which they accepted. The telephone was in Mr. Rattenbury's bedroom, which opened off the drawing room. Mr. Rattenbury remained in the drawing room, but Stoner came into the bedroom, and overheard the arrangements which Mrs. Rattenbury was making. He was frightfully angry and threatened Mrs. Rattenbury with an air pistol, which he was carrying in his hand, and which she took to be a revolver. He told Mrs. Rattenbury that he would kill her if they went to Bridport. Mrs. Rattenbury, nervous lest Mr. Rattenbury should overhear the conversation, though, as she said, "He never really took very much notice," urged Stoner into the dining room, and went there with him. Once there he accused her of having had connexion with her husband that afternoon—an accusation entirely baseless—and said that, if the Bridport plan were carried out, he would refuse to drive. Stoner said that at Mr. Jenks's house the Rattenburys would have to share a bedroom, but Mrs. Rattenbury assured him that would not be so, and what she said she knew to be the truth, for she and her husband had stayed with Mr. Jenks before, and had had two rooms. Stoner, though he appeared to be pacified, continued to brood over the matter in his mind, and at about eight o'clock that evening, he went to the house of his grandparents, sat and chatted, apparently normally, with his grandmother for some time, and borrowed a carpenter's mallet, but borrowed it perfectly openly. He went back to Villa Madeira and Mrs. Rattenbury noticed nothing abnormal about him.

That same evening Mrs. Rattenbury sat and played cards with her husband, kissed him good night and went upstairs. It was Irene's evening out, and Mrs. Rattenbury passed the time by getting together her things for Bridport. She had already put out Mr. Rattenbury's clothes in his bedroom downstairs. Irene came in at about ten fifteen, and went straight to her room. Some ten minutes later she went downstairs, either to see if all was well or to get something to eat—there seems a slight discrepancy in her evidence here. When she was downstairs, in the hall, she heard a sound of heavy breathing, and putting her head into Mr. Rattenbury's bedroom, she switched on the light. He was not there, and the sound of breathing came from the drawing room, the door between that and the bedroom being open. Miss Riggs concluded that he had, as he so often did, fallen asleep in his chair, and she went upstairs again into her bedroom. A few moments later she went out again to go to the lavatory, and found Stoner leaning over the banisters at the head of the stairs, looking down. She said, "What is the matter?" He replied, "Nothing, I was looking to see if the lights were out." Then about a quarter of an hour later Mrs. Rattenbury came to Irene's room and told her about the expedition to Bridport. Mrs. Rattenbury then went to her own room, and about ten minutes later Stoner came and slipped into her bed. He seemed very agitated and upset. She said, "What is the matter, darling?" He replied that he was in trouble, but that he could not tell her what it was about. She replied that he must tell her, that she was strong enough to bear anything and he then said, "You won't be going to Bridport tomorrow." He went on to say that he had hurt "Ratz." He said that he had hit him over the head with a mallet, which he had since hidden in the garden. Mrs. Rattenbury definitely conveyed the impression from the box that it was possible that the idea in Stoner's head was merely to injure Mr. Rattenbury, so that the proposed expedition could not take place. "I thought," she said, "he was frightened at what he had done, because he had hurt Mr. Rattenbury. . . . I thought he'd just hurt him badly enough to prevent him going to Bridport, and when I said 'I'll go and see him,' he said, 'No, you must not; the sight will upset you,' and I thought all I had to do was to fix Ratz up, and that would put him all right."

It may be that this was the only idea in Stoner's unbalanced and ill-educated mind, but that he found it impossible to stop after the first blow, and administered two more. Or it may be that, in his disturbed and jealous state, he would have done anything sooner than allow the Bridport trip to take place. If Stoner had driven the Rattenburys to Bridport, he would have had to do so in his capacity of chauffeur. He would have stayed there in the same capacity, eaten in the servants' hall, not had access to his mistress and ranked as a domestic with the other domestics. The thought of the expedition to Bridport, coming, as it would have, directly after the "orgy" in London, was unbearable. It may be argued that as a motive, this distaste for going to Bridport was very inadequate. But all motives for murder are inadequate. Men have murdered for smaller sums than an embezzler would plot to obtain. Directly the sense of what Stoner was telling her penetrated to Mrs. Rattenbury's mind, she jumped out of bed and ran downstairs as she was, in her pajamas and bare feet. A minute later, Irene Riggs, who had not yet fallen asleep, heard her mistress shrieking for her. Miss Riggs ran downstairs and found Mr. Rattenbury leaning back in an armchair, as though he were asleep. There was a large pool of blood on the floor, and one of his eyes was very swollen and discolored, and she thought he had a black eye. Mrs. Rattenbury asked Irene to telephone for the doctor at once, telling her to hurry and, to use Miss Riggs's own expression, went "raving about the house." "Oh! poor Ratz. Poor Ratz!" she kept repeating. "Can't somebody do something?" Mrs. Rattenbury drank some whisky; she was violently sick, and drank more whisky. She kept on telling Miss Riggs to wipe up the blood because she said little John must not see any blood.

Now there is no doubt Mrs. Rattenbury knew from the moment she set eyes on her husband that Stoner's talk upstairs had not been a mere attempt to attract her interest and attention. She knew that he had injured her husband in a terrible fashion, and that tragedy, which she could not control, had suddenly taken possession of her life. Her first thought was for her husband, her second for little John. Her third was for Stoner, and this thought persisted, and deepened in intensity, during the hours that followed.

Dr. O'Donnell arrived at Villa Madeira at about eleven forty-five, in answer to the telephone call. Mrs. Rattenbury was, in his opinion, already very drunk. Mr. Rooke, the surgeon, arrived at the house about five minutes after midnight, and he also was of the opinion that Mrs. Rattenbury was drunk. Dr. O'Donnell and Mr. Rooke decided that, largely owing to the excited condition of Mrs. Rattenbury, the only proper place for her husband was in a nursing home. They took him there, shaved his head and discovered three wounds, which were obviously the result of external violence, and of three separate blows. Dr. O'Donnell telephoned the Central Police Station, about ten minutes' walk from the nursing home and two minutes by car, and said: "Dr. O'Donnell speaking from Strathallen Nursing Home, Manor Road. Mr. Rooke and myself have just taken Mr. Rattenbury from 5 Manor Road to the nursing home. On examination we find three serious wounds on the back of his skull, due to external violence, which will most probably prove fatal." Central Police Station replied: "You want an officer?" Dr. O'Donnell said, "Yes, at once." But it was half an hour before the constable arrived. The constable then said he must get an inspector, and at about three fifteen A.M. Inspector Mills, who had already been at Villa Madeira, arrived. At three thirty Inspector Mills, Mr. Rooke and Dr. O'Donnell left the nursing home. Stoner was sleeping peacefully outside in the Rattenbury car, and he drove Dr. O'Donnell back to Villa Madeira following the police car.

When Dr. O'Donnell got out of the car, he was struck by the fact that every light in Villa Madeira was on, the door was open and the radio gramophone was playing. There were four police officers in the house. Mrs. Rattenbury was by now extremely drunk. A constable, who had arrived at three o'clock, had observed then that Mrs. Rattenbury was under the influence of alcohol, but, as he put it, "to a mild extent." One has, of course, to realize that the police standard of drunkenness is very high; as Mr. Justice Humphreys phrased it—"drunk in the police sense seems to mean hopelessly drunk."

At three thirty, according to Dr. O'Donnell, Mrs. Rattenbury was past knowing what she was thinking or saying. Dr. O'Donnell, very shocked, turned off the radio gramophone, and tried to explain to Mrs. Rattenbury the gravity of her husband's condition, but she could not take in what he was saying. Inspector Mills agreed that Mrs. Rattenbury was more under the influence of drink than when he had seen her at two A.M. He said to her: "Your husband has been seriously injured, and is now in the nursing home." To which Mrs. Rattenbury replied: "Will that be against me?" Inspector Mills then cautioned her, and apparently was satisfied that she understood the meaning of the caution. Then she made a statement. "I did it. He has lived too long. I will tell you in the morning where the mallet is. Have you told the Coroner yet? I shall make a better job of it next time. Irene does not know. I have made a proper muddle of it. I thought I was strong enough." Dr. O'Donnell, who considered that Mrs. Rattenbury was unable to understand what was said to her, or to know what she was saying, pointed out that she was in no fit condition to be asked anything, and took her up to bed. He administered half a grain of morphia—a large dose—and went downstairs again. After a few minutes he went into the sitting room and found that Mrs. Rattenbury had managed to get downstairs again and was again being questioned by the police. Inspector Mills said to her: "Do you suspect anyone?" and she replied: "Yes. I think so. His son."

Dr. O'Donnell, who was aware that Mr. Rattenbury's son lived abroad, knew that Mrs. Rattenbury had no idea of what she was saying, and he said to the inspector: "Look at her condition—she is full of whisky, and I have just given her a large dose of morphia. She is in no condition to make any statement." He then took her by the arm and helped her upstairs again. Then (it was by now after four A.M.), Dr. O'Donnell went home. At six A.M. Inspector Carter arrived at the house, where some members of the police had remained all night. He went into Mrs. Rattenbury's room and stated in evidence that she woke up. This was not unnatural, in view of the fact that the police had been in that very tiny house all night, perpetually going up and down stairs. Inspector Carter realized that Mrs. Rattenbury was ill, and in no fit condition to make a statement, and he told Miss Riggs to prepare some coffee. When the coffee came the saucer shook so in Mrs. Rattenbury's hand that she could not hold it. She managed to swallow it, but retched and said that she wanted to be sick. The Inspector telephoned for a police matron, who arrived and helped Mrs. Rattenbury downstairs to her bath and helped her to dress. This matron was not called as witness, but it is reasonable to conclude that she thought Mrs. Rattenbury a sick woman. Yet, according to Inspector Carter, Mrs. Rattenbury, who had been drinking steadily from about eleven o'clock the night before till three thirty in the morning (quite undeterred by the police), who had then been given half a grain of morphia which she had not been allowed to sleep off, was by eight fifteen competent to make a statement! The statement which she then made to him, after being duly cautioned, and which he wrote down in his notebook, read as follows: "About nine P.M. on the 24th March I was playing cards with my husband when he dared me to kill him, as he wanted to die. I picked up a mallet and he then said: 'You have not the guts to do it!' I then hit him with the mallet. I hid the mallet outside. I would have shot him if I had had a gun." Inspector Carter deposed that Mrs. Rattenbury read the statement over aloud and clearly and then signed it. He then took her to Bournemouth Police Station, where she was charged. Before she left the house she had a moment alone with Miss Riggs and said: "You must get Stoner to give me the mallet." This is important, and it will be found, on reading Mrs. Rattenbury's progressive statements all through the night, that, even in her befogged condition, there was one thread of continuity—a desire to help Stoner, and to get hold of the mallet with which he told her he had hit Mr. Rattenbury, and then hidden in the garden. At the Police Station, about eight forty-five, Mrs. Rattenbury was formally charged, and said: "That is right. I did it deliberately, and would do it again." The police did not, at the hearing at Petty Sessions, mention the fact that Mrs. Rattenbury had been drunk, and Mr. Rooke, noticing this omission, communicated the fact to Mrs. Rattenbury's solicitors. Had it not been for Mr. Rooke and Dr. O'Donnell, the fact that Mrs. Rattenbury had been in no fit condition to make a statement, to know what was said to her or to know what she herself was saying, would not have been given in evidence. Mr. O'Connor, in his cross-examination of Inspector Carter, said: "Dr. O'Donnell has told us in his evidence that no reliance can be placed on any statement made by Mrs. Rattenbury at eight fifteen in the morning." "No," agreed the Inspector. "Do you say she was normal at eight fifteen?"—"Yes. She was not normal when she first woke up, but I waited till eight fifteen." "Do you know that the medical officer at Holloway Prison has reported that she was still under the influence of drugs three days later?"—"He has never reported it to me." "Is your evidence to the jury that, from the time you began to take her statement until she left your charge, she did not appear to you to be under the influence of drugs?"—"She did not." "Not at any time?"—"Not at any time." Yet, Mrs. Rattenbury was, during the whole of the time Inspector Carter had to do with her, *non compos mentis* from morphia!

Later in the trial Mr. Justice Humphreys, turning over the pages of Inspector Carter's notebook, was struck by the fact that there was an entry that had not been put in evidence. This consisted of a statement that Mrs. Rattenbury made directly she woke up at six o'clock. The learned Judge drew Mr. O'Connor's attention to the fact that there was something which had not yet been observed in the notebook. Mr. O'Connor was handed the notebook, read the entry through to himself and expressed his gratitude to the learned Judge. Indeed, Mr. Justice Humphreys had made one of the most important points for the defense that was made in the case, as was shown when Inspector Carter was recalled to the box.

By the Judge: "Did Mrs. Rattenbury make any statement to you about this alleged crime before eight fifteen?"—"No statement to me, my lord. Mrs. Rattenbury said the words that I have written in that book, while she was lying on the bed, directly she woke up. I did not put them down in statement form. I did not refer to it in my evidence for this reason. When Mrs. Rattenbury woke up, I said in my evidence that, in my opinion, she was not then in a normal condition and I did not caution her, and for that reason I made no reference at all to these remarks that I put down in my book that she said. That is why I omitted to say anything at all about it in my evidence in chief. I was not entitled, in my opinion, to give anything in evidence if I had not previously administered a caution, and, in my opinion, she was not in a condition normally to make a statement." *By the Judge:* "Then in your opinion she was not in a condition to make a statement at six fifteen?"—"At six ten, no, my lord." *By the Judge:* "Then what was said at that time was something said by a woman who was not in a condition to make a statement that can be acted upon?"—"Not in my opinion, my lord."

There was no doubt that Inspector Carter was actuated by an admirable sense of fair play, and the learned Judge, in his summing up, said: "I think there is no ground for complaining of his conduct or saying that he acted improperly here, although, I think, he was mistaken . . . he made a mistake in not informing the Director of Public Prosecutions that that statement had been made by the accused, and that he had it in his notebook. It is not for the police officers to decide . . . what is admissible in evidence and what is not, or what should be given or what not. Their duty is to give all material to the authorities, and let them decide." Now, the important point about the first entry in Inspector Carter's notebook—the entry he did not put in evidence, that he wrote at six fifteen—and the one which he wrote down after cautioning her at eight fifteen, is this, the two statements are practically identical. At six fifteen when, according to Inspector Carter, she was not fit to make a statement, she said: "I picked up the mallet and he dared me to hit him. He said: 'You have not guts enough to do it.' I hit him. I hid the mallet. He is not dead, is he? Are you the Coroner?" At eight fifteen she said: "He dared me to kill him. He wanted to die. I picked up the mallet, and he said: 'You have not guts enough to do it.' I hid the mallet outside the house." It will be seen at once that, with the exception of the words, "He is not dead, is he? Are you the Coroner?" the statements are the same, except that at eight fifteen she used the word "kill," and at six fifteen the word "hit"! To put it concisely: she made the same statement when, according to the Inspector, she was fit to make a statement, that she had made two hours earlier, when even he had considered her totally unfit! It was to all intents and purposes the same statement. The importance of this is obvious—Mrs. Rattenbury no more knew what she was saying at eight fifteen than she did at six fifteen, and the second statement was of no more value than the first. At one o'clock of that day, when Dr. O'Donnell saw her at the police station, he says she was supported into the room, that she could not stand without swaying, that she looked dazed and had contracted pupils as a result of the morphia. Three days later Dr. Morton of Holloway Prison considered that she was still suffering from "confusion of mind, a result of alcohol, and possibly a large dose of morphia. She kept repeating the same sentences over and over again." From 28 March she was better and appeared to have forgotten what she had said and how she behaved on the previous days since her reception. It is perfectly obvious that police officers are not fit judges of when a person is under the influence of morphia or not. There is no reason why they should be. But they are judges of drunkenness, and Mrs. Rattenbury should not have been allowed to go on drinking, or have been questioned during the Sunday night. Dr. O'Donnell, as the learned Judge pointed out, knew much more of these matters than the police officer, and much later on Monday, after she had been taken to the Police Court, he declared that it would still be unsafe to attach any importance to anything that Mrs. Rattenbury said.

Now Mrs. Rattenbury was not used to drugs, in spite of suggestions made to the contrary; she had, indeed, a horror of drugs, and the only time previously in her life that any had been administered to her was when Dr. O'Donnell in July, 1934, had administered a quarter of a grain of morphia, when she was ill and excited. On that occasion she was allowed to have her sleep out, and she had indeed slept for some twelve hours. When the stronger dose of half a grain of morphia was given to her on the night of Sunday, 24 March, she had no chance of sleep. It is not suggested for a moment that the police tried to awaken her. But Villa Madeira is a tiny house. Stoner and the police were up and down and about it all night long. Now, anyone who has had to have morphia knows that if he is not allowed to sleep off the effects his condition is far worse than if it had never been administered. This was the case with Mrs. Rattenbury, and, according to the experienced Dr. Morton, she still was suffering from the effects of the morphia three days later. Many people felt that even if Mrs. Rattenbury did not know what she was saying when she was drunk and when she was drugged, yet what she said came from her subconscious self, and hence was true. This is an error, as any doctor knows. What does come through all her statements, if they are carefully analyzed, is her anxiety for Stoner, and her wish to take the blame. Another strong point for the defense, besides the undoubted one that Mrs. Rattenbury was quite unfit to make statements, was the complete blank in her memory when she emerged from her drugged state into ordinary consciousness at Holloway Prison. Mrs. Rattenbury remembered nothing from the time when she began to drink after discovering her wounded husband, until 28 March at Holloway Prison. Many people, as a result of drinking, "pass out," as it is called. Mrs. Rattenbury did so, and the result of the morphia's effect being thwarted was that she stayed "out" for a very long time. Mrs. Rattenbury remembered nothing from when she first became drunk on Sunday night. As far as her mind was concerned, she knew nothing about the interrogations, nothing about the injection of morphia, nothing about the police matron having helped to get her up. She did not remember being taken away from Villa Madeira in a car by the police; the only thing that swam up at all in her recollection was Stoner's farewell kiss in her room, and the face of little John at her door. Mr. Croom-Johnson, in cross-examination, asked her: "About conversations, your mind is a complete blank?"—"Absolutely." "About incidents?"—"Yes. It might be somebody else you are talking about." "Is your mind a complete blank about making the statement to Inspector Carter which he wrote down in this little book?"—"I cannot remember that. I have tried and tried and tried yesterday, and last night I tried to remember again." The notebook was handed to her, and Mr. Croom-Johnson asked her whether the signature at the bottom of the statement was hers, and she said that it was. "It is my signature, but I do not remember it." Now it is natural for the layman to feel that loss of memory is a convenient form of defense, but Mrs. Rattenbury could not have deceived medical men as highly trained and as astute as Mr. Rooke, Dr. O'Donnell and Dr. Morton —the last named accustomed to all the tricks of delinquent women.

The prosecution took the unusual step of allowing the defense to recall one of the Crown witnesses, Mr. Rooke, and this courteous gesture was a great help to Mrs. Rattenbury. Mr. Rooke deposed that in his experience patients often talked long and lucidly when under morphia, but when the effects of the drug had worn off their minds were a complete blank regarding anything they had said. When it is considered that Mrs. Rattenbury was not only suffering from the morphia, but that before the morphia had been administered she had temporarily lost her mind through drink, I think it is clear that no reliance can be placed on anything that she said.

Mrs. Rattenbury was removed to Holloway Prison in London, and Stoner and Miss Riggs were left in the house at Manor Road. But Miss Riggs had no intention of being left alone with Stoner. She knew that Mrs. Rattenbury was innocent, not only of striking the blows, but of complicity in the assault. One of Mrs. Rattenbury's most striking characteristics was her horror of cruelty. She could not have hurt anything. Therefore, Irene Riggs thought that either a burglar had broken in, or that Stoner must have been Mr. Rattenbury's assailant. Irene's mother and brother moved into Villa Madeira and stayed there with her until Stoner was arrested on Thursday, 28 March. The story of those days between the commission of the crime and the arrest of Stoner is a curious one. Dr. O'Donnell had been asked by relations of Mr. Rattenbury to keep Villa Madeira under his eye, and the doctor accordingly called there on the Monday, Tuesday, Wednesday and Thursday. On the first three days he tried to see Miss Riggs alone, but found it impossible as Stoner did not leave them. On Wednesday Miss Riggs was nearly distracted with anxiety, and felt she must talk about the case to someone. She still felt herself the custodian of Mrs. Rattenbury's secret love affair, and she never discussed her even with her relations. Although not a Catholic, she went to see a priest, because she knew that what she told a priest would be safe. She came back at about ten thirty that night and her mother opened the door to her. Mrs. Riggs told her that Stoner was very drunk, that he had been going up and down the road, shouting, "Mrs. Rattenbury is in jail, and I've put her there." He had been brought back by two taxi drivers. Irene Riggs telephoned to the police and two plain-clothes men arrived. Stoner was in bed and seemed very drunk. This was very unusual for him, for he not only never drank himself, but objected to Mrs. Rattenbury drinking, and had a good influence on her in this respect. On the morning of Thursday, 28 March, Dr. O'Donnell called at Villa Madeira. Irene Riggs opened the door. It had always been Stoner who had opened it up to then. Dr. O'Donnell asked where Stoner was, and she told him that he had gone to Holloway to see Mrs. Rattenbury. Dr. O'Donnell then said that Mrs. Rattenbury was the best mistress that Miss Riggs had ever had, or that she was ever likely to have, and if there was anything she could tell the police, it was her duty to do so. Poor Miss Riggs, still loyal to her employer, said she could not let Mrs. Rattenbury's secret out, but Dr. O'Donnell very sensibly said that a secret was nothing when a life was at stake. He pointed out that if she was put in the witness box, and then had the story of Mrs. Rattenbury's liaison dragged out of her, she herself would be implicated if she had concealed her knowledge. He asked Miss Riggs whether she thought Mrs. Rattenbury had murdered her husband, and Irene Riggs replied: "I know she did not do it." Dr. O'Donnell asked her how she knew, and she replied that Stoner had confessed it to her. He had also told her that there would be no fingerprints on the mallet as he had worn gloves. Dr. O'Donnell rang up Bournemouth Police Station, and said that Miss Riggs wished to make a statement, and that Stoner had confessed to her. Dr. O'Donnell added that Stoner had left for London, and that no time should be lost in taking Irene Riggs's statement. At two thirty the police arrived and Irene Riggs told them what she knew. Stoner was arrested at the station on his return to Bournemouth that evening, and this time the charge was murder, for Mr. Rattenbury had died.

The very fact that both Stoner and Mrs. Rattenbury refused to inculpate each other was a source of great difficulty to their defenders. Stoner further complicated his counsel's very difficult task by injecting into his defense the curious suggestion that he was a cocaine addict, which there was no evidence to bear out, and which Mr. Justice Humphreys disposed of in no uncertain fashion in his summing-up. The Judge pointed out that there was one human being, and one only, who knew whether Stoner was in the habit of taking cocaine, and whether he took it on the afternoon of Sunday, 24 March, and that was Stoner himself. Stoner was an available witness, and had he wished to prove that he had ever taken cocaine, or was under the influence of cocaine, he could have gone into the box to say so. "What," remarked the learned Judge, "seems to me in the circumstances of this case a fact of the utmost significance, is that Stoner prefers not to give evidence." Stoner had told Mrs. Rattenbury a long time before the murder that he took drugs. She was so worried about this that she confided it to Dr. O'Donnell, although she was not at all sure—for in spite of her headlong infatuation she had a certain shrewdness—that Stoner had not invented the whole thing so as to make himself interesting to her. Dr. O'Donnell, at Mrs. Rattenbury's request, had interviewed Stoner and asked him what drug he was taking. Stoner told him that it was cocaine, and that he had found it in his father's house. To anyone who had seen Stoner's father in the witness box, the suggestion was not only cruel, but absurd. Mr. Stoner was a self-respecting, honest, hard-working man. It detracts somewhat from what has been called the chivalry of Stoner's conduct that he should have been able to make such a suggestion about his father. Stoner was certainly not a drug addict. Whether he was a cinema addict I do not know, but this fantastic story might well have emanated from a cinema-nourished mind. Had he not confused his defense by insisting on this fairy tale, his counsel would have been able to present a much more sympathetic picture of a boy crazy with love and wild with unreasoning jealousy, who had hit without knowing what he did. The cocaine story was too far-fetched. When Stoner was asked to describe what cocaine looked like, he replied that it was brown with black specks in it, evidently describing the only sort of things he knew, such as household pepper or influenza snuff.

During the trial Stoner sat unmoved in his corner of the dock, with his elbow on the ledge, and his cheek on his hand. His eyes were downcast and his face remained immovable. Mrs. Rattenbury also was perfectly calm, but it was a frozen, and not an apathetic calm. Her physical aspect changed, without any movement on her part, in a curious manner. By Friday she looked twenty years older than she had on Monday. On the last day even her hands changed color, and were a livid greenish white. She was an excellent witness. Her voice was low and rich. She gave a great impression of truthfulness, and she was astonishingly self-controlled. Only a nervous tic in the side of her face, which jerked perpetually, betrayed the tension of her mind. Mr. R. Lewis-Manning, her solicitor, was impressed throughout all his conversations with her, by her veracity. He, as did Mr. O'Connor, felt a terrible responsibility. Mr. Lewis-Manning was certain that Mrs. Rattenbury was not pretending when for several weeks she insisted that she would not implicate Stoner, but preferred to hang rather than he should come to any harm. Unlike Mrs. Thompson, she had immense physical courage. It was the thought of her children, and what a fearful heritage would be theirs if she were found guilty, that eventually made her tell the truth. It is easy to say that all this could have been a pretense on her part, but it would not have been easy, indeed, it would not have been possible for her to make this pretense appear the truth to Mr. Lewis-Manning and Mr. O'Connor.

The behavior of a certain section of the press during the course of the trial, had it been made public, which for obvious reasons it was not, would have caused an uneasy feeling in the public mind. Someone engaged in the case was telephoned to on the Monday when the case opened, and offered £500 as his "rake-off," if he would get Mrs. Rattenbury to write her life story. Then, as the unexpected angle that the case was assuming became visible, the press raised its offer. By Thursday, this gentleman, engaged in the case, who was a man of honor, was offered £3,500 as his "rake-off," and one paper was foolish enough to put this offer in writing! It is needless to say that none of the offers was considered for a moment, and would not have been if the wealth of the world had been offered.

Mr. Casswell was handicapped in his defense of his client, Stoner, by the fantastic nature of the story which Stoner had told. Mr. O'Connor was in no such invidious position; he had a very clear notion of the mentality of his client, and he was able to give full play to his sympathetic interpretation of that mentality. There were cases, Mr. O'Connor pointed out, when the accused person had a record and history which might inspire the jury with a revulsion against that person's character. "It is in this case, perhaps," he continued, "that the task of the jury is most difficult of all—the task of separating from their minds the natural revulsion they feel against behavior which nobody would seek to condone or commend. I am not here to condone, still less to commend, her conduct. I am not here to cast one stone against that wretched boy whose position there in the dock may be due to folly and self-indulgence on her part, to which he fell a victim." Mr. O'Connor went on to say that the jury must not imagine that the two defenses had been arranged in concert—were connected in any way. Each defense was in its water-tight compartment. "I will say no more," continued Mr. O'Connor, "about what is past in Mrs. Rattenbury's life. I would only say that if you may be tempted to feel that she has sinned, that her sin has been great and has involved others who would never otherwise have been involved, that you should ask yourselves whether you or anybody of you are prepared first to cast a stone." Having pleaded one of the greatest of speeches for the defense ever uttered—and the deathless words "cast a stone" sounded through a hushed Court—Mr. O'Connor went on to give a very good description of the mentality of the accused person who was not his client. He said of Stoner: "Can you doubt seduced; raised out of his sphere; taken away to London; given a very high time there; a lad who was melodramatic and went about with a dagger, violent sometimes, impulsive, jealous, his first love; a lad whose antecedents had been quiet, whose associations had been prosaic; never mixed with girls; flung into the vortex of this illicit love; unbalanced enough, and, in addition to all these things, either endeavoring to sustain his passion with cocaine or already an addict of drugs. You may as moral men and women, as citizens, condemn her in your souls for the part she has played in raising this position. She will bear to her grave the brand of reprobation, and men and women will know how she has acted. That will be her sorrow and her disgrace so long as she lives. You may think of Mrs. Rattenbury as a woman, self-indulgent and willful, who by her own acts and folly had erected in this poor young man a Frankenstein of jealousy which she could not control."

Mr. Justice Humphreys' summing-up was a brilliant exposition of the law. There is no judge more capable of weighing evidence, and the right value was given to every piece of evidence that had come before the Court. But the Anglo-Saxon assumption, unfortunately, still is that women, whatever their circumstances, want to be married, and Mr. Justice Humphreys was no exception to this assumption. He spoke, in his summing-up, of the period (the "orgy") which Mrs. Rattenbury and Stoner spent in Kensington. The learned Judge said: "Do you believe that while they were in London the future was not discussed? What they were going to do when they got back? Could life go on in the same way? Would not something have to be done with—or to—Mr. Rattenbury? Would he not ask 'What about my £250? How much did the operation cost you? Did you have the operation? If so, where? I hope you are better for it.' Or, if he was so callous and disinterested a husband that he would not be expected even to ask about the operation, at least as a mean man would not you expect him, and would not they expect him—that is the point— to make some inquiries about the money? Do you think that these two persons in London imagined that life could go on just the same after their return, after an absence of four days, as before?"

The learned Judge went on to quote Mrs. Rattenbury's account of the events of Saturday. He quoted Mrs. Rattenbury's evidence: "I think we played cards. I think it was just the same as any other night." The learned Judge asked: "Do you believe that? Do you believe that after an absence of four days Mr. Rattenbury never asked a question as to what happened in London?"

Let us consider the history and mentality of these people as we know them through the medium of the trial. Ill-balanced as she was, Mrs. Rattenbury was a woman of the world. The last thing she would have wanted was to have married a chauffeur, twenty years younger than herself; she was—again to use a slang expression, but slang fits Mrs. Rattenbury's career—"sitting pretty." She had a kind husband who allowed her to live her own life. She had a young and ardent lover who satisfied her emotionally and physically. She had two children to whom she was passionately devoted. She was being supported as extravagantly as she could have hoped for, all the circumstances considered. She was, as she rather pathetically said in evidence, "happy then." For her husband, she had a maternal affection— it must be remembered that in all her loves Mrs. Rattenbury was essentially maternal. She spoiled and protected Stoner; she adored her children; she comforted her husband; she tried to give Irene Riggs as good a life as possible; she was kind to every stranger who came within her gates. The one thing that would have been impossible to Mrs. Rattenbury, amoral, casual, unbalanced and passionate as she was, would have been to have taken part in harming another human being. Mrs. Rattenbury, both as a humane woman and a completely amoral woman, did not desire her husband's death, and did not wish to marry her lover, and there is no evidence, and none was ever brought forward, that she had ever desired either of these things. The unfortunate Stoner, with a much simpler experience of life and with that adolescent urge to heroics, which is a hangover from infantilism, could not see that there was no need for any drama of jealousy at all. The boundary line between drama and reality was obscure for him, and living entirely in an unintelligent world of crude emotion, he hit out almost blindly. And this gesture, conceived in an unreal world, materialized in a world of actual facts. Our prisons are of course full of sufferers from infantilism, and what goes on in their heads bears no relation to real life, as it has to be lived, though it could not possibly be said they were not sane.

The jury were out for forty-seven minutes, and they returned the only possible verdict to which they had been admirably directed upon the evidence. They found Mrs. Rattenbury not guilty, and Stoner, guilty, adding a recommendation to mercy. Mrs. Rattenbury stood immovable while the verdict of not guilty was returned, but, when the foreman of the jury pronounced the word "guilty" in respect of Stoner, she gave a little moan and put out her hand. She was led away, and Stoner received his sentence without flinching. He spoke for the first time when asked by the clerk of the Court whether he had anything to say why the Court should not give him judgment of death according to law. Stoner replied in a low voice, "Nothing at all." He was then taken below, and Mrs. Rattenbury was brought back to plead to the accusation of being an accessory after the fact. She could not speak—she could not make any sound at all, her mouth moved a little and that was all. The Clerk of the Court informed the jury that the prisoner at the Bar had pleaded not guilty. The prosecution said that they proposed to offer no evidence, and Mr. Justice Humphreys instructed the jury to return a verdict of not guilty, which they did. Mrs. Rattenbury was discharged.

Mrs. Rattenbury had an admirably fair trial. She was not, of course, bullied by the prosecution, as she would have been in France or the United States. In fact, Mr. Croom-Johnson could, even within the limits allowed to the Crown, have been more severe than he was. Mr. Justice Humphreys told the jury unmistakably that even though they might feel they could not possibly have any sympathy for the woman, it should not make them any more ready to convict her of the crime. It should, if anything, make them less ready to accept evidence against her. This is admirable, and in the best tradition of the English law. Unfortunately, there is a custom in the Courts that is not nearly so admirable, to animadvert upon the moral qualities, or lack of them, in a person accused of a crime. I am, of course, using the word merely in the only sense Anglo-Saxons seem to use it, with reference to sexual morality. Mrs. Rattenbury, at the time the learned judge was making his remarks about her moral character, was a woman at the extreme edge of what it was possible to bear and go on living. But she had to listen to the dread voice of the Judge as he said: "Members of the jury, having heard her learned counsel, having regard to the facts of this case, it may be that you will say that you cannot possibly feel any sympathy for that woman; *you cannot have any feeling except disgust for her*." (My italics.) More could hardly be said of George Joseph Smith, or of a systematic poisoner, or a baby farmer.

This may show a very lofty and moral viewpoint, but we are often told that a criminal Court is not a court of morals. In this trial apparently it was. And strange as it may seem, there are some of us, though apparently regrettably few, who are so constituted that we cannot see a fellow human being in the extreme of remorse, shame and despair, without feeling pity as well as disgust. Indeed, it is quite

possible for the disgust to cease to exist because of the overwhelming
nature of the pity. Mrs. Rattenbury was in some ways a vulgar and a
silly woman, but she was a generous, kindly, lavish creature, capable
of great self-sacrifice. She was innocent of the crime of which, entirely on the strength of her own drunken maunderings, she was
accused, but, nevertheless, though her life was handed back to her, it
was handed back to her in such a shape that it was of no use to her.
"People"—that dread judgment bar of daily life known as "people"
—would always say: "Of course she told him to do it. And, anyway,
she was a dreadful woman." For the world has progressed very little
since Ezekiel wrote: "And I will judge thee as women that break
wedlock and shed blood are judged, and I will give thee blood in fury
and jealousy." Such was the judgment of society on Mrs. Rattenbury,
and she knew it.

Her husband's relatives took her away with them, but the press
besieged the flat where they gave her refuge. The doctor who had
been called in to attend her removed her to a nursing home, pursued
by newspapermen, one of whom called out to the doctor escorting
her: "If you take her to Bournemouth we'll follow you." A horrible
example of what the demands of his newspaper can do to a young
man who probably started as a decent human being.

Mrs. Rattenbury was by now very ill, physically and mentally.
And, in her fear and grief for Stoner, in her misery for her children,
in her remorse and shame, she wanted to be alone. She left the
nursing home; and of what she did during the nightmare hours
that followed we only know from the tragedy that followed. She
must have bought a knife and taken a train down to that part of
the world where she had been happy in what was stigmatized as an
"adulterous intercourse." And there, beside the placid waters of a
little stream, she sat and wrote, feverishly and passionately, on the
backs of envelopes and odd bits of paper, the reasons for the terrible
deed that she was about to do. She referred to the assumption that
she dominated Stoner, and declared that no one could dominate him,
and that whatever he wanted to do he always did. She repeated that
if she had not been made to tell the truth, she would never have given
Stoner away. She complained about the press dogging her footsteps,
and she wrote of the scathing attack on her character. How, indeed,
was it possible for her ever to make a home for her little boys, to
watch them at play, to invite other children to play with them? She
must have known it would be worse for her children if she lived than

if she died. Her writing finished, she thrust the knife six times into her breast. The blade penetrated her heart thrice. She fell forward into the water, dead. When an ancient Roman killed himself, he inserted the tip of the sword between two ribs, and fell upon it; he called it "falling upon the sword." He knew that the shrinking of the flesh was such that it was almost impossible to drive a knife steadily into the breast. Mrs. Rattenbury drove it in six times.

The Rattenbury case had revealed a strange and unlovely mode of life, but the woman's last act raised it sharply to higher issues. Most people in England, especially women, seem easily able to feel superior to Mrs. Rattenbury. She had had "adulterous intercourse"; she had taken for her lover a boy young enough to be her son; and the boy was a servant. That out of this unpromising material she had created something that to her was beautiful and made her happy was unforgivable to the people of England. Her life had been given back to her, but the whole world was too small a place, too bare of any sheltering rock, for her to find a refuge.

Stoner lost his appeal, but he was reprieved, and the sentence of death commuted to penal servitude. Blind and muddled humanity had been even more blind and muddled than usual, and everyone concerned had paid a terrible price for the sin of lack of intelligence.

SING A SONG OF SIXPENCE
By John Buchan

. . . .

*It was a rainy evening. Ned Leithen was walking home
through Hyde Park when a man in a shabby overcoat stopped him.
Leithen offered him sixpence.
But the man needed five million pounds.*

*The effect of night, of any flowing water, of lighted cities, of the peep of
day, of ships, of the open ocean, calls up in the mind an army of anonymous desires and pleasures. Something, we feel, should happen; we know
not what, yet we proceed in quest of it.*

—R. L. STEVENSON

Leithen's face had that sharp chiseling of the jaw and that compres-
sion of the lips which seem to follow upon high legal success. Also an
overdose of German gas in '18 had given his skin an habitual pallor,
so that he looked not unhealthy, but notably urban. As a matter of
fact he was one of the hardest men I have ever known, but a chance
observer might have guessed from his complexion that he rarely left
the pavements.

Burminster, who had come back from a month in the grass countries with a face like a deep-sea mariner's, commented on this one
evening.

"How do you manage always to look like the complete Cit, Ned?"
he asked. "You're as much a Londoner as a Parisian is a Parisian, if
you know what I mean."

Leithen said that he was not ashamed of it, and he embarked on a
eulogy of the metropolis. In London you met sooner or later everybody you had ever known; you could lay your hand on any knowl-

edge you wanted; you could pull strings that controlled the innermost Sahara and the topmost Pamirs. Romance lay in wait for you at every street corner. It was the true City of the Caliphs.

"That is what they say," said Sandy Arbuthnot sadly, "but I never found it so. I yawn my head off in London. Nothing amusing ever finds me out—I have to go and search for it, and it usually costs the deuce of a lot."

"I once stumbled upon a pretty generous allowance of romance," said Leithen, "and it cost me precisely sixpence."

Then he told us this story.

It happened a good many years ago, just when I was beginning to get on at the Bar. I spent busy days in court and chambers, but I was young and had a young man's appetite for society, so I used to dine out most nights and go to more balls than were good for me. It was pleasant after a heavy day to dive into a different kind of life. My rooms at the time were in Downs Street, the same house as my present one, only two floors higher up.

On a certain night in February I was dining in Bryanston Square with the Nantleys. Mollie Nantley was an old friend, and used to fit me as an unattached bachelor into her big dinners. She was a young hostess and full of ambition, and one met an odd assortment of people at her house. Mostly political, of course, but a sprinkling of art and letters, and any visiting lion that happened to be passing through. Mollie was a very innocent lion hunter, but she had a partiality for the breed.

I don't remember much about the dinner, except that the principal guest had failed her. Mollie was loud in her lamentations. He was a South American President who had engineered a very pretty *coup d'état* the year before, and was now in England on some business concerning the finances of his State. You may remember his name— Ramon Pelem—he made rather a stir in the world for a year or two. I had read about him in the papers, and had looked forward to meeting him, for he had won his way to power by extraordinary boldness and courage, and he was quite young. There was a story that he was partly English and that his grandfather's name had been Pelham. I don't know what truth there was in that, but he knew England well and Englishmen liked him.

Well, he had cried off on the telephone an hour before, and Mollie was grievously disappointed. Her other guests bore the loss with more fortitude, for I expect they thought he was a brand of cigar.

In those days dinners began earlier and dances later than they do today. I meant to leave soon, go back to my rooms and read briefs, and then look in at Lady Samplar's dance between eleven and twelve. So at nine thirty I took my leave.

Jervis, the old butler, who had been my ally from boyhood, was standing on the threshold, and in the square there was a considerable crowd, now thinning away. I asked what the trouble was.

"There's been an arrest, Mr. Edward," he said in an awestruck voice. "It 'appened when I was serving coffee in the dining room, but our Albert saw it all. Two foreigners, he said—proper rascals by their look—were took away by the police just outside this very door. The constables was very nippy and collared them before they could use their pistols—but they 'ad pistols on them and no mistake. Albert says he saw the weapons."

"Did they propose to burgle you?" I asked.

"I cannot say, Mr. Edwards. But I shall give instruction for a very careful lockup tonight."

There were no cabs about, so I decided to walk on and pick one up. When I got into Great Cumberland Place, it began to rain sharply, and I was just about to call a prowling hansom, when I put my hand into my pocket. I found that I had no more than one solitary sixpence.

I could, of course, have paid when I got to my flat. But as the rain seemed to be slacking off, I preferred to walk. Mollie's dining room had been stuffy, I had been in court all day and I wanted some fresh air.

You know how in little things, when you have decided on a course, you are curiously reluctant to change it. Before I got to the Marble Arch, it had begun to pour in downright earnest. But I still stumped on. Only I entered the Park, for even in February there is a certain amount of cover from the trees.

I passed one or two hurried pedestrians, but the place was almost empty. The occasional lamps made only spots of light in a dripping darkness, and it struck me that this was a curious patch of gloom and loneliness to be so near to crowded streets, for with the rain had come a fine mist. I pitied the poor devils to whom it was the only home. There was one of them on a seat which I passed. The collar of his thin, shabby overcoat was turned up, and his shameful old felt hat was turned down, so that only a few square inches of pale face were visible. His toes stuck out of his boots, and he seemed sunk in a sodden misery.

I passed him and then turned back. Casual charity is an easy dope for the conscience, and I indulge in it too often. When I approached him he seemed to stiffen and his hands moved in his pockets.

"A rotten night," I said. "Is sixpence any good to you?" And I held out my solitary coin.

He lifted his face, and I started. For the eyes that looked at me were not those of a waster. They were bright, penetrating, authoritative—and they were young. I was conscious that they took in more of me than mine did of him.

"Thank you very much," he said, as he took the coin, and the voice was that of a cultivated man. "But I'm afraid I need rather more than sixpence."

"How much?" I asked. This was clearly an original.

"To be accurate, five million pounds."

He was certainly mad, but I was fascinated by this wisp of humanity. I wished that he would show more of his face.

"Till your ship comes home," I said, "you want a bed, and you'd be the better of a change. Sixpence is all I have on me. But if you come to my rooms, I'll give you the price of a night's lodging, and I think I might find you some old clothes."

"Where do you live?" he asked.

"Close by—in Downs Street." I gave the number.

He seemed to reflect, and then he shot a glance on either side into the gloom behind the road. It may have been fancy, but I thought that I saw something stir in the darkness.

"What are you?" he asked.

I was getting abominably wet, and yet I submitted to be cross-examined by this waif.

"I am a lawyer," I said.

He looked at me again, very intently.

"Have you a telephone?" he asked.

I nodded.

"Right," he said. "You seem a good fellow and I'll take you at your word. I'll follow you. . . . Don't look back, please. It's important. . . . I'll be in Down Street as soon as you. . . . *Marchons.*"

It sounds preposterous, but I did exactly as I was bid. I never looked back, but I kept my ears open for the sound of following footsteps. I thought I heard them, and then they seemed to die away.

I turned out of the Park at Grosvenor Gate and went down Park Lane. When I reached the house which contained my flat, I looked up and down the street, but it was empty except for a waiting four-wheeler. But just as I turned in, I caught a glimpse of someone running at the Hertford Street end. The runner came to a sudden halt, and I saw that it was not the man I had left.

To my surprise I found the waif on the landing outside my flat. I was about to tell him to stop outside, but as soon as I unlocked the door he brushed past me and entered. My man, who did not sleep on the premises, had left the light burning in the little hall.

"Lock the door," he said in a tone of authority. "Forgive me taking charge, but I assure you it is important."

Then to my amazement he peeled off the sopping overcoat, and kicked off his disreputable shoes. They were odd shoes, for what looked like his toes sticking out was really part of the make-up. He stood up before me in underclothes and socks, and I noticed that his underclothing seemed to be of the finest material.

"Now for your telephone," he said.

I was getting angry at these liberties.

"Who the devil are you?" I demanded.

"I am President Pelem," he said, with all the dignity in the world. "And you?"

"I?—oh, I am the German Emperor."

He laughed. "You know you invited me here," he said. "You've brought this on yourself." Then he stared at me. "Hullo, I've seen you before. You're Leithen. I saw you play at Lords'. I was twelfth man for Harrow that year. . . . Now for the telephone."

There was something about the fellow, something defiant and debonair and young, that stopped all further protest on my part. He might or might not be President Pelem, but he was certainly not a wastrel. Besides, he seemed curiously keyed up, as if the occasion were desperately important, and he infected me with the same feeling. I said no more, but led the way into my sitting room. He flung himself on the telephone, gave a number, was instantly connected and began a conversation in monosyllables.

It was a queer jumble that I overheard. Bryanston Square was mentioned, and the Park, and the number of my house was given—to somebody. There was a string of foreign names—Pedro and Alejandro and Manuel and Alcaza—and short breathless inquiries. Then I heard—"a good fellow—looks as if he might be useful in a row"—

and I wondered if he was referring to me. Some rapid Spanish followed, and then, "Come round at once—they will be here before you. Have policemen below, but don't let them come up. We should be able to manage alone. Oh, and tell Burton to ring up here as soon as he has news." And he gave my telephone number.

I put some coals on the fire, changed into a tweed jacket and lit a pipe. I fetched a dressing gown from my bedroom and flung it on the sofa. "You'd better put that on," I said when he had finished.

He shook his head.

"I would rather be unencumbered," he said. "But I should dearly love a cigarette . . . and a liqueur brandy, if you have such a thing. That Park of yours is infernally chilly."

I supplied his needs, and he stretched himself in an armchair, with his stockinged feet to the fire.

"You have been very good-humored, Leithen," he said. "Valdez—that's my aide-de-camp—will be here presently, and he will probably be preceded by other guests. But I think I have time for the short explanation which is your due. You believed what I told you?"

I nodded.

"Good. Well, I came to London three weeks ago to raise a loan. That was a matter of life or death for my big stupid country. I have succeeded. This afternoon the agreement was signed. I think I mentioned the amount to you—five million sterling."

He smiled happily and blew a smoke ring into the air.

"I must tell you that I have enemies. Among my happy people there are many rascals, and I had to deal harshly with them. 'So foul a sky clears not without a storm'—that's Shakespeare, isn't it? I learned it at school. You see, I had the Holy Church behind me, and therefore I had against me all the gentry who call themselves liberators. Red Masons, anarchists, communists, that sort of crew. A good many are now reposing beneath the sod, but some of the worst remain. In particular, six followed me to England with instructions that I must not return.

"I don't mind telling you, Leithen, that I have had a peculiarly rotten time the last three weeks. It was most important that nothing should happen to me till the loan was settled, so I had to lead the sheltered life. It went against the grain, I assure you, for I prefer the offensive to the defensive. The English police were very amiable, and I never stirred without a cordon, your people and my own. The Six wanted to kill me, and as it is pretty easy to kill anybody if you don't mind being killed yourself, we had to take rather elaborate precautions. As it was, I was twice nearly done in. Once my carriage broke down mysteriously, and a crowd collected, and if I hadn't had the luck to board a passing cab, I should have had a knife in my ribs. The second was at a public dinner—something not quite right about the cayenne pepper served with the oysters. One of my staff is still seriously ill."

He stretched his arms.

"Well, that first stage is over. They can't wreck the loan, whatever happens to me. Now I am free to adopt different tactics and take the offensive. I have no fear of the Six in my own country. There I can take precautions, and they will find it difficult to cross the frontier or to live for six hours thereafter if they succeed. But here you are a free people, and protection is not so easy. I do not wish to leave England just yet—I have done my work and have earned a little play. I know your land and love it, and I look forward to seeing something of my friends. Also I want to attend the Grand National. Therefore, it is necessary that my enemies should be confined for a little, while I take my holiday. So for this evening I made a plan. I took the offensive. I deliberately put myself in their danger."

He turned his dancing eyes toward me, and I have rarely had such an impression of wild and mirthful audacity.

"We have an excellent intelligence system," he went on, "and the Six have been assiduously shadowed. But as I have told you, no precautions avail against the fanatic, and I do not wish to be killed on my little holiday. So I resolved to draw their fire—to expose myself as ground bait, so to speak, that I might have the chance of netting them. The Six usually hunt in couples, so it was necessary to have three separate acts in the play, if all were to be gathered in. The first—"

"Was in Bryanston Square," I put in, "outside Lady Nantley's house?"

"True. How did you know?"

"I have just been dining there, and heard that you were expected. I saw the crowd in the square as I came away."

"It seems to have gone off quite nicely. We took pains to let it be known where I was dining. The Six, who mistrust me, delegated only two of their number for the job. They never put all their eggs in one basket. The two gentlemen were induced to make a scene, and, since they proved to be heavily armed, were taken into custody and may get a six months' sentence. Very prettily managed, but unfortunately, it was the two that matter least—the ones we call Little Pedro and Alejandro the Scholar. Impatient, blundering children, both of them. That leaves four."

The telephone bell rang, and he made a long arm for the receiver. The news he got seemed to be good, for he turned a smiling face to me.

"I should have said two. My little enterprise in the Park has proved a brilliant success. . . . But I must explain. I was to be the bait for my enemies, so I showed myself to the remaining four. That was really rather a clever piece of business. They lost me at the Marble Arch and they did not recognize me as the scarecrow sitting on the seat in the rain. But they knew I had gone to earth there, and they stuck to the scent like terriers. Presently they would have found me, and there would have been shooting. Some of my own people were in the shadow between the road and the railings."

"When I saw you, were your enemies near?" I asked.

"Two were on the opposite side of the road. One was standing under the lamppost at the gate. I don't know where the fourth was at that moment. But all had passed me more than once. . . . By the way, you very nearly got yourself shot, you know. When you asked me if sixpence was any good to me. . . . That happens to be their password. I take great credit to myself for seeing instantly that you were harmless."

"Why did you leave the Park if you had your trap so well laid?" I asked.

"Because it meant dealing with all four together at once, and I do them the honor of being rather nervous about them. They are very quick with their guns. I wanted a chance to break up the covey, and your arrival gave it me. When I went off, two followed, as I thought they would. My car was in Park Lane, and gave me a lift; and one of them saw me in it. I puzzled them a little, but by now they must be certain. You see, my car has been waiting for some minutes outside this house."

"What about the other two?" I asked.

"Burton has just telephoned that they have been gathered in. Quite an exciting little scrap. To your police it must have seemed a bad case of highway robbery—two ruffianly-looking fellows hold up a peaceful elderly gentleman returning from dinner. The odds were not quite like that, but the men I had on the job are old soldiers of the

Indian wars and can move softly. . . . I only wish I knew which two they have got. Burton was not sure. Alcaza is one, but I can't be certain about the other. I hope it is not the Irishman."

My bell rang very loud and steadily.

"In a few seconds I shall have solved that problem," he said gaily. "I am afraid I must trouble you to open the door, Leithen."

"Is it your aide-de-camp?"

"No. I instructed Valdez to knock. It is the residuum of the Six. Now, listen to me, my friend. These two, whoever they are, have come here to kill me, and I don't mean to be killed. . . . My first plan was to have Valdez here—and others—so that my two enemies should walk into a trap. But I changed my mind before I telephoned. They are very clever men and by this time they will be very wary. So I have thought of something else."

The bell rang again and a third time insistently.

"Take these," and he held out a pair of cruel little blush revolvers. "When you open the door, you will say that the President is at home and, in token of his confidence, offers them these. '*Une espèce d'Irlandais, Messieurs. Vous commencez trop tard, et vous finissez trop tôt.*' Then bring them here. Quick, now. I hope Corbally is one of them."

I did exactly as I was told. I cannot say that I had any liking for the task, but I was a good deal under the spell of that calm young man, and I was resigned to my flat being made a rendezvous for desperadoes. I had locked and chained and bolted the door, so it took me a few moments to open it.

I found myself looking at emptiness.

"Who is it?" I called. "Who rang?"

I was answered from behind me. It was the quickest thing I have ever seen, for they must have slipped through the moment when my eyes were dazzled by the change from the dim light of the hall to the glare of the landing. That gave me some notion of the men we had to deal with.

"Here," said the voice. I turned and saw two men in waterproofs and felt hats, who kept their hands in their pockets and had a fraction of an eye on the two pistols I swung by the muzzles.

"Monsieur le Président will be glad to see you, gentlemen," I said. I held out the revolvers, which they seemed to grasp and flick into their pockets with a single movement. Then I repeated slowly the piece of rudeness in French.

One of the men laughed. "Ramon does not forget," he said. He was a young man with sandy hair and hot blue eyes and an odd break in his long drooping nose. The other was a wiry little fellow, with a grizzled beard and what looked like a stiff leg.

I had no guess at my friend's plan, and was concerned to do precisely as I was told. I opened the door of my sitting room, and noticed that the President was stretched on my sofa facing the door. He was smoking and was still in his underclothes. When the two men behind me saw that he was patently unarmed, they slipped into the room with a quick catlike movement and took their stand with their backs against the door.

"Hullo, Corbally," said the President pleasantly. "And you, Manuel. You're looking younger than when I saw you last. Have a cigarette?" and he nodded toward my box on the table behind him. Both shook their heads.

"I'm glad you have come. You have probably seen the news of the loan in the evening papers. That should give you a holiday, as it gives me one. No further need for the hectic oversight of each other, which is so wearing and takes up so much time."

"No," said the man called Manuel, and there was something very grim about his quiet tones. "We shall take steps to prevent any need for that in the future."

"Tut, tut—that is your old self, Manuel. You are too fond of melodrama to be an artist. You are a priest at heart."

The man snarled. "There will be no priest at your deathbed." Then to his companion, "Let us get this farce over."

The President paid not the slightest attention, but looked steadily at the Irishman. "You used to be a sportsman, Mike. Have you come to share Manuel's taste for potting the sitting rabbit?"

"We are not sportsmen; we are executioners of justice," said Manuel.

The President laughed merrily. "Superb! The best Roman manner." He still kept his eyes on Corbally.

"Damn you, what's your game, Ramon?" the Irishman asked. His freckled face had become very red.

"Simply to propose a short armistice. I want a holiday. If you must know, I want to go to the National."

"So do I."

"Well, let's call a truce. Say for two months or till I leave England —whichever period shall be the shorter. After that you can get busy again."

The one he had named Manuel broke into a spluttering torrent of

Spanish, and for a little they all talked that language. It sounded like a commination service on the President, to which he good-humoredly replied. I had never seen this class of ruffian before, to whom murder was as simple as shooting a partridge, and I noted curiously the lean hands, the restless, wary eyes and the ugly lips of the type. So far as I could make out, the President seemed to be getting on well with the Irishman, but to be having trouble with Manuel.

"Have ye really and truly nothing on ye?" Corbally asked.

The President stretched his arms and revealed his slim figure in its close-fitting pants and vest.

"Nor him there?" and he nodded toward me.

"He is a lawyer; he doesn't use guns."

"Then I'm damned if I touch ye. Two months it is. What's your fancy for Liverpool?"

This was too much for Manuel. I saw in what seemed to be one movement his hand slip from his pocket, Corbally's arm swing in a circle and a plaster bust of Julius Cæsar tumble off the top of my bookcase. Then I heard the report.

"Ye nasty little man," said Corbally as he pressed him to his bosom in a bear's hug.

"You are a traitor!" Manuel shouted. "How will we face the others? What will Alejandro say and Alcaza—?"

"I think I can explain," said the President pleasantly. "They won't know for quite a time, and then only if you tell them. You two gentlemen are all that remain for the moment of your patrotic company. The other four have been the victims of the English police—two in Bryanston Square, and two in the Park close to the Marble Arch."

"Ye don't say!" said Corbally, with admiration in his voice. "Faith, that's smart work!"

"They, too, will have a little holiday. A few months to meditate on politics, while you and I go to the Grand National."

Suddenly there was a sharp rat-tat at my door. It was like the knocking in *Macbeth* for dramatic effect. Corbally had one pistol at my ear in an instant, while a second covered the President.

"It's all right," said the latter, never moving a muscle. "It's General Valdez, whom I think you know. That was another argument which I was coming to if I hadn't had the good fortune to appeal to Mr. Corbally's higher nature. I know you have sworn to kill me, but I take it that the killer wants to have a sporting chance of escape. Well, there wouldn't have been the faintest shadow of a chance here. Valdez is at the door, and the English police are below. You are brave men, I know, but even brave men dislike the cold gallows."

The knocker fell again. "Let him in, Leithen," I was told, "or he will be damaging your valuable door. He has not the Northern phlegm of you and me and Mr. Corbally."

A tall man in an ulster, which looked as if it covered a uniform, stood on the threshold. Someone had obscured the lights on the landing so that the staircase was dark, but I could see in the gloom other figures. "President Pelem," he began . . .

"The President is here," I said. "Quite well and in great form. He is entertaining two other guests."

The General marched to my sitting room. I was behind him and did not see his face, but I can believe that it showed surprise when he recognized the guests. Manuel stood sulkily defiant, his hands in his waterproof pockets, but Corbally's light eyes were laughing.

"I think you know each other," said the President graciously.

"My God!" Valdez seemed to choke at the sight. "These swine! . . . Excellency, I have—"

"You have nothing of the kind. These are friends of mine for the next two months, and Mr. Corbally and I are going to the Grand National together. Will you have the goodness to conduct them downstairs and explain to the inspector of police below that all has gone well and that I am perfectly satisfied, and that he will hear from me in the morning. . . . One moment. What about a stirrup cup? Leithen, does your establishment run to a whisky-and-soda all round?"

It did. We all had a drink, and I believe I clinked glasses with Manuel.

I looked in at Lady Samplar's dance as I had meant to. Presently I saw a resplendent figure arrive—the President, with the ribbon of the Gold Star of Bolivar across his chest. He was no more the larky undergraduate, but the responsible statesman, the father of his country. There was a considerable crowd in his vicinity when I got near him and he was making his apologies to Mollie Nantley. She saw me and insisted on introducing me. "I so much wanted you two to meet. I had hoped it would be at my dinner—but anyhow I have managed it." I think she was a little surprised when the President took my hand in both of his. "I saw Mr. Leithen play at Lords' in '97," he said. "I was twelfth man for Harrow that year. It is delightful to make his acquaintance, I shall never forget this meeting."

"How English he is!" Mollie whispered to me as we made our way out of the crowd.

They got him next year. They were bound to, for in that kind of business you can have no real protection. But he managed to set his country on its feet before he went down. . . . No, it was neither Manuel nor Corbally. I think it was Alejandro the Scholar.

THE MURDER IN LE MANS
By Janet Flanner

. . . .

An alarming survey of a French jury's verdict
of sanity in a 1933 trial of two servant sisters who took
brutal care of their mistresses.

When, in February, 1933, the Papin sisters, cook and housemaid, killed Mme. and Mlle. Lancelin in the respectable provincial town of Le Mans, a half-dozen hours from Paris, it was not a murder but a revolution. It was only a minor revolution—minor enough to be fought in a front hall by four females, two on a side. The rebels won with horrible handiness. The lamentable Lancelin forces were literally scattered over a distance of ten bloody feet, or from the upper landing halfway down the stairs. The physical were the most chilling details, the conquered the only dull elements in a fiery, fantastic struggle that should have remained inside Christine Papin's head and which, when it touched earth, unfortunately broke into paranoiac poetry and one of the most graceless murders in French annals.

On the day he was to be made a widower, M. Lancelin, retired lawyer, spent his afternoon at his respectable provincial club; at six forty-five he reported to his brother-in-law, M. Renard, practicing lawyer, at whose table they were to dine at seven *en famille*, that, having gone by the Lancelin home in the Rue La Bruyère to pick up his wife and daughter Geneviève, he had found the doors bolted and the windows dark—except for the maids' room in the attic, where, until he started knocking, there was a feeble glow. It had appeared again only as he was leaving.

Two lawyers this time set off for the Lancelin dwelling, to observe again the mansard gleam fade, again creep back to life as the men retreated. Alarmed (for at the least a good dinner was drying up), the gentlemen procured a brace of policemen and a brigadier, who, by forcing Lancelin's window, invited Lancelin to walk into his parlor, where he discovered his electric lights did not work. Two of the police crept upstairs with one flashlight and the brother-in-law. Close to the second floor the trio humanely warned the husband not to follow.

On the third step from the landing, all alone, staring uniquely at the ceiling, lay an eye. On the landing itself the Lancelin ladies lay, at odd angles and with heads like blood puddings. Beneath their provincial petticoats their modest limbs had been knife-notched the way a fancy French baker notches his finer long loaves. Their fingernails had been uprooted, one of Geneviève's teeth was pegged in her own scalp. A second single orb—the mother's, this time, for both generations seemed to have been treated with ferocious nonpartisanship —rested shortsightedly gazing at nothing in the corner of the hall. Blood had softened the carpet till it was like an elastic red moss.

The youngest and third policeman (his name was Mr. Truth) was sent creeping toward the attic. Beneath the door a crack of light flickered. When he crashed the door, the light proved to be a candle, set on a plate so as not to drip, for the Papins were well-trained servants. The girls were in one bed in two blue kimonos. They had taken off their dresses which were stained. They had cleaned their hands and faces. They had, the police later discovered, also cleaned the carving knife, hammer and pewter pitcher which they had been using and put them neatly back where they belonged—though the pitcher was by now too battered to look tidy. Christine, the elder (Léa, the younger, was never after to speak intelligibly except once at the trial), did not confess; she merely made their mutual statement: they had done it. Truth took what was left of the candle—the short-circuiting electric iron had blown out the fuse again that afternoon and was at the bottom of everything, Christine kept saying, though the sensible Truth paid no attention—and lighted the girls downstairs, over the corpses, and out to the police station. They were still in their blue kimonos and in the February air their hair was wild, though ordinarily they were the tidiest pair of domestics in Le Mans.

Through a typographical error the early French press reports printed the girls' name not as Papin, which means nothing, but as Lapin, which means rabbit. It was no libel.

Waiting trial in the prison, Christine, who was twenty-eight years of age and the cathartic of the two, had extraordinary holy visions and unholy reactions. Léa, who was twenty-two and looked enough like her sister to be a too-long-delayed twin, had nothing, since the girls were kept separate and Léa thus had no dosage for her feeble brain.

Their trial at the local courthouse six months later was a national event, regulated by guards with bayonnets, ladies with lorgnettes and envoys from the Parisian press. As commentators *Paris-Soir* sent a pair of novelists, the Tharaud brothers, Jean and Jérôme, who, when they stoop to journalism, write of themselves as "I" and nearly even won the Goncourt Prize under this singular consolidation. Special scribes were posthasted by *Détective*, hebdomadal penny dreadful prosperously owned by the *Nouvelle Revue Française*, or France's *Atlantic Monthly*. *L'Œuvre*, as daily house organ for the Radical-Socialist Party (supposedly friendly to the working classes till they unfortunately shot a few of them in the Concorde riot), sent Bérard, or their best brain.

The diametric pleas of prosecution and defense facing these historians were clear: either (*a*) the Papins were normal girls who had murdered without a reason, murdering without reason apparently being a proof of normalcy in Le Mans, or else (*b*) the Rabbit sisters were as mad as March Hares, and so didn't have to have a reason. Though they claimed to have one just like anybody else, if the jury would only listen: their reason was that unreliable electric iron, or a mediocre cause for a revolution. . . . The iron had blown out on Wednesday, been repaired Thursday, blown again Friday, taking the houselights with it at five. By six the Lancelin ladies, in from their walk, had been done to death in the dark—for the dead do not scold.

While alive, Madame had once forced Léa to her housemaid knees to retrieve a morsel of paper overlooked on the parlor rug. Or, as the Tharauds ponderously wrote in their recapitulation of the crime, "God knows the Madame Lancelins exist on earth." This one, however, had been rare in that she corroborated Léa's dusting by donning a pair of white gloves, she commented on Christine's omelettes by formal notes delivered to the kitchen by Geneviève—both habits adding to the Papins' persecution complex, or their least interesting facet. Madame also gave the girls enough to eat and "even allowed them to have heat in their attic bedroom," though Christine did not know if Madame was kind, since in six years' service she had never spoken to them, and if people don't talk, how can you tell? As for the motive for their crime, it was again the Tharauds who, all on the girls' side, thus loyally made it clear as mud: "As good servants the girls had been highly contraried" when the iron blew once. Twice "it was still as jewels of servants who don't like to lose their time that they became irritated. Perhaps if the sisters had been less scrupulous as domestics the horror which followed would never have taken place. And I wish to say," added Jean and Jérôme, without logic and in unison, "that many people still belong to early periods of society."

Among others, the jury did. They were twelve good men and true, or quite incompetent to appreciate the Papin sisters. Also, the trial lasted only twenty-six hours, or not long enough to go into the girls' mental rating though the next forty or fifty years of their lives depended on it. The prosecution summoned three local insane-asylum experts who had seen the girls twice for a half hour, and swore on the stand that the *prisonnières* were "of unstained heredity"—i.e., their father having been a dipsomaniac who violated their elder sister, since become a nun; their mother having been an hysteric "crazy for money"; a cousin having died in a madhouse and an uncle having hanged himself "because his life was without joy." In other words, heredity O.K., legal responsibility 100 percent.

Owing to the girls' weak, if distinguished, defense—high-priced French lawyers work cheaply for criminals if bloody enough, the publicity being a fortune in itself—their equally distinguished psychiatrist's refutation carried no weight. Their lawyer was Pierre Chautemps, cousin to that Camille Chautemps who, as Prime Minister, so weakly defended the French republic in the 1933 Boulevard Saint-Germain riots; their expert was the brilliant Parisian professor, Logre, whose "colossal doubt on their sanity" failed to count since under cross-examination he had to admit he had never seen the girls before even for five minutes; just knew all about them by sitting back in his Paris study, ruminating. He did, too, but the jury sniffed at the stuck-up city man.

Thus, they also missed Logre's illuminating and delicate allusion to the girls as a "psychological couple," though they'd understood the insane-asylum chief's broader reference to Sappho. Of paramount interest to twelve good men and true, the girls' incest was really one of the slighter details of their dubious domesticity. On the jury's ears Christine's prison visions also fell flat. Indeed it was not until six months after she was sentenced to be beheaded that these hallucinations were appreciated for their literary value in a scholarly essay entitled "*Motifs du Crime Paranoïaque: ou Le Crime des Soeurs Papins,*" by Docteur Jacques Lacan, in a notable surrealist number of the intelligentsia quarterly *Minotaure.*

In court, however, Christine's poetic visions were passed over as a willful concoction of taradiddles that took in no one—except the defense, of course. Yet they had, in the limited data of lyrical paranoia and modern psychiatry, constituted an exceptional performance. Certain of the insane enjoy strange compensations; having lost sight of reality they see singular substitutes devoid of banal sequence, and before the rare spectacle of effect without cause are pushed to profound questions the rest of us are too sensible to bother with. "Where was I before I was in the belly of my mother?" Christine first inquired, and the fit was on. She next wished to know where the Lancelin ladies might now be, for, though dead, could they not have come back in other bodies? For a cook she showed, as the Tharauds said, "a bizarre interest in metempsychoses," further illuminated by her melancholy reflection, "Sometimes I think in former lives that I was my sister's husband." Then while the prison dormitory shuddered, Christine claimed to see that unholy bride hanging hanged to an apple tree, with her limbs and the tree's limbs broken. At the sad sight crazed Christine leapt in the air to the top of a ten-foot barred window where she maintained herself with muscular ease. It was then that Léa, whom she had not seen since their incarceration six months before, was called in as a sedative. And to her Christine cried with strange exultation, "Say yes, say yes," which nobody understands to this day. By what chance did this Sarthe peasant fall like the Irish Joyce in the last line of *Ulysses* on the two richest words in any tongue—those of human affirmation, Yes, yes. . . .

Thus ended the lyrical phase of Christine's seizure, which then became, maybe, political. At any rate she hunger-struck for three days, like someone with a cause, went into the silence, wept and prayed like a leader betrayed, traced holy signs with her tongue on the prison walls, tried to take Léa's guilt on her shoulders, and, when this failed, at least succeeded in freeing her own of her strait jacket.

"Wasn't all of that just make-believe?" the prison officials later asked her. (All except escaping from the strait jacket, of course, or a reality that had never occurred in French penal history before.) "If monsieur wishes," said Christine politely. Both the girls were very polite in prison and addressed their keepers in the formal third person, as if the guards were company who had just stepped into the Lancelins' parlor for tea.

During the entire court proceeding, report on visions, vices and all, from one thirty after lunch of one day to three thirty before breakfast of the next, Christine sat on the accused bench with eyes closed. She looked like someone asleep or a medium in a trance, except that she rose when addressed and blindly said nearly nothing. The judge, a kind man with ferocious mustaches was, in his interrogation, finally forced to examine his own conscience, since he couldn't get Christine to talk about hers.

"When you were reprimanded in your kitchen, you never answered back but you rattled your stove lids fiercely; I ask myself if this was not sinful pride. . . . Yet you rightly think work is no disgrace. No, you also have no class hatred," he said with relief to find that he and she were neither Bolsheviks. "Nor were you influenced by literature, apparently, since only books of piety were found in your room."

(Not that printed piety had taught the girls any Christian mercy once they started to kill. The demi-blinding of the Lancelins is the only criminal case on record where eyeballs were removed from the living head without practice of any instrument except the human finger. The duplicating of the tortures was also curiously cruel; Christine took Madame in charge, the dull Léa followed suit by tending to Mademoiselle; whatever the older sister did to the older woman, the younger sister repeated on fresher flesh in an orgy of obedience.)

As the trial proceeded, the spectators could have thought the court was judging one Papin cadaver seen double, so much the sisters looked alike and dead. Their sanity expert had called them Siamese souls. The Papins' was the pain of being two where some mysterious unity had been originally intended; between them was a schism which the dominant, devilish Christine had tried to resolve into one self-reflection, without ever having heard of Narcissus or thinking that the pallid Léa might thus be lost to view. For, if Christine's eyes were closed to the judge, Léa's were as empty in gaze as if she were invisible and incapable of sight. Her one comment on trial for her life was that, with the paring knife, she had "made little carvings" in poor spinster Geneviève's thighs. For there, as her Christine had said, lay the secret of life. . . .

When the jury came in with their verdict Christine was waiting for them, still somnambulant, her hands clasped not as in prayer but as if pointing down into the earth. In the chill predawn both sisters' coat

collars were turned up as if they had just come in from some domestic errand run in the rain. With their first effort at concentration
on Léa, whom all day the jury had tried to ignore, the foreman gave
her ten years' confinement and twenty of municipal exile. Christine
was sentenced to have her head cut off in the public square of Le
Mans which, since females are no longer guillotined, meant life—a
courtesy she, at the moment, was ignorant of.

When Christine heard her sentence of decapitation, in true belief
she fell to her knees. At last she had heard the voice of God.

SLEEPING BEAUTY
By John Collier

. . . .

She was the most beautiful girl in the world,
and she'd been asleep for five years, in a side show.
For twenty-five cents anyone could try to awaken her with a kiss.
One man tried too hard, perhaps.

Roger Paston had everything in the world that he wanted. He had a
very civilized little Regency house, whose ivory façade was reflected
in a lake of suitable proportions. There was a small park, as green as
moss, and well embowered with sober trees. Outside this, his estate
ran over some of the shaggiest hills in the south of England. The
ploughed fields lay locked in profound woods. A farm house and a
cottage or two sent their blue smoke curling up into the evening
sky.

With all this, his income was very small, but his land paid for
itself, and his tastes, being perfect, were simple in the extreme. His
dinner was a partridge roasted very plain, a bottle of Hermitage, an
apple pie and a mouthful of Cheshire cheese. His picture was a tiny
little Constable, left to him by his great-uncle. His gun was Father's
old Purdey, which fitted him to a hair; his dog a curly-coated re-
triever; his horse a cob, but a good one; he had the same three suits
made for him every year; and when his friends went abroad it did not
occur to him to find others.

In short, he was half a solitary, with a mild manner and a plain
face. He was obsessed by the placid beauty of his quiet house, and by
the rich, harsh beauty of the wild farmlands on the hills. Perhaps he
was a little precious in his insatiable devouring of these delights; at
all events he seldom left home, and, though he was thirty, he had
never fallen in love. Whenever he was attracted, he would think of

474

his woods and his hills, and then he would find something a little cheap or smart or tinny in the young woman who had caught his eye.

However, one day, just as he was congratulating himself on being the happiest man in all the world, the thought occurred to him that he had never experienced the rapture of returning to his paradise after a long absence abroad, and, being a connoisseur of sensations, this thought stuck in his mind, and before very long he had set off to America, where the best of his friends was settled in San Francisco.

On his way back across the Middle West he stopped off at Hugginsville in order to sharpen his homesickness to the keenest possible pitch. Hugginsville is the dreariest town that ever sweltered on the devastated prairie. Sickly trees, tipsy posts and rusty wire effectively dissipate all the grandeur of the endless plain. The soil was blown away in the droughts: the fields are nothing but hideous clay, with here and there the skeleton of a horse or a cow. A sunken creek, full of tin cans, oozes round a few hundred wooden shacks in the last stages of decay. The storekeepers have the faces of alligators; all the other people have the faces and the voices of frogs.

Roger deposited his bags in Mergler's Grand Hotel, which stank. He was regaled with a corned-beef hash more terrible than the town itself, because, after all, one did not have to eat the town. He toyed with the second half of a tin of fruit which had been opened for some departed guest, and went out to stroll a few yards along the main street.

When he had strolled a few yards along the main street he had the impression he was going mad, so he went back to Mergler's Grand Hotel.

When he had been another half an hour in Mergler's Hotel he began to bite at the ends of his fingers, so he went out into the main street again, but the sight of the people soon drove him back into Mergler's Grand Hotel. Thus he spent alternate half hours of the evening, and of the next three or four days. During this time he thought of his hushed woods and his rich fields, and particularly of his succulent partridges, and his homesickness was whetted to a razor edge.

On the fourth day his self-control broke, and with a terrible suddenness. He strapped up his bags, called for his bill. "What time is the next train?" he asked.

"Eight," said the hotel keeper.

"Eight o'clock tonight?" cried Roger in a panic. "Ten hours! What shall I do?"

"Better go along by the creek," said the hotel keeper.

"It's not deep enough!" cried Roger. "Ten hours!"

"You don't want to swim in that creek," said the hotel keeper. "That's leechy. You come to where them three alder trees are—"

"Their branches are not strong enough," said Roger.

"From there you'll see the fair-ground," said the hotel keeper.

"A fair?" cried Roger, as a man might cry, "A reprieve?"

"Yes, *sir*," returned the hotel keeper. "Scheduled to start at one P.M. this very afternoon. Boy, will ya find a fair at any of these goldarn hick towns hereabouts? No, *sir*."

Roger needed no greater incentive than the hotel keeper's recommendation, and the prospect of preserving his reason. At the stroke of one he was at the gate; the first blast of music engulfed him as he passed through.

I must restrain myself, he thought, from dashing too madly at the side shows. I have seven hours to fill in. I will see the Calf at half-past one, the Fat Lady at half-past two and the Pigtailed Boy at half-past three. At four thirty, by way of a central prop, I will indulge myself in the glamour of the fan dance, the memory of which will color the Giant Rat at five thirty, and at half-past six I will see the Sleeping Beauty, whatever she may be, and that will leave me half an hour to pick up my bags, and a happy hour on the place where the platform would be if there was one. I hope the train will not be late.

At the appointed hours Roger gravely inspected the heads of the two-headed Calf, the legs of the Fat Lady and the bottom of the Pigtailed Boy. He was glad of the fans when it came to the fan dance. He looked at the Giant Rat, and the Giant Rat looked at Roger. "I," said Roger under his breath, "am leaving on the eight o'clock train." The Giant Rat bowed its head and turned away.

The tent that housed the Sleeping Beauty was just filling as Roger approached. "Come on," cried the barker, "curtain just going up on the glamorous face and form of the girl who's a problem to modern science, celebrated in Ripley's *Believe It or Not*. In her night attire. See the most beautiful girl in America, passing away her youth and love time in unbroken sleep."

Roger paid his five cents and entered the crowded tent. An evil-looking rascal, dressed in a white surgical coat and with a stethoscope hung round his neck, was at that moment signaling for the curtain to be drawn aside.

A low dais was exposed: on it a hospital bed, at the head of which stood a sinister trollop tricked out in the uniform of a nurse.

"Here we have," said the pseudo-doctor, "the miracle that has baffled the scientists of the entire world." He continued his rigmarole. Roger gazed at the face on the pillow. It was, beyond any question at all, the most exquisite face he had ever seen in his life.

He was as staggered as if he had seen a milk-white unicorn. He had believed this sort of face had vanished utterly from the world. "This is the sort of thing Lely painted," he said. "This explains Nelson. Good Lord, it explains Troy. It is *the* face of beauty that used to come once in a hundred years, and I thought it had gone forever. I thought we had a film star's face instead."

"Well, folks," said the pseudo-doctor, "I just want you to know, for the sake of the reputation of the scientific profession, that there has been absolutely no deception in the announcement made to you that this is the most beautiful young lady in the world. Lest you should be speculating on whether her recumbert posture, maintained night and day for five years, has been the cause of shrinkage or wasting of the limbs, hips, or bust—Nurse, be so good as to turn back that sheet."

The nurse, with a simper, pulled back the grubby cotton and revealed the whole form of this wonderful creature, clad in a diaphanous nightgown, and lying in the most graceful, fawnlike posture you can possibly imagine.

Roger was shaken to his very heart's root by a sort of ecstasy. "I knew," said he to himself, "that my careful way of life had meaning. I knew that it led, or pointed, somewhere." He remembered he had been called an ostrich, an escapist. "This," said he, "is worth everything that has happened in the last two hundred years."

He could not rid himself of a feeling that this nymph, this Arcadian being, would open her eyes, and that when they were opened those eyes would be fixed on him. He trembled. Then he became angrily aware of other people in the booth. "To think she should be exposed to these!"

"Gentlemen," the hateful showman was saying, "the resources of world science have proved impotent to awaken this beautiful young lady from her trance that has lasted five years. Now, gents, the old fairy tale you heard around that dear old mamma's knee assures each and every one of us the Sleeping Beauty woke up when Prince Charming happened along with his kiss. In order to contribute to the expensive medical attention required by this young lady, we are prepared, for the fee of one quarter deposited in the bowl on the bedside table, to allow any gentleman in the audience to try his luck at being Prince Charming. Now, gentlemen, take your places in a queue to avoid the crush."

There was a shuffling of feet, a snigger or two and a good deal of muttering.

"Yeah? What's he think he's got—Marlene Dietrich?"

"O.K., Irving. You step up when I'm through."

Roger, stuck fast in the middle of the pack, cursed them as swine for hesitating over a pearl, which might, he thought, irradiate and transform their abject lives by its contact, if they were not struck dead in the profaning act. But as he saw a grinning sheik push forward toward the barrier, applauded by some and followed by others, it occurred to him that he might have to do the striking. He made a desperate clutch at reason. "I must get out of this," he said.

He rushed off toward his hotel, hurrying fast, then slowing up, as men do who try to tear themselves away from terrifying destinies. He came to a stop at the sight of Mergler's Grand Hotel. He found that he was actually grinding his teeth. "It is impossible," he said, "to bear the thought of that shy, wild, innocent face being ravaged by those lecherous reptiles. And what is a hundred times worse," he cried (for beauty is always ravaged), "those blind mouths have kissed her, and I have not!

"It is seven o'clock," he said. "I might still get back there, and yet catch my train."

Perhaps I had better not, he thought, as he set off faster than he had fled. Perhaps I am making a fool of myself. There is only one sensible thing for me to do: that is to get home as quickly as ever I can.

He thought of his home. "But what is it all made for," said he, "except to be a shell for such a creature as this? Or for the hope of her? Or the image of her? I could carry that kiss home, and live with the memory of it, and every shady oak would rejoice at the ghost of the goddess. . . ."

His thoughts were becoming rather wild, but then the day was hot and he was walking at a tremendous speed. He arrived, flushed and panting, at a propitious moment, just as a batch of people were coming out of the booth. How impossible it would have been, he thought, if I had had to kiss her in the midst of that hideous mob! Now the curtain will be lowered while the tent fills up. I shall have a chance to be alone with her for a moment.

He found the back entrance, and squeezed through a narrow flap in the canvas. The doctor and the nurse were taking a little refreshment between shows. Roger did not dare look at the bed.

"Other way in, buddy," said the doctor. "Unless you're the press, that is."

"I am not the press," said Roger.

"Then the other way in," said the doctor.

"Listen," said Roger. "How long is it between shows? I want to spend a few minutes alone with this girl."

"Yeah?" said the doctor, observing Roger's flushed face and breathless speech.

"I can pay you," said Roger.

"Stool pigeon—vice squad," observed the nurse in a level tone.

"Listen, buddy," said the doctor, "you don't want to muscle in here with a low-down immoral proposition like that."

"Can't you see I'm an Englishman?" cried Roger. "How can I be a member of the vice squad or anything else? This is nothing immoral. I just want . . ."

"I wonder," said the doctor.

The nurse examined Roger with prolonged and expert attention. "O.K.," she said at last.

"O.K. nothing," said the doctor.

"O.K. a hundred bucks," said the nurse.

"A hundred bucks?" said the doctor. "Listen, son, it's true what Will Rogers said: 'We all been young once.' You want a private interview—maybe you *are* the press—with this interesting young lady. Well, mebbe. Mebbe a hundred bucks, and—what do you say, Nurse?"

The nurse examined Roger again. "Ten minutes," said she.

"Ten minutes," continued the doctor to Roger. "After twelve o'clock tonight when we close down."

"No. Now," said Roger. "I've got to catch a train."

"Yeah?" said the doctor. "And have some guys snooping to see why we don't begin on time. No, *sir*. There's ethics in this profession —*the show goes on*. Scram. Twelve o'clock. Open up, Dave."

Roger filled in part of the time by watching the thickening crowds file into the booth. As the evening wore on an increasing proportion were repulsively drunk. In the end he went away and sat down by the stinking creek, holding his head in his hands and waiting for the endless hours to drag by. The sunken water oozed past, darkly. The night over the great flat of lifeless clay was heavy with a stale and sterile heat, the lights of the fair glared in the distance and the dark water crept on. Roger had the vague but dangerous impression that here was the end of the world.

At last the blaze of lights was extinguished. A few were left: even these began to wink out one by one, like sparks on a piece of smouldering paper. Roger got up like a somnambulist and made his way back to the fair.

The doctor and the nurse were eating silently and voraciously when he entered. The single harsh light in the tent, falling on their ill-colored faces and their fake uniforms, gave them the appearance of waxworks, or corpses come to life, while the girl lying in the bed, with the flush of health on her cheeks and her hair in a lovely disorder, looked like a creature of the fresh wind, caught in this hideous stagnation by some enchantment, waiting for a deliverer. Certainly the world seemed upside down.

"Say, you showed up!" said the doctor.

"Got the hundred simoleons?" asked the nurse.

"Here is the money," said Roger. "Where can I be alone with her?"

"Push the bed through the curtain," said the doctor. "We'll turn the radio on."

"Have you a light of any sort—a candle?" asked Roger, when this was done.

"You want a light?" said the doctor. "O.K. We'll pull the curtain down a bit at the top. Service, huh?"

"Ten minutes," said the nurse.

"Have a heart," said the doctor. "Give the poor guy fifteen."

"Ten minutes," said the nurse.

"Gee, it's tough!" observed the doctor. "O.K. Clock on."

Roger was alone with the beauty for which he, and his whole life, and his house, and his land, were made. He moistened his handkerchief and wiped away the blurred lipstick from her mouth. Fortunately they had not thought it necessary to add color to her cheeks.

He tried to clear his mind to make it as blank as a negative film, so that he could photograph upon it each infinitely fine curve of cheek and lip, the sweep of the dreaming lashes and the tendrils of the enchanted hair.

Suddenly, to his horror, he found his eyes were dimming with tears. He had made his mind a blank in order to photograph a goddess, and now his whole being was flooded with pity for a girl. But almost at once he ceased to struggle against this emotion, and, borne away by it, he leaned forward and kissed her on the lips.

The effect was astounding. If he had somewhere at the back of his mind a faint hope that his kiss might awaken her, he forgot it now. It is the fate of those who kiss sleeping beauties to be awakened themselves, and all Roger's previous emotions, though they had seemed to shake him to the core, were the merest stirrings in a long sleep compared with the sudden leap he now made into the broad daylight of complete and unquestioning love.

At that moment he heard an admonitory cough on the other side of the curtain. He jerked it aside and went through.

"On time," said the doctor approvingly.

"How much," said Roger, "will you take for that girl?"

"Hear that?" said the doctor to the nurse. "He wants to buy the act."

"Sell," said the nurse.

"Yeah? You're jealous," said the doctor.

"Sell," said the nurse.

"Not under ten grand," said the doctor.

"Twelve," said the nurse.

"Twelve thousand dollars?" said Roger.

"She says," said the doctor.

This was not a matter for haggling over. "I will pay you that," said Roger. "It will take me a few days to get the money."

"Do you know what she grosses?" said the doctor.

"I don't want to know," said Roger. "I don't want you to tell me anything about her."

"Sure," said the nurse. "If he don't want to know, you keep your trap shut."

"You can bring her to the hotel," said Roger, "and stay with her till I hand you the money."

"Mergler's Grand?" said the nurse. "That's extra."

In the end everything was arranged. Roger cabled his lawyer to raise the money. In due course it arrived. He paid the doctor and nurse, who at once bade him farewell, and that evening Roger and his wonderful charge set off for Chicago, New York and England.

The nurse had informed him that long stretches of travel were apparently not good for the sleeper. "Seems to give her the willies," she had said. "How do you know?" Roger had asked. "She squawks," the nurse had replied. "Sounds horrible."

This being so, Roger had determined to restrain his eagerness, and rest twenty-four hours in Chicago. When they arrived he went to a hotel, where Daphne, as he had decided to call her, was transferred to a comfortable bed, and Roger, who had spent most of the night journey in watching over her, took the liberty of snatching a little sleep in the twin to it.

In the afternoon he awoke, and went downstairs to the lounge. The man at the reception desk signaled to him. "There's been a couple of people asking for you," he said, "only you left orders not to be disturbed."

"Who can they be?" said Roger. He was not left to wonder very long. "This couple coming here now," said the receptionist. Roger looked round and saw a man and a woman approaching. He thought they looked extremely unsavory.

"This is the gentleman," said the receptionist.

"Mr. Paston?" said the man.

"We should like to have a word with you," said the woman.

"Better go somewhere quiet," said the man.

"What do you want to see me about?" said Roger.

"About my daughter!" cried the woman in a heartrending tone. "About my little girl. My baby."

"Tell me exactly what you mean," said Roger, moving with them to a deserted entrance hall.

"Kidnaping, white-slave trade and violation of the Mann Act," said the man.

"That doc sold her like a chattel!" cried the woman.

"What is the Mann Act?" asked Roger.

"You move a dame, any dame but your wife or daughter, outa one state into another," said the man, "and that's the Mann Act. Two years."

"Prove that she is your daughter," said Roger.

"Listen, wise guy," said the man, "if half a dozen of the hometown folks aren't enough for you, they'll be enough for the district attorney. Do you see that dick standing outside? Boy, I've only got to whistle."

"You want money," said Roger at last.

"I want my Rosie," said the woman.

"We drew twenty per for Rosie," said the man. "Yeah, she kept her folks."

Roger argued with them for a time. It became abundantly clear that, whether or not they were her parents, they could very effectively prevent his taking Daphne any farther. There was nothing for it but to forsake her, or to agree to their demand. Their demand was for twenty thousand dollars. This meant selling almost all the stock he had left, and at the most unfavorable possible moment. He cabled to England, and soon afterward paid over the money and received in exchange a document surrendering all parental rights and appointing him the true and legal guardian of the sleeping girl.

Roger was stunned. He moved on to New York in a sort of dream. The phrases of that first appalling interview repeated themselves constantly in his mind: it was with a horrible shock that he realized the same phrases, or others very like them, were being launched at him from outside. A seedy but very businesslike-looking clergyman had buttonholed him in the foyer of the Warwick Hotel.

He was talking about young American womanhood, purity, two humble members of his flock, the moral standards of the state of Tennessee and a girl called Susy-Mary. Behind him stood two figures, which, speechless themselves, were calculated to take away the power of speech from any man.

"It is true, then," said Roger, "about hillbillies?"

"That name, sir," said the clergyman, "is not appreciated in the mountain country of—"

"And their daughter is named Susy-Mary?" said Roger.

"These humble, homely folk . . ." began the clergyman.

"And I have her upstairs?" said Roger. "Then the other parents were crooks. I knew it. And these want their daughter back. How did they hear of it?"

"Your immoral act, sir," said the clergyman, "has had nationwide press publicity for the last three days."

"I should read the papers," said Roger. "So that is why the others were so eager to be paid. These people want to take the girl back to some filthy cabin. . . ."

"Humble," said the clergyman, "but pure."

". . . till they can sell her to the next rascally showman who passes. I'll tell you the circumstances in which I found her. No, I won't, though." He endeavored to convince the clergyman of his respectability and of the excellence of his intentions as far as Daphne-Rosy-Susy-Mary was concerned.

"That is all very well," said the clergyman, "but, Mr. Paston, have you ever thought what a mother's heart really means?"

"Last time," said Roger, "it meant twenty thousand dollars."

One should never be witty, even when in the depths of despair. The words "twenty thousand dollars" were rumblingly echoed, as from a mountain cavern, from the deep mouth of the male parent, whose aged eye took on a forbidding gleam.

From that moment the conversation was mere persiflage. Roger was faced with the choice of paying another twenty thousand dollars or leaving his Daphne behind him. He asked leave to walk up and down by himself for a little time, in order to think and breathe more freely.

This will take the last penny of my capital, he thought. I shall have nothing to live on. Daphne will need the most expensive doctors. Ah, well, I can be happy with her if I sell the estate and retain only the keeper's cottage. We shall then have four or five hundred a year, as many stars as before, and the deep woods all round us. I'll do it.

He did not do quite that, for he found that hasty sales do not usually result in prices proportionate to the beauty and the value of estates. There were also some legal fees to be paid, one or two little presents to be make in the interests of haste, and some heavy hotel and traveling expenses.

When all was done, Roger found his fortune had dwindled to a very little more than two hundred a year, but he had the cottage, with Orion towering above it, and the mighty woods all round.

He was almost too happy. The lonely spot where he lived seemed to him to be more English and more beautiful even than his lost house. He would walk up and down outside, and watch the treacly yellow candlelight shine through the tiny pane, and exult in knowing that all the beauty of the world was casketed there. He became dizzy with the poetry of it all, and forgot to shave.

There was only one fly in his ointment. His house, at its hasty auction, had been knocked down to the most hideous, brassy rascal imaginable: a big bookmaker, he was told.

Roger seemed always to be meeting this flashy and beefy swaggerer, and every time he did so he took longer to get over it. He began to be oppressed by the thought that he had sinned in allowing his beautiful piece of country to pass into such defiling hands: "If I were a god, I should take vengeance for that." However, he had only to sit a little while beside Daphne's bed to forget all his hate and fear, in contemplation of the poetry book of her sleeping face.

The doctor came down once a month. Roger trembled to think of his bill. "I have some good news for you," said the doctor, brushing a cobweb from his sleeve. "This sort of thing you know . . . very mysterious. Well, we've narrowed it down to a gland or two. . . . There's a johnny in Vienna. . . . I think he's hit on something."

"You think you can wake her?" said Roger.

"I think we can," said the doctor. "As a matter of fact, I've brought the extract down with me. I'll show you how to administer it. You'll have to keep up the dose, you know. This is the secretion itself, which her gland should be turning out but isn't. Miss one day and she'll relapse."

Roger took all the instructions. The doctor went off, brushing away more cobwebs as he did so.

Roger walked alone under the stars. I am going to wake her up, thought he. Her eyes will open, and look into mine, and I will take her by the hand and show her the apple tree and the tall edge of the woods and the hills rolling away, and Orion reeling over the dark blue. . . . He walked about half the night. In the morning, with reverent trembling hands, he gave her the first capsule.

The doctor had told him he might expect results on the third day. All that day, and all the next, Roger scarcely left the bedside. Now and then he bit at a crust of bread he had put on the chest of drawers, but he neither slept nor washed nor shaved nor did anything but watch her drooped eyelids, waiting for the faintest flicker.

The night wore on, the candle guttered and went out: the dawn was already pale at the window. Soon the first rays of the sun struck aslant across the bed. They reached the face of the sleeper; she stirred, blinked, opened her eyes wide and closed them again. She yawned.

"Gee-minnie-ikes!" she whined. "Gawd-amighty, what a hangover! What they done to me?"

She opened her eyes wide. "Who're you, moonshiner?" she asked. "Eh, what dump's this yere? What you done to me?"

"You are all right," said Roger in some confusion. He had

dreamed of various phrases that should be the first to drop from those perfect lips, but he had dreamed of nothing like this. What dismayed him most was the voice in which she spoke: it was the most grating, petulant, ill-conditioned whine he had ever heard in his life. "You are all right," he said again.

"Awright nuthin'!" replied his beloved cynically. "Paw'll blow yer liver out fer this. Say, hobo, what'll yer gimme not to tell Paw? Gimme a dollar?"

"Listen, my dear . . ." said Roger.

"Ow! My deeya!" cried she.

"You're in England now," said Roger. "And I have brought you here."

Her eyes rounded. "You a slaver?" she asked. " 'M I goin' to be a sportin'-house gal? With an evenin' dress?"

"I can see," said Roger, "that this is going to take a lot of explaining."

He told her of her beauty, doubtless the outcrop of some pure old English strain preserved for centuries in the mountain settlements. She listened to this with a complacent giggle or two, but when he described how he had given up all he had, and how they were to live in this secluded beauty forever, and she should love him if she could, and he would worship her anyway, her mouth took a downward turn.

"I wanna go home," she said. "I wanna go where there's fellers. I wanna go where Solly Bateson is; he said he'd get me into pichers."

"Listen," said Roger, with a sinking heart. "I'm your legal guardian now. Of course, you shall go home if you want to, but first of all you must give this place a trial. I'll do all I can to make you happy, and if it fails . . ."

His beloved cheered up a little. "Will ya gimme a nekkid-vamp dress?" said she. "One of them without no back?"

"If you're good," said Roger.

"Oky-doke," said she, opening her arms to him.

"Not that," said Roger. "But you shall get up and come and see the place, and I'll tell you all about it. Here's a dress and everything. I'll wait for you downstairs."

He went downstairs, and tried to escape his thoughts by building a fire, and setting out some breakfast. Soon his charmer joined him. Her method of eating was effective rather than delicate. Her further conversation was highly colored rather than refined. "Come on," said she, as Roger led her outside, "we'll catch a gopher and cut his front legs off."

This was not a very good beginning. Roger, however, had sunk his whole life in this creature; he dared not admit to himself that it was hopeless. During the days that followed he faced every new revelation with a steely calm, and dealt with sulks, hysterics, whines and screaming fits with exemplary patience.

Nevertheless, each new day added a little to his despondency. Daphne sulked more and more, and more and more frequently she demanded to be sent back to her home town. Finally, after a scene that lasted two days, Roger went to see his lawyer, to ask if he could raise money for her passage.

"It would not be wise," said the lawyer. "I put the little that was left into some excellent shares, which I knew would drop heavily for a little while, and then steady at their true figure. Well, they're just at bottom at the moment. If you can wait three months, now . . ."

"I don't know," said Roger. "I'll think it over and write to you."

He returned to the cottage, where he found two little surprises. One was a bill from the doctor, for more than two hundred pounds; the other, which far outweighed any such evil, was that Daphne was in an entirely new mood. She stroked his chin, sat on his knee and declared she didn't want to go home after all. "Mebbe I gonna like the old shack," said she.

Roger did not persist after explanations, at which in any case Daphne was hardly an adept. He just took it as a gift from the gods, and he began to build hopes that this marked a turning point. She is very young, he thought. As the lovely seasons go round, they are bound to influence her. Perhaps in a year or two . . .

His love sprang up in his heart again. He rejoiced over it, encouraged it, nourished it, for it was not only the most beautiful thing in the world, but the only thing he had. To raise it to its full ecstasy again, he made a practice of avoiding conversation with his beauty, and instead he took every opportunity of watching her when she thought herself alone. He would seat her under the apple tree in the hope that she would go to sleep there, for then her loveliness reached its height, or he would follow her into the woods, for which she showed an increasing fondness, and watch her scramble for nuts and blackberries, with her hair wild and a stained mouth—like the nymph he had dreamed of.

She went wild when she got into the woods, and often scampered so fast through the glades that Roger could not follow without betraying his presence, so generally he went back to the cottage, where there were a number of little household tasks awaiting his attention.

One day, however, he was so intoxicated by her wood-nymph loveliness that, after he had lost sight of her, he still persisted in the same direction, in the hope of finding her sleeping under a tree, or paddling in the brook, or making some similar picture without which he felt he could not live through the day.

He looked here and there, moving very cautiously. At last he got to the bottom end of the wood near where his old house was, and then he heard voices from an old quarry that had crumbled to a mossy dell on the very edge. There was no mistaking one of these voices.

"Yeah, he came snoopin' along after me agin. But I ditched him, baby. Pore critter, he's just plumb nuts. Say, honey, when yer gonna take me up to the city?"

Roger peered over the edge. There was his nymph, and there was the satyr. It was the beefy bookmaker from his old house.

There was a large stone lying at his feet. He thought a little of murder, but his brain was very cold. Good Lord! he thought. At last I am done with impulsiveness!

He walked quietly away, and returned to the cottage. Everything was as it was, except that the postman had called and left a duplicate of the doctor's bill which he had received a month ago.

Roger read the bill very carefully. "I shall soon have no money left at all," said he. "Yes, I've become practical all of a sudden. The question is, what shall I do?"

He saw a small box on the mantelpiece, and he eyed this small box for a long time. It contained the gland extract which kept Daphne awake. After a good deal of very matter-of-fact thinking, Roger took this small box and dropped it at the back of the fire.

Daphne came home and chattered a good deal. Roger was even more silent than usual. Next day Daphne yawned a great deal, and slept for a very long time under the apple tree. The day after that she did not come down to breakfast. She stirred and murmured a little in the afternoon, soon she ceased even to murmur or to stir.

Roger went downstairs and wrote to a firm that advertised motor caravans. Next summer he was at Blackpool, clad in a spotless white coat, addressing the multitude from under a sign that read:

THE SLEEPING BEAUTY
Dr. von Stangelberg exhibits the
Wonder of Modern Science
Adults only
THE SLEEPING BEAUTY
THREEPENCE

THE SHADOW OF THE SHARK
By G. K. Chesterton

. . . .

No one could have approached the body across the soft sand.
There was no weapon to be found.
But somehow a murder had been committed.

It is notable that the late Mr. Sherlock Holmes, in the course of those inspiring investigations for which we can never be sufficiently grateful to their ingenious author, seems only twice to have ruled out an explanation as intrinsically impossible. And it is curious to notice that in both cases the distinguished author himself has since come to regard that impossible thing as possible, and even as positively true. In the first case the great detective declared that he never knew a crime committed by a flying creature. Since the development of aviation, and especially the development of German aviation, Sir Arthur Conan Doyle, patriot and war historian, has seen a good many crimes committed by flying creatures. And in the other case the detective implied that no deed need be attributed to spirits or supernatural beings; in short, to any of the agencies to which Sir Arthur is now the most positive and even passionate witness. Presumably, in his present mood and philosophy the Hound of the Baskervilles might well have been a really ghostly hound; at least, if the optimism which seems to go with spiritualism would permit him to believe in such a thing as a hellhound. It may be worth while to note this coincidence, however, in telling a tale in which both these explanations necessarily played a part. The scientists were anxious to attribute it to aviation, and the spiritualists to attribute it to spirits; though it might be questioned whether either the spirit or the flying man should be congratulated on his utility as an assassin.

A mystery which may yet linger as a memory, but which was in its time a sensation, revolved round the death of a certain Sir Owen Cram, a wealthy eccentric, chiefly known as a patron of learning and the arts. And the peculiarity of the case was that he was found stabbed in the middle of a great stretch of yielding sand by the seashore, on which there was absolutely no trace of any footprints but his own. It was admitted that the wound could not have been self-inflicted; and it grew more and more difficult even to suggest how it could have been inflicted at all. Many theories were suggested, ranging, as we have said, from that of the enthusiasts for aviation to that of the enthusiasts for psychical research; it being evidently regarded as a feather in the cap either of science or spiritualism to have effected so neat an operation. The true story of this strange business has never been told; it certainly contained elements which, if not supernatural, were at least supernormal. But to make it clear, we must go back to the scene with which it began; the scene on the lawn of Sir Owen's seaside residence, where the old gentleman acted as a sort of affable umpire in the disputes of the young students who were his favorite company; the scene which led up to the singular silence and isolation, and ultimately to the rather eccentric exit of Mr. Amos Boon.

Mr. Amos Boon had been a missionary, and still dressed like one; at any rate, he dressed like nothing else. His sturdy, full-bearded figure carried a broad-brimmed hat combined with a frock coat; which gave him an air at once outlandish and dowdy. Though he was no longer a missionary, he was still a traveler. His face was brown and his long beard was black; there was a furrow of thought in his brow and a rather strained look in his eyes, one of which sometimes looked a little larger than the other, giving a sinister touch to what was in some ways so commonplace. He had ceased to be a missionary through what he himself would have called the broadening of his mind. Some said there had been a broadening of his morals as well as of his mind; and that the South Sea Islands, where he had lived, had seen not a little of such ethical emancipation. But this was possibly a malicious misrepresentation of his very human curiosity and sympathy in the matter of the customs of the savages; which to the ordinary prejudice was indistinguishable from a white man going *fantée*. Anyhow, traveling about alone with nothing but a big Bible, he had learned to study it minutely, first for oracles and commandments, and afterward for errors and contradictions; for the Bible-smasher is only the Bible-worshipper turned upside down. He pursued the not very arduous task of proving that David and Saul did not on all occasions merit the Divine favor; and always concluded by roundly declaring that he preferred the Philistines. Boon and his Philistines were already a byword of some levity among the young men who, at that moment, were arguing and joking around him.

At that moment Sir Owen Cram was playfully presiding over a dispute between two or three of his young friends about science and poetry. Sir Owen was a little restless man, with a large head, a bristly gray mustache and a gray fan of hair like the crest of a cockatoo. There was something sprawling and splayfooted about his continuous movement which was compared by thoughtless youth to that of a crab; and it corresponded to a certain universal eagerness which was really ready to turn in all directions. He was a typical amateur, taking up hobby after hobby with equal inconsistency and intensity. He had impetuously left all his money to a museum of natural history, only to become immediately swallowed up in the single pursuit of landscape painting; and the groups around him largely represented the stages of his varied career. At the moment a young painter, who was also by way of being a poet, was defending some highly poetical notions against the smiling resistance of a rising doctor, whose hobby was biology. The data of agreement would have been difficult to find, and few save Sir Owen could have claimed any common basis of sympathy; but the important matter just then was the curious effect of the young men's controversy upon Mr. Boon.

"The subject of flowers is hackneyed, but the flowers are not," the poet was insisting. "Tennyson was right about the flower in the crannied wall; but most people don't look at flowers in a wall, but only in a wallpaper. If you generalize them, they are dull, but if you simply see them they are always startling. If there's a special providence in a falling star, there's more in a rising star; and a live star at that."

"Well, I can't see it," said the man of science good-humoredly; he was a red-haired, keen-faced youth in pince-nez, by the name of Wilkes. "I'm afraid we fellows grow out of the way of seeing it like that. You see, a flower is only a growth like any other, with organs and all that; and its inside isn't any prettier or uglier than an animal's. An insect is much the same pattern of rings and radiations. I'm interested in it as I am in an octopus or any sea beast you would think a monster."

"But why should you put it that way round?" retorted the poet. "Why isn't it quite as logical the other way round? Why not say the octopus is as wonderful as the flower, instead of the flower as ordinary as the octopus? Why not say that crackens and cuttles and all the sea-monsters are themselves flowers; fearful and wonderful flowers in that terrible twilight garden of God. I do not doubt that God can be as fond of a shark as I am of a buttercup."

"As to God, my dear Gale," began the other quietly, and then he seemed to change his form of words. "Well, I am only a man—nay, only a scientific man, which you may think lower than a sea beast. And the only interest I have in a shark is to cut him up; always on the preliminary supposition that I have prevented him from cutting me up."

"Have you ever met a shark?" asked Amos Boon, intervening suddenly.

"Not in society," replied the poet with a certain polite discomposure, looking round with something like a flush under his fair hair; he was a long, loose-limbed man named Gabriel Gale, whose pictures were more widely known than his poems.

"You've seen them in the tanks, I suppose," said Boon; "but I've seen them in the sea. I've seen them where they are lords of the sea, and worshipped by the people as great Gods. I'd as soon worship those gods as any other."

Gale the poet was silent, for his mind always moved in a sort of sympathy with merely imaginative pictures; and he instantly saw, as in a vision, boiling purple seas and plunging monsters. But another young man standing near him, who had hitherto been rather primly silent, cut in quietly; a theological student, named Simon, the deposit of some epoch of faith in Sir Owen's stratified past. He was a slim man with sleek, dark hair and darting, mobile eyes, in spite of his compressed lips. Whether in caution or contempt, he had left the attack on medical materialism to the poet, who was always ready to plunge into an endless argument with anybody. Now he intervened merely to say:

"Do they worship only a shark? It seems rather a limited sort of religion."

"Religion!" repeated Amos Boon rudely; "what do you people know about religion? You pass the plate round, and when Sir Owen puts a penny in it, you put up a shed where a curate can talk to a congregation of maiden aunts. These people have got something like a religion. They sacrifice things to it—their beasts, their babies, their lives. I reckon you'd turn green with fear if you'd ever so much as caught a glimpse of religion. Oh, it's not just a fish in the sea; rather it's the sea round a fish. The sea is the blue cloud he moves in, or the green veil or curtain hung about him, the skirts of which trail with thunder."

All faces were turned toward him, for there was something about him beyond his speech. Twilight was spreading over the garden, which lay near the edge of a chalk cliff above the shore, but the last light of sunset still lay on a part of the lawn, painting it yellow rather than green, and glowing almost like gold against the last line of the sea, which was a somber indigo and violet, changing nearer land to a lurid, pale green. A long cloud of a jagged shape happened to be trailing across the sun; and the broad-hatted, hairy man from the South Seas suddenly pointed at it.

"I know where the shape of that cloud would be called the shadow of the shark," he cried, "and a thousand men would fall on their faces ready to fast or fight, or die. Don't you see the great black dorsal fin, like the peak of a moving mountain? And then you lads discuss him as if he were a stroke at golf; and one of you says he would cut him up like birthday cake; and the other says your Jewish Jehovah would condescend to pat him like a pet rabbit."

"Come, come," said Sir Owen, with a rather nervous waggishness, "we mustn't have any of your broad-minded blasphemies."

Boon turned on him a baneful eye; literally an eye, for one of his eyes grew larger till it glowed like the eye of the Cyclops. His figure was black against the fiery turf, and they could almost hear his beard bristling.

"Blasphemy!" he cried in a new voice, with a crack in it. "Take care it is not you who blaspheme."

And then, before anyone could move, the black figure against the patch of gold had swung round and was walking away from the house, so impetuously that they had a momentary fear that he would walk over the cliff. However, he found the little wooden gate that led to a flight of wooden steps; and they heard him stumbling down the path to the fishing village below.

Sir Owen seemed suddenly to shake off a paralysis like a fit of slumber. "My old friend is a little eccentric," he said. "Don't go, gentlemen; don't let him break up the party. It is early yet."

But growing darkness and a certain social discomfort had already begun to dissolve the group on the lawn; and the host was soon left with a few of the most intimate of his guests. Simon and Gale, and his late antagonist, Dr. Wilkes, were staying to dinner; the darkness drove them indoors, and eventually found them sitting round a flask of green Chartreuse on the table; for Sir Owen had his expensive conventions as well as his expensive eccentricities. The talkative poet, however, had fallen silent, and was staring at the green liquid in his glass as if it were the green depth of the sea. His host attacked with animation the other ordinary topics of the day.

"I bet I'm the most industrious of the lot of you," he said. "I've been at my easel on the beach all day, trying to paint this blessed cliff, and make it look like chalk and not cheese."

"I saw you, but I didn't like to disturb you," said Wilkes. "I generally try to put in an hour or so looking for specimens at high tide: I suppose most people think I'm shrimping or only paddling and doing it for my health. But I've got a pretty good nucleus of that museum we were talking about, or at least the aquarium part of it. I put in most of the rest of the time arranging the exhibits; so I deny the implication of idleness. Gale was on the seashore too. He was doing nothing as usual; and now he's saying nothing, which is much more uncommon."

"I have been writing letters," said Simon, in his precise way, "but letters are not always trivial. Sometimes they are rather tremendous."

Sir Owen glanced at him for a moment, and a silence followed, which was broken by a thud and a rattle of glasses as Gale brought his fist down on the table like a man who had thought of something suddenly.

"Dagon!" he cried, in a sort of ecstasy.

Most of the company seemed but little enlightened; perhaps they thought that saying "Dagon" was his poetical and professional fashion of saying "Damn." But the dark eyes of Simon brightened, and he nodded quickly.

"Why, of course you're right," he said. "That must be why Mr. Boon is so fond of the Philistines."

In answer to a general stare of inquiry, he said smoothly: "The Philistines were a people from Crete, probably of Hellenic origin, who settled on the coast of Palestine, carrying with them a worship which may very well have been that of Poseidon, but which their enemies, the Israelites, described as that of Dagon. The relevant matter here is that the carved or painted symbol of the god seems always to have been a fish."

The mention of the new matter seemed to reawaken the tendency of the talk to turn into a wrangle between the poet and the professional scientist.

"From my point of view," said the latter, "I must confess myself somewhat disappointed with your friend Mr. Boon. He represented himself as a rationalist like myself, and seemed to have made some scientific studies of folklore in the South Seas. But he seemed a little unbalanced; and surely he made a curious fuss about some sort of a fetish, considering it was only a fish."

"No, no, no!" cried Gale, almost with passion. "Better make a fetish of the fish. Better sacrifice yourself and everybody else on the horrible huge altar of the fish. Better do anything than utter the star-blasting blasphemy of saying it is *only* a fish. It's as bad as saying the other thing is only a flower."

"All the same, it *is* only a flower," answered Wilkes, "and the advantage of looking at these things in a cool and rational way from the outside is that you can—"

He stopped a moment and remained quite still, as if he was watching something. Some even fancied that his pale, aquiline face looked paler as well as sharper.

"What was that at the window?" he asked. "Is anybody outside this house?"

"What's the matter? What did you see?" asked his host in abrupt agitation.

"Only a face," replied the doctor, "but it was not—it was not like a man's face. Let's get outside and look into this."

Gabriel Gale was only a moment behind the doctor, who had impetuously dashed out of the room. Despite his lounging demeanor, the poet had already leaped to his feet with his hand on the back of the chair, when he stiffened where he stood; for he had seen it. The faces of the others showed that they had seen it too.

Pressed against the dark window pane, but only wanly luminous as it protruded out of the darkness, was a large face looking at first rather like a green goblin mask in a pantomime. Yet it was in no sense human; its eyes were set in large circles, rather in the fashion of an owl. But the glimmering covering that faintly showed on it was not of feathers, but of scales.

The next moment it had vanished. The mind of the poet, which made images as rapidly as a cinema, even in a crisis of action, had already imagined a string of fancies about the sort of creature he saw it to be. He had thought involuntarily of some great flying fish winging its way across the foam, and the flat sand and the spire and roofs of the fishing village. He had half-imagined the moist sea air thickening in some strange way to a greener and more liquid atmosphere in which the marine monsters could swim about in the streets. He had entertained the fancy that the house itself stood in the depths of the sea, and that the great goblin-headed fishes were nosing round it, as round the cabin windows of a wreck.

At that moment a loud voice was heard outside crying in distinct accents: "The fish has legs."

For that instant, it seemed to give the last touch to the monstrosity. But the meaning of it came back to them, a returning reality, with the laughing face of Dr. Wilkes as he reappeared in the doorway, panting.

"Our fish had two legs, and used them," he said. "He ran like a hare when he saw me coming; but I could see plainly enough it was a man, playing you a trick of some sort. So much for that psychic phenomenon."

He paused and looked at Sir Owen Cram with a smile that was keen and almost suspicious.

"One thing is very clear to me," he said. "You have an enemy."

The mystery of the human fish, however, did not long remain even a primary topic of conversation in a social group that had so many topics of conversation. They continued to pursue their hobbies and pelt each other with their opinions; even the smooth and silent Simon being gradually drawn into the discussions, in which he showed a dry and somewhat cynical dexterity. Sir Owen continued to paint with all the passion of an amateur. Gale continued to neglect to paint, with all the nonchalance of a painter. Mr. Boon was presumably still as busy with his wicked Bible and his good Philistines as Dr. Wilkes with his museum and his microscopic marine animals, when the little seaside town was shaken as by an earthquake with the incomprehensible calamity which spread its name over all the newspapers of the country.

Gabriel Gale was scaling the splendid swell of turf that terminated in the great chalk cliff above the shore, in a mood consonant to the sunrise that was storming the skies above him. Clouds haloed with sunshine were already sailing over his head as if sent flying from a flaming wheel; and when he came to the brow of the cliff he saw one of those rare revelations when the sun does not seem to be merely the most luminous object in a luminous landscape, but itself the solitary focus and streaming fountain of all light. The tide was at the ebb, and the sea was only a strip of delicate turquoise over which rose the tremendous irradiation. Next to the strip of turquoise was a strip of orange sand, still wet, and nearer the sand was a desert of a more dead yellow or brown, growing paler in the increasing light. And as he looked down from the precipice upon that plain of pale gold, he saw two black objects lying in the middle of it. One was a small easel, still standing, with a campstool fallen beside it; the other was the flat and sprawling figure of a man.

The figure did not move, but as he stared he became conscious that another human figure was moving, was walking over the flat sands toward it from under the shadow of the cliff. Looking at it steadily, he saw that it was the man called Simon; and in an instant he seemed to realize that the motionless figure was that of Sir Owen Cram. He hastened to the stairway down the cliff and so to the sands; and soon stood face to face with Simon; for they both looked at each other for a moment before they both looked down at the body. The conviction was already cold in his heart that it was a dead body. Nevertheless, he said sharply: "We must have a doctor; where is Dr. Wilkes?"

"It is no good, I fear," said Simon, looking away at the sea.

"Wilkes may only confirm our fears that he is dead," said Gale, "but he may have something to say about how he died."

"True," said the other, "I will go for him myself." And he walked back rapidly toward the cliff in the track of his own footprints.

Indeed, it was at the footprints that Gale was gazing in a bemused fashion at that moment. The tracks of his own coming were clear enough, and the tracks of Simon's coming and going; and the third rather more rambling track of the unmistakable boots of the unfortunate Sir Owen, leading up to the spot where his easel was planted. And that was all. The sand was soft, so that the lightest foot would disturb it; it was well above the tides; and there was not the faintest trace of any other human being having been near the body. Yet the body had a deep wound under the angle of the jaw; and there was no sign of any weapon of suicide.

Gabriel Gale was a believer in common sense, in theory if not always in practice. He told himself repeatedly that these things were the practical clues in such a case; the wound, the weapon or absence of weapon, the footprints or absence of footprints. But there was also a part of his mind which was always escaping from his control and playing tricks; fixing on his memory meaningless things as if they were symbols, and then haunting him with them as mysteries. He made no point of it; it was rather subconscious than self-conscious; but the parts of any living picture that he saw were seldom those that others saw, or that it seemed sensible to see. And there were one or two details in the tragedy before him that haunted him then and long afterward. Cram had fallen backward in a rather twisted fashion, with his feet toward the shore; and a few inches from the left foot lay a starfish. He could not say whether it was merely the bright orange color of the creature that irrationally riveted his eye, or merely some obscure fancy of repetition, in that the human figure was itself spread and sprawling flat like a starfish, with four limbs instead of five. Nor did he attempt to analyze this æsthetic antic of his psychology; it was a suppressed part of his mind which still repeated that the mystery of the untrodden sands would turn out to be something quite simple; but that the starfish possessed the secret.

He looked up to see Simon returning with the doctor, indeed with two doctors; for there was more than one medical representative in the mob of Sir Owen's varied interests. The other was a Dr. Garth, a little man with an angular and humorous face; he was an old friend of Gale's, but the poet's greeting was rather *distrait*. Garth and his colleagues, however, got to work on a preliminary examination, which made further talk needless. It could not be a full examination till the arrival of the police, but it was sufficient to extinguish any hope of life, if any such had lingered. Garth, who was bent over the body in a crouching posture, spoke to his fellow physician without raising his head.

"There seems to be something rather odd about this wound. It goes almost straight upward, as if it was struck from below. But Sir Owen was a very small man; and it seems queer that he should be stabbed by somebody smaller still."

Gale's subconsciousness exploded with a strange note of harsh mockery.

"What," he cried, "you don't think the starfish jumped up and killed him?"

"No, of course not," said Garth, with his gruff good humor. "What on earth is the matter with you?"

"Lunacy, I think," said the poet, and began to walk slowly toward the shore.

As time went on he almost felt disposed to fancy that he had correctly diagnosed his own complaint. The image began to figure even in his dreams, but not merely as a natural nightmare about the body on the seashore. The significant sea creature seemed more vivid even than the body. As he had originally seen the corpse from above, spread flat out beneath him, he saw it in his visions as something standing, as if propped against a wall or even merely drawn or graven on a wall. Sometimes the sandy ground had become a ground of old gold in some decoration of the Dark Ages, with the figure in the stiff agonies of a martyr, but the red star always showed like a lamp by his feet. Sometimes it was a hieroglyphic of a more Eastern sort, as of some stone god rigidly dancing; but the five-pointed star was always in the same place below. Sometimes it seemed a rude, red-sandstone sort of drawing; yet more archaic; but the star was always the reddest spot in it. Now and again, while the human figure was as dry and dark as a mummy, the star would seem to be literally alive, waving its flaming fingers as if it were trying to tell him something. Now and then even the whole figure was upside down, as if to restore the star to its proper place in the skies.

"I told Wilkes that a flower was a living star," he said to himself. "A starfish is more literally a living star. But this is like going crazy. And if there is one thing I strongly object to, it is going crazy. What use should I be to all my brother lunatics, if I once really lost my balance on the tightrope over the abyss?"

He sat staring into vacancy for some time, trying to fit in this small and stubborn fancy with a much steadier stream of much deeper thoughts that were already driving in a certain direction. At last, the light of a possibility began to dawn in his eyes; and it was evidently something very simple when it was realized; something which he felt he ought to have thought of before; for he laughed shortly and scornfully at himself as he rose to his feet.

"If Boon goes about everywhere introducing his shark and I go into society always attended by my starfish," he murmured to himself, "we shall turn the world into an aquarium bigger and better than Dr. Wilkes is fixing up. I'm going down to make some inquiries in the village."

Returning thence across the sands at evening, after several conversations with skippers and fishermen, he wore a more satisfied expression.

I always did believe, he reflected, that the footprint business would be the simplest thing in the affair. But there are some things in it that are by no means simple.

Then he looked up, and saw far off on the sands, lonely and dark against the level evening light, the strange hat and stumpy figure of Amos Boon.

He seemed to consider for a moment the advisability of a meeting; then he turned away and moved toward the stairway up the cliff. Mr. Boon was apparently occupied in idly drawing lines on the sand with his shabby umbrella; like one drawing plans for a child's sand castle, but apparently without any such intelligent object or excuse. Gale had often seen the man mooning about with equally meaningless and automatic gestures; but as the poet mounted the rocky steps, climbing higher and higher, he had a return of the irrational feeling of a visionary vertigo. He told himself again, as if in warning, that it was his whole duty in life to walk on a tightrope above a void in which many imaginative men were swallowed up. Then he looked down again at the drop of the dizzy cliffs to the flats that seemed to be swimming below him like a sea. And he saw the long, loose lines drawn in the sand unified into a shape, as flat as a picture on a wall. He had often seen a child, in the same fashion, draw on the sand a pig as large as a house. But in this case he could not shake off his former feeling of something archaic, like a palæolithic drawing, about the scratching of the brown sand. And Mr. Boon had not drawn a pig, but a shark; conspicuous with its jagged teeth and fin like a horn exalted.

But he was not the only person overlooking this singular decorative scheme. When he came to the short railings along the brow of the cliff in which the stairway terminated, he found three figures leaning on it and looking down; and instantly realized how the case was closing in. For even in their outlines against the sky he had recognized the two doctors and an inspector of police.

"Hullo, Gale," observed Wilkes, "may I present you to Inspector Davies; a very active and successful officer."

Garth nodded. "I understand the inspector will soon make an arrest," he said.

"The inspector must be getting back to his work and not talking about it,'" said that official good-humoredly. "I'm going down to the village. Anybody coming my way?"

Dr. Wilkes assented and followed him, but Dr. Garth stopped a moment, being detained by the poet, who caught hold of his sleeve with unusual earnestness.

"Garth," he said, "I want to apologize. I'm afraid I was woolgathering when we met the other day, and didn't hail you as I ought to hail an old friend. You and I have been in one or two queer affairs together, and I want to talk to you about this one. Shall we sit down on that seat over there?"

They seated themselves on an iron seat set up on the picturesque headland; and Gale added, "I wish you could tell me roughly how you got as far as you seem to have got."

Garth gazed silently out to sea, and said at last: "Do you know that man Simon?"

"Yes," replied the poet, "that's the way it works, is it?"

"Well, the investigation soon began to show that Simon knew rather more than he said. He was on the spot before you; and for some time he wouldn't admit what it was he saw before you turned up. We guessed it was because he was afraid to tell the truth; and in one sense he was."

"Simon doesn't talk enough," said Gale thoughtfully. "He doesn't talk about himself enough; so he thinks about himself too much. A man like that always gets secretive; not necessarily in the sense of being criminal, or even of being malicious, but merely of being morbid. He is the sort that is ill-treated at school and never says so. As long as a thing terrified him, he couldn't talk about it."

"I don't know how you guessed it," said Garth, "but that is something like the line of discoveries. At first they thought that Simon's silence was guilt, but it was only a fear of something more than guilt; of some diabolic destiny and entanglement. The truth is that when he went up before you to the cliff head at daybreak, he saw something that hag-rode his morbid spirit ever since. He saw the figure of this man Boon poised on the brink of the precipice, black against the dawn, and waving his arms in some unearthly fashion as if he were going to fly. Simon thought the man was talking to himself, and perhaps even singing. Then the strange creature passed on toward the village and was lost in the twilight; but when Simon came to the edge of the cliff he saw Sir Owen lying dead far out on the sands below, beside his easel."

"And ever since, I suppose," observed Gale, "Simon has seen sharks everywhere."

"You are right again," said the doctor. "He has admitted since that a shadow on the blind or a cloud on the moon would have the unmistakable shape of the fish with the fin erect. But in fact, it is a very mistakable shape; anything with a triangular top to it would suggest it to a man in his state of nerves. But the truth is that so long as he thought Boon had dealt death from a distance by some sort of curse or spell, we could get nothing out of him. Our only chance was to show him that Boon might have done it even by natural means. And we did show it, after all."

"What is your theory, then?" asked the other.

"It is too general to be called a theory yet," replied the doctor; "but honestly, I do not think it at all impossible that Boon might have killed a man on the sands from the top of a cliff, without falling back on any supernatural stuff. You've got to consider it like this: Boon has been very deep in the secrets of savages, especially in that litter of islands that lie away toward Australia. Now, we know that such savages, for all they are called ignorant, have developed many dexterities and many unique tools. They have blowpipes that kill at a considerable distance; they harpoon and lasso things, and draw them in on a line. Above all, the Australian savages have discovered the boomerang, that actually returns to the hand. Is it quite so inconceivable that Boon might know some way of sending a penetrating projectile from a distance, and even possibly of recovering it in some way? Dr. Wilkes and I, on examining the wound, found it a very curious one: it was made by some tapering, pointed tool, with a slight curve; and it not only curved upward, but even slightly outward, as if the curve were returning on itself. Does not that suggest to you some outlandish weapon of a strange shape, and possibly with strange properties? And always remember that such an explanation would explain something else as well, which is generally regarded as the riddle. It would explain why the murderer left no footprints round the body."

Gale gazed out to sea in silence, as if considering; then he said simply: "An extremely shrewd argument. But I know why he left no footprints. It is a much simpler explanation than that."

Garth stared at him for a few moments; and then observed gravely: "May I then ask, in return, what is your theory?"

"My theory will seem a maze of theories, and nothing else," said Gale. "It is, as many would say, of such stuff as dreams are made of. Most modern people have a curious contradiction; they abound in theories, yet they never see the part that theories play in practical life. They are always talking about temperament and circumstances and accident; but most men are what their theories make them; most men go in for murder or marriage, or mere lounging because of some theory of life, asserted or assumed. So I can never manage to begin my ex-

planations in that brisk, pointed, practical way that you doctors and
detectives do. I see a man's mind first, sometimes almost without any
particular man attached to it. I could only begin this business by
describing a mental state—which can't be described. Our murderer
or maniac, or whatever you call him, is certainly affected by some of
the elements attributed to him. His view has reached an insane degree of simplicity, and in that sense of savagery. But I doubt whether
he would necessarily transfer the savagery from the end to the
means. In one sense, indeed, his view might be compared to the
barbaric. He saw every creature and even every object naked. He did
not understand that what clothes a thing is sometimes the most real
part of it. Have you ever noticed how true is that old phrase, 'clothed
and in his right mind'? Man is not in his right mind when he is not
clothed with the symbols of his social dignity. Humanity is not even
human when it is naked. But in a lower sense it is so of lesser things,
even of lifeless things. A lot of nonsense is talked about auras; but
this is the truth behind it. Everything has a halo. Everything has a
sort of atmosphere of what it signifies, which makes it sacred. Even
the little creatures he studied had each of them its halo; but he would
not see it."

"But what little creatures did Boon study?" asked Garth in some
wonder. "Do you mean the cannibals?"

"I was not thinking about Boon," replied Gabriel Gale.

"What do you mean?" cried the other, in sudden excitement.
"Why, Boon is almost in the hands of the police."

"Boon is a good man," said Gale calmly; "he is very stupid; that is
why he is an atheist. There are intelligent atheists, as we shall see
presently; but that stunted, stupid sort is much commoner, and much
nicer. But he is a good man; his motive is good; he originally talked
all that tosh of the superiority of the savage because he thought he
was the underdog. He may be a trifle cracked, by now, about sharks
and other things; but that's only because his travels have been too
much for his intellect. They say travel broadens the mind; but you
must have the mind. He had a mind for a suburban chapel, and there
passed before it all the panorama of gilded nature worship and
purple sacrifice. He doesn't know if he's on his head or his heels, any
more than a good many others. But I shouldn't wonder if heaven is
largely populated with atheists of that sort, scratching their heads
and wondering where they are.

"But Boon is a parenthesis; that is all he is. The man I am talking

about is very much the point, and a sharp one at that. He dealt in
something very different from muddled mysticism about human sacrifice. Human sacrifice is quite a human weakness. He dealt in assassination; direct, secret, straight from a head as inhuman as hell. And I
knew it when I first talked to him over the teacups and he said he
saw nothing pretty in a flower."

"My dear fellow!" remonstrated Dr. Garth.

"I don't mean that a man merely dissecting a daisy must be on the
road to the gallows," conceded the poet, magnanimously, "but I do
say that to mean it as he meant it is to be on a straight road of logic
that leads there if he chooses to follow it. God is inside everything.
But this man wanted to be outside everything; to see everything hung
in a vacuum, simply its own dead self. It's not only not the same, it's
almost the opposite of skepticism in the sense of Boon or the Book
of Job. That's a man overwhelmed by the mysteries; but this man
denies that there are any mysteries. It's not, in the ordinary sense, a
matter of theology, but psychology. Most good pagans and pantheists
might talk of the miracles of nature; but this man denies that there
are any miracles, even in the sense of marvels. Don't you see that
dreadful dry light shed on things must at last wither up the moral
mysteries as illusions, respect for age, respect for property, and that
the sanctity of life will be a superstition? The men in the street are
only organisms, with their organs more or less displayed. For such a
one there is no longer any terror in the touch of human flesh, nor does
he see God watching him out of the eyes of a man."

"He may not believe in miracles, but he seems to work them,"
remarked the doctor. "What else was he doing, when he struck a man
down on the sand without leaving a mark to show where he stood?"

"He was paddling," answered Gale.

"As high up on the shore as that?" inquired the other.

Gale nodded. "That was what puzzled me; till something I saw on
the sand started a train of thought that led to my asking the seafaring
people about the tides. It's very simple; the night before we found the
body was a flood tide, and the sea came up higher than usual; not
quite to where Cram was sitting, but pretty near. So that was the way
that the real human fish came out of the sea. That was the way the
divine shark really devoured the sacrifice. The man came paddling in
the foam, like a child on a holiday."

"Who came?" asked Garth; but he shuddered.

"Who did go dredging for sea beasts with a sort of shrimping net along the shore every evening? Who did inherit the money of the old man for his ambitious museum and his scientific career? Who did tell me in the garden that a cowslip was only a growth like a cancer?"

"I am compelled to understand you," said the doctor gloomily. "You mean that very able young man named Wilkes?"

"To understand Wilkes you must understand a good deal," continued his friend. "You must reconstruct the crime, as they say. Look out over that long line of darkening sea and sand, where the last light runs red as blood; that is where he came dredging every day, in the same bloodshot dusk, looking for big beasts and small; and in a true sense everything was fish that came to his net. He was constructing his museum as a sort of cosmos; with everything traced from the fossil to the flying fish. He had spent enormous sums on it, and had got quite disinterestedly into debt; for instance he had had magnificent models made, in wax or papier-mâché, of small fish magnified, or extinct fish restored; things that South Kensington cannot afford, and certainly Wilkes could not afford. But he had persuaded Cram to leave his money to the museum, as you know; and for him Cram was simply a silly old fool, who painted pictures he couldn't paint, and talked of sciences he didn't understand; and whose only natural function was to die and save the museum. Well, when every morning Wilkes had done polishing the glass cases of his masks and models, he came round by the cliff and took a turn at the fossils in the chalk with his geological hammer; then he put it back in that great canvas bag of his, and unslung his long shrimping net and began to wade. This is where I want you to look at that dark red sand and see the picture; one never understands anything till one sees the picture. He went for miles along the shallows of that desolate shore, long inured to seeing one queer creature or another stranded on the sand; here a sea hedgehog, and there a starfish, and then a crab, and then another creature. I have told you he had reached a stage when he would have looked at an angel with the eye of an ornithologist. What would he think of a man, and a man looking like that? Don't you see that poor Cram must have looked like a crab or a sea urchin; his dwarfed, hunched figure seen from behind, with his fan of bristling whiskers, his straggling bow legs and restless twisting feet all tangled up with the three legs of his stool; making him look as if he had five limbs like a starfish? Don't you see he looked like a Common Object of the Seashore? And Wilkes had only to collect this specimen, and all his other specimens were safe. Everything was fish that came to his net, and . . .

"He stretched out the long pole in his hand to its full extent, and drew the net over the old man's head as if he were catching a great gray moth. He plucked him backward off his stool so that he lay kicking on his back on the sand; and doubtless looking more like a large insect than ever. Then the murderer bent forward, propped by one hand upon his pole, and the other armed with his geological hammer. With the pick at the back of that instrument he struck in what he well knew to be a vital spot. The curve you noticed in the wound is due to that sharp side of the hammer being shaped like a pickaxe. But the unusual position of it, and the puzzle of how such a blow could be struck upward, was due to the queer posture of the two figures. The murderer struck at a head that was upside down. It could only occur as a rule if the victim were standing on his head, a posture in which few persons await the assassin. But with the flourish and sweep of the great net, I fancy a starfish caught in it fell out of it, just beyond the dead man's foot. At any rate, it was that starfish and the accident of its lying so high on the shore, that set my mind drifting in the general direction of tides; and the possibility of the murderer having been moving about in the water. If he made any prints the breakers washed them out; and I should never have begun to think of it but for that red five-fingered little monster."

"Then do you mean to tell me," demanded Garth, "that all this business about the shadow of the shark had nothing to do with it?"

"The shadow of the shark had everything to do with it," replied Gale. "The murderer hid in the shadow of the shark, and struck from under the shadow of the shark. I doubt if he would have struck at all, if he had not had the shadow of that fantastic fin in which to hide. And the proof is that he himself took the trouble to emphasize and exaggerate the legend of poor Boon dancing before Dagon. Do you remember that queer incident of the fish's face at the window? How did anybody merely playing a practical joke get hold of a fish's face? It was very lifelike; for it was one of the masks modeled for the Wilkes museum; and Wilkes had left it in the hall in his great canvas bag. It seems simple, doesn't it, for a man to raise an alarm inside a house, walk out to see, and instantly put on a mask and look in at a window? That's all he did; and you can see his idea, from the fact that he proceeded to warn Sir Owen of an enemy. He wanted all this idolatrous and mystical murder business worked for all it was worth, that his own highly reasonable murder might not be noticed. And you see he has succeeded. You tell me that Boon is in the hands of the police."

Garth sprang to his feet. "What is to be done?" he said.

"You will know what to do," said the poet. "You are a good and just man, and a practical man, too. I am not a practical man." He rose with a certain air of apology. "You see, you want an unpractical man for finding out this sort of thing."

And once more he gazed down from the precipice into the abysses below.

A SMALL BURIED TREASURE
By John Fischer

. . . .

Grave robbers are imaginative fellows, especially in Greece.

Aleko became a grave robber mostly out of boredom, though hunger had something to do with it.

He is not a talkative man, so I learned about his profession only obliquely and over a considerable period of time. (His former profession, that is. Now he is a businessman of monumental respectability, the owner of a cherished second-hand Cadillac in which he will drive you anywhere in Europe for quite a reasonable fee.) The first hint came in Salonika, after we had been traveling for days over the rutted, dusty roads of northern Greece.

We had stopped at a sidewalk café for a cup of coffee. On the way back to the car we passed one of those little open-front shops which seem to be the commonest form of enterprise in Macedonia. Its counter was piled with canvas shoes, old clothes, battered lamps and similar castoffs. At one end was a tray of jewelry. I wouldn't have given it a second glance if Aleko hadn't stopped and begun to poke around among the earrings and bangles. Most of them looked as if they had come originally from the Greek equivalent of a dime store, and the one he pointed out to me—a copper-colored bracelet—was even more tarnished than the rest.

"You might buy that," he said. "It won't cost much."

There was nothing I needed less, but I had learned to follow Aleko's suggestions, however odd. He conducted the mandatory haggling and bought it in the end for a few drachmas.

When we were on the road again I asked him why.

"It's old," he said. "Probably about eighth century B.C. I think it came, maybe, from the grave of a little girl. Because it wasn't gold, the grave robbers sold it cheap. They are ignorant fellows mostly." He was silent for a couple of miles, and then added: "I know a little about such things."

(At the time all this sounded unlikely, but weeks later I found out that Aleko was right. Museum people told me that the bracelet was bronze, not copper; its incised decorations were Early Geometric; a few similar pieces are in the Binaki collection in Athens.)

Two days later Aleko asked, diffidently, if I would mind our making a short detour. We were driving east, toward the Turkish border, along the narrow strip of coastal plain at the top of the Aegean Sea. The road originally had been built by the Roman emperors to link their two great seats of power, Constantinople and Rome, but it had deteriorated considerably since their time. A few miles to the north rose the long crest of mountains that mark the Bulgarian border. In their foothills, Aleko said, was the village of Moustheni. No, I wouldn't find it on the map—just a dozen or so stone huts.

"When I left there twenty years ago," he said, "I wore handcuffs. I never expected to go back—but now that we are so close, I would like to drop by and see if they remember me. It would be good for them to see me traveling in my own car and with an American friend."

As we turned onto the rocky track that led toward the foothills, he told me about his boyhood in Moustheni. His family, like most of the others, were tobacco farmers. Except for the few weeks each year when he helped plant, hoe and harvest their three-acre patch, he had no work. Nor was there much else to do—no school, no movies, not even any girls; for in this part of the country, so long under Turkish rule, the women are still secluded. (Many of the older ones never appear in public without their heavy, tentlike veils; the younger ones, never without a chaperon.) So Aleko spent much time with a few other idle youngsters at a table in front of the town's only café, playing cards, nursing a thimbleful of coffee through the long hot afternoons, grumbling about their poverty and boredom.

He doesn't remember who first thought of the tumuli. These are mounds, about ten feet high, which rise like pimples all over the Macedonian plain; along some stretches of road you pass one about every quarter of a mile. Each of them covers a tomb, usually a rough stone enclosure which contains (or once did) the bones of some Bronze Age chief, and sometimes those of his family, servants and horses. (Common people were, presumably, buried with less pretension.) A stranger finds it hard to believe that there could have been so many of them; but, as Aleko pointed out, people as bellicose as the Achaeans and Dorians could manage over a few thousand years of tribal warfare to run through quite a few chiefs.

The young men of Moustheni had heard that archaeologists from Athens recently had been digging in such a mound near the ancient ruins of Amphipolis, not far away. Nobody knew for sure what, if anything, they had found; but there were rumors of much treasure—jeweled sword hilts, necklaces, armlets, statues of solid gold. Why shouldn't the boys do a little digging on their own?

Such enterprises are of course illegal in Greece, and the penalties are severe. But policemen are scarce in the country districts; besides, the Moustheni explorers planned to work at night. As an extra precaution they organized themselves into two shifts of four men each—one to stand sentry while the other dug.

"For the next year," Aleko said, "I labored harder than I ever have in my life. We would tackle a grave just like the archaeologists do—cutting a trench about two feet wide straight through the middle of the mound. If we hit anything promising, we would then open branch trenches to the left or right. And always we would try to finish the job and fill in the trenches before daybreak. We even replaced the sod and bushes as best we could, to avoid attracting attention to our business.

"We must have opened a hundred tumuli without finding a thing except bones and bits of useless pottery. Other grave robbers, you see, had got there first, maybe hundreds of years ago. So all we got for our trouble was calloused palms and aching backs, and naturally we began to get discouraged. Then one night we found it.

"This mound looked exactly like all the others, but somehow the earlier diggers had missed it. Alongside the bones of the old warrior we found all the equipment his people had given him for his last journey—three pots that must have held food and wine, a bronze spearhead, a wreath of gold leaves and a little statue of Hercules. It was only about six inches high, but it was gold—probably from the ancient mines near the headwaters of the Strymon River—and to us the workmanship seemed very fine. None of us had ever seen anything like it.

"But what could we do with it? If we tried to sell such a rarity anywhere in Greece, the authorities would begin to ask questions at once. And how could we find out what it was worth? After so much labor, you understand, we didn't propose to let ourselves be cheated.

"We stopped our nighttime ventures, and for days we sat around the café and talked about this problem. In the end we worked out a very clever scheme. . . ."

At this point Aleko's account was interrupted by our arrival at Moustheni. It looked even grimmer than he had led me to expect—a single cobbled street twisting up the hillside between two rows of gray hovels. But there was nothing grim about the people. As we came abreast of the first house, Aleko began to honk his horn, and the whole village—including a remarkable number of dogs and babies—poured out to follow. The appearance of any automobile here was cause for excitement enough, but when they recognized the man at the wheel the uproar really cut loose. If St. Demetrios himself had ridden into town on his spectral white stallion, he couldn't have produced more astonishment, or noise.

Aleko inched the car along to the café, where he had plotted with his friends so many years ago, and stopped to receive homage. At this place the street widens a little, to form a sort of village square. Though it was crowded to the walls, somebody managed to drag a couple of tables out to the center, and after Aleko had introduced me to what I took to be the village elders, we sat down with them for a ceremonial round of *ouzo* and thick, bitter coffee. Aleko insisted on paying for everything. While I couldn't understand a word of the conversation, it was clear that he was enacting—with great dignity—the Prodigal's Return.

His sense of timing was flawless. In precisely twenty minutes he rose, shook hands again with everybody, and led the procession back to his car—the very image of the man of affairs who has to be off to the pressing business of the outside world. A swarm of children and dogs, in full cry, raced beside us until we passed the last house.

All the way back to the main road Aleko grinned in silent satisfaction. I had a hard time getting him to pick up the thread of his story.

"One of the men you met back there—the one who passed around the tobacco and cigarette papers—is Philip Galas," he said. "He is a farmer now, but in the old days he was one of our diggers. He had relatives in Kavala, and there he had met a jeweler and pawnbroker—a rich man but trustworthy. To get our scheme under way, Philip took the statue to him and persuaded him to make an exact copy.

Naturally we had to promise him a share—a full one-ninth—of the wealth we expected to have before long.

"The jeweler then carried his copy to the local museum and tried to sell it, saying that it had been pawned in his shop over a year ago and that the owner had never reclaimed it. The curator, of course, refused. He explained that it was only a modern reproduction, though a good one, and therefore worth little more than the metal it contained. Our friend pretended great disappointment. But if it *had* been genuine, he asked, what price would it have brought? At least a million drachmas, the museum man told him. Perhaps more, for such works of art from the archaic period were very rare indeed.

"Once we had that information, we knew just what to do next. From our fathers and the jeweler we borrowed enough money to send one member of our band—you will forgive me if I don't mention his name—to Paris. He carried the little Hercules, the real one, baked inside a loaf of bread. It was a safe hiding place, since nearly all peasants carry a parcel of bread and sausage when they go traveling, and the customs guards never pay it any attention.

"In Paris our messenger had no great trouble in finding a dealer willing to pay a fair price and ask no questions."

Aleko lapsed into one of his long silences; I thought the story was finished. When he began talking again, it was about Greek history.

"The habit of betrayal has always been our great weakness," he said. "Remember Alcibiades? Remember Ephialtes, who sold the pass at Thermopylae? Such men are more typical than you might think. Every city in Greece has its legend of at least one betrayer. So has Moustheni.

"Our agent didn't come home. Instead he went to Athens with our money in his pocket, and wrote an unsigned letter to the national police, telling them all about our little venture in midnight archaeology. So a truckload of policemen pulled into the village one morning, and arrested all seven of us. They took us to the Kavala court, where the judge sentenced us to a big fine and many years in jail. If the war hadn't broken out that fall, I might have been in prison yet."

What happened, he explained, was that the royal government had opened the jail doors for every man who wanted to fight the invaders. Aleko and his friends set off for the mountains, with no equipment except a rifle and a belt of cartridges apiece, and fought for five years against Italians, Germans and Bulgarians. When the war was over, nobody felt inclined to remember the old charges.

"But the archaeologists didn't forget our statue," he added. "With the help of the French police they eventually got their hands on the little Hercules. You can see it any day you like in the Kavala museum—the finest piece in its collection. We never got a penny for it, of course."

Did he know, I asked, what had become of the man who turned them in?

"Yes," Aleko said, "he came back to Macedonia after the war. Perhaps he too thought that old scores would be forgotten. He was mistaken."

For a long while we had met no one along the road. Now we saw ahead of us two old women on minute donkeys, riding sidesaddle in the fashion of the country. Aleko pulled up beside them to ask about the turnoff for Keramoti, the fishing village where he was to leave me and where I hoped to find some sort of boat to take me on the next leg of my journey. When we were on our way again, he said:

"There is one thing about these old graves. When everybody knows that one of them has been opened—as, for example, the one where we found the treasure—it is no longer of interest. Nobody else is likely to look inside it again, maybe not for centuries. It makes an ideal place to hide a body."

THE HORLA
By Guy de Maupassant

· ·

"I was sure, as sure as I am that day follows night,
that there lived at my side an invisible being
who fed on milk and water."

May 8. What a glorious day! I have spent the whole morning lying on the grass in front of my house, under the enormous plane tree that forms a complete covering, shelter and shade for it. I love this country, and I love living here because it is here I have my roots, those deep-down slender roots that hold a man to the place where his forefathers were born and died, hold him to ways of thought and habits of eating, to customs as to particular foods, to local fashions of speech, to the intonations of country voices, to the scent of the soil, the villages and the very air itself.

I love this house of mine where I grew up. From my windows I see the Seine flowing alongside my garden, beyond the high road, almost at my door, the great wide Seine, running from Rouen to Havre, covered with passing boats.

Away to the left, Rouen, the vast city, with its blue roofs lying under the bristling host of Gothic belfries. They are beyond number, frail or sturdy, dominated by the leaden steeples of the cathedral, and filled with bells that ring out in the limpid air of fine mornings, sending me the sweet and far-off murmur of their iron tongues, a brazen song borne to me on the breeze, now louder, now softer, as it swells or dies away.

How beautiful this morning has been!

Toward eleven o'clock a long convoy of boats followed each other past my gate, behind a squat tug looking like a fly, and wheezing painfully as it vomited thick clouds of smoke.

After two English yachts, whose red flags waved against the sky, came a splendid three-master, all white, gloriously clean and glittering. The sight of this ship filled me with such joy that I saluted her, I don't know why.

May 11. I have had a slight fever for the last few days; I feel ill or rather unhappy.

Whence come these mysterious influences that change our happiness to dejection and our self-confidence to discouragement? It is as if the air, the unseen air, were full of unknowable powers whose mysterious nearness we endure. I wake full of joy, my throat swelling with a longing to sing. Why? I go down to the waterside; and suddenly, after a short walk, I come back home wretched, as if some misfortune were waiting me there. Why? Has a chill shudder, passing lightly over my skin, shaken my nerves and darkened my spirit? Have the shapes of the clouds or the color of the day, the ever-changing color of the visible world, troubled my mind as they slipped past my eyes? Does anyone know? Everything that surrounds us, everything that we see unseeing, everything that we brush past unknowing, everything that we touch impalpably, everything that we meet unnoticing, has on us, on the organs of our bodies, and through them on our thoughts, on our very hearts, swift, surprising and inexplicable effects.

How deep it is, this mystery of the Invisible! We cannot fathom it with our miserable senses, with our eyes that perceive neither the too small, nor the too great, nor the too near, nor the too distant, nor the inhabitants of a star, nor the inhabitants of a drop of water . . . with our ears that deceive us, transmitting the vibrations of the air to us as sonorous sounds. They are fairies who by a miracle transmute movement into sound, from which metamorphosis music is born, and make audible in song the mute quivering of nature . . . with our smell, feebler than a dog's . . . with our taste, that can only just detect the age of a wine.

If only we had other organs to work other miracles on our behalf, what things we could discover round us!

May 16. I am certainly ill, I was so well last month. I have a fever, a terrible fever, or rather a feverish edginess that oppresses my mind as much as my body. All day and every day I suffer this frightful sense of threatened danger, this apprehension of coming ill or approaching death, this presentiment which is doubtless the warning signal of a lurking disease germinating in my blood and my flesh.

May 18. I have just consulted my doctor, for I was not getting any sleep. He found that my pulse is rapid, my eyes dilated, my nerves on edge, but no alarming symptom of any kind. I am to take cold showers and drink bromide of potassium.

May 25. No change. My case is truly strange. As night falls, an incomprehensible uneasiness fills me, as if the night concealed a frightful menace directed at me. I dine in haste, then I try to read; but I don't understand the words: I can hardly make out the letters. So I walk backward and forward in my drawing room, oppressed by a vague fear that I cannot throw off, fear of sleeping and fear of my bed.

About ten o'clock I go up to my room. The instant I am inside the room I double-lock the door and shut the windows; I am afraid . . . of what? I never dreaded anything before. . . . I open my cupboards, I look under my bed; I listen . . . listen . . . to what? It's a queer thing that a mere physical ailment, some disorder in the blood perhaps, the jangling of a nerve thread, a slight congestion, the least disturbance in the functioning of this living machine of ours, so imperfect and so frail, can make a melancholic of the happiest of men and a coward of the bravest. Then I lie down, and wait for sleep as if I were waiting to be executed. I wait for it, dreading its approach; my heart beats, my legs tremble; my whole body shivers in the warmth of the bed-clothes, until the moment I fall suddenly on sleep, like a man falling into deep and stagnant waters, there to drown. Nowadays I never feel the approach of this perfidious sleep, that lurks near me, spying on me, ready to take me by the hand, shut my eyes, steal my strength.

I sleep—for a long time—two or three hours—then a dream—no—a nightmare seizes me. I feel that I am lying down and that I am asleep. . . . I feel it and I know it . . . and I feel too that someone approaches me, looks at me, touches me, climbs on my bed, kneels on my chest, takes my neck between his hands and squeezes . . . squeezes . . . with all his might, strangling me.

I struggle madly, in the grip of the frightful impotence that paralyzes us in dreams; I try to cry out—I can't; I try to move—I can't;

panting, with the most frightful efforts, I try to turn round, to fling off this creature who is crushing and choking me—I can't do it.

And suddenly I wake up, terrified, covered with sweat. I light a candle. I am alone.

The crisis over—a crisis that happens every night—I fall at last into a quiet sleep, until daybreak.

June 2. My case has grown worse. What can be the matter with me? Bromide is useless; showers are useless. Lately, by way of wearying a body already quite exhausted, I went for a tramp in the forest of Roumare. At first I thought that the fresh air, the clear sweet air, full of the scents of grass and trees, was pouring a new blood into my veins and a new strength into my heart. I followed a broad glade, then I turned toward Boville, by a narrow walk between two ranks of immensely tall trees that flung a thick green roof, almost a black roof, between the sky and me.

A sudden shudder ran through me, not a shudder of cold but a strange shudder of anguish.

I quickened my pace, uneasy at being alone in this wood, unreasonably, stupidly, terrified by the profound solitude. Abruptly I felt that I was being followed, that someone was on my heels, very close, close enough to touch me.

I swung round. I was alone. I saw behind me only the straight open walk, empty, high, terrifyingly empty; it stretched out in front of me too, as far as the eye could see, as empty, and frightening.

I shut my eyes. Why? And I began to turn round on my heel at a great rate like a top. I almost fell; I opened my eyes again; the trees were dancing; the earth was swaying; I was forced to sit down. Then, ah! I didn't know now which way I had been walking. Strange thought! Strange! Strange thought! I didn't know anything at all now. I took the right-hand way, and found myself back in the avenue that had led me into the middle of the forest.

June 3. The night has been terrible. I am going to go away for several weeks. A short journey will surely put me right.

July 2. Home again. I am cured. I have had, moreover, a delightful holiday. I visited Mont-Saint-Michel, which I didn't know.

What a vision one gets, arriving at Avranches as I did, toward dusk! The town lies on a slope, and I was taken into the public garden, at the end of the city. A cry of astonishment broke from me. A shoreless bay stretched before me, as far as eye could see: it lay between opposing coasts that vanished in distant mist; and in the midst of this vast tawny bay, under a gleaming golden sky, a strange hill, somber and peaked, thrust up from the sands at its feet. The sun had just sunk, and on a horizon still riotous with color was etched the outline of this fantastic rock that bore on its summit a fantastic monument.

At daybreak I went out to it. The tide was low, as on the evening before, and as I drew near it, the miraculous abbey grew in height before my eyes. After several hours' walking I reached the monstrous pile of stones that supports the little city dominated by the great church. I clambered up the steep narrow street, I entered the most wonderful Gothic dwelling made for God on this earth, as vast as a town, with innumerable low rooms hollowed out under the vaults and high galleries slung over slender columns. I entered this gigantic granite jewel, as delicate as a piece of lace, pierced everywhere by towers and airy belfries where twisting stairways climb, towers and belfries that by day against a blue sky and by night against a dark sky lift strange heads, bristling with chimeras, devils, fantastic beasts and monstrous flowers, and are linked together by slender carved arches.

When I stood on the top I said to the monk who accompanied me: "What a glorious place you have here, Father!"

"We get strong winds," he answered, and we fell into talk as we watched the incoming sea run over the sand and cover it with a steel cuirass.

The monk told me stories, all the old stories of this place, legends, always legends.

One of them particularly impressed me. The people of the district, those who lived on the Mount, declared that at night they heard voices on the sands, followed by the bleating of two goats, one that called loudly and one calling softly. Unbelievers insisted that it was the crying of sea birds which at one and the same time resembled bleatings and the wailing of human voices: but late-returning fishermen swore that they had met an old shepherd wandering on the dunes, between two tides, round the little town flung so far out of the world. No one ever saw the head hidden in his cloak: he led, walking in front of them, a goat with the face of a man and a she-goat with the face of a woman; both of them had long white hair and talked incessantly, disputing in an unknown tongue, then abruptly ceased shouting to begin a loud bleating.

"Do you believe it?" I asked the monk.

He murmured: "I don't know."

"If," I went on, "there existed on the earth beings other than ourselves, why have we not long ago learned to know them; why have you yourself not seen them? Why have I not seen them myself?"

He answered: "Do we see the hundred thousandth part of all that exists? Think, there's the wind, the greatest force in nature, which throws down men, shatters buildings, uproots trees, stirs up the sea into watery mountains, destroys cliffs and tosses the tall ships against the shore, the wind that kills, whistles, groans, roars—have you seen it, can you see it? Nevertheless, it exists."

Before his simple reasoning I fell silent. This man was either a seer or a fool. I should not have cared to say which; but I held my peace. What he had just said, I had often thought.

July 3. I slept badly; I am sure there is a feverish influence at work here, for my coachman suffers from the same trouble as myself. When I came home yesterday, I noticed his strange pallor.

"What's the matter with you, Jean?" I demanded.

"I can't rest any more, sir; my nights are eating up my days. Since you went away, sir, this has been on me like a spell."

The other servants are all right, however, but I am terrified of getting caught by it again.

July 4. It has surely caught me again. My old nightmares have come back. Last night I felt crouching on me someone who presses his mouth on mine and drinks my life between my lips. Yes, he sucked it from my throat like a leech. Then he rose from me, replete, and I awoke, so battered, bruised, enfeebled, that I could not move. If this goes on for many days more, I shall certainly go away again.

July 5. Have I lost my reason? What has just happened, what I saw last night, is so strange that my head reels when I think of it.

Following my invariable custom in the evenings, I had locked my door; then, feeling thirsty, I drank half a glass of water and I happened to notice that my carafe was filled up right to its crystal stopper.

I lay down after this and fell into one of my dreadful slumbers, from which I was jerked about two hours later by a shock more frightful than any of the others.

Imagine a sleeping man, who has been assassinated, and who wakes with a knife through his lung, with the death rattle in his throat, covered with blood, unable to breathe, and on the point of death, understanding nothing—and there you have it.

When I finally recovered my sanity, I was thirsty again; I lit a candle and went toward the table where I had placed my carafe. I lifted it and held it over my glass; not a drop ran out. It was empty! It was completely empty. At first, I simply didn't understand; then all at once I was so overcome that I was forced to sit down, or say rather that I fell into a chair! Then I leaped up again and looked round me! Then I sat down again, lost in surprise and fear, in front of the transparent crystal. I gazed at it with a fixed stare, seeking an answer to the riddle. My hands were trembling. Had someone drunk the water? Who? I? It must have been me. Who could it have been but me? So I was a somnambulist, all unaware I was living the mysterious double life that raises the doubt whether there be not two selves in us, or whether, in moments when the spirit lies unconscious, an alien self, unknowable and unseen, inhabits the captive body that obeys this other self as it obeys us, obeys it more readily than it obeys us.

Oh, can anyone understand my frightful agony? Can anyone understand the feelings of a sane-minded, educated, thoroughly rational man, staring in abject terror through the glass of his carafe, where the water has disappeared while he slept? I remained there until daylight, not daring to go back to bed.

July 6. I am going mad. My carafe was emptied again last night— or rather, I emptied it.

But is it I? Is it I? Who can it be? Who? Oh, my God! Am I going mad? Who will save me?

July 10. I have just made some astonishing experiments.

Decidedly. I am mad! And yet . . .

On the sixth of July, before lying down in bed, I placed on my table wine, milk, water, bread and strawberries.

Someone drank—I drank—all the water, and a little of the milk. Neither the wine, nor the bread, nor the strawberries were touched.

On the 7th of July, I made the same experiment and got the same result.

On the 8th of July, I omitted the water and the milk. Nothing was touched.

Finally, on the 9th of July, I placed only the water and milk on my table, taking care to wrap the carafes in white muslin cloths and to tie down the stoppers. Then I rubbed my lips, my beard and my hands with a charcoal pencil and lay down.

The usual overpowering sleep seized me, followed shortly by the frightful wakening. I had not moved, my bedclothes themselves bore no marks. I rushed toward my table. The cloths wrapped around the bottles remained spotless. I untied the cords, shaking with fear. All the water had been drunk! All the milk had been drunk! Oh, my God! . . .

I am leaving for Paris at once.

July 12. Paris. I suppose I lost my head during the last few days! I must have been the sport of my disordered imagination, unless I really am a somnambulist or have fallen under one of those indubitable but hitherto inexplicable influences that we call suggestions. However that may be, my disorder came very near to lunacy, and twenty-four hours in Paris have been enough to restore my balance.

Yesterday I went to the races and made various calls. I felt myself endowed with new vital strength, and I ended my evening at the Théâtre Français. They were presenting a play by the younger Dumas; and his alert forceful intelligence completed my cure. There can be no doubt that loneliness is dangerous to active minds. We need round us men who think and talk. When we live alone for long periods, we people the void with phantoms.

I returned to the hotel in high spirits, walking along the boulevards. Amid the jostling of the crowd, I thought ironically on my terrors, on my hallucinations of a week ago, when I had believed, yes, believed that an invisible being dwelt under my roof. How weak and shaken and speedily unbalanced our brains are immediately they are confronted by a tiny incomprehensible fact!

Instead of coming to a conclusion in these simple words: "I do not understand because the cause eludes me," at once we imagine frightening mysteries and supernatural powers.

July 14. Fête de la République. I walked through the streets. The firecrackers and the flags filled me with a childish joy. At the same time, it is vastly silly to be joyous on a set day by order of the government. The mob is an imbecile herd, as stupid in its patience as it is savage when roused. You say to it: "Enjoy yourself," and it enjoys itself. You say to it: "Go and fight your neighbor." It goes to fight. You say to it: "Vote for the Emperor." It votes for the Emperor. Then you say to it: "Vote for the Republic." And it votes for the Republic.

Its rulers are just as stupid; but instead of obeying men they obey principles, which can only be half-baked, sterile and false in so much as they are principles, that is to say, ideas reputed certain and immutable, in this world where nothing is sure, since light and sound are both illusions.

July 16. Yesterday I saw some things that have profoundly disturbed me.

I dined with my cousin, Mme. Sablé, whose husband commands the 76th Light Horse at Limoges. At her house I met two young women, one of whom has married a doctor, Dr. Parent, who devotes himself largely to nervous illnesses and the extraordinary discoveries that are the outcome of the recent experiments in hypnotism and suggestion.

He told us at length about the amazing results obtained by English scientists and by the doctors of the Nancy school.

The facts that he put forward struck me as so fantastic that I confessed myself utterly incredulous.

"We are," he declared, "on the point of discovering one of the most important secrets of nature, I mean one of the most important secrets on this earth; for there are certainly others as important, away yonder, in the stars. Since man began to think, since he learned to express and record his thoughts, he has felt the almost impalpable touch of a mystery impenetrable by his clumsy and imperfect senses, and he has tried to supplement the impotence of his organic powers by the force of his intelligence. While this intelligence was still in a rudimentary stage, this haunting sense of invisible phenomena clothed itself in terrors such as occur to simple minds. Thus are born popular theories of the supernatural, the legends of wandering spirits, fairies, gnomes, ghosts. I'll add the God-myth itself, since our conceptions of the artificer-creator, to whatever religion they belong, are really the most uninspired, the most unintelligent, the most inacceptable products of the fear-clouded brain of human beings. Nothing is truer than that saying of Voltaire's: 'God has made man in His image, but man has retorted upon Him in kind.'

"But for a little over a century we have had glimpse of a new knowledge. Mesmer and others have set our feet on a fresh path, and, more specially during the last four or five years, we have actually reached surprising results."

My cousin, as incredulous as I, smiled. Dr. Parent said to her: "Shall I try to put you to sleep, Madame?"

"Yes, do."

She seated herself in an armchair, and he looked fixedly into her eyes, proceeding to fascinate her. As for me, I felt suddenly uneasy: my heart thumped, my throat contracted. I saw Mme. Sablé's eyes grow heavy, her mouth twitch, her bosom rise and fall with her quick breathing.

Within ten minutes she was asleep.

"Go behind her," said the doctor.

I seated myself behind her. He put a visiting card in her hands and said to her: "Here is a looking glass: what can you see in it?"

"I see my cousin," she answered.

"What is he doing?"

"He is twisting his mustache."

"And now?"

"He is drawing a photograph from his pocket."

"Whose photograph is it?"

"His."

She was right! And this photograph had been sent me at my hotel only that very evening.

"What is he doing in the photograph?"

"He is standing, with his hat in his hand."

Evidently she saw, in this card, this piece of white pasteboard, as she would have seen in a glass.

The young women, terrified, cried: "That's enough! Enough! Enough!"

But the doctor said authoritatively: "You will get up tomorrow at eight o'clock; then you will call on your cousin at his hotel and you will beg him to lend you five thousand francs that your husband has asked you to get and will exact on his next leave."

Then he woke her up.

On my way back to the hotel, I thought about this curious séance, and I was assailed by doubts, not of the absolutely unimpeachable good faith of my cousin, whom since our childhood I had looked upon as my sister, but of the possibility of trickery on the doctor's part. Had he concealed a looking glass in his hand and held it before the slumbering young woman when he was holding before her his visiting card? Professional conjurers do things as strange.

I had reached the hotel by now and I went to bed.

Then in the morning, towards half-past eight, I was roused by my man, who said to me:

"Mme. Sablé wishes to speak to you at once, sir."

I got hurriedly into my clothes and had her shown in.

She seated herself, very agitated, her eyes downcast, and, without lifting her veil, said:

"I have a great favor to ask you, my dear cousin."

"What is it, my dear?"

"I hate to ask it of you, and yet I must. I need, desperately, five thousand francs."

"You? You need it?"

"Yes, I, or rather my husband, who has told me to get it."

I was so astounded that I stammered as I answered her. I wondered whether she and Dr. Parent were not actually making fun of me, whether it weren't a little comedy they had prepared beforehand and were acting very well.

But as I watched her closely my doubts vanished entirely. The whole affair was so painful to her that she was trembling with distress, and I saw that her throat was quivering with sobs.

I knew that she was very rich and I added:

"What! do you mean to say that your husband can't call on five thousand francs! Come, think. Are you sure he told you to ask me for it?"

She hesitated for a few moments as if she were making a tremendous effort to search her memory, then she answered:

"Yes . . . yes . . . I'm quite sure."

"Has he written to you?"

She hesitated again, reflecting. I guessed at the tortured striving of her mind. She didn't know. She knew nothing except that she had to borrow five thousand francs from me for her husband. Then she plucked up courage to lie.

"Yes, he has written to me."

"But when? You didn't speak to me about it yesterday."

"I got his letter this morning."

"Can you let me see it?"

"No . . . no . . . no . . . it is very intimate . . . too personal. . . . I've . . . I've burned it."

"Your husband must be in debt, then."

Again she hesitated, then murmured: "I don't know."

I told her abruptly: "The fact is I can't lay my hands on five thousand francs at the moment, my dear."

A kind of agonized wail broke from her.

"Oh, I implore you, I implore you, get it for me."

She grew dreadfully excited, clasping her hands as if she were praying to me. The tone of her voice changed as I listened: she wept, stammering, torn with grief, goaded by the irresistible command that had been laid on her.

"Oh, I implore you to get it. . . . If you knew how unhappy I am! . . . I must have it today."

I took pity on her.

"You shall have it at once, I promise you."

"Thank you, thank you," she cried. "How kind you are!"

"Do you remember," I went on, "what happened at your house yesterday evening?"

"Yes."

"Do you remember that Dr. Parent put you to sleep?"

"Yes."

"Very well, he ordered you to come this morning and borrow five thousand francs from me, and you are now obeying the suggestion."

She considered this for a moment and answered: "Because my husband wants it."

I spent an hour trying to convince her, but I did not succeed in doing so.

When she left, I ran to the doctor's house. He was just going out, and he listened to me with a smile. Then he said: "Now do you believe?"

"I must."

"Let's go and call on your cousin."

She was already dozing on a day bed, overwhelmed with weariness. The doctor felt her pulse, and looked at her for some time, one hand lifted toward her eyes that slowly closed under the irresistible compulsion of his magnetic force.

When she was asleep:

"Your husband has no further need for five thousand francs. You will forget that you begged your cousin to lend it to you, and if he speaks to you about it, you will not understand."

Then he woke her up. I drew a wallet from my pocket.

"Here is what you asked me for this morning, my dear."

She was so dumfounded that I dared not press the matter. I did, however, try to rouse her memory, but she denied it fiercely, thought I was making fun of her and at last was ready to be angry with me.

Back at the hotel. The experience has disturbed me so profoundly that I could not bring myself to take lunch.

July 19. I have told several people about this adventure and been laughed at for my pains. I don't know what to think now. The wise man says: Perhaps?

July 21. I dined at Bougival, then I spent the evening at the rowing-club dance. There's no doubt that everything is a question of places and persons. To believe in the supernatural on the island of La Grenouillère would be the height of folly . . . but at the top of Mont-Saint-Michel? . . . in the Indies? We are terrified under the influence of our surroundings. I am going home next week.

July 30. I have been home since yesterday. All is well.

August 2. Nothing new. The weather has been glorious. I spend my days watching the Seine run past.

August 4. The servants are quarrelling among themselves. They declare that someone breaks the glasses in the cupboard at night. My man blames the cook, who blames the housemaid, who blames the other two. Who is the culprit? It would take a mighty clever man to find out.

August 6. This time, I am not mad. I've seen . . . I've seen . . . I've seen! . . . I have no more doubts. . . . I've seen. . . . I'm still cold to my fingertips. . . . I'm still penetrated with fear to the marrow of my bones . . . I have seen! . . .

At two o'clock, in broad daylight, I was walking in my rose garden . . . between the autumn roses that are just coming out.

As I paused to look at a *Géant des Batailles,* which bore three superb flowers, I saw, I distinctly saw, right under my eye, the stem of one of these roses bend as if an invisible hand had twisted it, then break as if the hand had plucked it. Then the flower rose, describing in the air the curve that an arm would have made carrying it toward a mouth, and it hung suspended in the clear air, quite alone, motionless, a terrifying scarlet splash three paces from my eyes.

I lost my head and flung myself on it, grasping at it. My fingers closed on nothing: it had disappeared. Then I was filled with a savage rage against myself; a rational, serious-minded man simply does not have such hallucinations.

But was it really an hallucination? I turned to look for the stem, and I perceived it immediately, on the bush, freshly broken off, between two other roses that still remained on the branch.

Then I went back to the house, my senses reeling: now I was sure, as sure as I am that day follows night, that there lived at my side an invisible being who fed on milk and water, who could touch things, take them, move them from one place to another, endowed therefore with a material nature, imperceptible to our senses though it was, and living, as I live, under my roof. . . .

August 7. I slept quietly. He has drunk the water from my carafe, but he did not disturb my sleep.

I wonder if I am mad. Sometimes as I walk in the blazing sunshine along the river bank, I am filled with doubts of my sanity, not the vague doubts I have been feeling, but precise and uncompromising doubts. I have seen madmen; I have known men who were intelligent, lucid, even exceptionally clear-headed in everything in life but on one point. They talked quite clearly, easily and profoundly about everything, until suddenly their mind ran on to the rocks of their madness and was there rent in pieces, strewn to the winds and foundered in the fearful raging sea, filled with surging waves, fogs, squalls, that we call "insanity."

I should certainly have thought myself mad, absolutely mad, if I were not conscious, if I were not perfectly aware of my state of mind, if I did not get to the bottom of it and analyze it with such complete clearness. I must be, in fact, no worse than a sane man troubled with hallucinations. There must be some unknown disturbance in my brain, one of those disturbances that modern physiologists are trying to observe and elucidate; and this disturbance has opened a deep gulf in my mind, in the orderly and logical working of my thoughts. Similar phenomena take place in a dream that drags us through the most unreal phantasmagoria without sowing the least surprise in our minds because the mechanism of judgment, the controlling censor, is asleep, while the imaginative faculty wakes and works. Can one of the invisible strings that control my mental keyboard have become muted?

Sometimes, after an accident, a man loses his power to remember proper names or verbs or figures or only dates. The localization of all the different faculties of the mind is now proved. Is there anything surprising, therefore, in the idea that my power of examining the unreality of certain hallucinations has ceased to function in my brain just now?

I thought of all this as I walked by the side of the water. The sunlight flung a mantle of light across the river, clothing the earth with beauty, filling my thoughts with love of life, of the swallows whose swift flight is a joy to my eyes, of the riverside grasses whose shuddering whisper contents my ears.

Little by little, however, I fell prey to an inexplicable uneasiness. I felt as though some force, an occult force, were paralyzing my movements, halting me, hindering me from going on any further, calling me back. I was oppressed by just such an unhappy impulse to turn back as one feels when a beloved person has been left at home ill and one is possessed by a foreboding that the illness has taken a turn for the worse.

So, in spite of myself, I turned back, sure that I should find bad news waiting in my house, a letter or a telegram. There was nothing; and I was left more surprised and uneasy than if I had had yet another fantastic vision.

August 8. Yesterday I spent a frightful evening. He did not manifest himself again, but I felt him near me, spying on me, watching me, taking possession of me, dominating me and more to be feared when he hid himself in this way than if he gave notice of his constant invisible presence by supernatural phenomena.

However, I slept.

August 9. Nothing, but I am afraid.

August 10. Nothing; what will happen tomorrow?

August 11. Still nothing: I can't remain in my home any longer, with this fear and these thoughts in my mind: I shall go away.

August 12. Ten o'clock in the evening. I have been wanting to go away all day. I can't. I have been wanting to carry out the easy simple act that will set me free—go out—get into my carriage to go to Rouen—I can't. Why?

August 13. Under the affliction of certain maladies, all the resources of one's physical being seem crushed, all one's energy exhausted, one's muscles relaxed, one's bones grown as soft as flesh and one's flesh turned to water. In a strange and wretched fashion I suffer all these pains in my spiritual being. I have no strength, no courage, no control over myself, no power even to summon up my will. I can will nothing; but someone wills for me—and I obey.

August 14. I am lost. Someone has taken possession of my soul and is master of it; someone orders all my acts, all my movements, all my thoughts. I am no longer anything, I am only a spectator, enslaved, and terrified by all the things I do. I wish to go out. I cannot. He does not wish it; and I remain, dazed, trembling, in the armchair where he keeps me seated. I desire no more than to get up, to raise myself, so that I can think I am master of myself again. I can't do it. I am riveted to my seat; and my seat is fast to the ground, in such fashion that no force could lift us.

Then, all at once, I must, must, must go to the bottom of my garden and pick strawberries and eat them. And I go. I pick strawberries and I eat them. Oh, my God! my God! my God! Is there a God? If there is one, deliver me, save me, help me! Pardon me! Pity me! Have mercy on me! How I suffer! How I am tortured! How terrible this is!

August 15. Well, think how my poor cousin was possessed and overmastered when she came to borrow five thousand francs from me. She submitted to an alien will that had entered into her, as if it were another soul, a parasitic tyrannical soul. Is the world coming to an end?

But what is this being, this invisible being who is ruling me? This unknowable creature, this wanderer from a supernatural race.

So Unseen Ones exist? Then why is it that since the world began they have never manifested themselves in so unmistakable a fashion as they are now manifesting themselves to me? I have never read of anything like the things that are happening under my roof. If I could only leave it, if I could go away, fly far away and return no more, I should be saved, but I can't.

August 16. Today I was able to escape for two hours, like a prisoner who finds the door of his cell accidentally left open. I felt that I was suddenly set free, that he had withdrawn himself. I ordered the horses to be put in the carriage as quickly as possible and I reached Rouen. Oh, what a joy it was to find myself able to tell a man: "Go to Rouen," and be obeyed!

I stopped at the library and I asked them to lend me the long treatise of Dr. Hermann Herestauss on the unseen inhabitants of the antique and modern worlds.

Then, just as I was getting back into my carriage, with the words, "To the station," on my lips, I shouted—I didn't speak, I shouted—in a voice so loud that the passers-by turned round: "Home," and I fell, overwhelmed with misery, onto the cushions of my carriage. He had found me again and taken possession once more.

August 17. What a night! what a night! Nevertheless it seems to me that I ought to congratulate myself. I read until one o'clock in the morning. Hermann Herestauss, a doctor of philosophy and theogony, has written an account of all the invisible beings who wander among men or have been imagined by men's minds. He describes their origins, their domains, their power. But none of them is the least like the being who haunts me. It is as if man, the thinker, has had a foreboding vision of some new being, mightier than himself, who shall succeed him in this world; and, in his terror, feeling him draw near, and unable to guess at the nature of this master, he has created all the fantastic crowd of occult beings, dim phantoms born of fear.

Well, I read until one o'clock and then I seated myself near my open window to cool my head and my thoughts in the gentle air of night.

It was fine and warm. In other days how I should have loved such a night!

No moon. The stars wavered and glittered in the black depths of the sky. Who dwells in these worlds? What forms of life, what living creatures, what animals or plants do they hold? What more than we do the thinkers in those far-off universes know? What more can they do than we? What do they see that we do not know of? Perhaps one of them, some day or other, will cross the gulf of space and appear on our earth as a conqueror, just as in olden days the Normans crossed the sea to subdue weaker nations.

We are so infirm, so defenseless, so ignorant, so small, on this grain of dust that revolves and crumbles in a drop of water.

So dreaming, I fell asleep, in the fresh evening air.

I slept for about forty minutes and opened my eyes again without moving, roused by I know not what vague and strange emotions. At first I saw nothing, then all at once I thought that the page of a book lying open on my table had turned over of itself. Not a breath of air came in at the window. I was surprised and I sat waiting. About four minutes later, I saw, I saw, yes, I saw with my own eyes another page come up and turn back on the preceding one, as if a finger had folded it back. My armchair was empty, seemed empty; but I realized that he was there, he, sitting in my place and reading. In one wild spring, like the spring of a mutinous beast resolved to eviscerate his trainer, I crossed the room to seize him and crush him and kill him. But before I had reached it my seat turned right over as if he had fled before me . . . my table rocked, my lamp fell and was extinguished, and my window slammed shut as if I had surprised a malefactor who had flung himself out into the darkness, tugging at the sashes with all his force.

So he had run away; he had been afraid, afraid of me, me!

Then . . . then . . . tomorrow . . . or the day after or someday . . . I should be able to hold him under my fists, and crush him against the ground. Don't dogs sometimes bite and fly at their masters' throats?

August 18. I've been thinking things over all day. Oh, yes, I'll obey him, satisfy his impulses, do his will, make myself humble, submissive, servile. He is the stronger. But an hour will come. . . .

August 19. I know now. . . . I know. . . . I know everything! I have just read the following in the *Revue du Monde Scientifique*: "A strange piece of news reaches us from Rio de Janeiro. Madness, an epidemic of madness, comparable to the contagious outbursts of dementia that attacked the peoples of Europe in the Middle Ages, is raging at this day in the district of San Paulo. The distracted inhabitants are quitting their homes, deserting their villages, abandoning their fields, declaring themselves to be pursued, possessed and ordered about like a human herd by certain invisible but tangible beings, vampires of some kind, who feed on their vitality while they sleep, in addition to drinking milk and water without, apparently, touching any other form of food.

"Professor Don Pedro Henriquez, accompanied by several learned doctors, has set out for the district of San Paulo, to study on the spot the origins and the forms taken by this surprising madness, and to suggest to the Emperor such measures as appear to him most likely to restore the delirious inhabitants to sanity."

Ah! I remember, I remember the lovely Brazilian three-master that sailed past my windows on the eighth of last May, on her way up the Seine. I thought her so pretty, so white, so gay. The Being was on board her, come from over the sea, where his race is born. He saw me. He saw my house, white like the ship, and he jumped from the vessel to the bank. Oh, my God!

Now I know, I understand. The reign of man is at an end.

He is here, whom the dawning fears of primitive peoples taught them to dread. He who was exorcised by troubled priests, evoked in the darkness of night by wizards who yet never saw him materialize, to whom the foreboding vision of the masters who have passed through this world lent all the monstrous or gracious forms of gnomes, spirits, jinns, fairies and hobgoblins. Primitive terror visualized him in the crudest forms; later wiser men have seen him more clearly. Mesmer foresaw him, and it is ten years since doctors made the most exact inquiries into the nature of his power, even before he exercised it himself. They have been making a plaything of this weapon of the new God, this imposition of a mysterious will on the enslaved soul of man. They called it magnetism, hypnotism, suggestion . . . anything you like. I have seen them amusing themselves with this horrible power like foolish children. Woe to us! Cursed is man! He is here . . . the . . . the . . . what is his name? . . . the . . . it seems as if he were shouting his name in my ear and I cannot hear it . . . the . . . yes . . . he is shouting it. . . . I am listening. . . . I can't hear . . . again, tell me again . . . the . . . Horla. . . . I heard . . . the Horla . . . it is he . . . the Horla . . . he is here!

Oh, the vulture has eaten the dove, the wolf has eaten the sheep: the lion has devoured the sharp-horned buffalo; man has killed the lion with arrow, spear and gun: but the Horla is going to make of man what we have made of the horse and the cow: his thing, his servant and his food, by the mere force of his will. Woe to us!

But sometimes the beast rebels and kills his tamer . . . I too want . . . I could . . . but I must know him, touch him, see him. Scientists say that the eye of the beast is not like ours and does not see as ours does. . . . And my eye fails to show me this newcomer who is oppressing me.

Why? Oh, the words of the monk of Mont-Saint-Michel come to my mind: "Do we see the hundred thousandth part of all that exists? Think, there's the wind, the greatest force in nature, which throws down men, shatters buildings, uproots trees, stirs up the sea into watery mountains, destroys cliffs and tosses the tall ships against the shore, the wind that kills, whistles, groans, roars—have you seen it, can you see it? Nevertheless, it exists."

And I considered further: my eye is so weak, so imperfect, that it does not distinguish even solid bodies that have the transparency of glass. If a looking glass that has no foil backing bars my path, I hurl myself against it as a bird that has got into a room breaks its head on the window pane. How many other things deceive and mislead my eye? Then what is there to be surprised at in its failure to see a new body that offers no resistance to the passage of light?

A new being! why not? He must assuredly come! why should we be the last? Why is he not seen of our eyes as are all the beings created before us? Because his form is nearer perfection, his body finer and completer than ours—ours, which is so weak, so clumsily conceived, encumbered by organs always tired, always breaking down like a too complex mechanism, which lives like a vegetable or a beast, drawing its substance with difficulty from the air, the herbs of the field and meat, an animal machine subject to sickness, deformity and corruption, drawing its breath in pain, ill-regulated, simple and fantastic, ingeniously ill-made, clumsily and delicately erected, the mere rough sketch of a being who could become intelligent and noble.

There have been so few kinds created in the world, from the oyster to man. Why not one more, when we reach the end of the period of time that separates each successive appearance of a species from that which appeared before it?

Why not one more? Why not also new kinds of trees bearing monstrous flowers, blazing with color and filling all the countryside with their perfume? Why not other elements than fire, air, earth and water? There are four, only those four sources of our being! What a pity! Why not forty, four hundred, four thousand? How poor, niggardly and brutish everything is: grudgingly given, meanly conceived, stupidly executed. Consider the grace of the elephant, the hippopotamus! The elegance of the camel!

You bid me consider the butterfly! a winged flower! I can imagine one vast as a hundred worlds, with wings for whose shape, beauty, color, and sweep I cannot find any words. But I see it ... it goes from star to star, refreshing and perfuming them with the soft, gracious wind of its passing. And the people of the upper air watch it pass, in an ecstasy of joy!

What is the matter with me? It is he, he, the Horla, who is haunting me, filling my head with these absurdities! He is in me, he has become my soul; I will kill him.

August 19. I will kill him. I have seen him! I was sitting at my table yesterday evening, making a great show of being very absorbed in writing. I knew quite well that he would come and prowl round me, very close to me, so close that I might be able to touch him, seize him, perhaps? And then! ... then, I should be filled with the strength of desperation; I should have hands, knees, chest, face, teeth to strangle him, crush him, tear him, rend him.

With every sense quiveringly alert, I watched for him.

I had lit both my lamps and the eight candles on my chimney piece, as if I thought I should be more likely to discover him by this bright light.

In front of me was my bed, an old oak four-poster; on my right, the fireplace; on my left, my door carefully shut, after I had left it open for a long time to attract him; behind me, a very tall cupboard with a mirror front, which I used every day to shave and dress by, and in which I always regarded myself from head to foot whenever I passed in front of it.

Well, I pretended to write to deceive him, because he was spying on me too; and, all at once, I felt, I was certain, that he was reading over my shoulder, that he was there, brushing against my ear.

I stood up, my hand outstretched, and turned round, so quickly that I almost fell. What do you think? ... the room was as light as day, and I could not see myself in my looking glass! It was empty, transparent, deep, filled with light! I was not reflected in it . . . and I was standing in front of it. I could see the tall limpid expanse of glass from top to bottom. And I stared at it with a distraught gaze: I daren't move another step, I daren't make another movement; nevertheless I felt that he was there, whose immaterial body had swallowed up my reflection, but that he would elude me still.

How frightened I was! A moment later my reflection began to appear in the depths of the looking glass, in a sort of mist, as if I were looking at it through water; this water seemed to flow from left to right, slowly, so that moment by moment my reflection emerged more distinctly. It was like the passing of an eclipse. The thing that was concealing me appeared to possess no sharply defined outlines, but a kind of transparent opacity that gradually cleared.

At last I could see myself from head to foot, just as I saw myself every day when I looked in the glass.

I had seen him! The horror of it is still on me, making me shudder.

August 20. How can I kill him? Since I can't touch him? Poison? But he would see me put it in the water; and besides, would our poisons affect an immaterial body? No . . . no, they certainly would not. . . . Then how ? . . . how?

August 21. I have sent for a locksmith from Rouen, and ordered him to fit my room with iron shutters, such as they have in certain private houses in Paris, on the ground-floor windows, to keep out robbers. He is to make me a door, too, of the same kind. Everyone thinks me a coward, but much I care!

September 10. Rouen, Hôtel Continental. It is done . . . it is done . . . but is he dead? My brain reels with what I have seen.

Yesterday the locksmith put up my iron shutters and my iron door, and I left everything open until midnight, although it began to get cold.

All at once I felt his presence, and I was filled with joy, a mad joy. I rose slowly to my feet, and walked about the room for a long time, so that he should suspect nothing; then I took off my boots and carelessly drew on my slippers; then I closed my iron shutters, and sauntering back toward the door, I double-locked it too. Then I walked back to the window and secured it with a padlock, putting the key in my pocket.

Suddenly I realized that he was prowling anxiously round me, he was afraid now, and commanding me to open them for him. I almost yielded: I did not yield, but, leaning on the door, I set it ajar, just wide enough for me to slip out backward; and as I am very tall my head touched the lintel. I was sure that he could not have got out and I shut him in, alone, all alone. Oh joy! I had him! Then I ran downstairs; in the drawing room which is under my room, I took both my lamps and emptied the oil all over the carpet and the furniture, everything; then I set it on fire and I fled after having double-locked the main door.

And I went and hid myself at the bottom of my garden, in a grove of laurels. How long it took, how long! Everything was dark, silent, still, not a breath of air, not a star, mountains of unseen clouds that lay so heavily, so heavily, on my spirit.

I kept my gaze fixed on my house, and waited. How long it took! I was beginning to think that the fire had died out of itself, or that he, He, had put it out, when one of the lower windows fell in under the fierce breath of the fire and a flame, a great red and yellow flame, a long, curling, caressing flame, leaped up the white wall and pressed its kiss on the roof itself. A flood of light poured over trees, branches, leaves and with that a shudder, a shudder of fear, ran through them. The birds woke; a dog howled: I thought the dawn was at hand. In a moment two more windows burst into flame and I saw that the lower half of my house was now one frightful furnace. But a cry, a frightful piercing agonized cry, a woman's cry, stabbed the night, and two skylights opened. I had forgotten my servants. I saw their distraught faces and their wildly waving arms. . . .

Then, frantic with horror, I began to run toward the village, shouting: "Help! help! fire! fire!" I met people already on their way to the house and I turned back with them to look at it.

By now the house was no more than a horrible and magnificent funeral pyre, a monstrous pyre lighting up the whole earth, a pyre that was consuming men, and consuming Him, Him, my prisoner, the new Being, the new Master, the Horla!

The whole roof fell in with a sudden crash, and a volcano of flames leaped to the sky. Through all the windows open on the furnace, I saw the fiery vat, and I reflected that he was there, in this oven, dead. . . .

Dead? Perhaps? . . . His body? Perhaps that body through which light fell could not be destroyed by the methods that kill our bodies?

Suppose he is not dead? . . . Perhaps only time has power over the

Invisible and Dreadful One. Why should this transparent, unknowable body, this body of the spirit, fear sickness, wounds, infirmity, premature destruction?

Premature destruction? The source of all human dread! After man, the Horla. After him who can die any day, any hour, any moment, by accidents of all kinds, comes he who can only die in his appointed day, hour and moment, when he has attained the limit of his existence.

No . . . no . . . I know, I know . . . he is not dead . . . so . . . so . . . I shall have to kill myself, myself! . . .

SCRAWNS

By Dorothy L. Sayers

• •

Miss Susan Tabbit was no Lord Peter Wimsey,
but eventually she was able to solve the mystery
of the Scrawns.

The gate, on whose peeled and faded surface the name SCRAWNS was just legible in the dim light, fell to with a clap that shook the rotten gatepost and scattered a shower of drops from the drenched laurels. Susan Tabbit set down the heavy suitcase which had made her arm ache, and peered through the drizzle toward the little house.

It was a curious, lopsided, hunch-shouldered building, seeming not so much to preside over its patch of wintry garden as to be eaves-dropping behind its own hedges. Against a streak of watery light in the west, its chimneystacks—one at either end—suggested pricked ears, intensely aware; the more so, that its face was blind.

Susan shivered a little, and thought regretfully of the cheerful bus that she had left at the bottom of the hill. The conductor had seemed just as much surprised as the station porter had been when she mentioned her destination. He had opened his mouth as though about to make some comment, but had thought better of it. She wished she had had the courage to ask him what sort of place she was coming to. Scrawns. It was a queer name; she had thought so when she had first seen it on Mrs. Wispell's notepaper. Susan Tabbit, care of Mrs. Wispell, Scrawns, Roman Way, Dedcaster.

Her married sister had pursed up her lips when Susan gave her the address, reading it aloud with an air of disapproval. "What's she like, this Mrs. Wispell of Scrawns?" Susan had to confess that she did not know; she had taken the situation without an interview.

Now the house faced her, aloof, indifferent, but on the watch. No house should look so. She had been a fool to come; but it had been so evident that her sister was anxious to get her out of the house. There was no room for her, with all her brother-in-law's family coming. And she was short of money. She had thought it might be pleasant at Scrawns. House-parlormaid, to work with married couple; that had sounded all right. Three in family; that was all right, too. In her last job there had been only herself and eight in family; she had looked forward to a light place and a lively kitchen.

"And what am I thinking about?" said Susan, picking up the suitcase. "The family'll be out, as like as not, at a party or something of that. There'll be a light in the kitchen all right, I'll be bound."

She plodded over the sodden gravel, between two squares of lawn, flanked by empty beds and backed by a huddle of shrubbery; then turned along a path to the right, following the front of the house with its blank unwelcoming windows. The sidewalk was as dark as the front. She made out the outline of a French window, opening upon the path and, to her right, a wide herbaceous border, where tin labels, attached to canes, flapped forlornly. Beyond this there seemed to be a lawn, but the tall trees which surrounded it on all three sides drowned it in blackness and made its shape and extent a mystery. The path led on, through a half-open door that creaked as she pushed it back, and she found herself in a small, paved courtyard, across which the light streamed in a narrow beam from a small, lighted window.

She tried to look in at this window, but a net curtain veiled its lower half. She could only see the ceiling, low, with black rafters, from one of which there hung a paraffin lamp. Passing the window she found a door and knocked.

With the first fall of the old-fashioned iron knocker, a dog began to bark, loudly, incessantly, and furiously. She waited, her heart hammering, but nobody came. After a little she summoned up resolution to knock afresh. This time she thought she could distinguish, through the clamor, a movement within. The barking ceased, she heard a key turn and bolts withdrawn, and the door opened.

The light within came from a doorway on the left, and outlined against it, she was only aware of an enormous bulk and a dim triangle of whiteness, blocking her entrance to the house.

"Who is it?"

The voice was unlike any she had ever heard; curiously harsh and husky and sexless, like the voice of something strangled.

"My name's Tabbit—Susan Tabbit."

"Oh, you're the new girl!" There was a pause, as though the speaker were trying, in the uncertain dusk, to sum her up and reckon out her possibilities.

"Come in."

The looming bulk retreated, and Susan again lifted her suitcase and carried it inside.

"Mrs. Wispell got my letter, saying I was coming?"

"Yes; she got it. But one can't be too careful. It's a lonely place. You can leave your bag for Jarrock. This way."

Susan stepped into the kitchen. It was a low room, not very large but appearing larger than it was because of the shadows thrown into the far corners by the wide shade of the hanging lamp. There was a good fire, which Susan was glad to see, and over the mantelpiece an array of polished copper pans winked reassuringly. Behind her she again heard the jarring of shot bolts and turned key. Then her jailer—why did that word leap uncalled into her mind?—came back and stepped for the first time into the light.

As before, her first overwhelming impression was of enormous height and size. The flat, white, wide face, the billowing breasts, the enormous girth of white-aproned haunch seemed to fill the room and swim above her. Then she forgot everything else in the shock of realizing that the huge woman was cross-eyed.

It was no mere cast; not even an ordinary squint. The left eye was swiveled so horribly far inward that half the iris was invisible, giving to that side of the face a look of blind and cunning malignity. The other eye was bright and dark and small, and fixed itself acutely on Susan's face.

"I'm Mrs. Jarrock," said the woman in her odd, hoarse voice.

It was incredible to Susan that any man who was not blind and deaf should have married a woman so hideously disfigured and with such a raven croak. She said: "How do you do?" and extended a reluctant hand, which Mrs. Jarrock's vast palm engulfed in a grasp unexpectedly hard and masculine.

"You'll like a cup of tea before you change," said Mrs. Jarrock. "You can wait at table, I suppose?"

"Oh, yes, I'm used to that."

"Then you'd better begin tonight. Jarrock's got his hands full with Mr. Alistair. It's one of his bad days. We was both upstairs, that's why you had to wait." She again glanced sharply at the girl, and the swivel eye rolled unpleasantly and uncontrollably in its socket. She turned and bent to lift the kettle from the range, and Susan could not rid herself of the notion that the left eye was still squinting at her from its ambush behind the cook's flat nose.

"Is it a good place?" asked Susan.

"It's all right," said Mrs. Jarrock, "for them as isn't nervous. *She* don't trouble herself much, but that's only to be expected, as things are, and *he's* quiet enough if you don't cross him. Mr. Alistair won't trouble you, that's Jarrock's job. There's your tea. Help yourself to milk and sugar. I wonder if Jarrock—"

She broke off short; set down the teapot and stood with her large head cocked sideways, as though listening to something going on above. Then she moved hastily across the kitchen, with a lightness of step surprising in so unwieldy a woman, and disappeared into the darkness of the passage. Susan, listening anxiously, thought she could hear a sound like moaning and a movement of feet across the raftered ceiling. In a few minutes, Mrs. Jarrock came back, took the kettle from the fire and handed it out to some unseen person in the passage. A prolonged whispering followed, after which Mrs. Jarrock again returned and, without offering any comment, began to make buttered toast.

Susan ate without relish. She had been hungry when she left the bus, but the atmosphere of the house disconcerted her. She had just refused a second slice of toast when she became aware that a man had entered the kitchen.

He was a tall man and powerfully built, but he stood in the doorway as though suspicious or intimidated; she realized that he had probably been standing there for some time before she observed him. Mrs. Jarrock, seeing Susan's head turn and remain arrested, looked round also.

"Oh, there you are, Jarrock. Come and take your tea."

The man moved then, skirting the wall with a curious, crablike movement, and so coming by reluctant degrees to the opposite side of the fire, where he stood, his head averted, shooting a glance at Susan from the corner of his eye.

"This here's Susan," said Mrs. Jarrock. "It's to be hoped she'll settle down and be comfortable with us. I'll be glad to have her to help with the work, *as you* know, with one thing and another."

"We'll do our betht to make things eathy for her," said the man.

He lisped oddly and, though he held out his hand, he still kept his head half averted, like a cat that refuses to take notice. He retreated into an armchair, drawn rather far back from the hearth, and sat gazing into the fire. The dog which had barked when Susan knocked had followed him into the room, and now came over and sniffed at the girl's legs, uttering a menacing growl.

"Be quiet, Crippen," said the man. "Friends."

The dog, a large brindled bull terrier, was apparently not reassured. He continued to growl, till Jarrock, hauling him back by the collar, gave him a smart cuff on the head and ordered him under the table, where he went, sullenly. In bending to beat the dog, Jarrock for the first time turned his full face upon Susan, and she saw, with horror, that the left side of it, from the cheekbone downward, could scarcely be called a face, for it was seamed and puckered by a horrible scar, which had dragged the mouth upward into the appearance of a ghastly grin, while the left-hand side of the jaw seemed shapeless and boneless, a mere bag of wrinkled flesh.

Is everybody in this house maimed and abnormal? she thought, desperately. As though in answer to her thoughts, Mrs. Jarrock spoke to her husband.

"Has he settled down now?"

"Oh, he's quiet enough," replied the man, lisping through his shattered teeth. "He'll do all right." He retired again to his corner and began sucking in his buttered toast, making awkward sounds.

"If you've finished your tea," said Mrs. Jarrock, "I'd better show you your room. Have you taken Susan's bag up, Jarrock?"

The man nodded without speaking, and Susan, in some trepidation, followed the huge woman, who had lit a candle in a brass candlestick.

"You'll find the stairs awkward at first," said the hoarse voice, "and you'll have to mind your head in these passages. Built in the year one, this place was, and by a crazy builder at that, if you ask me."

She glided noiselessly along a narrow corridor and out into a square flagged hall, where a small oil lamp, heavily shaded, seemed to make darkness deeper; then mounted a flight of black oak stairs with twisted banisters of polished oak and shining oak treads, in which the candlelight was reflected on wavering yellow pools.

"There's only the one staircase," said Mrs. Jarrock. "Unhandy, I calls it, but you'll have to do your best. You'll have to wait till he's shut himself up of a morning before you bring down the slops; he don't like to see pails about. This here's their bedroom and that's the spare and this is Mr. Alistair's room. Jarrock sleeps in with him, of course, in case—" She stopped at the door, listening; then led the way up a narrow attic staircase.

"You're in here. It's small, but you're by yourself. And I'm next door to you."

The candle threw their shadows, gigantically distorted, upon the sloping ceiling, and Susan thought, fantastically: If I stay here, I shall grow the wrong shape, too.

"And the big attic's the master's place. You don't have nothing to do with that. Much as your place or ours is worth to poke your nose round the door. He keeps it locked, anyway." The cook laughed, a hoarse, throaty chuckle. "Queer things he keeps in there, I must say. I've seen 'em—when he brings 'em downstairs, that is. He's a funny one, is Mr. Wispell. Well, you'd better get changed into your black, then I'll take you to the mistress."

Susan dressed hurriedly before the little heart-shaped mirror with its old, greenish glass that seemed to absorb more of the candlelight than it reflected. She pulled aside the check window curtain and looked out. It was almost night, but she contrived to make out that the attic looked over the garden at the side of the house. Beneath her lay the herbaceous border, and beyond that, the tall trees stood up like a wall. The room itself was comfortably furnished, though, as Mrs. Jarrock had said, extremely small and twisted into a curious shape by the slanting flue of the great chimney, which ran up on the left-hand side and made a great elbow beside the bed head. There was a minute fireplace cut into the chimney, but it had an unused look. Probably, thought Susan, it would smoke.

At the head of the stairs she hesitated, candle in hand. She was divided between a dread of solitude and a dread of what she was to meet below. She tiptoed down the attic stair and emerged upon the landing. As she did so, she saw the back of Jarrock flitting down the lower flight, and noticed that he had left the door of "Mr. Alistair's" room open behind him. Urged by a curiosity powerful enough to overcome her uneasiness, she crept to the door and peeped in.

Facing her was an old-fashioned tester bed with dull green hangings; a shaded reading lamp burned beside it on a small table. The man on the bed lay flat on his back with closed eyes; his face was yellow and transparent as wax, with pinched, sharp nostrils; one hand, thin as a claw, lay passive upon the green counterpane; the other was hidden in the shadows of the curtain. Certainly, if Jarrock had been speaking of Mr. Alistair, he was right; this man was quiet enough now.

"Poor gentleman," whispered Susan, "He's passed away." And while the words were still on her lips a great bellow of laughter burst forth from somewhere on the floor below. It was monstrous, gargantuan, fantastic; it was an outrage upon the silent house. Susan started back, and the snuffer, jerking from the candlestick, leaped into the air and went ringing and rolling down the oak staircase to land with a brazen clang on the flags below.

Somewhere a door burst open and a loud voice, with a hint of that preposterous mirth still lurking in its depths, bawled out:

"What's that? What the devil's that? Jarrock! Did you make that filthy noise?"

"I beg your pardon, sir," said Susan, advancing in some alarm to the stairhead. "It was my fault, sir. I shook the candlestick and the snuffer fell down. I am very sorry, sir."

"You?" said the man. "Who the devil are you? Come down and let's have a look at you. Oh!" as Susan's black dress and muslin apron came into his view at the turn of the stair, "the new housemaid, hey! That's a pretty way to announce yourself. A damned good beginning! Don't you do it again, that's all. I won't have noise, d'you understand? All the noise in this house is made by me. That's my prerogative, if you know what the word means. Hey? Do you understand?"

"Yes, sir. I won't let it happen again, sir."

"That's right. And look here. If you've made a dent in those boards, d'you know what I'll do? Hey? I'll have the insides out of you, d'you hear?" He jerked back his big, bearded head, and his great guffaw seemed to shake the old house like a gust of wind. "Come on, girl, I won't eat you this time. Let's see your face. Your legs are all right, anyway. I won't have a housemaid with thick legs. Come in here and be vetted. Sidonia, here's the new girl, chucking the furniture all over the place the minute she's in the house. Did you hear it? Did you ever hear anything like it? Hey? Ha, ha!"

He pushed Susan in front of him into a sitting room furnished in deep orange and rich blues and greens like a peacock's tail, and with white walls that caught and flung back the yellow lamplight. The windows were closely shuttered and barred.

On a couch drawn up near the fire a girl was lying. She had a little, white, heart-shaped face, framed and almost drowned in a mass of heavy red hair, and on her long fingers were several old and heavy rings. At her husband's boisterous entry she rose rather awkwardly and uncertainly.

"Walter, dear, don't shout so. My head aches, and you'll frighten the poor girl. So you're Susan. How are you? I hope you had a good journey. Are Mr. and Mrs. Jarrock looking after you?"

"Yes, thank you, madam."

"Oh! then that's all right." She looked a little helplessly at her husband, and then back to Susan. "I hope you'll be a good girl, Susan."

"I shall try to give satisfaction, madam."

"Yes, yes, I'm sure you will." She laughed, on a high, silver note like a bird's call. "Mrs. Jarrock will put you in the way of things. I hope you'll be happy and stay with us." Her pretty, aimless laughter tinkled out again.

"I hope Susan won't disappear like the last one," said Mr. Wispell. Susan caught a quick glance darted at him by his wife, but before she could decide whether it was one of fear or of warning, they were interrupted. A bell pealed sharply with a jangling of wires, and in the silence that followed the two Wispells stared uneasily at each other.

"What the devil's that?" said Mr. Wispell. "I only hope to heaven—"

Jarrock came in. He held a telegram in his hand. Wispell snatched it from him and tore it open. With an exclamation of distaste and alarm he handed it to his wife, who uttered a sharp cry.

"Walter, we can't! She mustn't! Can't we stop her?"

"Don't be a fool, Sidonia. How can we stop her?"

"Yes, Walter. But don't you understand? She'll expect to find Helen here."

"Oh, Lord!" said Mr. Wispell.

Susan went early to bed. Dinner had been a strained and melancholy meal. Mrs. Wispell talked embarrassed nothings at intervals; Mr. Wispell seemed sunk in a savage gloom, from which he only roused himself to bark at Susan for more potatoes or another slice of bread. Nor were things much better in the kitchen, for it seemed that a visitor was expected.

"Motoring down from York," muttered Mrs. Jarrock. "Goodness knows when they'll get here. But that's her all over. No consideration, and never had. I'm sorry for the mistress, that's all."

Jarrock's distorted mouth twisted into a still more ghastly semblance of a grin.

"Rich folks must have their way," he said. "Four years ago it was the same thing. A minute's notice and woe betide if everything's not right. But we'll be ready for her, oh! we'll be ready for her, you'll see." He chuckled gently to himself.

Mrs. Jarrock gave a curious, sly smile. "You'll have to help me with the spare room, Susan," she said.

Later, coming down into the scullery to fill a hot-water bottle, Susan found the Jarrocks in close confabulation beside the sink.

"And see you make no noise about it," the cook was saying. "These girls have long tongues, and I wouldn't trust—"

She turned and saw Susan.

"If you've finished," she said, taking the bottle from her, "you'd best be off to bed. You've had a long journey."

The words were softly spoken, but they had an undertone of command. Susan took up her candlestick from the kitchen. As she passed the scullery on her way upstairs, she heard the Jarrocks whispering together and noticed, just inside the back door, two spades standing, with an empty sack beside them. They had not been there before, and she wondered idly what Jarrock could be wanting with them.

She fell asleep quickly, for she was tired; but an hour or two later she woke with a start and a feeling that people were talking in the room. The rain had ceased, for through the window she could see a star shining, and the attic was lit by the diffused grayness of moonlight. Nobody was there, but the voices were no dream. She could hear their low rumble, close beside her head. She sat up and lit her candle; then slipped out of bed and crept across to the door.

The landing was empty; from the room next her own she could hear the deep and regular snoring of the cook. She came back and stood for a moment, puzzled. In the middle of the room, she could hear nothing, but as she returned to the bed, she heard the voices again, smothered, as though the speakers were at the bottom of a well. Stooping, she put her ear to the empty fireplace. At once the voices became more distinct, and she realized that the great chimney was acting as a speaking tube from the room below. Mr. Wispell was talking. ". . . better be getting on with it . . . here at any time . . ."

"The ground's soft enough." That was Jarrock speaking. She lost a few words, and then:

". . . bury her four feet deep, because of the rose trees."

There came a silence. Then came the muffled echo of Mr. Wispell's great laugh; it rumbled with a goblin sound in the hollow chimney.

Susan crouched by the fireplace, feeling herself grow rigid with cold. The voices dropped to a subdued murmur. Then she heard a door shut and there was complete silence. She stretched her cramped limbs and stood a moment listening. Then, with fumbling haste she began to drag on her clothes. She must get out of this horrible house.

Suddenly a soft step sounded on the gravel beneath her window; it was followed by the chink of iron. Then a man's voice said: "Here, between Betty Uprichard and Evelyn Thornton." There followed the thick sound of a spade driven into heavy soil.

Susan stole to the window and looked out. Down below, in the moonlight, Mr. Wispell and Jarrock were digging, fast and feverishly, flinging up the soil about a shallow trench. A rose tree was lifted and laid to one side, and as she watched them, the trench deepened and widened to a sinister shape.

She huddled on the last of her clothing, pulled on her coat and hat, sought for and found the handbag that held her money and set the door gently ajar. There was no sound but the deep snoring from the next-door room.

She picked up her suitcase, which she had not unpacked before tumbling into bed. She hesitated a moment; then, as swiftly and silently as she could, she tiptoed across the landing and down the steep stair. The words of Mr. Wispell came back to her with sudden sinister import. "I hope she won't disappear like the last one." Had the last one, also, seen that which she was not meant to see, and scuttled on trembling feet down the stair with its twisted black banisters? Or had she disappeared still more strangely, to lie forever four feet deep under the rose trees? The old boards creaked beneath her weight; on the lower landing the door of Mr. Alistair's room stood ajar, and a faint light came from within it. Was he to be the tenant of the grave in the garden? Or was it meant for her, or for the visitor who was expected that night?

Her flickering candle flame showed her the front door chained and bolted. With a caution and control inspired by sheer terror, she pulled back the complaining bolts, lowered the chain with her hand, so that it should not jangle against the door, and turned the heavy key. The garden lay still and sodden under the moonlight. Drawing the door very gently to behind her, she stood on the threshold, free. She took a deep breath and slipped down the path as silently as a shadow.

A few yards down the hill road she came to a clump of thick bushes. Inside this she thrust the suitcase. Then, relieved of its weight, she ran. At four o'clock the next morning a young policeman was repeating a curious tale to the police sergeant at Dedcaster.

"The young woman is pretty badly frightened," he said, "but she tells her story straight enough. Do you think we ought to look into it?"

"Sounds queerish," said the sergeant. "Maybe you'd better go and have a look. Wait a minute, I'll come with you myself. They're odd people, those Wispells. Man's an artist, isn't he? Loose-living gentry they are, as often as not. Get the car out, Blaycock; you can drive us."

"What the devil is all this?" demanded Mr. Wispell. He stood upright in the light of the police lantern, leaning upon his spade, and wiped the sweat from his forehead with an earthy hand. "Is that our girl you've got with you? What's wrong with her? Hey? Thief, hey? If you've been bagging the silver, you young besom, it'll be the worse for you."

"This young woman's come to us with a queer tale, Mr. Wispell," said the sergeant. "I'd like to know what you're a-digging of here for."

Mr. Wispell laughed. "Of here for? What should I be digging of here for? Can't I dig in my own garden without your damned interference?"

"Now, that won't work, Mr. Wispell. That's a grave, that is. People don't dig graves in their gardens in the middle of the night for fun. I want that there grave opened. What've you got inside it? Now, be careful."

"There's nobody inside it at the moment," said Mr. Wispell, "and I should be obliged if you'd make rather less noise. My wife's in a delicate state of health, and my brother-in-law, who is an invalid with an injured spine, has had a very bad turn. We've had to keep him under morphia and we've only just got him off into a natural sleep. And now you come bellowing round—"

"What's that there in that sack?" interrupted the young policeman. As they all pressed forward to look, he found Susan beside him, and reassured her with a friendly pat on the arm.

"That?" Mr. Wispell laughed again. "That's Helen. Don't damage her, I implore you—if my aunt—"

The sergeant had bent down and slit open the sacking with a penknife. Soiled and stained, the pale face of a woman glimmered up at him. There was earth in her eyelids.

"Marble!" said the sergeant. "Well, I'll be hanged!"

There was the sound of a car stopping at the gate.

"Heaven almighty!" ejaculated Mr. Wispell. "We're done for! Get this into the house quickly, Jarrock."

"Wait a bit, sir. What I want to know—"

Steps sounded on the gravel. Mr. Wispell flung his hands to heaven. "Too late!" he groaned.

An elderly lady, very tall and upright, was coming round the side of the house.

"What on earth are you up to out here, Walter?" she demanded in a piercing voice. "Policemen? A nice welcome for your aunt, I must say. And what—*what* is my wedding present doing in the garden?" she added, as her eye fell on the naked marble figure.

"Oh, Lor'!" said Mr. Wispell. He flung down the spade and stalked away into the house.

"I'm afraid," said Mrs. Wispell, "you will have to take your month's money and go, Susan. Mr. Wispell is very much annoyed. You see, it was such a hideous statue, he wouldn't have it in the house, and nobody would buy it, and besides, Mrs. Glassover might turn up at any time, so we buried it and when she wired, of course we had to dig it up. But I'm afraid Mrs. Glassover will never forgive Walter, and she's sure to alter her will and—well, he's very angry, and really I don't know how you could be so silly."

"I'm sure I'm very sorry, madam. I was a bit nervous, some-how—"

"Maybe," said Mrs. Jarrock in her hoarse voice, "the poor girl was upset-like, by Jarrock. I did ought to have explained about him and poor Mr. Alistair getting blown up in the war and you being so kind to us—but there! Being used to his poor face myself I didn't think, somehow—and what with being all upset and one thing and another . . ."

The voice of Mr. Wispell came booming down the staircase. "Has that fool of a girl cleared off?"

The young policeman took Susan by the arm. He had pleasant brown eyes and curly hair, and his voice was friendly.

"Seems to me, miss," he said, "Scrawns ain't no place for you. You'd better come along of us and eat your dinner with Mother and me."

BIOGRAPHICAL NOTES

. . . .

(Compiled by Onica Friend)

ALSOP, STEWART (1914-   ), American.
Billy: The Seal Mission, page 88 (with Thomas Braden).
Editor, reporter, writes a syndicated column of political opinion with his brother, Joseph. He served in the Office of Special Services during World War II, parachuted into France shortly after D-Day and was decorated with the *Croix de guerre*. He and Thomas Braden, who was also in the OSS, wrote of their experiences in *Sub Rosa: The OSS and American Espionage* (1946); "Billy: The Seal Mission" is a chapter from this book. Mr. Alsop is now Washington editor of *The Saturday Evening Post*.

AUMONIER, STACY (1887-1928), British.
Old Fags, page 360.
Careers included those of designer, painter, entertainer and journalist. Private in World War I. His wife is concert pianist Gertrude Peppercorn. Best-known novel *The Querrils* (1919). Rebecca West said of him: "Mr. Aumonier's creations are dyed in the fast dyes of authentic imagination."

BIERCE, AMBROSE GWINNETT (1842-c.1914), American.
A Watcher by the Dead, page 109.
From a mad Ohio family with a father sternly religious, weak and poetry-loving, Ambrose at nineteen joined up with the Indiana Regulars at the first call of the Civil War. In later life, he insisted that everyone call him "Major," an appellation well suited to his tall, dignified frame and irascible though gentlemanly nature. His closest friends disliked him, his wife left him, he knew he had never made it in literature (most of his published writing was done as "a paid skunk who stinks for gold," as a friend once described Bierce's long journalistic association with William Randolph Hearst), so, at age seventy-one, he disappeared into Mexico and was never heard of again.

BIERSTADT, EDWARD HALE (1891-   ), American.
Death Draws a Triangle, page 124.
One-time editor of *Opera Magazine, Travel,* and *The Levant Review,* associate director of the Foreign Language Information Service, and executive secretary of the Emergency Committee on Near East Refugees (1922-23). Mr. Bierstadt's present activities are unknown.

BRADBURY, RAY (1930-   ), American.
The Last Night of the World, page 302.
Through his many stories, novels, and his stage and television plays, he is one of the best-known living writers of science fiction and has done much to elevate the genre. Buck Rogers, Flash Gordon, and Tarzan introduced him at age eight to the world of fantasy, and an ancestor, Mary Bradbury, tried as a witch in Salem in the seventeenth century, gave him, he says, a "dedicated interest in freedom from fear and a detestation of thought investigation or thought control of any sort." He writes "in order to make people leave people alone."

BRADEN, THOMAS W. (1918-   ), American.
Billy: The Seal Mission, page 88 (with Stewart Alsop).
Graduate of Dartmouth College, where he later taught English. With Stewart Alsop (*vid.*), he served during World War II as a parachutist for the Office of Special Services. After the war, he was executive secretary of the Museum of Modern Art in New York City, and is now a member of the Council on Foreign Relations and editor and publisher of the Oceanside (Calif.) *Blade-Tribune.*

BUCHAN, JOHN, 1st Baron Tweedsmuir (1875-1940), Scottish.
Sing a Song of Sixpence, page 454.
A novelist, he was also a biographer, historian, publisher, lawyer and diplomat. A baron, he was also a conservative member of Parliament (1927), Lord High Commissioner of the Church of Scotland in London, and Governor-General of Canada (1935). One of his novels, *The 39 Steps,* Alfred Hitchcock turned into a classic suspense film.

CASTELOT, ANDRÉ (1911-   ), French.
The Last Inhabitant of the Tuileries, page 211.
Historian and biographer, author of many books, all based on research in original, unedited documents. His books have been translated into several languages, and his *Marie Antoinette* (published here in 1957 as *Queen of France*) was awarded a prize by the Académie Française. Monsieur Castelot, who was instrumental in beginning the "Sons et Lumières" productions in France, broadcasts weekly on the French radio and has a show on Luxembourg television. He and his wife winter in Paris and

spend their summers in a lovely old farm house in Normandy. His *Josephine* is soon to be published in the United States.

CHESTERTON, GILBERT KEITH (1874-1936), British.
The Shadow of the Shark, page 490.
A known journalist, reviewer and essayist before he was twenty-one; also poet and novelist. His tales of a quiet little Roman Catholic priest, Father Brown, his detective hero, definitely enhanced the detective story. Chesterton, himself a staunch Catholic, once said: "I am one of those people who believe that you've got to be dominated by your moral slant." But he was also a liberal who believed in a supersocialism he called Distributism and who detested teetotalism and vegetarianism.

CHRISTIE, AGATHA (1891?-   ), British.
The Adventure of the Clapham Cook, page 289.
Wrote sad sentimental stories as a child, turned to detective novels toward the end of World War I while working in a French hospital. She found detection "excellent to take one's mind off one's worries." She loves to write in the deserts of Syria and Iraq, where she doubles as a photographer for her second husband, archaeologist Max Mallowan.

COATES, ROBERT MYRON (1897-   ), American.
The Net, page 156.
Expatriated in the twenties to France, where he introduced Ernest Hemingway to Gertrude Stein, he returned to the United States, and was until recently art critic for *The New Yorker* magazine, where he started work under the aegis of James Thurber. Among his many short stories and novels are *Wisteria Cottage* (1948) and *The Eater of Darkness* (1926), said to be the first American Dada novel. Mr. Coates now lives in Connecticut.

COLLIER, JOHN (1901-   ), British.
Sleeping Beauty, page 474.
Novelist (*His Monkey Wife*, 1930) and short-story writer. Poetry editor of *Time and Tide* for several years before coming in the thirties to Hollywood, where he lives with his second American wife. Basil Davenport called him "the master of an irony so perfectly balanced that his horror is hardly ever quite free of humor, nor his humor of horror."

DOYLE, SIR ARTHUR CONAN (1859-1930), British.
How the Brigadier Lost His Ear, page 390.
An unsuccessful doctor who wrote many of his stories while waiting for patients who never came. Medicine did, however, introduce him to Edinburgh surgeon Joseph Bell, from whose thin person and diagnostic per-

sonality Sir Arthur Conan Doyle distilled Sherlock Holmes, best-known and best-loved of all fictional detectives. A prolific writer of both fiction and nonfiction, he was also a defender of the defenseless. The death of his son during World War I converted him to Spiritualism, and he spent the latter part of his life and fortune spreading his beliefs in Europe, Australia and America.

ELLIN, STANLEY (1916-   ), American.
Fool's Mate, page 14.
His classic short-story collection, *Mystery Stories* (1956), was chosen as "one of the 200 best and most important titles published in the United States" for the permanent White House Library. He tried dairy farming, teaching, and steelworking, then entered the army in World War II. After the war, his wife encouraged him to write, and he was immediately successful. He lives in Brooklyn with her and his daughter.

FAULKNER, WILLIAM (1897-1962), American.
Dry September, page 409.
Until his death, Faulkner hunted, fished and wrote in Oxford, Mississippi, much as he did before his "revival" in 1945, when people such as Robert Penn Warren began saying: "The study of Faulkner is the most challenging single task in contemporary American literature for criticism to undertake." Faulkner received the Nobel Prize for Literature in 1949 for his novel *The Sound and the Fury*, saying, "Man will endure because he has a soul, a spirit capable of compassion and sacrifice and endurance." He considered his most important novel to be A *Fable* (1945), the retelling of Christ's passion in modern terms.

FISCHER, JOHN (1910-   ), American.
A *Small Buried Treasure*, page 509.
First a reporter and foreign correspondent, then economist with the Department of Agriculture, he spent a year in India as chief representative of the Board of Economic Warfare. Came to *Harper's Magazine* in 1944 as associate editor, was editor in chief for twenty years, and is now a contributing editor. Mr. Fischer wrote "A Small Buried Treasure" as part of his column "The Easy Chair." He has also written several books, including *Why They Behave Like Russians* (1947) and *The Stupidity Problem* (1964).

FLANNER, JANET (1892-   ), American.
The Murder in Le Mans, page 467.
Miss Flanner lives in Paris, visiting the United States frequently, and since 1925 has written the "Letter from Paris" column for *The New*

Yorker magazine under the name "Genêt." In 1940 some of her *New Yorker* profiles were collected under the title *An American in Paris*. She has received the French Legion of Honor and is a Member of the National Institute of Arts and Letters.

FREEMAN, KATHLEEN (deceased), British.
On the Killing of Eratosthenes the Seducer, page 278.
Greek scholar, Doctor of Literature, and also writer of mystery novels under the name Mary Fitt.

GAISER, GERD (1908-   ), German.
The Game of Murder, page 272.
Studied art and art history, served in the German Air Force in World War II. Winner of many literary prizes, and member of the Academy of Arts in Berlin.

GREENE, GRAHAM (1904-   ), British.
The End of the Party, page 202.
Master of portrayal of the hunter and the hunted, as seen from his early novels and from the film version of his *The Third Man* (1950). Reviewing *The End of the Affair* (1951), Louise Bogan said that the fear, mystery, pursuit and flight of his "entertainments" have "a close parallel to the religious drama of salvation and redemption," and recently his novels have dealt directly with the problems of Catholic dogma in the twentieth century. A Catholic himself, Greene has flirted with communism and opium smoking, the latter when covering the war in Indochina in 1954.

JESSE, FRYNIWYD TENNYSON (-1958), British.
Rattenbury and Stoner, page 421.
First a journalist and war correspondent, then a novelist, dramatist, and criminologist, she once said: "I am fond of flying and my chief passion is murder." She believed there were both "born murderers" and "murderees" born to be murdered. In 1918 she married H. M. Harwood, doctor, businessman, and well-known British playwright.

KIPLING, RUDYARD (1865-1936), British.
"They," page 306.
Born in Bombay, lived most of his early life in India, assimilating its peculiar character which he recreated so well in his works like the *Jungle Books* (1884) and *Kim* (1901). Finding journalism unsatisfying, the young Kipling turned to poetry, short stories, novels, and political nonfiction, all of which he mastered. He took an American wife and lived

for several years in Vermont, but remained always the epitome of the English imperialist, whose political epigrams such as "white man's burden" were household words. He was awarded the Nobel Prize for Literature in 1907.

LONDON, JACK (1876-1916), American.
A *Piece of Steak*, page 255.
Illegitimate son of an Irish astrologer and a Welsh girl, London moved from poverty to riches, from tramp to seafarer to Klondike prospector, to author of fifty books which earned him over $1,000,000, all of which he spent. A wild romantic and a socialist (he once ran for the office of mayor of Oakland, California), he took an overdose of morphine at age forty, ending his life as he had ended that of his autobiographical hero Martin Eden.

MARTIN, JOHN BARTLOW (1915-   ), American.
The Chair, page 326.
A free-lance writer from 1938 to 1962, when he was appointed ambassador to the Dominican Republic for two years. Campaigned for Stevenson, Kennedy, and Johnson. Spent two years in the army in the Criminal Investigation Division.

MAUPASSANT, GUY DE (1850-1893), French.
The Horla, page 515.
Novelist and poet, master of the naturalistic short story. Wrote of nothing but what he had seen and in none but the precise and simple style of a true seer whose mind was uncluttered by any philosophical or moral systems. "The Horla" (1887) shows the beginning of disintegration and hallucination brought about by the excessive exercise and drug consumption that led to his death at forty-three.

PADGETT, LEWIS (pseudonym for Henry Kuttner) (1914-1958), American.
Jesting Pilot, page 218.
First wrote Gothic tales for the pulps, was a fan of C. L. Moore, writer of fantasy and science fiction, until he found out the "C." stood for Catharine, where upon they married and formed a writing team under dozens of pseudonyms. As Lewis Padgett, Mr. Kuttner's detective novels include *The Brass Ring* (1947) and *The Day He Died* (1948).

PEARSON, EDMUND (1880-1937), American.
The Sixth Capsule; or, Proof by Circumstantial Evidence, page 3.
By profession a librarian and bibliophile, Pearson began exploring murder

cases. His best-known work is *Studies in Murder* (1924). *Murder at Smutty Nose*, which contains "The Sixth Capsule," followed in 1926. By 1927 he had given up library work to devote himself to studying murder. "The study of murder," he wrote, "is the study of the human heart in its darkest, strangest moments. Nothing surpasses it in interest."

PINTER, HAROLD (1930-   ), British.
Tea Party, page 120.
Once an actor, now primarily a playwright for stage, television, and cinema. "Tea Party" was presented on British television in 1964. Mr. Pinter lives in London with his wife, actress Vivien Merchant, who was for a time the female lead in his controversial, prize-winning play, "The Homecoming." He lists his recreation as drinking.

PUSHKIN, ALEXANDER (1799-1837), Russian.
The Queen of Spades, page 63.
Aristocrat, novelist, and poet, inspired by Lord Byron, the beauty of the Caucasus, and Shakespeare. Member of a secret society (of which there were many in Russia at that time), friend of conspirators and advocate of atheism, he was in and out of trouble until mortally wounded in a duel. "The Queen of Spades" (1834), his most famous short story, was made into an opera by Tschaikowsky.

SAINT-EXUPÉRY, ANTOINE DE (1900-1944), French.
Prisoner of the Sand, page 165.
Poet-philosopher who "extolled the values of friendship, love, responsibility, compassion and beauty." Fulfilling a youthful desire, he became first a commercial pilot, then during World War II a captain in the French Air Corps Reserve. His plane was shot down and he escaped only to be finally downed again four years later while flying reconnaissance over Italy and Southern France.

SAYERS, DOROTHY LEIGH (1893-1957), British.
Scrawns, page 539.
One of the most literate of detective fiction writers, an Oxford graduate with honors in Medieval Literature, she created her detective hero Lord Peter Wimsey because "there was no very hopeful market in those days [1923-37] for poetry or theology, and I had to make money somehow. . . ." She made it and dropped mystery for translation (Dante's *Inferno* and *Purgatorio*), literary criticism and theological writing.

SEABROOK, WILLIAM (1886-1945), American.
"*. . . Dead Men Working in the Cane Fields*," page 380.

Began writing as a journalist, joined the French army in 1915 and was invalided out with the *Croix de guerre*. He traveled all over the world, writing of his experiences such as dancing voodoo in Haiti and eating human flesh in Africa, only to wind up in a New York mental hospital as an alcoholic in 1933. His adventures ended with the taking of an overdose of sleeping pills at his home in Rhinebeck, New York.

SHEPHERD, WILLIAM GUNN (1878-1933), American
Shattering the Myth of John Wilkes Booth's Escape, page 231.
From reporter in St. Paul, Minnesota, to revolutionary in Mexico, to European war correspondent and free-lance writer.

TALLANT, ROBERT (1909-1957), American.
The Axeman Wore Wings, page 29.
Began work caged as a bank teller until the Depression. Then he odd-jobbed until finally, at twenty-eight, he decided to become a writer, bought a writers' magazine, a five-dollar typewriter and wrote. Most of his work is set in the South, particularly around New Orleans, his birthplace and home.

ZHURAVLEVA, ALEXANDRA, Russian.
Stone from the Stars, page 50.
Soviet science-fiction writer.